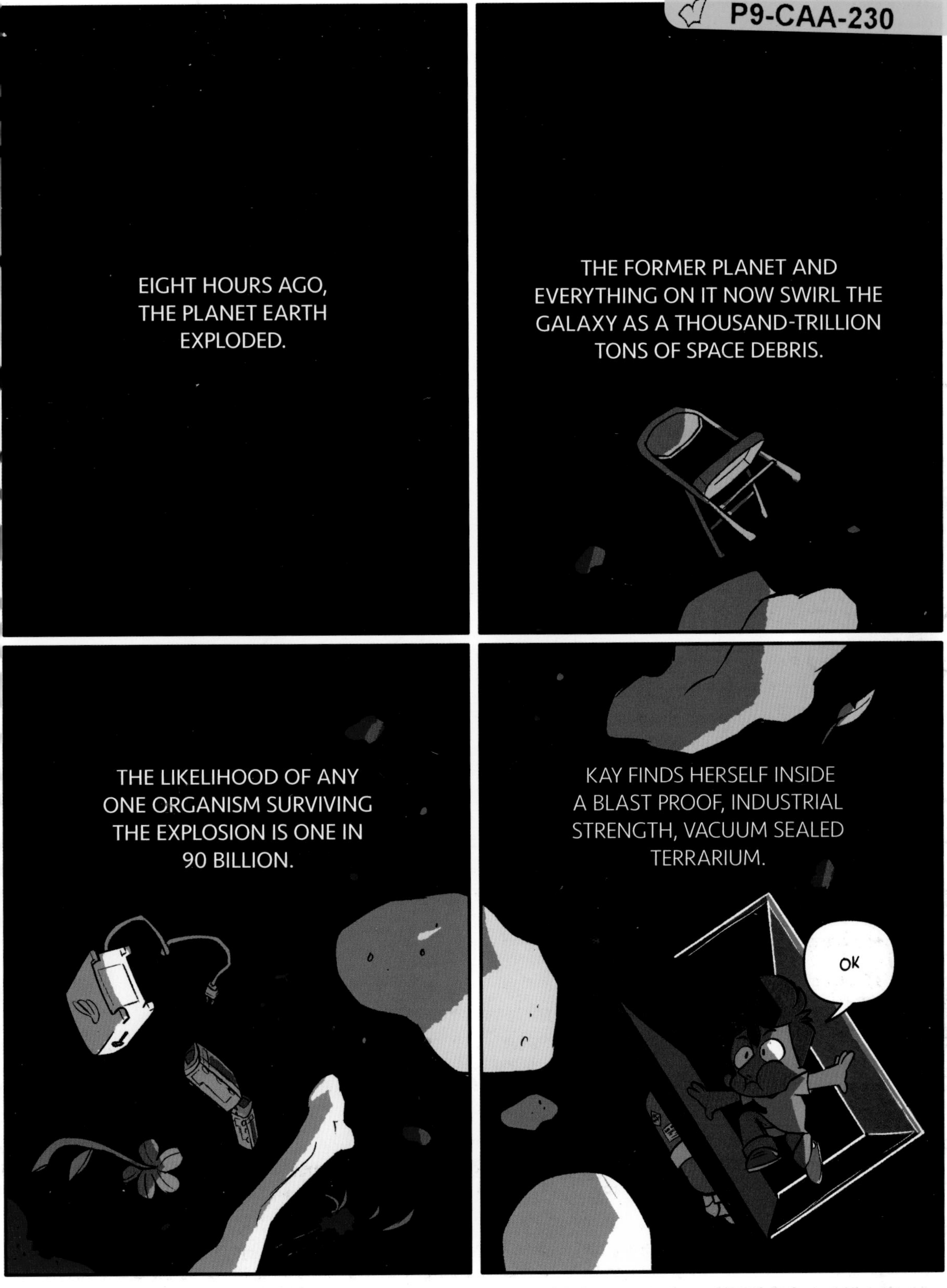

EIGHT HOURS AGO,
THE PLANET EARTH
EXPLODED.

THE FORMER PLANET AND
EVERYTHING ON IT NOW SWIRL THE
GALAXY AS A THOUSAND-TRILLION
TONS OF SPACE DEBRIS.

THE LIKELIHOOD OF ANY
ONE ORGANISM SURVIVING
THE EXPLOSION IS ONE IN
90 BILLION.

KAY FINDS HERSELF INSIDE
A BLAST PROOF, INDUSTRIAL
STRENGTH, VACUUM SEALED
TERRARIUM.

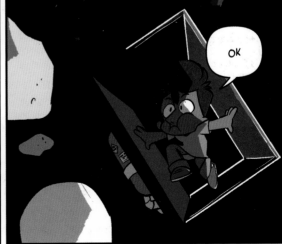

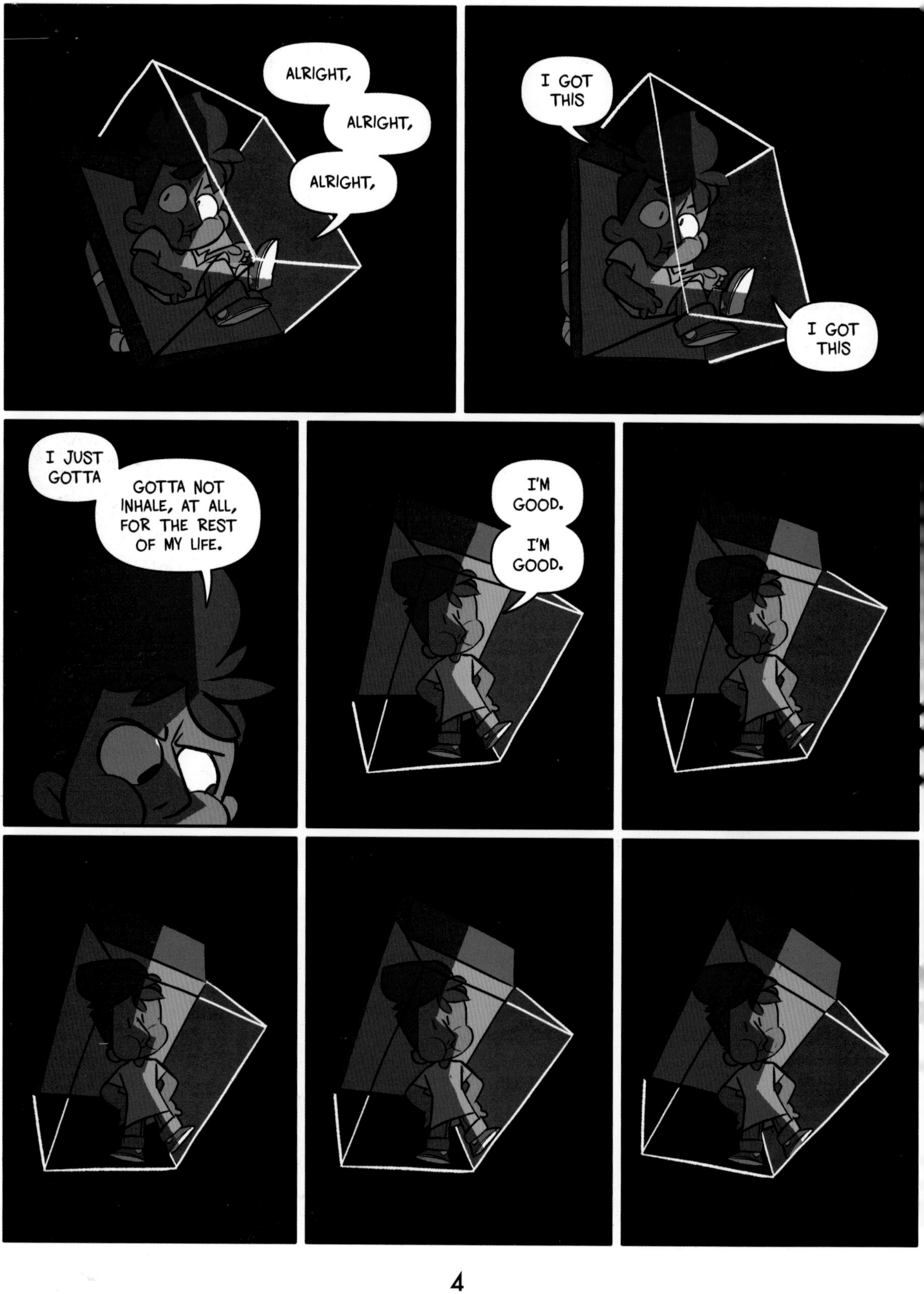
ALRIGHT,
ALRIGHT,
ALRIGHT,
I GOT THIS
I GOT THIS
I JUST GOTTA
GOTTA NOT INHALE, AT ALL, FOR THE REST OF MY LIFE.
I'M GOOD.
I'M GOOD.

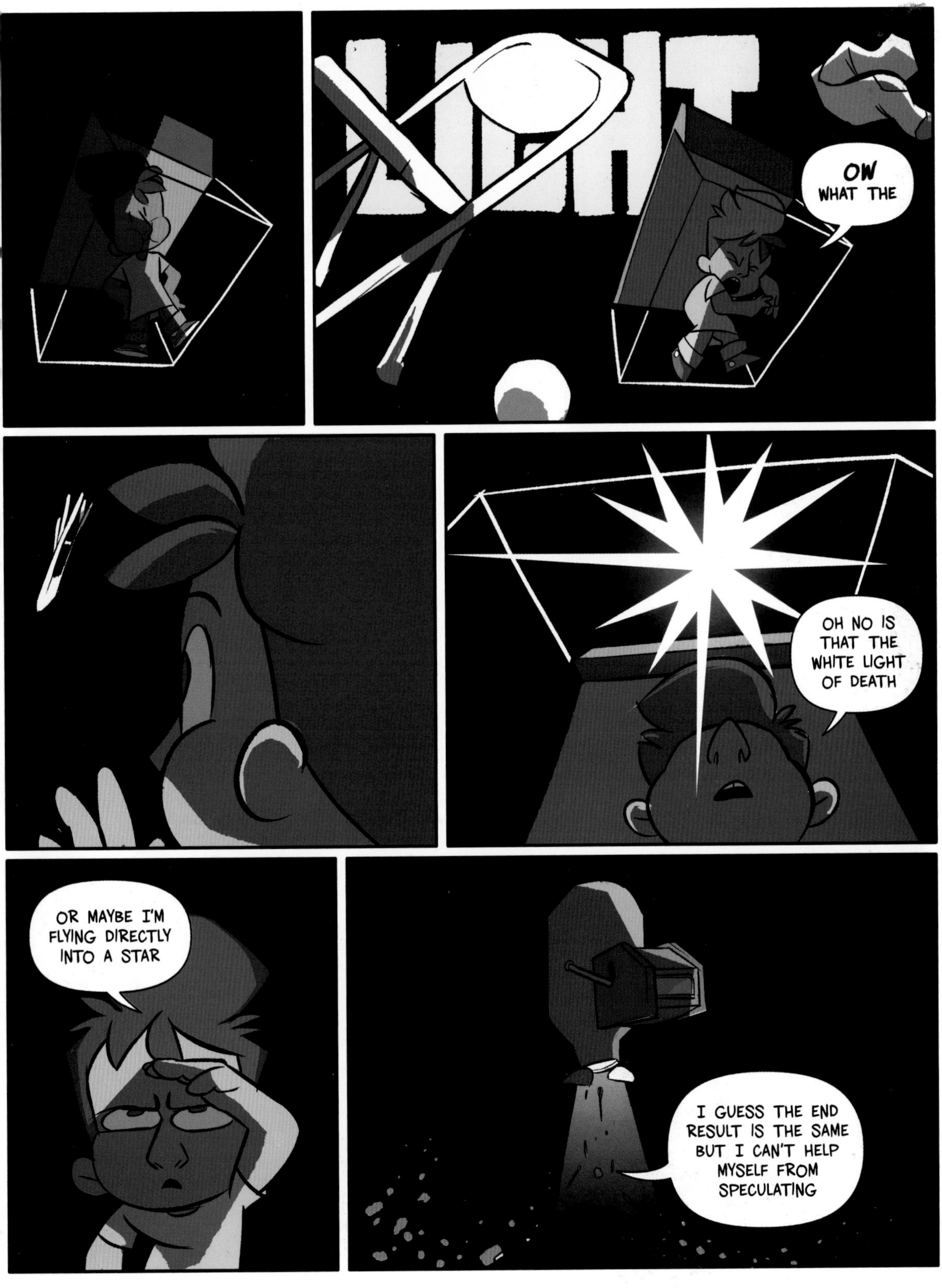
LIGHT
OW WHAT THE
OH NO IS THAT THE WHITE LIGHT OF DEATH
OR MAYBE I'M FLYING DIRECTLY INTO A STAR
I GUESS THE END RESULT IS THE SAME BUT I CAN'T HELP MYSELF FROM SPECULATING

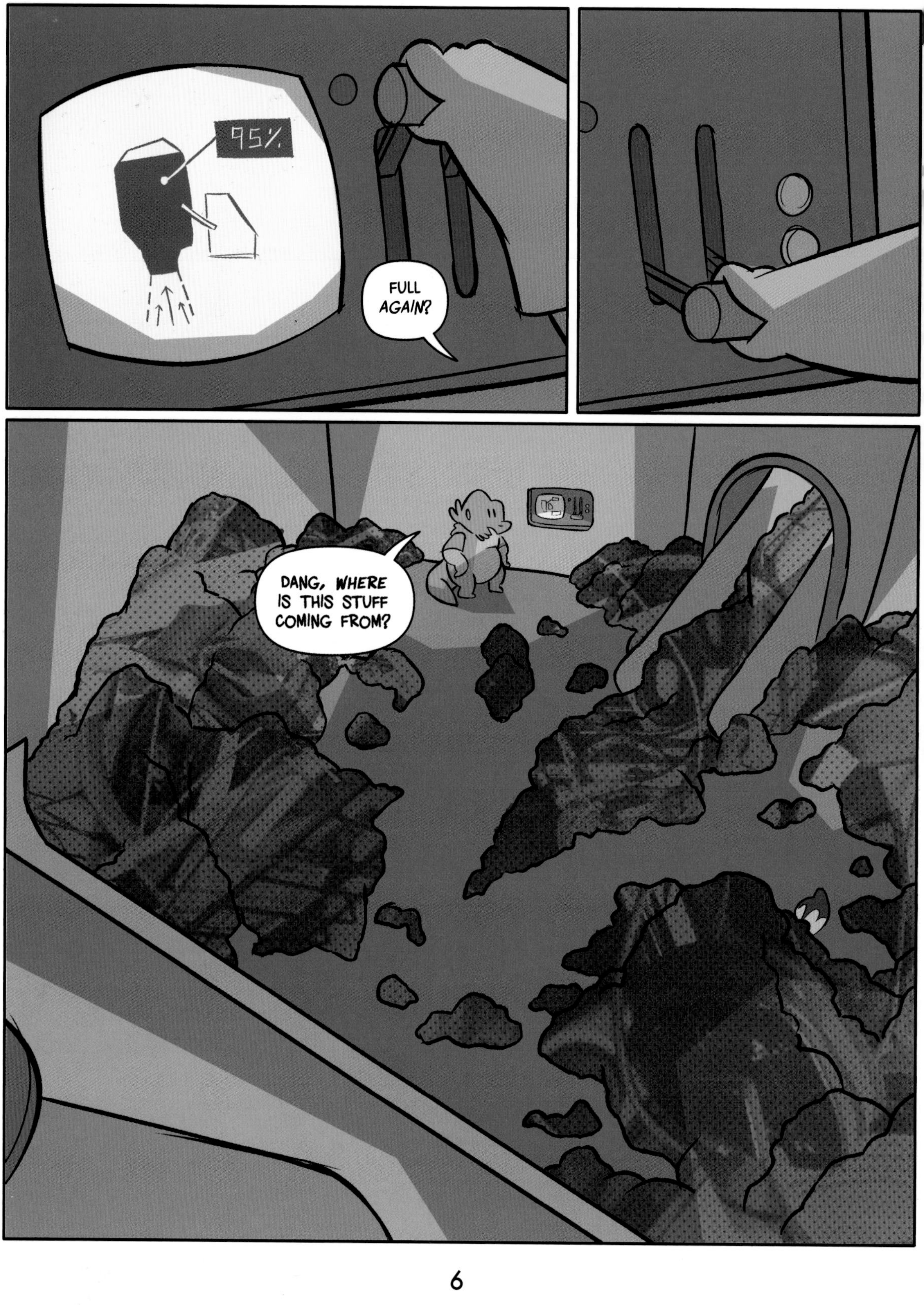
95%
FULL AGAIN?
DANG, WHERE IS THIS STUFF COMING FROM?

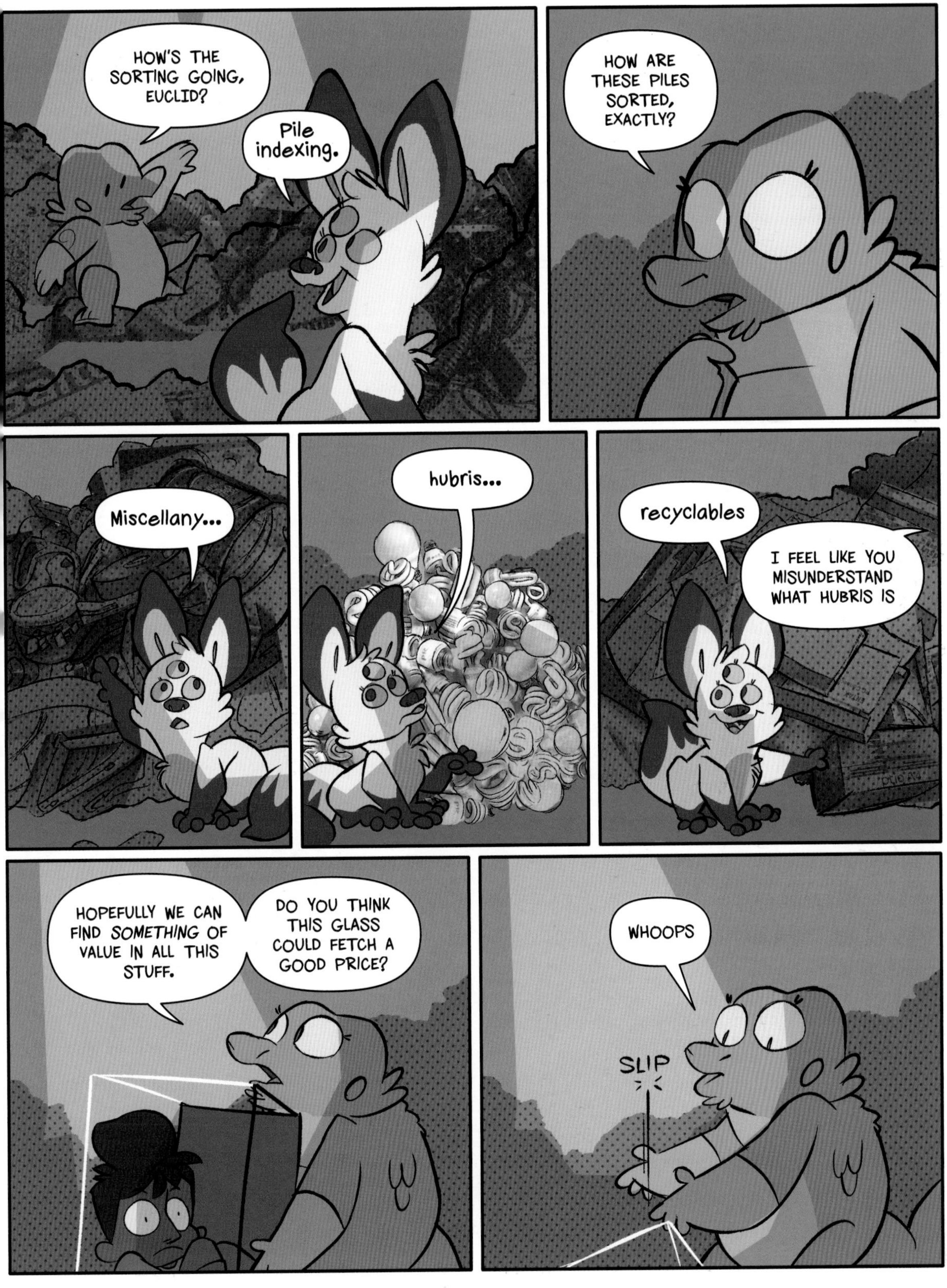
HOW'S THE SORTING GOING, EUCLID?
Pile indexing.
HOW ARE THESE PILES SORTED, EXACTLY?
Miscellany...
hubris...
recyclables
I FEEL LIKE YOU MISUNDERSTAND WHAT HUBRIS IS
HOPEFULLY WE CAN FIND SOMETHING OF VALUE IN ALL THIS STUFF.
DO YOU THINK THIS GLASS COULD FETCH A GOOD PRICE?
WHOOPS
SLIP

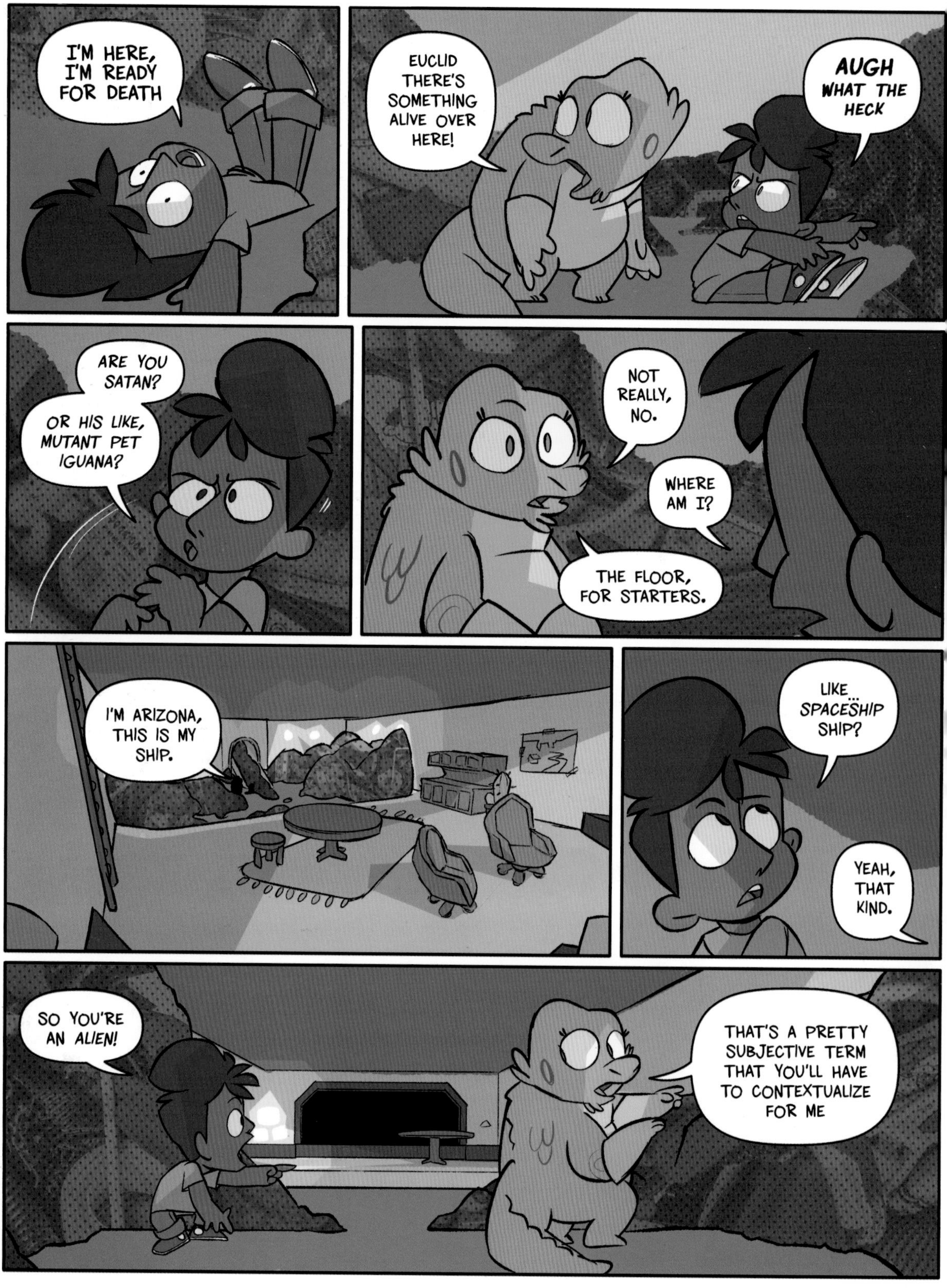
I'M HERE, I'M READY FOR DEATH
EUCLID THERE'S SOMETHING ALIVE OVER HERE!
AUGH WHAT THE HECK
ARE YOU SATAN?
OR HIS LIKE, MUTANT PET IGUANA?
NOT REALLY, NO.
WHERE AM I?
THE FLOOR, FOR STARTERS.
I'M ARIZONA, THIS IS MY SHIP.
LIKE... SPACESHIP SHIP?
YEAH, THAT KIND.
SO YOU'RE AN ALIEN!
THAT'S A PRETTY SUBJECTIVE TERM THAT YOU'LL HAVE TO CONTEXTUALIZE FOR ME

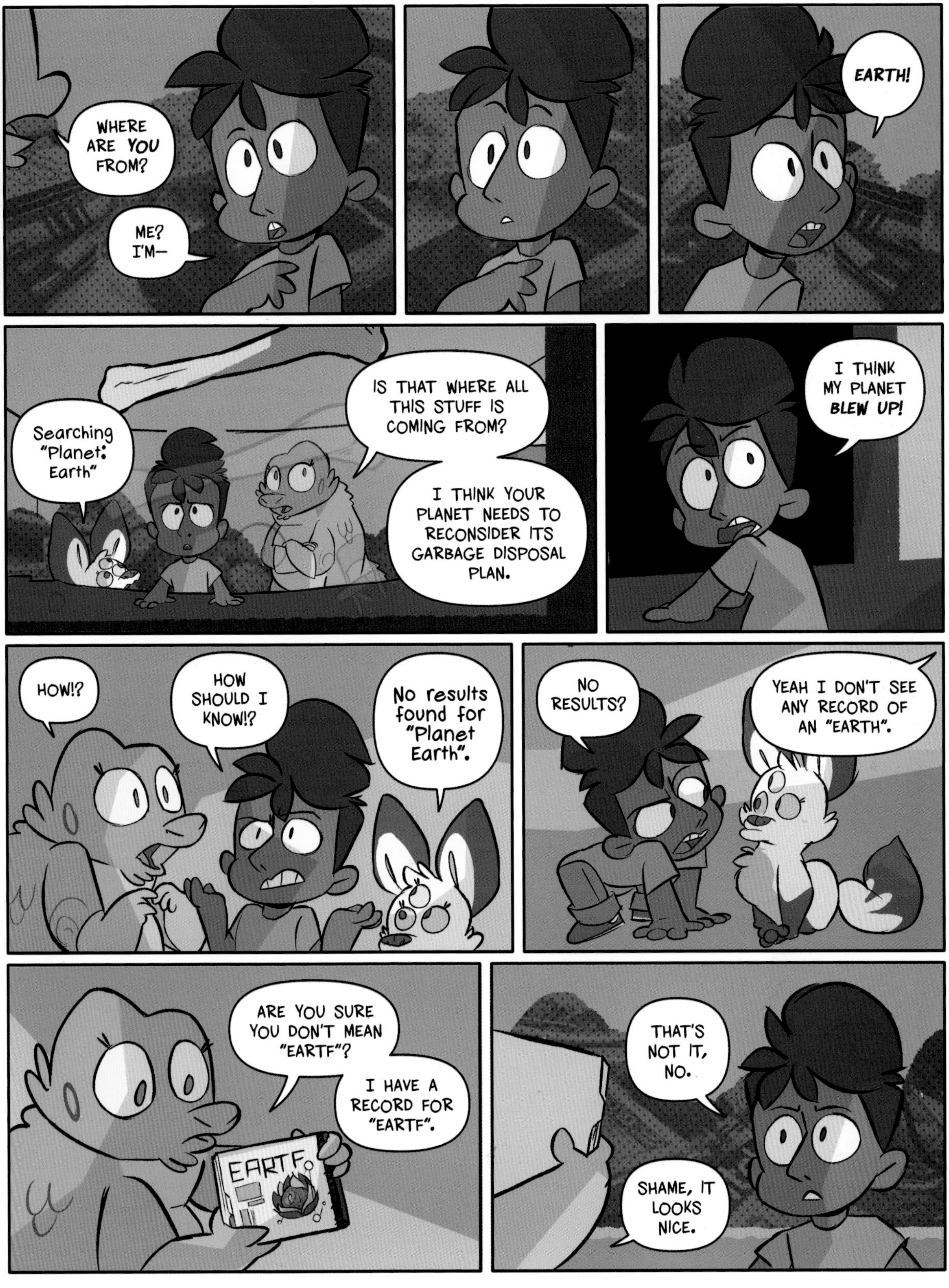
WHERE ARE YOU FROM?
ME? I'M—
EARTH!
Searching "Planet: Earth"
IS THAT WHERE ALL THIS STUFF IS COMING FROM?
I THINK YOUR PLANET NEEDS TO RECONSIDER ITS GARBAGE DISPOSAL PLAN.
I THINK MY PLANET BLEW UP!
HOW!?
HOW SHOULD I KNOW!?
No results found for "Planet Earth".
NO RESULTS?
YEAH I DON'T SEE ANY RECORD OF AN "EARTH".
ARE YOU SURE YOU DON'T MEAN "EARTF"?
I HAVE A RECORD FOR "EARTF".
EARTF
THAT'S NOT IT, NO.
SHAME, IT LOOKS NICE.

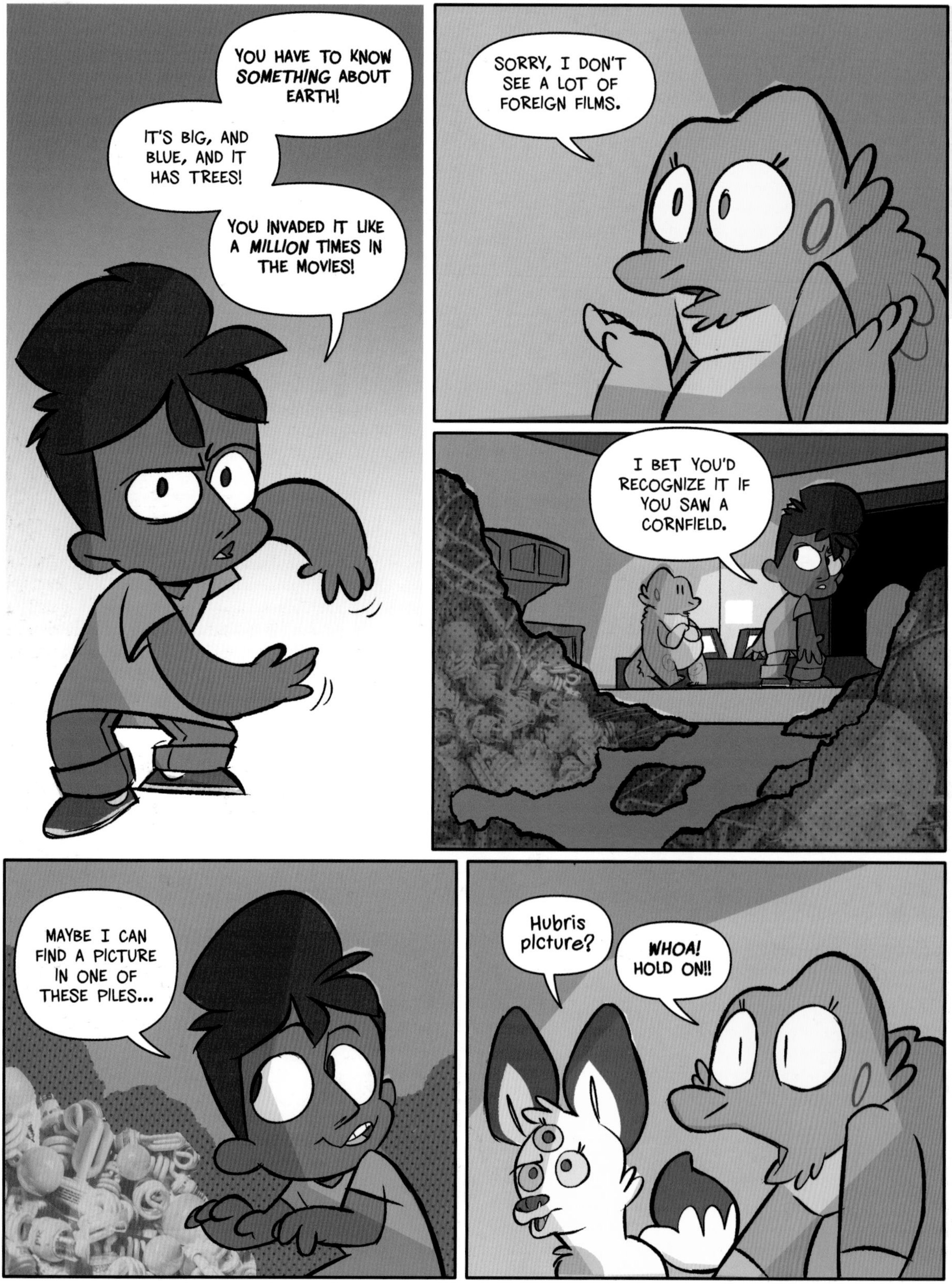
YOU HAVE TO KNOW *SOMETHING* ABOUT EARTH!
IT'S BIG, AND BLUE, AND IT HAS TREES!
YOU INVADED IT LIKE A *MILLION* TIMES IN THE MOVIES!
SORRY, I DON'T SEE A LOT OF FOREIGN FILMS.
I BET YOU'D RECOGNIZE IT IF YOU SAW A CORNFIELD.
MAYBE I CAN FIND A PICTURE IN ONE OF THESE PILES...
Hubris picture?
WHOA! HOLD ON!!

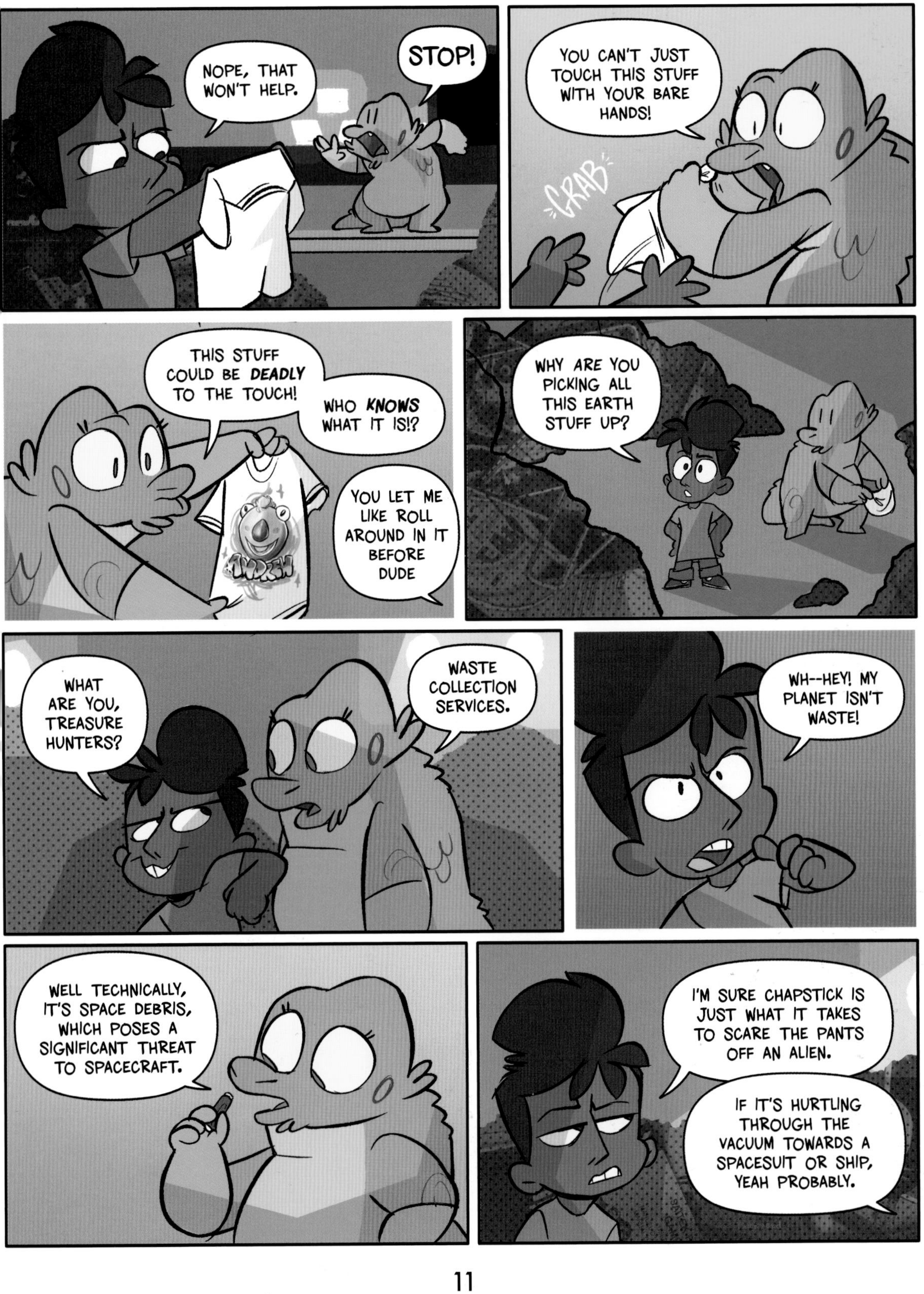
NOPE, THAT WON'T HELP.
STOP!
YOU CAN'T JUST TOUCH THIS STUFF WITH YOUR BARE HANDS!
GRAB
THIS STUFF COULD BE **DEADLY** TO THE TOUCH!
WHO **KNOWS** WHAT IT IS!?
YOU LET ME LIKE ROLL AROUND IN IT BEFORE DUDE
WHY ARE YOU PICKING ALL THIS EARTH STUFF UP?
WHAT ARE YOU, TREASURE HUNTERS?
WASTE COLLECTION SERVICES.
WH--HEY! MY PLANET ISN'T WASTE!
WELL TECHNICALLY, IT'S SPACE DEBRIS, WHICH POSES A SIGNIFICANT THREAT TO SPACECRAFT.
I'M SURE CHAPSTICK IS JUST WHAT IT TAKES TO SCARE THE PANTS OFF AN ALIEN.
IF IT'S HURTLING THROUGH THE VACUUM TOWARDS A SPACESUIT OR SHIP, YEAH PROBABLY.

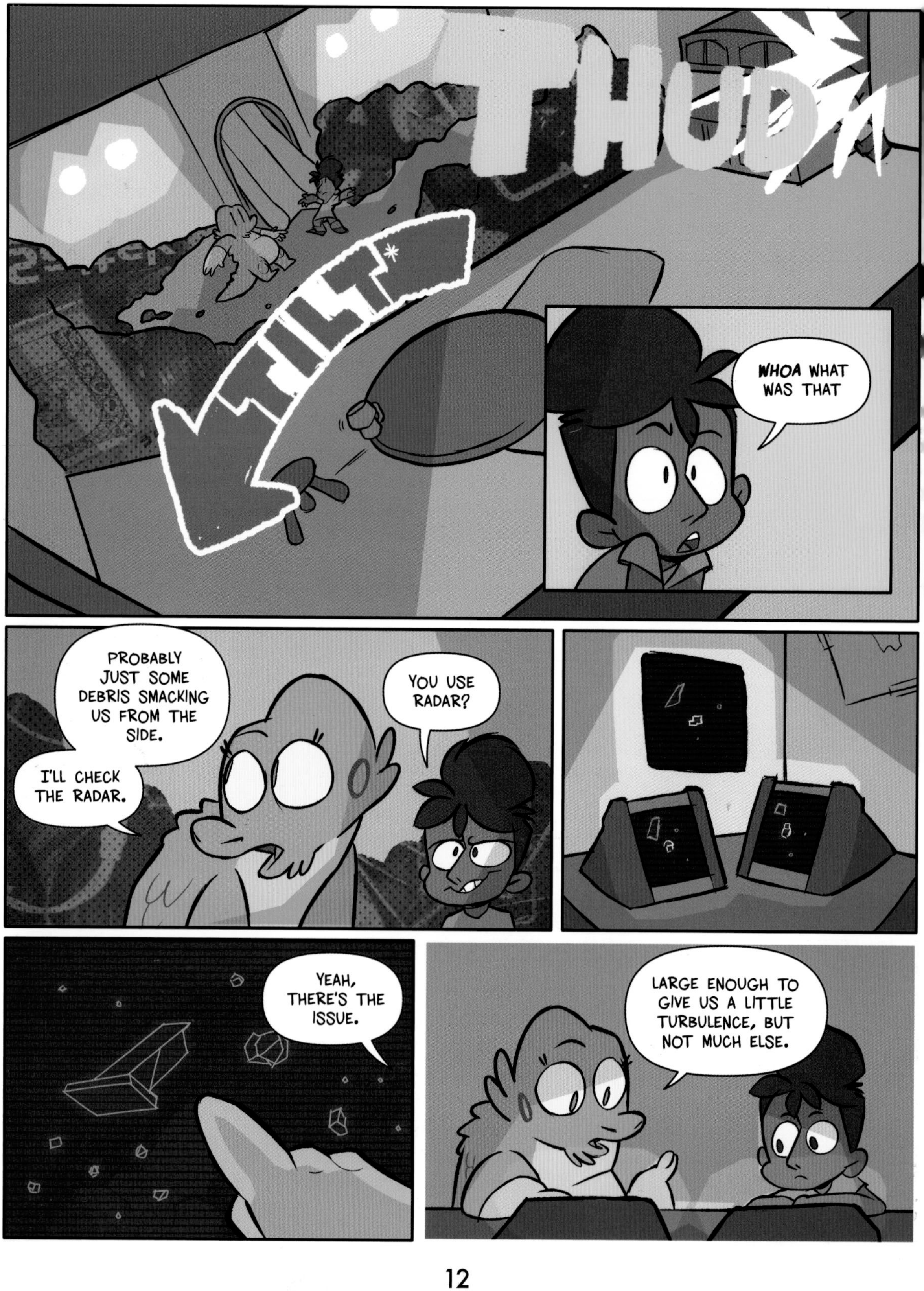
THUD
TILT
WHOA WHAT WAS THAT
PROBABLY JUST SOME DEBRIS SMACKING US FROM THE SIDE.
I'LL CHECK THE RADAR.
YOU USE RADAR?
YEAH, THERE'S THE ISSUE.
LARGE ENOUGH TO GIVE US A LITTLE TURBULENCE, BUT NOT MUCH ELSE.

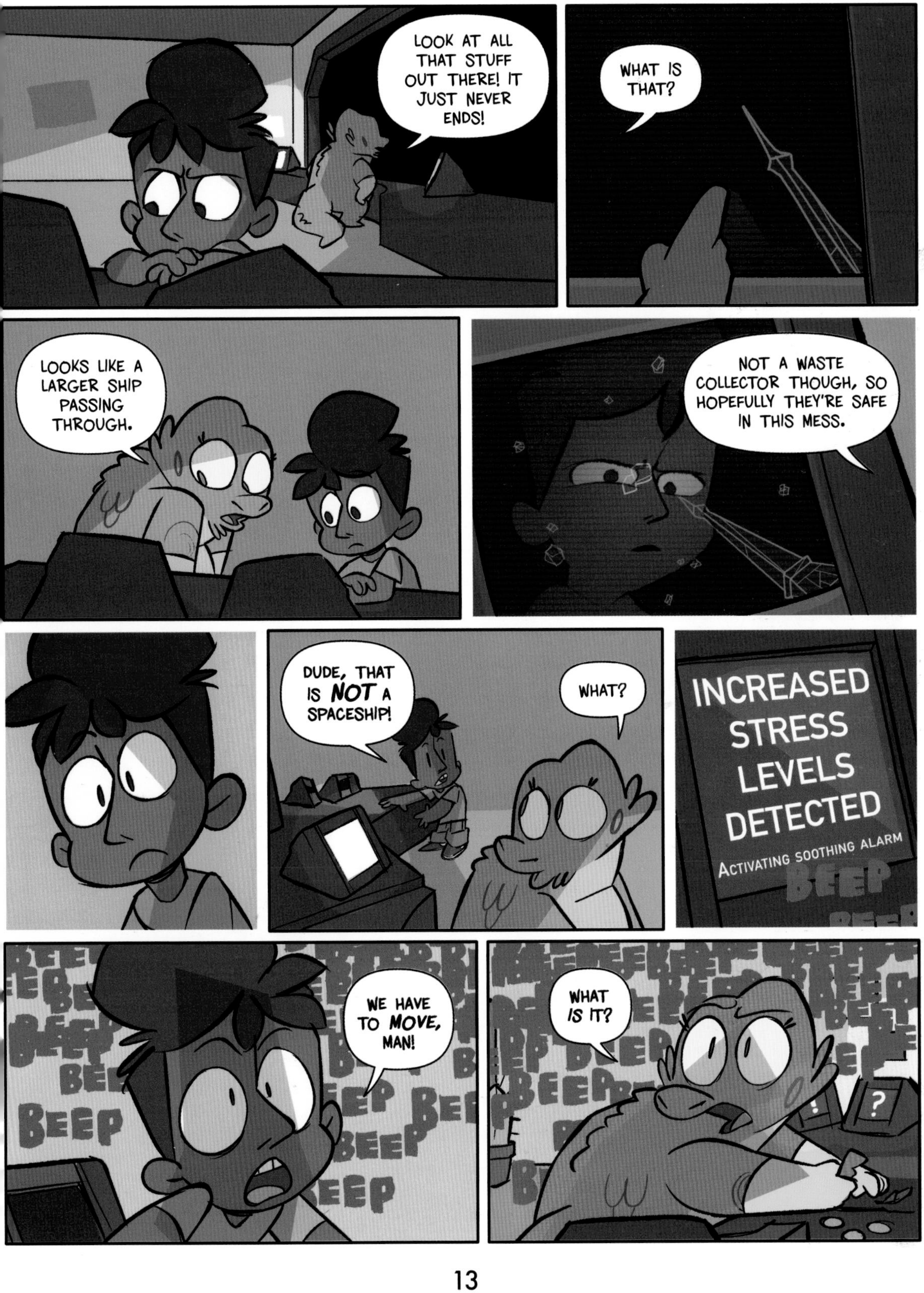

LOOK AT ALL THAT STUFF OUT THERE! IT JUST NEVER ENDS!
WHAT IS THAT?
LOOKS LIKE A LARGER SHIP PASSING THROUGH.
NOT A WASTE COLLECTOR THOUGH, SO HOPEFULLY THEY'RE SAFE IN THIS MESS.
DUDE, THAT IS NOT A SPACESHIP!
WHAT?
INCREASED STRESS LEVELS DETECTED
ACTIVATING SOOTHING ALARM
BEEP
WE HAVE TO MOVE, MAN!
WHAT IS IT?

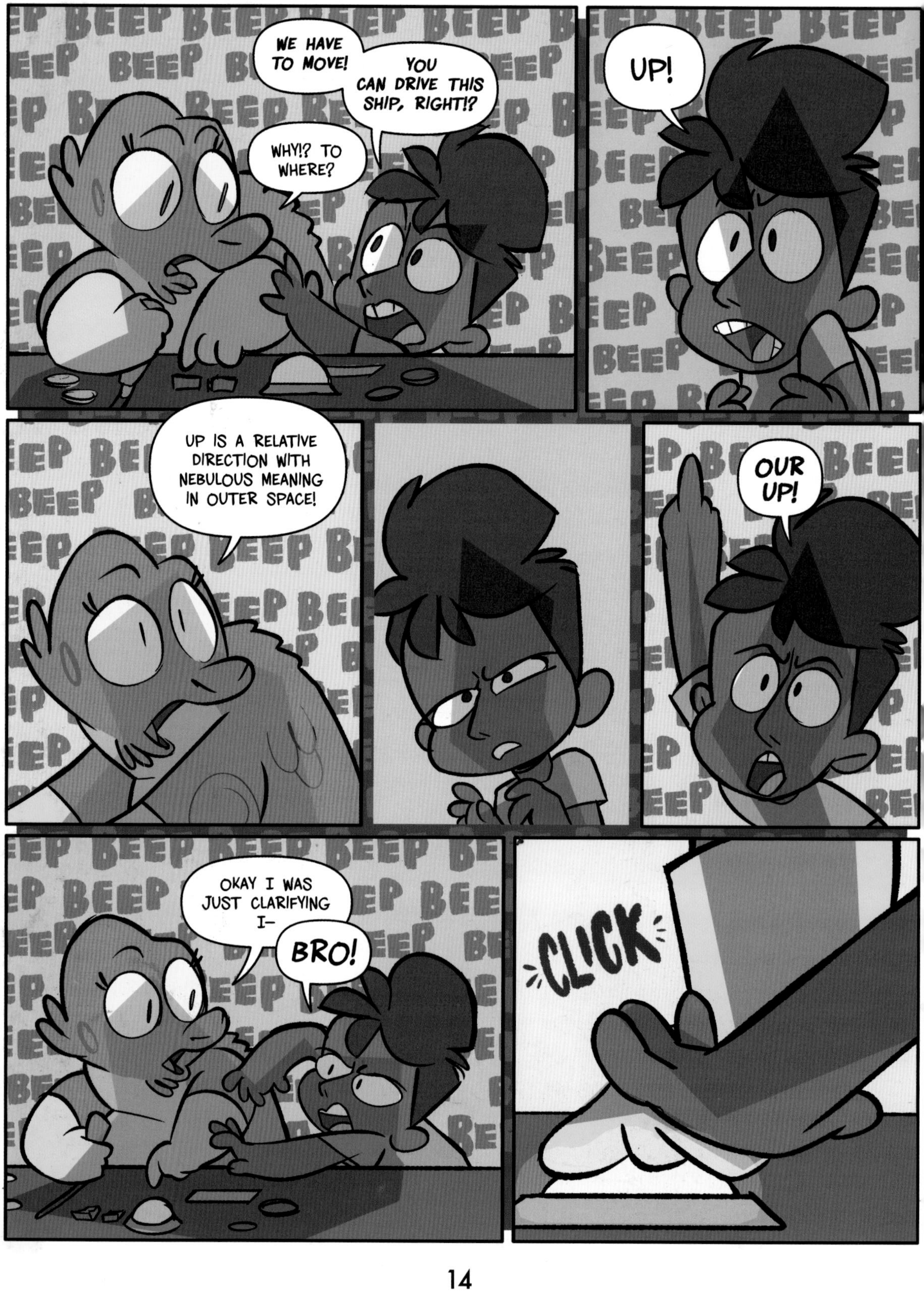
BEEP
WE HAVE TO MOVE!
YOU CAN DRIVE THIS SHIP, RIGHT!?
WHY!? TO WHERE?
UP!
UP IS A RELATIVE DIRECTION WITH NEBULOUS MEANING IN OUTER SPACE!
OUR UP!
OKAY I WAS JUST CLARIFYING I–
BRO!
CLICK

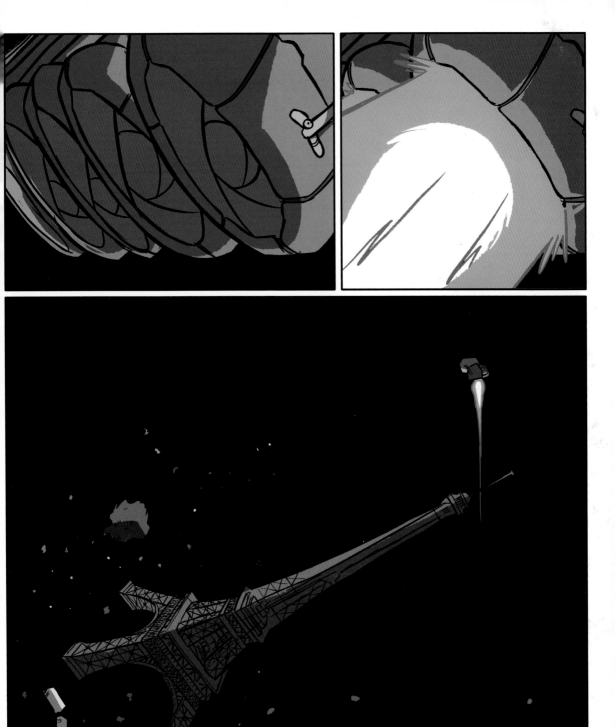

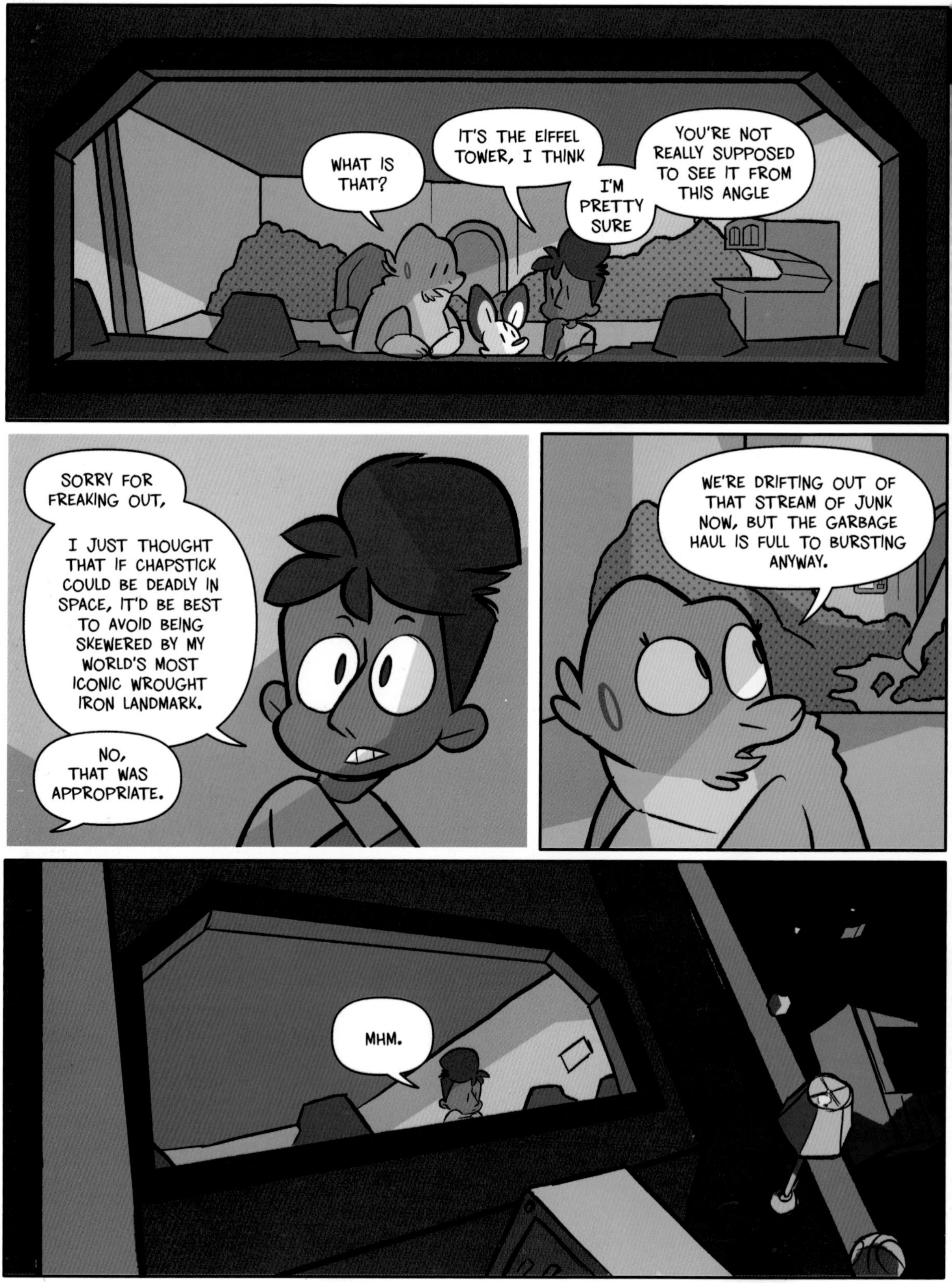
WHAT IS THAT?
IT'S THE EIFFEL TOWER, I THINK
I'M PRETTY SURE
YOU'RE NOT REALLY SUPPOSED TO SEE IT FROM THIS ANGLE
SORRY FOR FREAKING OUT,
I JUST THOUGHT THAT IF CHAPSTICK COULD BE DEADLY IN SPACE, IT'D BE BEST TO AVOID BEING SKEWERED BY MY WORLD'S MOST ICONIC WROUGHT IRON LANDMARK.
NO, THAT WAS APPROPRIATE.
WE'RE DRIFTING OUT OF THAT STREAM OF JUNK NOW, BUT THE GARBAGE HAUL IS FULL TO BURSTING ANYWAY.
MHM.

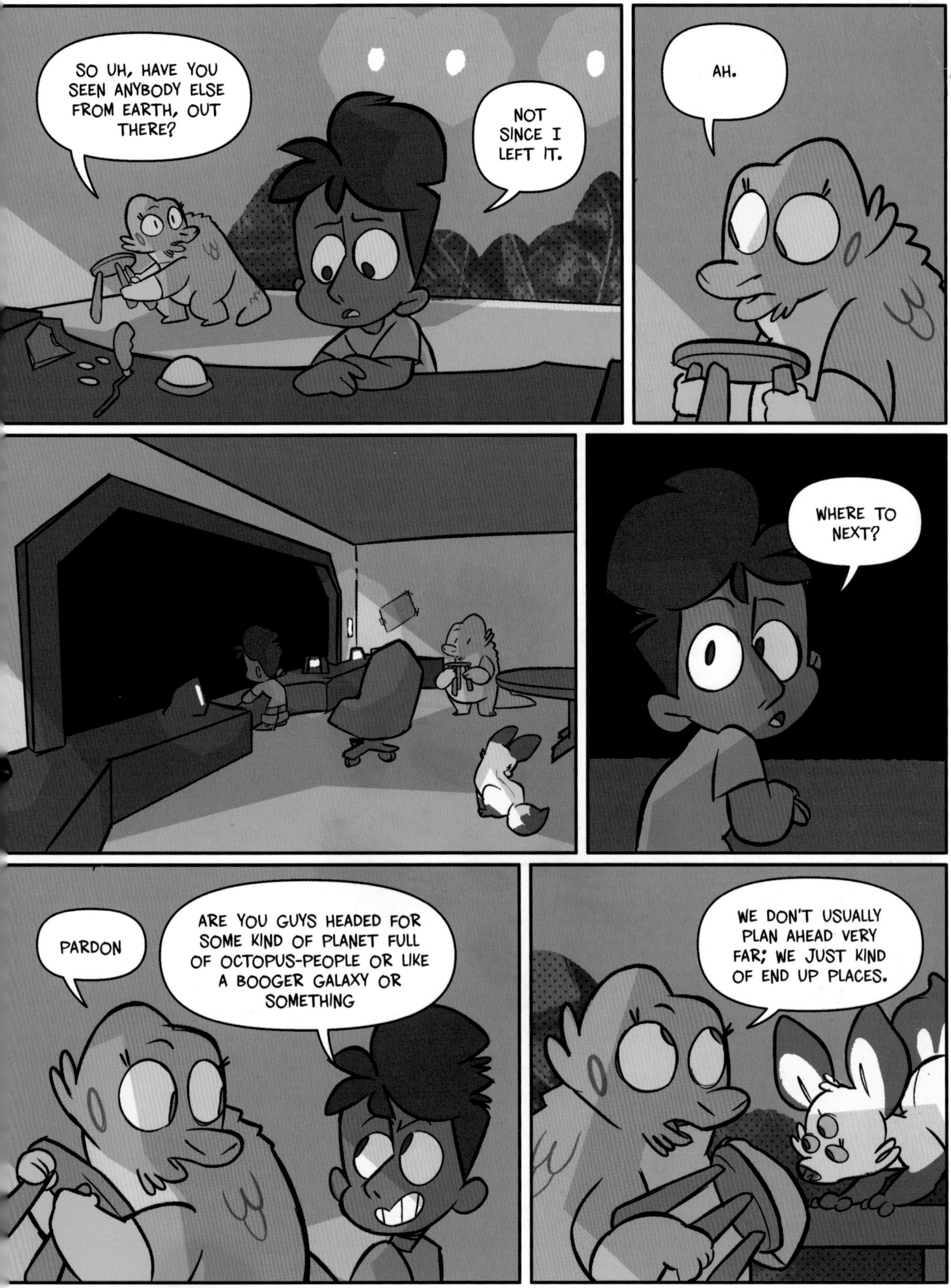
SO UH, HAVE YOU SEEN ANYBODY ELSE FROM EARTH, OUT THERE?
NOT SINCE I LEFT IT.
AH.
WHERE TO NEXT?
PARDON
ARE YOU GUYS HEADED FOR SOME KIND OF PLANET FULL OF OCTOPUS-PEOPLE OR LIKE A BOOGER GALAXY OR SOMETHING
WE DON'T USUALLY PLAN AHEAD VERY FAR; WE JUST KIND OF END UP PLACES.

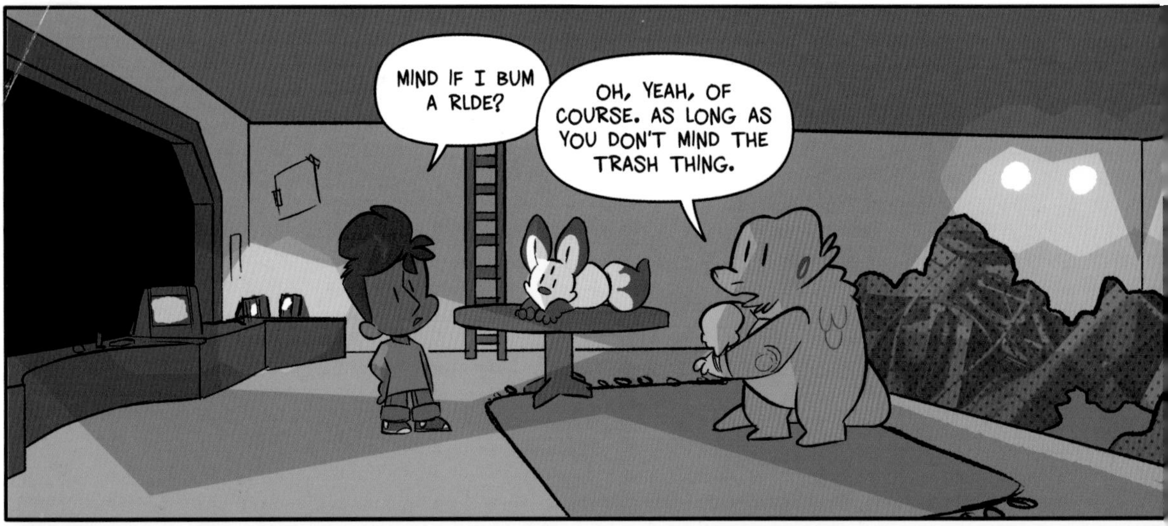
MIND IF I BUM A RLDE?
OH, YEAH, OF COURSE. AS LONG AS YOU DON'T MIND THE TRASH THING.

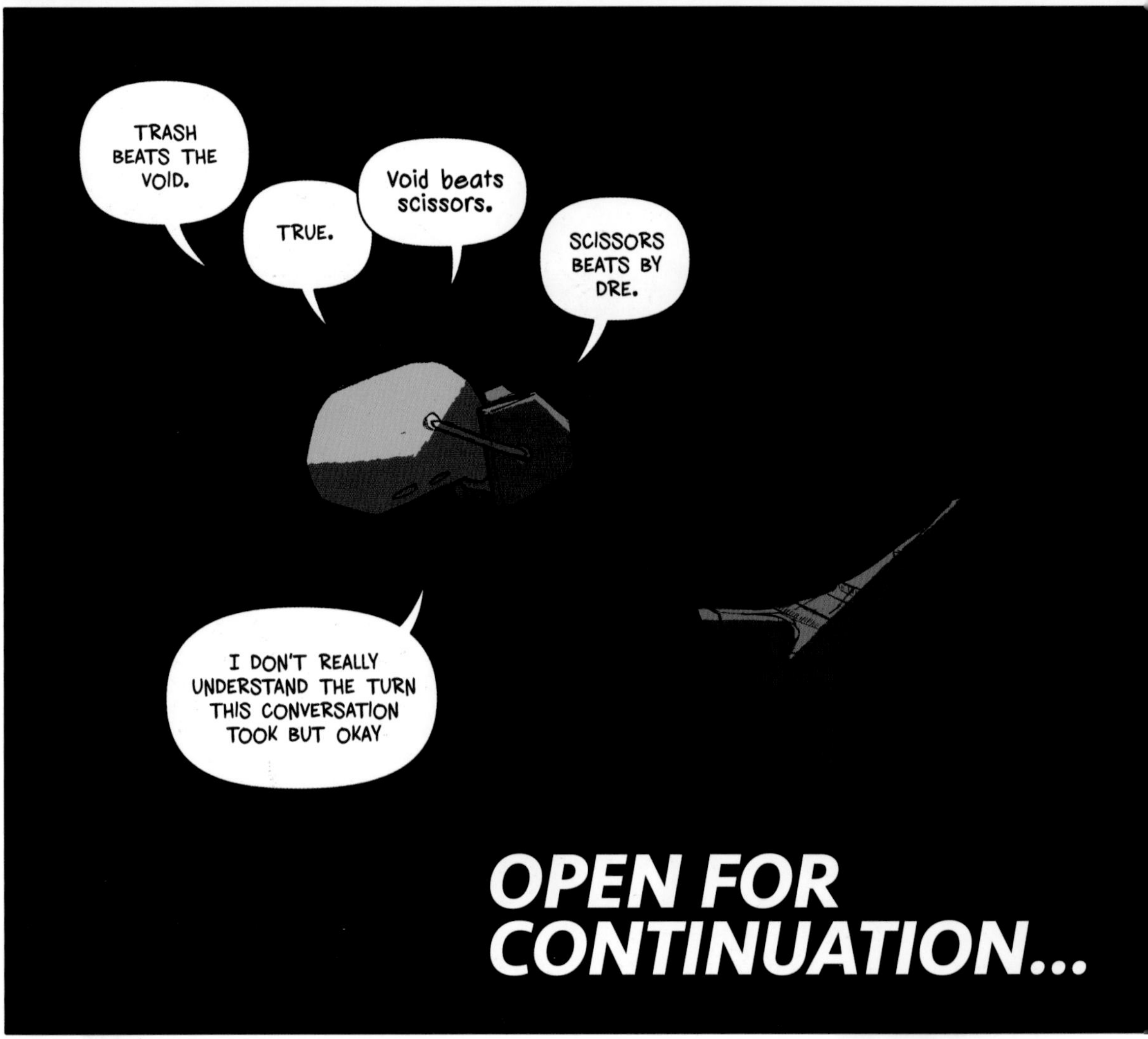
TRASH BEATS THE VOID.
TRUE.
Void beats scissors.
SCISSORS BEATS BY DRE.
I DON'T REALLY UNDERSTAND THE TURN THIS CONVERSATION TOOK BUT OKAY
OPEN FOR CONTINUATION...

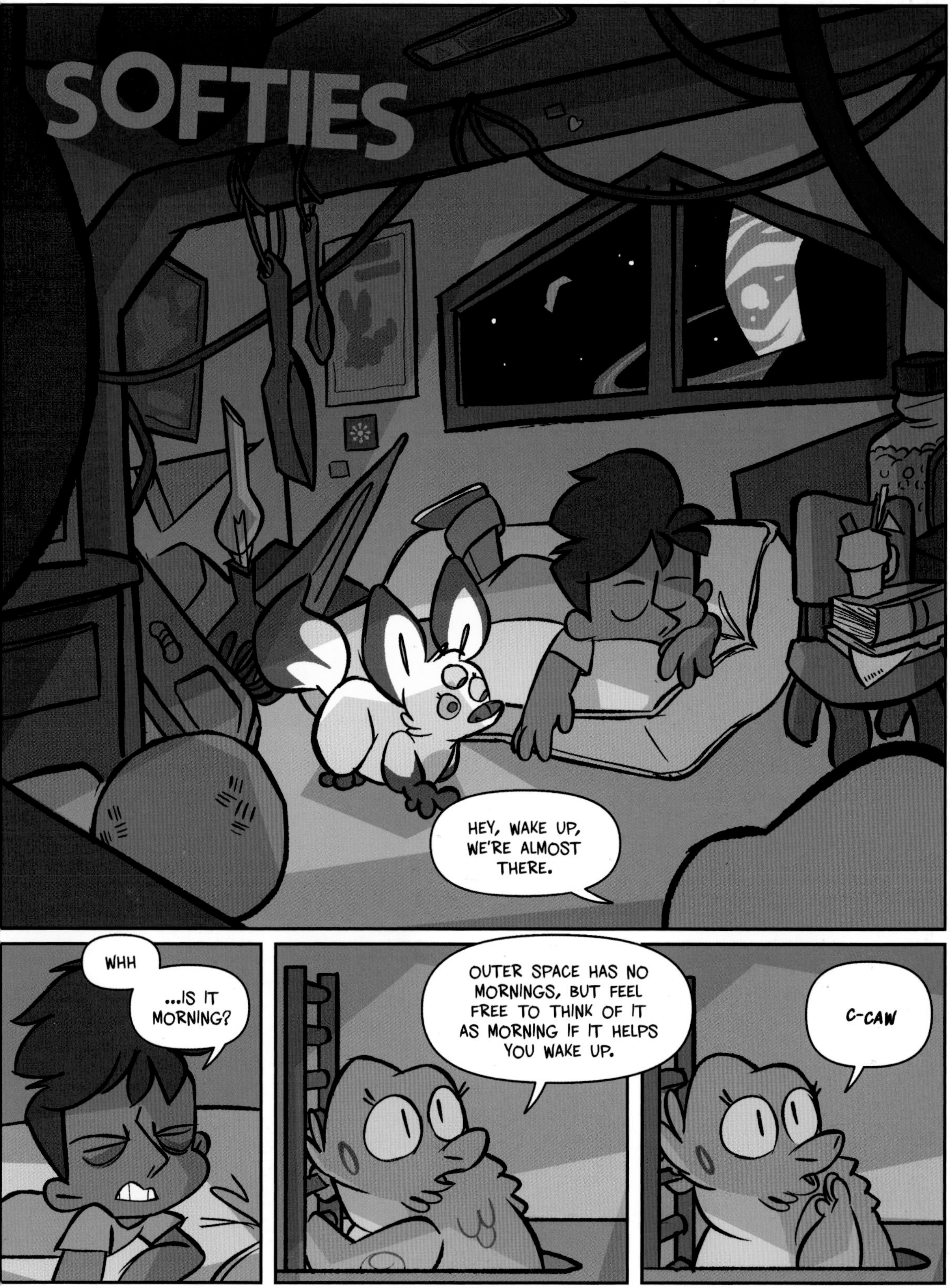
SOFTIES
HEY, WAKE UP, WE'RE ALMOST THERE.
WHH
...IS IT MORNING?
OUTER SPACE HAS NO MORNINGS, BUT FEEL FREE TO THINK OF IT AS MORNING IF IT HELPS YOU WAKE UP.
C-CAW

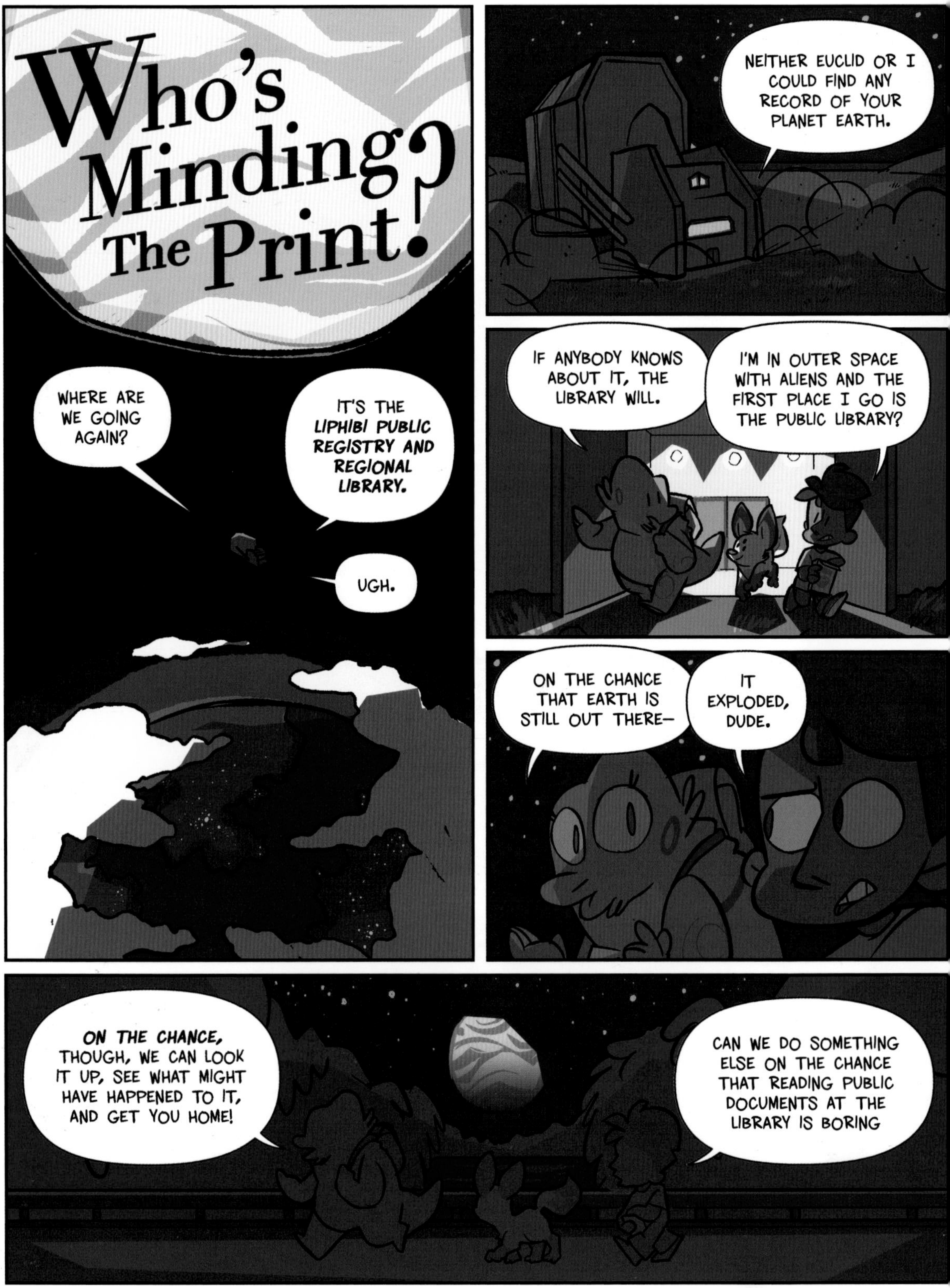
Who's Minding The Print?
WHERE ARE WE GOING AGAIN?
IT'S THE LIPHIBI PUBLIC REGISTRY AND REGIONAL LIBRARY.
UGH.
NEITHER EUCLID OR I COULD FIND ANY RECORD OF YOUR PLANET EARTH.
IF ANYBODY KNOWS ABOUT IT, THE LIBRARY WILL.
I'M IN OUTER SPACE WITH ALIENS AND THE FIRST PLACE I GO IS THE PUBLIC LIBRARY?
ON THE CHANCE THAT EARTH IS STILL OUT THERE–
IT EXPLODED, DUDE.
ON THE CHANCE, THOUGH, WE CAN LOOK IT UP, SEE WHAT MIGHT HAVE HAPPENED TO IT, AND GET YOU HOME!
CAN WE DO SOMETHING ELSE ON THE CHANCE THAT READING PUBLIC DOCUMENTS AT THE LIBRARY IS BORING

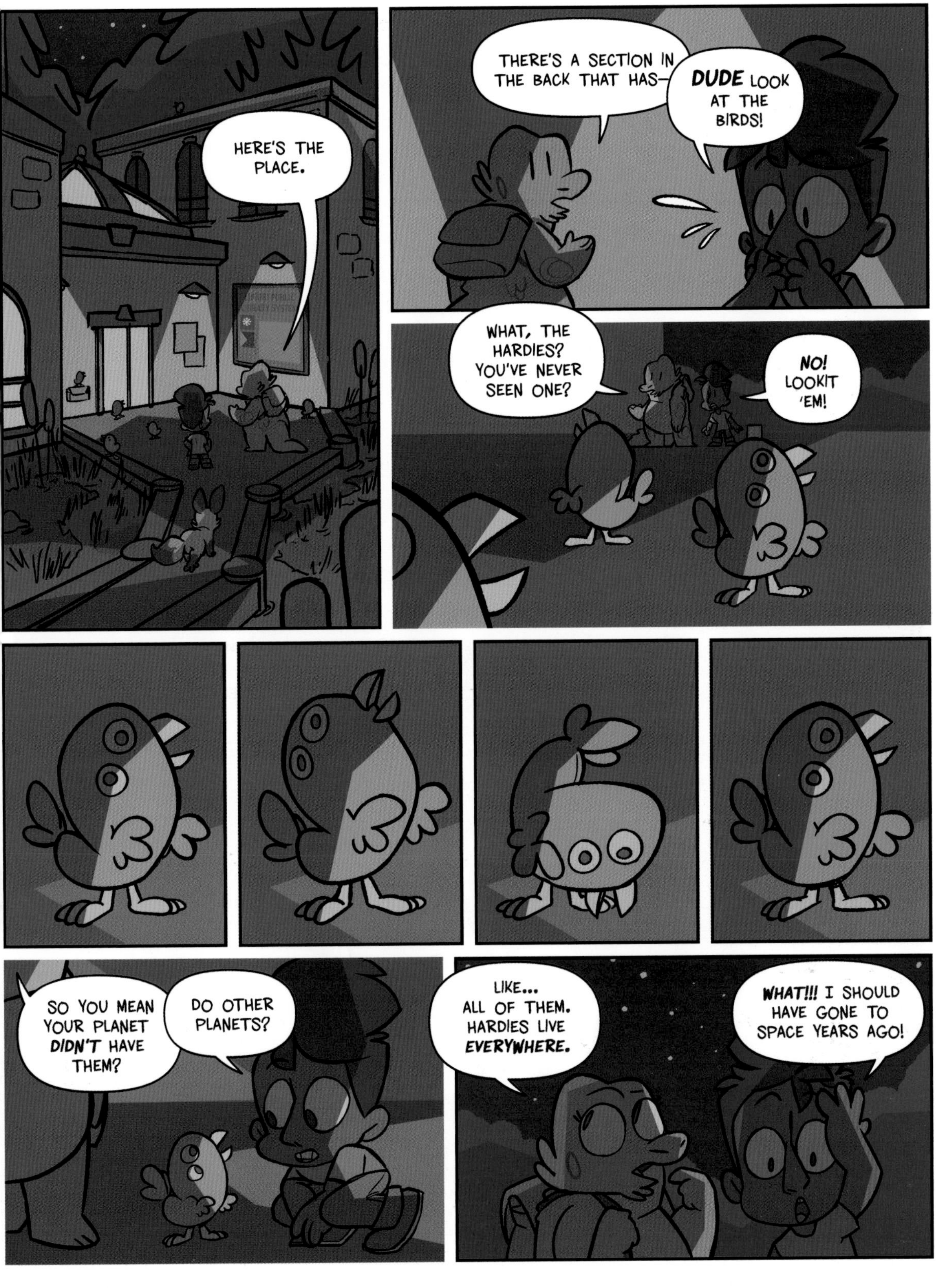
HERE'S THE PLACE.
THERE'S A SECTION IN THE BACK THAT HAS—
DUDE LOOK AT THE BIRDS!
WHAT, THE HARDIES? YOU'VE NEVER SEEN ONE?
NO! LOOKIT 'EM!
SO YOU MEAN YOUR PLANET DIDN'T HAVE THEM?
DO OTHER PLANETS?
LIKE... ALL OF THEM. HARDIES LIVE EVERYWHERE.
WHAT!!! I SHOULD HAVE GONE TO SPACE YEARS AGO!

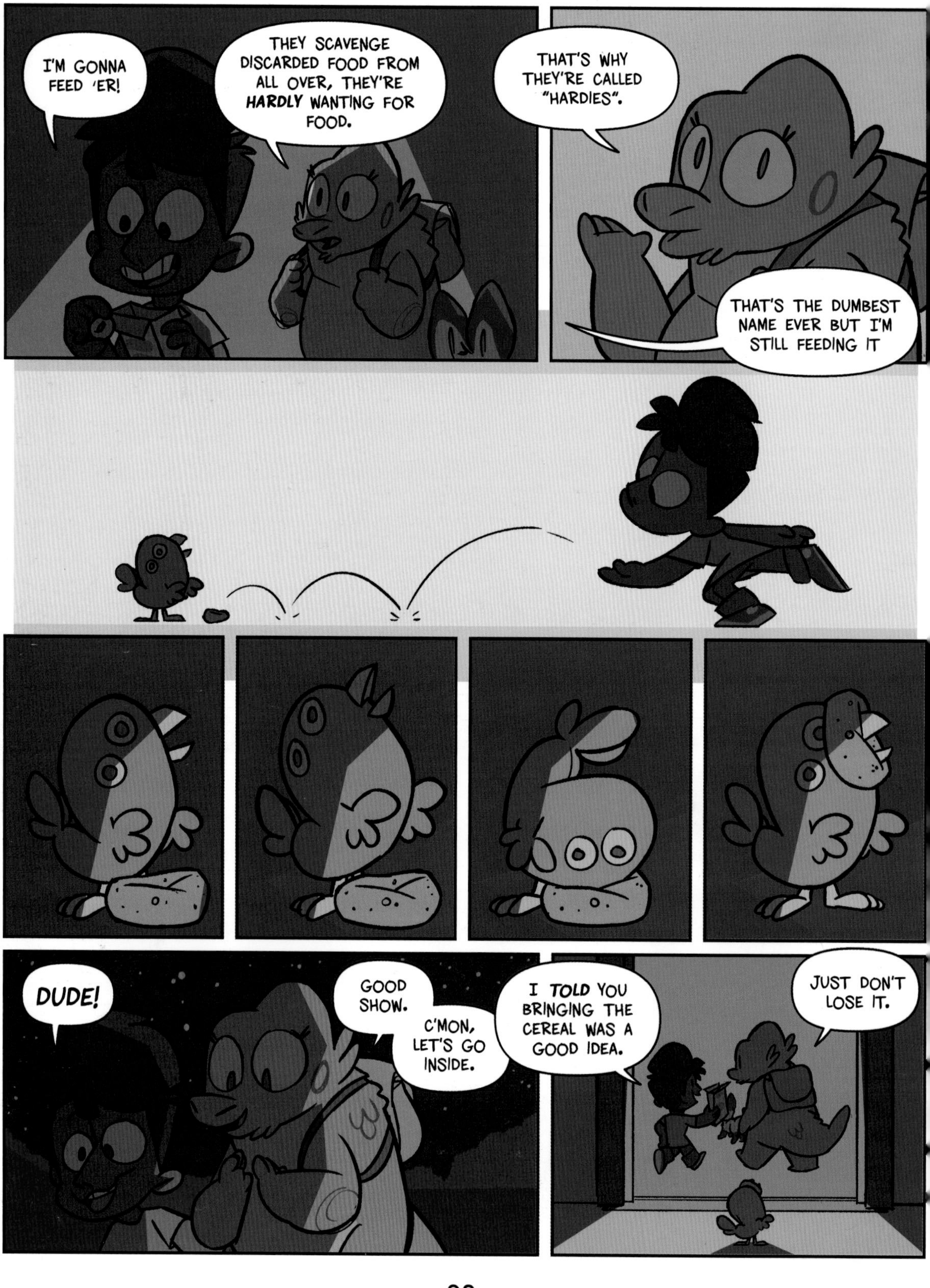
I'M GONNA FEED 'ER!
THEY SCAVENGE DISCARDED FOOD FROM ALL OVER, THEY'RE HARDLY WANTING FOR FOOD.
THAT'S WHY THEY'RE CALLED "HARDIES".
THAT'S THE DUMBEST NAME EVER BUT I'M STILL FEEDING IT
DUDE!
GOOD SHOW.
C'MON, LET'S GO INSIDE.
I TOLD YOU BRINGING THE CEREAL WAS A GOOD IDEA.
JUST DON'T LOSE IT.

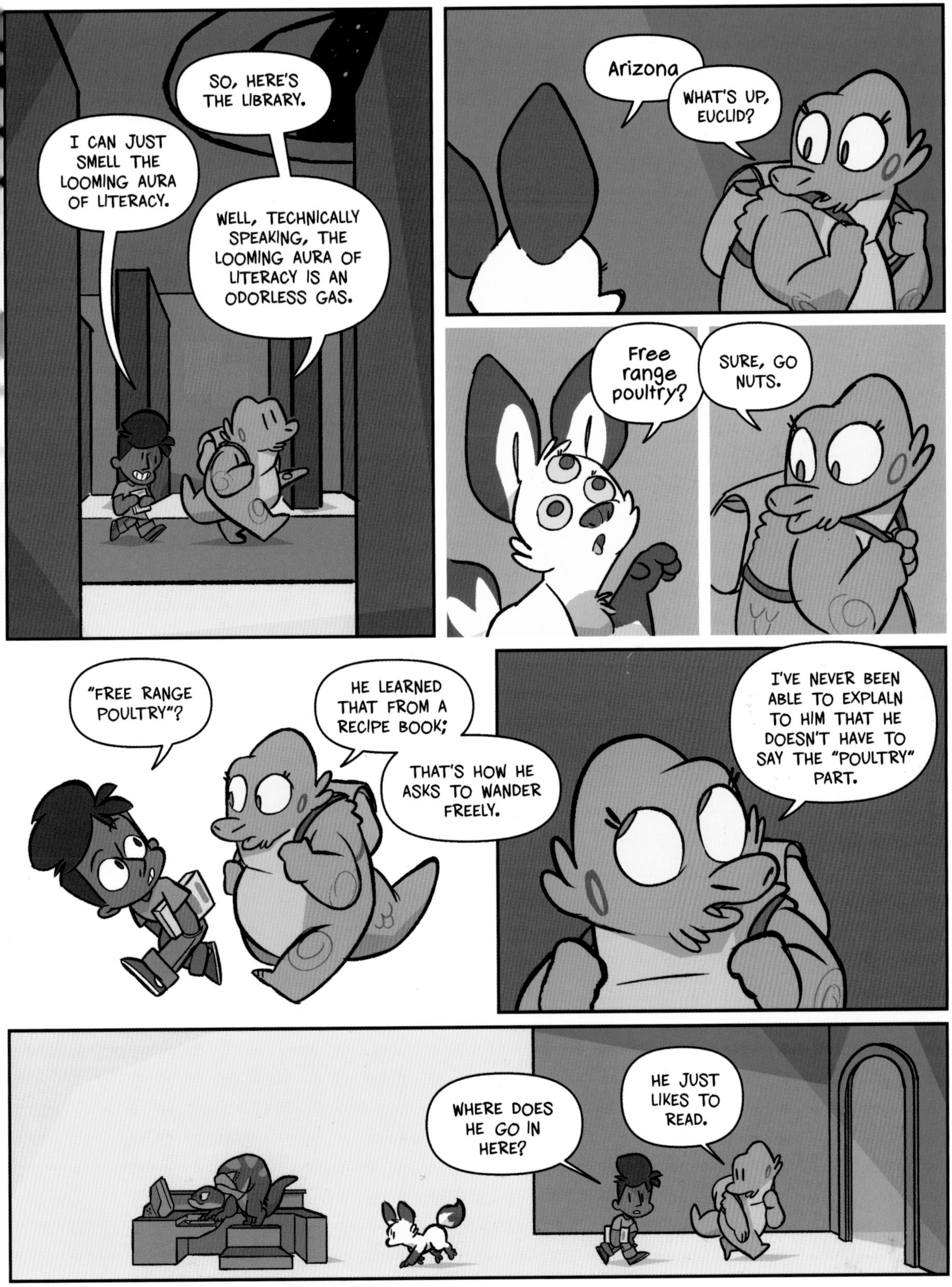

SO, HERE'S THE LIBRARY.
I CAN JUST SMELL THE LOOMING AURA OF LITERACY.
WELL, TECHNICALLY SPEAKING, THE LOOMING AURA OF LITERACY IS AN ODORLESS GAS.
Arizona
WHAT'S UP, EUCLID?
Free range poultry?
SURE, GO NUTS.
"FREE RANGE POULTRY"?
HE LEARNED THAT FROM A RECIPE BOOK;
THAT'S HOW HE ASKS TO WANDER FREELY.
I'VE NEVER BEEN ABLE TO EXPLALN TO HIM THAT HE DOESN'T HAVE TO SAY THE "POULTRY" PART.
WHERE DOES HE GO IN HERE?
HE JUST LIKES TO READ.

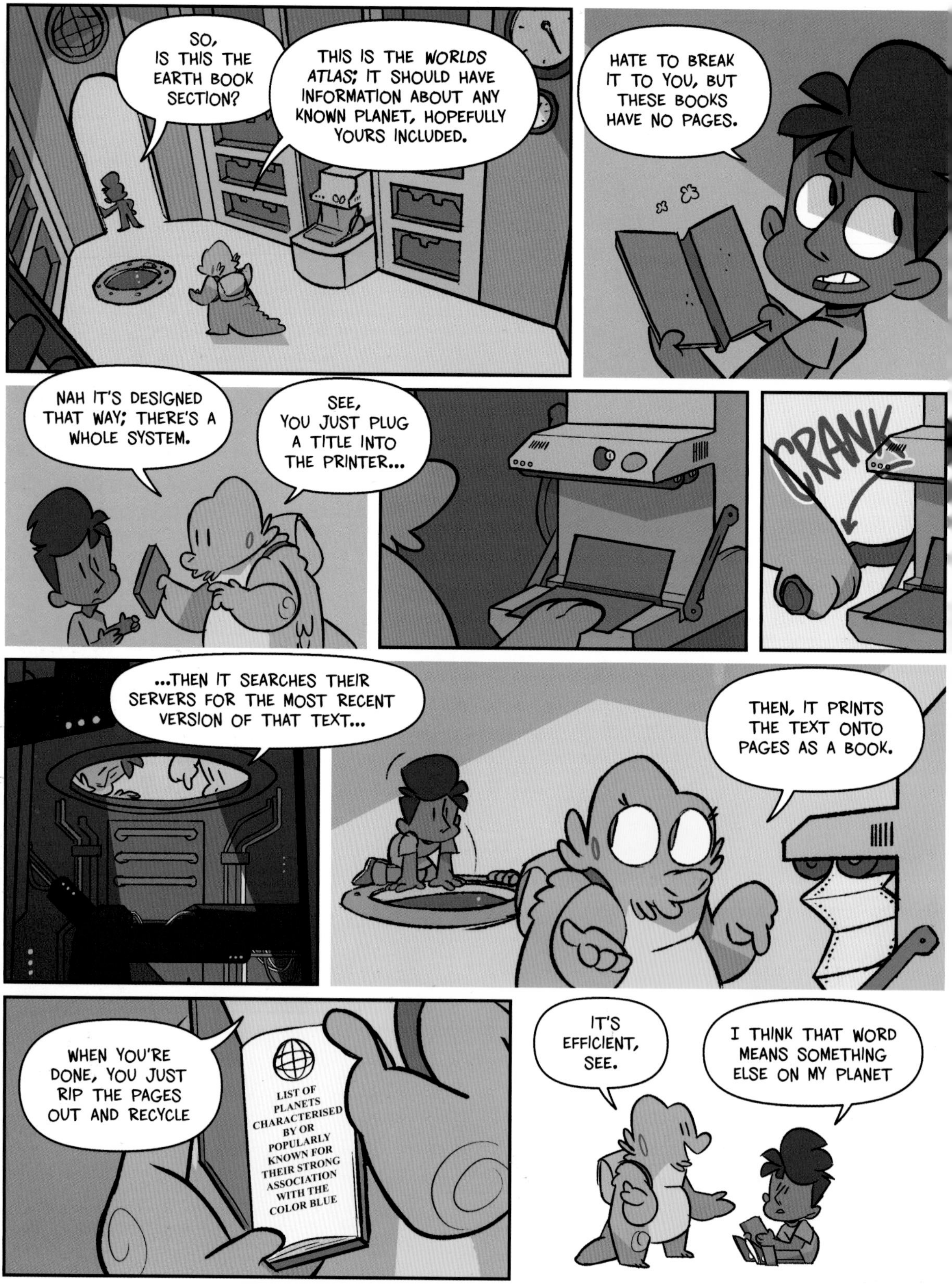
SO, IS THIS THE EARTH BOOK SECTION?
THIS IS THE *WORLDS ATLAS*; IT SHOULD HAVE INFORMATION ABOUT ANY KNOWN PLANET, HOPEFULLY YOURS INCLUDED.
HATE TO BREAK IT TO YOU, BUT THESE BOOKS HAVE NO PAGES.
NAH IT'S DESIGNED THAT WAY; THERE'S A WHOLE SYSTEM.
SEE, YOU JUST PLUG A TITLE INTO THE PRINTER...
CRANK
...THEN IT SEARCHES THEIR SERVERS FOR THE MOST RECENT VERSION OF THAT TEXT...
THEN, IT PRINTS THE TEXT ONTO PAGES AS A BOOK.
WHEN YOU'RE DONE, YOU JUST RIP THE PAGES OUT AND RECYCLE
LIST OF PLANETS CHARACTERISED BY OR POPULARLY KNOWN FOR THEIR STRONG ASSOCIATION WITH THE COLOR BLUE
IT'S EFFICIENT, SEE.
I THINK THAT WORD MEANS SOMETHING ELSE ON MY PLANET

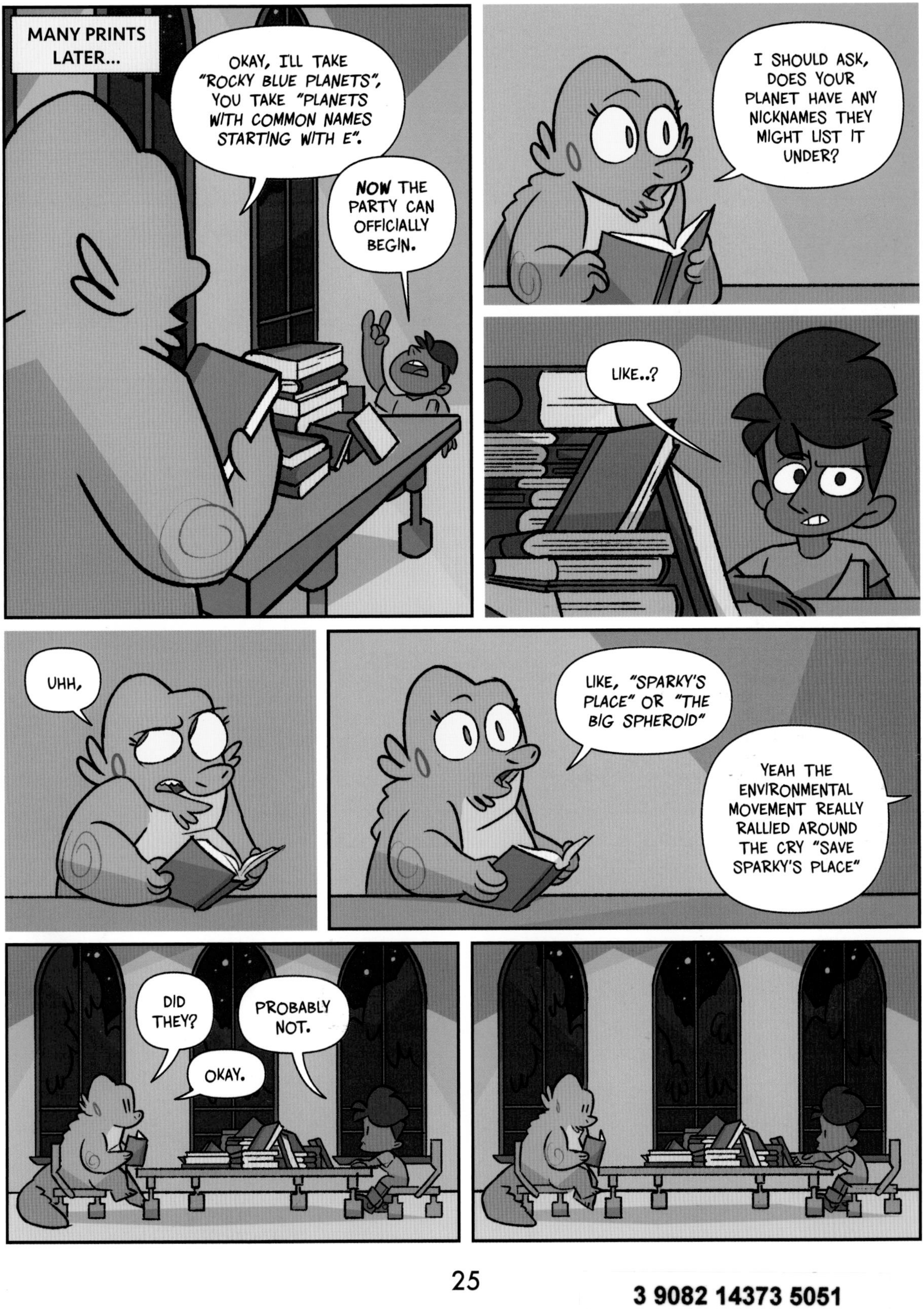
MANY PRINTS LATER...
OKAY, I'LL TAKE "ROCKY BLUE PLANETS", YOU TAKE "PLANETS WITH COMMON NAMES STARTING WITH E".
NOW THE PARTY CAN OFFICIALLY BEGIN.
I SHOULD ASK, DOES YOUR PLANET HAVE ANY NICKNAMES THEY MIGHT LIST IT UNDER?
LIKE..?
UHH,
LIKE, "SPARKY'S PLACE" OR "THE BIG SPHEROID"
YEAH THE ENVIRONMENTAL MOVEMENT REALLY RALLIED AROUND THE CRY "SAVE SPARKY'S PLACE"
DID THEY?
PROBABLY NOT.
OKAY.

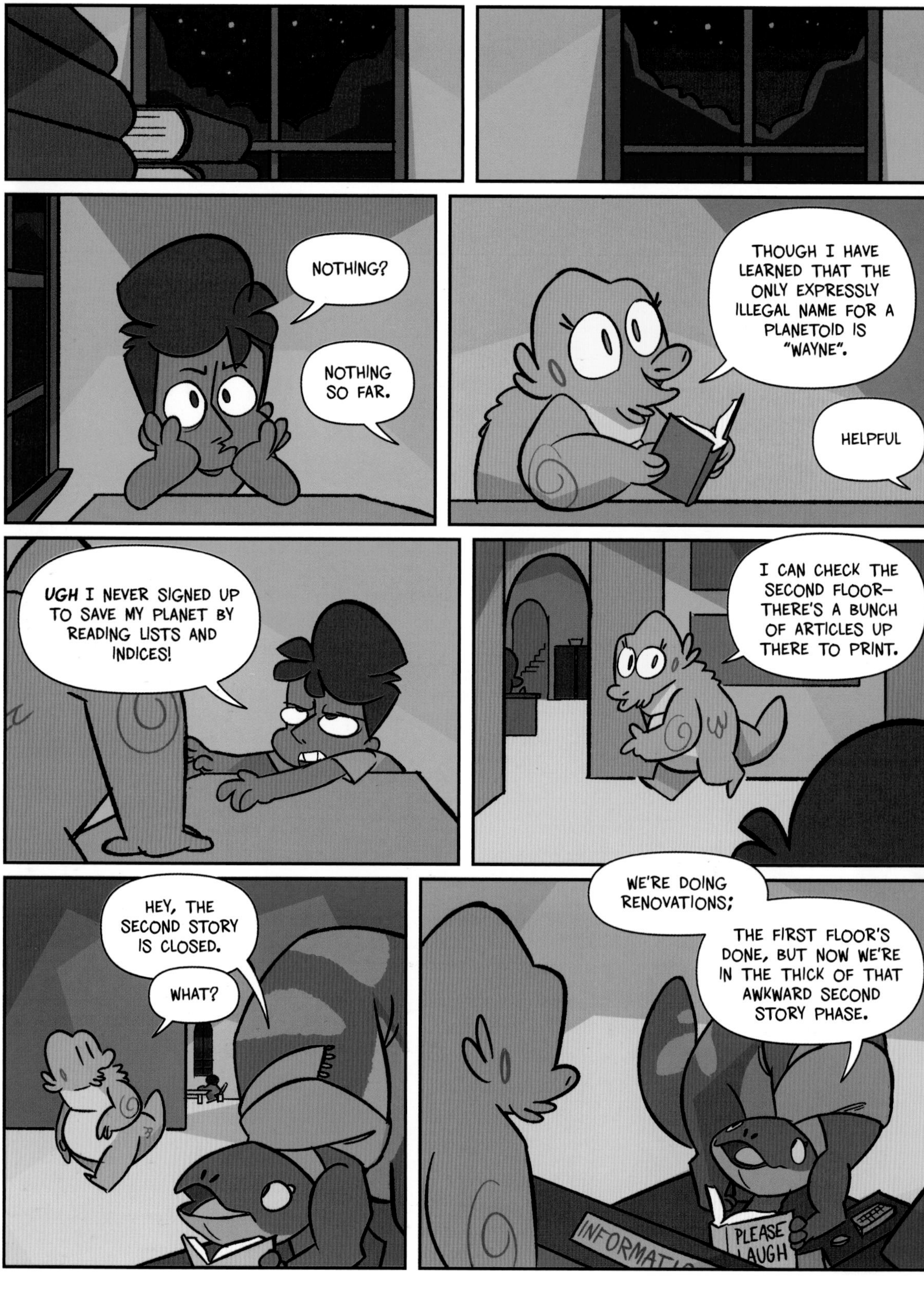
NOTHING?
NOTHING SO FAR.
THOUGH I HAVE LEARNED THAT THE ONLY EXPRESSLY ILLEGAL NAME FOR A PLANETOID IS "WAYNE".
HELPFUL
UGH I NEVER SIGNED UP TO SAVE MY PLANET BY READING LISTS AND INDICES!
I CAN CHECK THE SECOND FLOOR— THERE'S A BUNCH OF ARTICLES UP THERE TO PRINT.
HEY, THE SECOND STORY IS CLOSED.
WHAT?
WE'RE DOING RENOVATIONS;
THE FIRST FLOOR'S DONE, BUT NOW WE'RE IN THE THICK OF THAT AWKWARD SECOND STORY PHASE.
PLEASE LAUGH

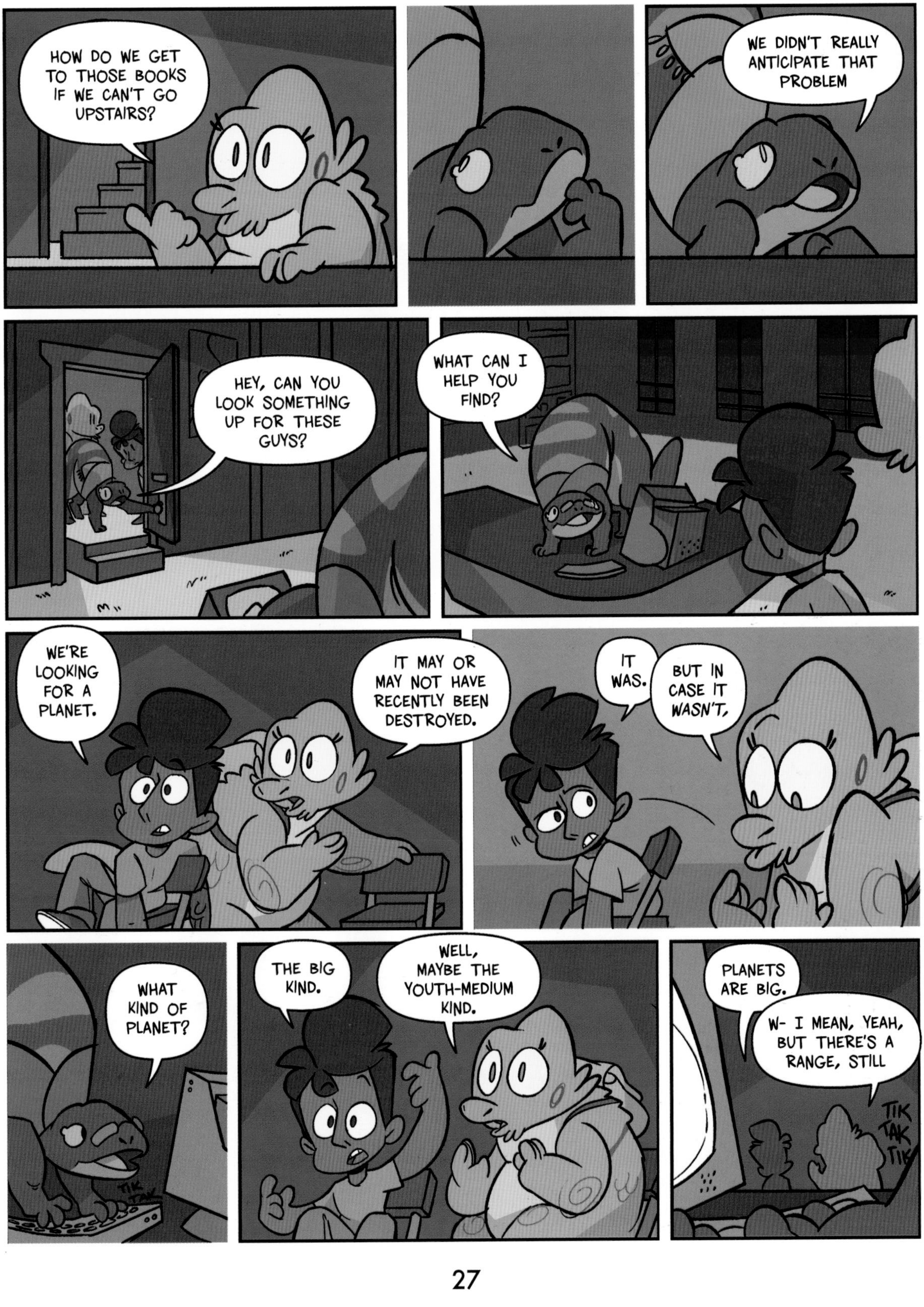

HOW DO WE GET TO THOSE BOOKS IF WE CAN'T GO UPSTAIRS?
WE DIDN'T REALLY ANTICIPATE THAT PROBLEM
HEY, CAN YOU LOOK SOMETHING UP FOR THESE GUYS?
WHAT CAN I HELP YOU FIND?
WE'RE LOOKING FOR A PLANET.
IT MAY OR MAY NOT HAVE RECENTLY BEEN DESTROYED.
IT WAS.
BUT IN CASE IT WASN'T,
WHAT KIND OF PLANET?
TIK TAK
THE BIG KIND.
WELL, MAYBE THE YOUTH-MEDIUM KIND.
PLANETS ARE BIG.
W- I MEAN, YEAH, BUT THERE'S A RANGE, STILL
TIK TAK TIK

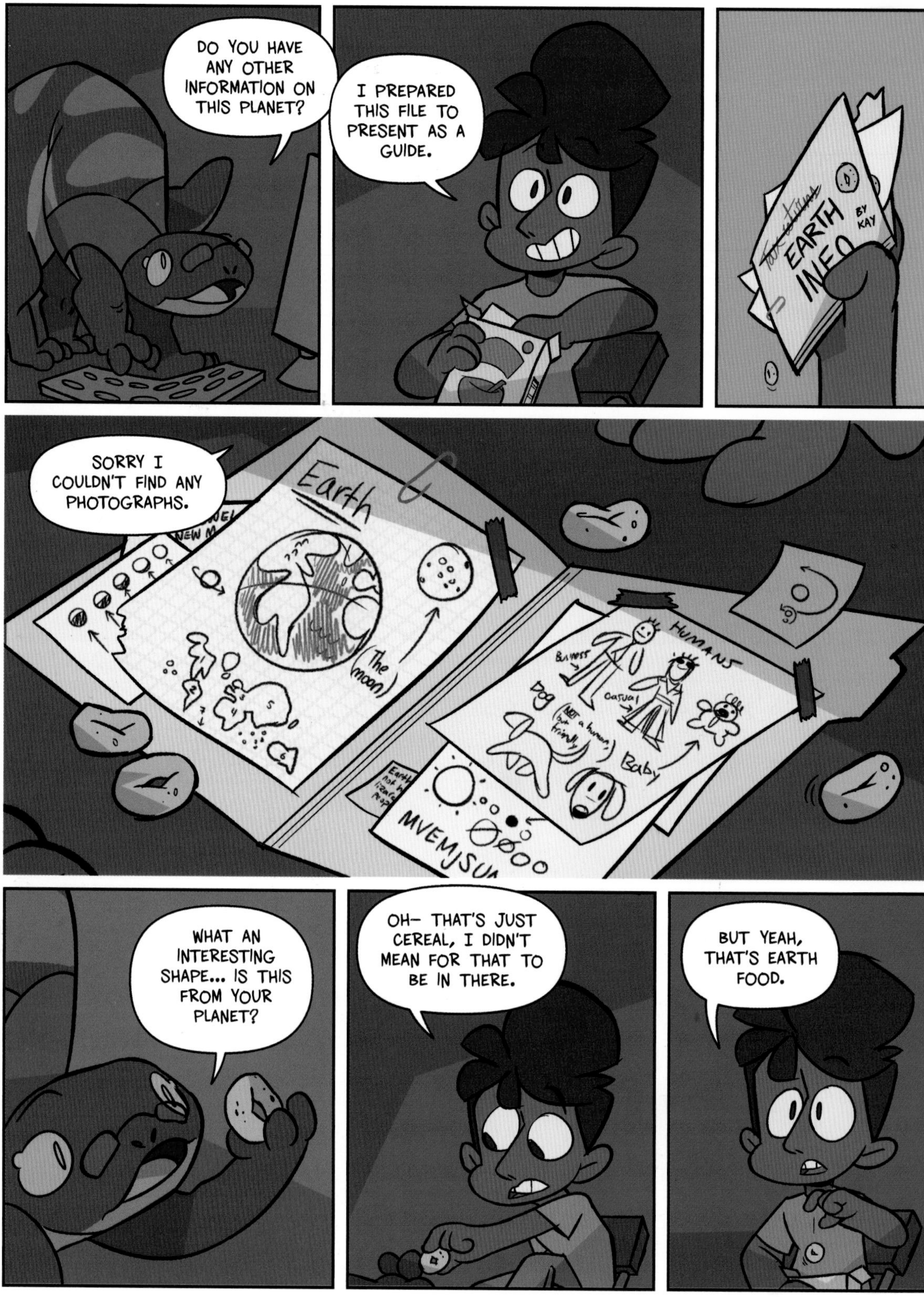
DO YOU HAVE ANY OTHER INFORMATION ON THIS PLANET?
I PREPARED THIS FILE TO PRESENT AS A GUIDE.
EARTH INFO
BY KAY
SORRY I COULDN'T FIND ANY PHOTOGRAPHS.
Earth
(The moon)
HUMANS
casual
Dog
Baby
WHAT AN INTERESTING SHAPE... IS THIS FROM YOUR PLANET?
OH– THAT'S JUST CEREAL, I DIDN'T MEAN FOR THAT TO BE IN THERE.
BUT YEAH, THAT'S EARTH FOOD.

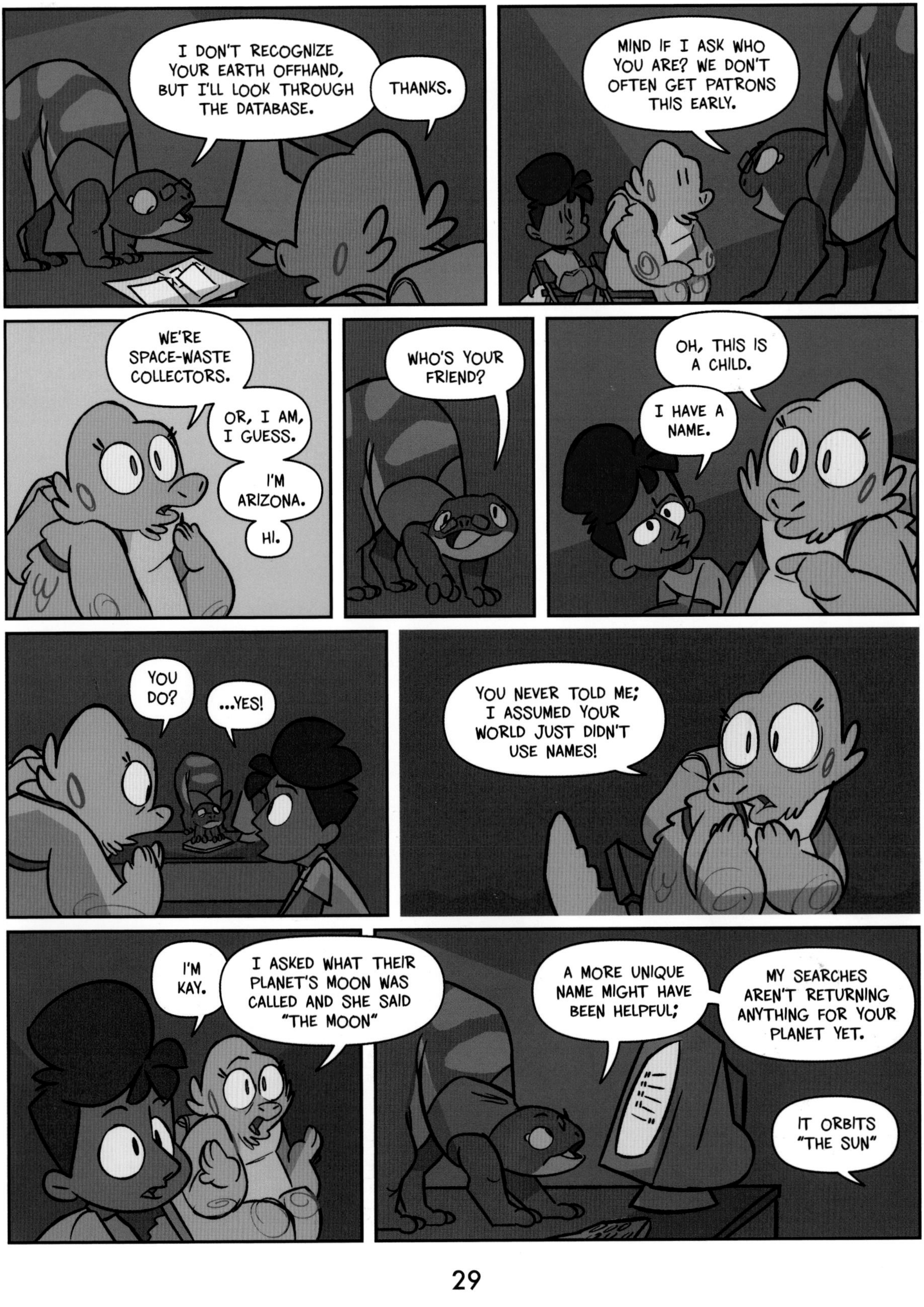
I DON'T RECOGNIZE YOUR EARTH OFFHAND, BUT I'LL LOOK THROUGH THE DATABASE.
THANKS.
MIND IF I ASK WHO YOU ARE? WE DON'T OFTEN GET PATRONS THIS EARLY.
WE'RE SPACE-WASTE COLLECTORS.
OR, I AM, I GUESS.
I'M ARIZONA.
HI.
WHO'S YOUR FRIEND?
OH, THIS IS A CHILD.
I HAVE A NAME.
YOU DO?
...YES!
YOU NEVER TOLD ME; I ASSUMED YOUR WORLD JUST DIDN'T USE NAMES!
I'M KAY.
I ASKED WHAT THEIR PLANET'S MOON WAS CALLED AND SHE SAID "THE MOON"
A MORE UNIQUE NAME MIGHT HAVE BEEN HELPFUL;
MY SEARCHES AREN'T RETURNING ANYTHING FOR YOUR PLANET YET.
IT ORBITS "THE SUN"

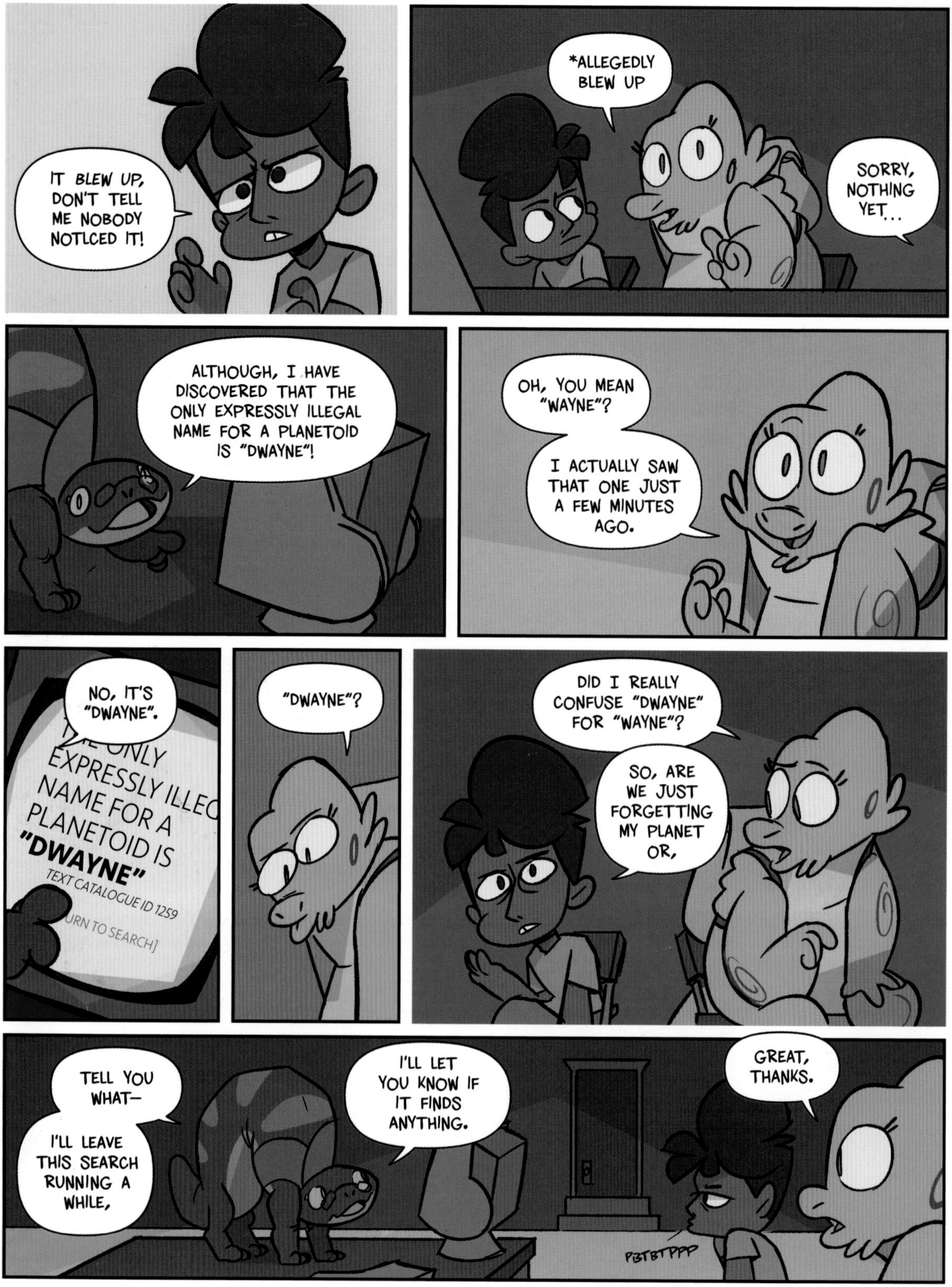
IT BLEW UP, DON'T TELL ME NOBODY NOTlCED IT!
*ALLEGEDLY BLEW UP
SORRY, NOTHING YET...
ALTHOUGH, I HAVE DISCOVERED THAT THE ONLY EXPRESSLY ILLEGAL NAME FOR A PLANETOID IS "DWAYNE"!
OH, YOU MEAN "WAYNE"?
I ACTUALLY SAW THAT ONE JUST A FEW MINUTES AGO.
NO, IT'S "DWAYNE".
EXPRESSLY ILLEG
NAME FOR A
PLANETOID IS
"DWAYNE"
TEXT CATALOGUE ID 1259
"DWAYNE"?
DID I REALLY CONFUSE "DWAYNE" FOR "WAYNE"?
SO, ARE WE JUST FORGETTING MY PLANET OR,
TELL YOU WHAT—
I'LL LEAVE THIS SEARCH RUNNING A WHILE,
I'LL LET YOU KNOW IF IT FINDS ANYTHING.
GREAT, THANKS.
PBTBTPPP

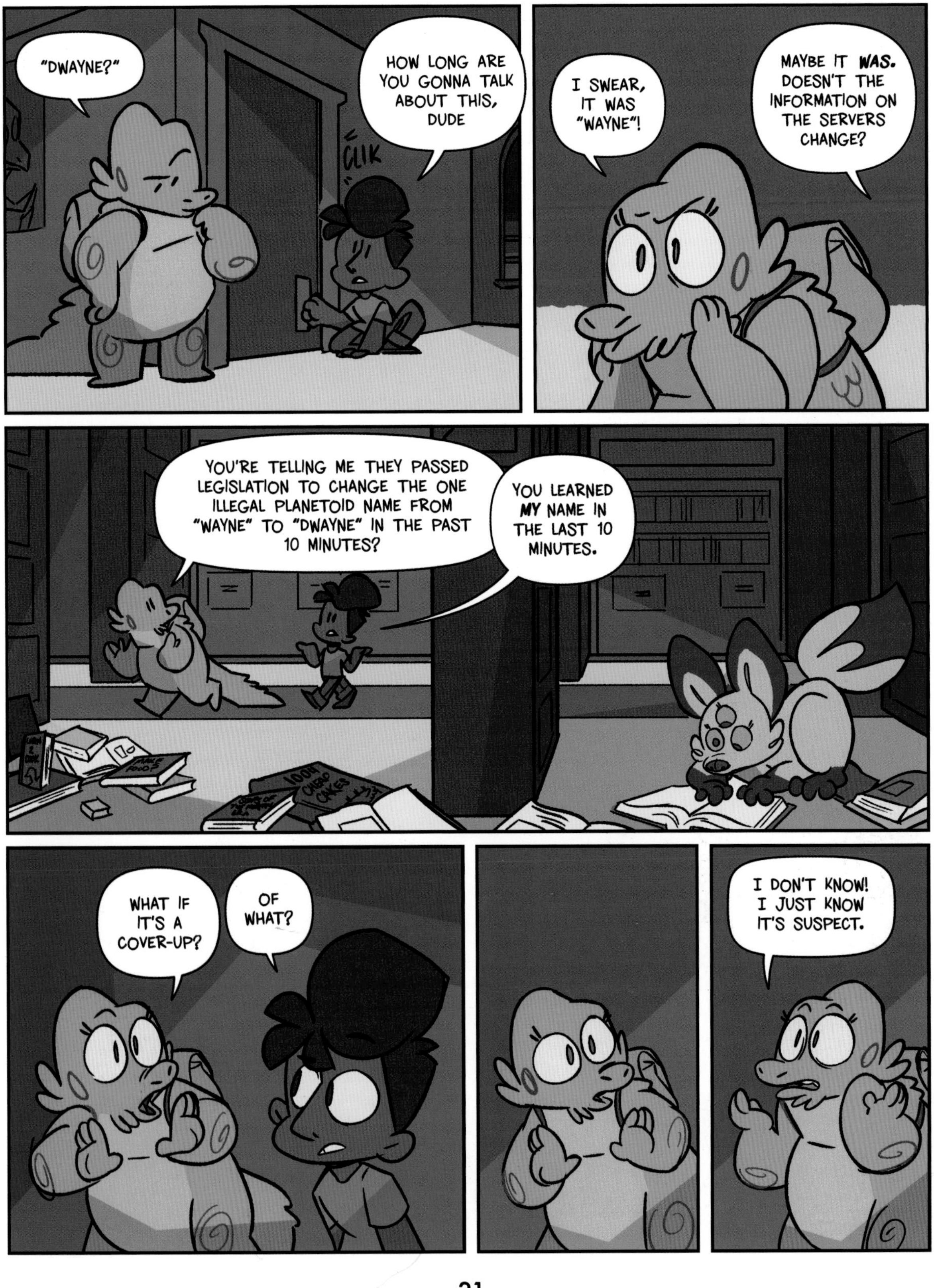
"DWAYNE?"
HOW LONG ARE YOU GONNA TALK ABOUT THIS, DUDE
CLIK
I SWEAR, IT WAS "WAYNE"!
MAYBE IT **WAS.** DOESN'T THE INFORMATION ON THE SERVERS CHANGE?
YOU'RE TELLING ME THEY PASSED LEGISLATION TO CHANGE THE ONE ILLEGAL PLANETOID NAME FROM "WAYNE" TO "DWAYNE" IN THE PAST 10 MINUTES?
YOU LEARNED **MY** NAME IN THE LAST 10 MINUTES.
100% CHEAP CAKES
WHAT IF IT'S A COVER-UP?
OF WHAT?
I DON'T KNOW! I JUST KNOW IT'S SUSPECT.

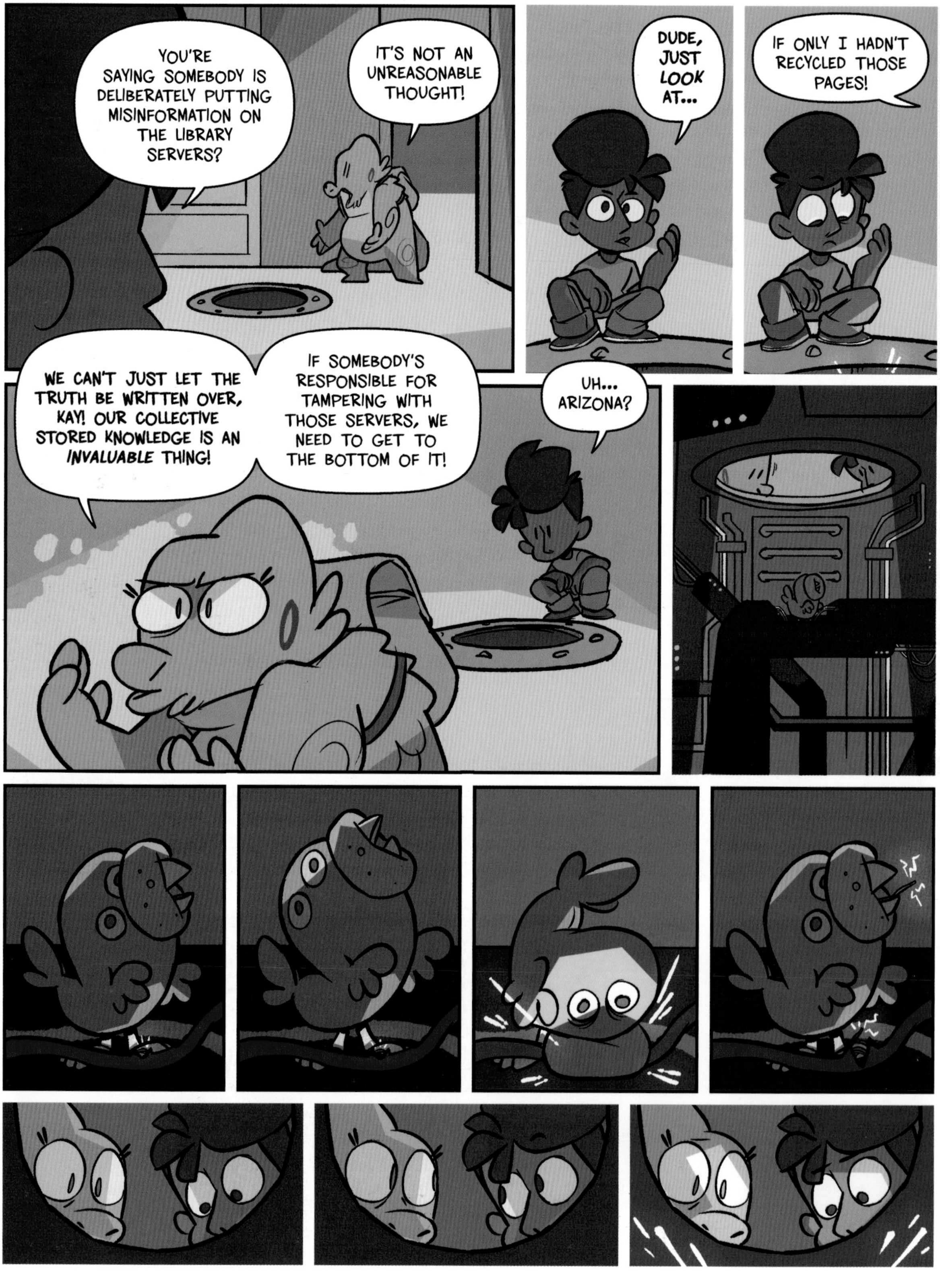
YOU'RE SAYING SOMEBODY IS DELIBERATELY PUTTING MISINFORMATION ON THE LIBRARY SERVERS?
IT'S NOT AN UNREASONABLE THOUGHT!
DUDE, JUST LOOK AT...
IF ONLY I HADN'T RECYCLED THOSE PAGES!
WE CAN'T JUST LET THE TRUTH BE WRITTEN OVER, KAY! OUR COLLECTIVE STORED KNOWLEDGE IS AN INVALUABLE THING!
IF SOMEBODY'S RESPONSIBLE FOR TAMPERING WITH THOSE SERVERS, WE NEED TO GET TO THE BOTTOM OF IT!
UH... ARIZONA?

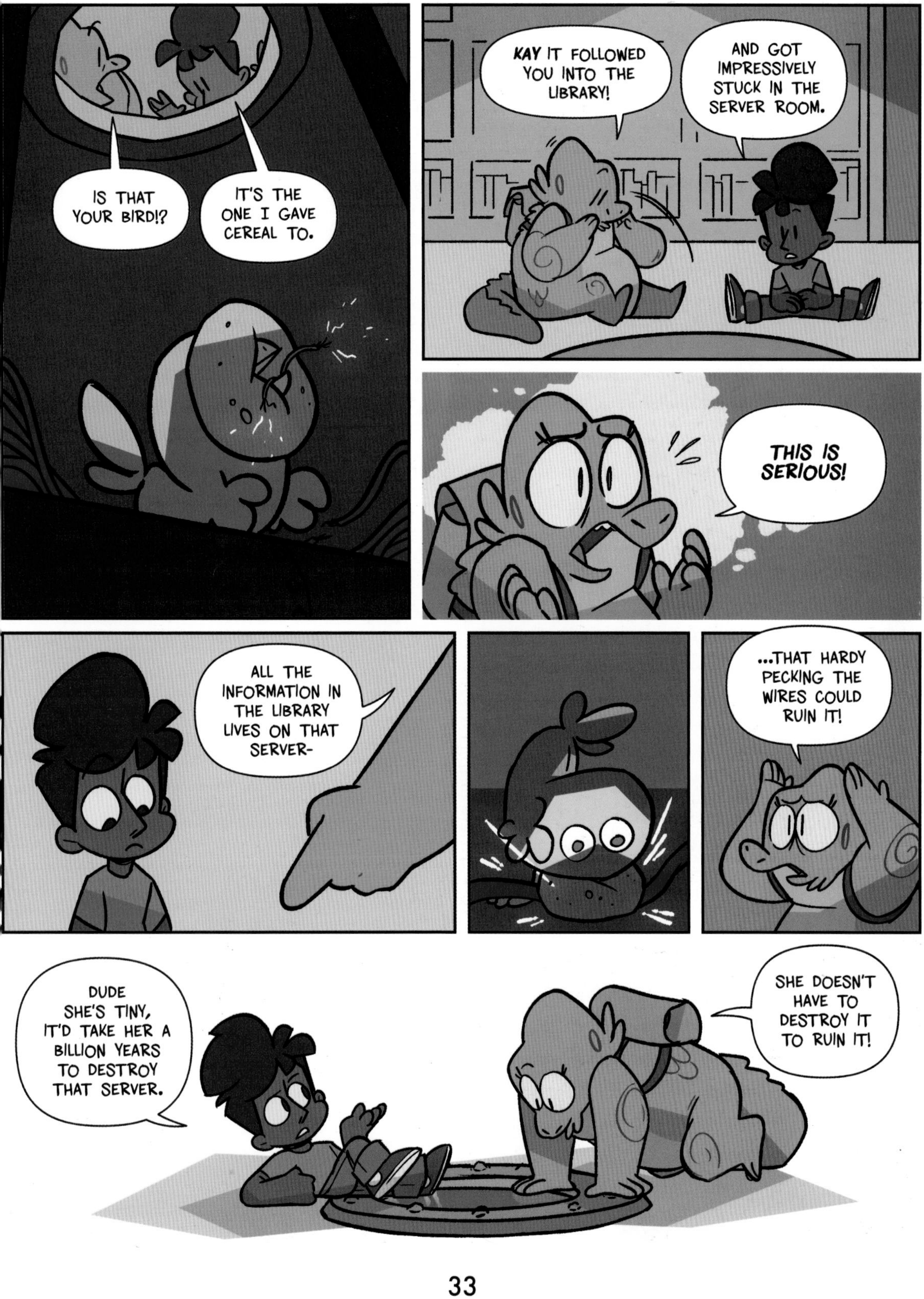

IS THAT YOUR BIRD!?
IT'S THE ONE I GAVE CEREAL TO.
KAY IT FOLLOWED YOU INTO THE LIBRARY!
AND GOT IMPRESSIVELY STUCK IN THE SERVER ROOM.
THIS IS SERIOUS!
ALL THE INFORMATION IN THE LIBRARY LIVES ON THAT SERVER-
...THAT HARDY PECKING THE WIRES COULD RUIN IT!
DUDE SHE'S TINY, IT'D TAKE HER A BILLION YEARS TO DESTROY THAT SERVER.
SHE DOESN'T HAVE TO DESTROY IT TO RUIN IT!

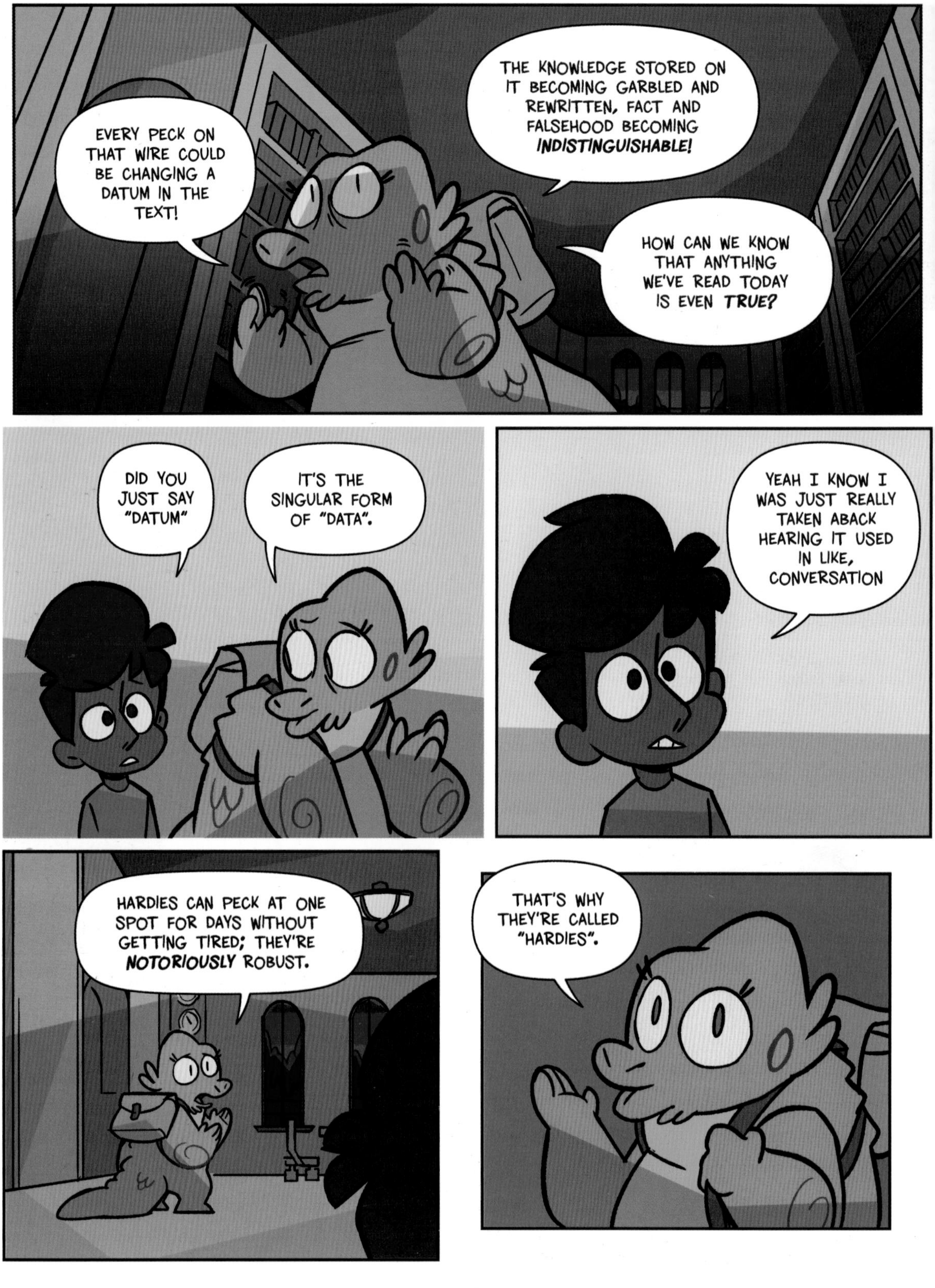
EVERY PECK ON THAT WIRE COULD BE CHANGING A DATUM IN THE TEXT!
THE KNOWLEDGE STORED ON IT BECOMING GARBLED AND REWRITTEN, FACT AND FALSEHOOD BECOMING ***INDISTINGUISHABLE!***
HOW CAN WE KNOW THAT ANYTHING WE'VE READ TODAY IS EVEN ***TRUE?***
DID YOU JUST SAY "DATUM"
IT'S THE SINGULAR FORM OF "DATA".
YEAH I KNOW I WAS JUST REALLY TAKEN ABACK HEARING IT USED IN LIKE, CONVERSATION
HARDIES CAN PECK AT ONE SPOT FOR DAYS WITHOUT GETTING TIRED; THEY'RE ***NOTORIOUSLY*** ROBUST.
THAT'S WHY THEY'RE CALLED "HARDIES".

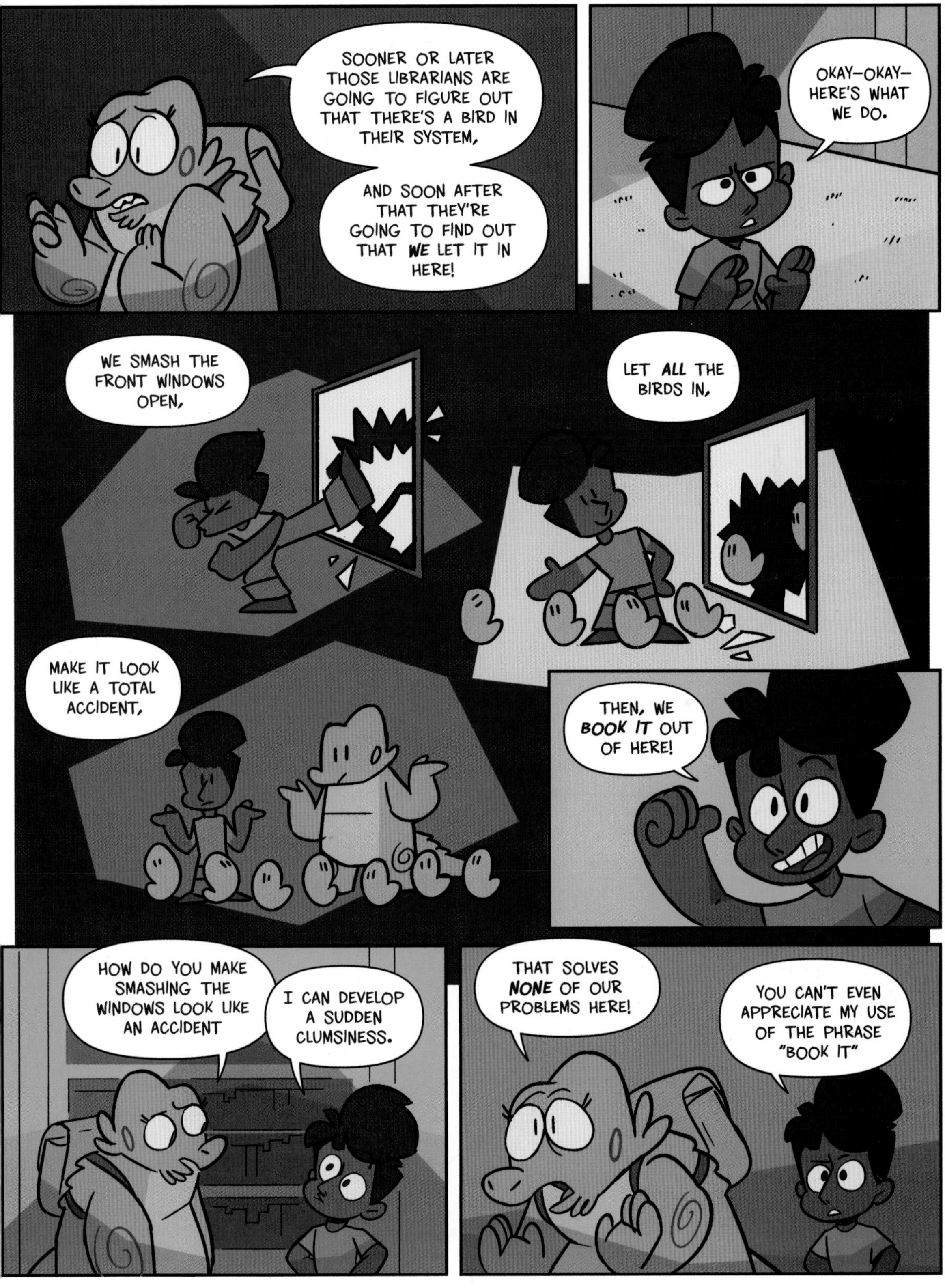
SOONER OR LATER THOSE LIBRARIANS ARE GOING TO FIGURE OUT THAT THERE'S A BIRD IN THEIR SYSTEM,
AND SOON AFTER THAT THEY'RE GOING TO FIND OUT THAT WE LET IT IN HERE!
OKAY—OKAY— HERE'S WHAT WE DO.
WE SMASH THE FRONT WINDOWS OPEN,
LET ALL THE BIRDS IN,
MAKE IT LOOK LIKE A TOTAL ACCIDENT,
THEN, WE BOOK IT OUT OF HERE!
HOW DO YOU MAKE SMASHING THE WINDOWS LOOK LIKE AN ACCIDENT
I CAN DEVELOP A SUDDEN CLUMSINESS.
THAT SOLVES NONE OF OUR PROBLEMS HERE!
YOU CAN'T EVEN APPRECIATE MY USE OF THE PHRASE "BOOK IT"

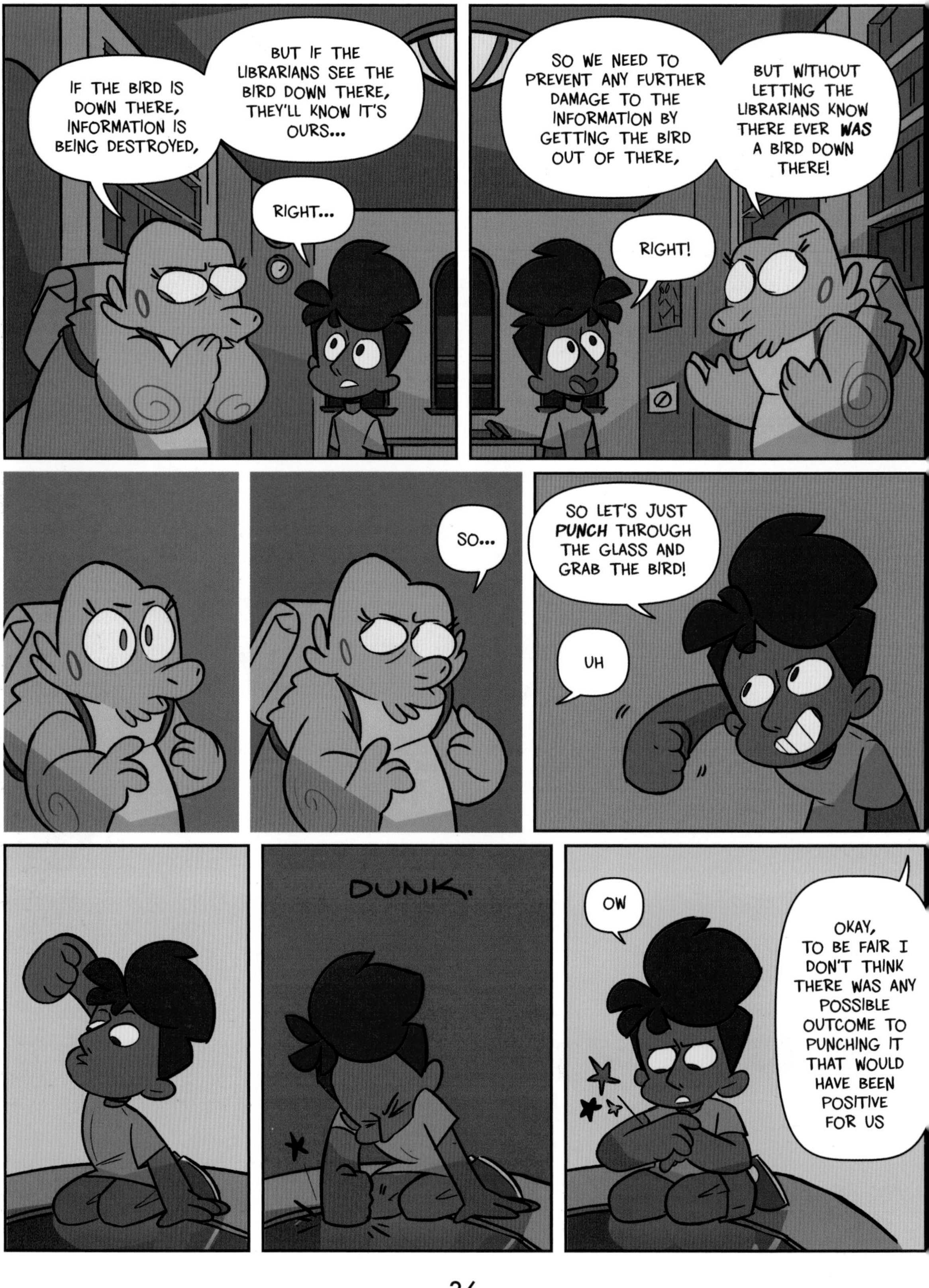
IF THE BIRD IS DOWN THERE, INFORMATION IS BEING DESTROYED,
BUT IF THE LIBRARIANS SEE THE BIRD DOWN THERE, THEY'LL KNOW IT'S OURS...
RIGHT...
SO WE NEED TO PREVENT ANY FURTHER DAMAGE TO THE INFORMATION BY GETTING THE BIRD OUT OF THERE,
BUT WITHOUT LETTING THE LIBRARIANS KNOW THERE EVER **WAS** A BIRD DOWN THERE!
RIGHT!
SO...
SO LET'S JUST **PUNCH** THROUGH THE GLASS AND GRAB THE BIRD!
UH
DUNK.
OW
OKAY, TO BE FAIR I DON'T THINK THERE WAS ANY POSSIBLE OUTCOME TO PUNCHING IT THAT WOULD HAVE BEEN POSITIVE FOR US

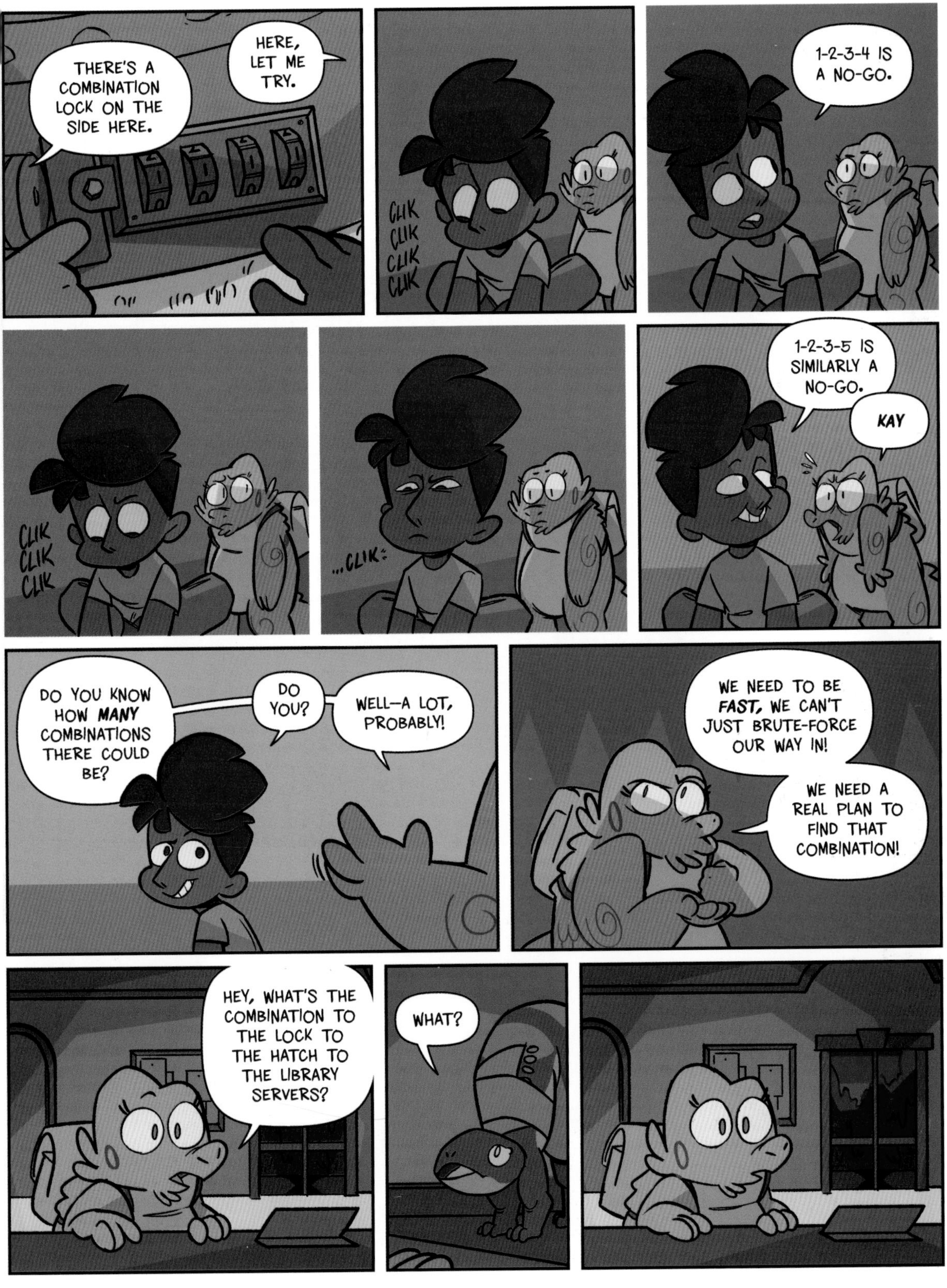
THERE'S A COMBINATION LOCK ON THE SIDE HERE.
HERE, LET ME TRY.
CLIK CLIK CLIK CLIK
1-2-3-4 IS A NO-GO.
CLIK CLIK CLIK
...CLIK
1-2-3-5 IS SIMILARLY A NO-GO.
KAY
DO YOU KNOW HOW MANY COMBINATIONS THERE COULD BE?
DO YOU?
WELL—A LOT, PROBABLY!
WE NEED TO BE FAST, WE CAN'T JUST BRUTE-FORCE OUR WAY IN!
WE NEED A REAL PLAN TO FIND THAT COMBINATION!
HEY, WHAT'S THE COMBINATION TO THE LOCK TO THE HATCH TO THE LIBRARY SERVERS?
WHAT?

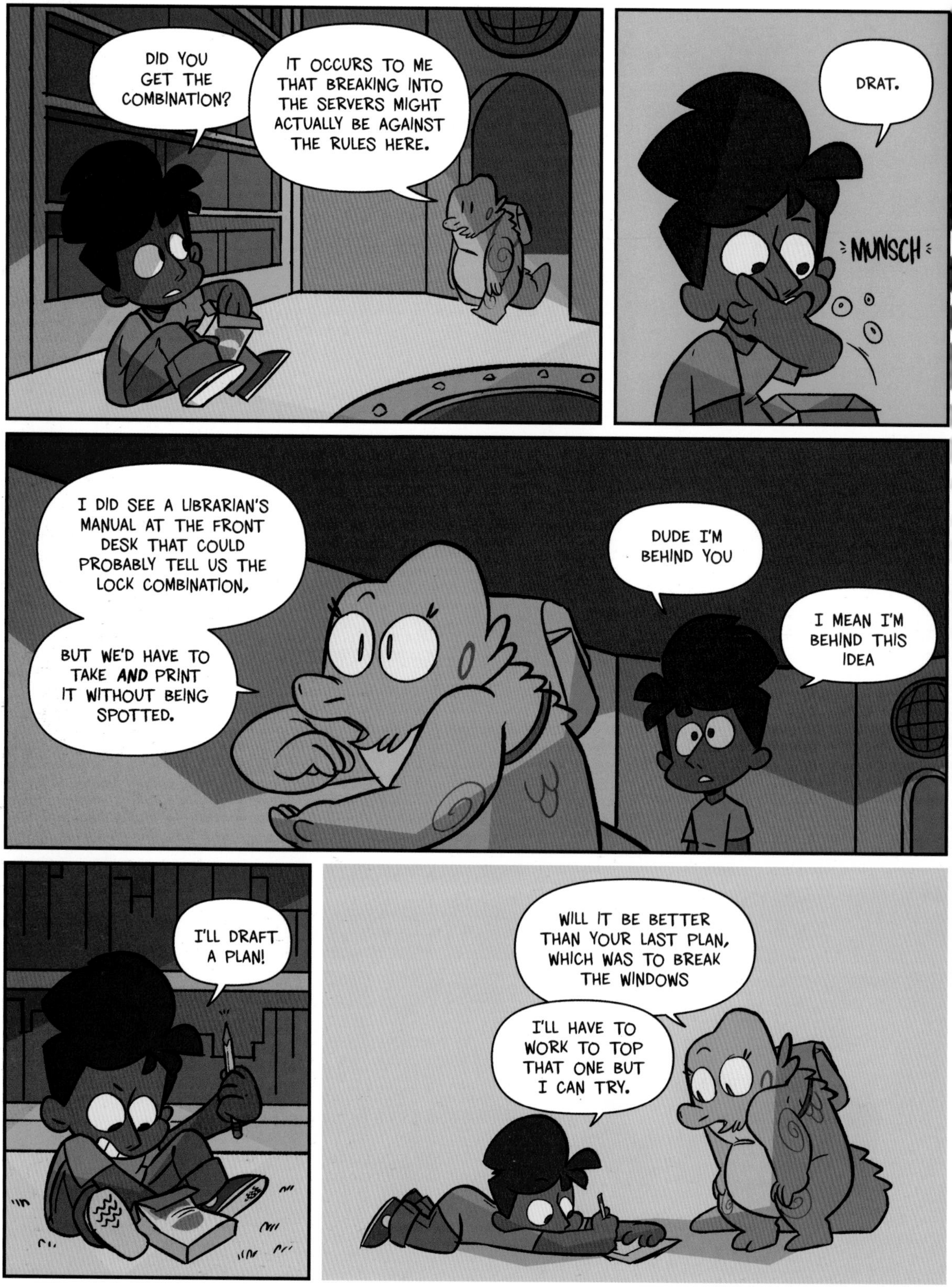
DID YOU GET THE COMBINATION?
IT OCCURS TO ME THAT BREAKING INTO THE SERVERS MIGHT ACTUALLY BE AGAINST THE RULES HERE.
DRAT.
MUNSCH
I DID SEE A LIBRARIAN'S MANUAL AT THE FRONT DESK THAT COULD PROBABLY TELL US THE LOCK COMBINATION,
BUT WE'D HAVE TO TAKE **AND** PRINT IT WITHOUT BEING SPOTTED.
DUDE I'M BEHIND YOU
I MEAN I'M BEHIND THIS IDEA
I'LL DRAFT A PLAN!
WILL IT BE BETTER THAN YOUR LAST PLAN, WHICH WAS TO BREAK THE WINDOWS
I'LL HAVE TO WORK TO TOP THAT ONE BUT I CAN TRY.

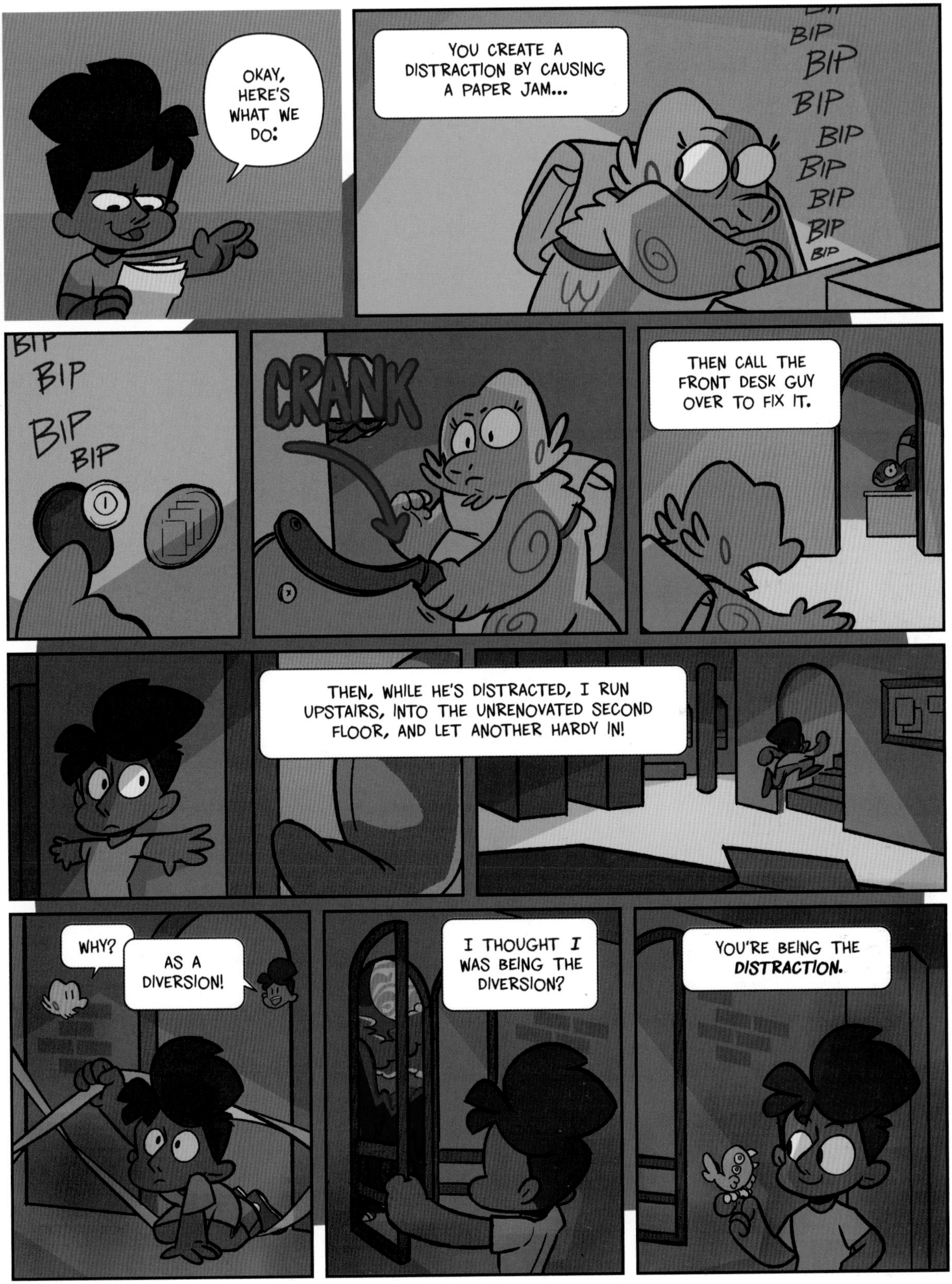
OKAY, HERE'S WHAT WE DO:
YOU CREATE A DISTRACTION BY CAUSING A PAPER JAM...
BIP BIP BIP BIP BIP BIP BIP BIP BIP
BIP BIP BIP BIP
CRANK
THEN CALL THE FRONT DESK GUY OVER TO FIX IT.
THEN, WHILE HE'S DISTRACTED, I RUN UPSTAIRS, INTO THE UNRENOVATED SECOND FLOOR, AND LET ANOTHER HARDY IN!
WHY?
AS A DIVERSION!
I THOUGHT I WAS BEING THE DIVERSION?
YOU'RE BEING THE DISTRACTION.

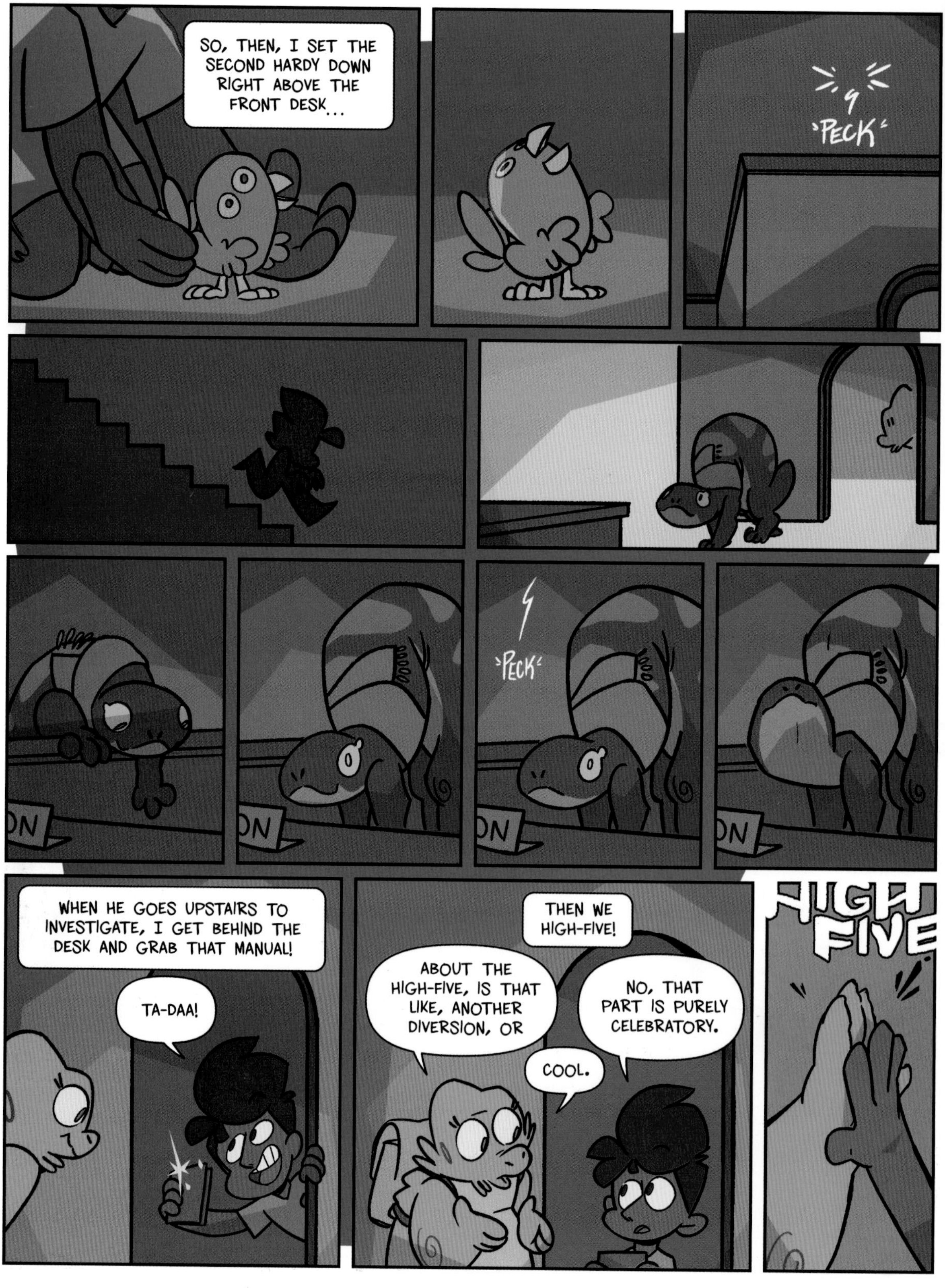
SO, THEN, I SET THE SECOND HARDY DOWN RIGHT ABOVE THE FRONT DESK...
PECK
PECK
WHEN HE GOES UPSTAIRS TO INVESTIGATE, I GET BEHIND THE DESK AND GRAB THAT MANUAL!
TA-DAA!
THEN WE HIGH-FIVE!
ABOUT THE HIGH-FIVE, IS THAT LIKE, ANOTHER DIVERSION, OR
NO, THAT PART IS PURELY CELEBRATORY.
COOL.
HIGH FIVE

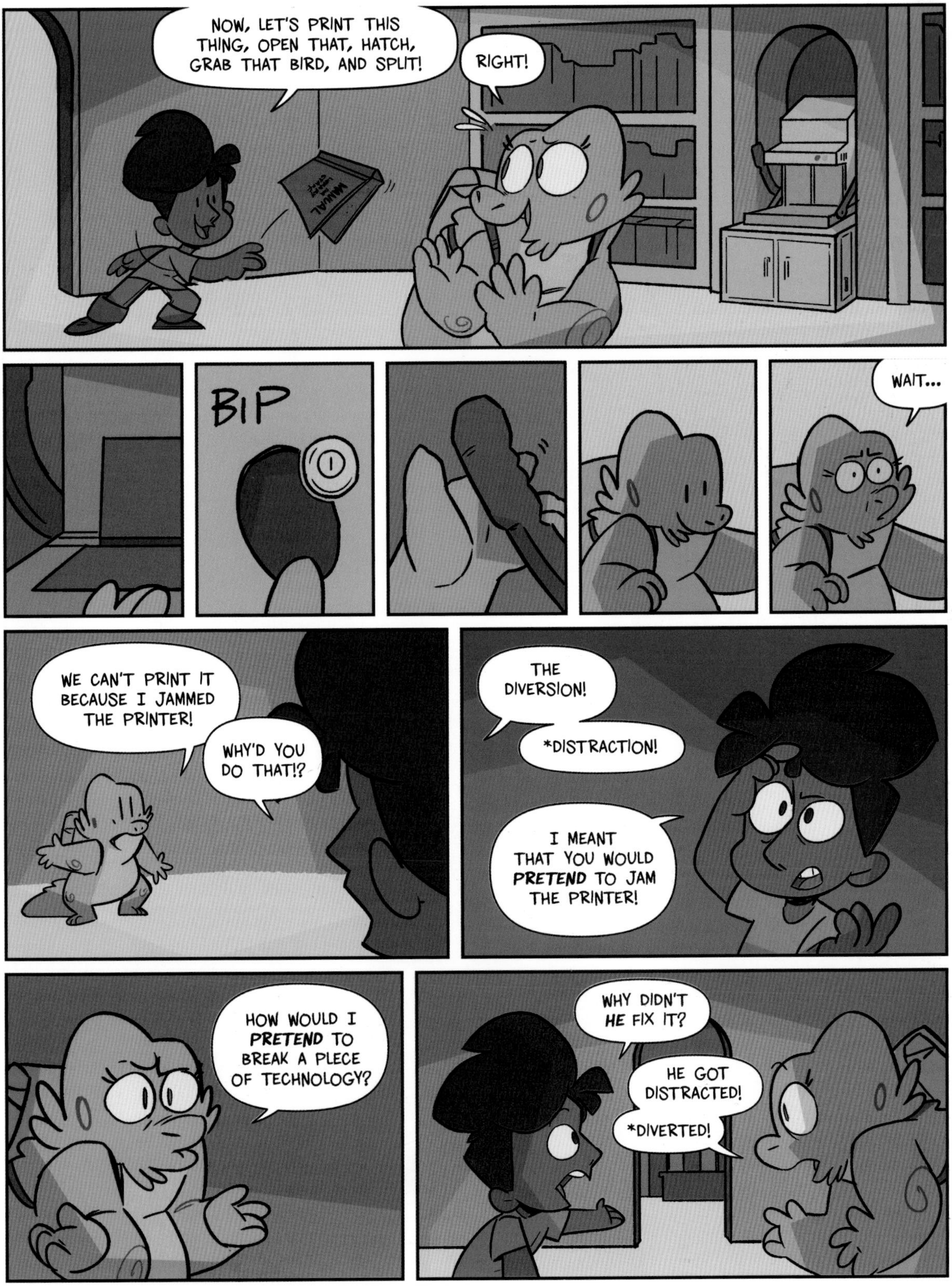
NOW, LET'S PRINT THIS THING, OPEN THAT, HATCH, GRAB THAT BIRD, AND SPLIT!
RIGHT!
BIP
WAIT...
WE CAN'T PRINT IT BECAUSE I JAMMED THE PRINTER!
WHY'D YOU DO THAT!?
THE DIVERSION!
*DISTRACTION!
I MEANT THAT YOU WOULD **PRETEND** TO JAM THE PRINTER!
HOW WOULD I **PRETEND** TO BREAK A PIECE OF TECHNOLOGY?
WHY DIDN'T **HE** FIX IT?
HE GOT DISTRACTED!
*DIVERTED!

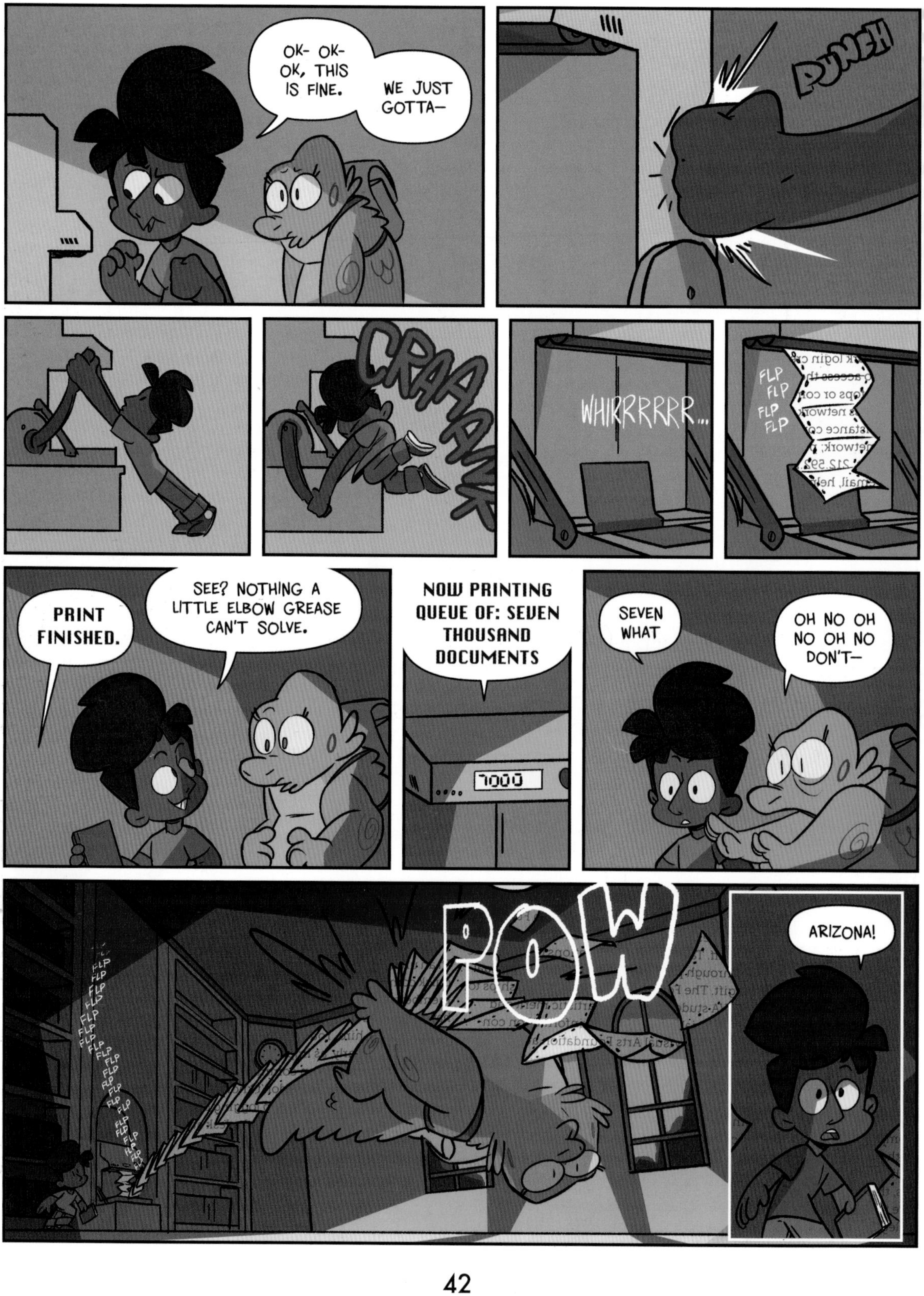
OK- OK- OK, THIS IS FINE.
WE JUST GOTTA—
PUNCH
CRAAAANK
WHIRRRRRR...
FLP FLP FLP FLP
PRINT FINISHED.
SEE? NOTHING A LITTLE ELBOW GREASE CAN'T SOLVE.
NOW PRINTING QUEUE OF: SEVEN THOUSAND DOCUMENTS
7000
SEVEN WHAT
OH NO OH NO OH NO DON'T—
POW
ARIZONA!

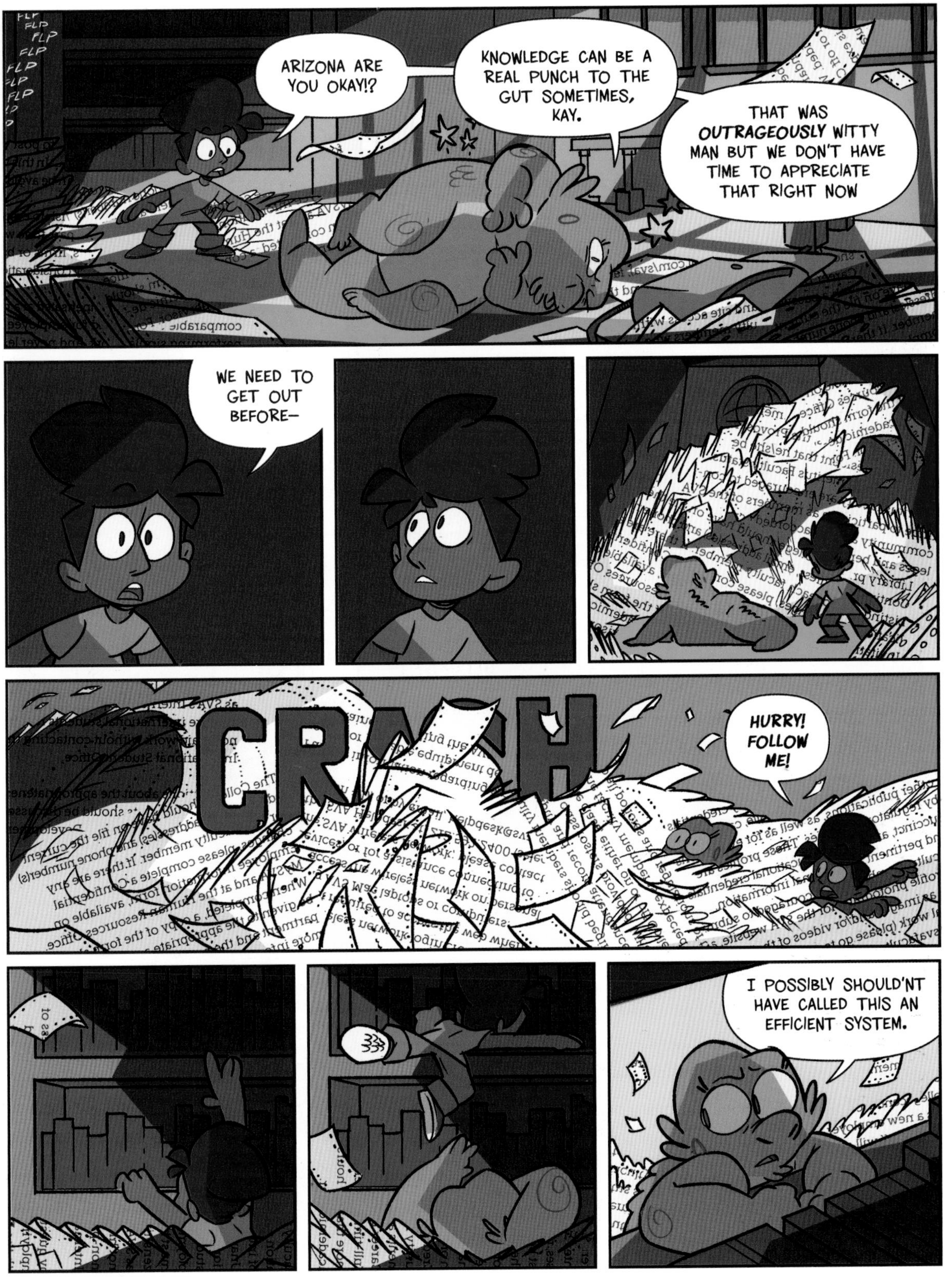
FLP FLP FLP FLP FLP FLP FLP
ARIZONA ARE YOU OKAY!?
KNOWLEDGE CAN BE A REAL PUNCH TO THE GUT SOMETIMES, KAY.
THAT WAS **OUTRAGEOUSLY** WITTY MAN BUT WE DON'T HAVE TIME TO APPRECIATE THAT RIGHT NOW
WE NEED TO GET OUT BEFORE–
CRASH
HURRY! FOLLOW ME!
I POSSIBLY SHOULD'NT HAVE CALLED THIS AN EFFICIENT SYSTEM.

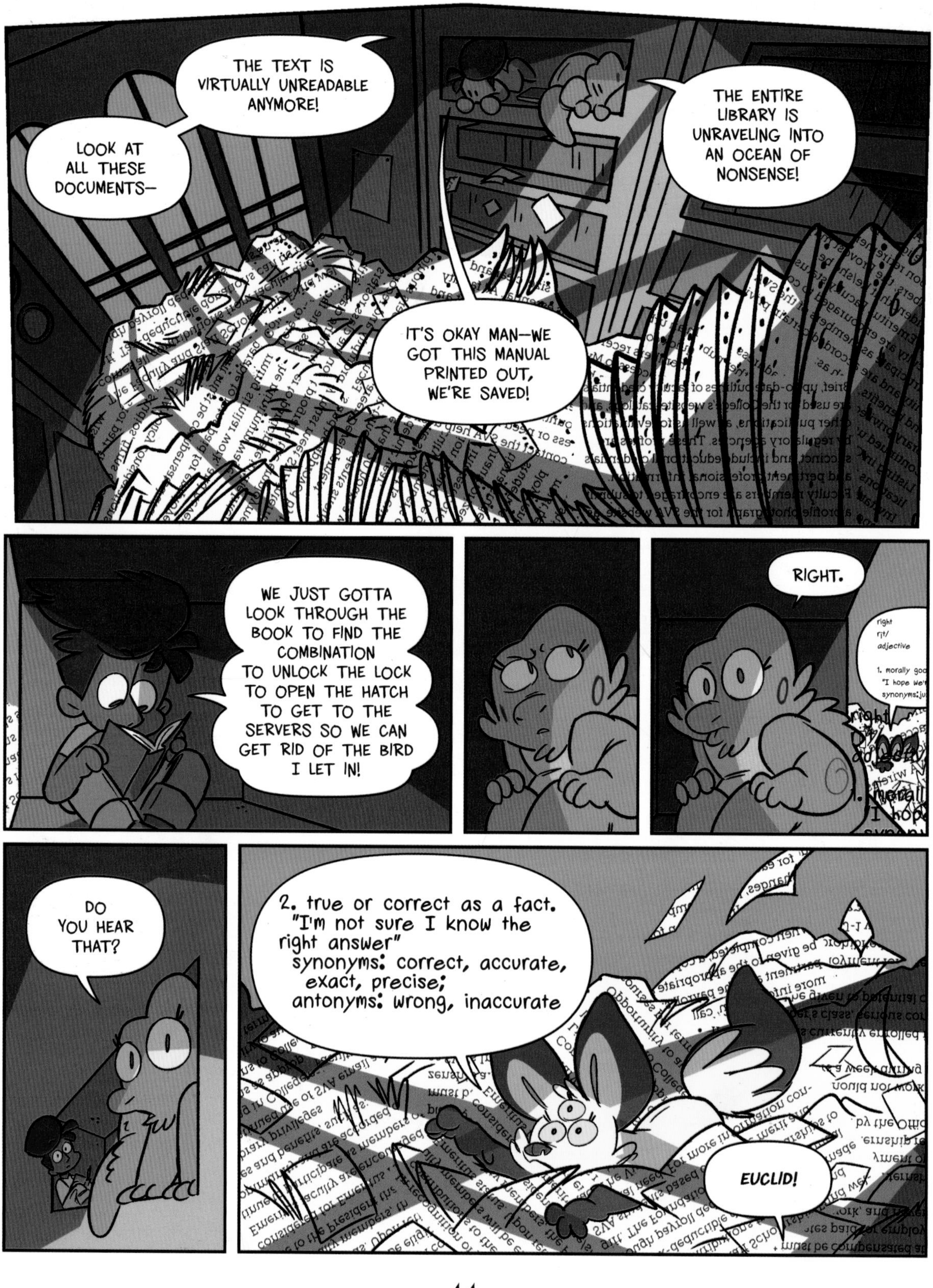
LOOK AT ALL THESE DOCUMENTS—
THE TEXT IS VIRTUALLY UNREADABLE ANYMORE!
THE ENTIRE LIBRARY IS UNRAVELING INTO AN OCEAN OF NONSENSE!
IT'S OKAY MAN—WE GOT THIS MANUAL PRINTED OUT, WE'RE SAVED!
WE JUST GOTTA LOOK THROUGH THE BOOK TO FIND THE COMBINATION TO UNLOCK THE LOCK TO OPEN THE HATCH TO GET TO THE SERVERS SO WE CAN GET RID OF THE BIRD I LET IN!
RIGHT.
DO YOU HEAR THAT?
2. true or correct as a fact. "I'm not sure I know the right answer" synonyms: correct, accurate, exact, precise; antonyms: wrong, inaccurate
EUCLID!

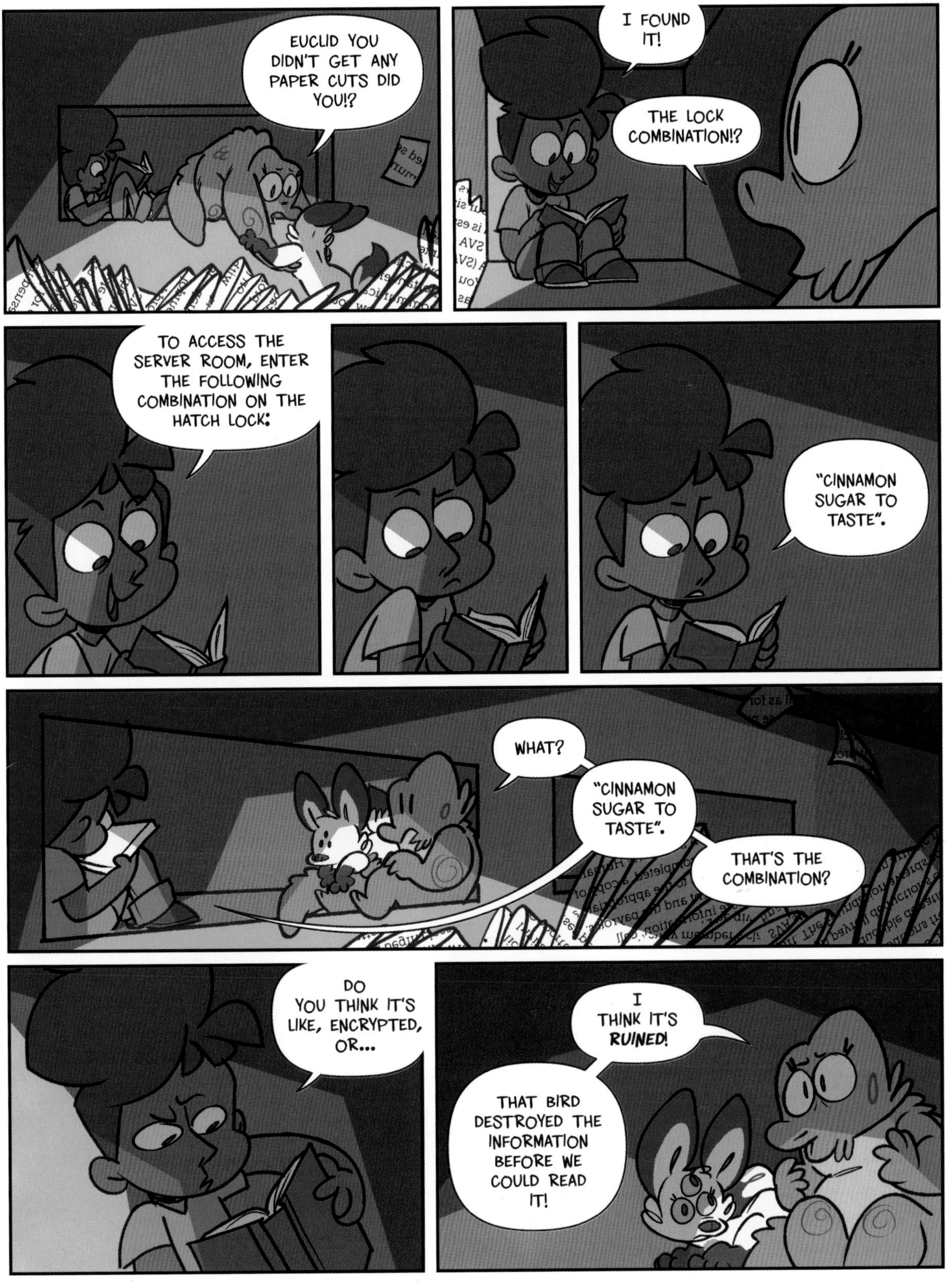
EUCLID YOU DIDN'T GET ANY PAPER CUTS DID YOU!?
I FOUND IT!
THE LOCK COMBINATION!?
TO ACCESS THE SERVER ROOM, ENTER THE FOLLOWING COMBINATION ON THE HATCH LOCK:
"CINNAMON SUGAR TO TASTE".
WHAT?
"CINNAMON SUGAR TO TASTE".
THAT'S THE COMBINATION?
DO YOU THINK IT'S LIKE, ENCRYPTED, OR...
I THINK IT'S RUINED!
THAT BIRD DESTROYED THE INFORMATION BEFORE WE COULD READ IT!

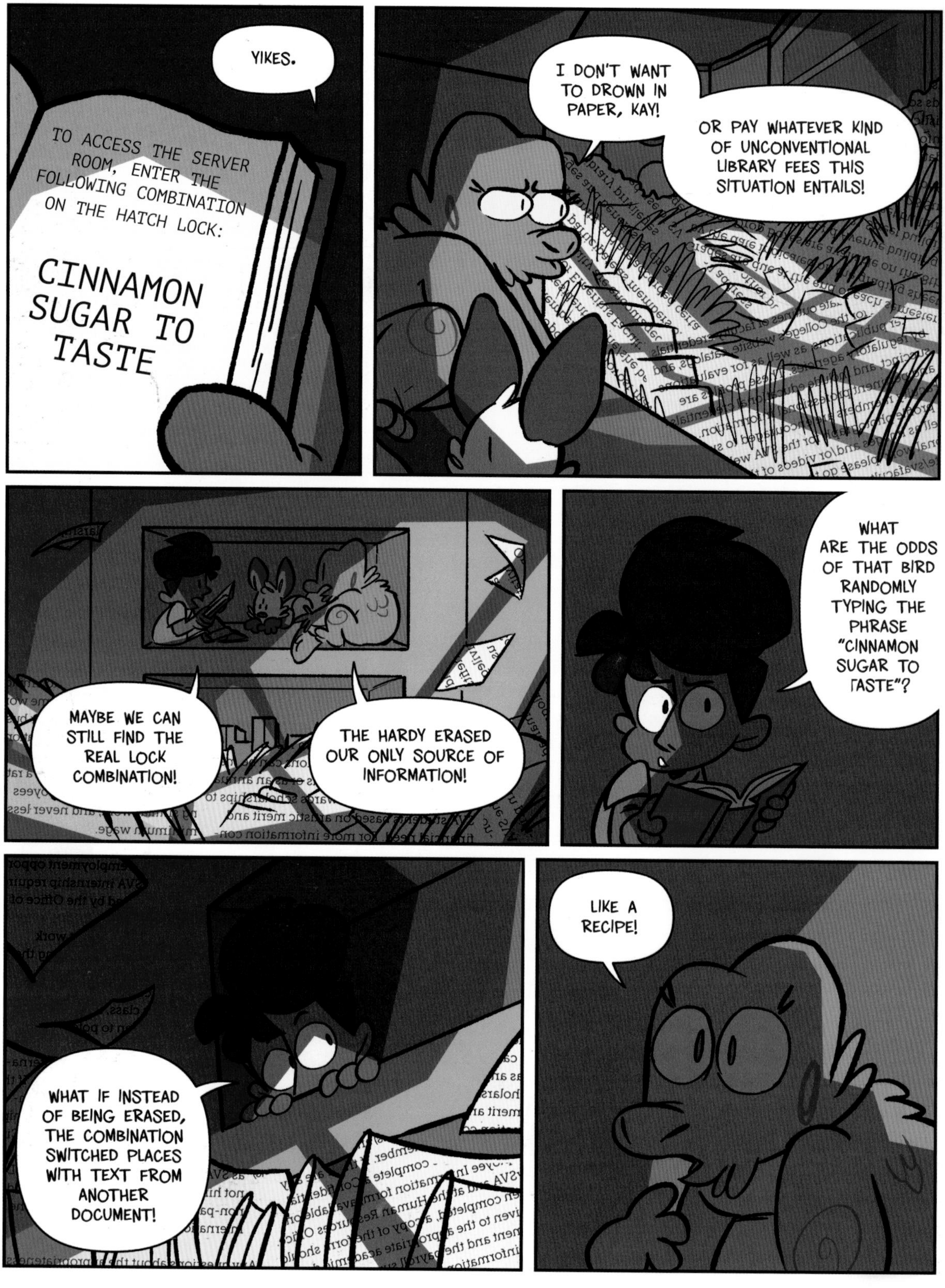
YIKES.
TO ACCESS THE SERVER ROOM, ENTER THE FOLLOWING COMBINATION ON THE HATCH LOCK:
CINNAMON SUGAR TO TASTE
I DON'T WANT TO DROWN IN PAPER, KAY!
OR PAY WHATEVER KIND OF UNCONVENTIONAL LIBRARY FEES THIS SITUATION ENTAILS!
MAYBE WE CAN STILL FIND THE REAL LOCK COMBINATION!
THE HARDY ERASED OUR ONLY SOURCE OF INFORMATION!
WHAT ARE THE ODDS OF THAT BIRD RANDOMLY TYPING THE PHRASE "CINNAMON SUGAR TO TASTE"?
WHAT IF INSTEAD OF BEING ERASED, THE COMBINATION SWITCHED PLACES WITH TEXT FROM ANOTHER DOCUMENT!
LIKE A RECIPE!

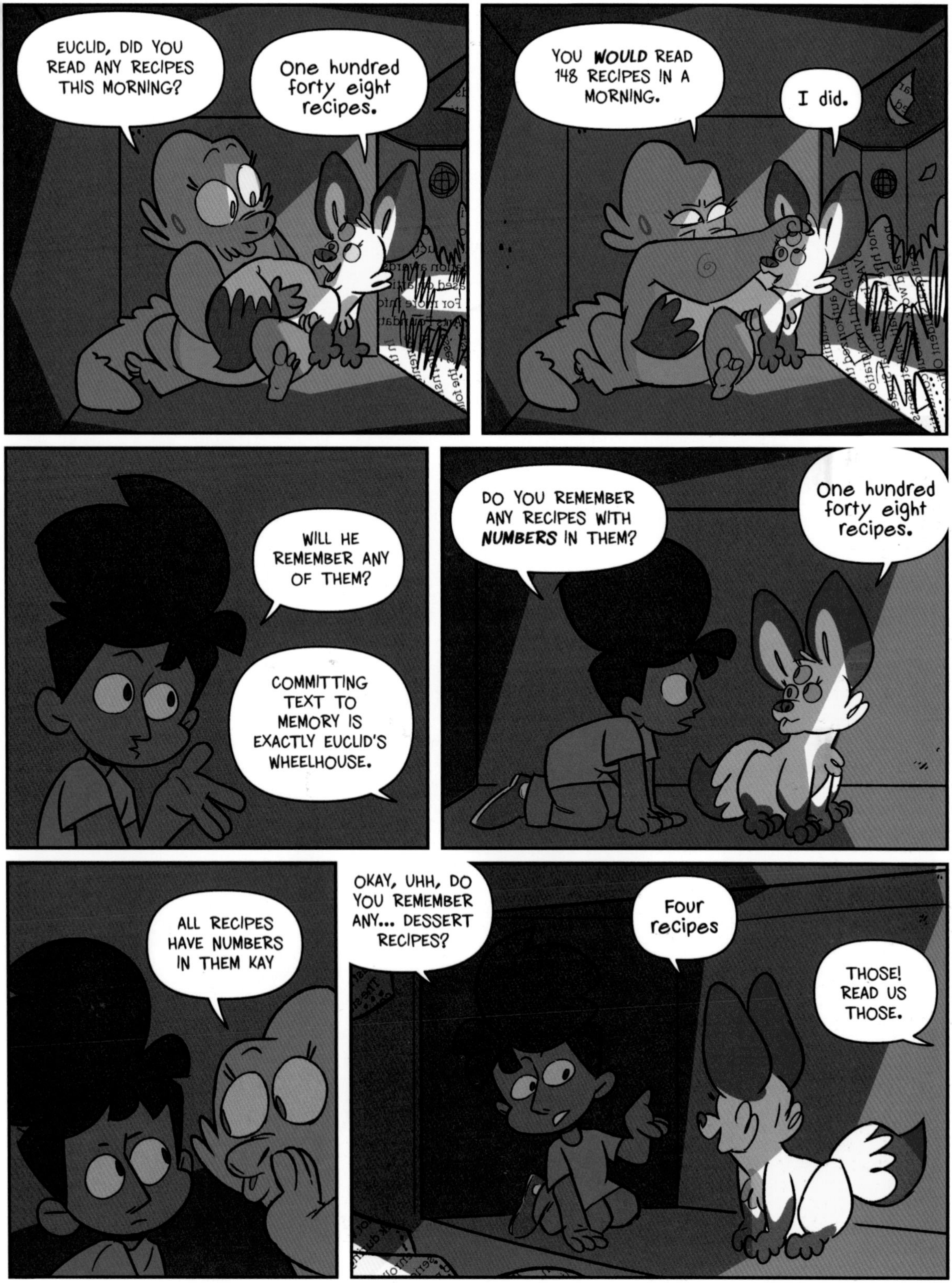
EUCLID, DID YOU READ ANY RECIPES THIS MORNING?
One hundred forty eight recipes.
YOU WOULD READ 148 RECIPES IN A MORNING.
I did.
WILL HE REMEMBER ANY OF THEM?
COMMITTING TEXT TO MEMORY IS EXACTLY EUCLID'S WHEELHOUSE.
DO YOU REMEMBER ANY RECIPES WITH NUMBERS IN THEM?
One hundred forty eight recipes.
ALL RECIPES HAVE NUMBERS IN THEM KAY
OKAY, UHH, DO YOU REMEMBER ANY... DESSERT RECIPES?
Four recipes
THOSE! READ US THOSE.

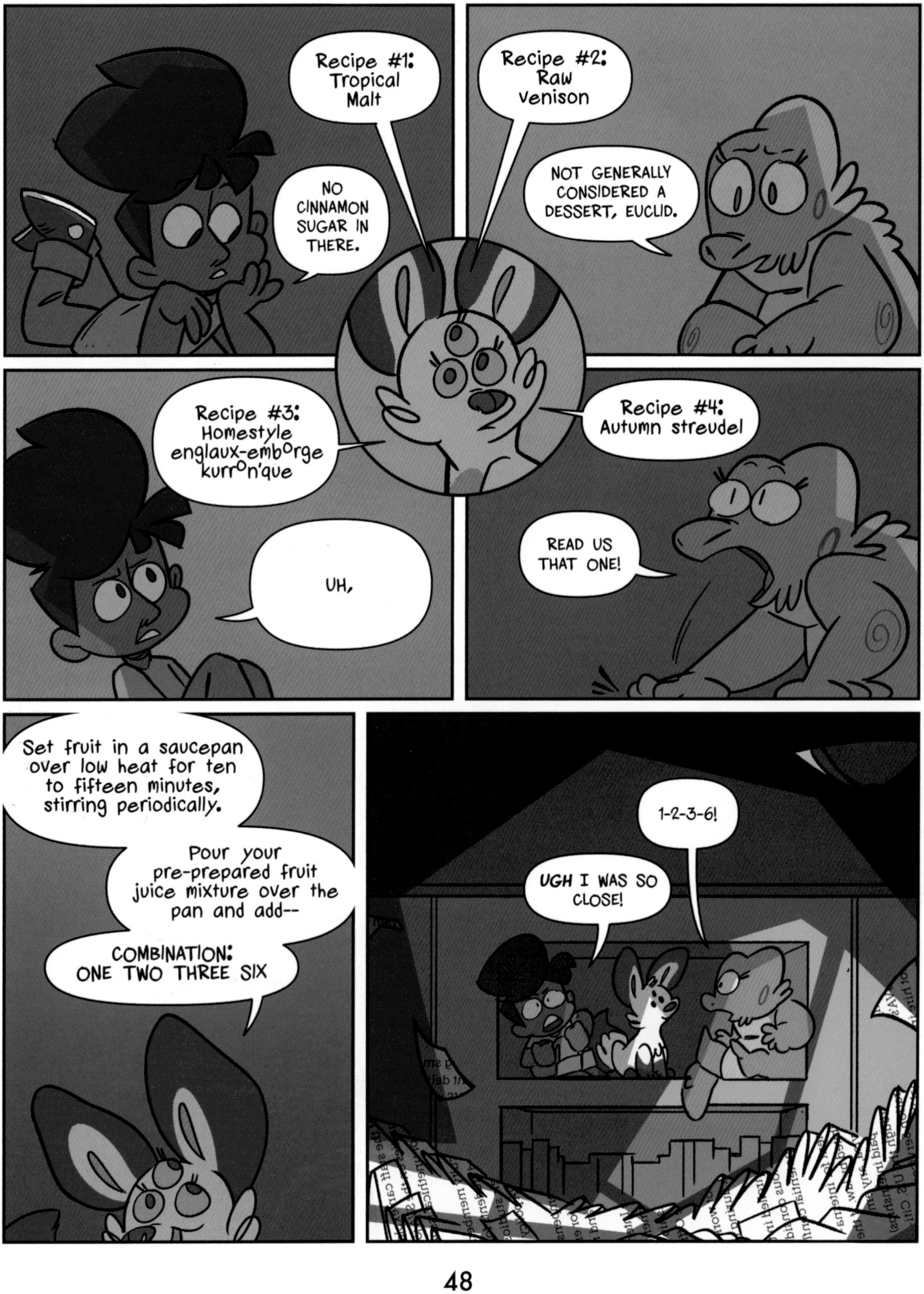
Recipe #1: Tropical Malt
NO CINNAMON SUGAR IN THERE.
Recipe #2: Raw venison
NOT GENERALLY CONSIDERED A DESSERT, EUCLID.
Recipe #3: Homestyle englaux-emborge kurron'que
UH,
Recipe #4: Autumn streudel
READ US THAT ONE!
Set fruit in a saucepan over low heat for ten to fifteen minutes, stirring periodically.
Pour your pre-prepared fruit juice mixture over the pan and add--
COMBINATION: ONE TWO THREE SIX
1-2-3-6!
UGH I WAS SO CLOSE!

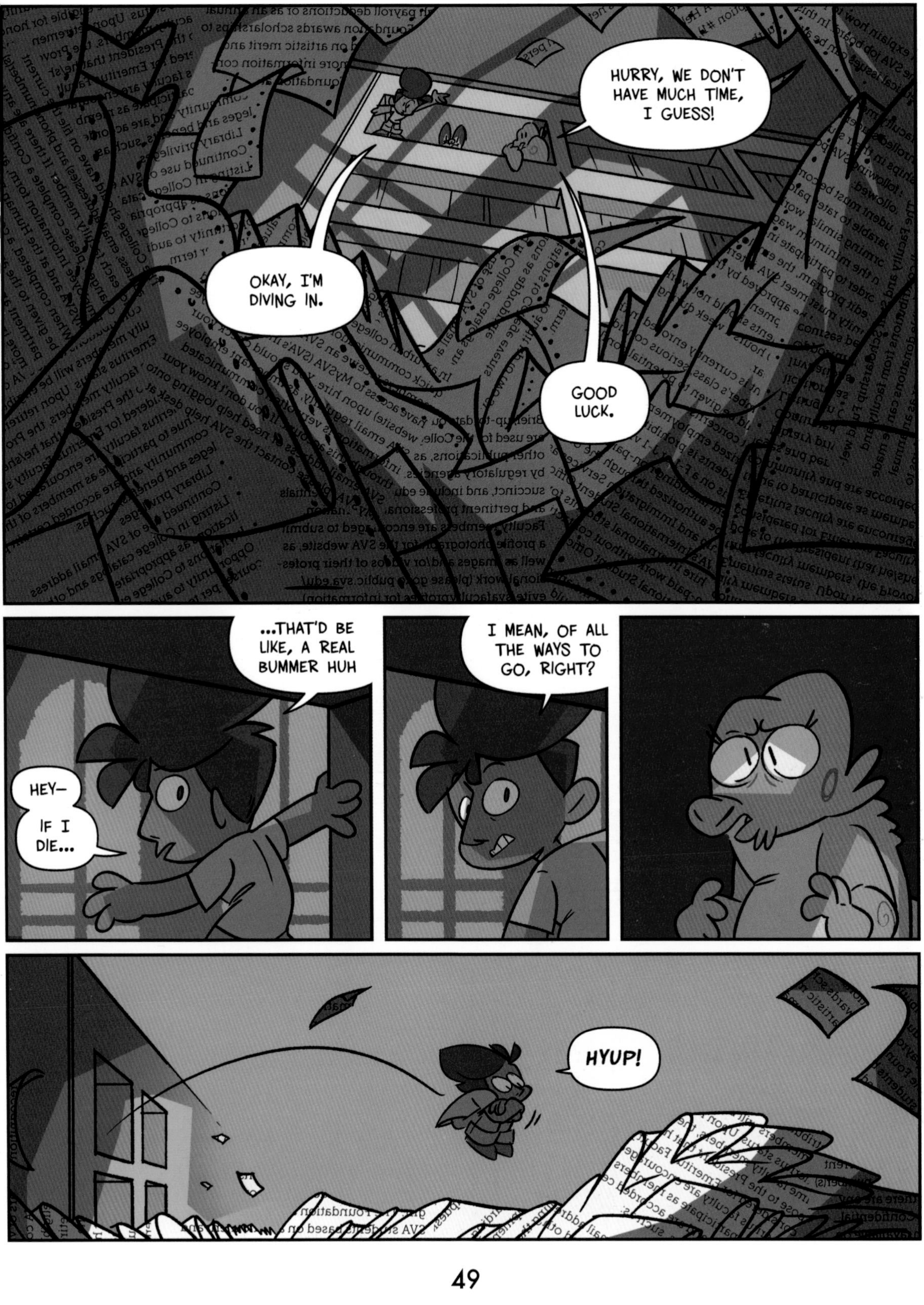
HURRY, WE DON'T HAVE MUCH TIME, I GUESS!
OKAY, I'M DIVING IN.
GOOD LUCK.
HEY—
IF I DIE...
...THAT'D BE LIKE, A REAL BUMMER HUH
I MEAN, OF ALL THE WAYS TO GO, RIGHT?
HYUP!

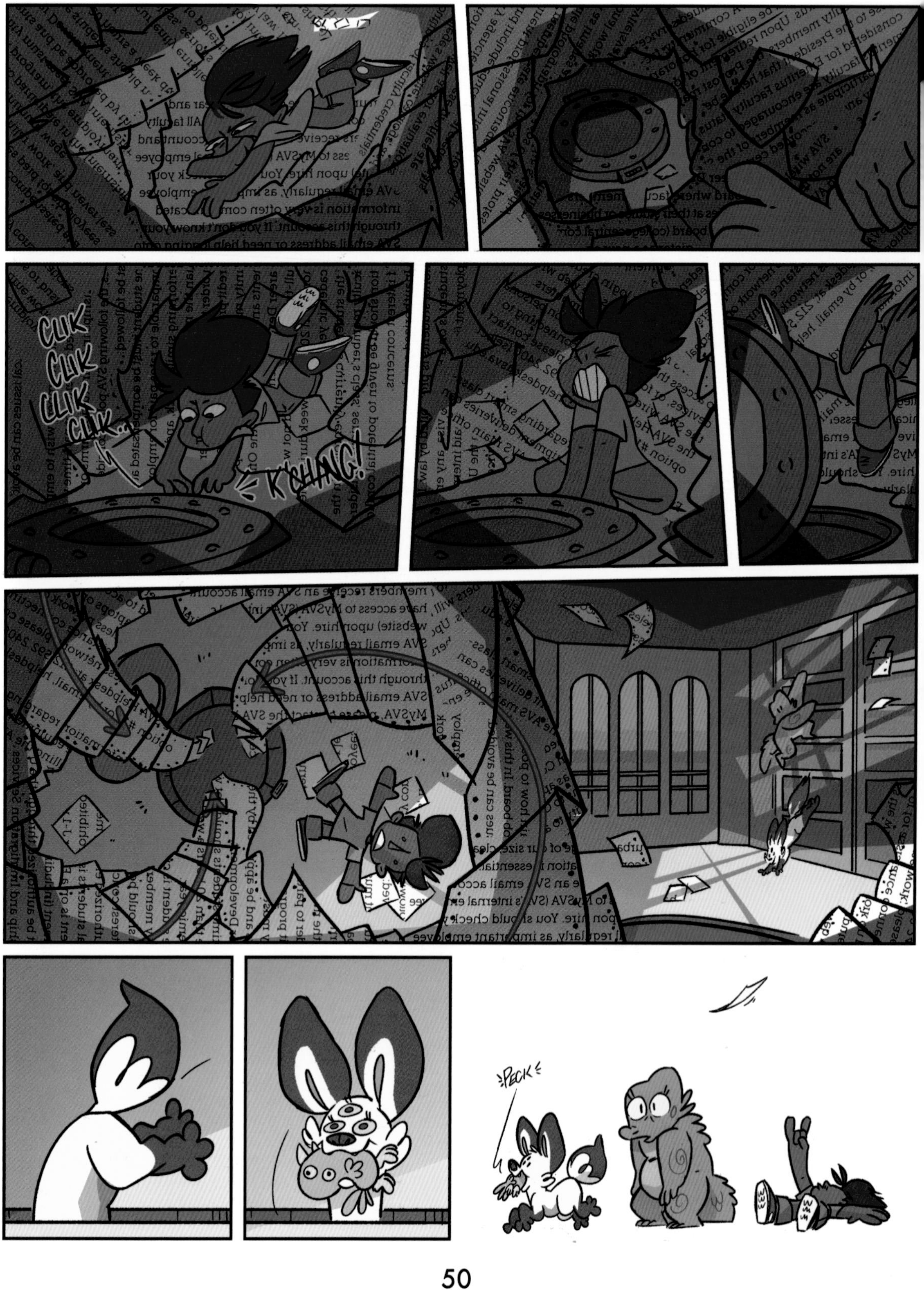
CLIK
CLIK
CLIK
CLIK..
K'CHANG!
PECK

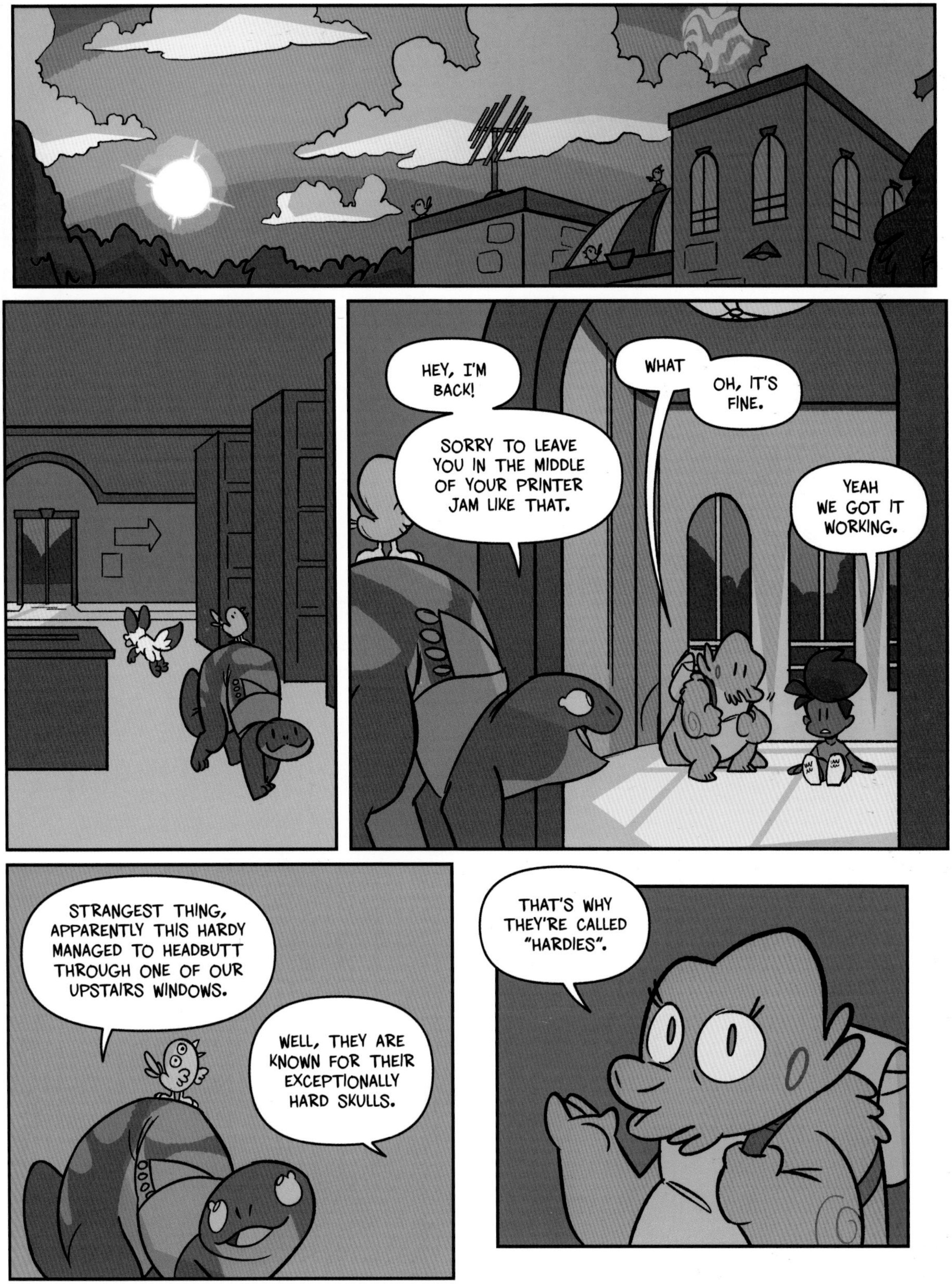
HEY, I'M BACK!
SORRY TO LEAVE YOU IN THE MIDDLE OF YOUR PRINTER JAM LIKE THAT.
WHAT
OH, IT'S FINE.
YEAH WE GOT IT WORKING.
STRANGEST THING, APPARENTLY THIS HARDY MANAGED TO HEADBUTT THROUGH ONE OF OUR UPSTAIRS WINDOWS.
WELL, THEY ARE KNOWN FOR THEIR EXCEPTIONALLY HARD SKULLS.
THAT'S WHY THEY'RE CALLED "HARDIES".

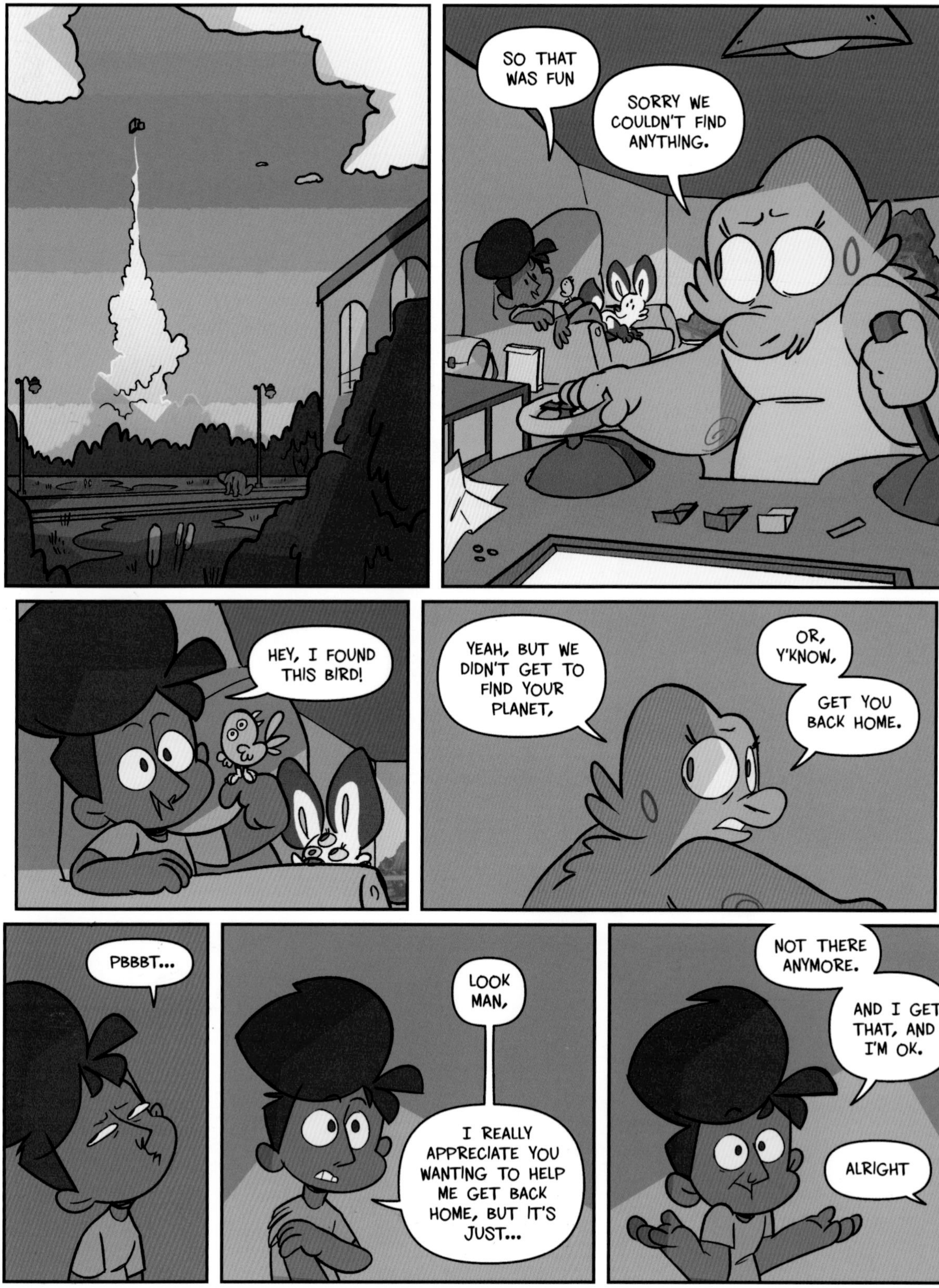
SO THAT WAS FUN
SORRY WE COULDN'T FIND ANYTHING.
HEY, I FOUND THIS BIRD!
YEAH, BUT WE DIDN'T GET TO FIND YOUR PLANET,
OR, Y'KNOW,
GET YOU BACK HOME.
PBBBT...
LOOK MAN,
I REALLY APPRECIATE YOU WANTING TO HELP ME GET BACK HOME, BUT IT'S JUST...
NOT THERE ANYMORE.
AND I GET THAT, AND I'M OK.
ALRIGHT

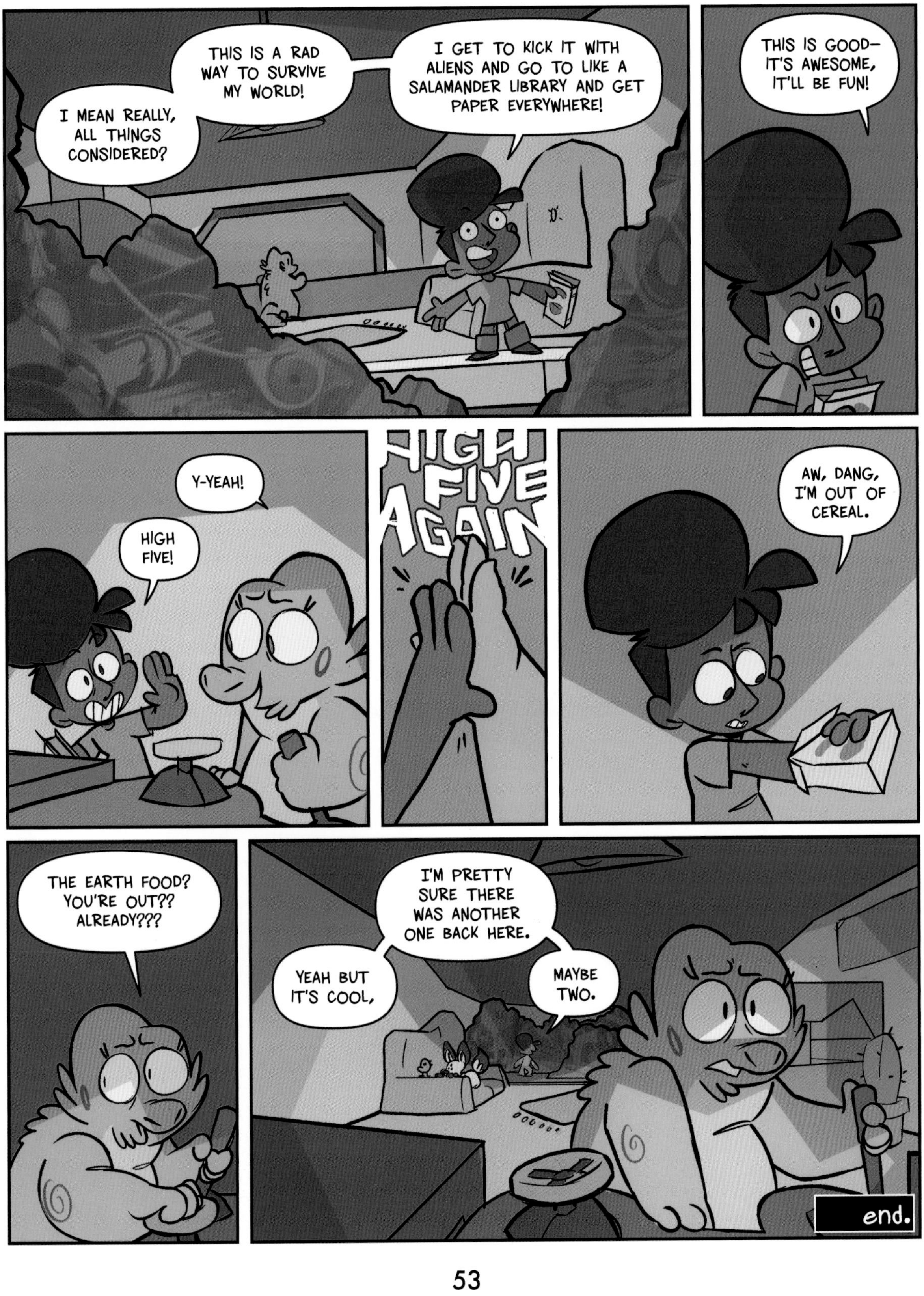
I MEAN REALLY, ALL THINGS CONSIDERED?
THIS IS A RAD WAY TO SURVIVE MY WORLD!
I GET TO KICK IT WITH ALIENS AND GO TO LIKE A SALAMANDER LIBRARY AND GET PAPER EVERYWHERE!
THIS IS GOOD— IT'S AWESOME, IT'LL BE FUN!
HIGH FIVE!
Y-YEAH!
HIGH FIVE AGAIN
AW, DANG, I'M OUT OF CEREAL.
THE EARTH FOOD? YOU'RE OUT?? ALREADY???
YEAH BUT IT'S COOL,
I'M PRETTY SURE THERE WAS ANOTHER ONE BACK HERE.
MAYBE TWO.
end.

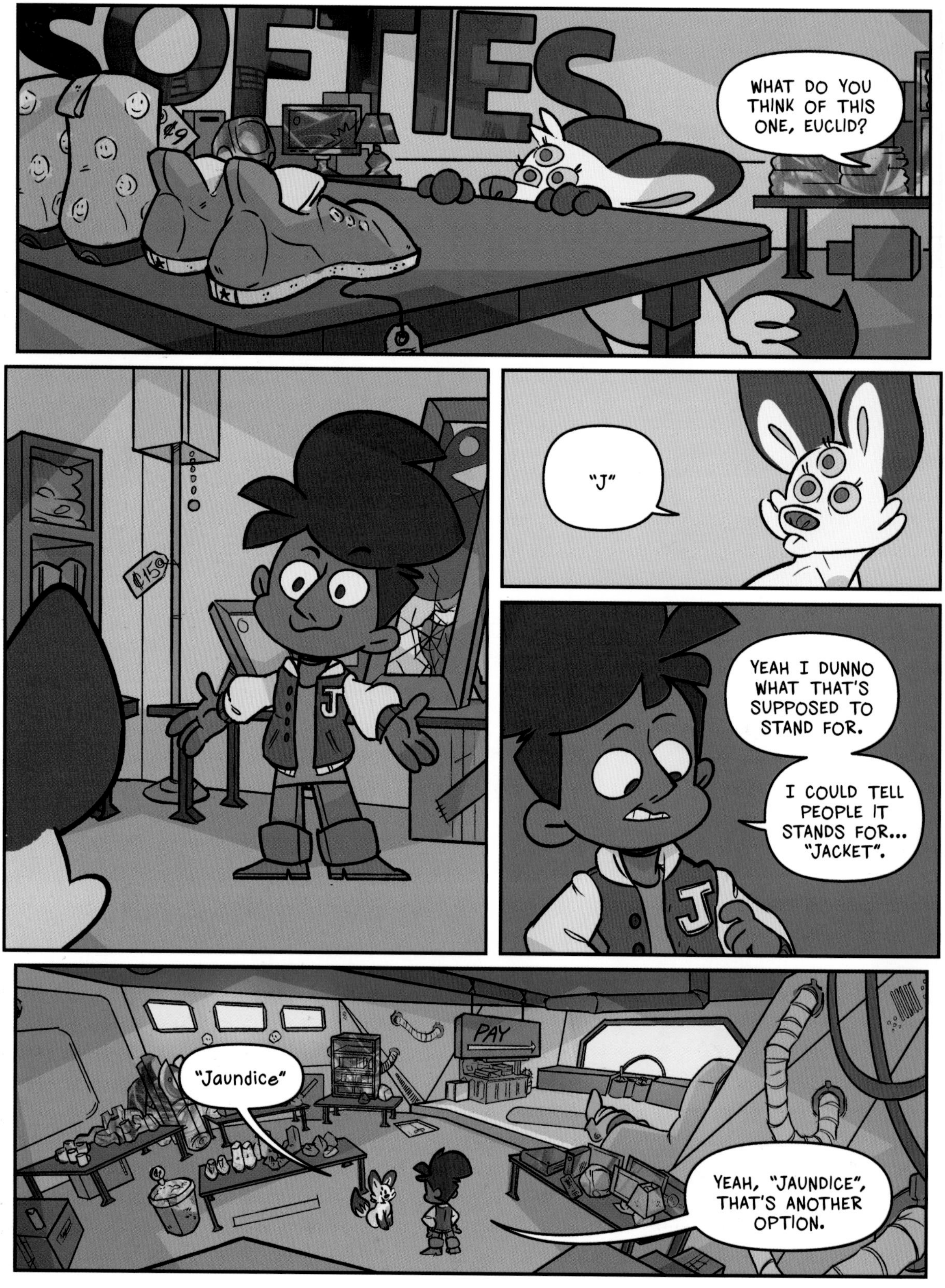
SOFTIES
¢9
WHAT DO YOU THINK OF THIS ONE, EUCLID?
¢15
"J"
YEAH I DUNNO WHAT THAT'S SUPPOSED TO STAND FOR.
I COULD TELL PEOPLE IT STANDS FOR... "JACKET".
PAY
"Jaundice"
YEAH, "JAUNDICE", THAT'S ANOTHER OPTION.

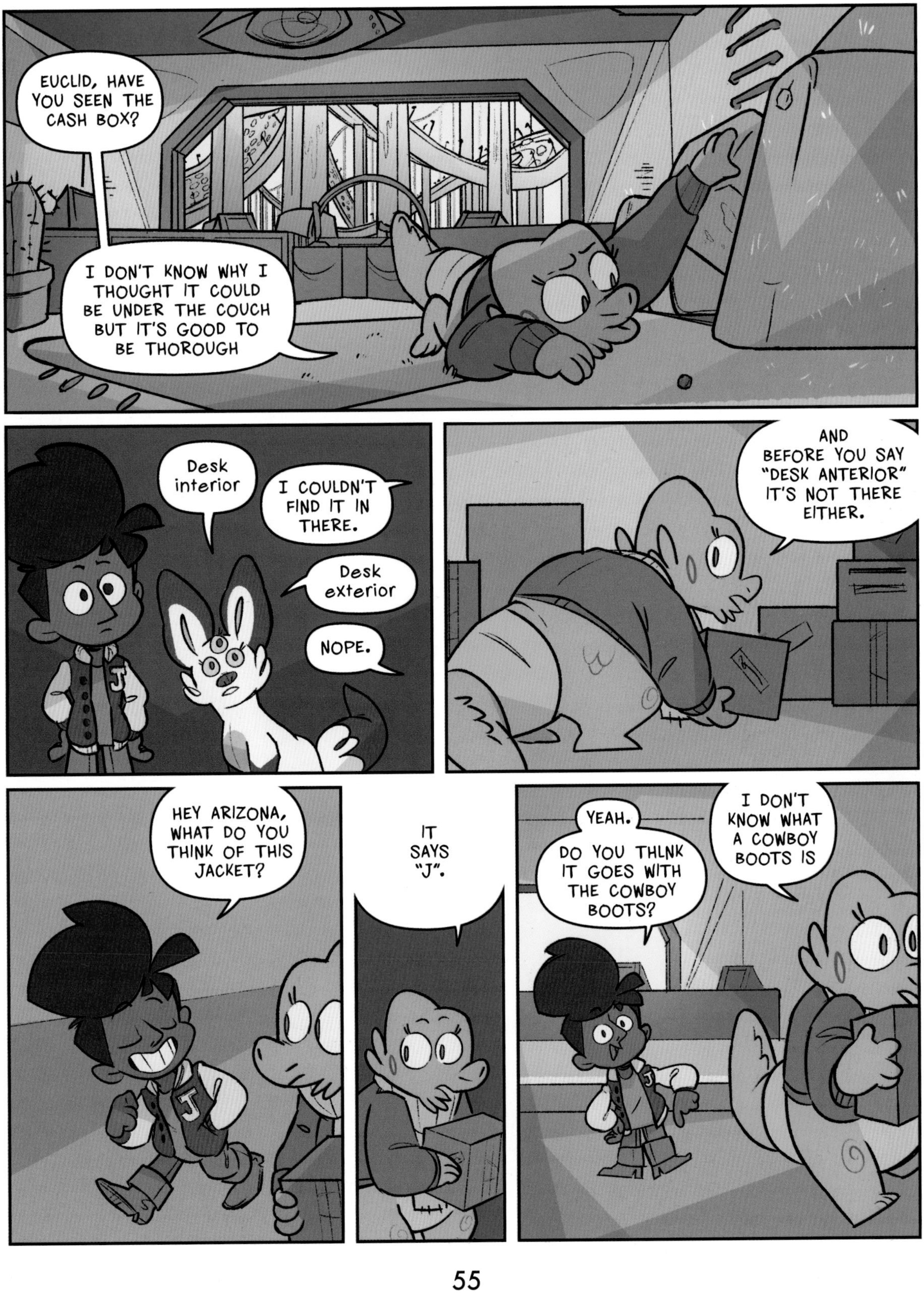
EUCLID, HAVE YOU SEEN THE CASH BOX?
I DON'T KNOW WHY I THOUGHT IT COULD BE UNDER THE COUCH BUT IT'S GOOD TO BE THOROUGH
Desk interior
I COULDN'T FIND IT IN THERE.
Desk exterior
NOPE.
AND BEFORE YOU SAY "DESK ANTERIOR" IT'S NOT THERE EITHER.
HEY ARIZONA, WHAT DO YOU THINK OF THIS JACKET?
IT SAYS "J".
YEAH.
DO YOU THINK IT GOES WITH THE COWBOY BOOTS?
I DON'T KNOW WHAT A COWBOY BOOTS IS

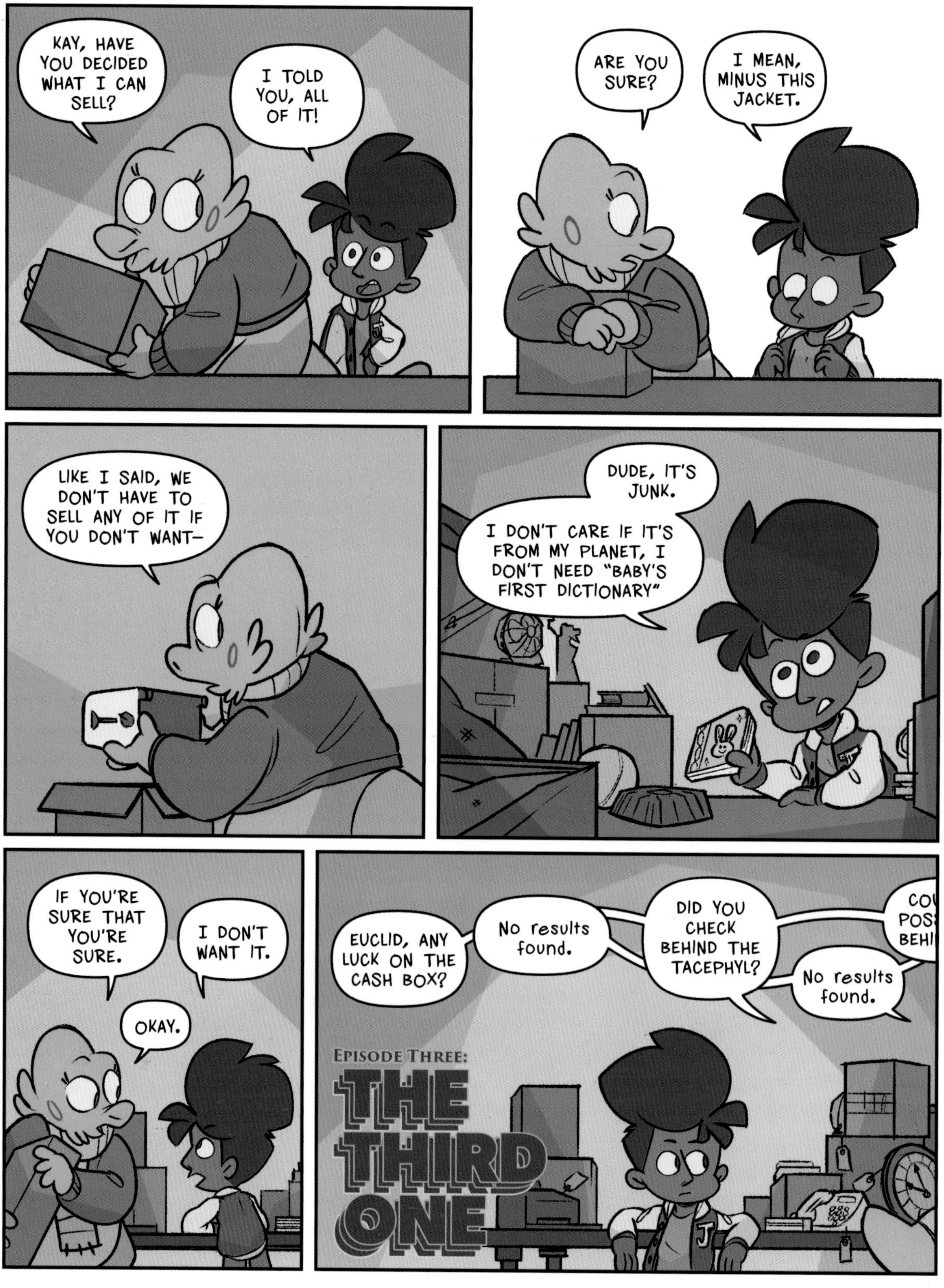
KAY, HAVE YOU DECIDED WHAT I CAN SELL?
I TOLD YOU, ALL OF IT!
ARE YOU SURE?
I MEAN, MINUS THIS JACKET.
LIKE I SAID, WE DON'T HAVE TO SELL ANY OF IT IF YOU DON'T WANT—
DUDE, IT'S JUNK.
I DON'T CARE IF IT'S FROM MY PLANET, I DON'T NEED "BABY'S FIRST DICTIONARY"
IF YOU'RE SURE THAT YOU'RE SURE.
I DON'T WANT IT.
OKAY.
EUCLID, ANY LUCK ON THE CASH BOX?
No results found.
DID YOU CHECK BEHIND THE TACEPHYL?
No results found.
EPISODE THREE:
THE THIRD ONE

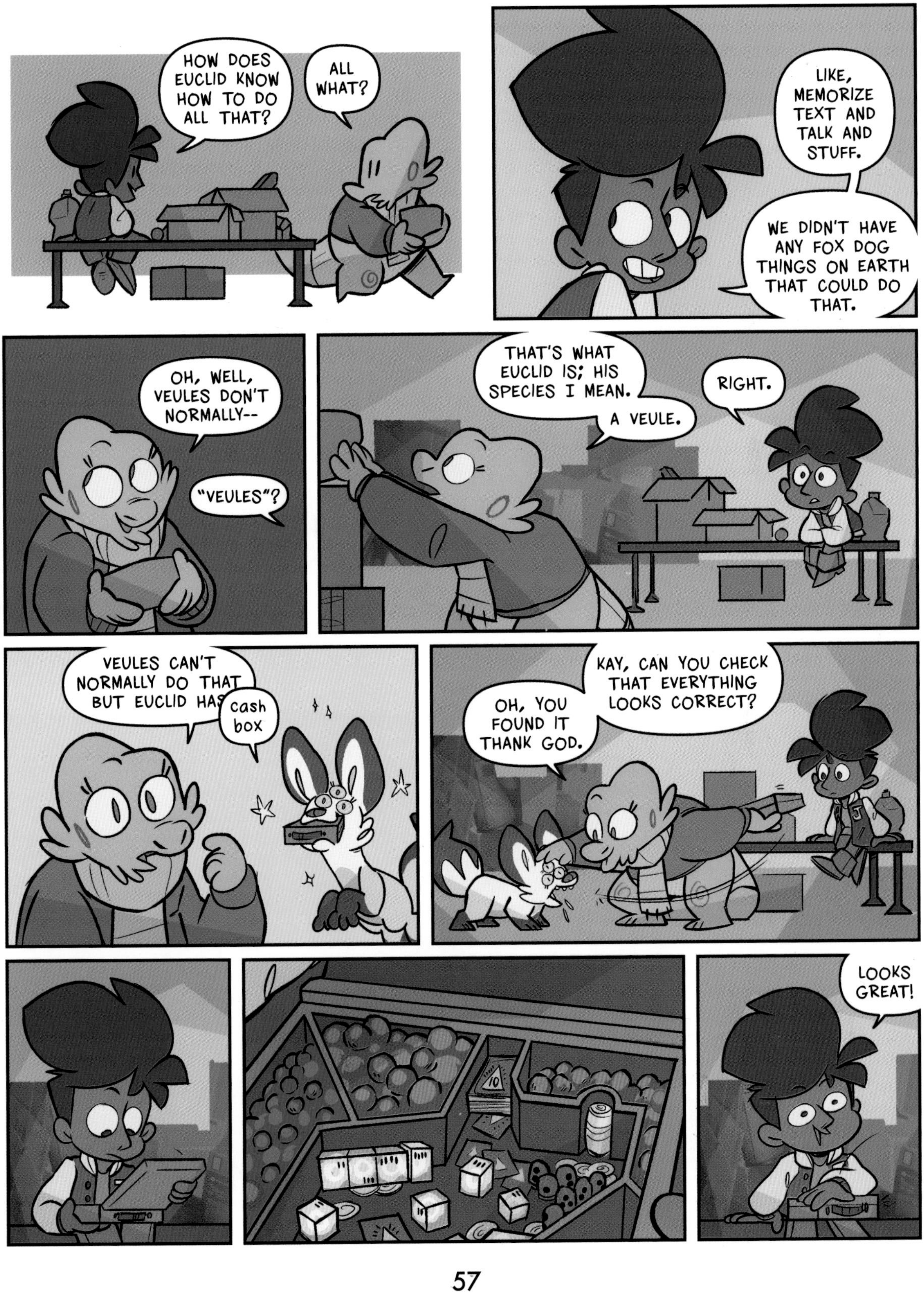
HOW DOES EUCLID KNOW HOW TO DO ALL THAT?
ALL WHAT?
LIKE, MEMORIZE TEXT AND TALK AND STUFF.
WE DIDN'T HAVE ANY FOX DOG THINGS ON EARTH THAT COULD DO THAT.
OH, WELL, VEULES DON'T NORMALLY--
"VEULES"?
THAT'S WHAT EUCLID IS; HIS SPECIES I MEAN.
A VEULE.
RIGHT.
VEULES CAN'T NORMALLY DO THAT BUT EUCLID HAS
cash box
OH, YOU FOUND IT THANK GOD.
KAY, CAN YOU CHECK THAT EVERYTHING LOOKS CORRECT?
10
LOOKS GREAT!

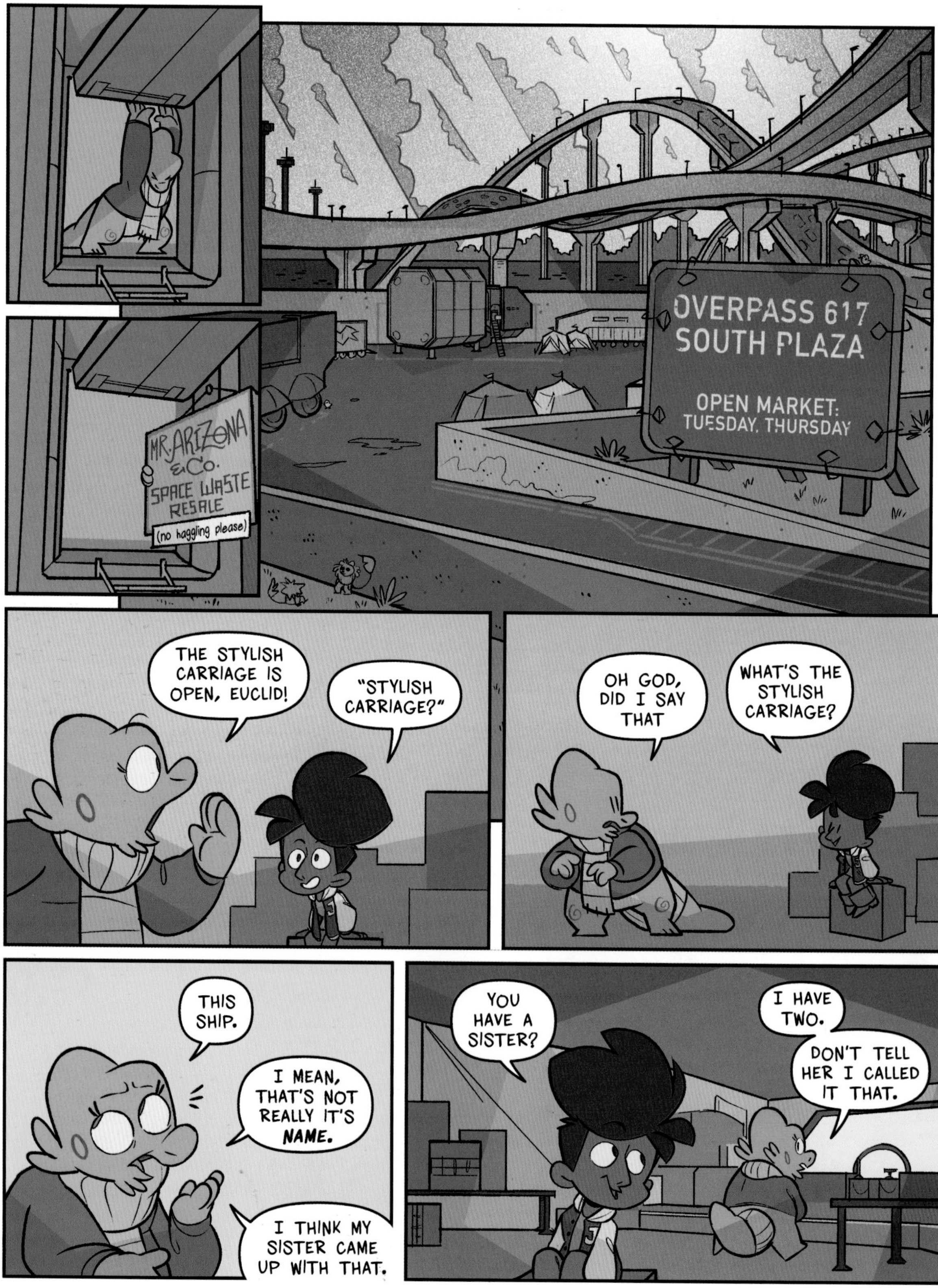
MR. ARIZONA & Co.
SPACE WASTE RESALE
(no haggling please)
OVERPASS 617
SOUTH PLAZA
OPEN MARKET:
TUESDAY, THURSDAY
THE STYLISH CARRIAGE IS OPEN, EUCLID!
"STYLISH CARRIAGE?"
OH GOD, DID I SAY THAT
WHAT'S THE STYLISH CARRIAGE?
THIS SHIP.
I MEAN, THAT'S NOT REALLY IT'S **NAME.**
I THINK MY SISTER CAME UP WITH THAT.
YOU HAVE A SISTER?
I HAVE TWO.
DON'T TELL HER I CALLED IT THAT.

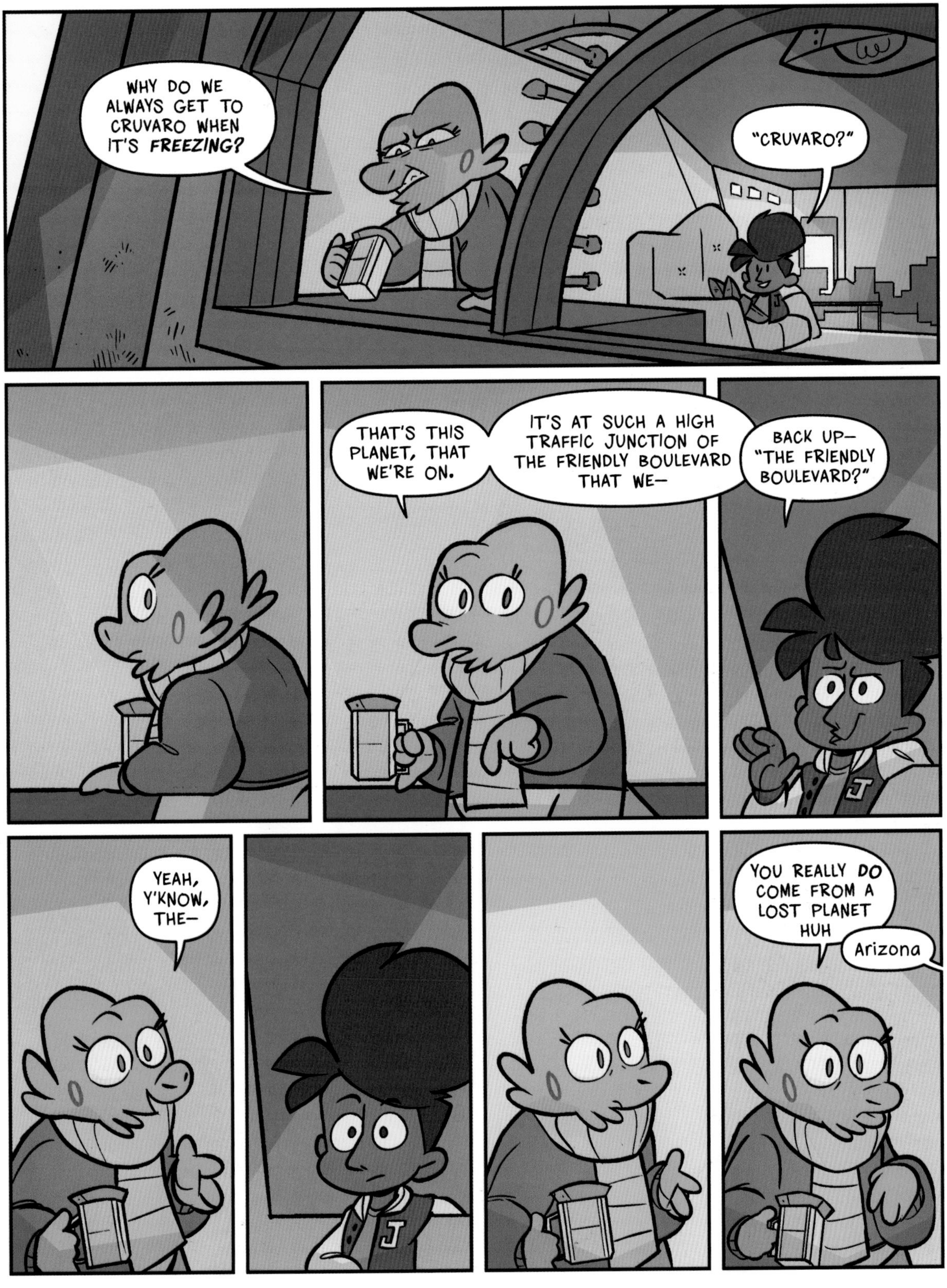
WHY DO WE ALWAYS GET TO CRUVARO WHEN IT'S FREEZING?
"CRUVARO?"
THAT'S THIS PLANET, THAT WE'RE ON.
IT'S AT SUCH A HIGH TRAFFIC JUNCTION OF THE FRIENDLY BOULEVARD THAT WE—
BACK UP— "THE FRIENDLY BOULEVARD?"
YEAH, Y'KNOW, THE—
YOU REALLY DO COME FROM A LOST PLANET HUH
Arizona

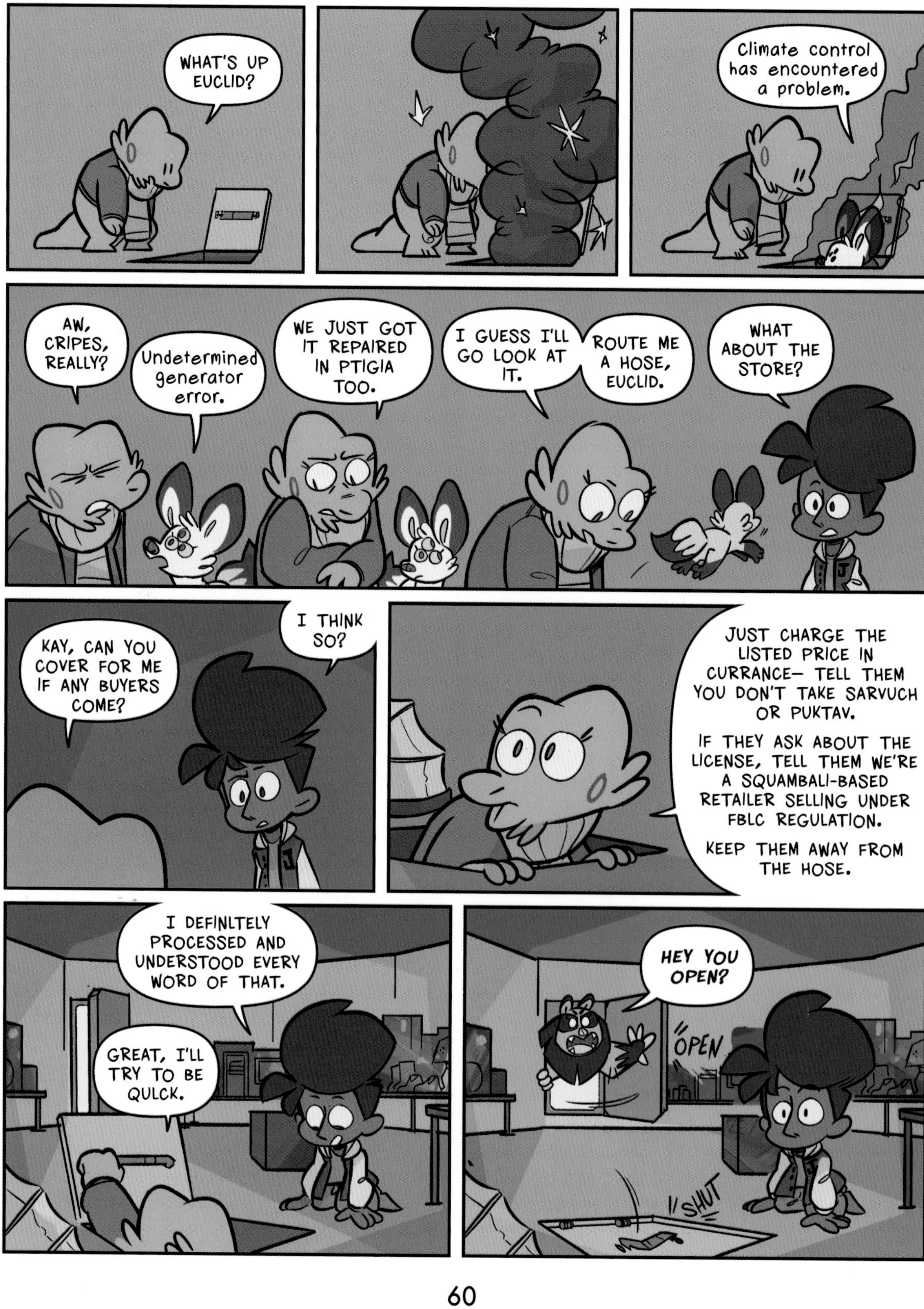
WHAT'S UP EUCLID?
Climate control has encountered a problem.
AW, CRIPES, REALLY?
Undetermined generator error.
WE JUST GOT IT REPAIRED IN PTIGIA TOO.
I GUESS I'LL GO LOOK AT IT.
ROUTE ME A HOSE, EUCLID.
WHAT ABOUT THE STORE?
KAY, CAN YOU COVER FOR ME IF ANY BUYERS COME?
I THINK SO?
JUST CHARGE THE LISTED PRICE IN CURRANCE— TELL THEM YOU DON'T TAKE SARVUCH OR PUKTAV.
IF THEY ASK ABOUT THE LICENSE, TELL THEM WE'RE A SQUAMBALI-BASED RETAILER SELLING UNDER FBLC REGULATION.
KEEP THEM AWAY FROM THE HOSE.
I DEFINITELY PROCESSED AND UNDERSTOOD EVERY WORD OF THAT.
GREAT, I'LL TRY TO BE QUICK.
HEY YOU OPEN?
OPEN
SHUT

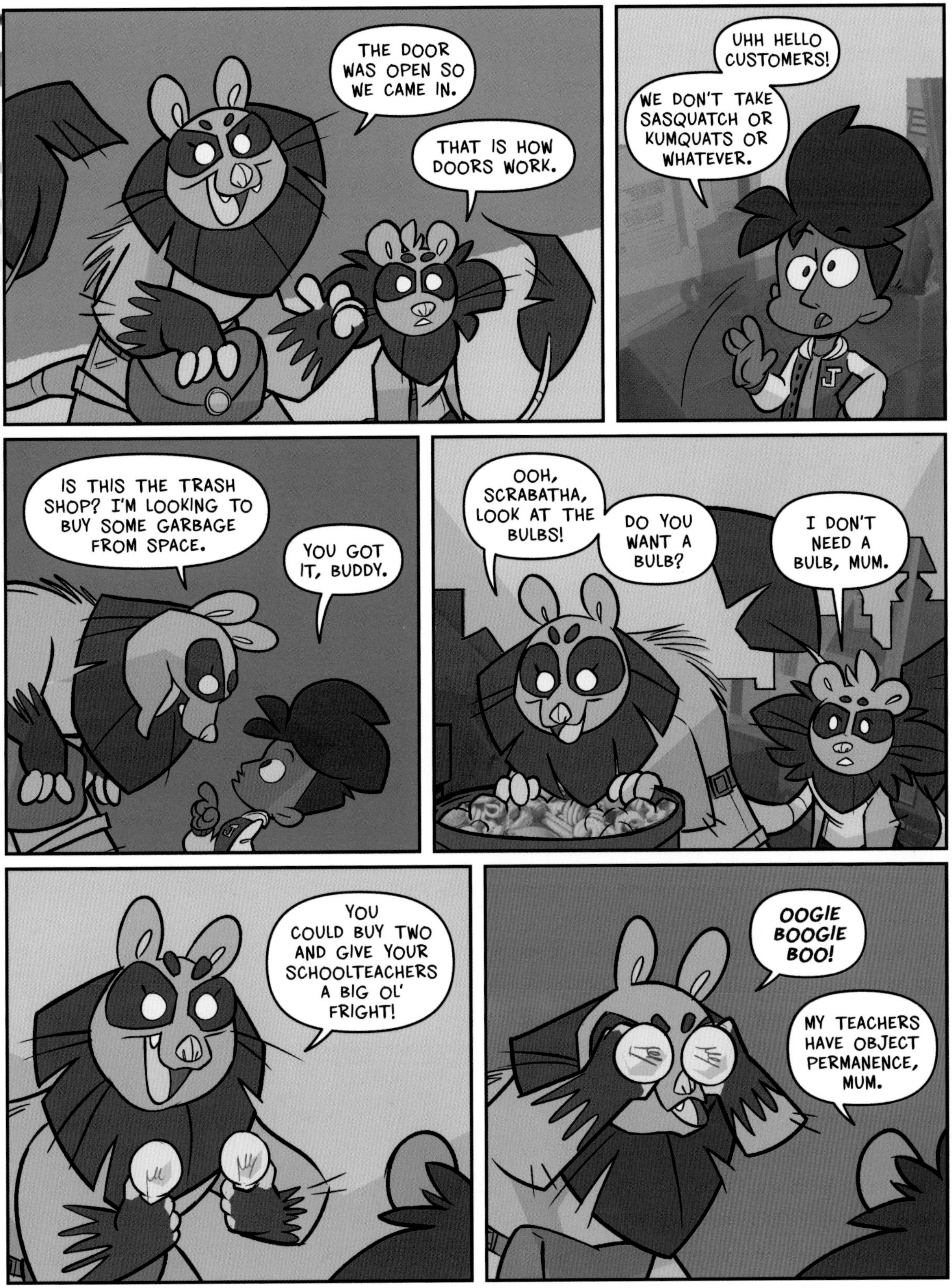
THE DOOR WAS OPEN SO WE CAME IN.
THAT IS HOW DOORS WORK.
UHH HELLO CUSTOMERS!
WE DON'T TAKE SASQUATCH OR KUMQUATS OR WHATEVER.
IS THIS THE TRASH SHOP? I'M LOOKING TO BUY SOME GARBAGE FROM SPACE.
YOU GOT IT, BUDDY.
OOH, SCRABATHA, LOOK AT THE BULBS!
DO YOU WANT A BULB?
I DON'T NEED A BULB, MUM.
YOU COULD BUY TWO AND GIVE YOUR SCHOOLTEACHERS A BIG OL' FRIGHT!
OOGIE BOOGIE BOO!
MY TEACHERS HAVE OBJECT PERMANENCE, MUM.

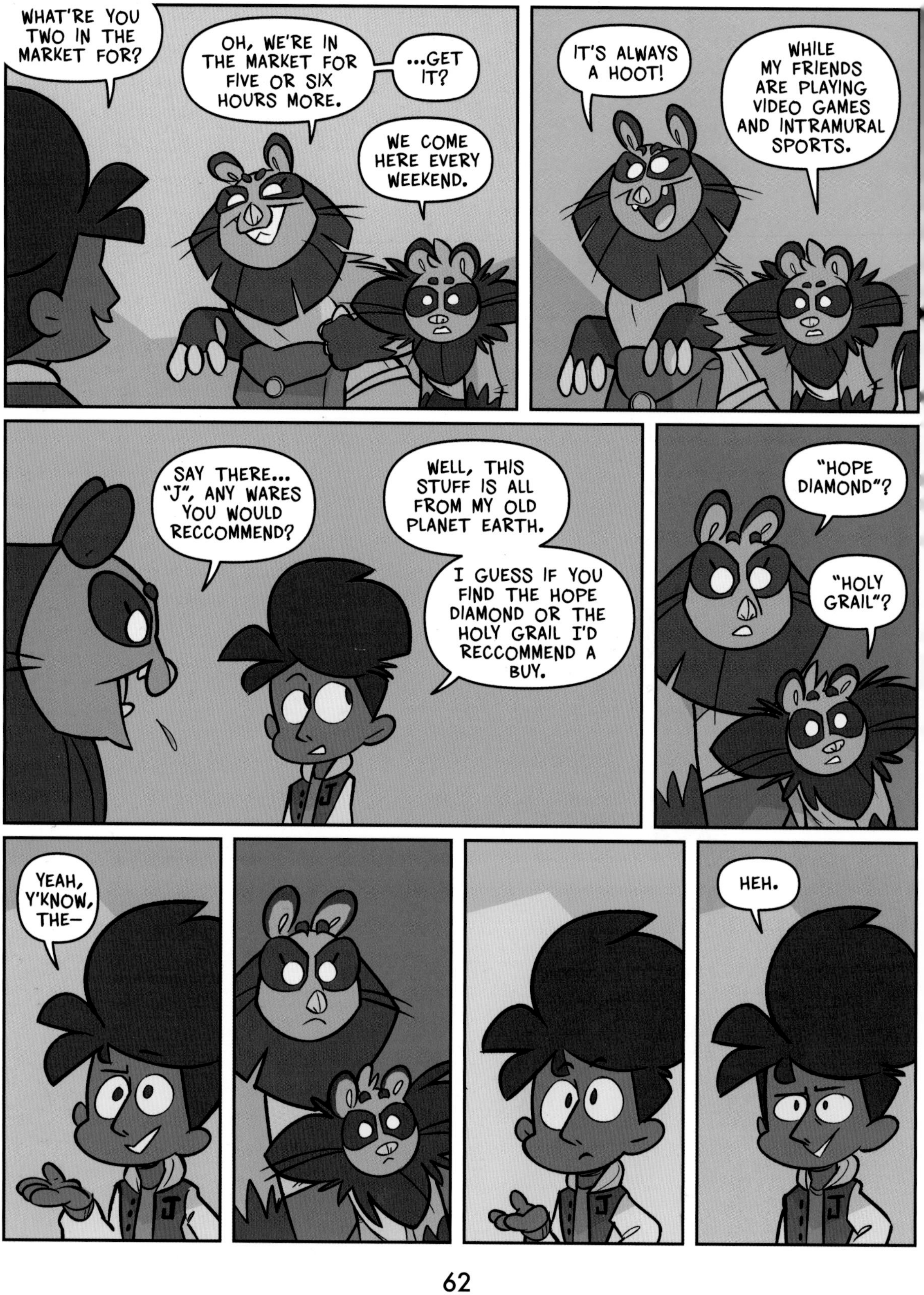
WHAT'RE YOU TWO IN THE MARKET FOR?
OH, WE'RE IN THE MARKET FOR FIVE OR SIX HOURS MORE.
...GET IT?
WE COME HERE EVERY WEEKEND.
IT'S ALWAYS A HOOT!
WHILE MY FRIENDS ARE PLAYING VIDEO GAMES AND INTRAMURAL SPORTS.
SAY THERE... "J", ANY WARES YOU WOULD RECCOMMEND?
WELL, THIS STUFF IS ALL FROM MY OLD PLANET EARTH.
I GUESS IF YOU FIND THE HOPE DIAMOND OR THE HOLY GRAIL I'D RECCOMMEND A BUY.
"HOPE DIAMOND"?
"HOLY GRAIL"?
YEAH, Y'KNOW, THE—
HEH.

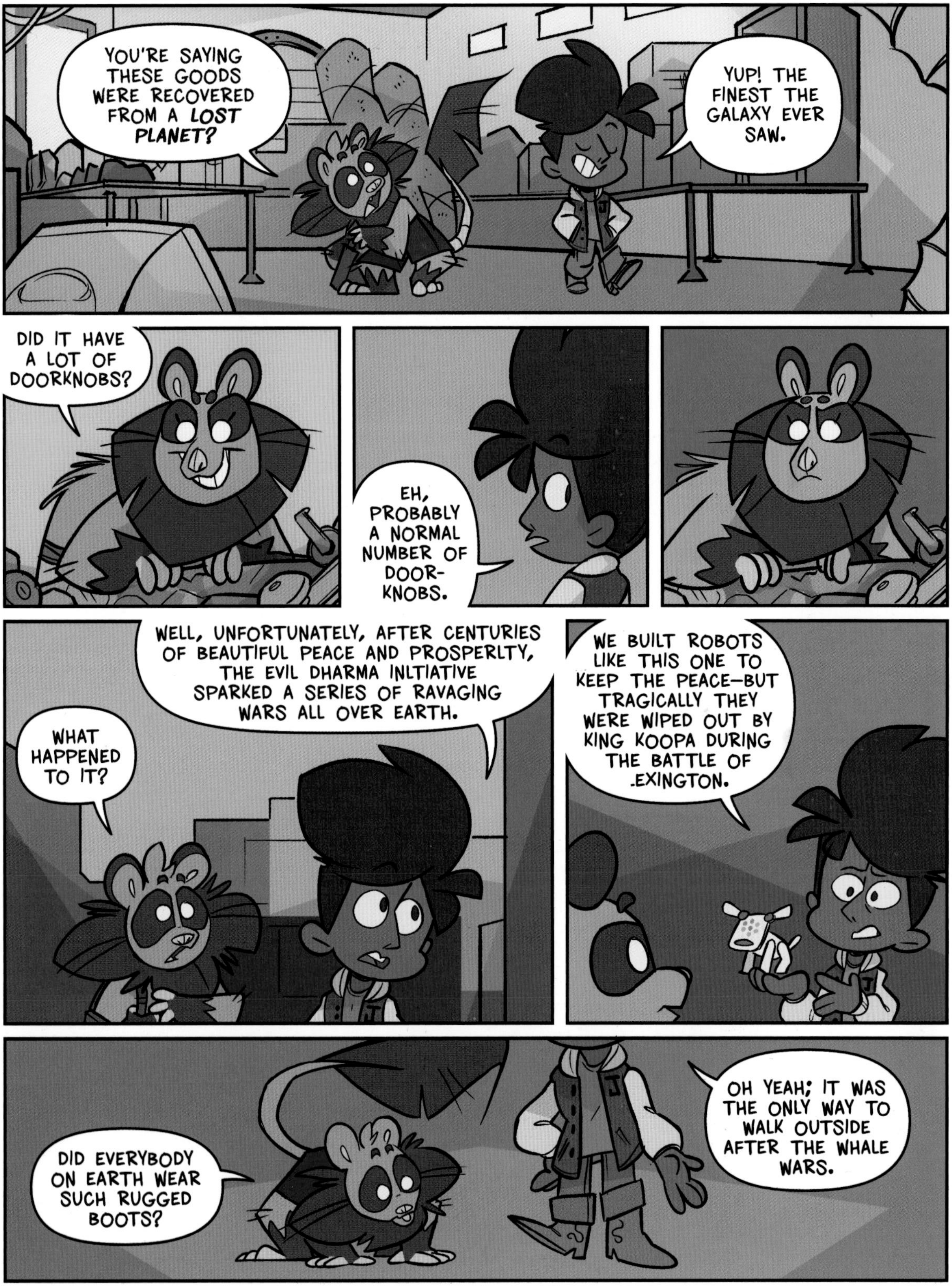
YOU'RE SAYING THESE GOODS WERE RECOVERED FROM A **LOST PLANET?**
YUP! THE FINEST THE GALAXY EVER SAW.
DID IT HAVE A LOT OF DOORKNOBS?
EH, PROBABLY A NORMAL NUMBER OF DOOR-KNOBS.
WHAT HAPPENED TO IT?
WELL, UNFORTUNATELY, AFTER CENTURIES OF BEAUTIFUL PEACE AND PROSPERLTY, THE EVIL DHARMA INLTIATIVE SPARKED A SERIES OF RAVAGING WARS ALL OVER EARTH.
WE BUILT ROBOTS LIKE THIS ONE TO KEEP THE PEACE—BUT TRAGICALLY THEY WERE WIPED OUT BY KING KOOPA DURING THE BATTLE OF .EXINGTON.
DID EVERYBODY ON EARTH WEAR SUCH RUGGED BOOTS?
OH YEAH; IT WAS THE ONLY WAY TO WALK OUTSIDE AFTER THE WHALE WARS.

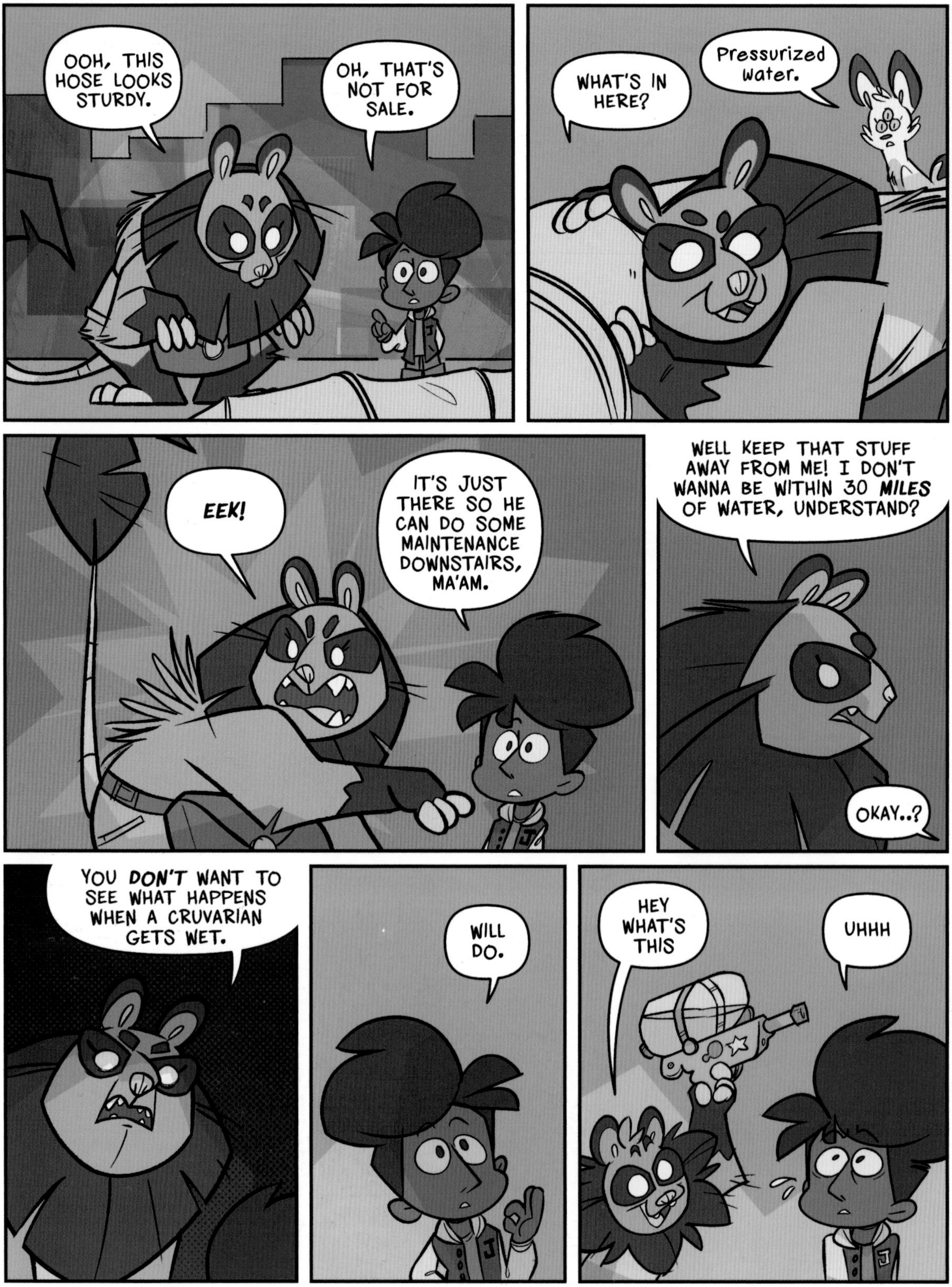

OOH, THIS HOSE LOOKS STURDY.
OH, THAT'S NOT FOR SALE.
WHAT'S IN HERE?
Pressurized water.
EEK!
IT'S JUST THERE SO HE CAN DO SOME MAINTENANCE DOWNSTAIRS, MA'AM.
WELL KEEP THAT STUFF AWAY FROM ME! I DON'T WANNA BE WITHIN 30 MILES OF WATER, UNDERSTAND?
OKAY..?
YOU DON'T WANT TO SEE WHAT HAPPENS WHEN A CRUVARIAN GETS WET.
WILL DO.
HEY WHAT'S THIS
UHHH

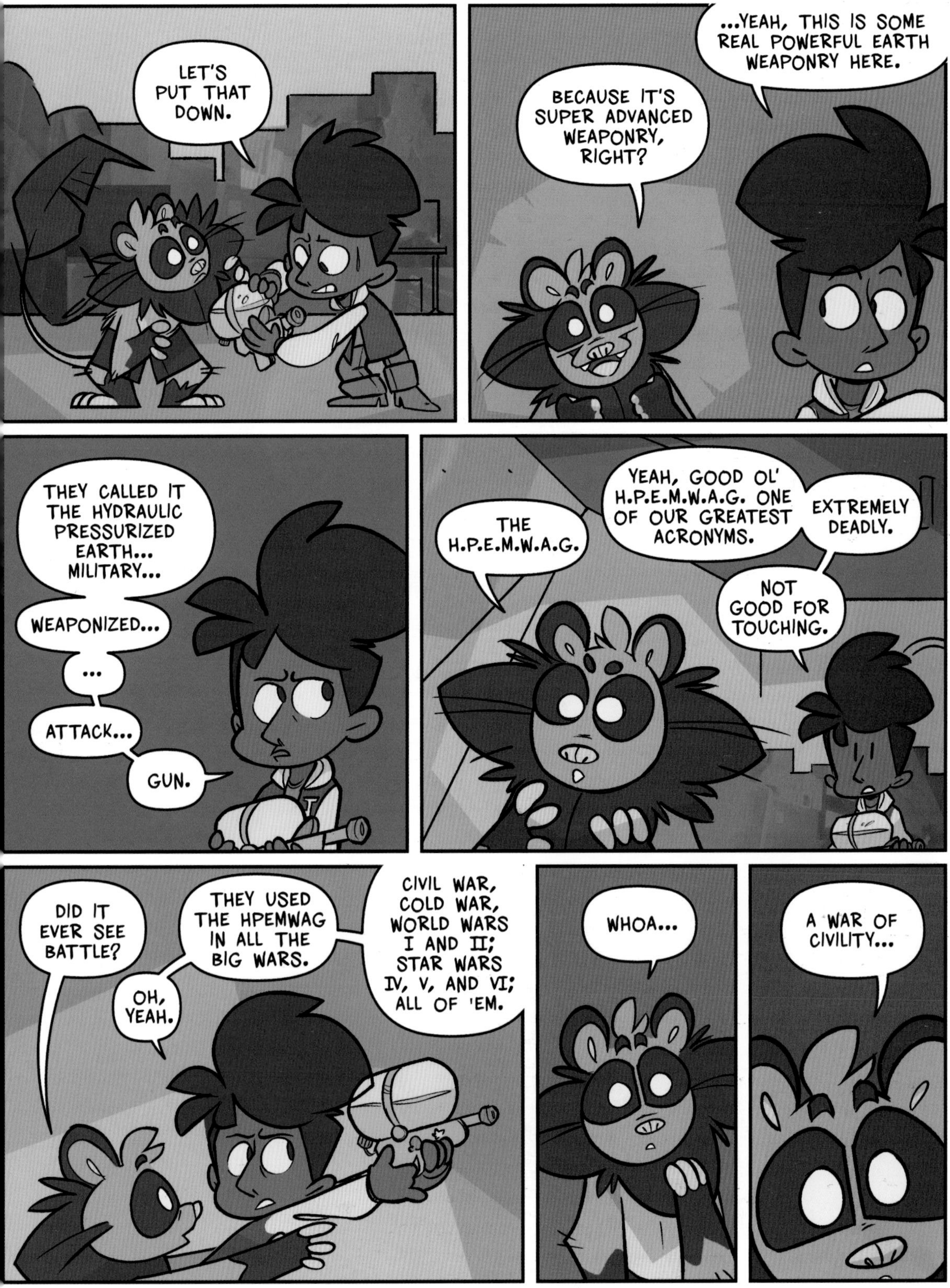
LET'S PUT THAT DOWN.
BECAUSE IT'S SUPER ADVANCED WEAPONRY, RIGHT?
...YEAH, THIS IS SOME REAL POWERFUL EARTH WEAPONRY HERE.
THEY CALLED IT THE HYDRAULIC PRESSURIZED EARTH... MILITARY...
WEAPONIZED...
...
ATTACK...
GUN.
THE H.P.E.M.W.A.G.
YEAH, GOOD OL' H.P.E.M.W.A.G. ONE OF OUR GREATEST ACRONYMS.
EXTREMELY DEADLY.
NOT GOOD FOR TOUCHING.
DID IT EVER SEE BATTLE?
OH, YEAH.
THEY USED THE HPEMWAG IN ALL THE BIG WARS.
CIVIL WAR, COLD WAR, WORLD WARS I AND II; STAR WARS IV, V, AND VI; ALL OF 'EM.
WHOA...
A WAR OF CIVILITY...

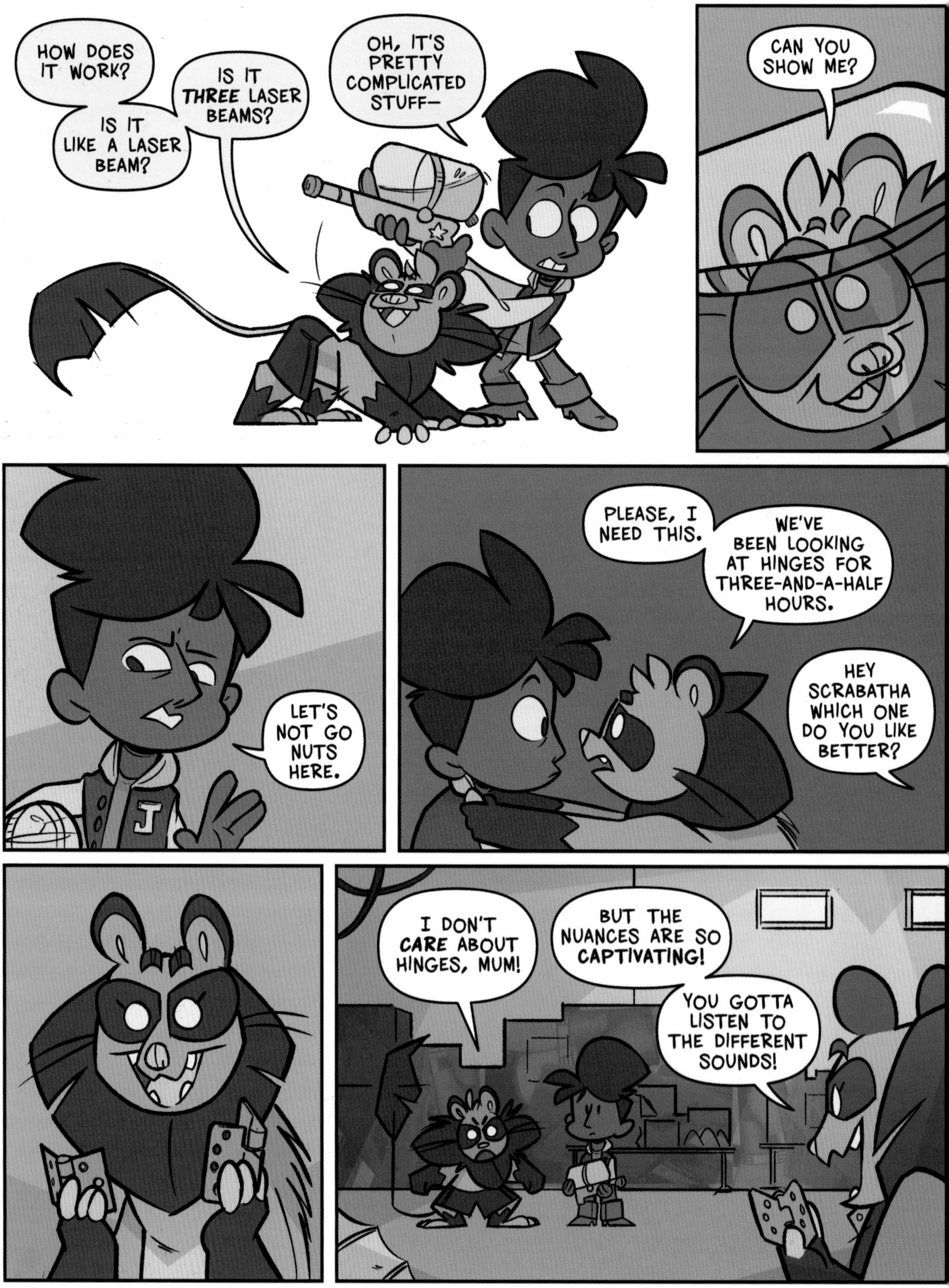

HOW DOES IT WORK?
IS IT LIKE A LASER BEAM?
IS IT **THREE** LASER BEAMS?
OH, IT'S PRETTY COMPLICATED STUFF—
CAN YOU SHOW ME?
LET'S NOT GO NUTS HERE.
PLEASE, I NEED THIS.
WE'VE BEEN LOOKING AT HINGES FOR THREE-AND-A-HALF HOURS.
HEY SCRABATHA WHICH ONE DO YOU LIKE BETTER?
I DON'T **CARE** ABOUT HINGES, MUM!
BUT THE NUANCES ARE SO **CAPTIVATING!**
YOU GOTTA LISTEN TO THE DIFFERENT SOUNDS!

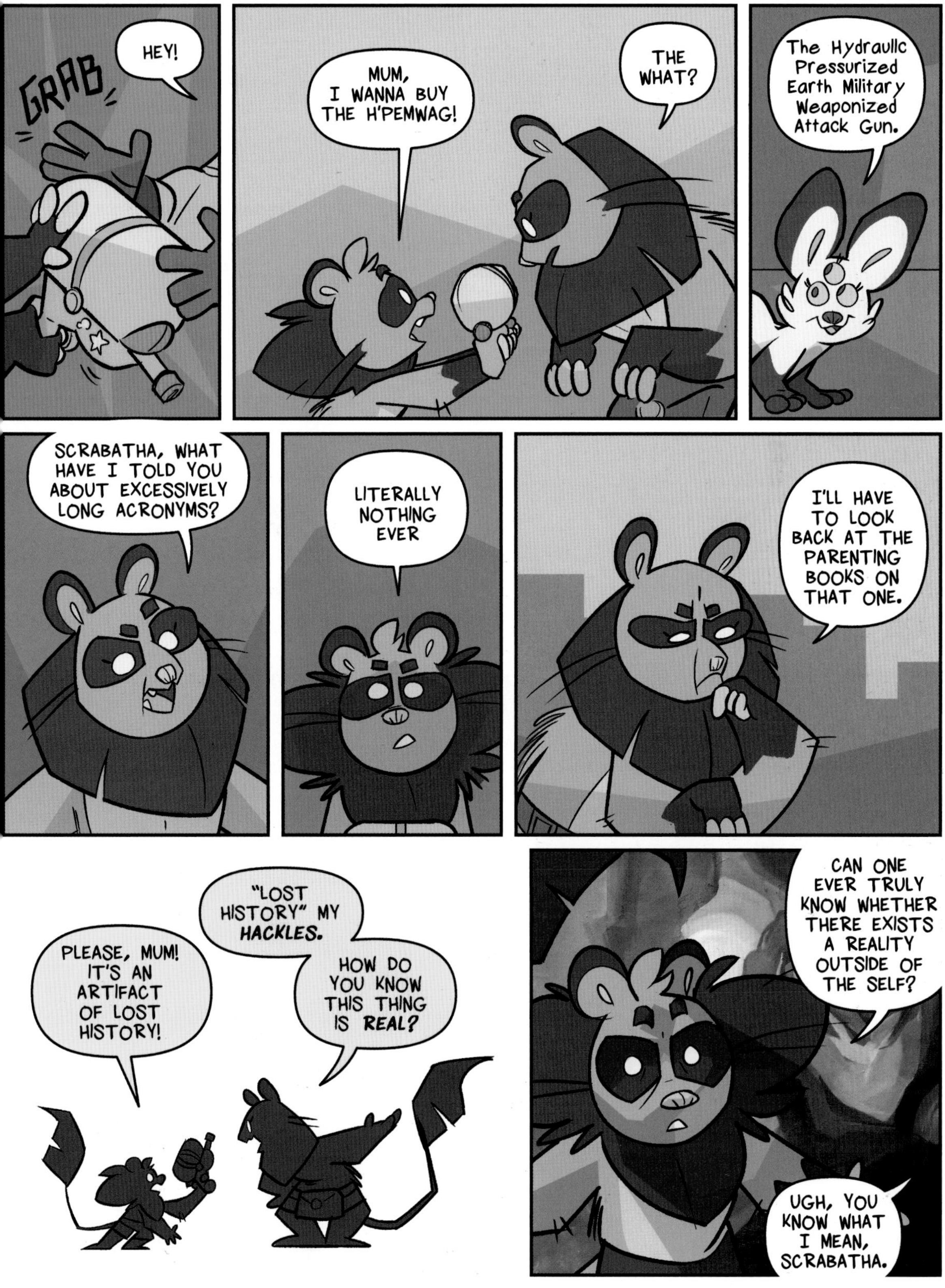

GRAB
HEY!
MUM, I WANNA BUY THE H'PEMWAG!
THE WHAT?
The Hydraulic Pressurized Earth Military Weaponized Attack Gun.
SCRABATHA, WHAT HAVE I TOLD YOU ABOUT EXCESSIVELY LONG ACRONYMS?
LITERALLY NOTHING EVER
I'LL HAVE TO LOOK BACK AT THE PARENTING BOOKS ON THAT ONE.
PLEASE, MUM! IT'S AN ARTIFACT OF LOST HISTORY!
"LOST HISTORY" MY **HACKLES.**
HOW DO YOU KNOW THIS THING IS **REAL?**
CAN ONE EVER TRULY KNOW WHETHER THERE EXISTS A REALITY OUTSIDE OF THE SELF?
UGH, YOU KNOW WHAT I MEAN, SCRABATHA.

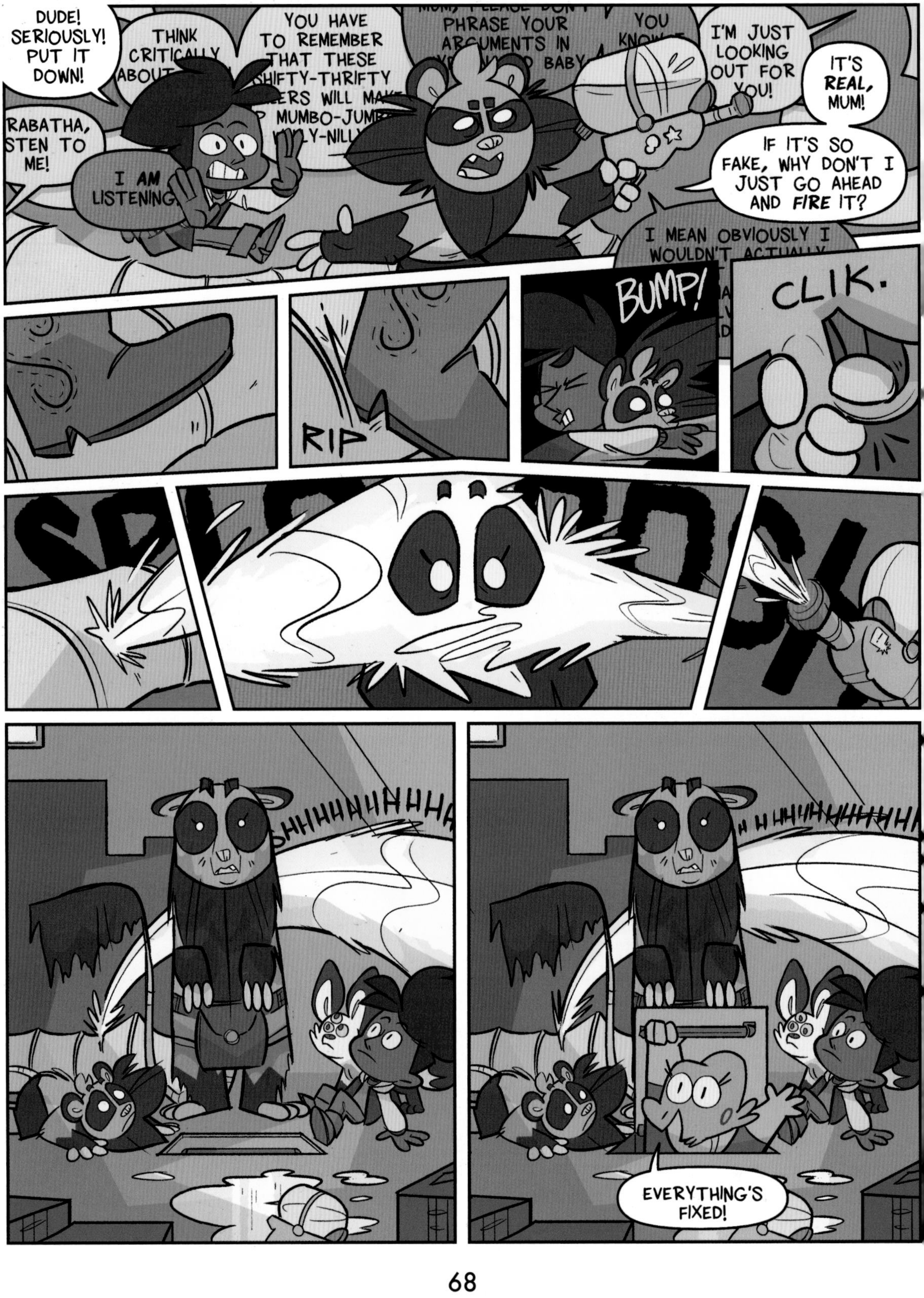
DUDE! SERIOUSLY! PUT IT DOWN!
THINK CRITICALLY
YOU HAVE TO REMEMBER THAT THESE SHIFTY-THRIFTY
PHRASE YOUR ARGUMENTS IN
I'M JUST LOOKING OUT FOR YOU!
IT'S **REAL,** MUM!
IF IT'S SO FAKE, WHY DON'T I JUST GO AHEAD AND **FIRE** IT?
I MEAN OBVIOUSLY I
I **AM** LISTENING.
BUMP!
RIP
CLIK.
EVERYTHING'S FIXED!

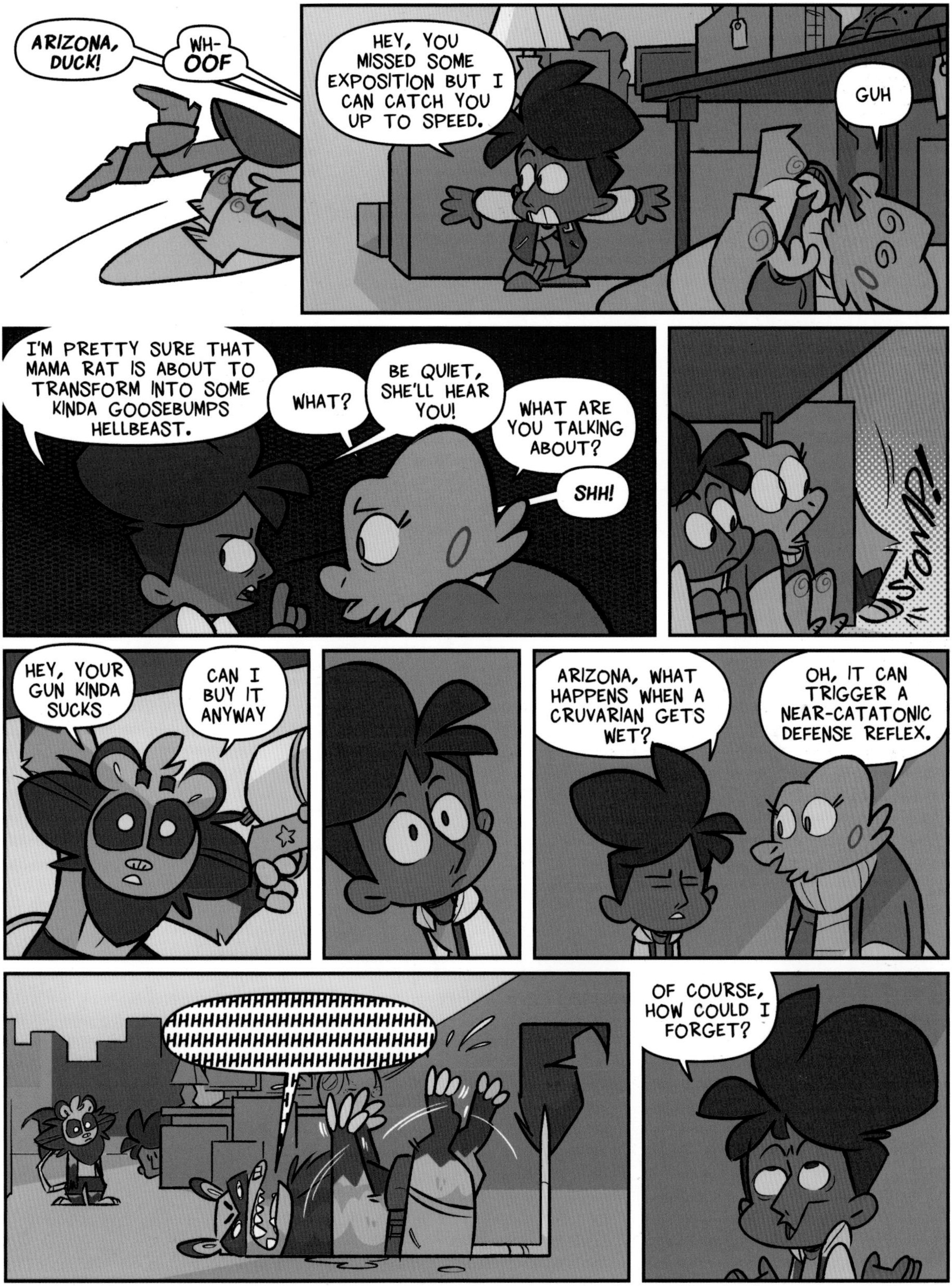
ARIZONA, DUCK!
WH-OOF
HEY, YOU MISSED SOME EXPOSITION BUT I CAN CATCH YOU UP TO SPEED.
GUH
I'M PRETTY SURE THAT MAMA RAT IS ABOUT TO TRANSFORM INTO SOME KINDA GOOSEBUMPS HELLBEAST.
WHAT?
BE QUIET, SHE'LL HEAR YOU!
WHAT ARE YOU TALKING ABOUT?
SHH!
STOMP!
HEY, YOUR GUN KINDA SUCKS
CAN I BUY IT ANYWAY
ARIZONA, WHAT HAPPENS WHEN A CRUVARIAN GETS WET?
OH, IT CAN TRIGGER A NEAR-CATATONIC DEFENSE REFLEX.
AHHHHHHHHHHHHHHHHHHHHHHHHHHHHHHHHHHHHHHHHHHHHHHHHHHHHHHHHHHHHHHHHHHHHHHHHHHHHHHHHHH
OF COURSE, HOW COULD I FORGET?

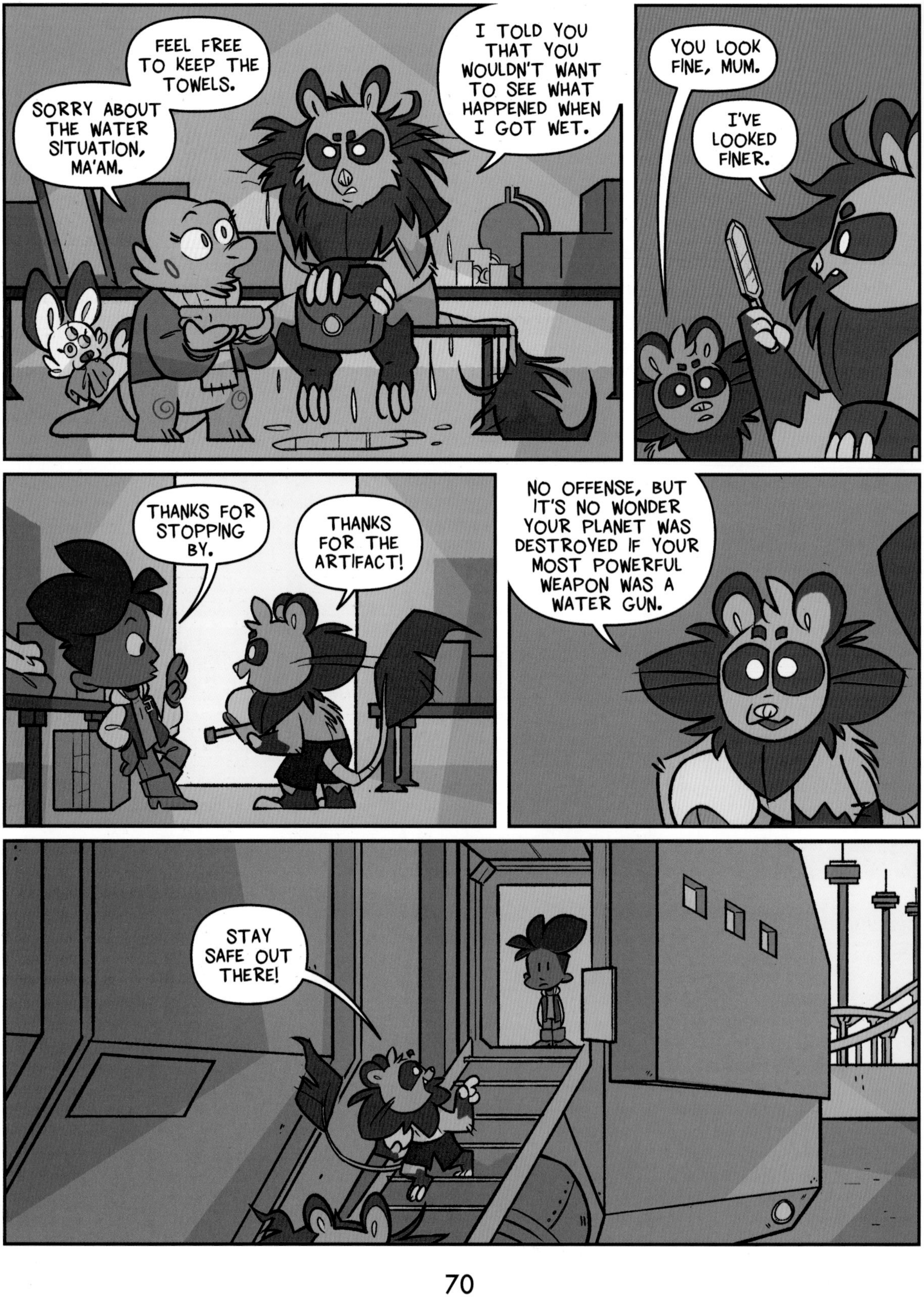
SORRY ABOUT THE WATER SITUATION, MA'AM.
FEEL FREE TO KEEP THE TOWELS.
I TOLD YOU THAT YOU WOULDN'T WANT TO SEE WHAT HAPPENED WHEN I GOT WET.
YOU LOOK FINE, MUM.
I'VE LOOKED FINER.
THANKS FOR STOPPING BY.
THANKS FOR THE ARTIFACT!
NO OFFENSE, BUT IT'S NO WONDER YOUR PLANET WAS DESTROYED IF YOUR MOST POWERFUL WEAPON WAS A WATER GUN.
STAY SAFE OUT THERE!

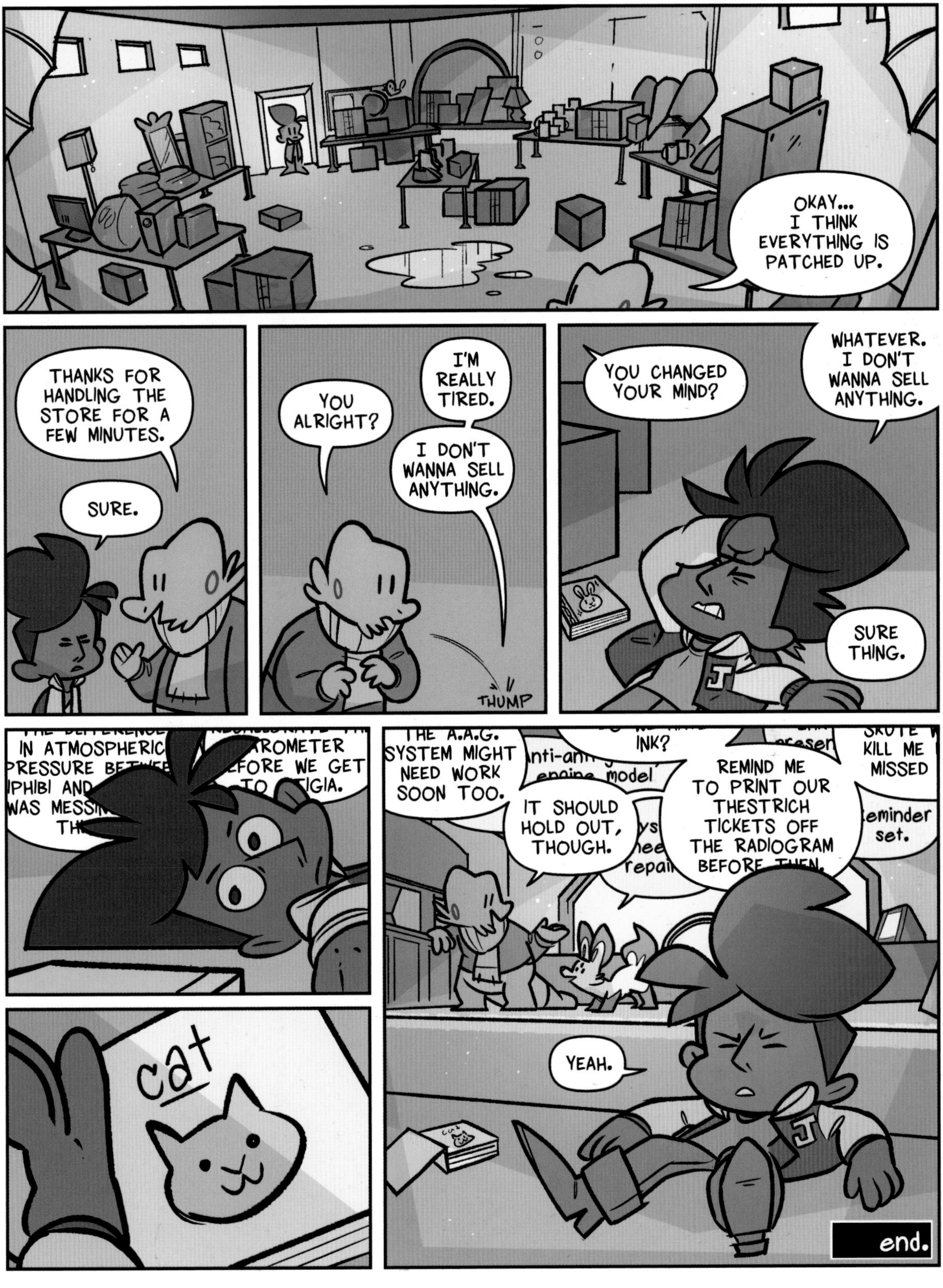
OKAY... I THINK EVERYTHING IS PATCHED UP.
THANKS FOR HANDLING THE STORE FOR A FEW MINUTES.
SURE.
YOU ALRIGHT?
I'M REALLY TIRED.
I DON'T WANNA SELL ANYTHING.
THUMP
YOU CHANGED YOUR MIND?
WHATEVER. I DON'T WANNA SELL ANYTHING.
SURE THING.
IN ATMOSPHERIC
THE A.A.G. SYSTEM MIGHT NEED WORK SOON TOO.
INK?
KILL ME
MISSED
REMIND ME TO PRINT OUR THESTRICH TICKETS OFF THE RADIOGRAM
IT SHOULD HOLD OUT, THOUGH.
set.
cat
YEAH.
end.

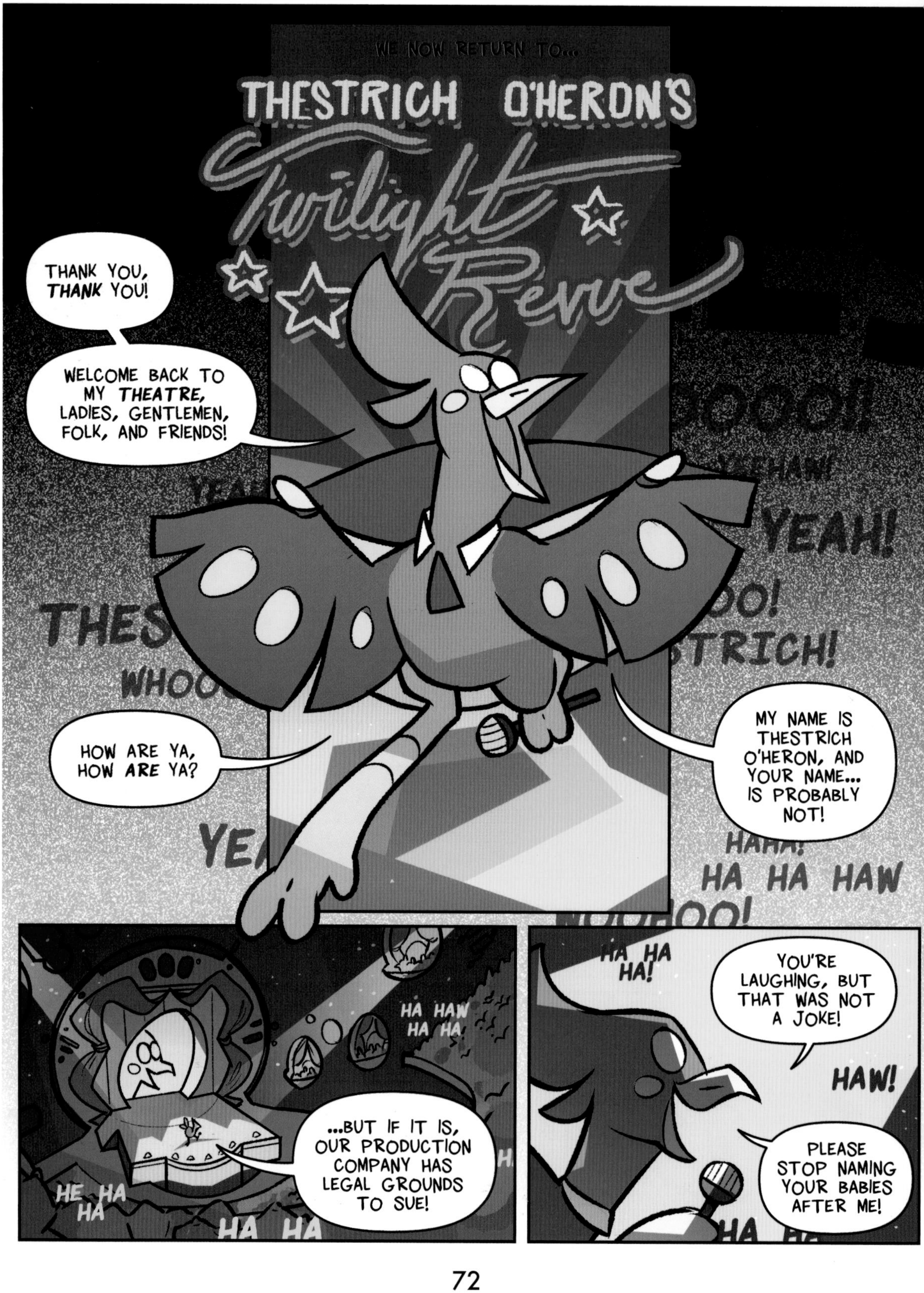
WE NOW RETURN TO...
THESTRICH O'HERON'S
Twilight Revue
THANK YOU, THANK YOU!
WELCOME BACK TO MY THEATRE, LADIES, GENTLEMEN, FOLK, AND FRIENDS!
YEAH!
HOW ARE YA, HOW ARE YA?
MY NAME IS THESTRICH O'HERON, AND YOUR NAME... IS PROBABLY NOT!
HAHA!
HA HA HAW
HA HAW HA HA
...BUT IF IT IS, OUR PRODUCTION COMPANY HAS LEGAL GROUNDS TO SUE!
HE HA HA
HA HA
HA HA HA!
YOU'RE LAUGHING, BUT THAT WAS NOT A JOKE!
HAW!
PLEASE STOP NAMING YOUR BABIES AFTER ME!

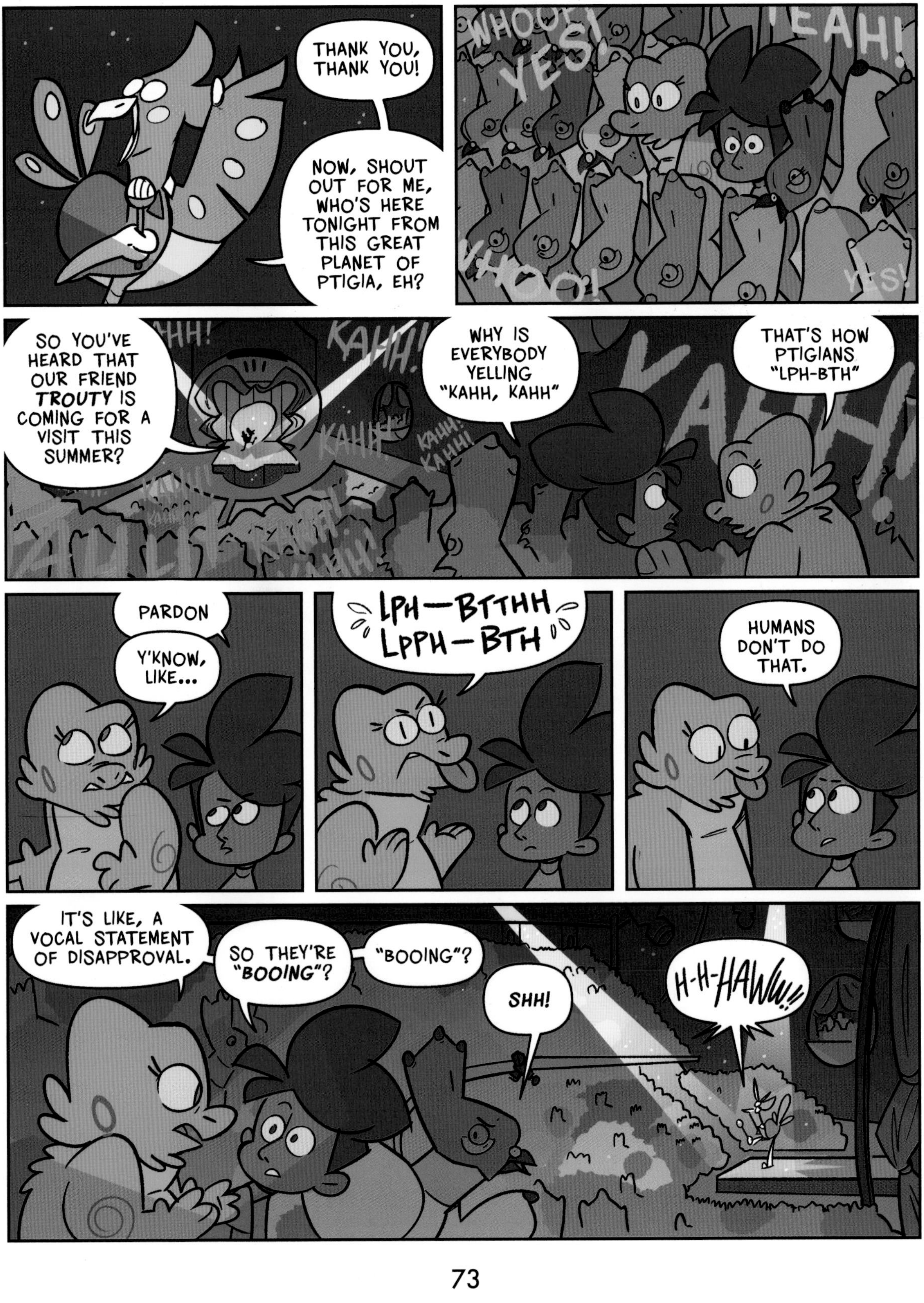

THANK YOU, THANK YOU!
NOW, SHOUT OUT FOR ME, WHO'S HERE TONIGHT FROM THIS GREAT PLANET OF PTIGIA, EH?
WHOOP! YES! YEAH! WHOO! YES!
SO YOU'VE HEARD THAT OUR FRIEND TROUTY IS COMING FOR A VISIT THIS SUMMER?
KAHH! KAHH! KAHH, KAHH!
WHY IS EVERYBODY YELLING "KAHH, KAHH"
THAT'S HOW PTIGIANS "LPH-BTH"
PARDON
Y'KNOW, LIKE...
LPH—BTTHH LPPH—BTH
HUMANS DON'T DO THAT.
IT'S LIKE, A VOCAL STATEMENT OF DISAPPROVAL.
SO THEY'RE "BOOING"?
"BOOING"?
SHH!
H-H-HAWW!!

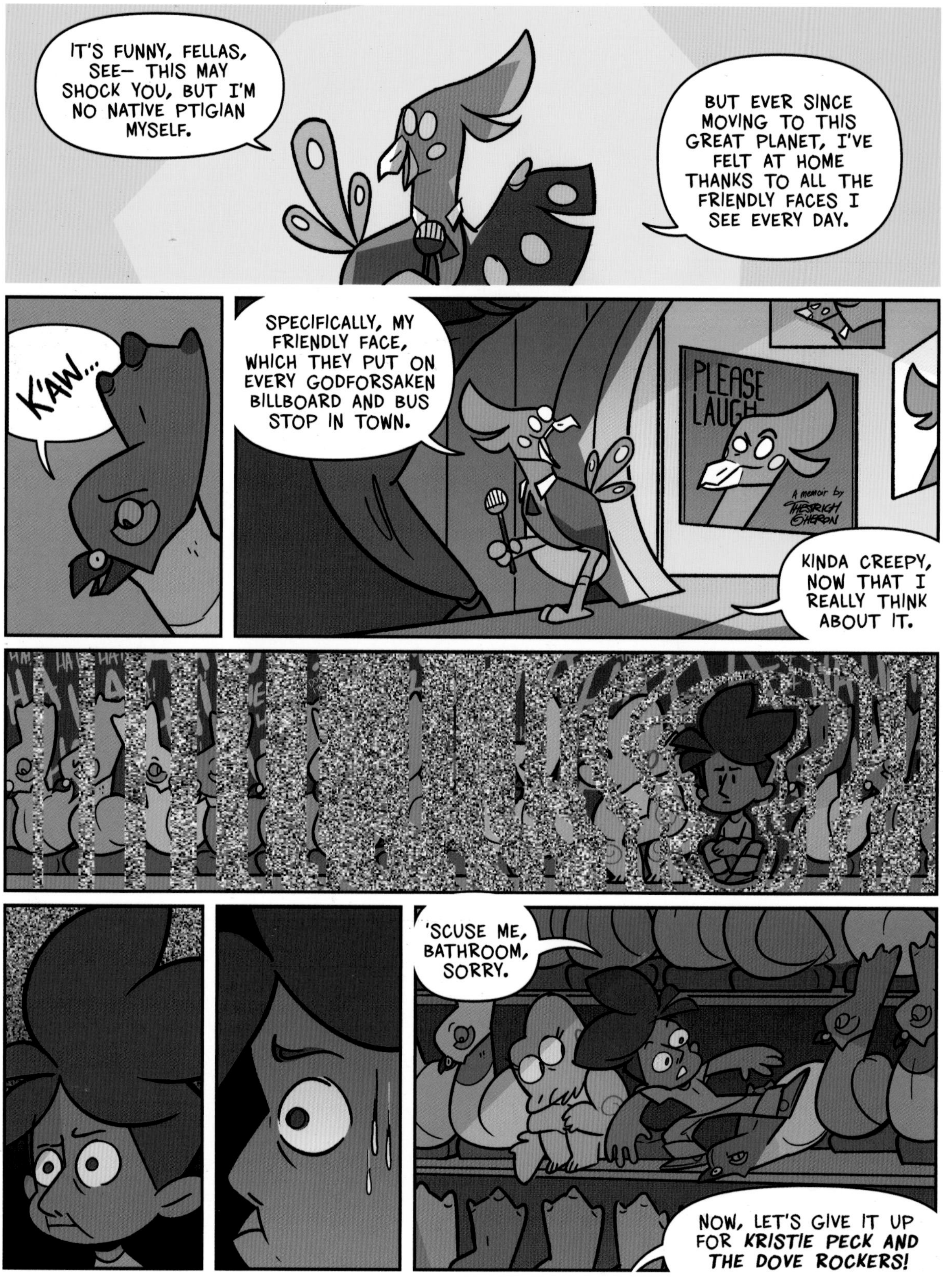
IT'S FUNNY, FELLAS, SEE— THIS MAY SHOCK YOU, BUT I'M NO NATIVE PTIGIAN MYSELF.
BUT EVER SINCE MOVING TO THIS GREAT PLANET, I'VE FELT AT HOME THANKS TO ALL THE FRIENDLY FACES I SEE EVERY DAY.
K'AW...
SPECIFICALLY, MY FRIENDLY FACE, WHICH THEY PUT ON EVERY GODFORSAKEN BILLBOARD AND BUS STOP IN TOWN.
PLEASE LAUGH
A memoir by
KINDA CREEPY, NOW THAT I REALLY THINK ABOUT IT.
'SCUSE ME, BATHROOM, SORRY.
NOW, LET'S GIVE IT UP FOR *KRISTIE PECK AND THE DOVE ROCKERS!*

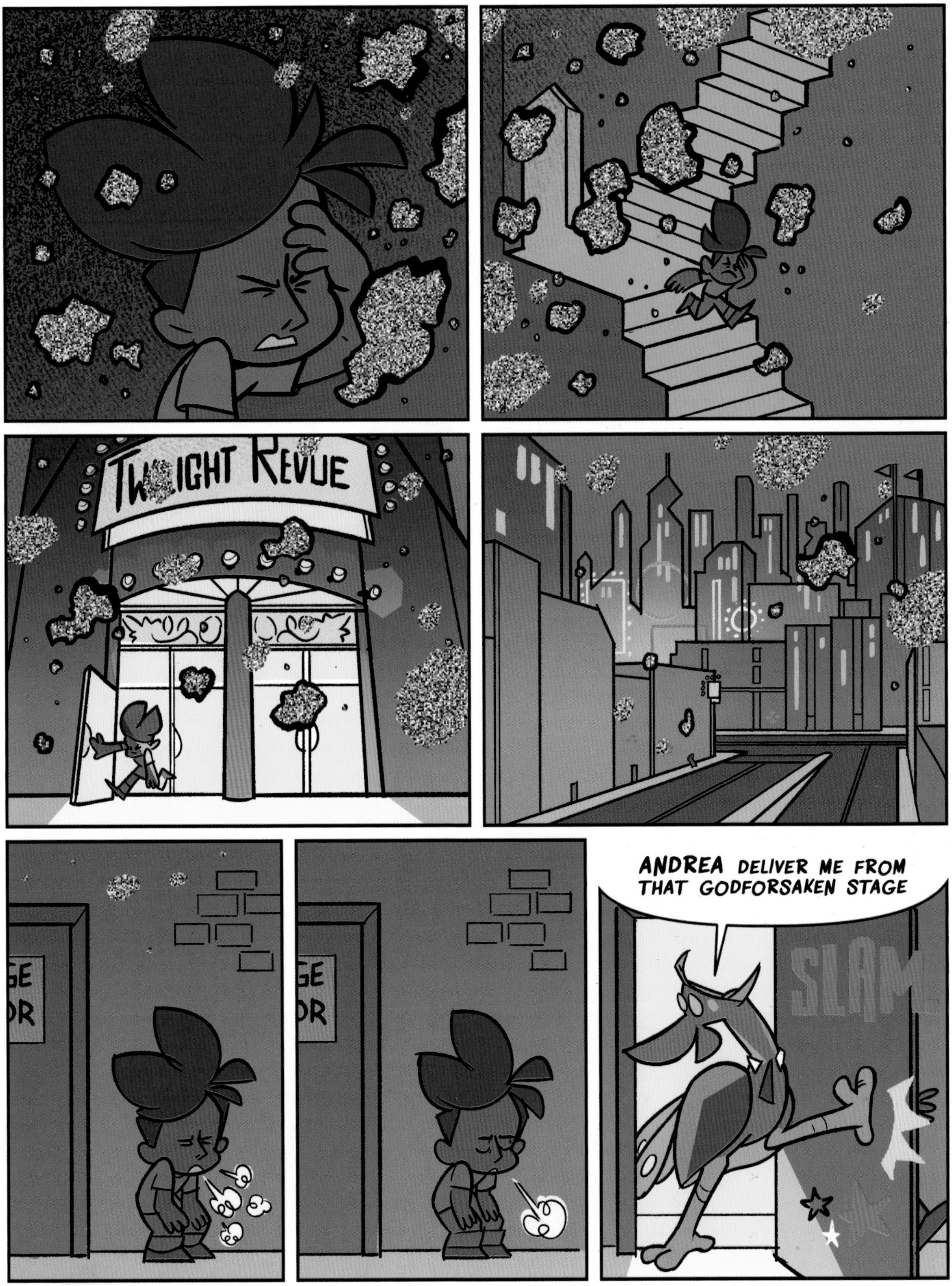
TWILIGHT REVUE
GE
OR
ANDREA DELIVER ME FROM THAT GODFORSAKEN STAGE
SLAM

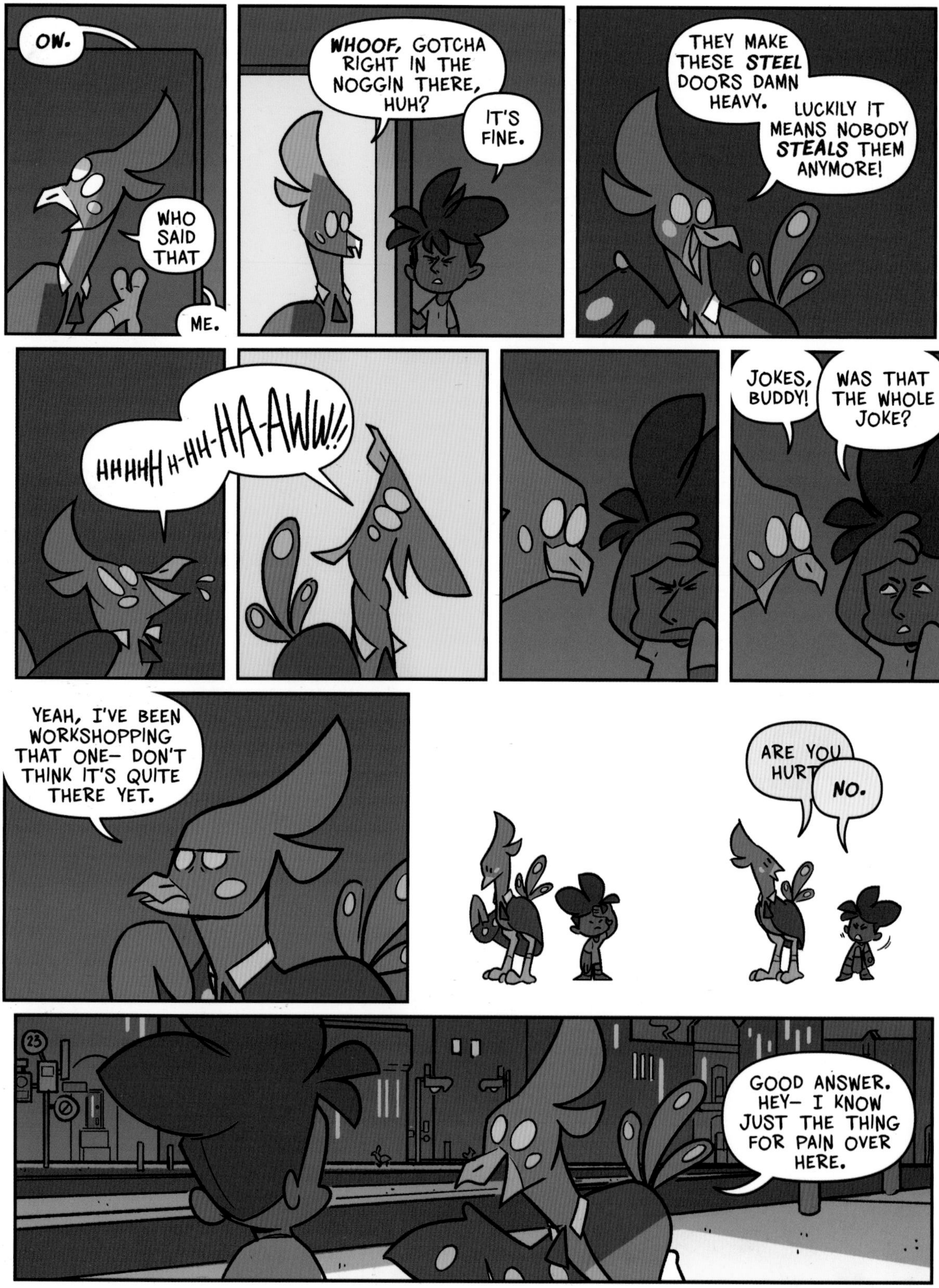
OW.
WHO SAID THAT
ME.
WHOOF, GOTCHA RIGHT IN THE NOGGIN THERE, HUH?
IT'S FINE.
THEY MAKE THESE STEEL DOORS DAMN HEAVY.
LUCKILY IT MEANS NOBODY STEALS THEM ANYMORE!
HHHHH H-HH-HA-AWW!!
JOKES, BUDDY!
WAS THAT THE WHOLE JOKE?
YEAH, I'VE BEEN WORKSHOPPING THAT ONE— DON'T THINK IT'S QUITE THERE YET.
ARE YOU HURT
NO.
GOOD ANSWER. HEY— I KNOW JUST THE THING FOR PAIN OVER HERE.

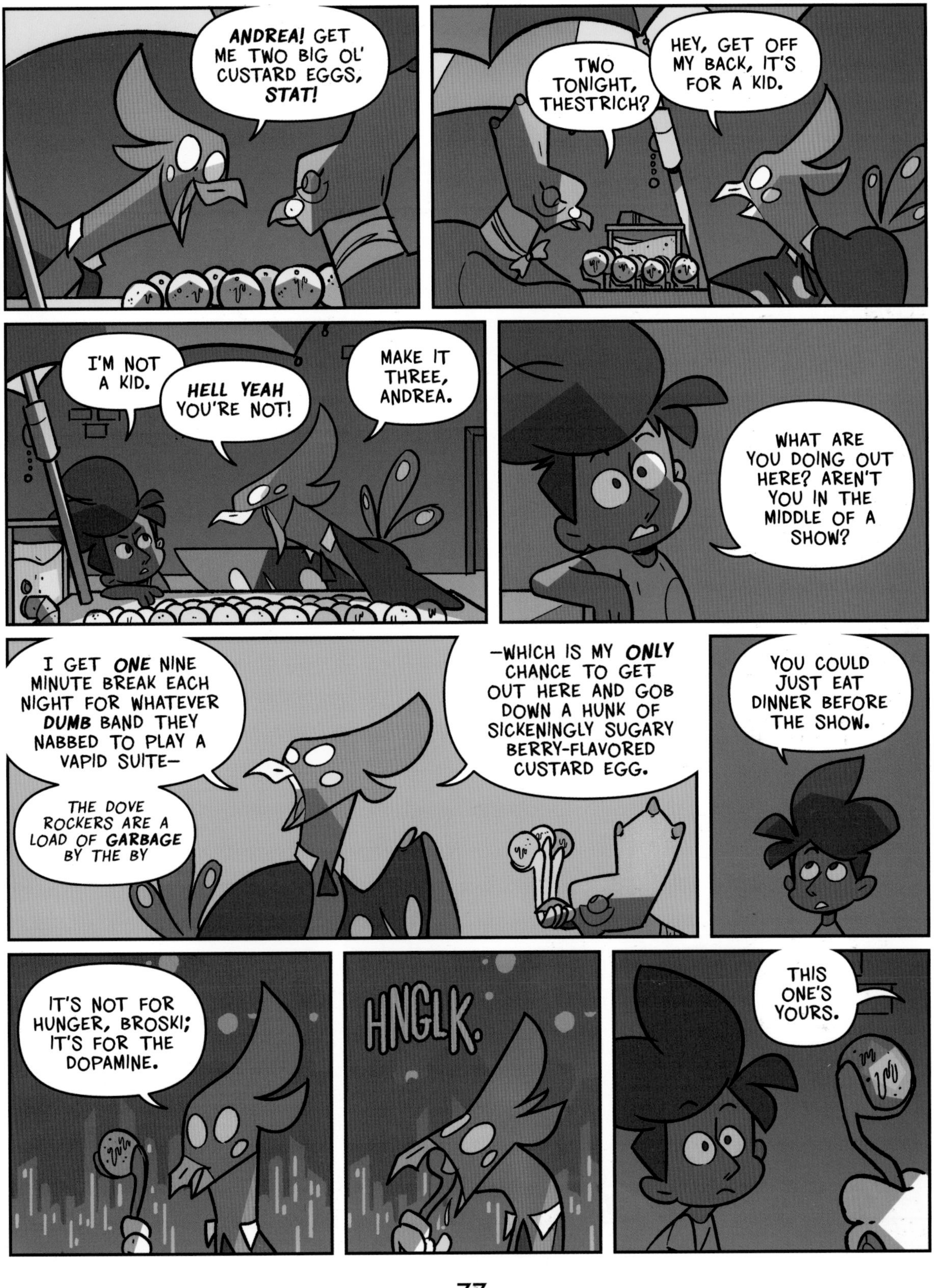
ANDREA! GET ME TWO BIG OL' CUSTARD EGGS, STAT!
TWO TONIGHT, THESTRICH?
HEY, GET OFF MY BACK, IT'S FOR A KID.
I'M NOT A KID.
HELL YEAH YOU'RE NOT!
MAKE IT THREE, ANDREA.
WHAT ARE YOU DOING OUT HERE? AREN'T YOU IN THE MIDDLE OF A SHOW?
I GET ONE NINE MINUTE BREAK EACH NIGHT FOR WHATEVER DUMB BAND THEY NABBED TO PLAY A VAPID SUITE–
THE DOVE ROCKERS ARE A LOAD OF GARBAGE BY THE BY
–WHICH IS MY ONLY CHANCE TO GET OUT HERE AND GOB DOWN A HUNK OF SICKENINGLY SUGARY BERRY-FLAVORED CUSTARD EGG.
YOU COULD JUST EAT DINNER BEFORE THE SHOW.
IT'S NOT FOR HUNGER, BROSKI; IT'S FOR THE DOPAMINE.
HNGLK.
THIS ONE'S YOURS.

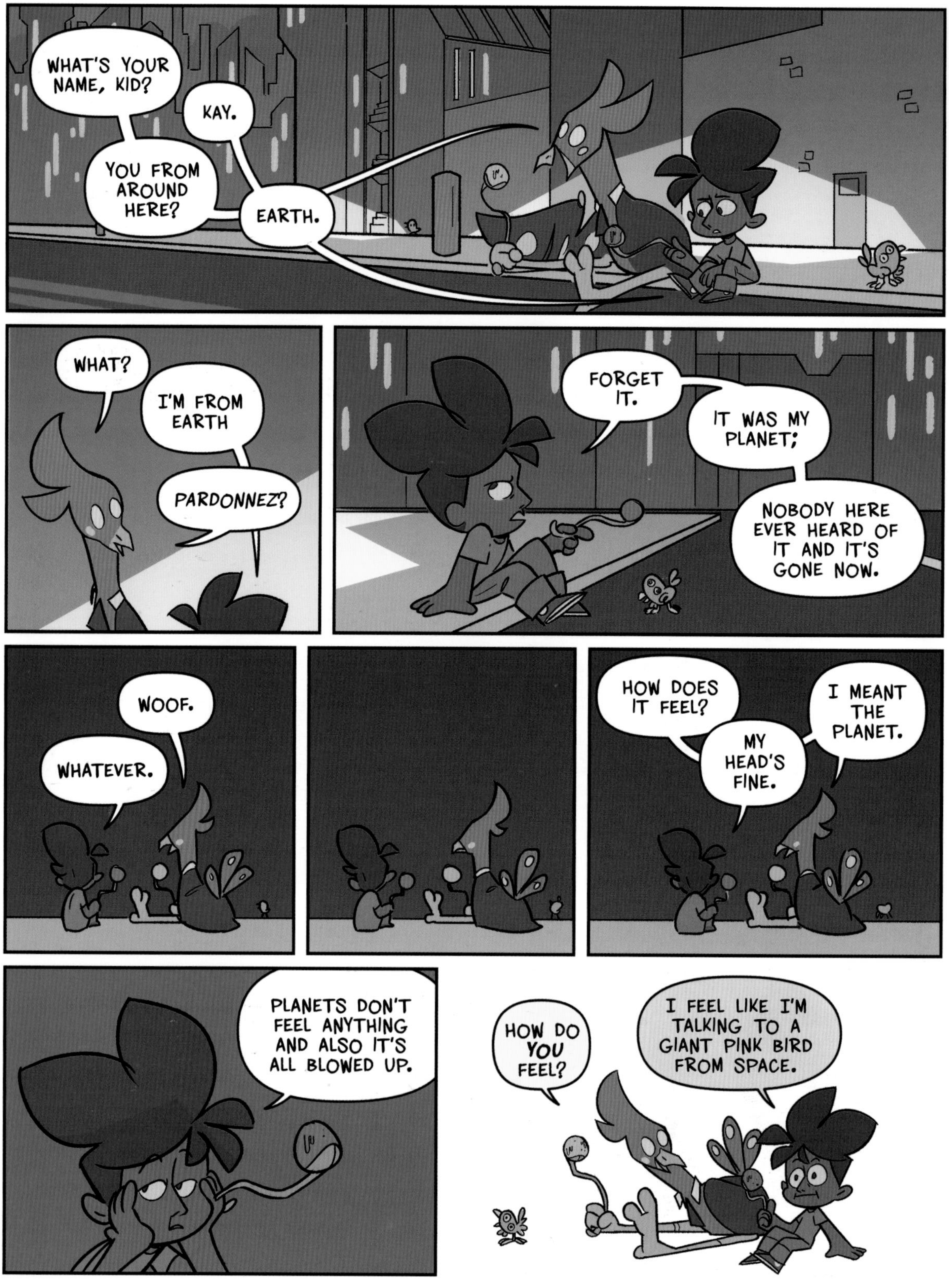
WHAT'S YOUR NAME, KID?
KAY.
YOU FROM AROUND HERE?
EARTH.
WHAT?
I'M FROM EARTH
PARDONNEZ?
FORGET IT.
IT WAS MY PLANET;
NOBODY HERE EVER HEARD OF IT AND IT'S GONE NOW.
WHATEVER.
WOOF.
HOW DOES IT FEEL?
MY HEAD'S FINE.
I MEANT THE PLANET.
PLANETS DON'T FEEL ANYTHING AND ALSO IT'S ALL BLOWED UP.
HOW DO YOU FEEL?
I FEEL LIKE I'M TALKING TO A GIANT PINK BIRD FROM SPACE.

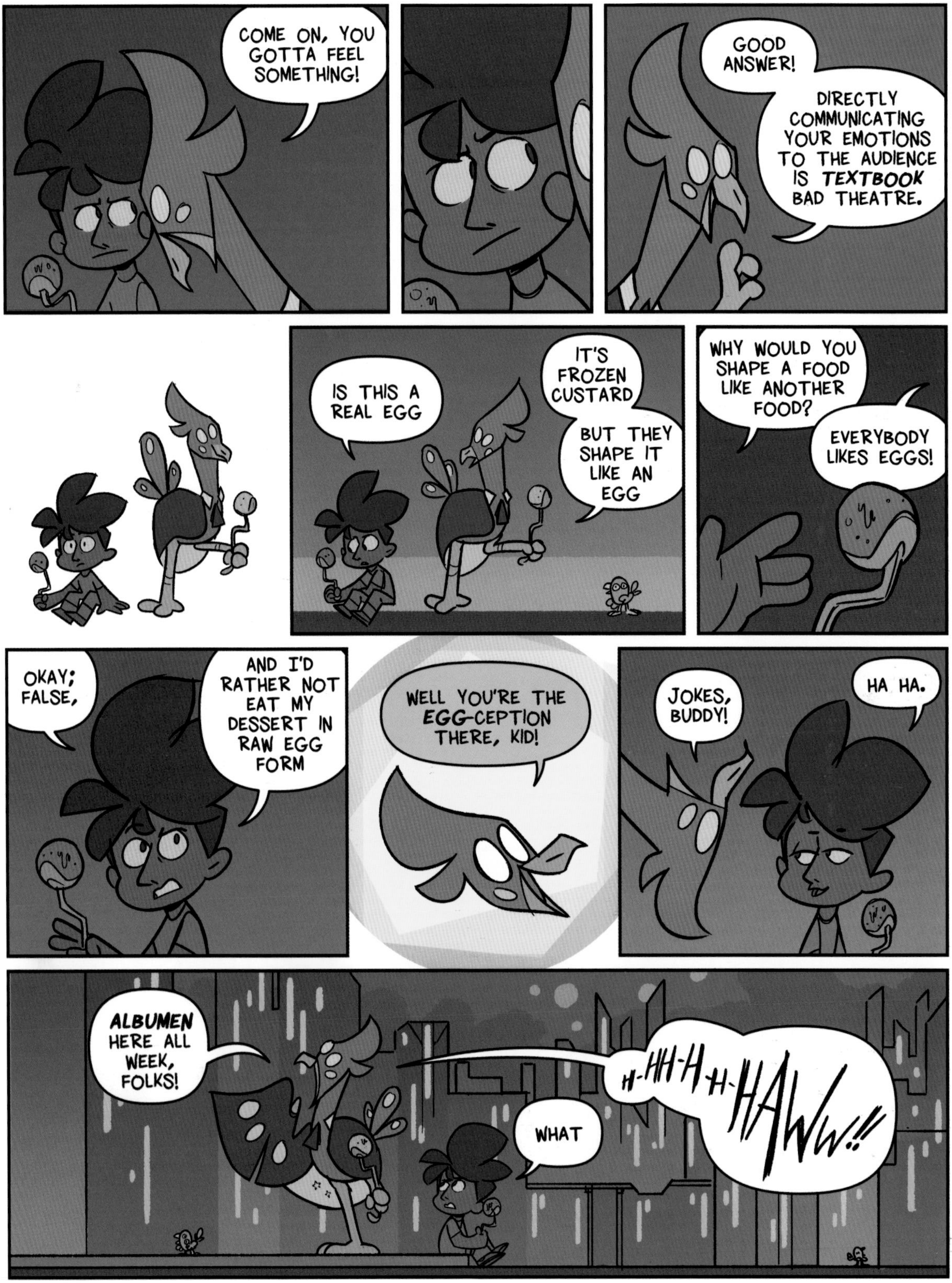

COME ON, YOU GOTTA FEEL SOMETHING!
GOOD ANSWER!
DIRECTLY COMMUNICATING YOUR EMOTIONS TO THE AUDIENCE IS **TEXTBOOK** BAD THEATRE.
IS THIS A REAL EGG
IT'S FROZEN CUSTARD
BUT THEY SHAPE IT LIKE AN EGG
WHY WOULD YOU SHAPE A FOOD LIKE ANOTHER FOOD?
EVERYBODY LIKES EGGS!
OKAY; FALSE,
AND I'D RATHER NOT EAT MY DESSERT IN RAW EGG FORM
WELL YOU'RE THE **EGG**-CEPTION THERE, KID!
JOKES, BUDDY!
HA HA.
ALBUMEN HERE ALL WEEK, FOLKS!
H-HH-H-H-HAWW!!
WHAT

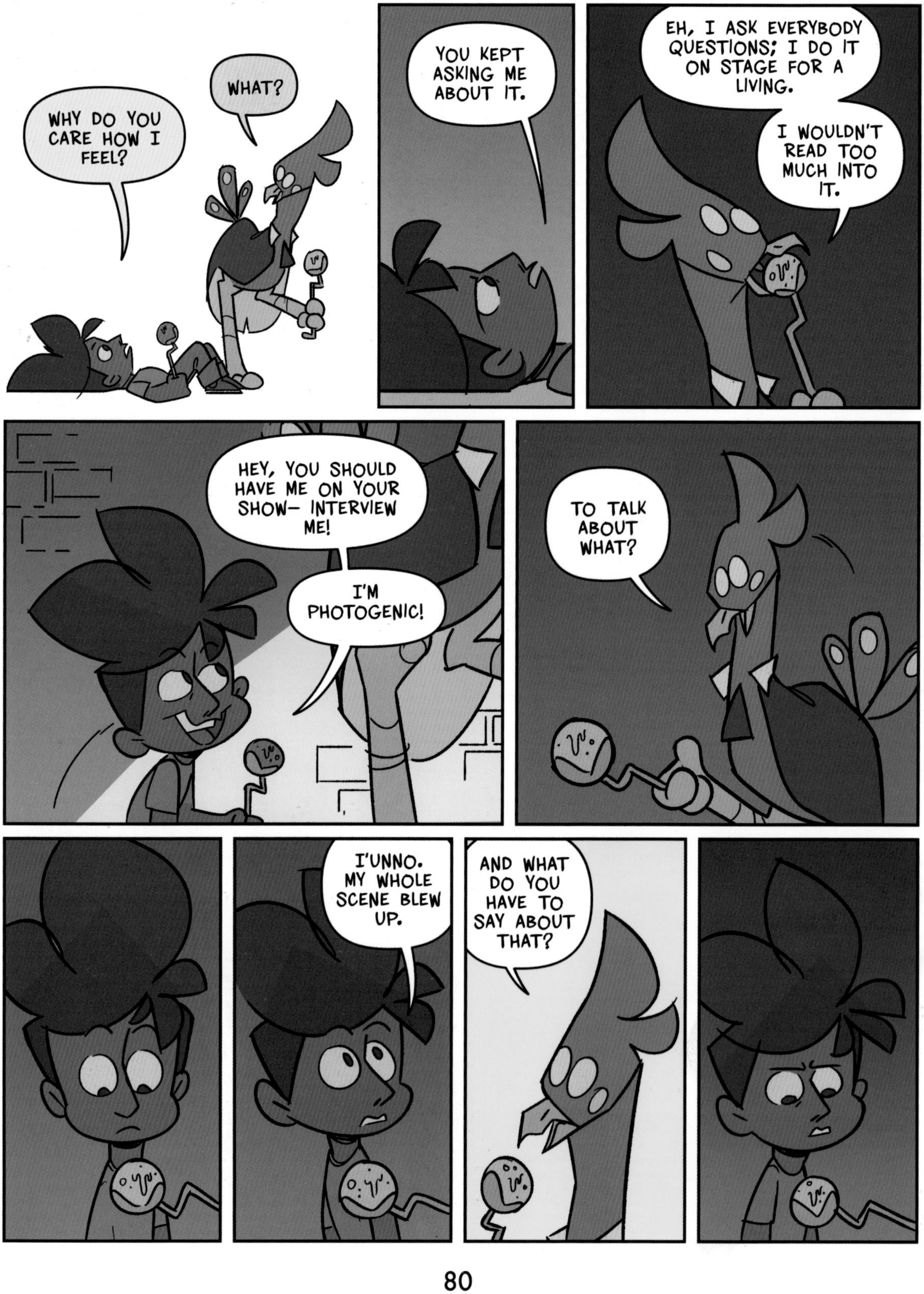
WHY DO YOU CARE HOW I FEEL?
WHAT?
YOU KEPT ASKING ME ABOUT IT.
EH, I ASK EVERYBODY QUESTIONS; I DO IT ON STAGE FOR A LIVING.
I WOULDN'T READ TOO MUCH INTO IT.
HEY, YOU SHOULD HAVE ME ON YOUR SHOW– INTERVIEW ME!
I'M PHOTOGENIC!
TO TALK ABOUT WHAT?
I'UNNO. MY WHOLE SCENE BLEW UP.
AND WHAT DO YOU HAVE TO SAY ABOUT THAT?

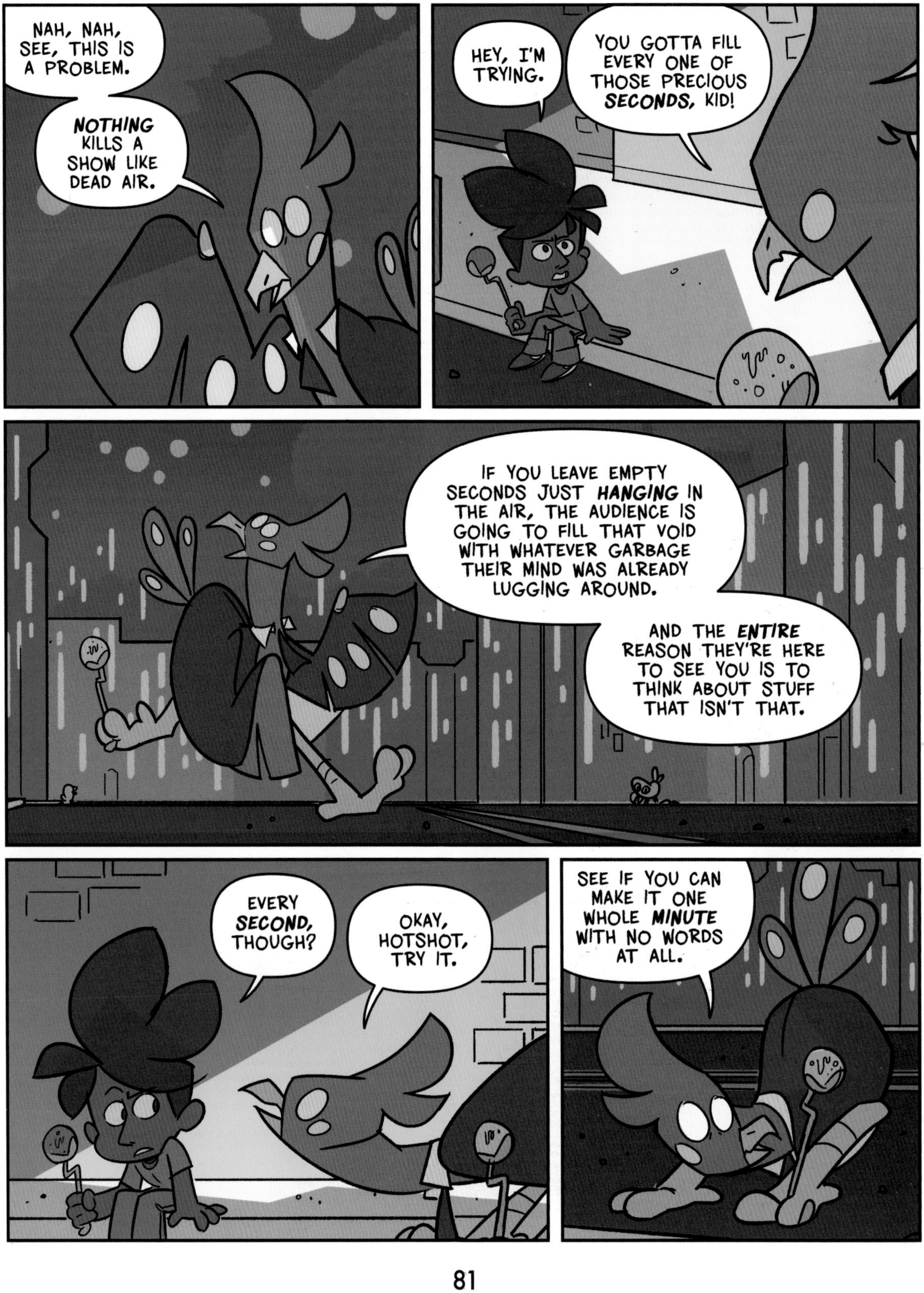
NAH, NAH, SEE, THIS IS A PROBLEM.
NOTHING KILLS A SHOW LIKE DEAD AIR.
HEY, I'M TRYING.
YOU GOTTA FILL EVERY ONE OF THOSE PRECIOUS SECONDS, KID!
IF YOU LEAVE EMPTY SECONDS JUST HANGING IN THE AIR, THE AUDIENCE IS GOING TO FILL THAT VOID WITH WHATEVER GARBAGE THEIR MIND WAS ALREADY LUGGING AROUND.
AND THE ENTIRE REASON THEY'RE HERE TO SEE YOU IS TO THINK ABOUT STUFF THAT ISN'T THAT.
EVERY SECOND, THOUGH?
OKAY, HOTSHOT, TRY IT.
SEE IF YOU CAN MAKE IT ONE WHOLE MINUTE WITH NO WORDS AT ALL.

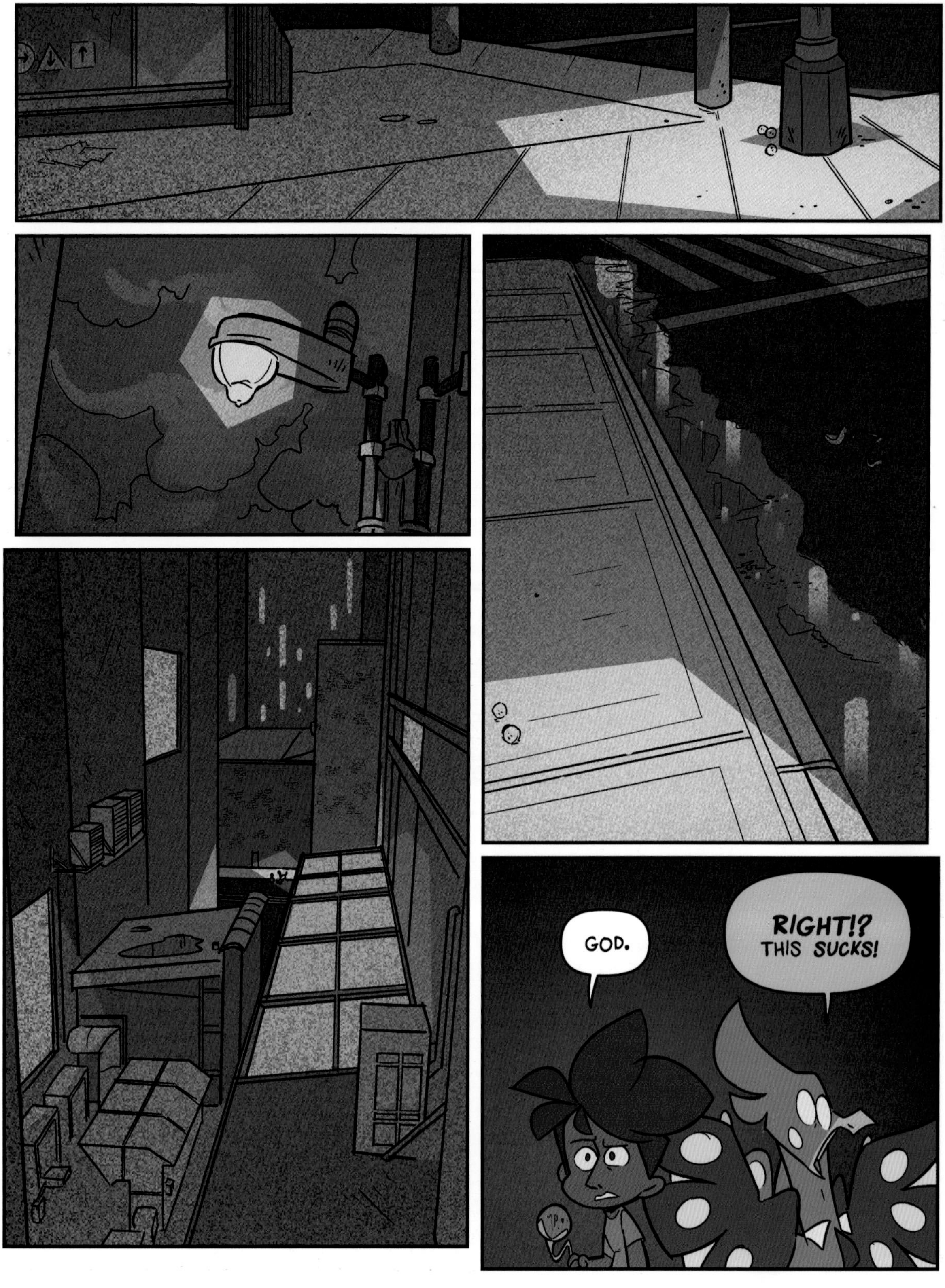
GOD.
RIGHT!? THIS SUCKS!

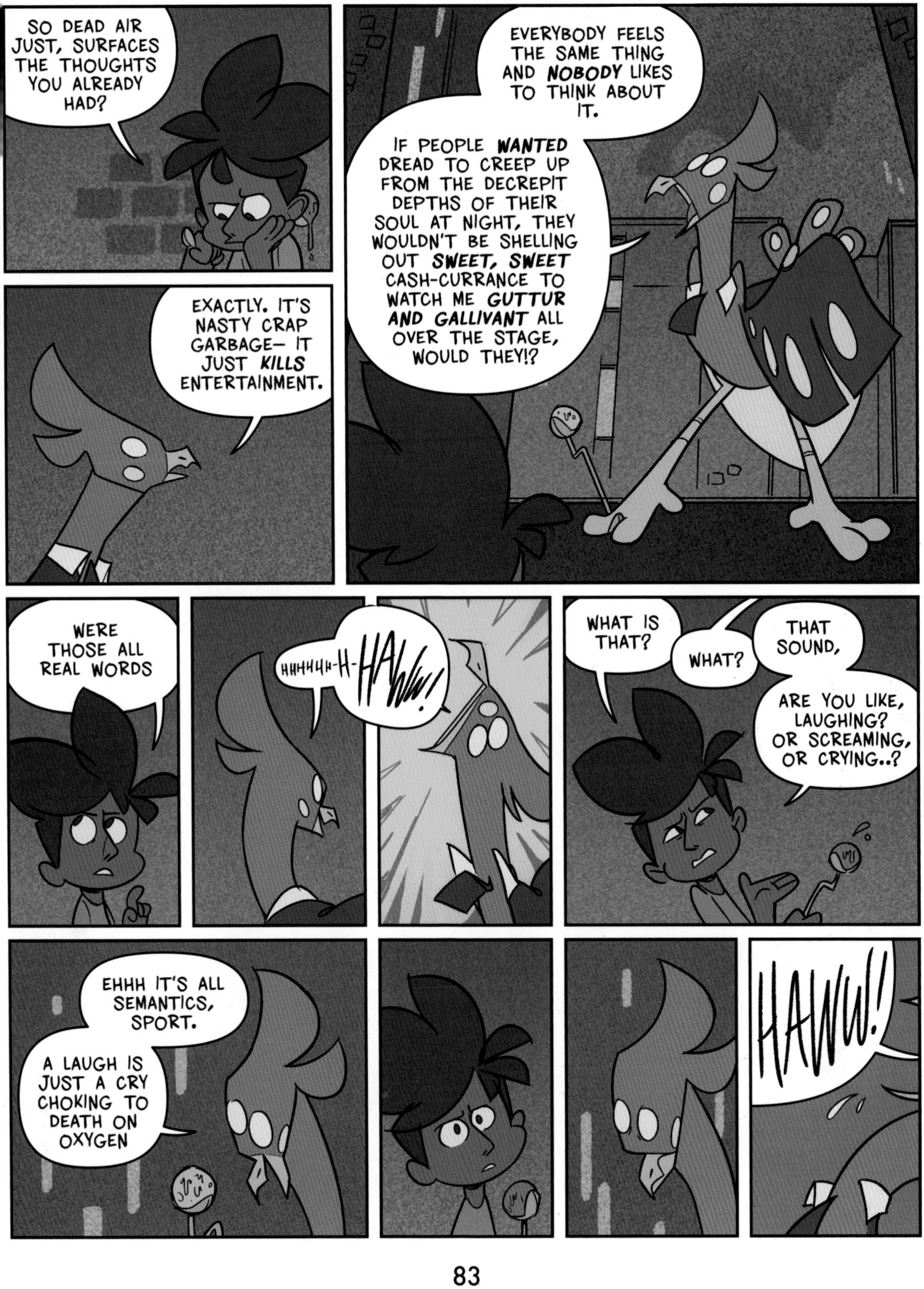
SO DEAD AIR JUST, SURFACES THE THOUGHTS YOU ALREADY HAD?
EXACTLY. IT'S NASTY CRAP GARBAGE– IT JUST KILLS ENTERTAINMENT.
EVERYBODY FEELS THE SAME THING AND NOBODY LIKES TO THINK ABOUT IT.
IF PEOPLE WANTED DREAD TO CREEP UP FROM THE DECREPIT DEPTHS OF THEIR SOUL AT NIGHT, THEY WOULDN'T BE SHELLING OUT SWEET, SWEET CASH-CURRANCE TO WATCH ME GUTTUR AND GALLIVANT ALL OVER THE STAGE, WOULD THEY!?
WERE THOSE ALL REAL WORDS
HHHHHH-H-HAWW!
WHAT IS THAT?
WHAT?
THAT SOUND,
ARE YOU LIKE, LAUGHING? OR SCREAMING, OR CRYING..?
EHHH IT'S ALL SEMANTICS, SPORT.
A LAUGH IS JUST A CRY CHOKING TO DEATH ON OXYGEN
HAWW!

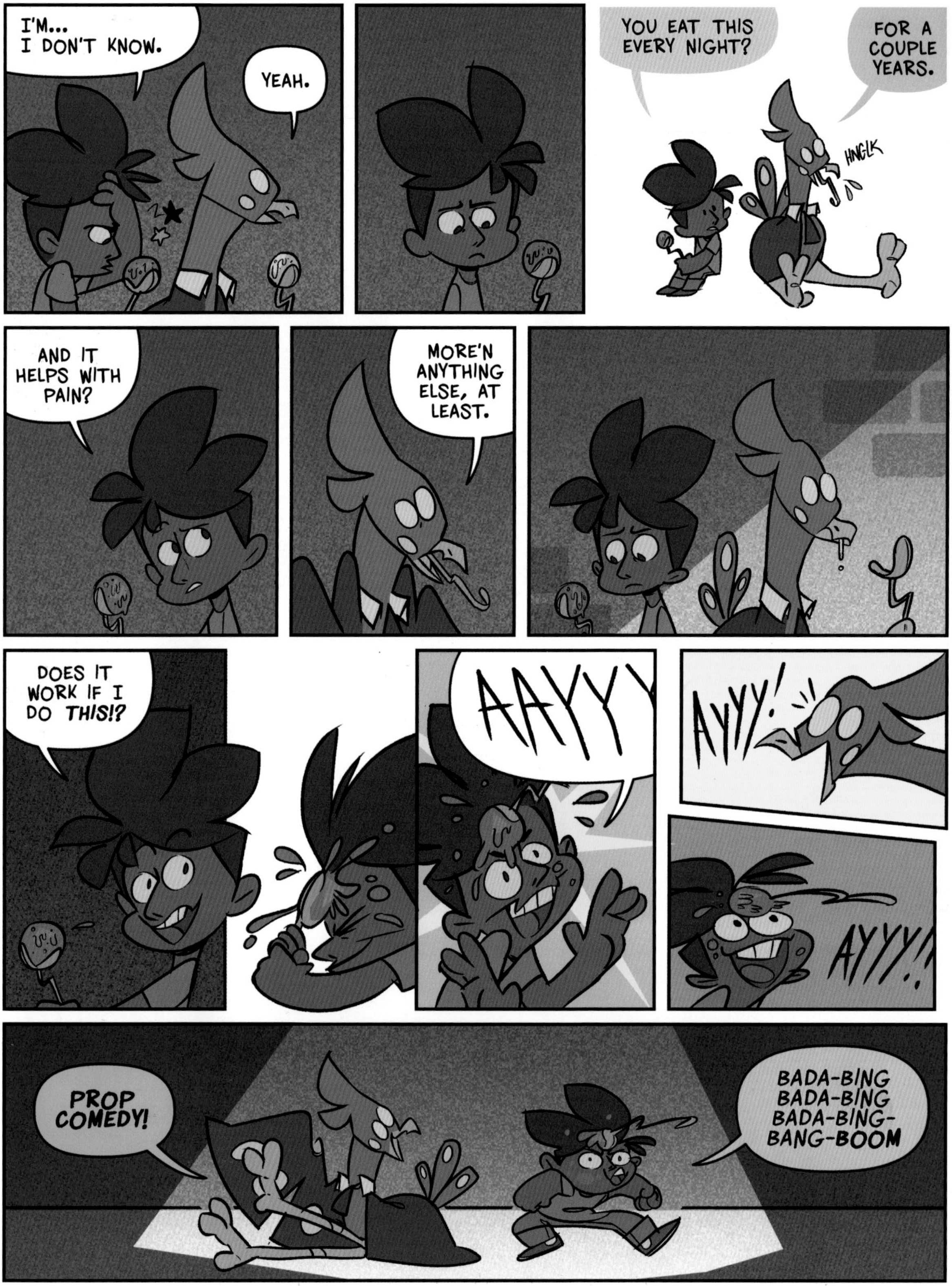
I'M... I DON'T KNOW.
YEAH.
YOU EAT THIS EVERY NIGHT?
FOR A COUPLE YEARS.
HNGLK
AND IT HELPS WITH PAIN?
MORE'N ANYTHING ELSE, AT LEAST.
DOES IT WORK IF I DO *THIS!?*
AAYYY
AYYY!
AYYY!!
PROP COMEDY!
BADA-BING BADA-BING BADA-BING-BANG-**BOOM**

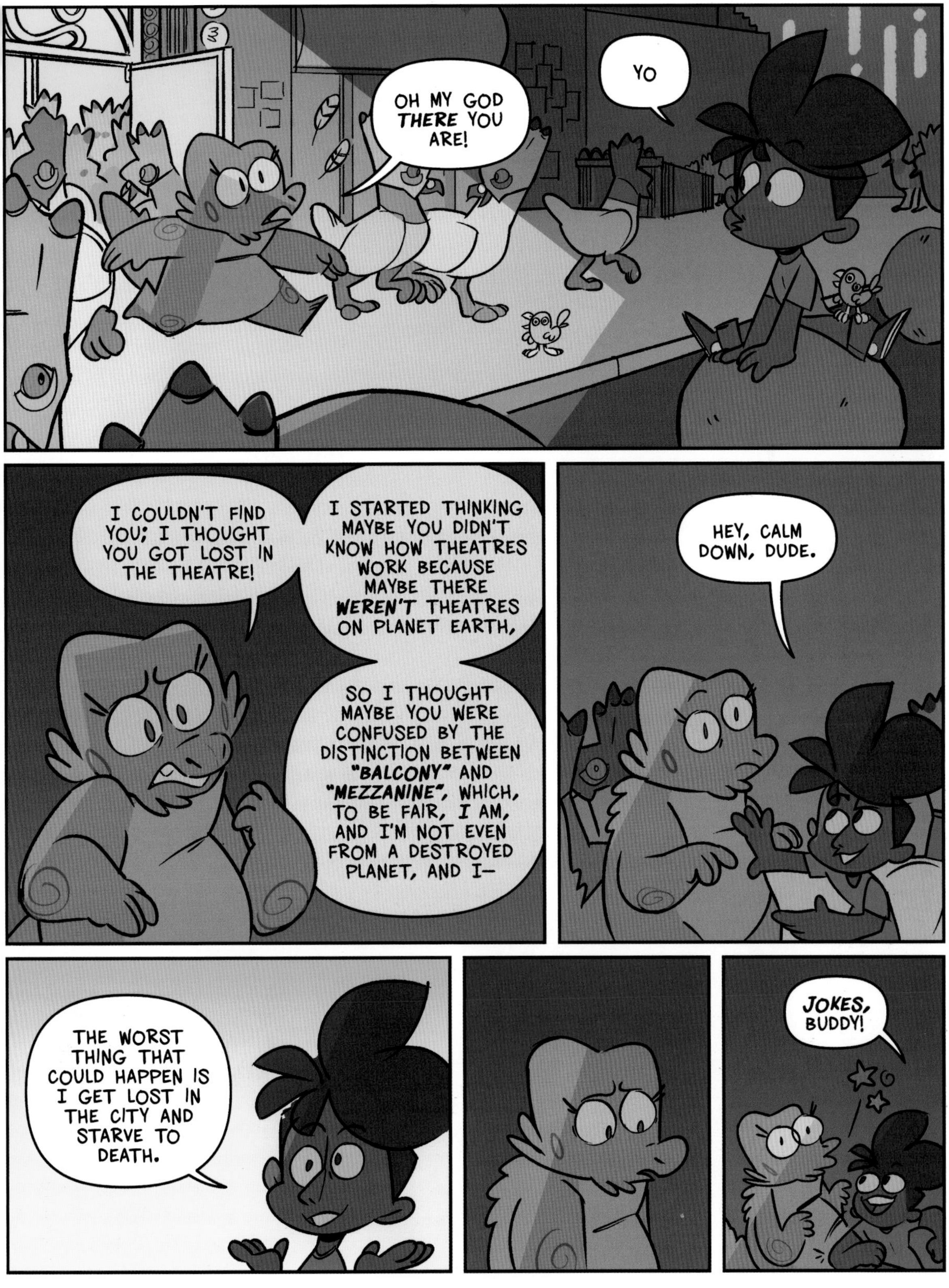
OH MY GOD THERE YOU ARE!
YO
I COULDN'T FIND YOU; I THOUGHT YOU GOT LOST IN THE THEATRE!
I STARTED THINKING MAYBE YOU DIDN'T KNOW HOW THEATRES WORK BECAUSE MAYBE THERE WEREN'T THEATRES ON PLANET EARTH,
SO I THOUGHT MAYBE YOU WERE CONFUSED BY THE DISTINCTION BETWEEN "BALCONY" AND "MEZZANINE", WHICH, TO BE FAIR, I AM, AND I'M NOT EVEN FROM A DESTROYED PLANET, AND I—
HEY, CALM DOWN, DUDE.
THE WORST THING THAT COULD HAPPEN IS I GET LOST IN THE CITY AND STARVE TO DEATH.
JOKES, BUDDY!

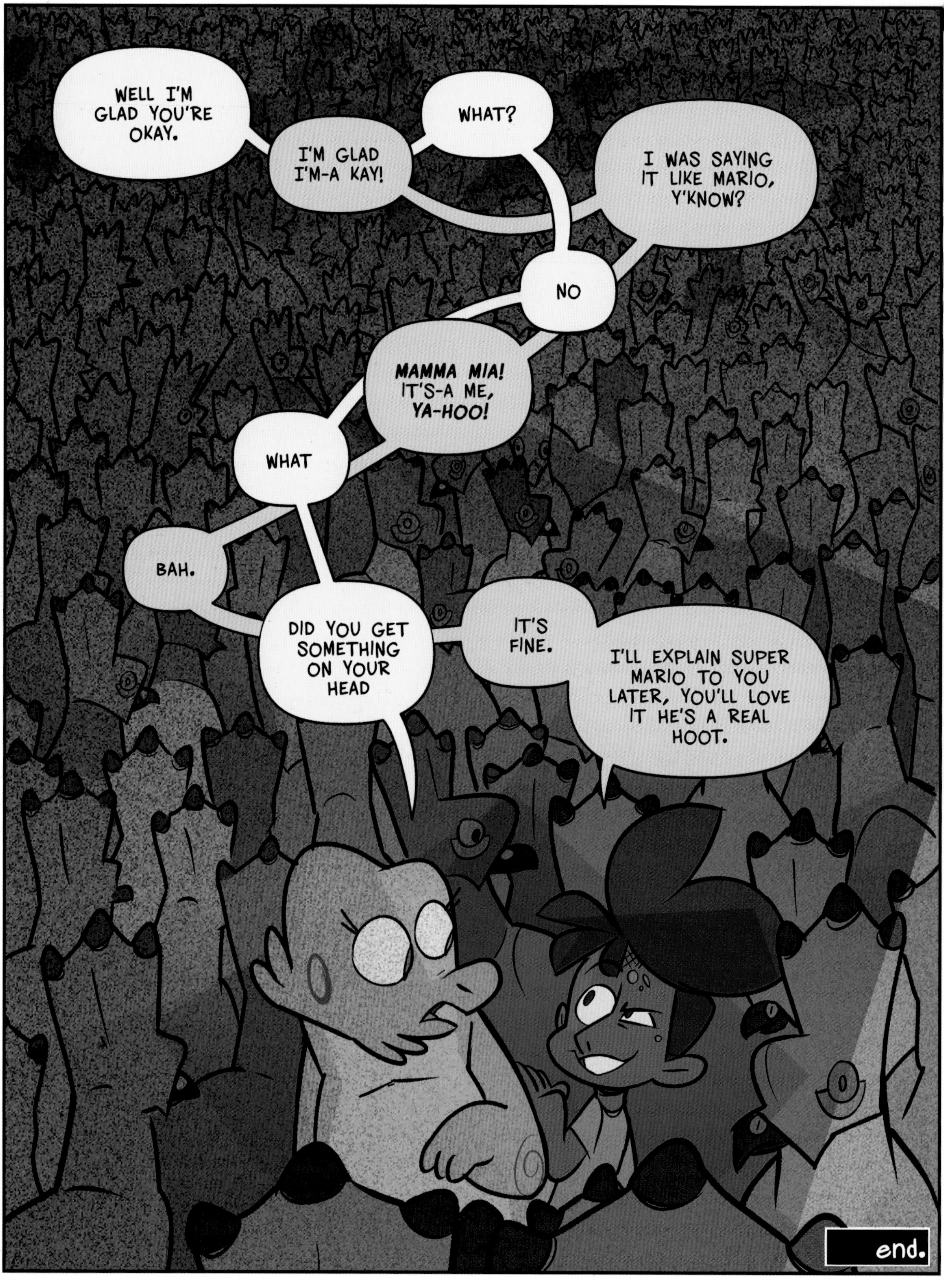
WELL I'M GLAD YOU'RE OKAY.
I'M GLAD I'M-A KAY!
WHAT?
I WAS SAYING IT LIKE MARIO, Y'KNOW?
NO
MAMMA MIA! IT'S-A ME, YA-HOO!
WHAT
BAH.
DID YOU GET SOMETHING ON YOUR HEAD
IT'S FINE.
I'LL EXPLAIN SUPER MARIO TO YOU LATER, YOU'LL LOVE IT HE'S A REAL HOOT.
end.

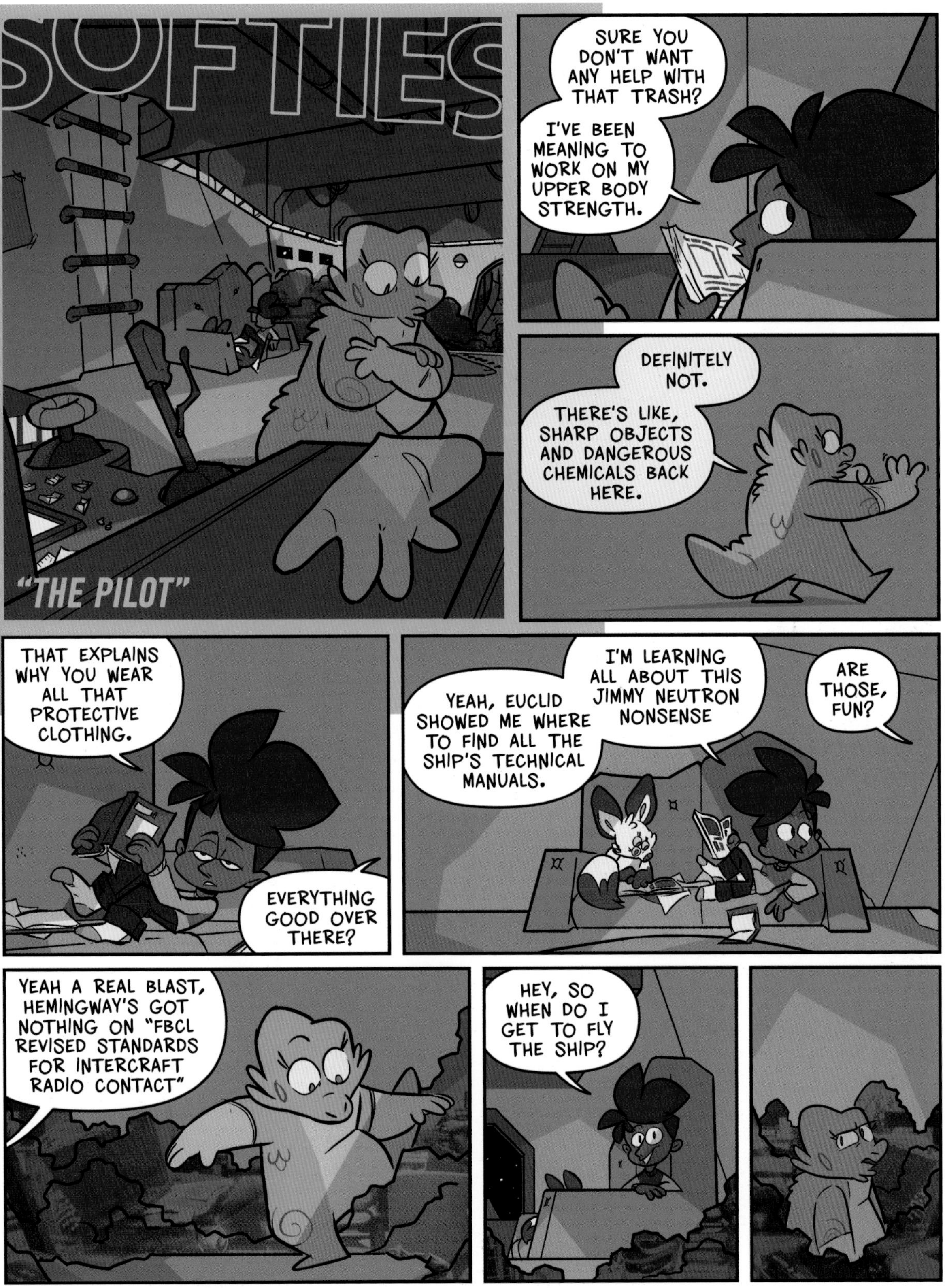
SOFTIES
"THE PILOT"
SURE YOU DON'T WANT ANY HELP WITH THAT TRASH?
I'VE BEEN MEANING TO WORK ON MY UPPER BODY STRENGTH.
DEFINITELY NOT.
THERE'S LIKE, SHARP OBJECTS AND DANGEROUS CHEMICALS BACK HERE.
THAT EXPLAINS WHY YOU WEAR ALL THAT PROTECTIVE CLOTHING.
EVERYTHING GOOD OVER THERE?
YEAH, EUCLID SHOWED ME WHERE TO FIND ALL THE SHIP'S TECHNICAL MANUALS.
I'M LEARNING ALL ABOUT THIS JIMMY NEUTRON NONSENSE
ARE THOSE, FUN?
YEAH A REAL BLAST, HEMINGWAY'S GOT NOTHING ON "FBCL REVISED STANDARDS FOR INTERCRAFT RADIO CONTACT"
HEY, SO WHEN DO I GET TO FLY THE SHIP?

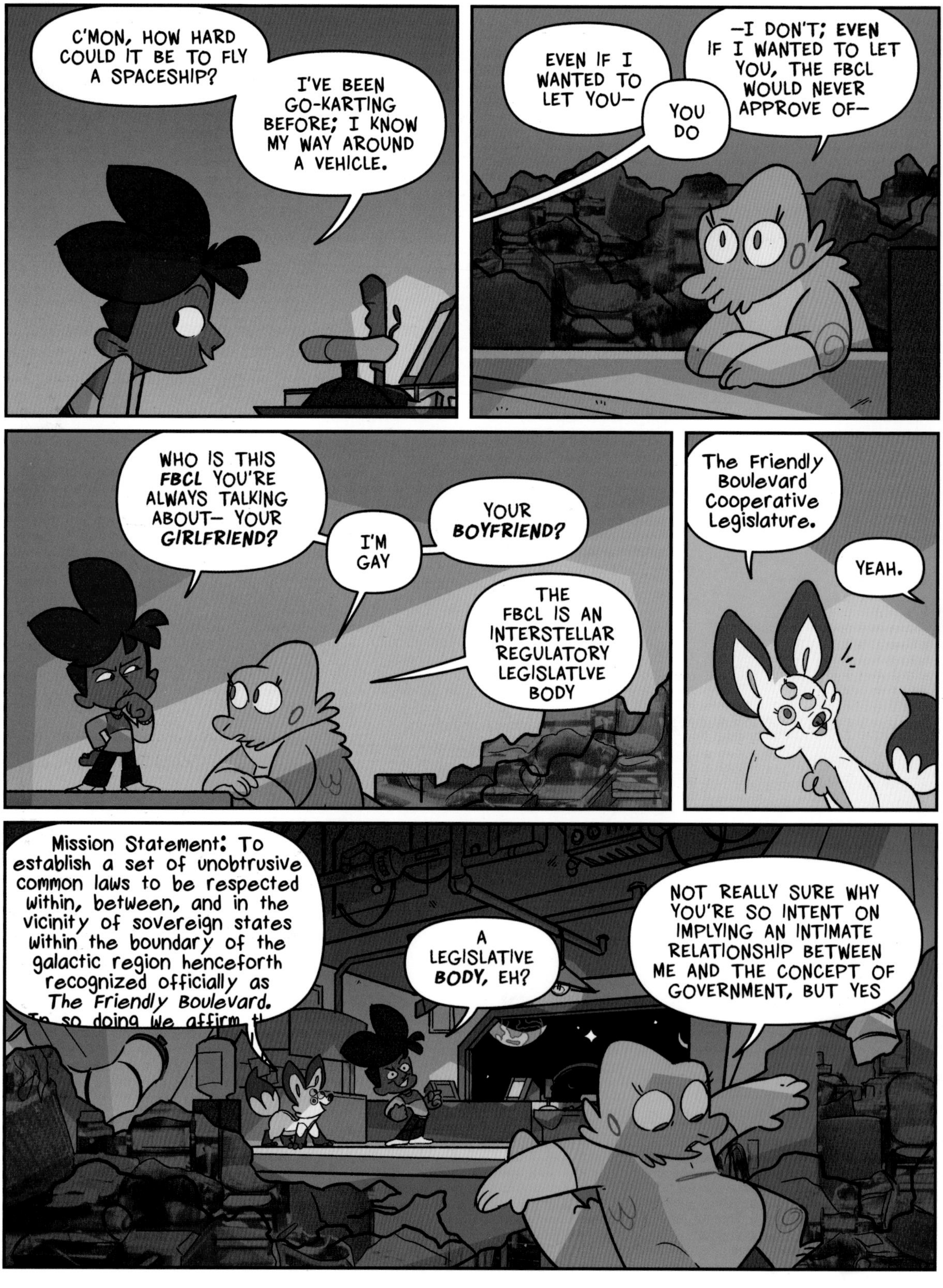

C'MON, HOW HARD COULD IT BE TO FLY A SPACESHIP?
I'VE BEEN GO-KARTING BEFORE; I KNOW MY WAY AROUND A VEHICLE.
EVEN IF I WANTED TO LET YOU—
YOU DO
—I DON'T; EVEN IF I WANTED TO LET YOU, THE FBCL WOULD NEVER APPROVE OF—
WHO IS THIS **FBCL** YOU'RE ALWAYS TALKING ABOUT— YOUR ***GIRLFRIEND?***
I'M GAY
YOUR ***BOYFRIEND?***
THE FBCL IS AN INTERSTELLAR REGULATORY LEGISLATLVE BODY
The Friendly Boulevard Cooperative Legislature.
YEAH.
Mission Statement: To establish a set of unobtrusive common laws to be respected within, between, and in the vicinity of sovereign states within the boundary of the galactic region henceforth recognized officially as *The Friendly Boulevard.*
A LEGISLATIVE ***BODY,*** EH?
NOT REALLY SURE WHY YOU'RE SO INTENT ON IMPLYING AN INTIMATE RELATIONSHIP BETWEEN ME AND THE CONCEPT OF GOVERNMENT, BUT YES

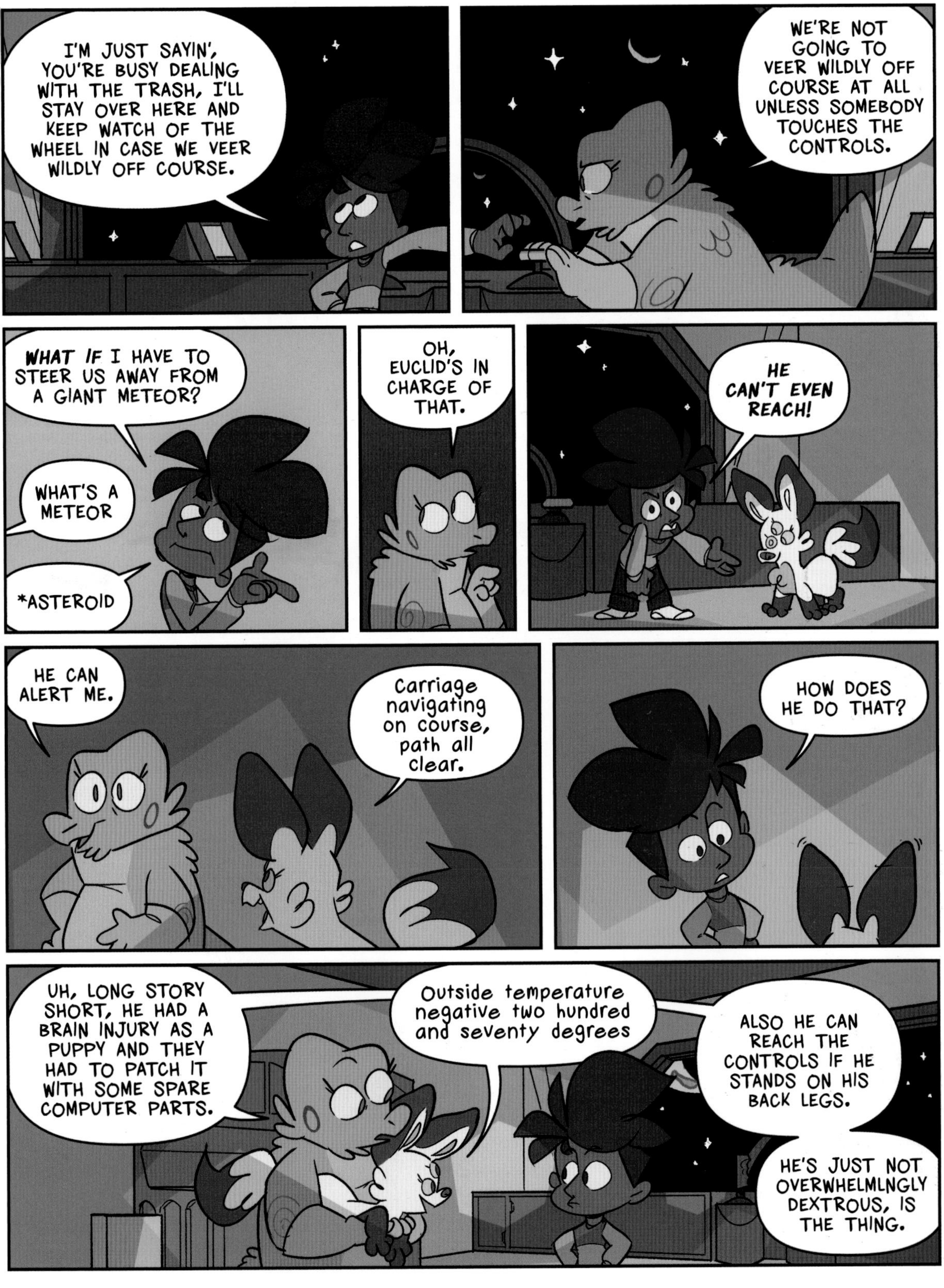
I'M JUST SAYIN', YOU'RE BUSY DEALING WITH THE TRASH, I'LL STAY OVER HERE AND KEEP WATCH OF THE WHEEL IN CASE WE VEER WILDLY OFF COURSE.
WE'RE NOT GOING TO VEER WILDLY OFF COURSE AT ALL UNLESS SOMEBODY TOUCHES THE CONTROLS.
WHAT IF I HAVE TO STEER US AWAY FROM A GIANT METEOR?
WHAT'S A METEOR
*ASTEROID
OH, EUCLID'S IN CHARGE OF THAT.
HE CAN'T EVEN REACH!
HE CAN ALERT ME.
Carriage navigating on course, path all clear.
HOW DOES HE DO THAT?
UH, LONG STORY SHORT, HE HAD A BRAIN INJURY AS A PUPPY AND THEY HAD TO PATCH IT WITH SOME SPARE COMPUTER PARTS.
Outside temperature negative two hundred and seventy degrees
ALSO HE CAN REACH THE CONTROLS IF HE STANDS ON HIS BACK LEGS.
HE'S JUST NOT OVERWHELMLNGLY DEXTROUS, IS THE THING.

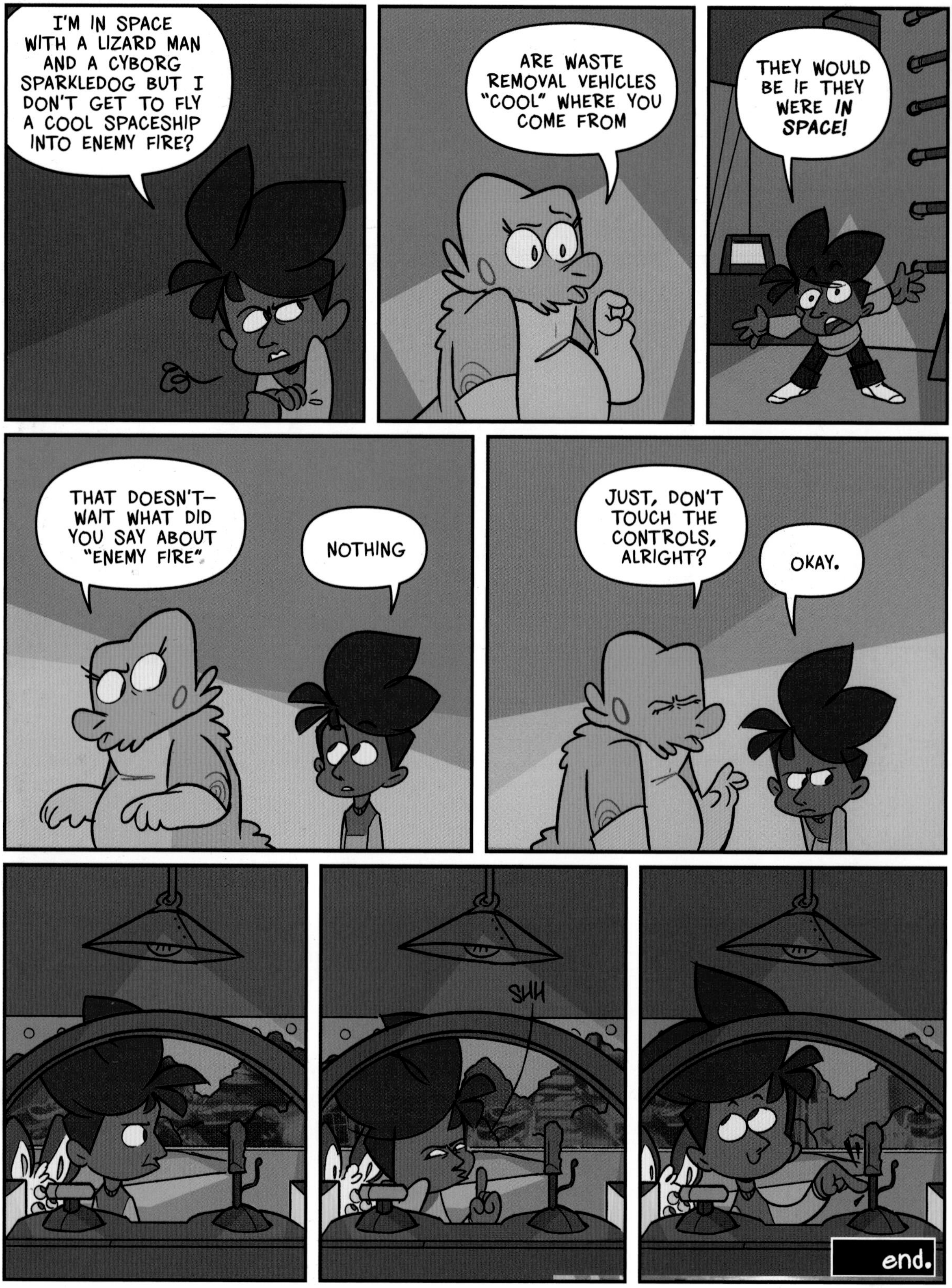
I'M IN SPACE WITH A LIZARD MAN AND A CYBORG SPARKLEDOG BUT I DON'T GET TO FLY A COOL SPACESHIP INTO ENEMY FIRE?
ARE WASTE REMOVAL VEHICLES "COOL" WHERE YOU COME FROM
THEY WOULD BE IF THEY WERE IN SPACE!
THAT DOESN'T— WAIT WHAT DID YOU SAY ABOUT "ENEMY FIRE"
NOTHING
JUST, DON'T TOUCH THE CONTROLS, ALRIGHT?
OKAY.
SHH
end.

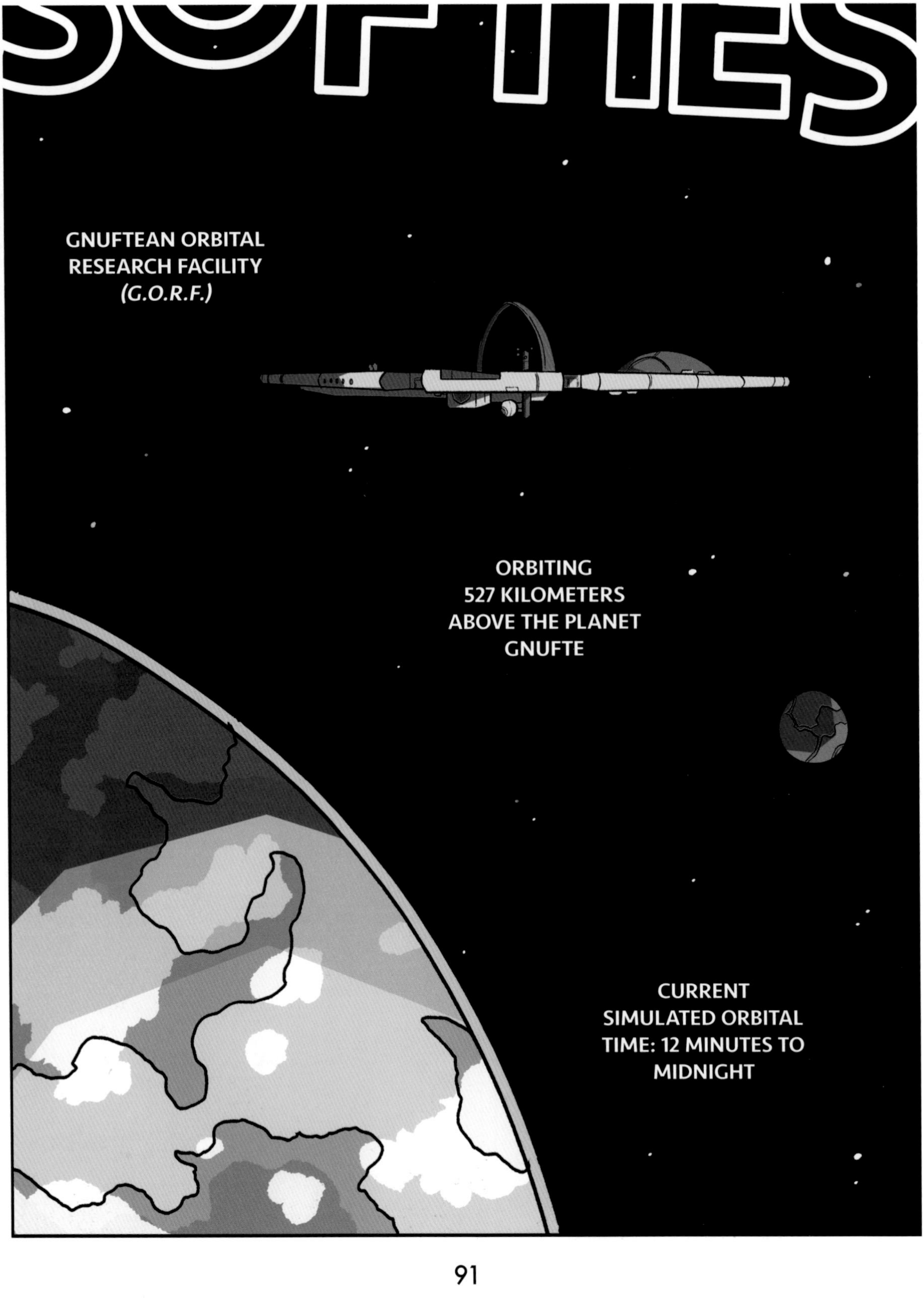
SOFTIES
GNUFTEAN ORBITAL
RESEARCH FACILITY
(G.O.R.F.)
ORBITING
527 KILOMETERS
ABOVE THE PLANET
GNUFTE
CURRENT
SIMULATED ORBITAL
TIME: 12 MINUTES TO
MIDNIGHT

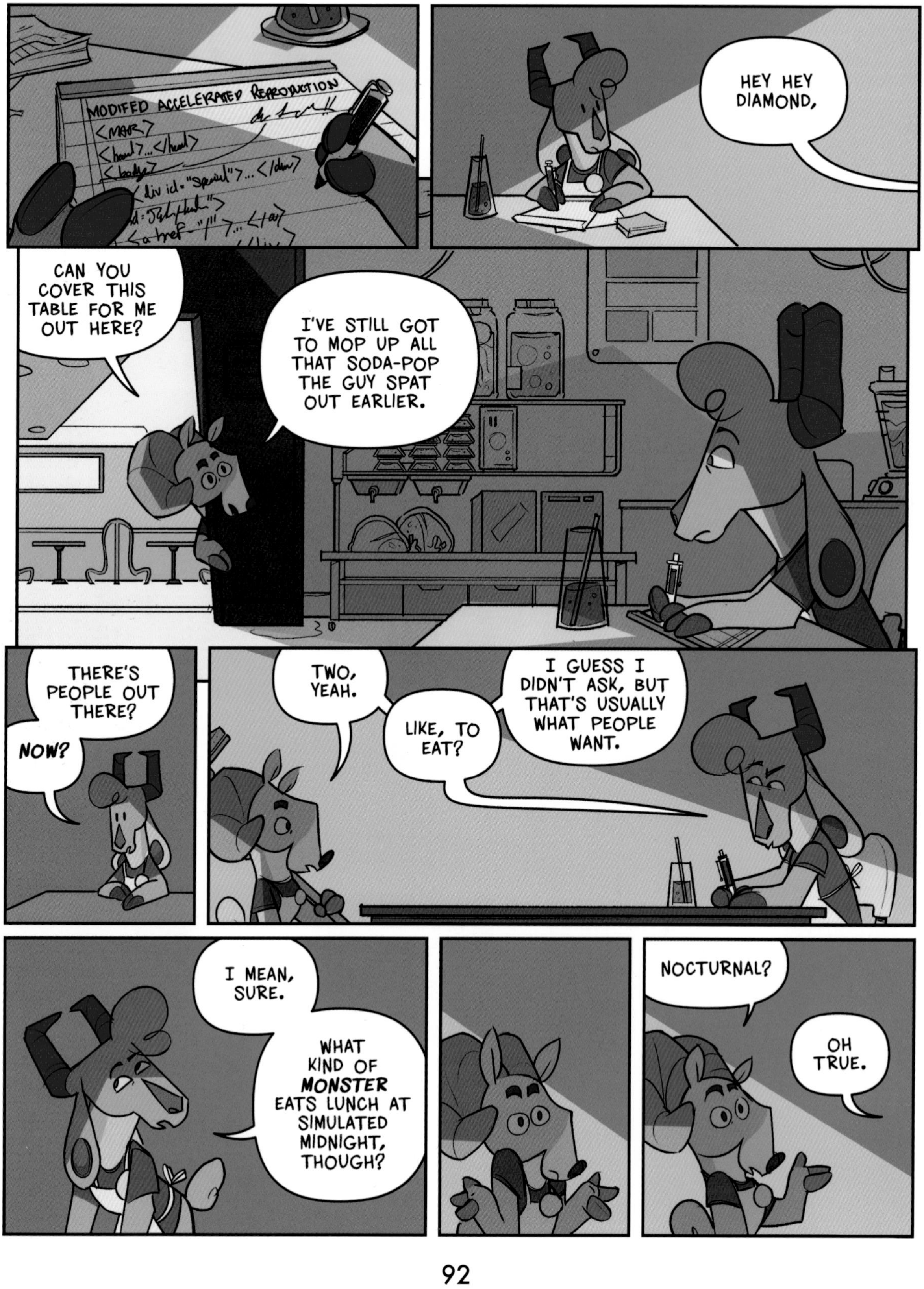
MODIFED ACCELERATED REPRODUCTION
HEY HEY DIAMOND,
CAN YOU COVER THIS TABLE FOR ME OUT HERE?
I'VE STILL GOT TO MOP UP ALL THAT SODA-POP THE GUY SPAT OUT EARLIER.
THERE'S PEOPLE OUT THERE?
NOW?
TWO, YEAH.
LIKE, TO EAT?
I GUESS I DIDN'T ASK, BUT THAT'S USUALLY WHAT PEOPLE WANT.
I MEAN, SURE.
WHAT KIND OF MONSTER EATS LUNCH AT SIMULATED MIDNIGHT, THOUGH?
NOCTURNAL?
OH TRUE.

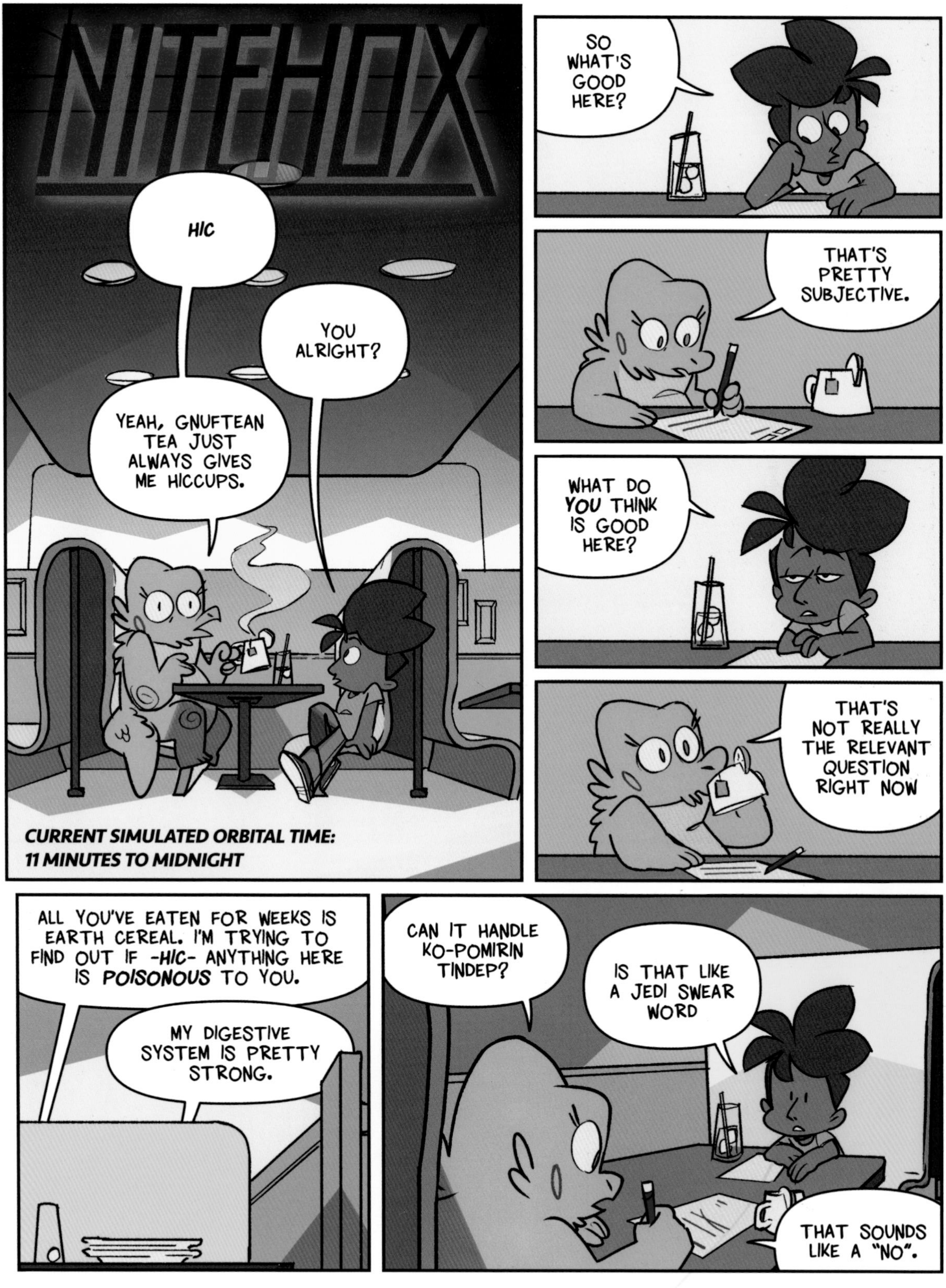
NITEHOX
HIC
YOU ALRIGHT?
YEAH, GNUFTEAN TEA JUST ALWAYS GIVES ME HICCUPS.
CURRENT SIMULATED ORBITAL TIME: 11 MINUTES TO MIDNIGHT
SO WHAT'S GOOD HERE?
THAT'S PRETTY SUBJECTIVE.
WHAT DO *YOU* THINK IS GOOD HERE?
THAT'S NOT REALLY THE RELEVANT QUESTION RIGHT NOW
ALL YOU'VE EATEN FOR WEEKS IS EARTH CEREAL. I'M TRYING TO FIND OUT IF -*HIC*- ANYTHING HERE IS *POISONOUS* TO YOU.
MY DIGESTIVE SYSTEM IS PRETTY STRONG.
CAN IT HANDLE KO-POMIRIN TINDEP?
IS THAT LIKE A JEDI SWEAR WORD
THAT SOUNDS LIKE A "NO".

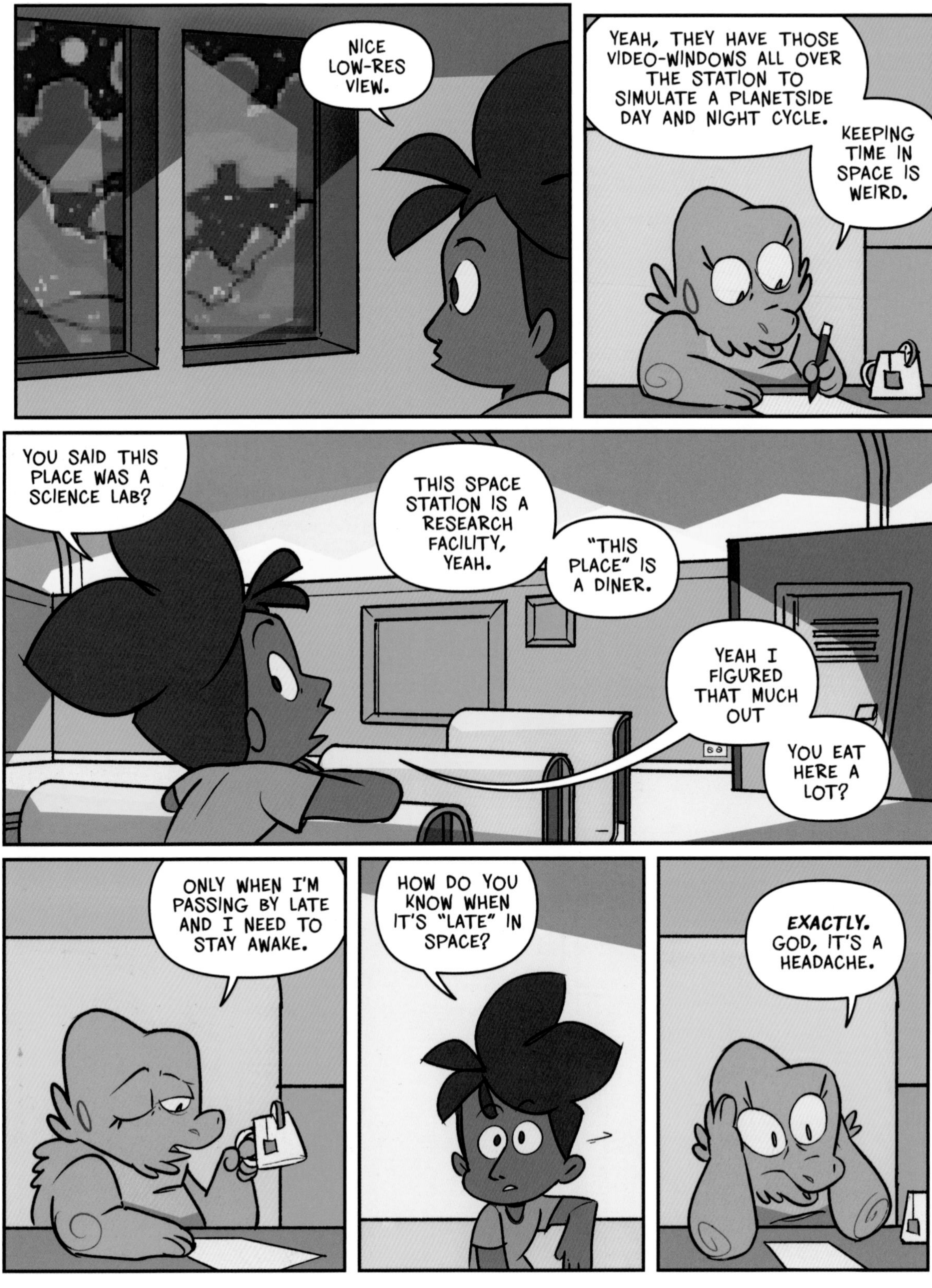
NICE LOW-RES VIEW.
YEAH, THEY HAVE THOSE VIDEO-WINDOWS ALL OVER THE STATION TO SIMULATE A PLANETSIDE DAY AND NIGHT CYCLE.
KEEPING TIME IN SPACE IS WEIRD.
YOU SAID THIS PLACE WAS A SCIENCE LAB?
THIS SPACE STATION IS A RESEARCH FACILITY, YEAH.
"THIS PLACE" IS A DINER.
YEAH I FIGURED THAT MUCH OUT
YOU EAT HERE A LOT?
ONLY WHEN I'M PASSING BY LATE AND I NEED TO STAY AWAKE.
HOW DO YOU KNOW WHEN IT'S "LATE" IN SPACE?
EXACTLY. GOD, IT'S A HEADACHE.

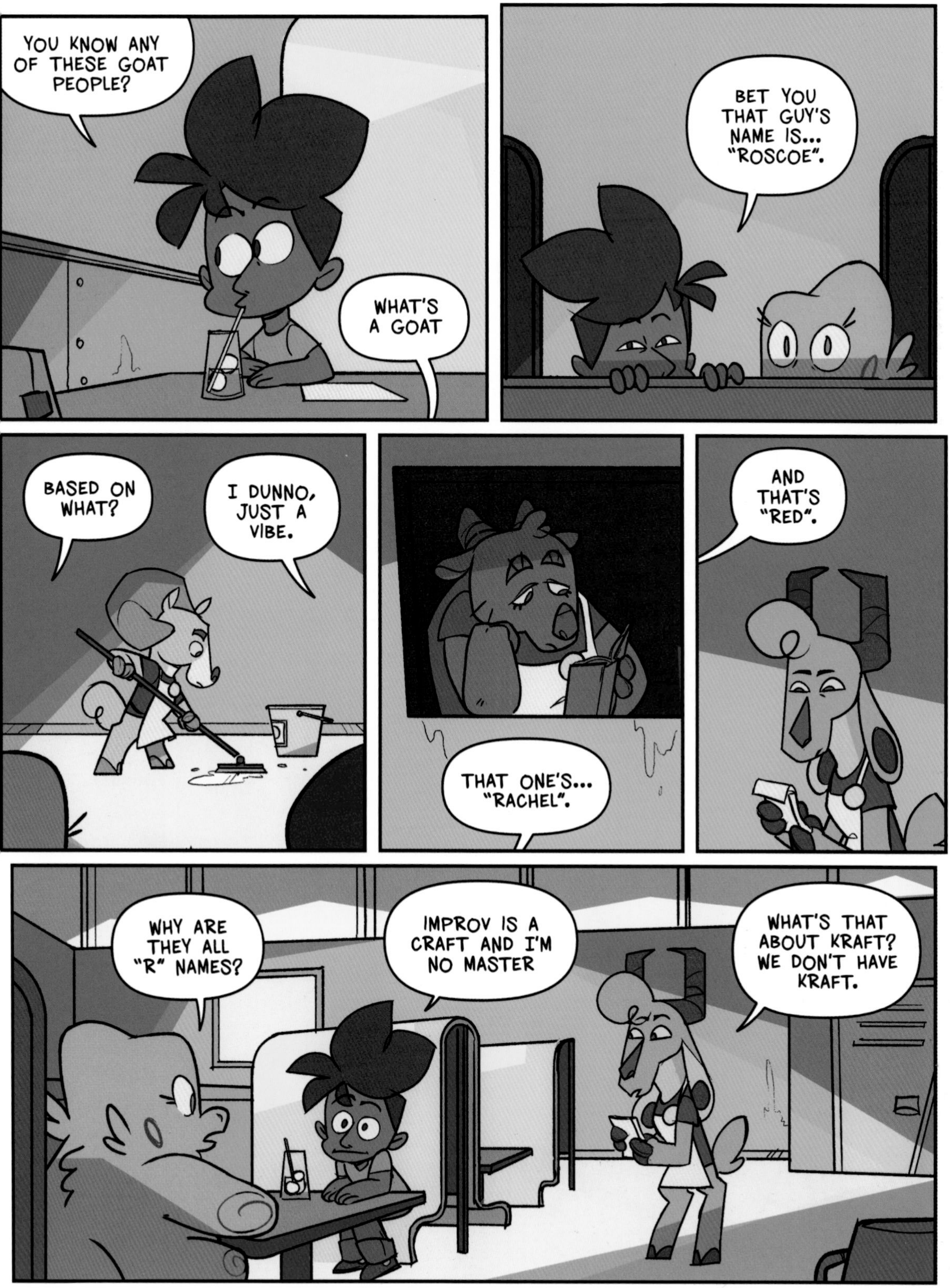
YOU KNOW ANY OF THESE GOAT PEOPLE?
WHAT'S A GOAT
BET YOU THAT GUY'S NAME IS... "ROSCOE".
BASED ON WHAT?
I DUNNO, JUST A VIBE.
THAT ONE'S... "RACHEL".
AND THAT'S "RED".
WHY ARE THEY ALL "R" NAMES?
IMPROV IS A CRAFT AND I'M NO MASTER
WHAT'S THAT ABOUT KRAFT? WE DON'T HAVE KRAFT.

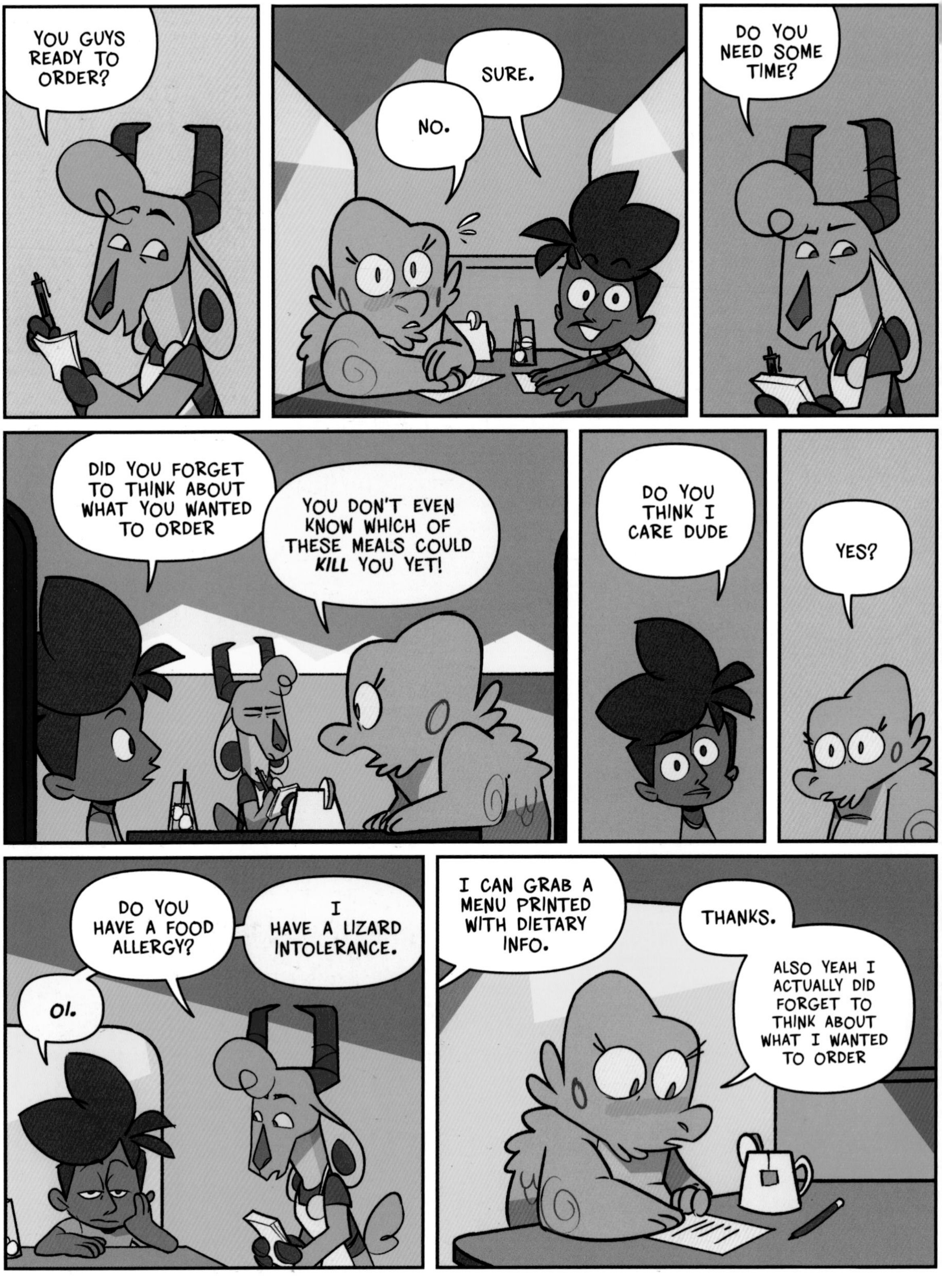
YOU GUYS READY TO ORDER?
SURE.
NO.
DO YOU NEED SOME TIME?
DID YOU FORGET TO THINK ABOUT WHAT YOU WANTED TO ORDER
YOU DON'T EVEN KNOW WHICH OF THESE MEALS COULD KILL YOU YET!
DO YOU THINK I CARE DUDE
YES?
DO YOU HAVE A FOOD ALLERGY?
I HAVE A LIZARD INTOLERANCE.
OI.
I CAN GRAB A MENU PRINTED WITH DIETARY INFO.
THANKS.
ALSO YEAH I ACTUALLY DID FORGET TO THINK ABOUT WHAT I WANTED TO ORDER

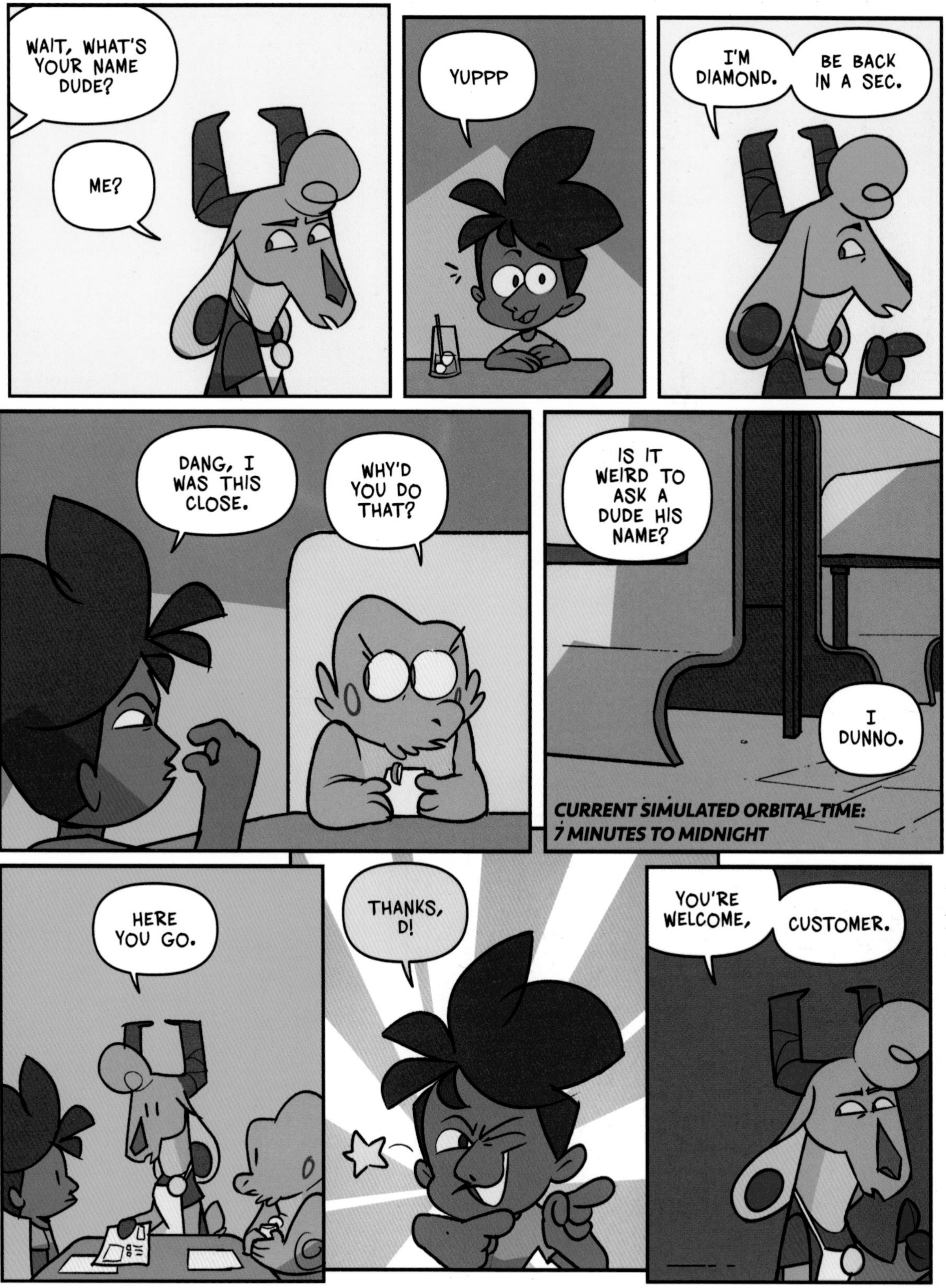
WAIT, WHAT'S YOUR NAME DUDE?
ME?
YUPPP
I'M DIAMOND.
BE BACK IN A SEC.
DANG, I WAS THIS CLOSE.
WHY'D YOU DO THAT?
IS IT WEIRD TO ASK A DUDE HIS NAME?
I DUNNO.
CURRENT SIMULATED ORBITAL TIME: 7 MINUTES TO MIDNIGHT
HERE YOU GO.
THANKS, D!
YOU'RE WELCOME,
CUSTOMER.

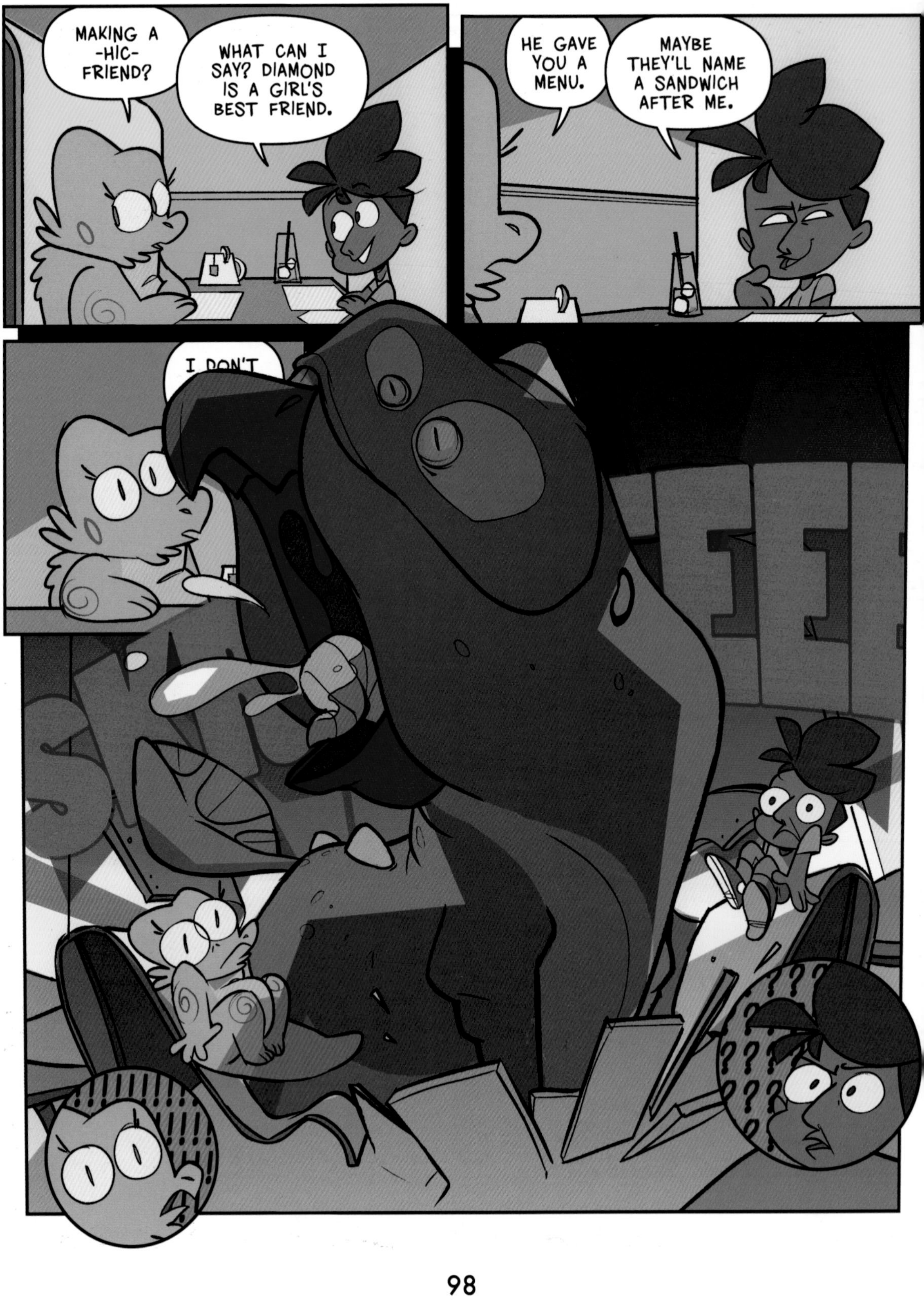
MAKING A -HIC- FRIEND?
WHAT CAN I SAY? DIAMOND IS A GIRL'S BEST FRIEND.
HE GAVE YOU A MENU.
MAYBE THEY'LL NAME A SANDWICH AFTER ME.
I DON'T

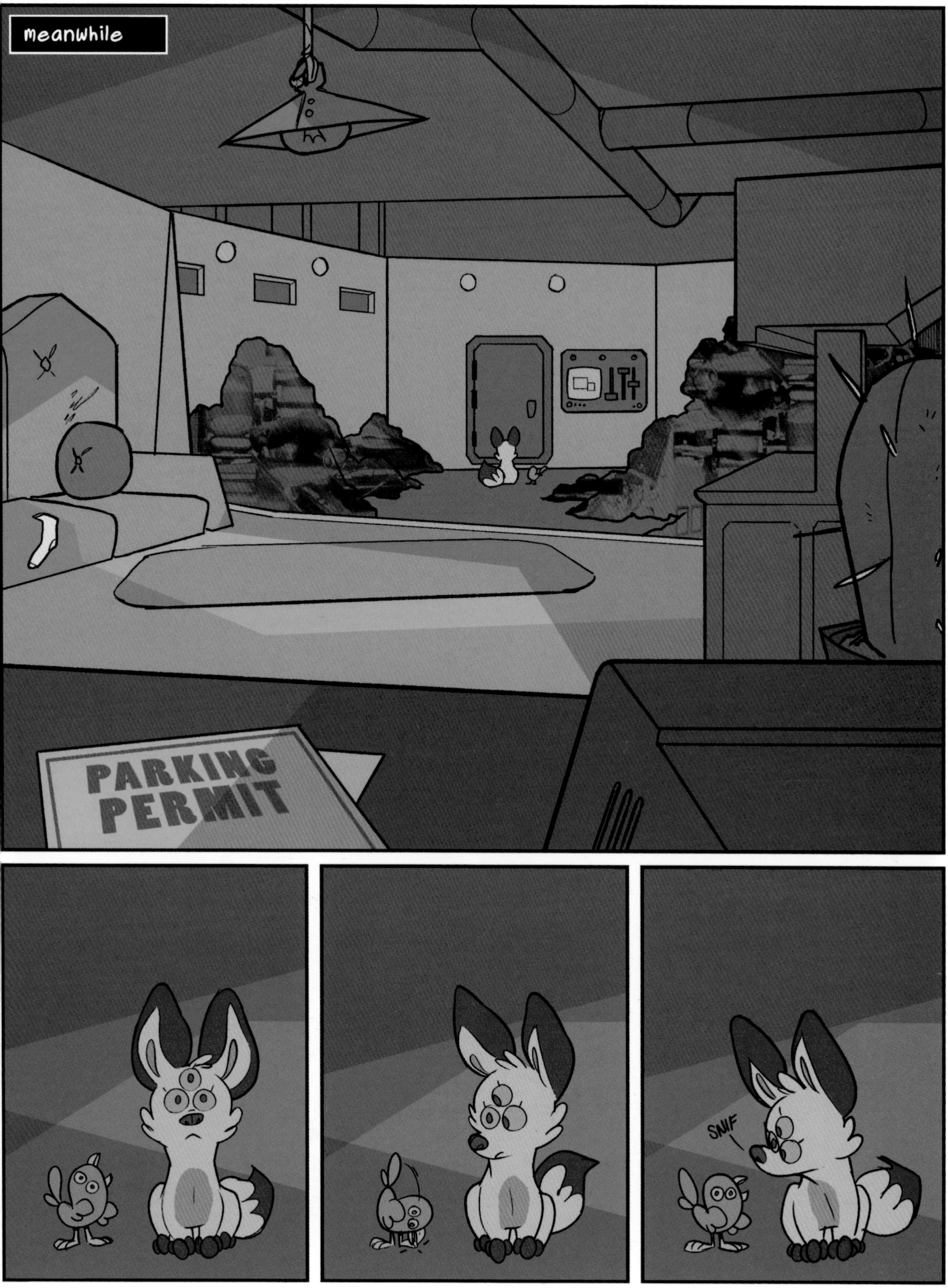
meanwhile
PARKING PERMIT
SNIFF

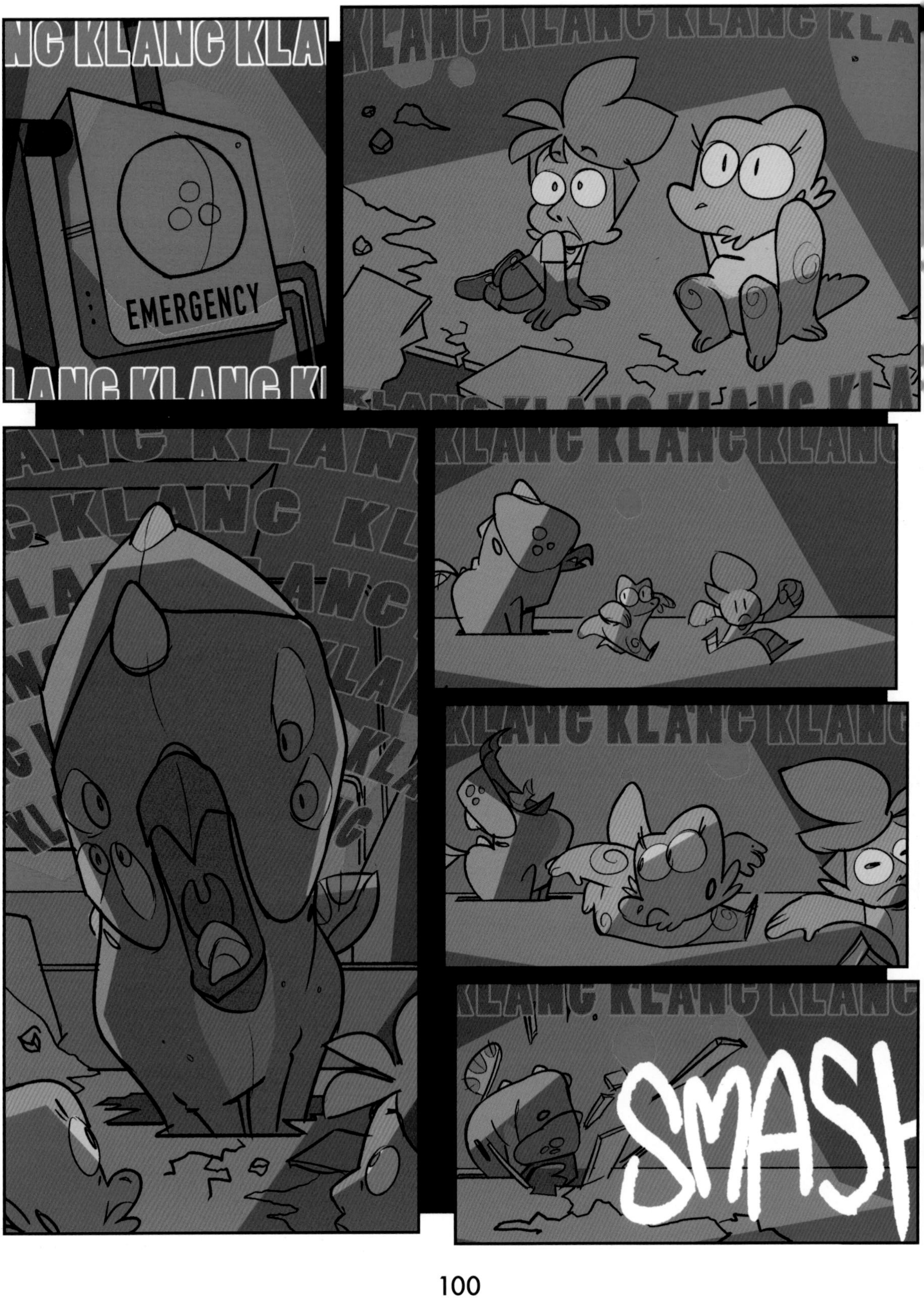
KLANG KLANG
EMERGENCY
KLANG KLANG
KLANG KLANG
KLANG KLANG
KLANG KLANG
KLANG KLANG
SMASH

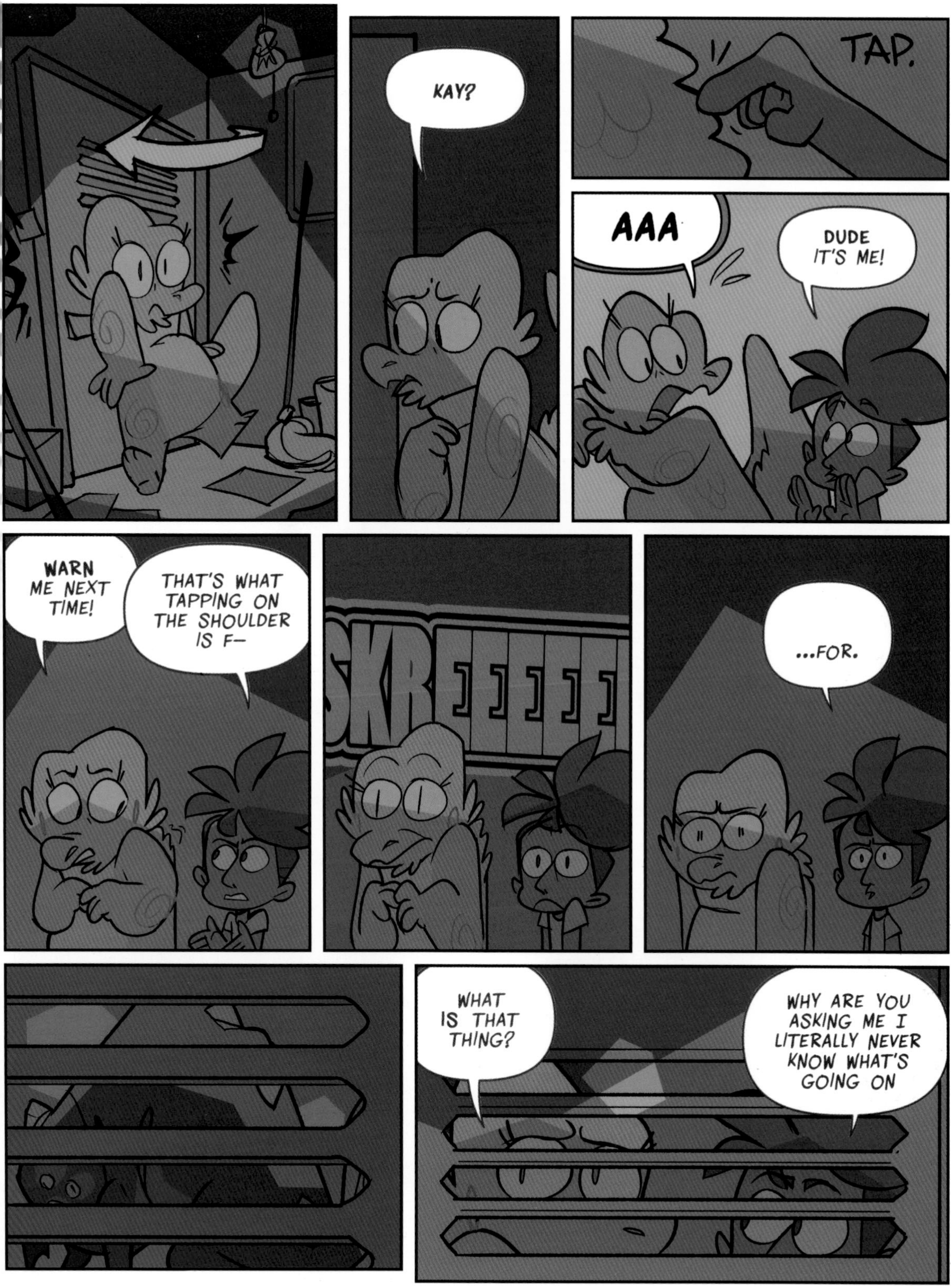
KAY?
TAP.
AAA
DUDE IT'S ME!
WARN ME NEXT TIME!
THAT'S WHAT TAPPING ON THE SHOULDER IS F—
SKREEEEEE
...FOR.
WHAT IS THAT THING?
WHY ARE YOU ASKING ME I LITERALLY NEVER KNOW WHAT'S GOING ON

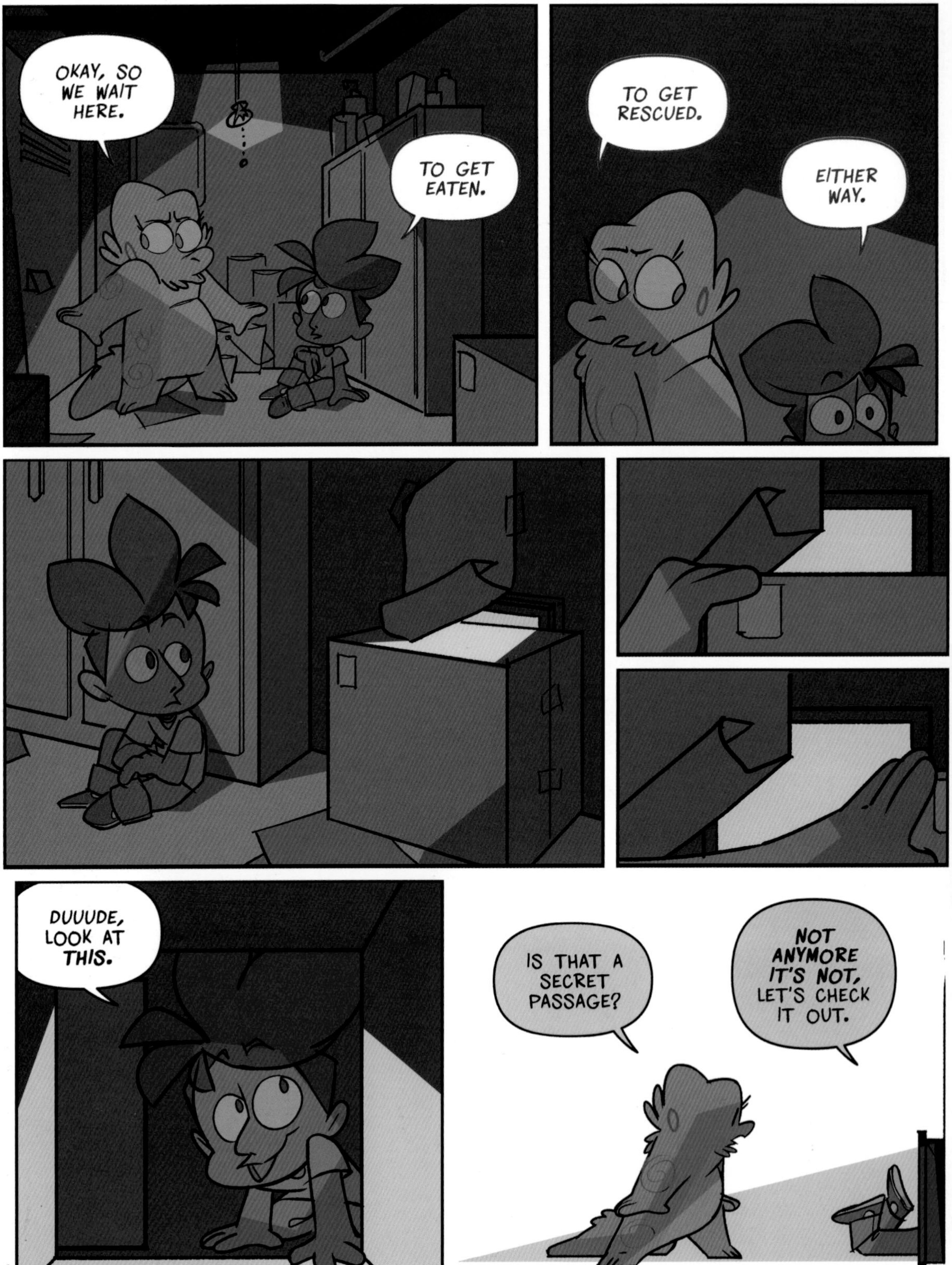
OKAY, SO WE WAIT HERE.
TO GET EATEN.
TO GET RESCUED.
EITHER WAY.
DUUUDE, LOOK AT THIS.
IS THAT A SECRET PASSAGE?
NOT ANYMORE IT'S NOT, LET'S CHECK IT OUT.

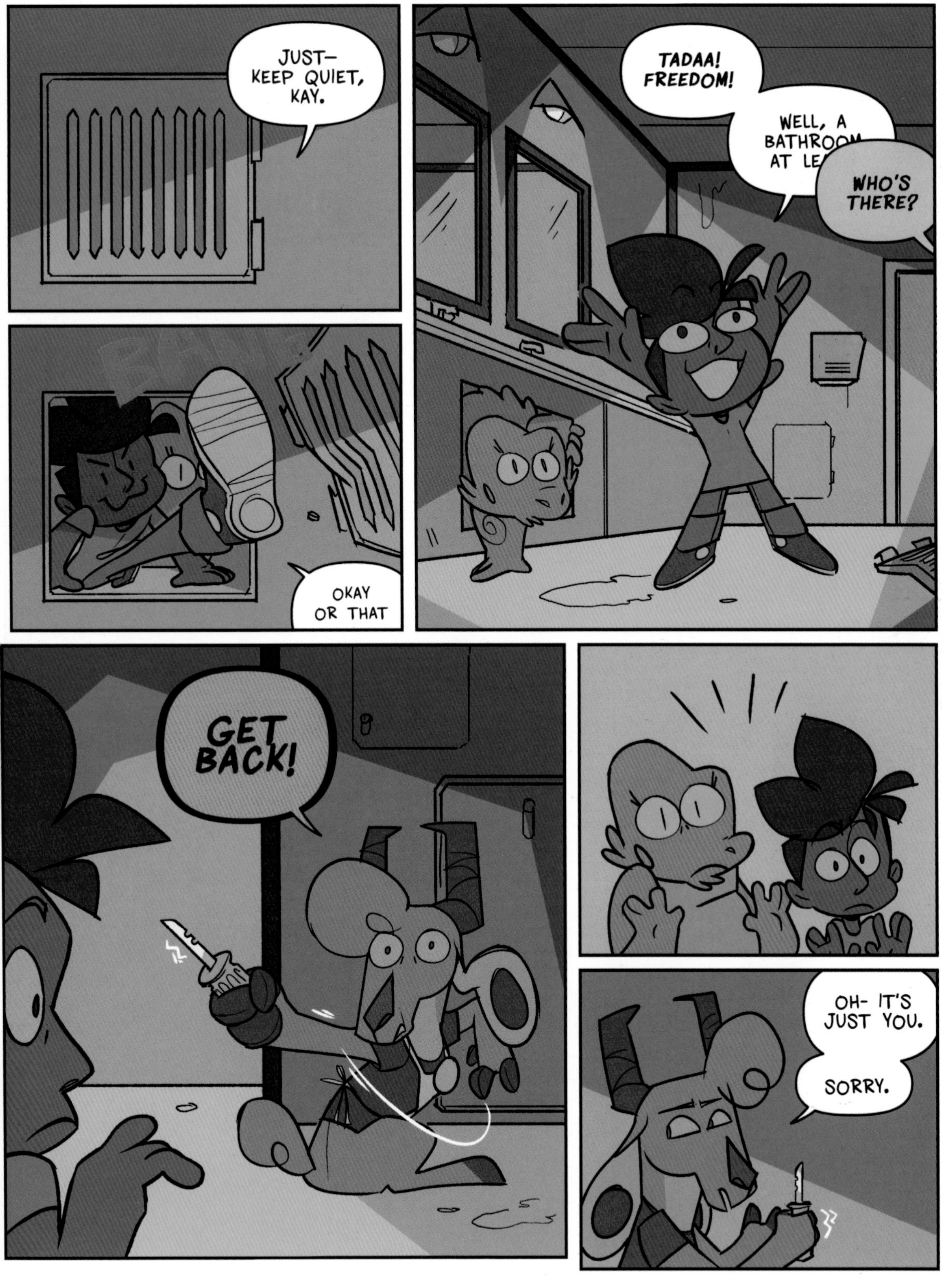
JUST— KEEP QUIET, KAY.
OKAY OR THAT
TADAA! FREEDOM!
WELL, A BATHROOM AT LE
WHO'S THERE?
GET BACK!
OH- IT'S JUST YOU.
SORRY.

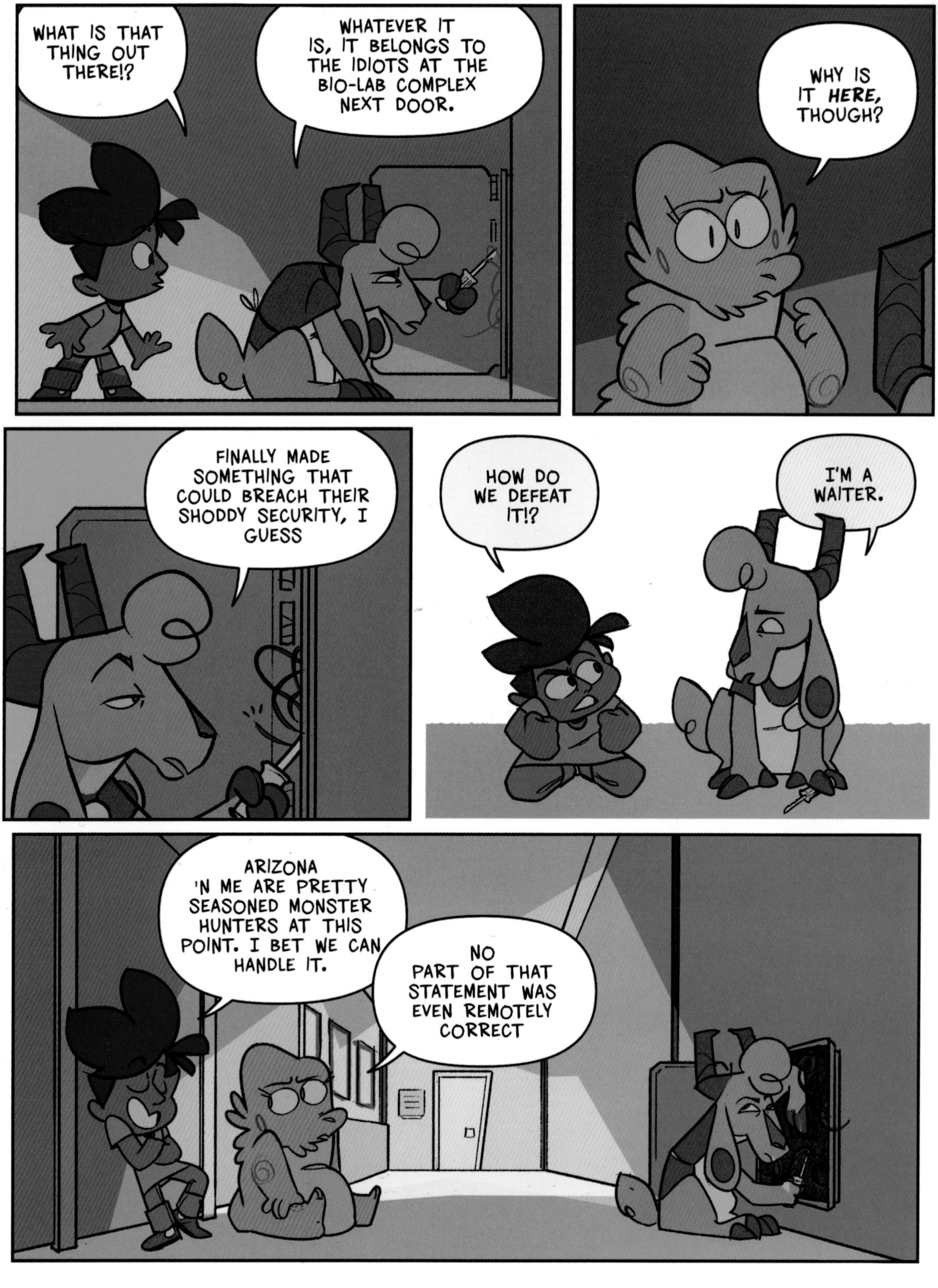
WHAT IS THAT THING OUT THERE!?
WHATEVER IT IS, IT BELONGS TO THE IDIOTS AT THE BIO-LAB COMPLEX NEXT DOOR.
WHY IS IT *HERE,* THOUGH?
FINALLY MADE SOMETHING THAT COULD BREACH THEIR SHODDY SECURITY, I GUESS
HOW DO WE DEFEAT IT!?
I'M A WAITER.
ARIZONA 'N ME ARE PRETTY SEASONED MONSTER HUNTERS AT THIS POINT. I BET WE CAN HANDLE IT.
NO PART OF THAT STATEMENT WAS EVEN REMOTELY CORRECT

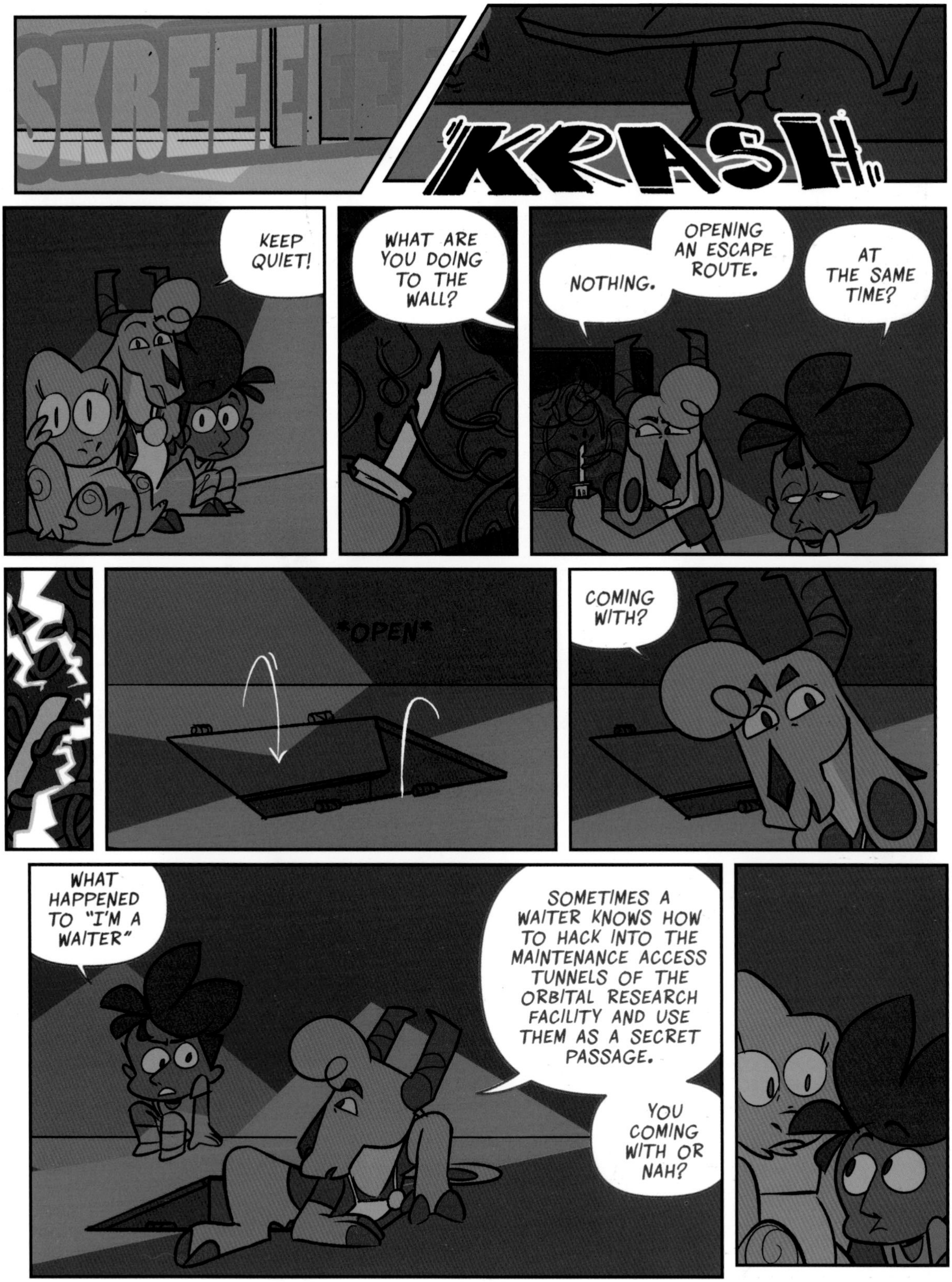
SKREEEEE
KRASH
KEEP QUIET!
WHAT ARE YOU DOING TO THE WALL?
NOTHING.
OPENING AN ESCAPE ROUTE.
AT THE SAME TIME?
OPEN
COMING WITH?
WHAT HAPPENED TO "I'M A WAITER"
SOMETIMES A WAITER KNOWS HOW TO HACK INTO THE MAINTENANCE ACCESS TUNNELS OF THE ORBITAL RESEARCH FACILITY AND USE THEM AS A SECRET PASSAGE.
YOU COMING WITH OR NAH?

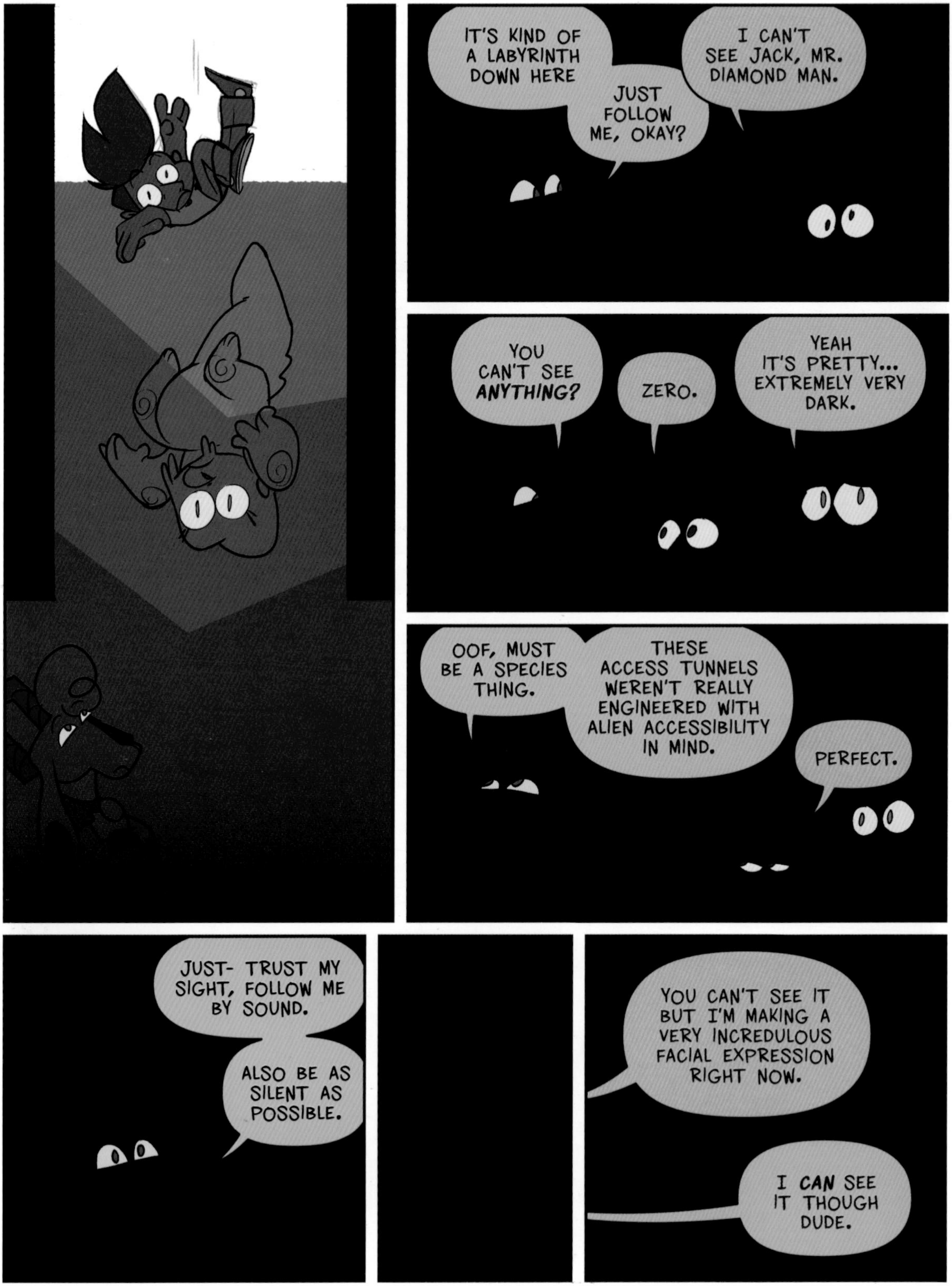
IT'S KIND OF A LABYRINTH DOWN HERE
JUST FOLLOW ME, OKAY?
I CAN'T SEE JACK, MR. DIAMOND MAN.
YOU CAN'T SEE ANYTHING?
ZERO.
YEAH IT'S PRETTY... EXTREMELY VERY DARK.
OOF, MUST BE A SPECIES THING.
THESE ACCESS TUNNELS WEREN'T REALLY ENGINEERED WITH ALIEN ACCESSIBILITY IN MIND.
PERFECT.
JUST- TRUST MY SIGHT, FOLLOW ME BY SOUND.
ALSO BE AS SILENT AS POSSIBLE.
YOU CAN'T SEE IT BUT I'M MAKING A VERY INCREDULOUS FACIAL EXPRESSION RIGHT NOW.
I CAN SEE IT THOUGH DUDE.

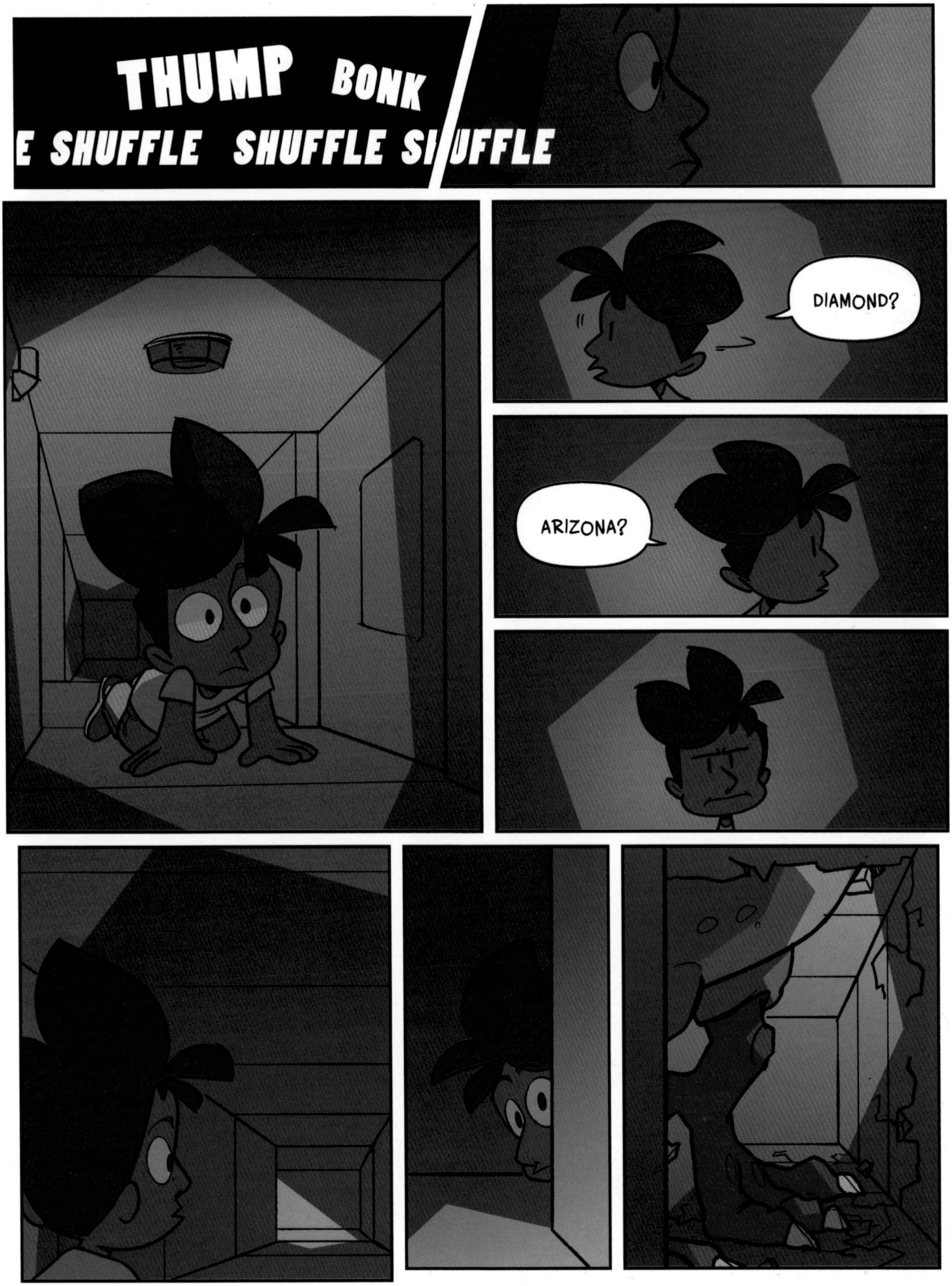

THUMP
BONK
E SHUFFLE SHUFFLE SHUFFLE
DIAMOND?
ARIZONA?

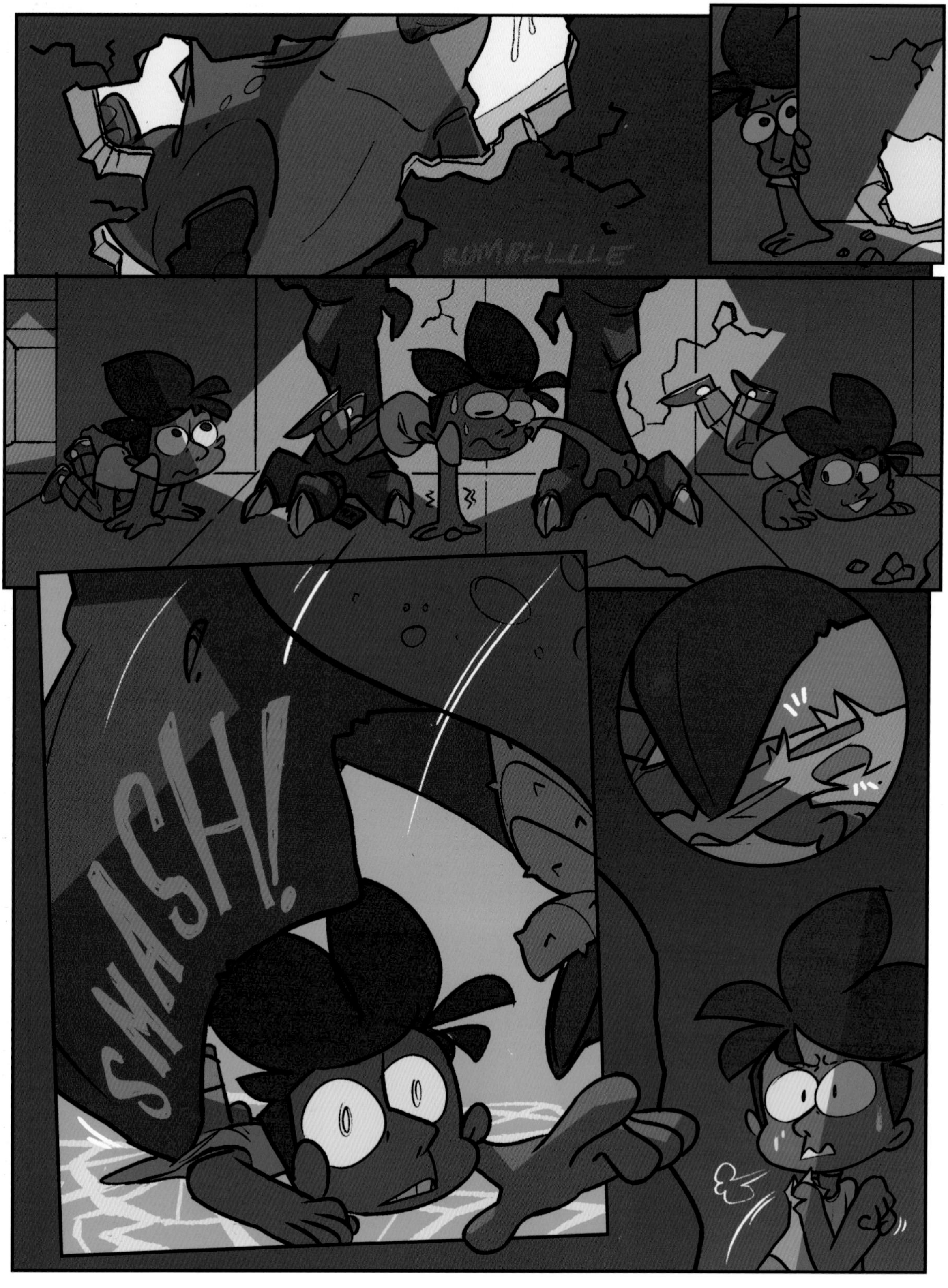
RUMBLLLLE
SMASH!

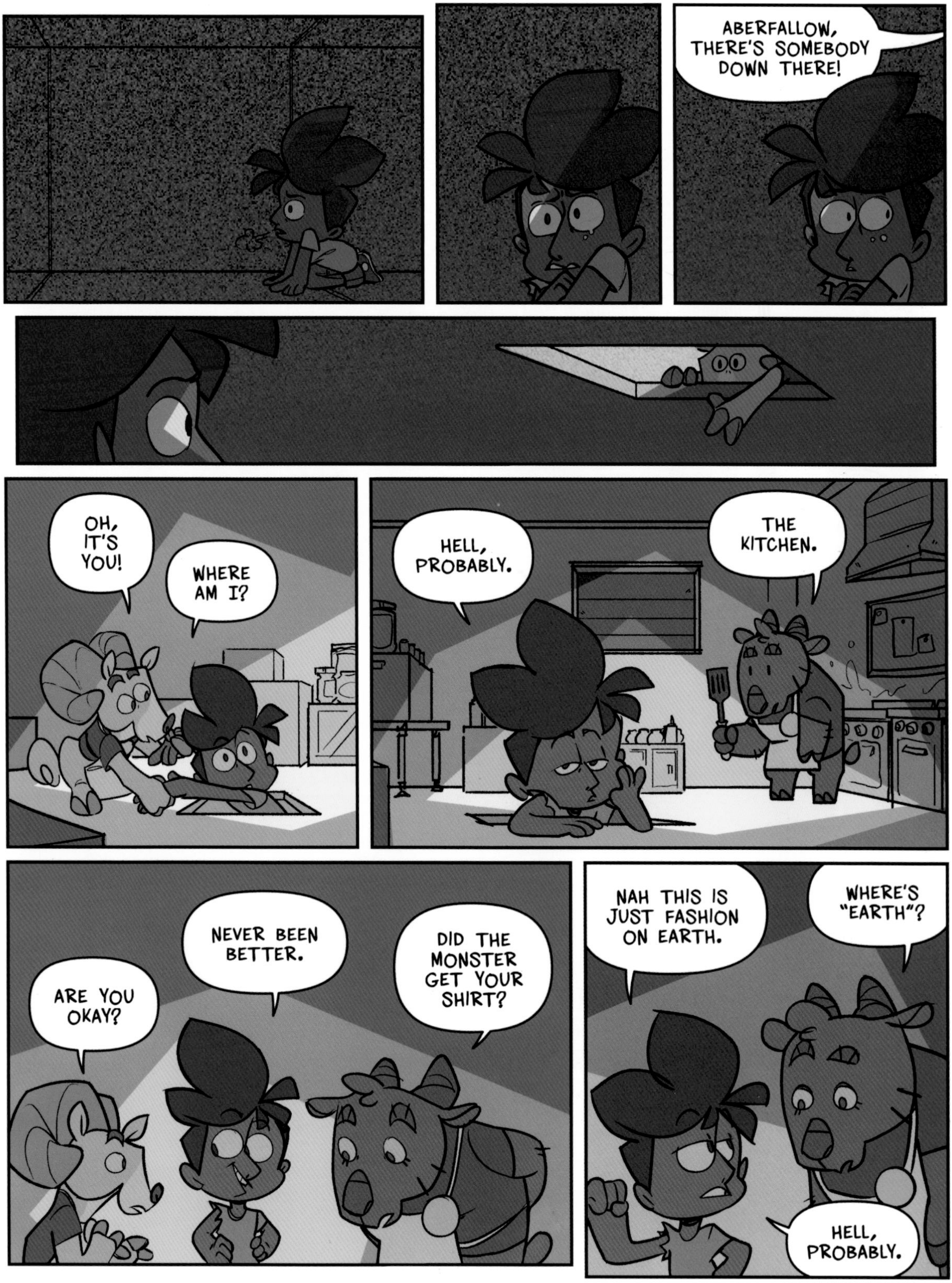
ABERFALLOW, THERE'S SOMEBODY DOWN THERE!
OH, IT'S YOU!
WHERE AM I?
HELL, PROBABLY.
THE KITCHEN.
ARE YOU OKAY?
NEVER BEEN BETTER.
DID THE MONSTER GET YOUR SHIRT?
NAH THIS IS JUST FASHION ON EARTH.
WHERE'S "EARTH"?
HELL, PROBABLY.

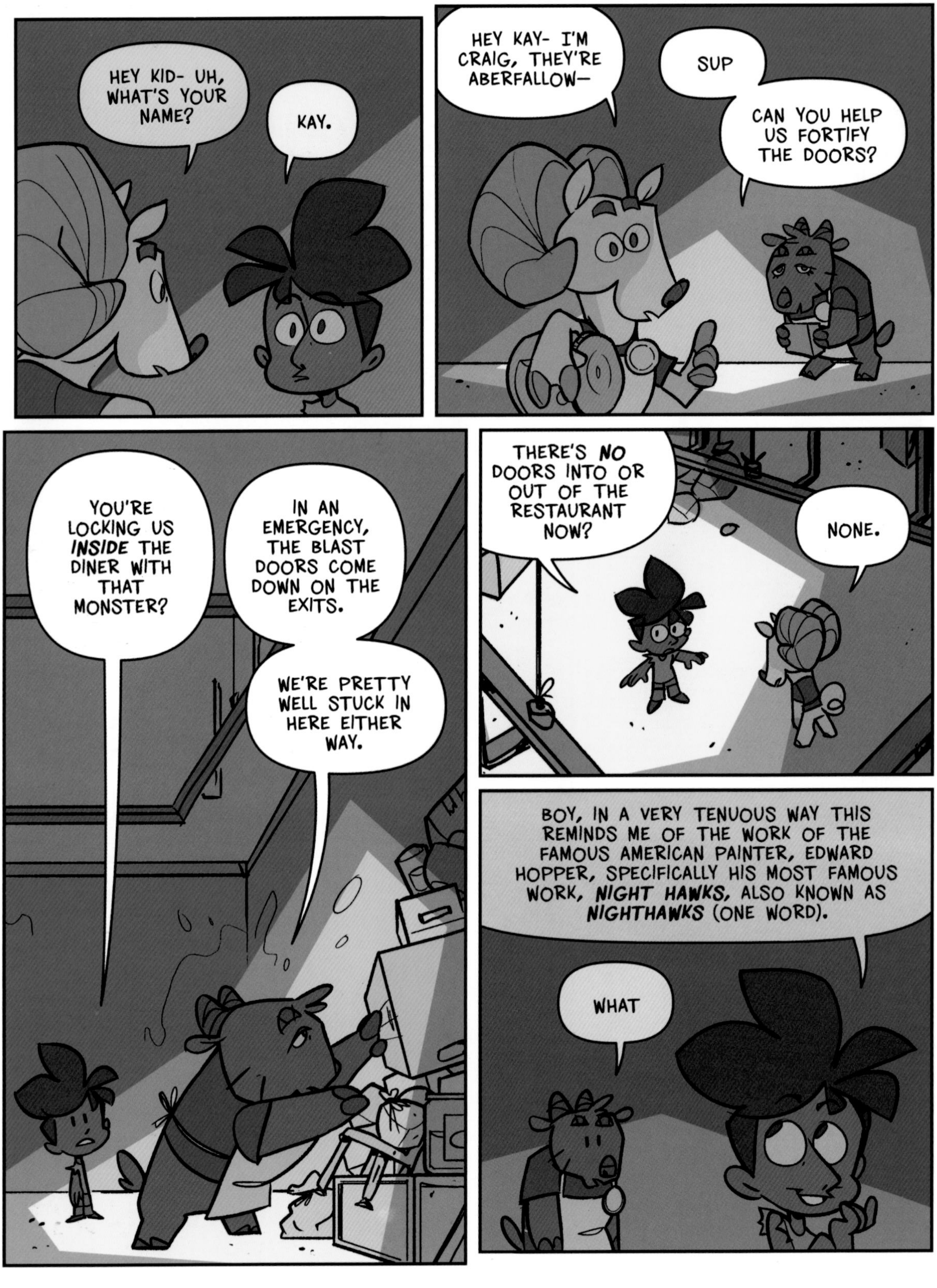
HEY KID- UH, WHAT'S YOUR NAME?
KAY.
HEY KAY- I'M CRAIG, THEY'RE ABERFALLOW—
SUP
CAN YOU HELP US FORTIFY THE DOORS?
YOU'RE LOCKING US **INSIDE** THE DINER WITH THAT MONSTER?
IN AN EMERGENCY, THE BLAST DOORS COME DOWN ON THE EXITS.
WE'RE PRETTY WELL STUCK IN HERE EITHER WAY.
THERE'S **NO** DOORS INTO OR OUT OF THE RESTAURANT NOW?
NONE.
BOY, IN A VERY TENUOUS WAY THIS REMINDS ME OF THE WORK OF THE FAMOUS AMERICAN PAINTER, EDWARD HOPPER, SPECIFICALLY HIS MOST FAMOUS WORK, ***NIGHT HAWKS,*** ALSO KNOWN AS ***NIGHTHAWKS*** (ONE WORD).
WHAT

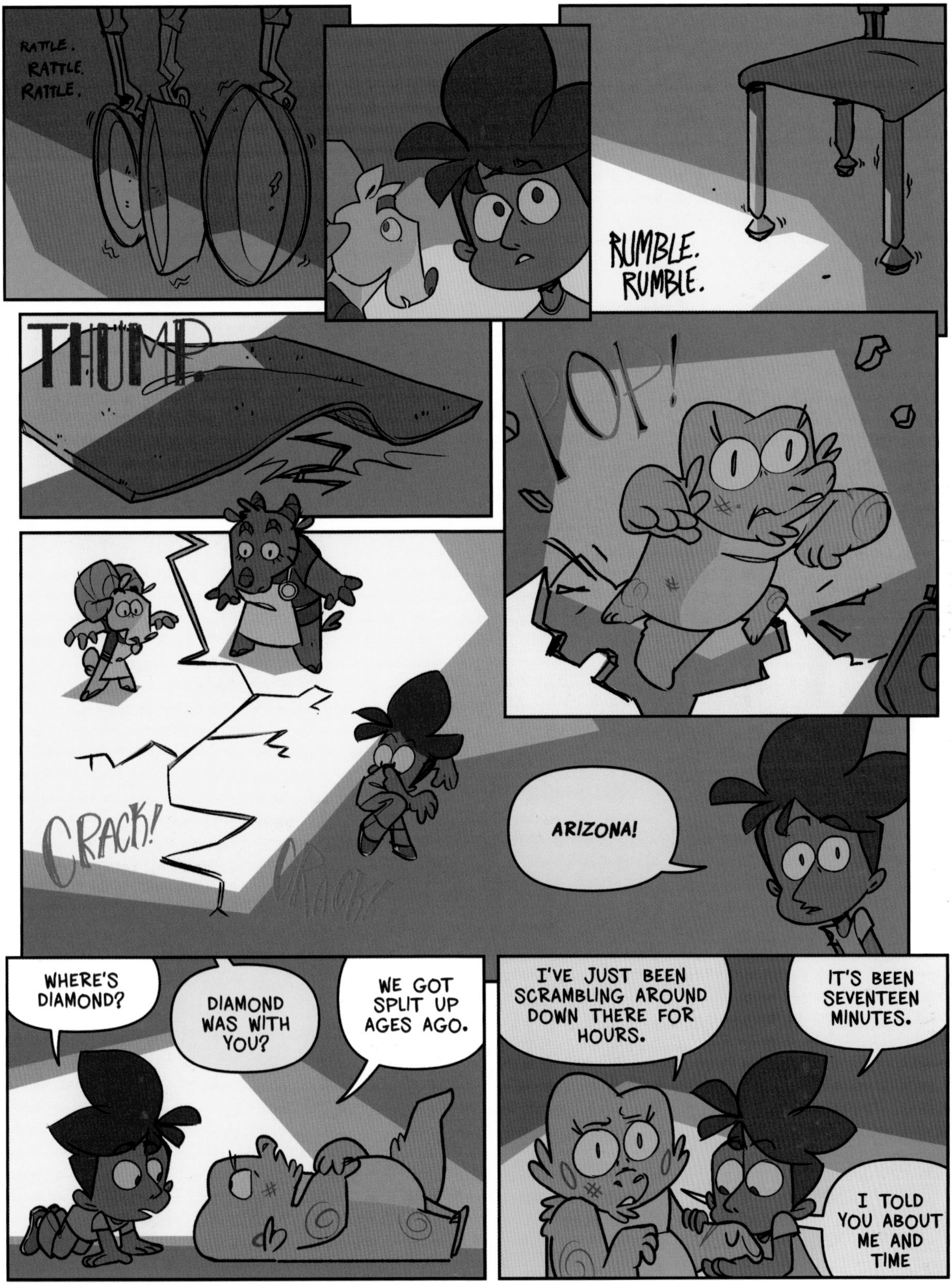
RATTLE.
RATTLE.
RATTLE.
RUMBLE.
RUMBLE.
THUMP.
POP!
CRACK!
CRACK!
ARIZONA!
WHERE'S DIAMOND?
DIAMOND WAS WITH YOU?
WE GOT SPLIT UP AGES AGO.
I'VE JUST BEEN SCRAMBLING AROUND DOWN THERE FOR HOURS.
IT'S BEEN SEVENTEEN MINUTES.
I TOLD YOU ABOUT ME AND TIME

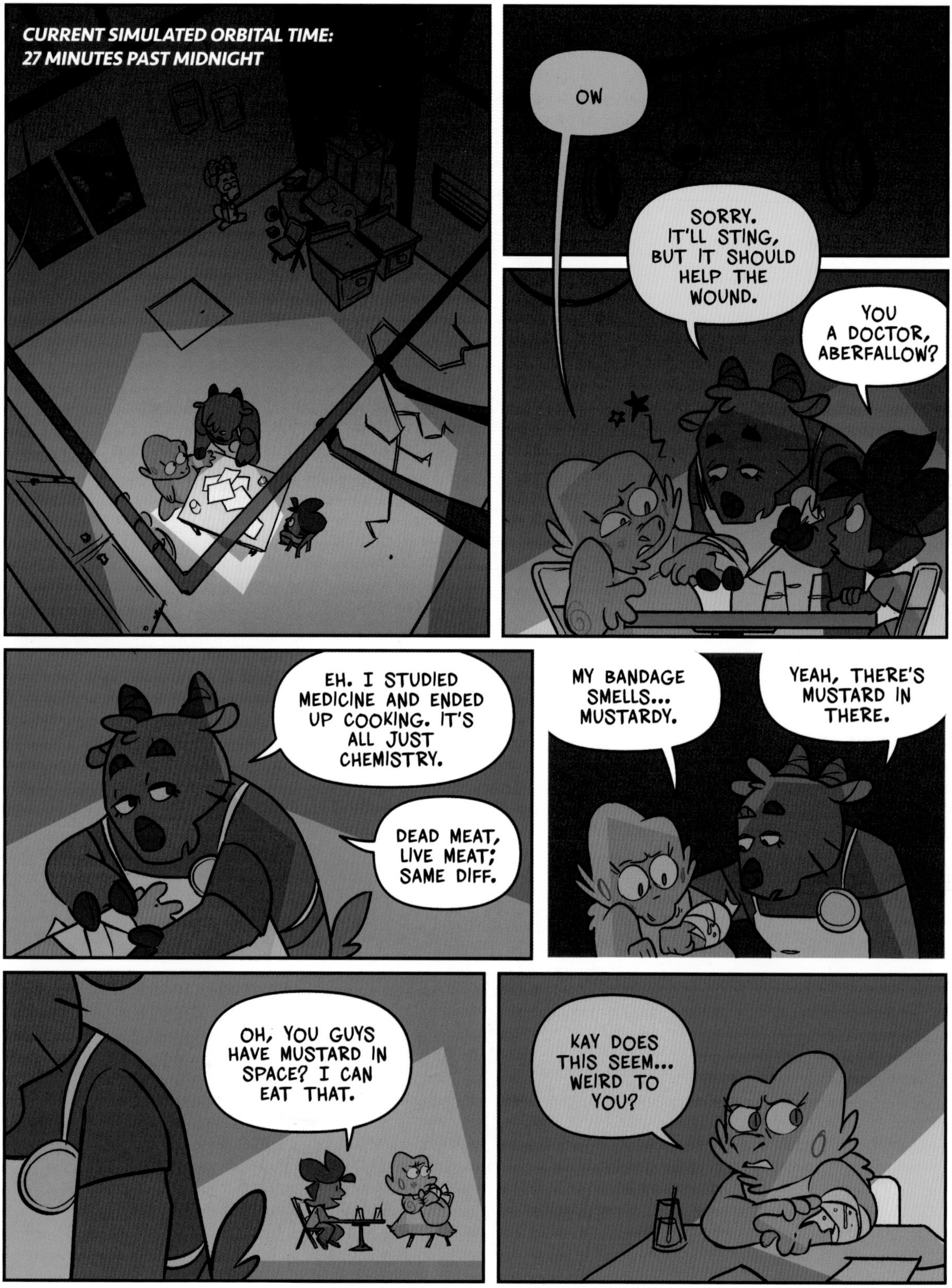
CURRENT SIMULATED ORBITAL TIME:
27 MINUTES PAST MIDNIGHT
OW
SORRY. IT'LL STING, BUT IT SHOULD HELP THE WOUND.
YOU A DOCTOR, ABERFALLOW?
EH. I STUDIED MEDICINE AND ENDED UP COOKING. IT'S ALL JUST CHEMISTRY.
DEAD MEAT, LIVE MEAT; SAME DIFF.
MY BANDAGE SMELLS... MUSTARDY.
YEAH, THERE'S MUSTARD IN THERE.
OH, YOU GUYS HAVE MUSTARD IN SPACE? I CAN EAT THAT.
KAY DOES THIS SEEM... WEIRD TO YOU?

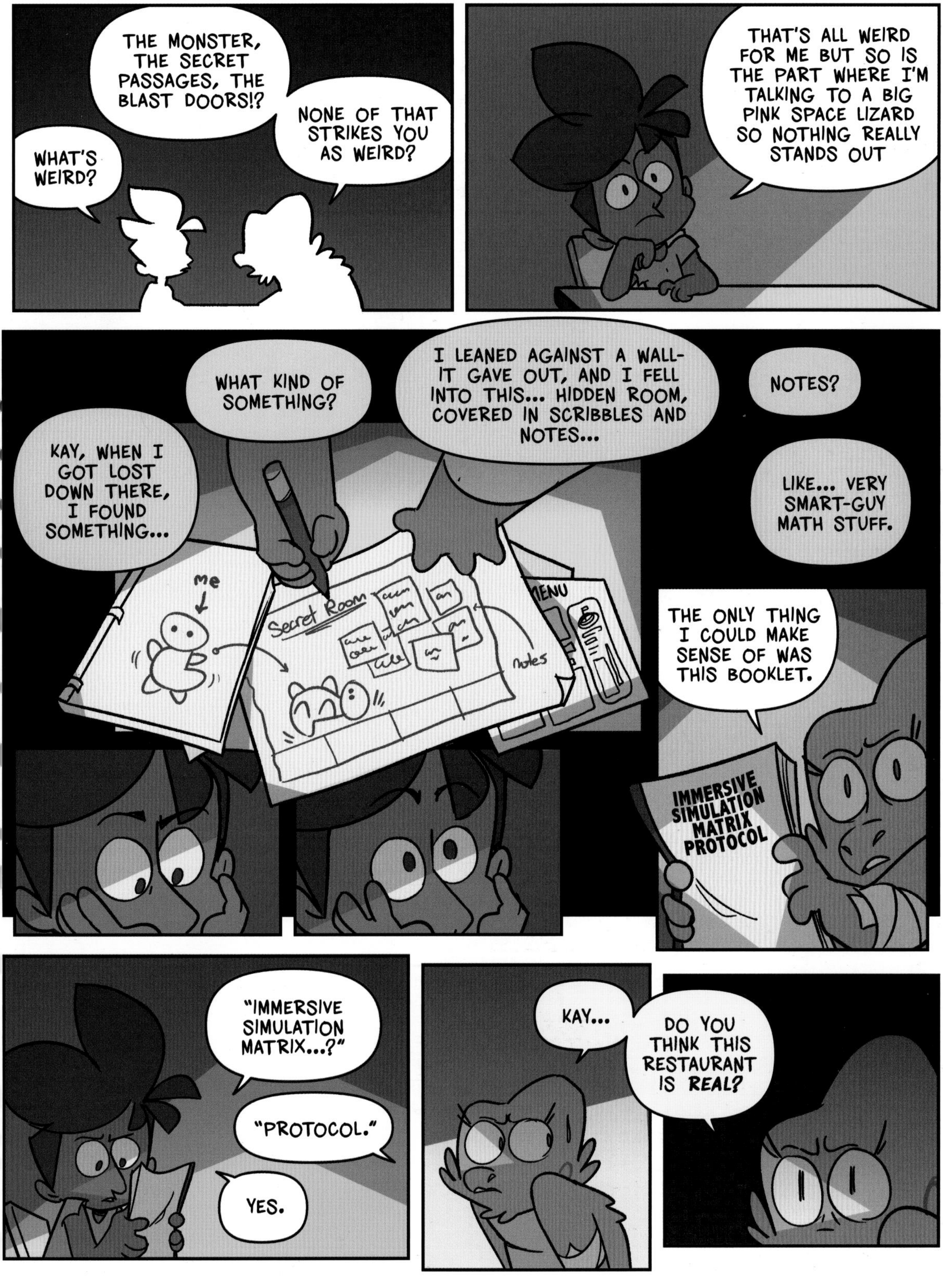
THE MONSTER, THE SECRET PASSAGES, THE BLAST DOORS!?
WHAT'S WEIRD?
NONE OF THAT STRIKES YOU AS WEIRD?
THAT'S ALL WEIRD FOR ME BUT SO IS THE PART WHERE I'M TALKING TO A BIG PINK SPACE LIZARD SO NOTHING REALLY STANDS OUT
KAY, WHEN I GOT LOST DOWN THERE, I FOUND SOMETHING...
WHAT KIND OF SOMETHING?
I LEANED AGAINST A WALL- IT GAVE OUT, AND I FELL INTO THIS... HIDDEN ROOM, COVERED IN SCRIBBLES AND NOTES...
NOTES?
LIKE... VERY SMART-GUY MATH STUFF.
me
Secret Room
notes
MENU
THE ONLY THING I COULD MAKE SENSE OF WAS THIS BOOKLET.
IMMERSIVE SIMULATION MATRIX PROTOCOL
"IMMERSIVE SIMULATION MATRIX...?"
"PROTOCOL."
YES.
KAY...
DO YOU THINK THIS RESTAURANT IS *REAL*?

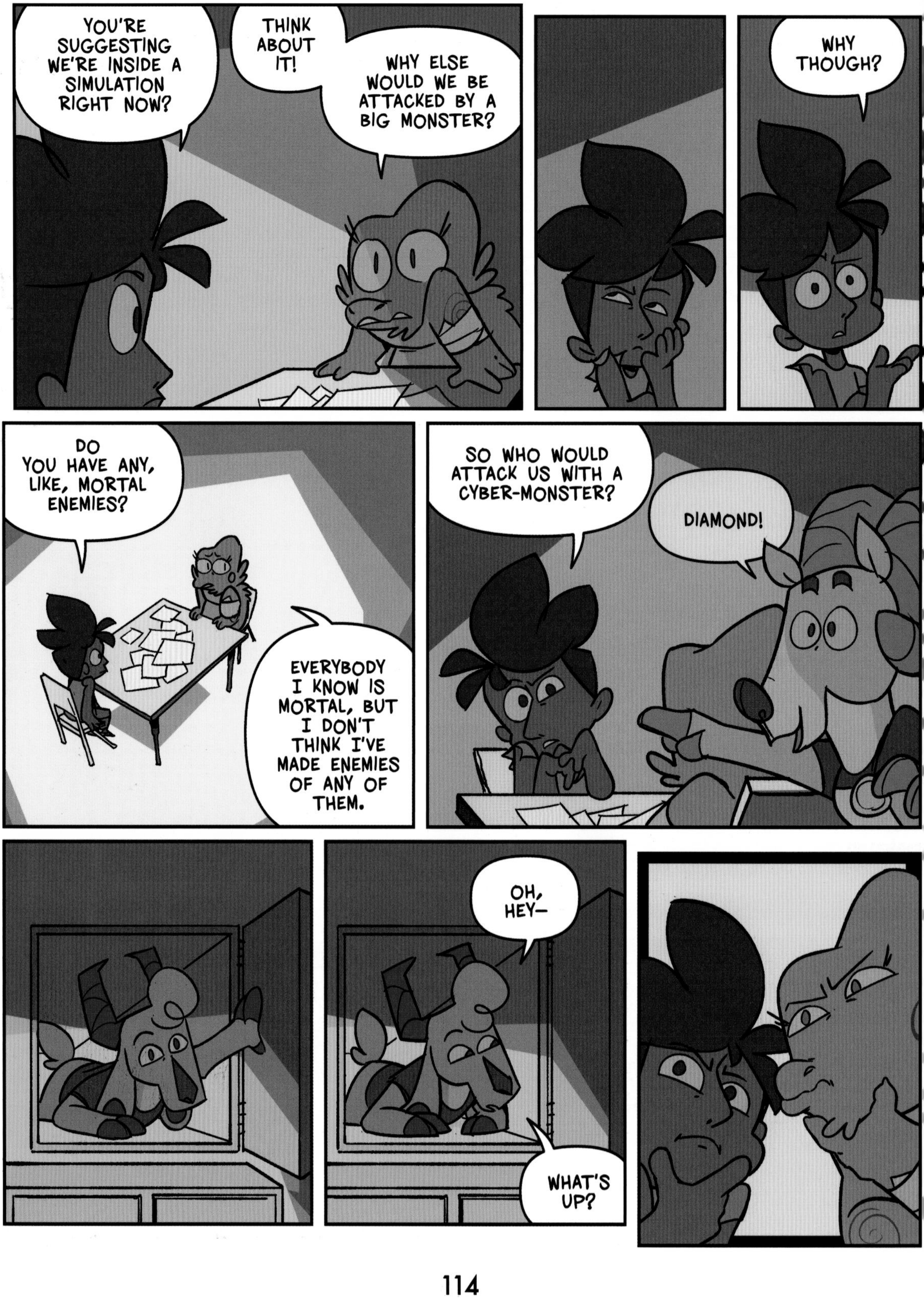
YOU'RE SUGGESTING WE'RE INSIDE A SIMULATION RIGHT NOW?
THINK ABOUT IT!
WHY ELSE WOULD WE BE ATTACKED BY A BIG MONSTER?
WHY THOUGH?
DO YOU HAVE ANY, LIKE, MORTAL ENEMIES?
EVERYBODY I KNOW IS MORTAL, BUT I DON'T THINK I'VE MADE ENEMIES OF ANY OF THEM.
SO WHO WOULD ATTACK US WITH A CYBER-MONSTER?
DIAMOND!
OH, HEY—
WHAT'S UP?

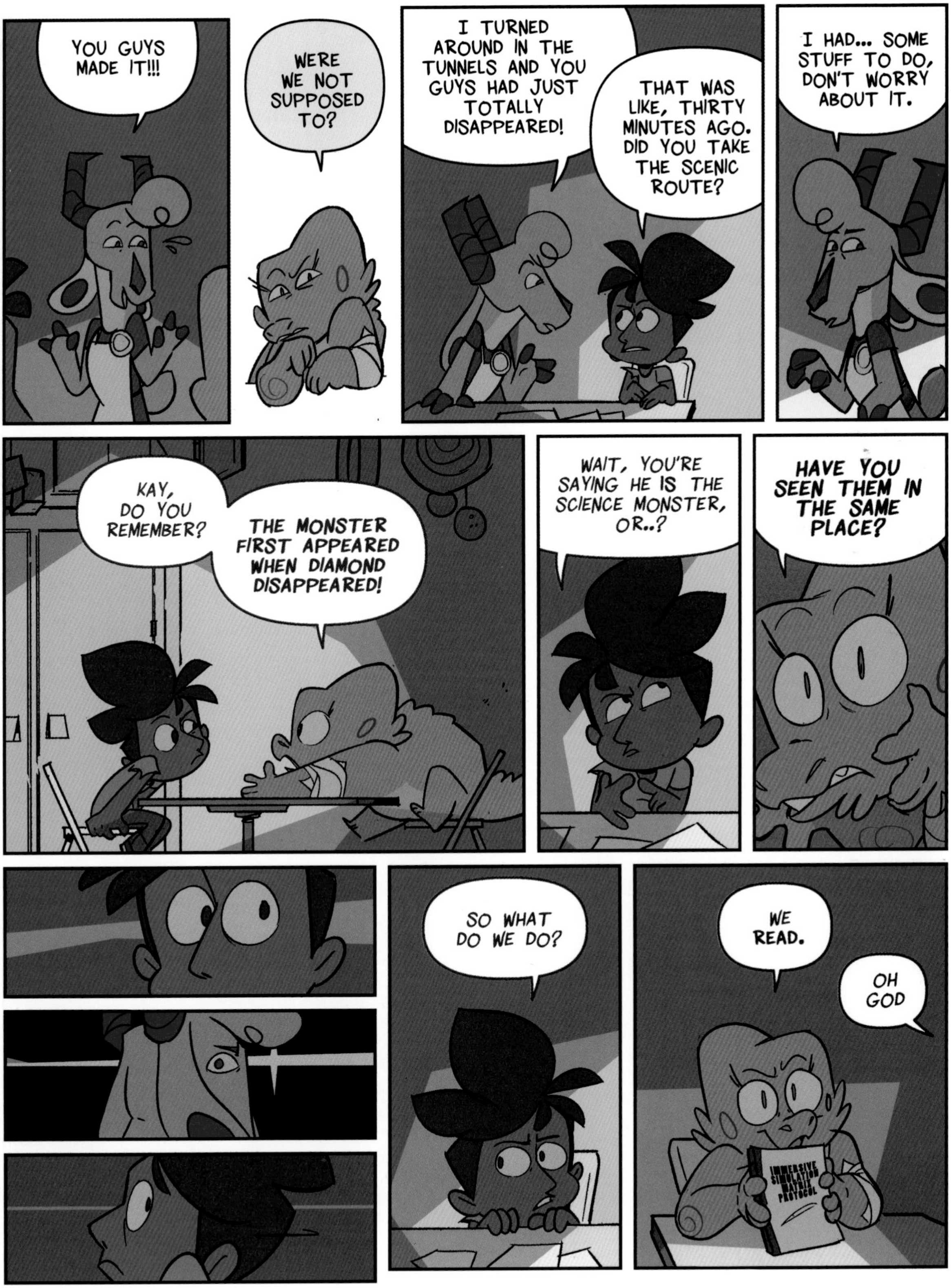

YOU GUYS MADE IT!!!
WERE WE NOT SUPPOSED TO?
I TURNED AROUND IN THE TUNNELS AND YOU GUYS HAD JUST TOTALLY DISAPPEARED!
THAT WAS LIKE, THIRTY MINUTES AGO. DID YOU TAKE THE SCENIC ROUTE?
I HAD... SOME STUFF TO DO, DON'T WORRY ABOUT IT.
KAY, DO YOU REMEMBER?
THE MONSTER FIRST APPEARED WHEN DIAMOND DISAPPEARED!
WAIT, YOU'RE SAYING HE IS THE SCIENCE MONSTER, OR..?
HAVE YOU SEEN THEM IN THE SAME PLACE?
SO WHAT DO WE DO?
WE READ.
OH GOD
IMMERSIVE SIMULATION MATRIX PROTOCOL

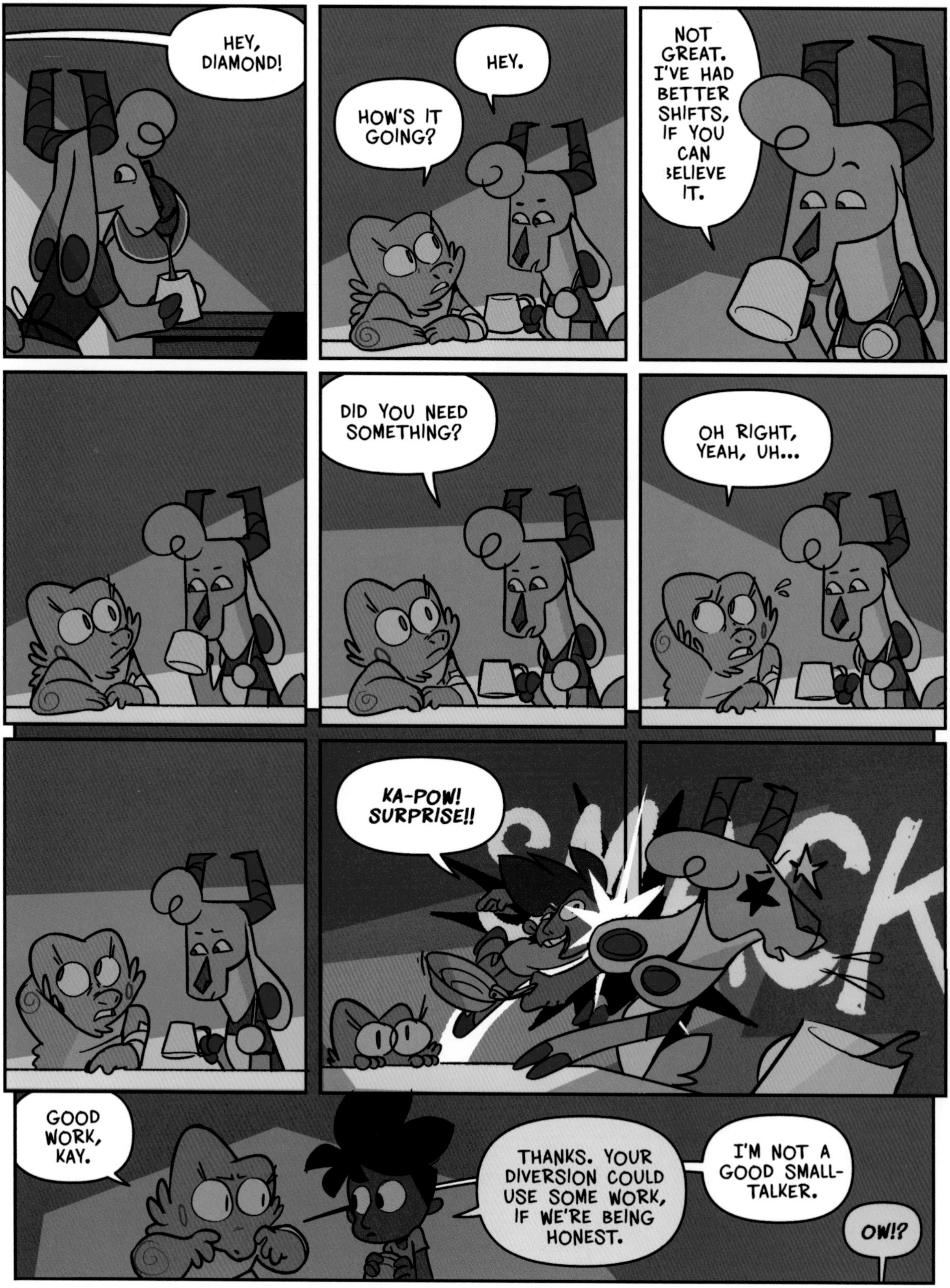
HEY, DIAMOND!
HEY.
HOW'S IT GOING?
NOT GREAT. I'VE HAD BETTER SHIFTS, IF YOU CAN BELIEVE IT.
DID YOU NEED SOMETHING?
OH RIGHT, YEAH, UH...
KA-POW! SURPRISE!!
GOOD WORK, KAY.
THANKS. YOUR DIVERSION COULD USE SOME WORK, IF WE'RE BEING HONEST.
I'M NOT A GOOD SMALL-TALKER.
OW!?

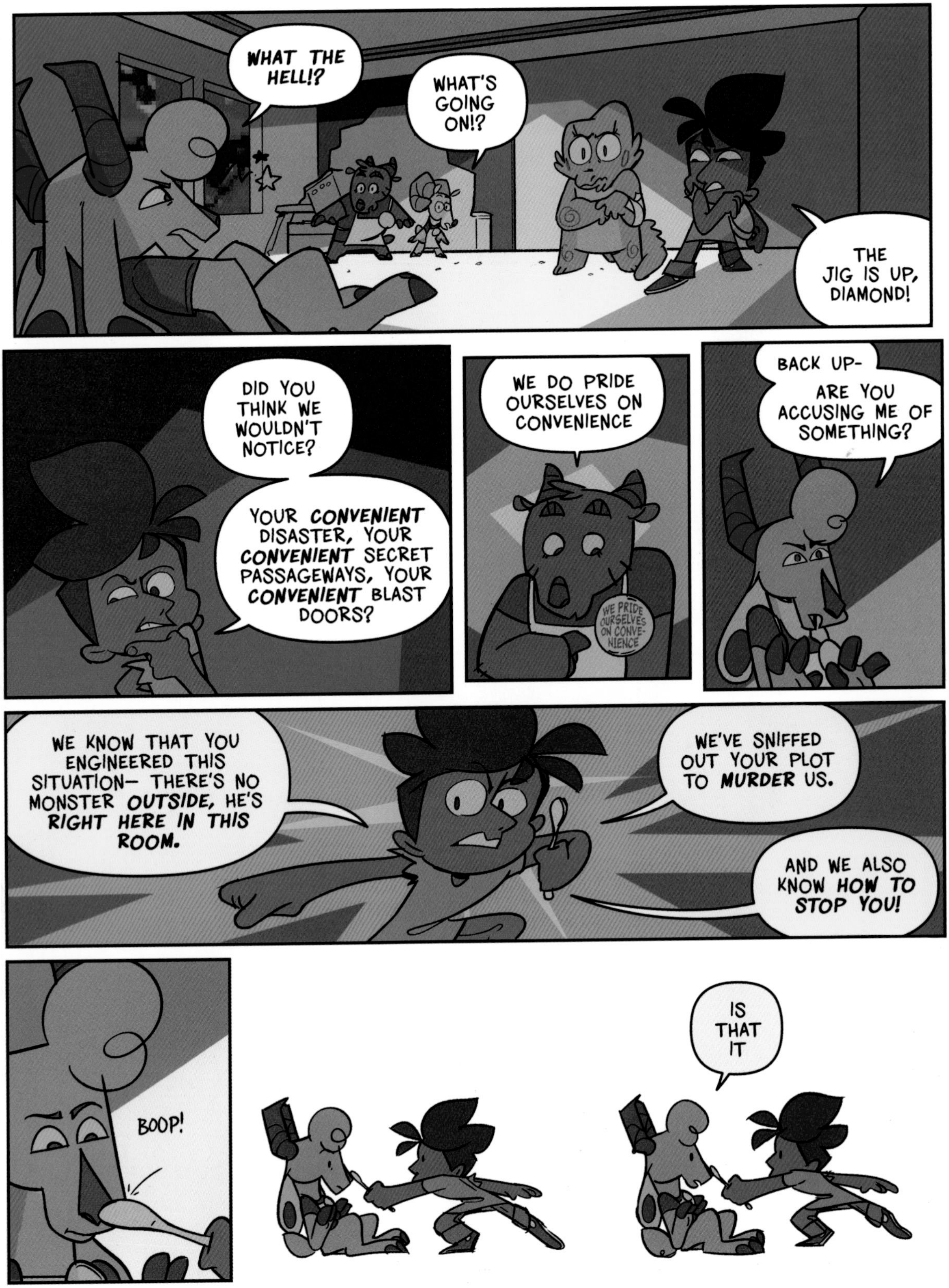
WHAT THE HELL!?
WHAT'S GOING ON!?
THE JIG IS UP, DIAMOND!
DID YOU THINK WE WOULDN'T NOTICE?
YOUR CONVENIENT DISASTER, YOUR CONVENIENT SECRET PASSAGEWAYS, YOUR CONVENIENT BLAST DOORS?
WE DO PRIDE OURSELVES ON CONVENIENCE
WE PRIDE OURSELVES ON CONVENIENCE
BACK UP-
ARE YOU ACCUSING ME OF SOMETHING?
WE KNOW THAT YOU ENGINEERED THIS SITUATION— THERE'S NO MONSTER OUTSIDE, HE'S RIGHT HERE IN THIS ROOM.
WE'VE SNIFFED OUT YOUR PLOT TO MURDER US.
AND WE ALSO KNOW HOW TO STOP YOU!
BOOP!
IS THAT IT

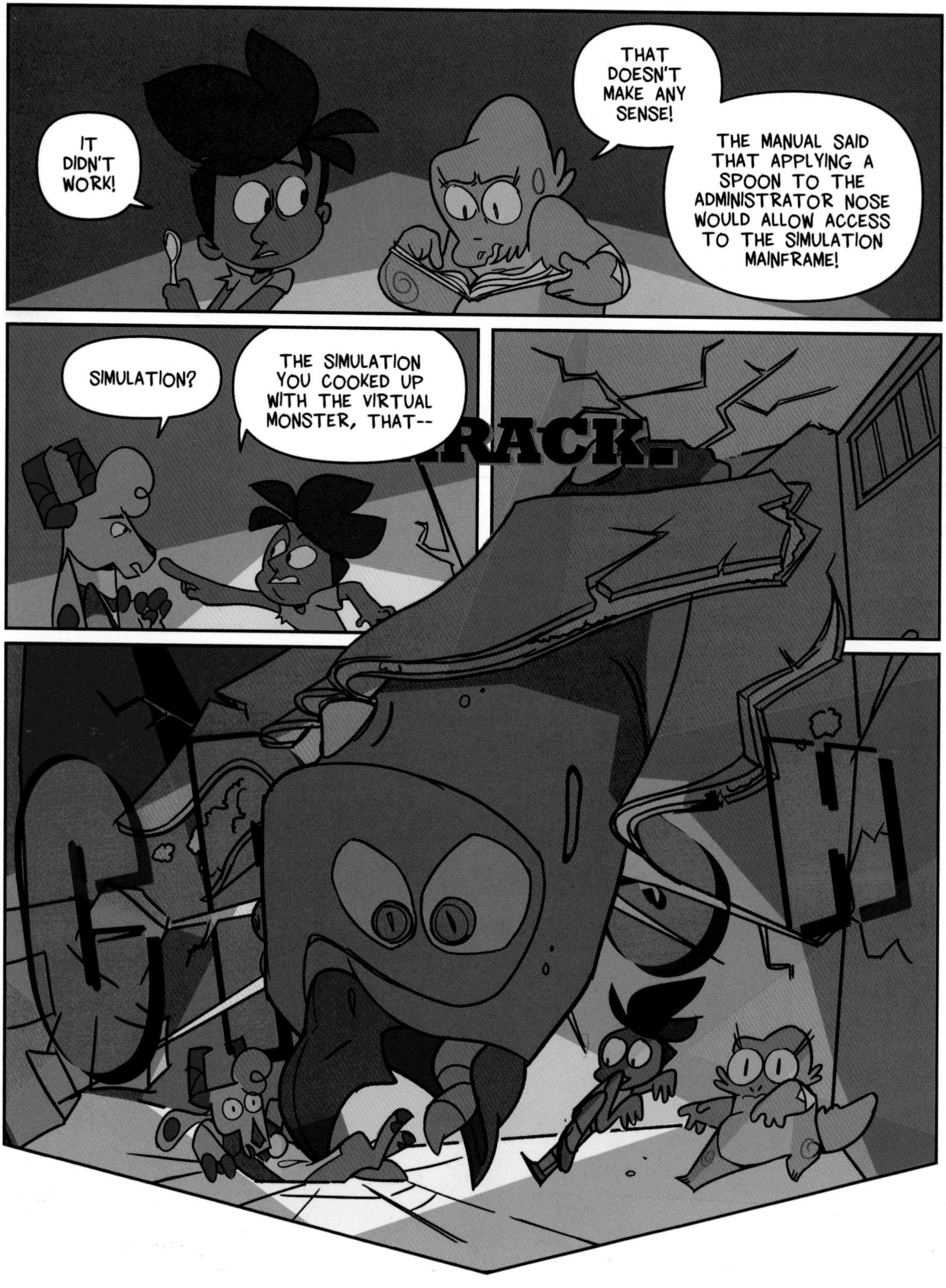
IT DIDN'T WORK!
THAT DOESN'T MAKE ANY SENSE!
THE MANUAL SAID THAT APPLYING A SPOON TO THE ADMINISTRATOR NOSE WOULD ALLOW ACCESS TO THE SIMULATION MAINFRAME!
SIMULATION?
THE SIMULATION YOU COOKED UP WITH THE VIRTUAL MONSTER, THAT--
RACK.

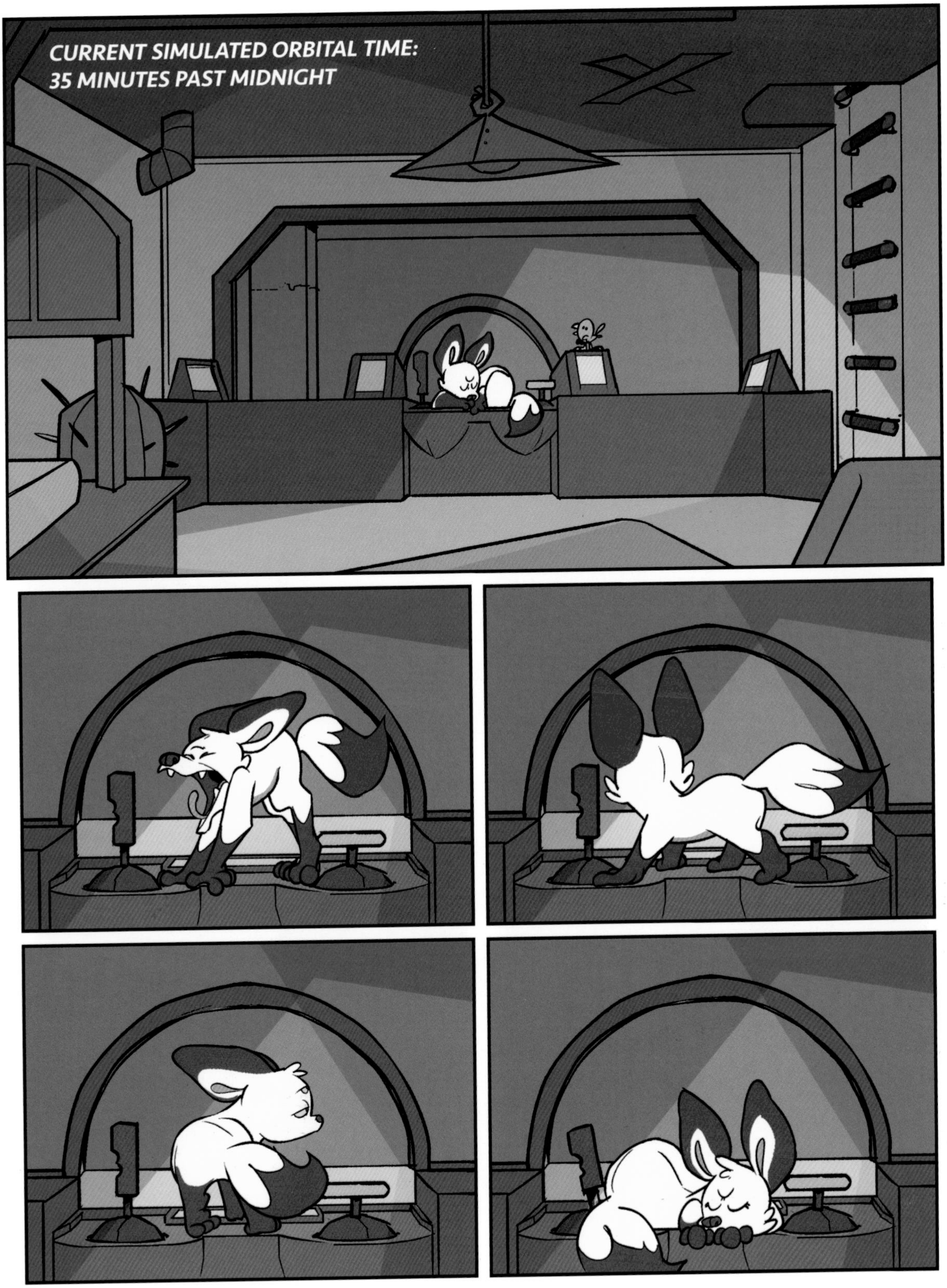
CURRENT SIMULATED ORBITAL TIME:
35 MINUTES PAST MIDNIGHT

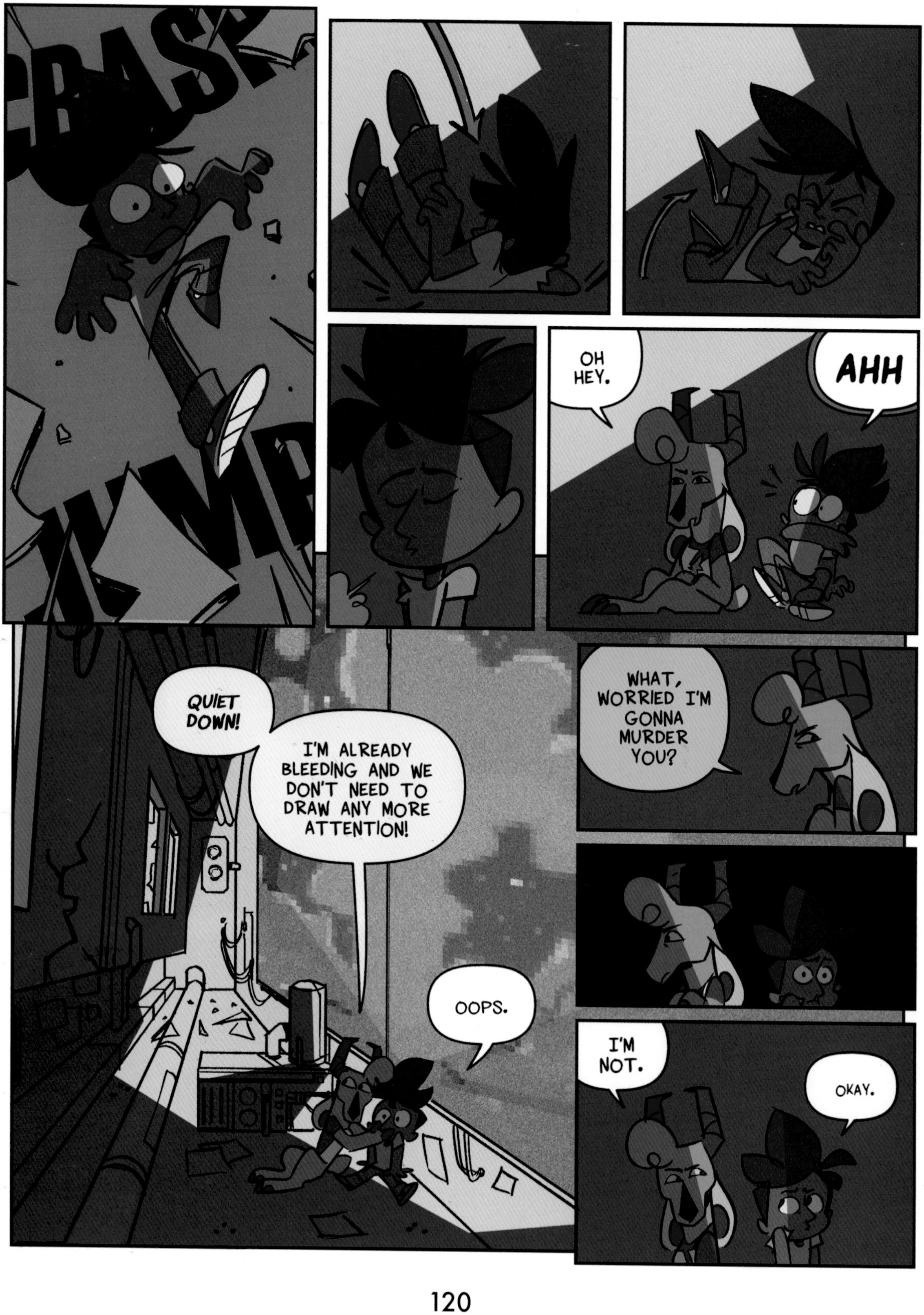
OH HEY.
AHH
QUIET DOWN!
I'M ALREADY BLEEDING AND WE DON'T NEED TO DRAW ANY MORE ATTENTION!
OOPS.
WHAT, WORRIED I'M GONNA MURDER YOU?
I'M NOT.
OKAY.

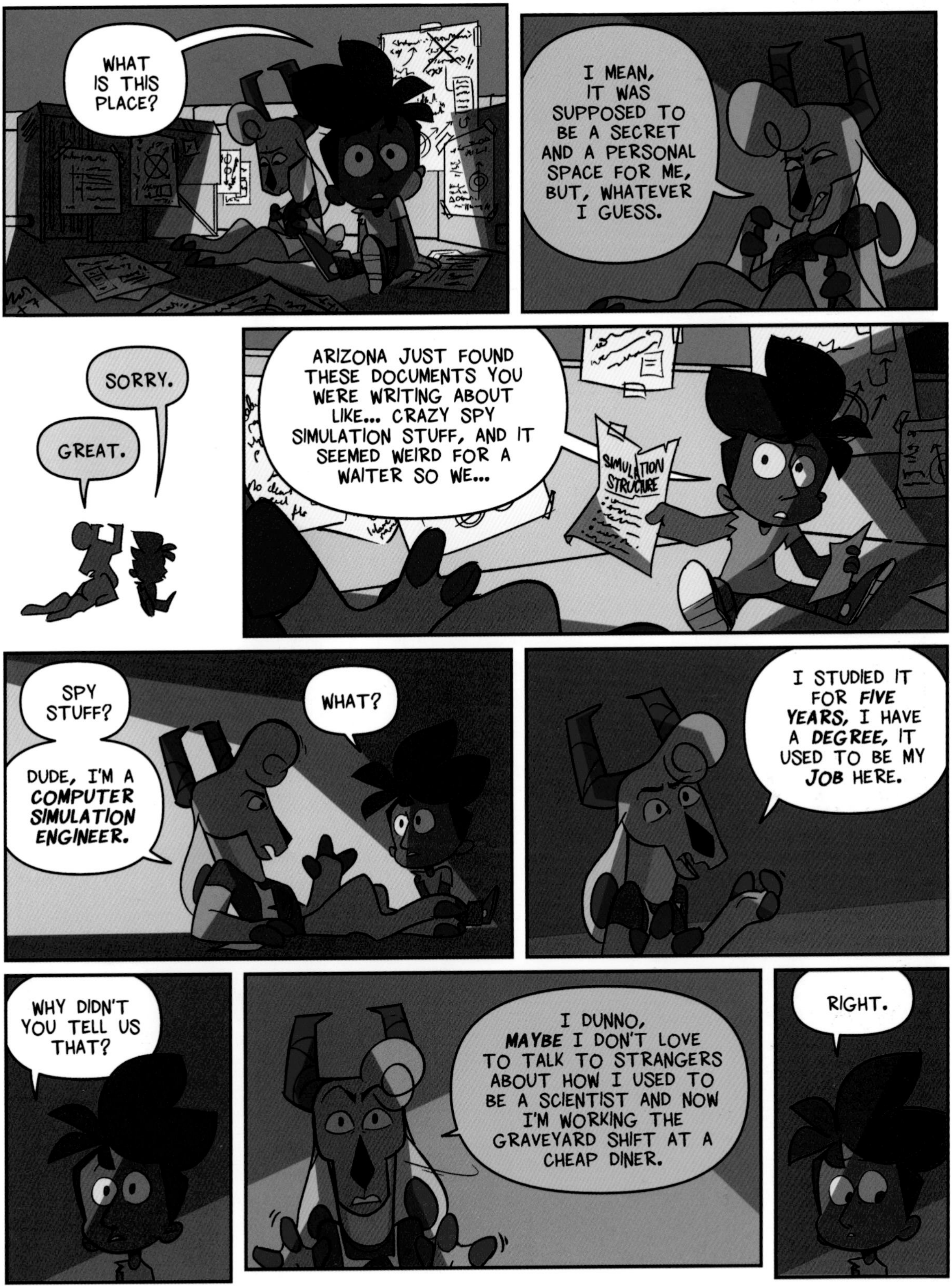
WHAT IS THIS PLACE?
I MEAN, IT WAS SUPPOSED TO BE A SECRET AND A PERSONAL SPACE FOR ME, BUT, WHATEVER I GUESS.
GREAT.
SORRY.
ARIZONA JUST FOUND THESE DOCUMENTS YOU WERE WRITING ABOUT LIKE... CRAZY SPY SIMULATION STUFF, AND IT SEEMED WEIRD FOR A WAITER SO WE...
SIMULATION STRUCTURE
SPY STUFF?
DUDE, I'M A **COMPUTER SIMULATION ENGINEER.**
WHAT?
I STUDIED IT FOR ***FIVE YEARS,*** I HAVE A ***DEGREE,*** IT USED TO BE MY ***JOB*** HERE.
WHY DIDN'T YOU TELL US THAT?
I DUNNO, ***MAYBE*** I DON'T LOVE TO TALK TO STRANGERS ABOUT HOW I USED TO BE A SCIENTIST AND NOW I'M WORKING THE GRAVEYARD SHIFT AT A CHEAP DINER.
RIGHT.

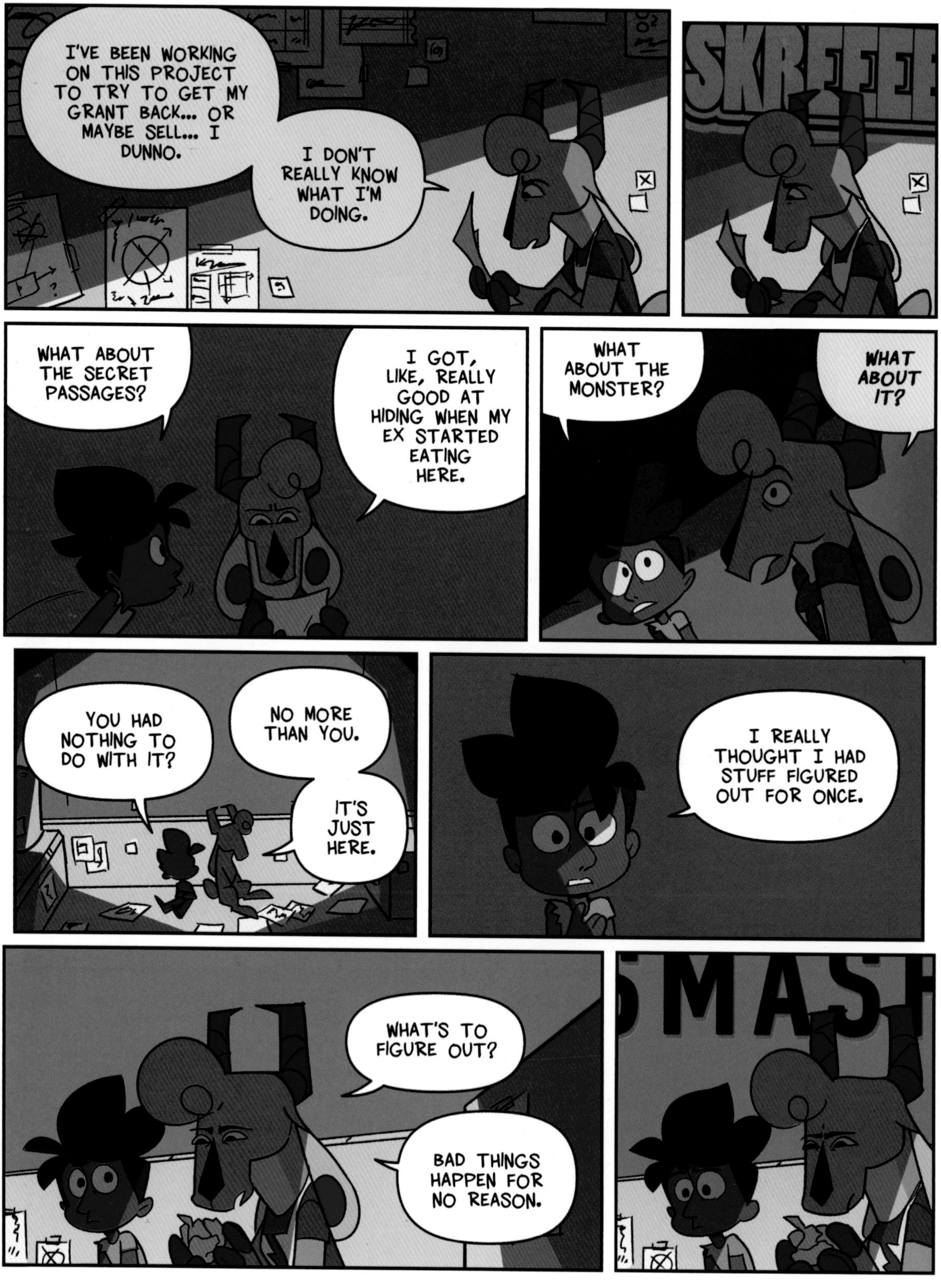
I'VE BEEN WORKING ON THIS PROJECT TO TRY TO GET MY GRANT BACK... OR MAYBE SELL... I DUNNO.
I DON'T REALLY KNOW WHAT I'M DOING.
SKREEEE
WHAT ABOUT THE SECRET PASSAGES?
I GOT, LIKE, REALLY GOOD AT HIDING WHEN MY EX STARTED EATING HERE.
WHAT ABOUT THE MONSTER?
WHAT ABOUT IT?
YOU HAD NOTHING TO DO WITH IT?
NO MORE THAN YOU.
IT'S JUST HERE.
I REALLY THOUGHT I HAD STUFF FIGURED OUT FOR ONCE.
WHAT'S TO FIGURE OUT?
BAD THINGS HAPPEN FOR NO REASON.
SMASH

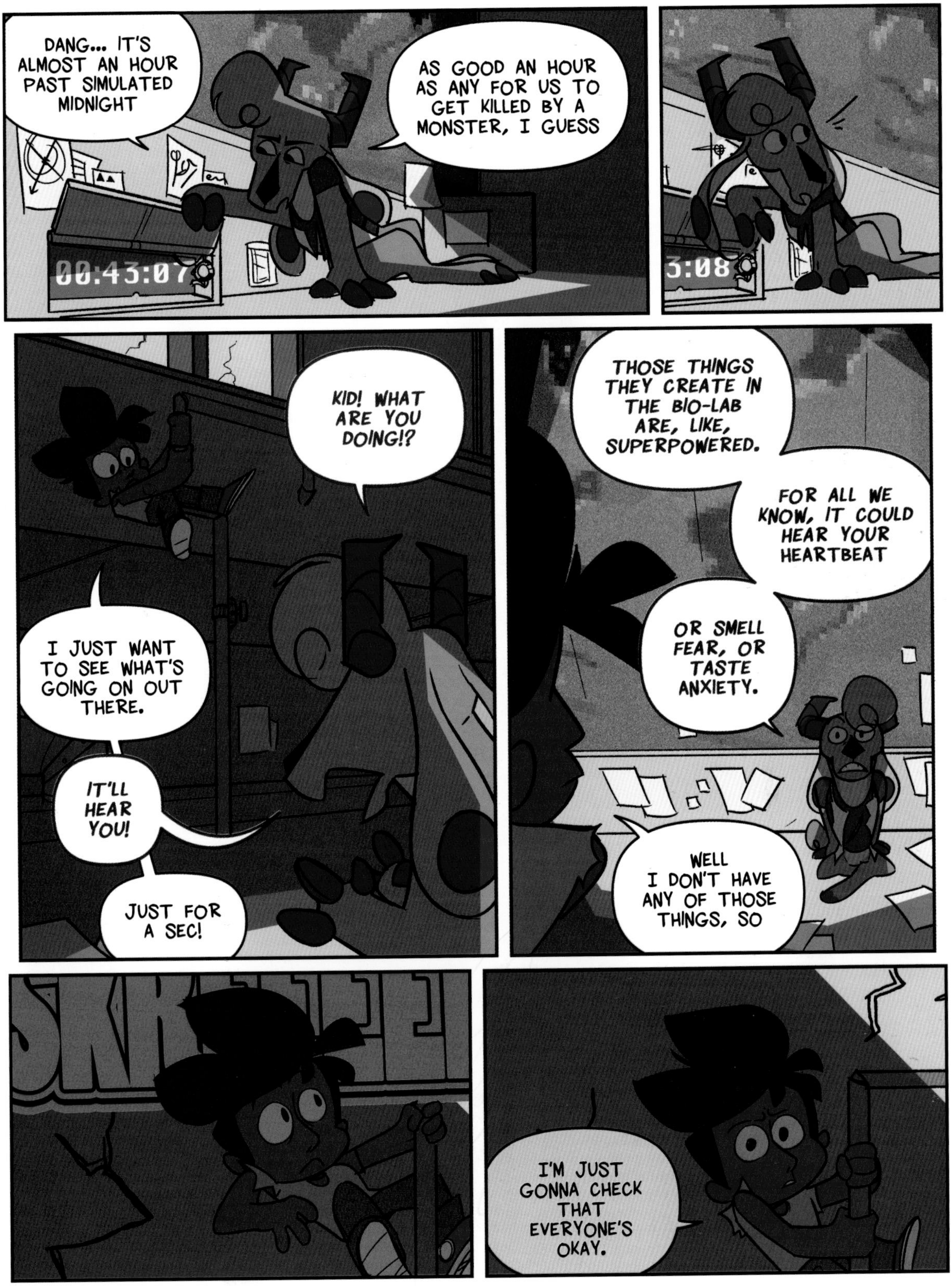
DANG... IT'S ALMOST AN HOUR PAST SIMULATED MIDNIGHT
AS GOOD AN HOUR AS ANY FOR US TO GET KILLED BY A MONSTER, I GUESS
00:43:07
3:08
KID! WHAT ARE YOU DOING!?
I JUST WANT TO SEE WHAT'S GOING ON OUT THERE.
IT'LL HEAR YOU!
JUST FOR A SEC!
THOSE THINGS THEY CREATE IN THE BIO-LAB ARE, LIKE, SUPERPOWERED.
FOR ALL WE KNOW, IT COULD HEAR YOUR HEARTBEAT
OR SMELL FEAR, OR TASTE ANXIETY.
WELL I DON'T HAVE ANY OF THOSE THINGS, SO
I'M JUST GONNA CHECK THAT EVERYONE'S OKAY.

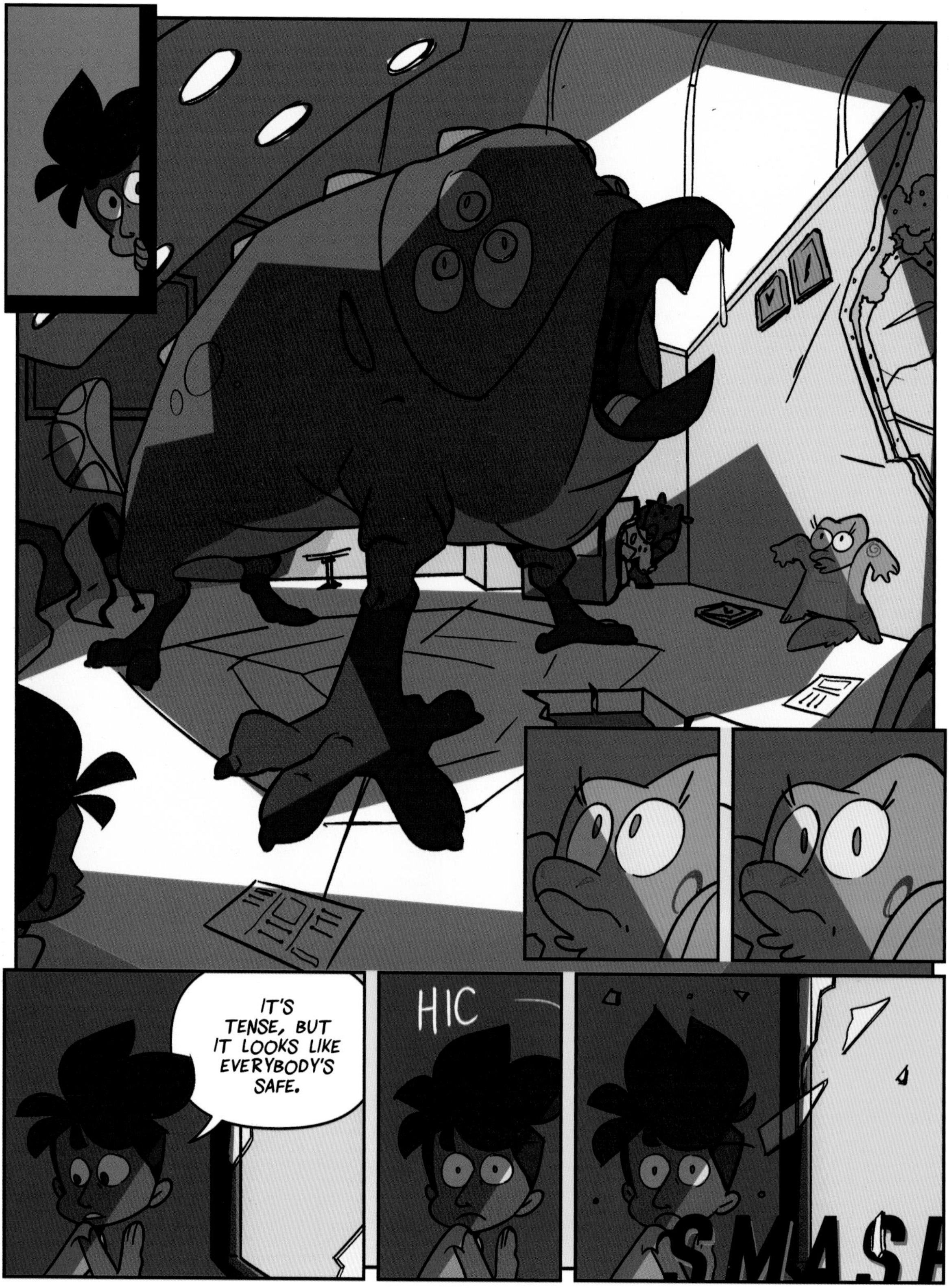
IT'S TENSE, BUT IT LOOKS LIKE EVERYBODY'S SAFE.
HIC
SMASH

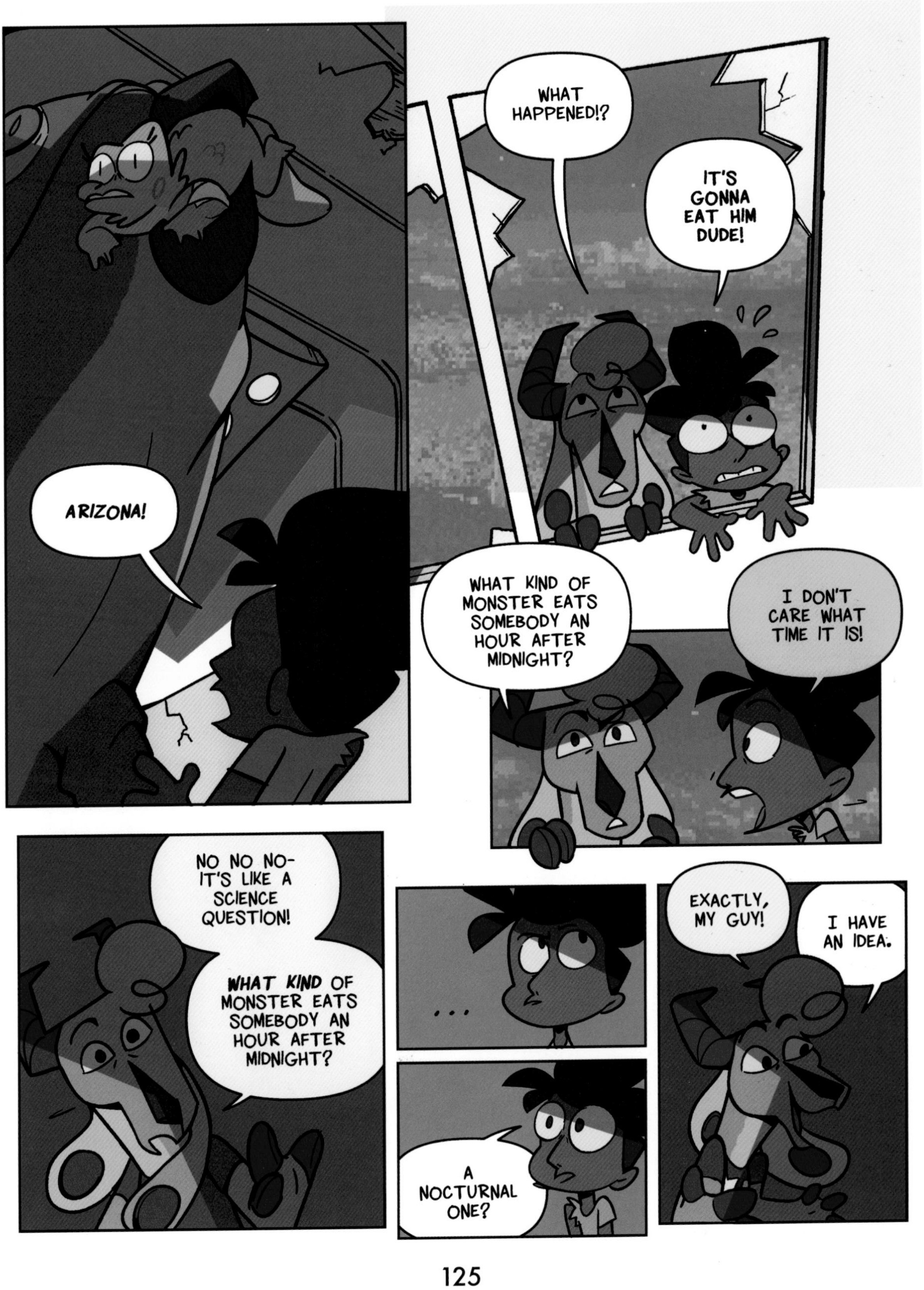
ARIZONA!
WHAT HAPPENED!?
IT'S GONNA EAT HIM DUDE!
WHAT KIND OF MONSTER EATS SOMEBODY AN HOUR AFTER MIDNIGHT?
I DON'T CARE WHAT TIME IT IS!
NO NO NO- IT'S LIKE A SCIENCE QUESTION!
WHAT KIND OF MONSTER EATS SOMEBODY AN HOUR AFTER MIDNIGHT?
...
A NOCTURNAL ONE?
EXACTLY, MY GUY!
I HAVE AN IDEA.

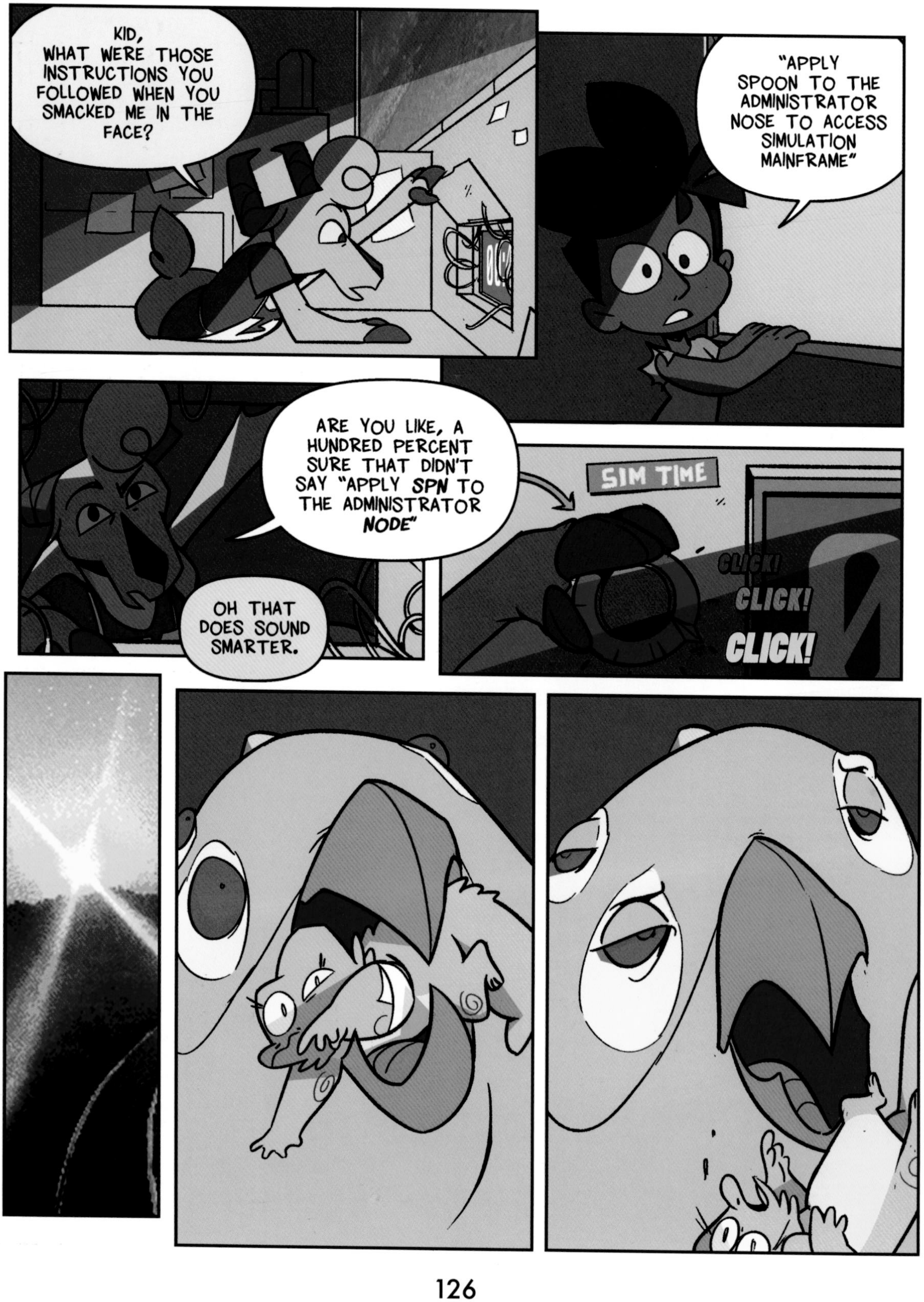
KID, WHAT WERE THOSE INSTRUCTIONS YOU FOLLOWED WHEN YOU SMACKED ME IN THE FACE?
"APPLY SPOON TO THE ADMINISTRATOR NOSE TO ACCESS SIMULATION MAINFRAME"
ARE YOU LIKE, A HUNDRED PERCENT SURE THAT DIDN'T SAY "APPLY **SPN** TO THE ADMINISTRATOR ***NODE***"
OH THAT DOES SOUND SMARTER.
SIM TIME
CLICK!
CLICK!
CLICK!

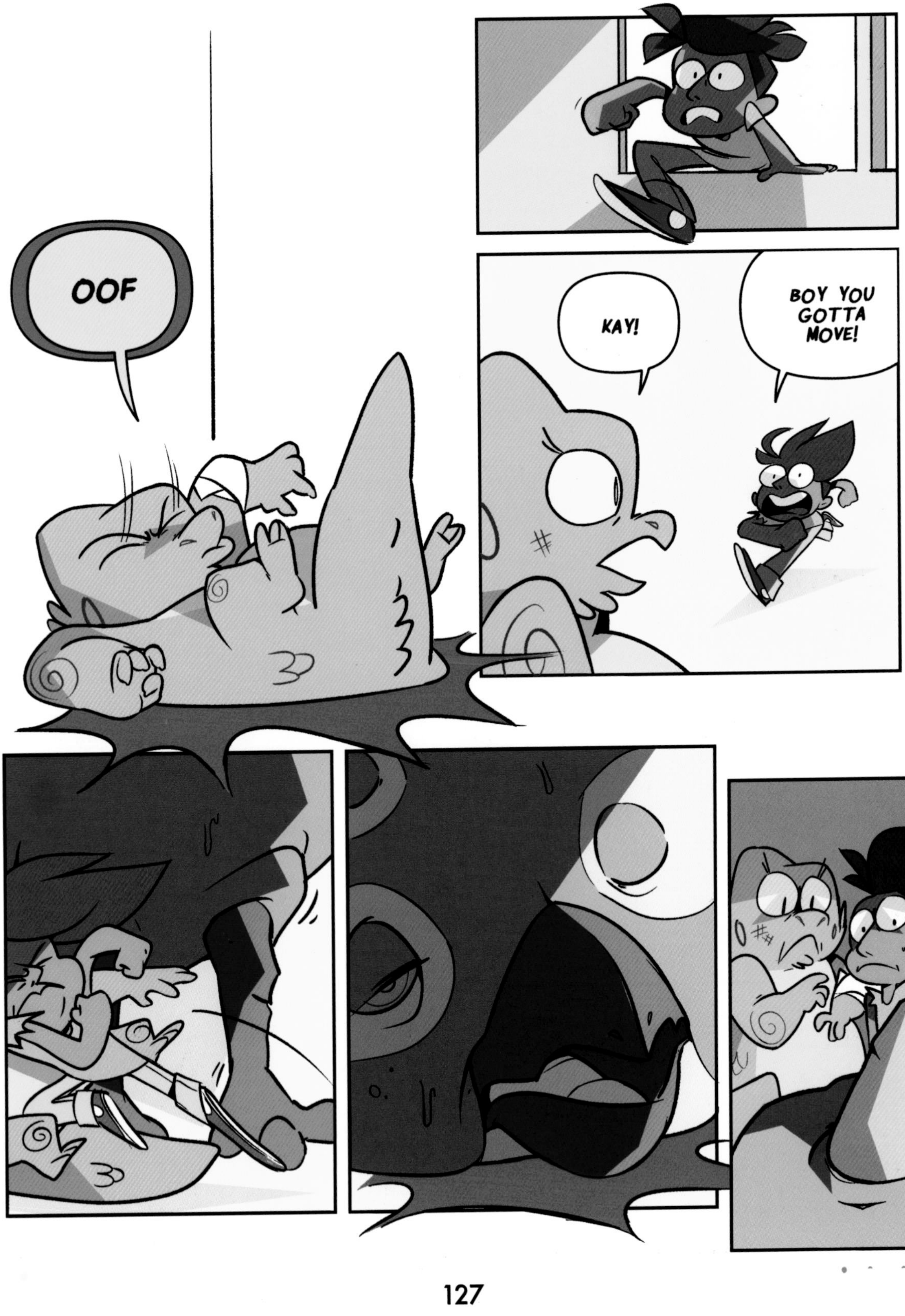

OOF
KAY!
BOY YOU GOTTA MOVE!

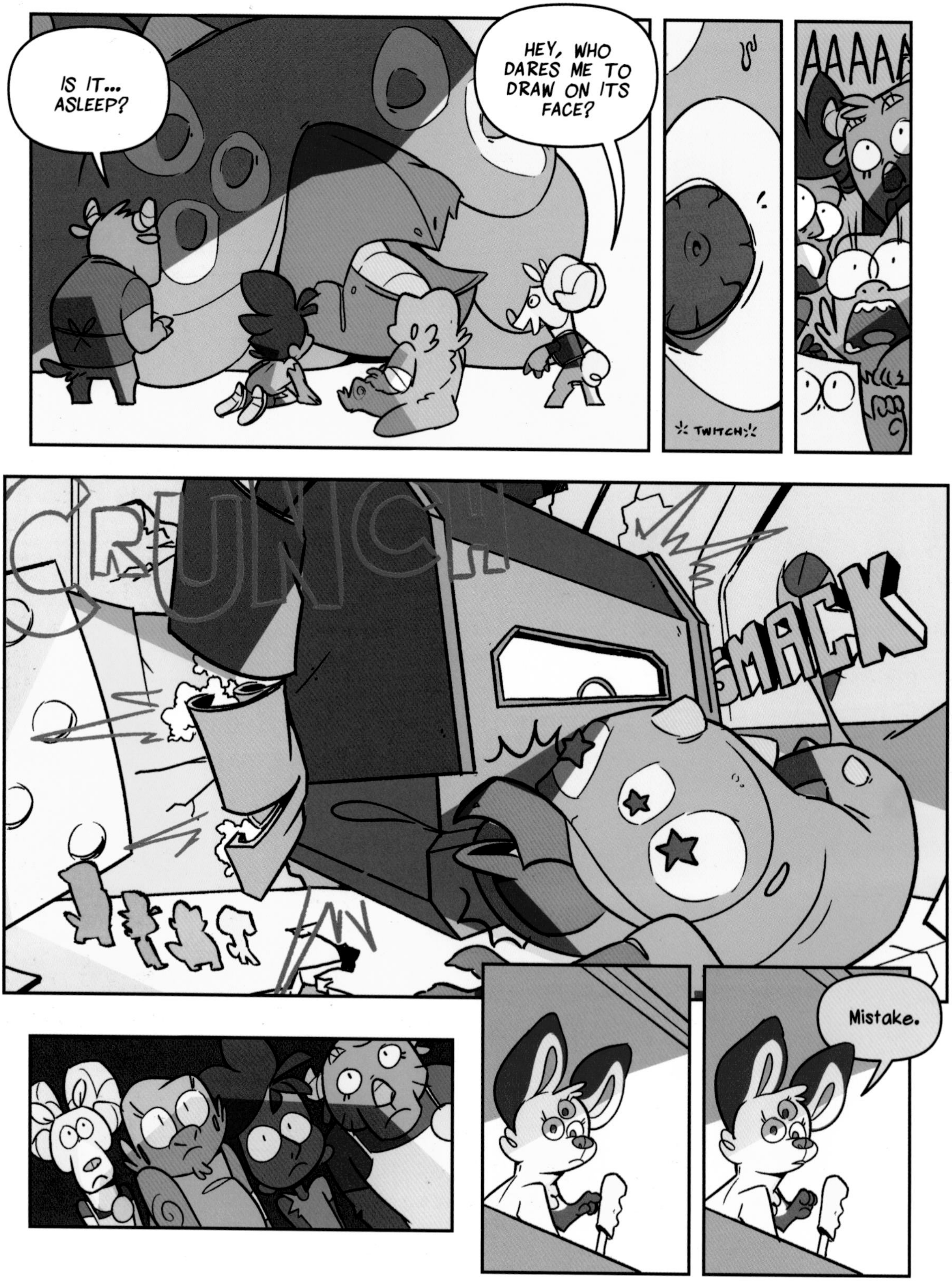
IS IT... ASLEEP?
HEY, WHO DARES ME TO DRAW ON ITS FACE?
TWITCH
AAAAA
CRUNCH
SMACK
Mistake.

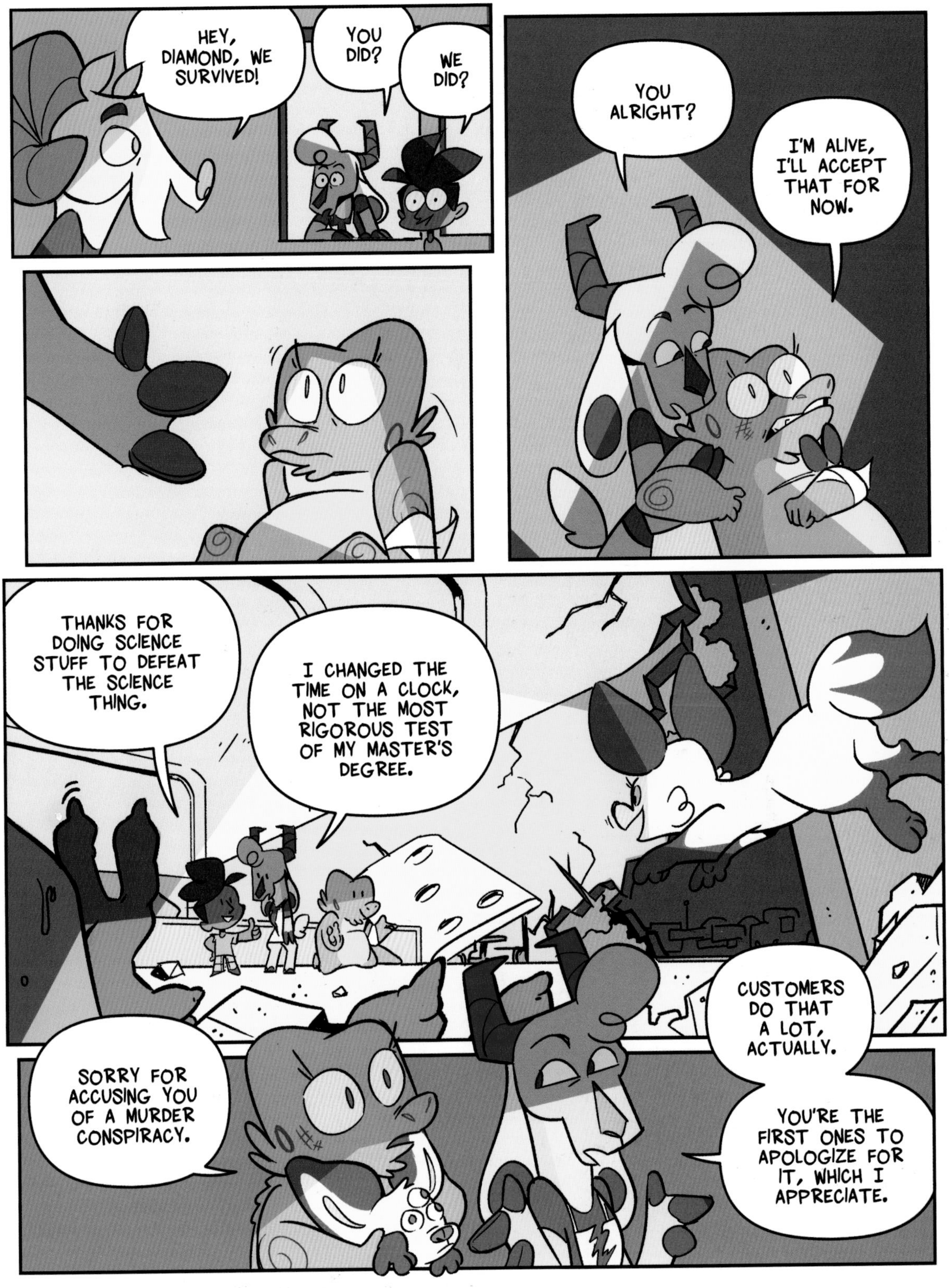

HEY, DIAMOND, WE SURVIVED!
YOU DID?
WE DID?
YOU ALRIGHT?
I'M ALIVE, I'LL ACCEPT THAT FOR NOW.
THANKS FOR DOING SCIENCE STUFF TO DEFEAT THE SCIENCE THING.
I CHANGED THE TIME ON A CLOCK, NOT THE MOST RIGOROUS TEST OF MY MASTER'S DEGREE.
SORRY FOR ACCUSING YOU OF A MURDER CONSPIRACY.
CUSTOMERS DO THAT A LOT, ACTUALLY.
YOU'RE THE FIRST ONES TO APOLOGIZE FOR IT, WHICH I APPRECIATE.

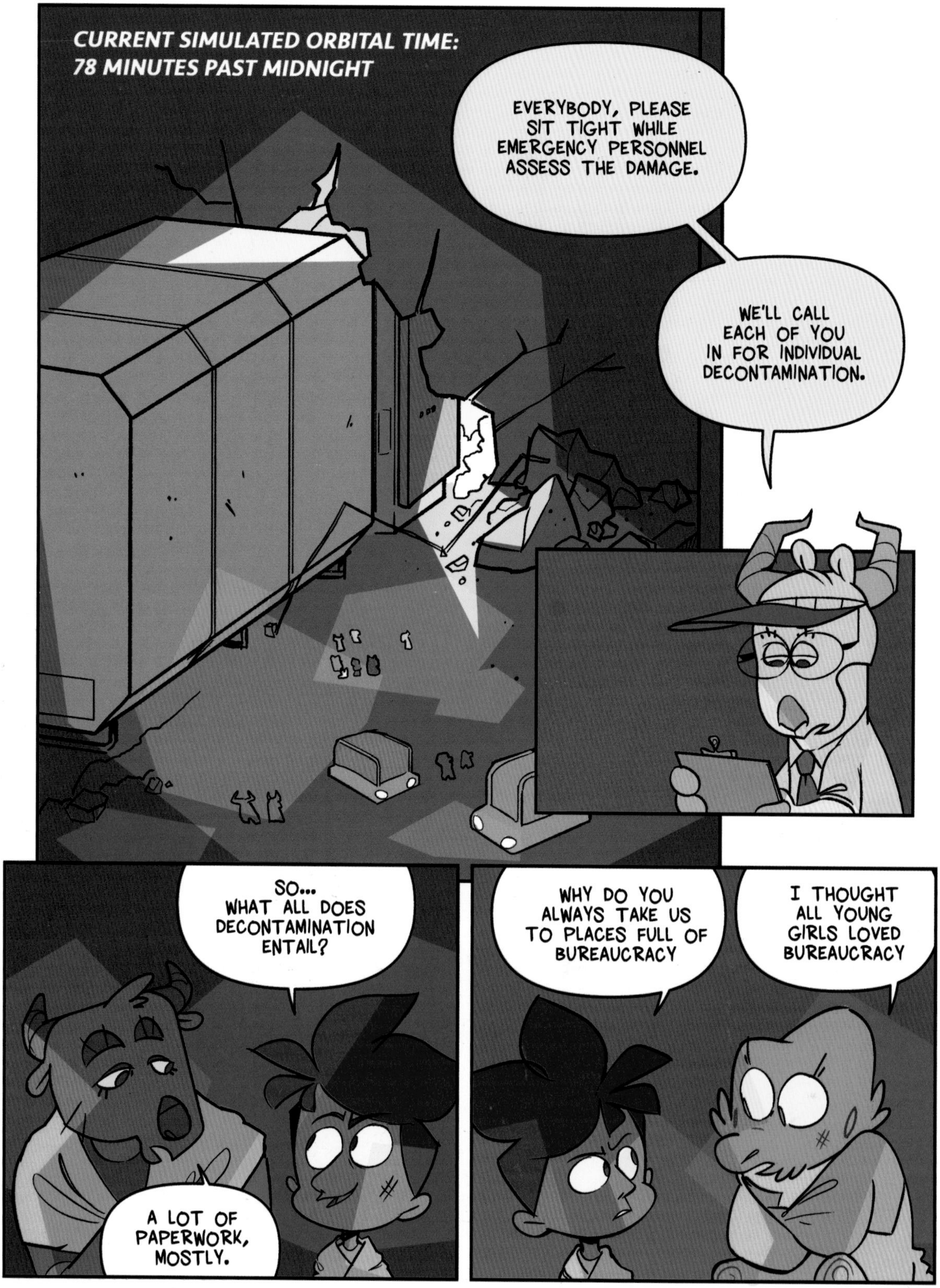
CURRENT SIMULATED ORBITAL TIME:
78 MINUTES PAST MIDNIGHT
EVERYBODY, PLEASE SIT TIGHT WHILE EMERGENCY PERSONNEL ASSESS THE DAMAGE.
WE'LL CALL EACH OF YOU IN FOR INDIVIDUAL DECONTAMINATION.
SO... WHAT ALL DOES DECONTAMINATION ENTAIL?
A LOT OF PAPERWORK, MOSTLY.
WHY DO YOU ALWAYS TAKE US TO PLACES FULL OF BUREAUCRACY
I THOUGHT ALL YOUNG GIRLS LOVED BUREAUCRACY

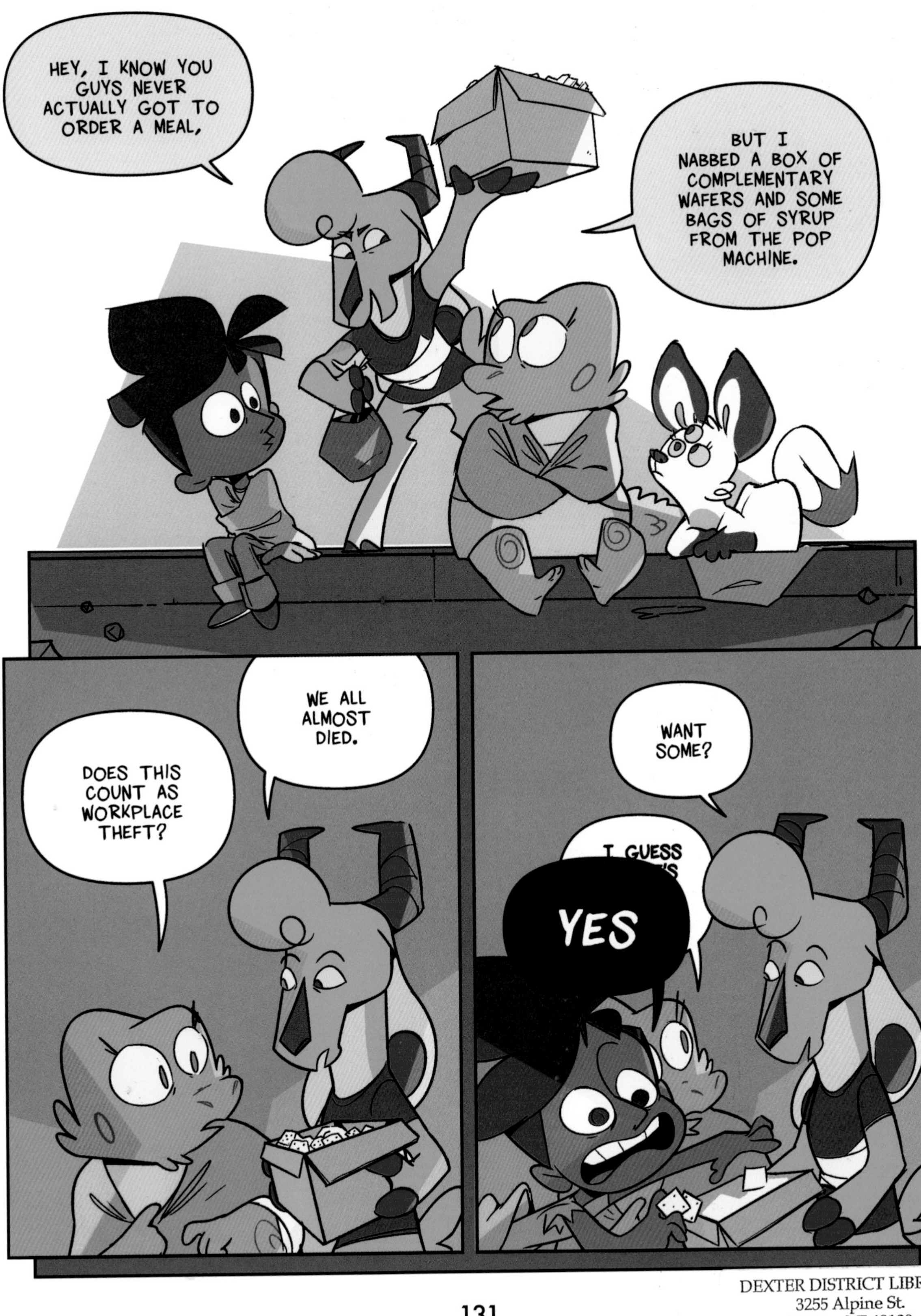
HEY, I KNOW YOU GUYS NEVER ACTUALLY GOT TO ORDER A MEAL,
BUT I NABBED A BOX OF COMPLEMENTARY WAFERS AND SOME BAGS OF SYRUP FROM THE POP MACHINE.
DOES THIS COUNT AS WORKPLACE THEFT?
WE ALL ALMOST DIED.
WANT SOME?
I GUESS
YES

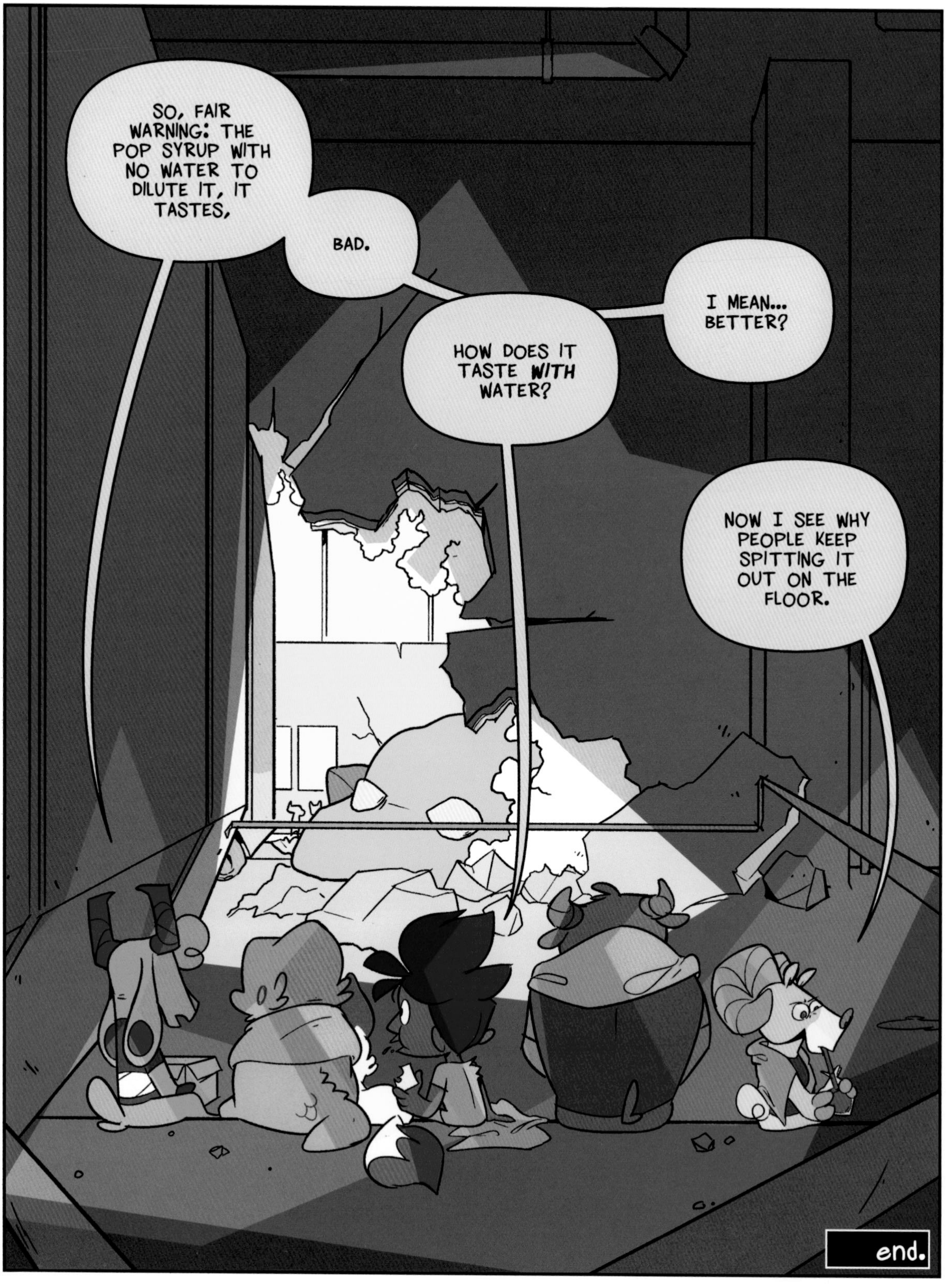
SO, FAIR WARNING: THE POP SYRUP WITH NO WATER TO DILUTE IT, IT TASTES,
BAD.
HOW DOES IT TASTE WITH WATER?
I MEAN... BETTER?
NOW I SEE WHY PEOPLE KEEP SPITTING IT OUT ON THE FLOOR.
end.

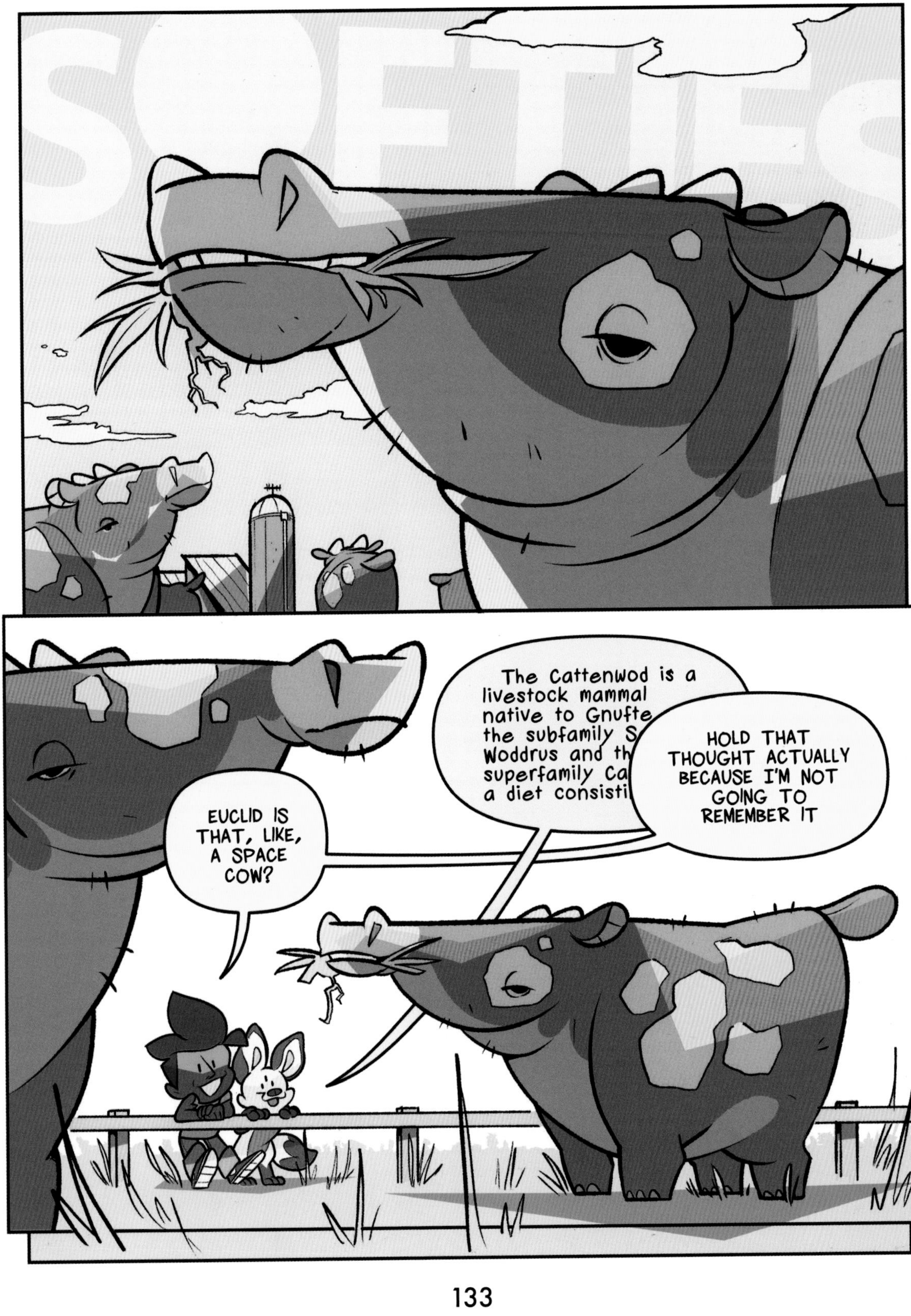
EUCLID IS THAT, LIKE, A SPACE COW?
The Cattenwod is a livestock mammal native to Gnufte the subfamily S Woddrus and th superfamily Ca a diet consisti
HOLD THAT THOUGHT ACTUALLY BECAUSE I'M NOT GOING TO REMEMBER IT

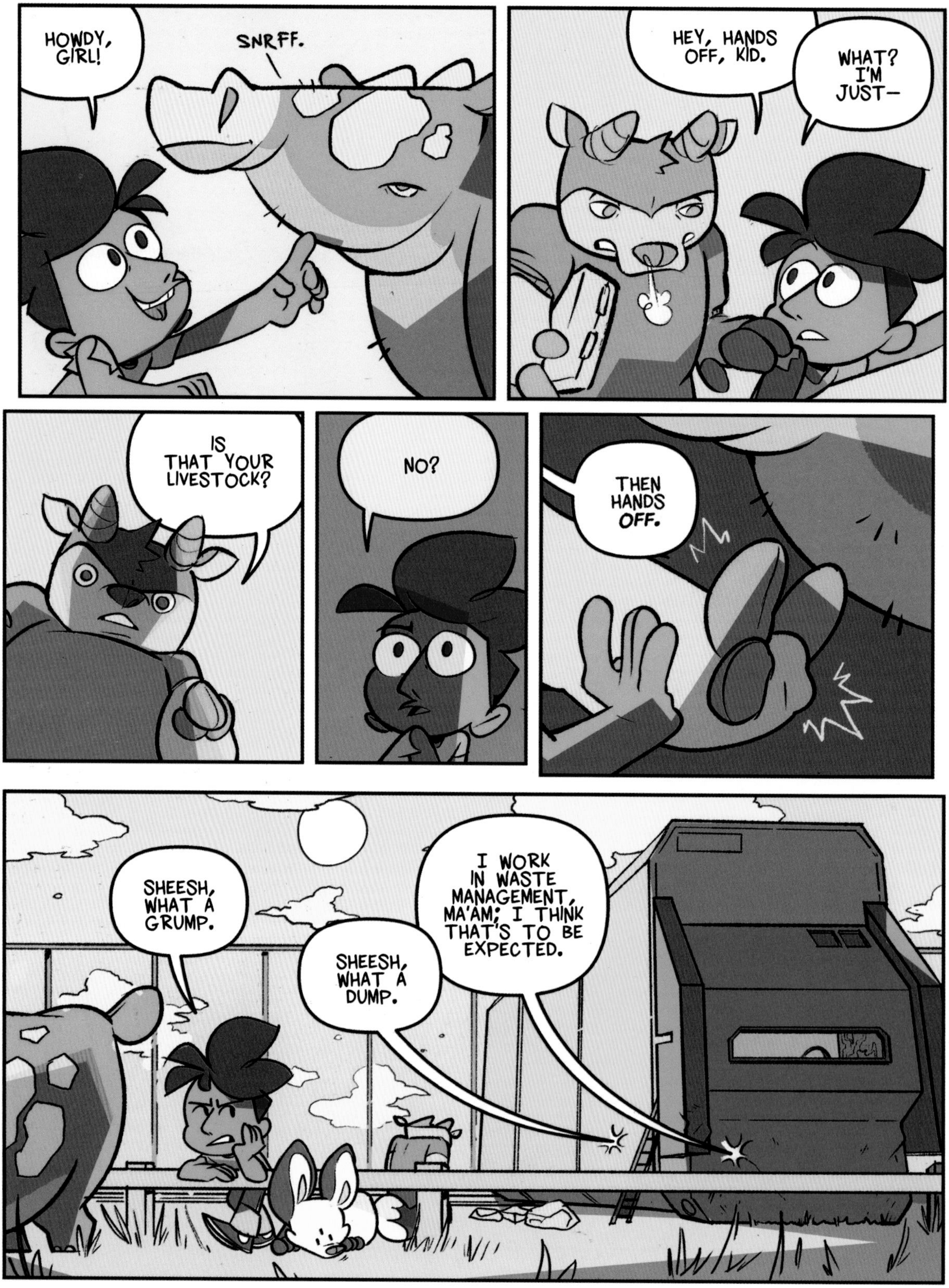
HOWDY, GIRL!
SNRFF.
HEY, HANDS OFF, KID.
WHAT? I'M JUST—
IS THAT YOUR LIVESTOCK?
NO?
THEN HANDS OFF.
SHEESH, WHAT A GRUMP.
SHEESH, WHAT A DUMP.
I WORK IN WASTE MANAGEMENT, MA'AM; I THINK THAT'S TO BE EXPECTED.

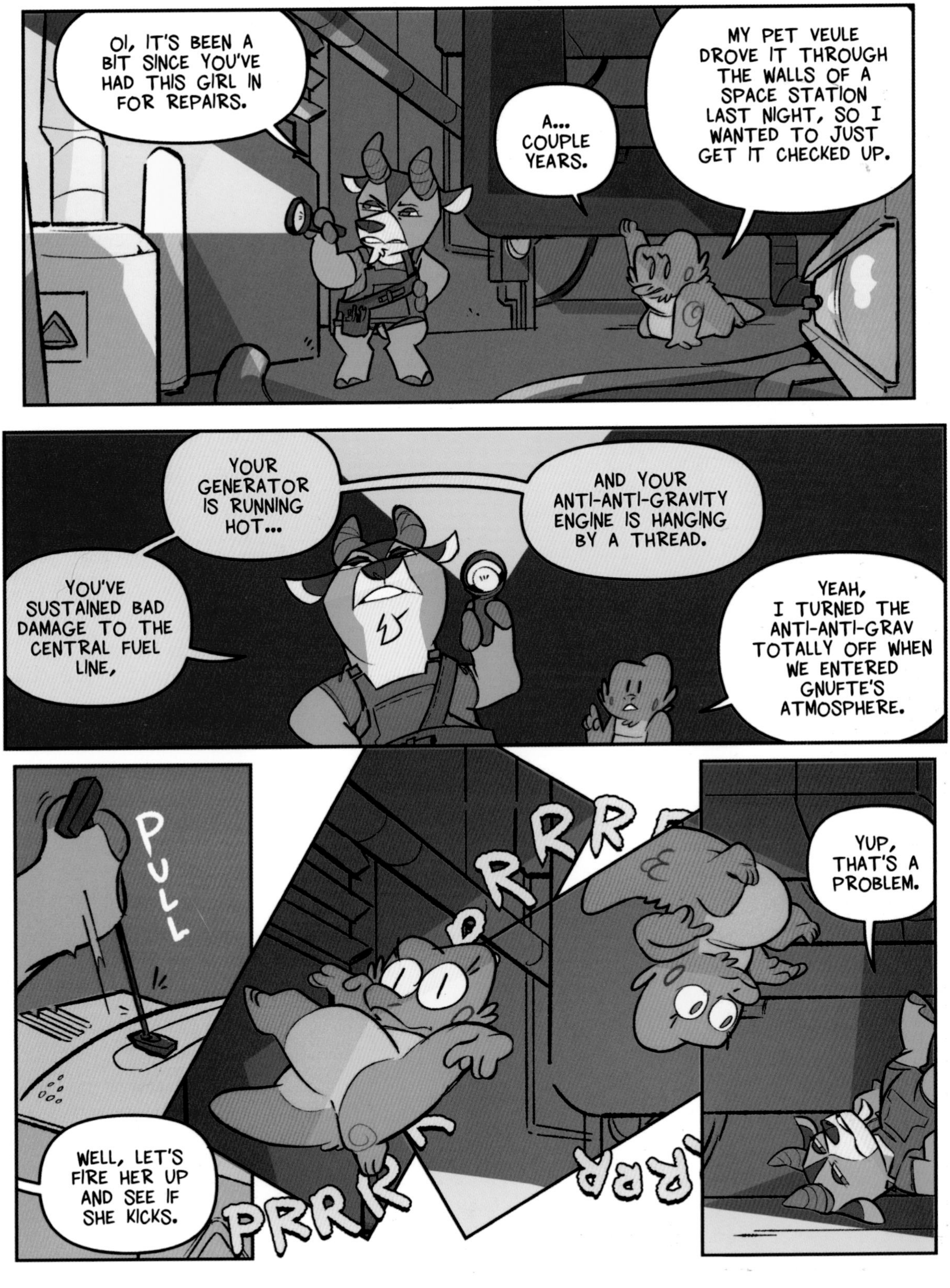
OI, IT'S BEEN A BIT SINCE YOU'VE HAD THIS GIRL IN FOR REPAIRS.
A... COUPLE YEARS.
MY PET VEULE DROVE IT THROUGH THE WALLS OF A SPACE STATION LAST NIGHT, SO I WANTED TO JUST GET IT CHECKED UP.
YOUR GENERATOR IS RUNNING HOT...
AND YOUR ANTI-ANTI-GRAVITY ENGINE IS HANGING BY A THREAD.
YOU'VE SUSTAINED BAD DAMAGE TO THE CENTRAL FUEL LINE,
YEAH, I TURNED THE ANTI-ANTI-GRAV TOTALLY OFF WHEN WE ENTERED GNUFTE'S ATMOSPHERE.
PULL
WELL, LET'S FIRE HER UP AND SEE IF SHE KICKS.
PRRR
RRRR
YUP, THAT'S A PROBLEM.

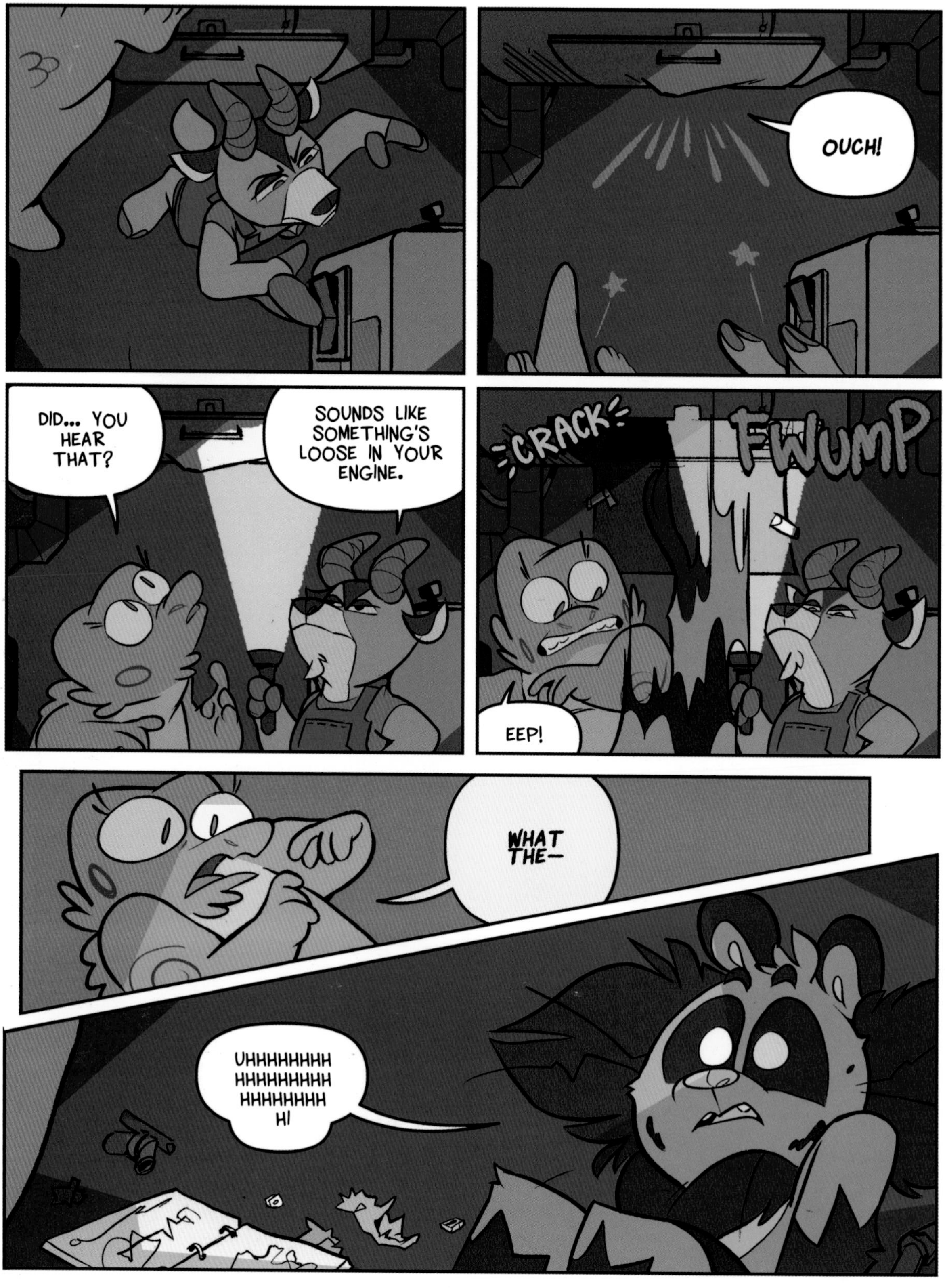
OUCH!
DID... YOU HEAR THAT?
SOUNDS LIKE SOMETHING'S LOOSE IN YOUR ENGINE.
CRACK
FWUMP
EEP!
WHAT THE—
UHHHHHHHH HHHHHHHHH HHHHHHHH H!

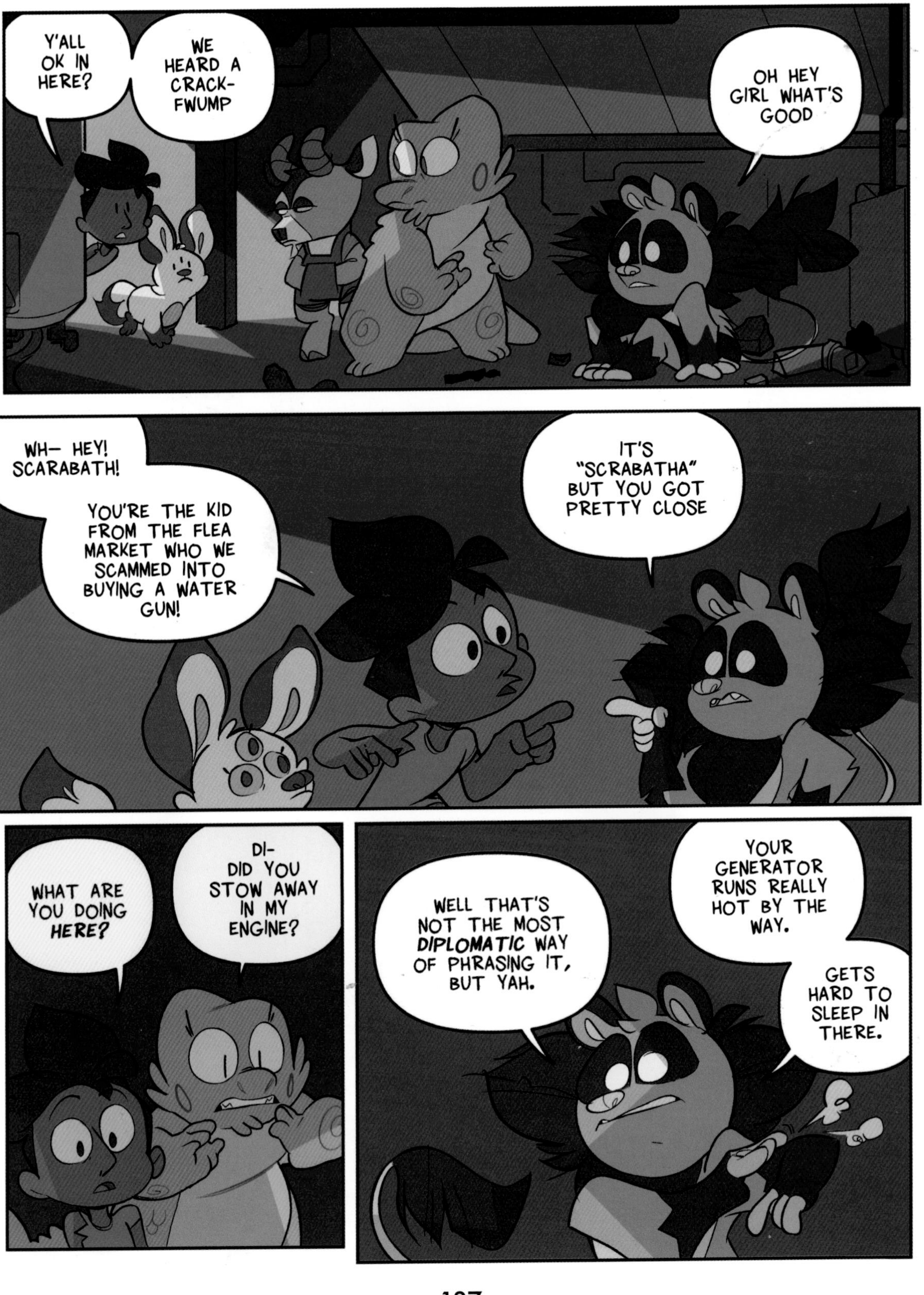
Y'ALL OK IN HERE?
WE HEARD A CRACK-FWUMP
OH HEY GIRL WHAT'S GOOD
WH— HEY! SCARABATH!
YOU'RE THE KID FROM THE FLEA MARKET WHO WE SCAMMED INTO BUYING A WATER GUN!
IT'S "SCRABATHA" BUT YOU GOT PRETTY CLOSE
WHAT ARE YOU DOING HERE?
DI- DID YOU STOW AWAY IN MY ENGINE?
WELL THAT'S NOT THE MOST DIPLOMATIC WAY OF PHRASING IT, BUT YAH.
YOUR GENERATOR RUNS REALLY HOT BY THE WAY.
GETS HARD TO SLEEP IN THERE.

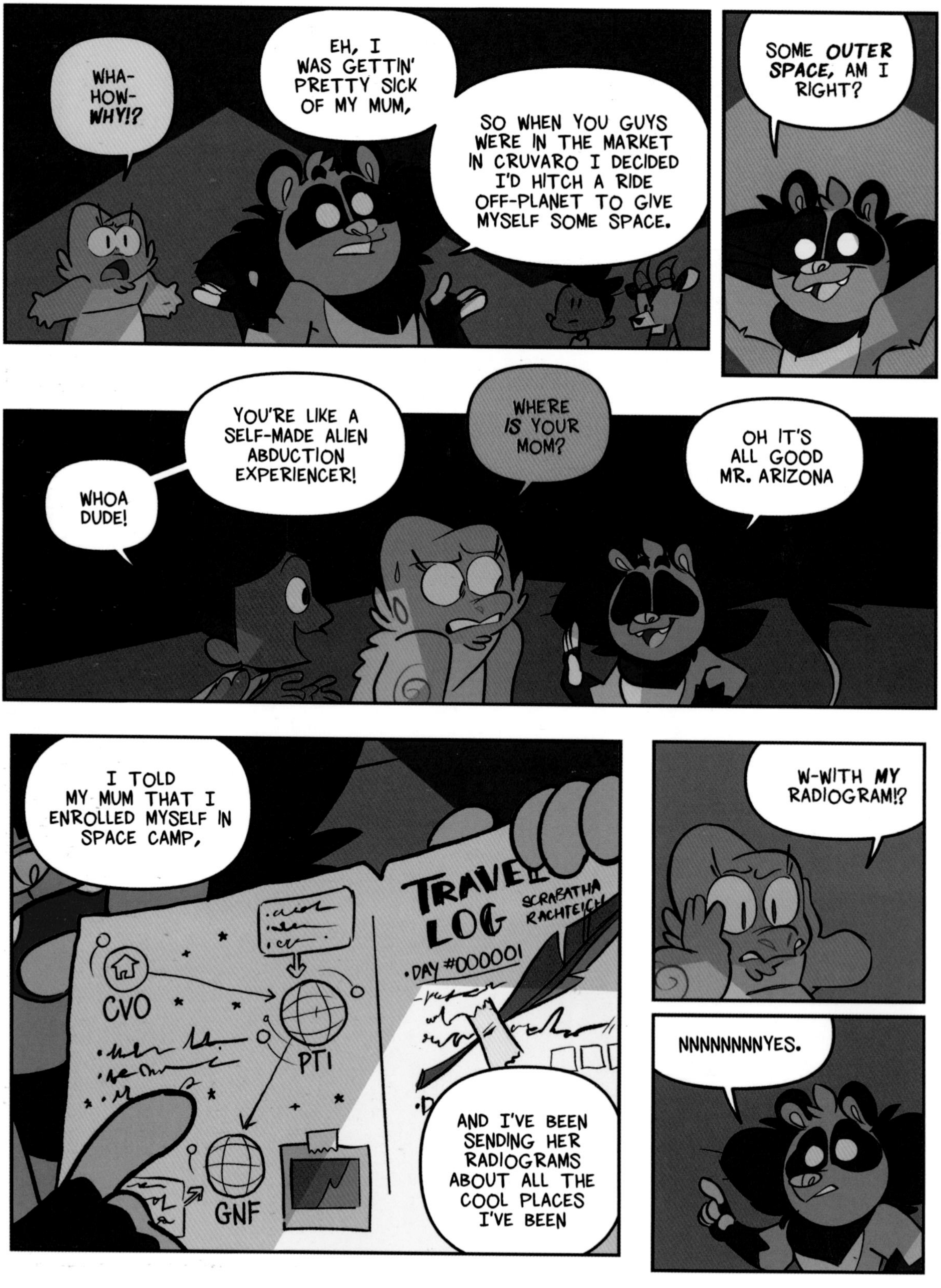
WHA-HOW-WHY!?
EH, I WAS GETTIN' PRETTY SICK OF MY MUM,
SO WHEN YOU GUYS WERE IN THE MARKET IN CRUVARO I DECIDED I'D HITCH A RIDE OFF-PLANET TO GIVE MYSELF SOME SPACE.
SOME OUTER SPACE, AM I RIGHT?
WHOA DUDE!
YOU'RE LIKE A SELF-MADE ALIEN ABDUCTION EXPERIENCER!
WHERE IS YOUR MOM?
OH IT'S ALL GOOD MR. ARIZONA
I TOLD MY MUM THAT I ENROLLED MYSELF IN SPACE CAMP,
TRAVE
LOG
SCRABATHA
DAY #000001
CVO
PTI
GNF
AND I'VE BEEN SENDING HER RADIOGRAMS ABOUT ALL THE COOL PLACES I'VE BEEN
W-WITH MY RADIOGRAM!?
NNNNNNNNYES.

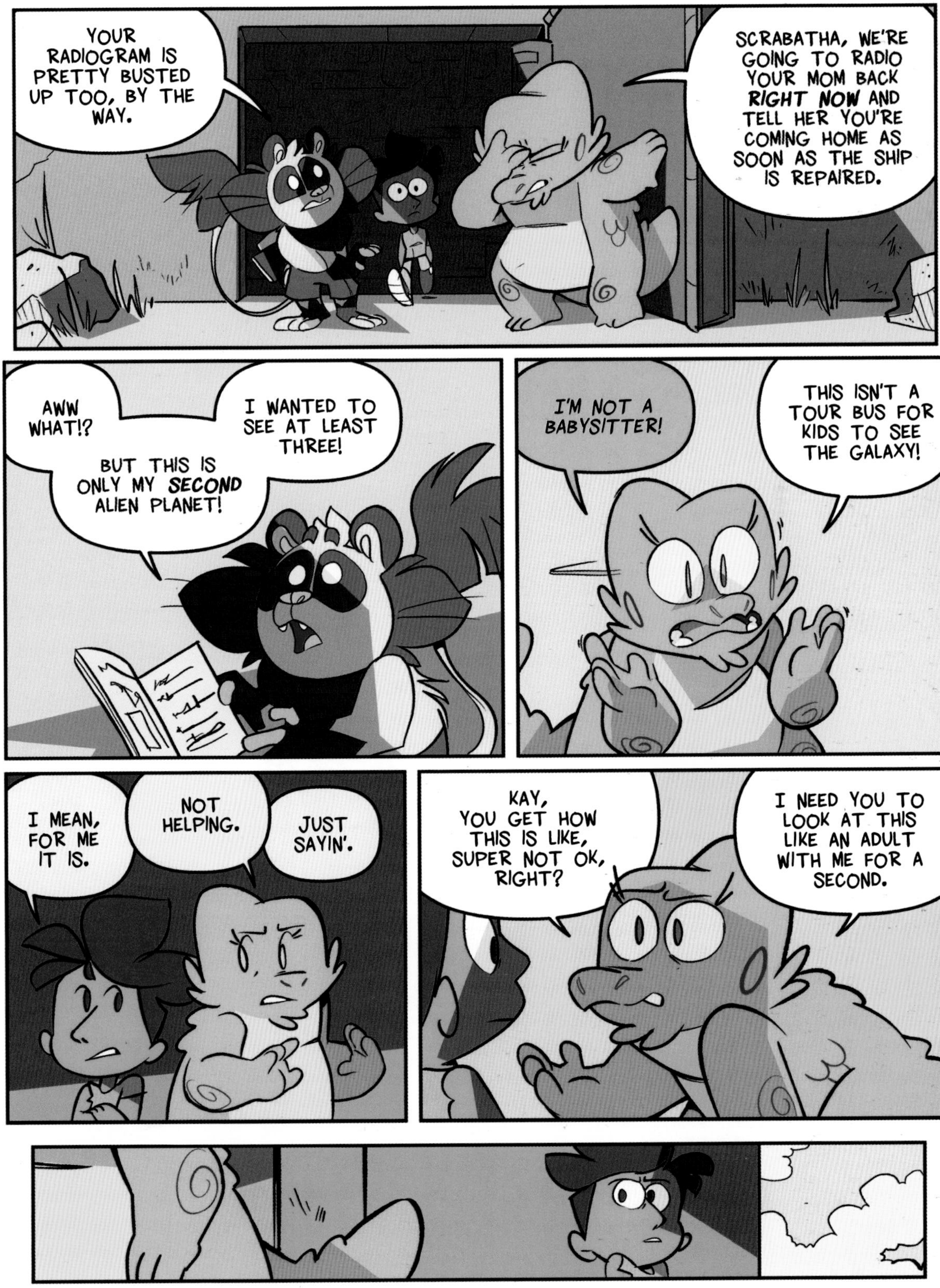

YOUR RADIOGRAM IS PRETTY BUSTED UP TOO, BY THE WAY.
SCRABATHA, WE'RE GOING TO RADIO YOUR MOM BACK **RIGHT NOW** AND TELL HER YOU'RE COMING HOME AS SOON AS THE SHIP IS REPAIRED.
AWW WHAT!?
BUT THIS IS ONLY MY **SECOND** ALIEN PLANET!
I WANTED TO SEE AT LEAST THREE!
I'M NOT A BABYSITTER!
THIS ISN'T A TOUR BUS FOR KIDS TO SEE THE GALAXY!
I MEAN, FOR ME IT IS.
NOT HELPING.
JUST SAYIN'.
KAY, YOU GET HOW THIS IS LIKE, SUPER NOT OK, RIGHT?
I NEED YOU TO LOOK AT THIS LIKE AN ADULT WITH ME FOR A SECOND.

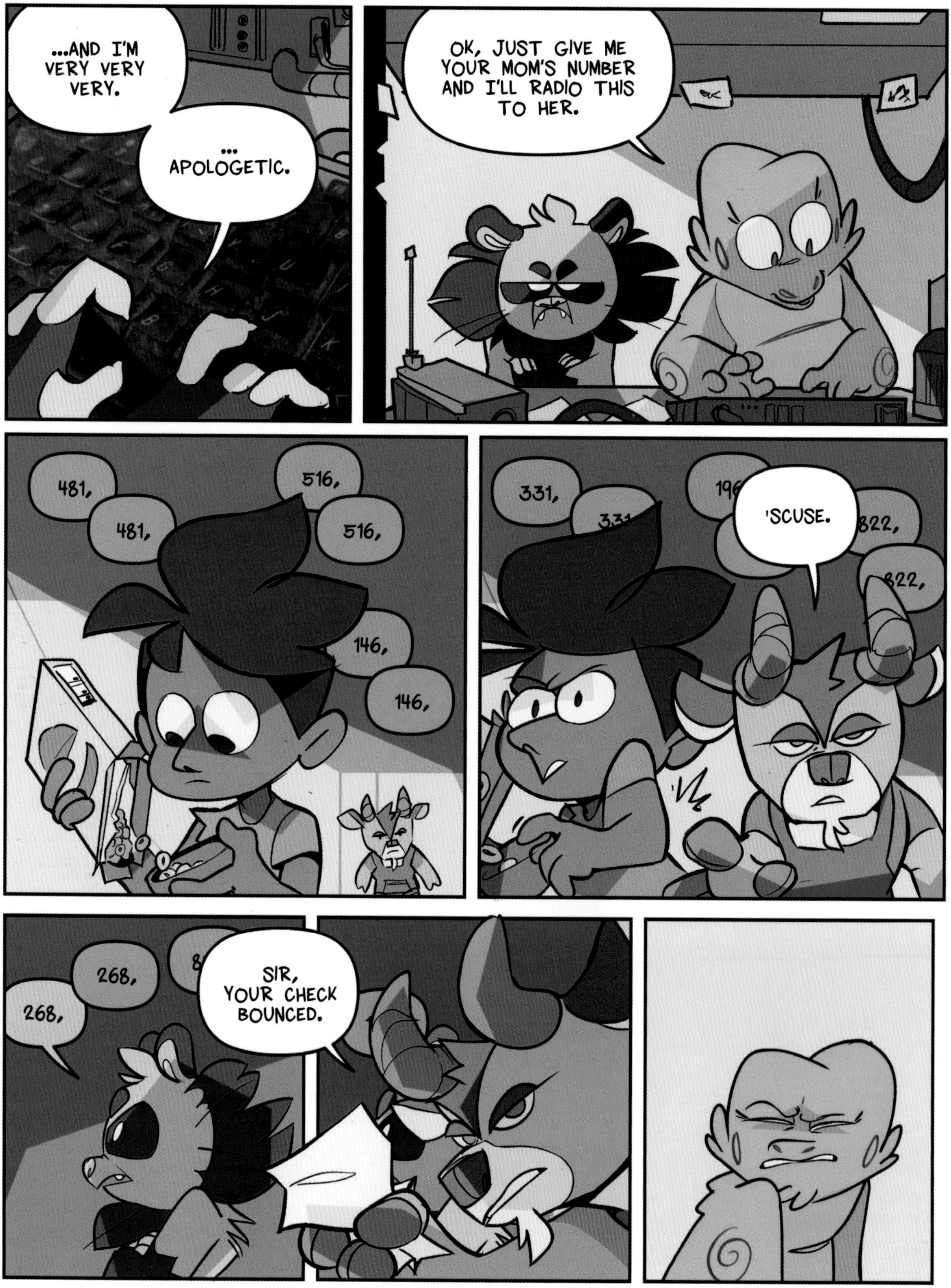
...AND I'M VERY VERY VERY.
... APOLOGETIC.
OK, JUST GIVE ME YOUR MOM'S NUMBER AND I'LL RADIO THIS TO HER.
481,
481,
516,
516,
146,
146,
331,
'SCUSE.
822,
822,
268,
268,
SIR, YOUR CHECK BOUNCED.

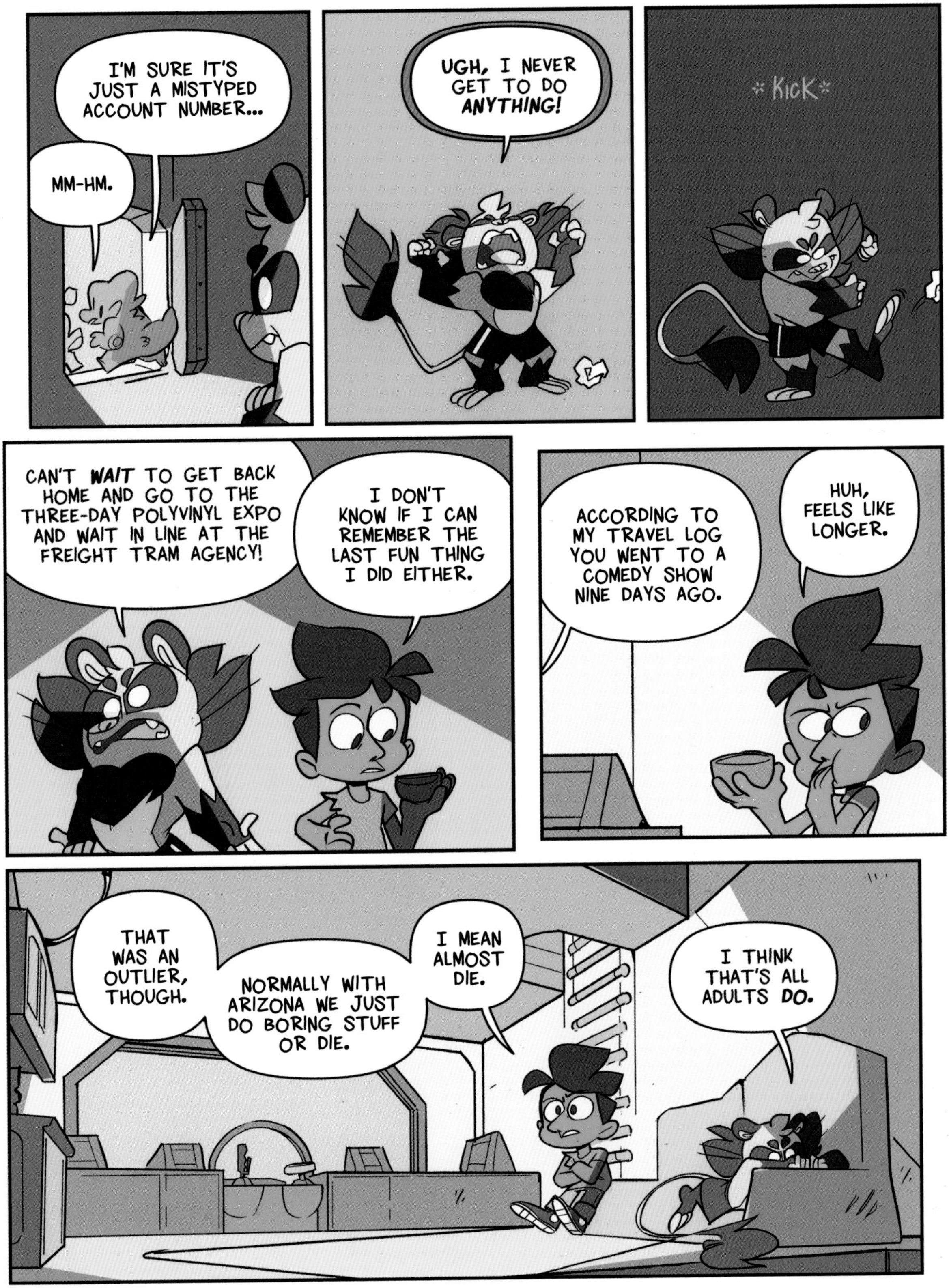

I'M SURE IT'S JUST A MISTYPED ACCOUNT NUMBER...
MM-HM.
UGH, I NEVER GET TO DO ANYTHING!
KICK
CAN'T WAIT TO GET BACK HOME AND GO TO THE THREE-DAY POLYVINYL EXPO AND WAIT IN LINE AT THE FREIGHT TRAM AGENCY!
I DON'T KNOW IF I CAN REMEMBER THE LAST FUN THING I DID EITHER.
ACCORDING TO MY TRAVEL LOG YOU WENT TO A COMEDY SHOW NINE DAYS AGO.
HUH, FEELS LIKE LONGER.
THAT WAS AN OUTLIER, THOUGH.
NORMALLY WITH ARIZONA WE JUST DO BORING STUFF OR DIE.
I MEAN ALMOST DIE.
I THINK THAT'S ALL ADULTS DO.

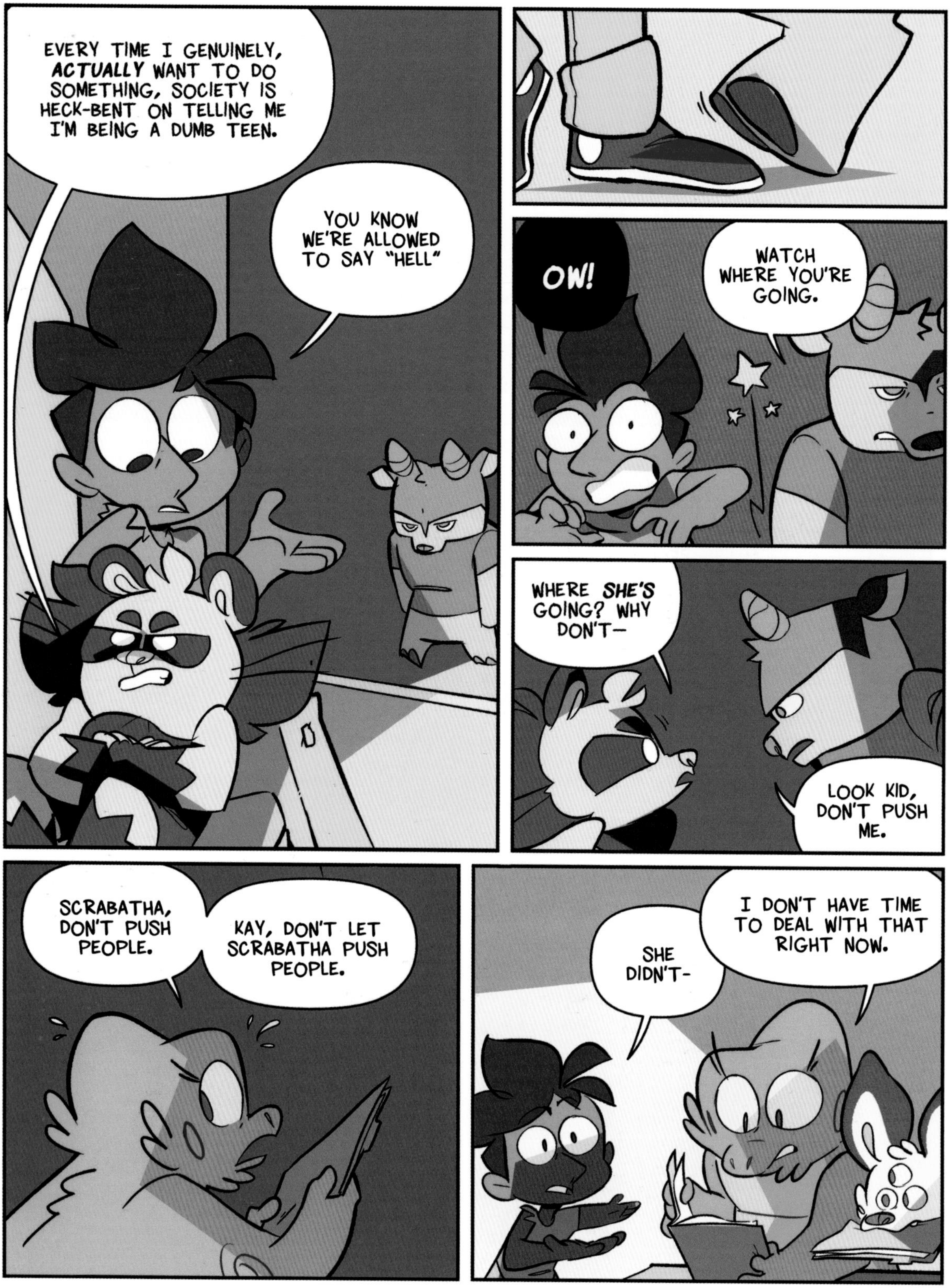
EVERY TIME I GENUINELY, ACTUALLY WANT TO DO SOMETHING, SOCIETY IS HECK-BENT ON TELLING ME I'M BEING A DUMB TEEN.
YOU KNOW WE'RE ALLOWED TO SAY "HELL"
OW!
WATCH WHERE YOU'RE GOING.
WHERE SHE'S GOING? WHY DON'T–
LOOK KID, DON'T PUSH ME.
SCRABATHA, DON'T PUSH PEOPLE.
KAY, DON'T LET SCRABATHA PUSH PEOPLE.
SHE DIDN'T-
I DON'T HAVE TIME TO DEAL WITH THAT RIGHT NOW.

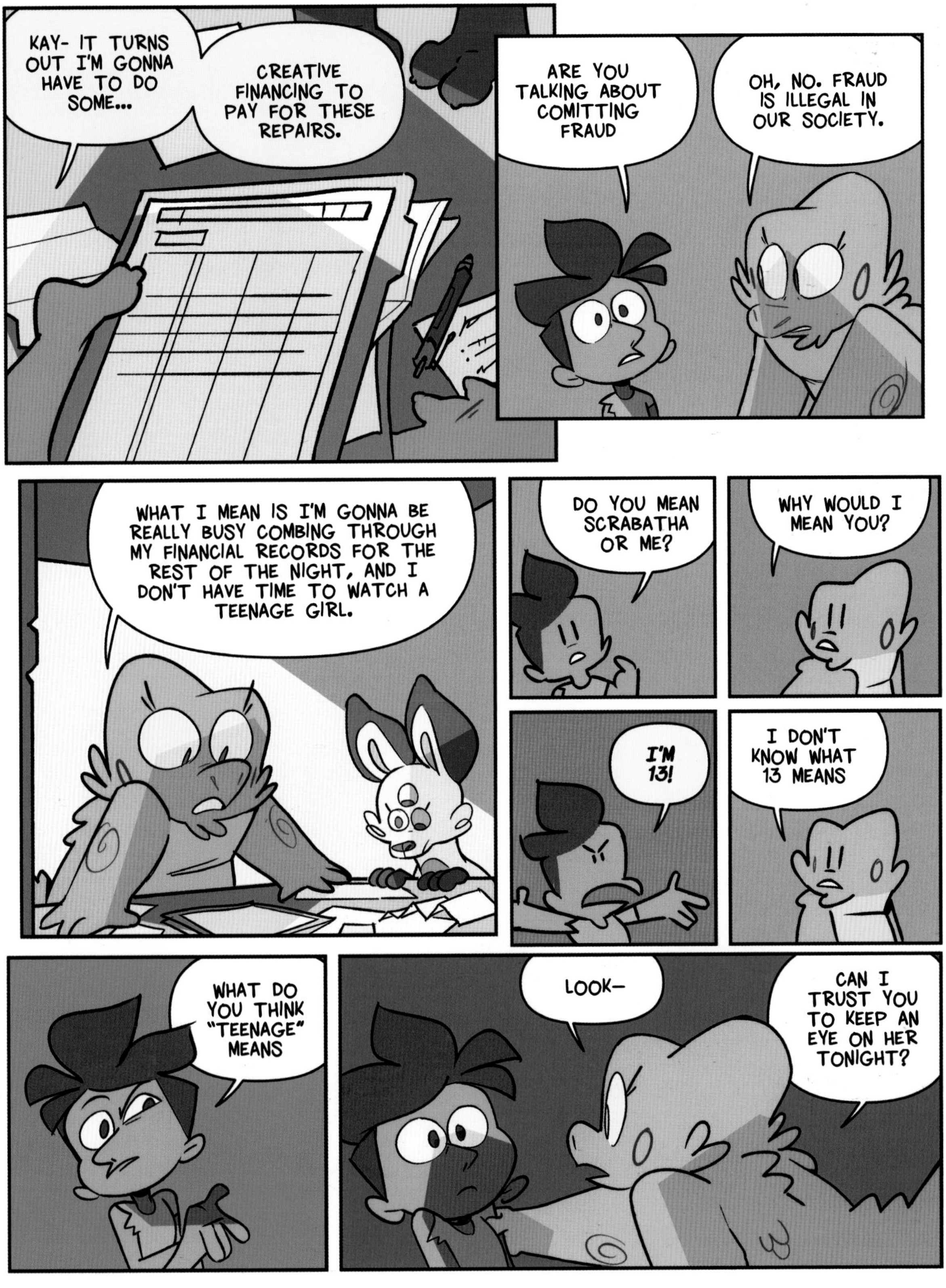
KAY- IT TURNS OUT I'M GONNA HAVE TO DO SOME...
CREATIVE FINANCING TO PAY FOR THESE REPAIRS.
ARE YOU TALKING ABOUT COMITTING FRAUD
OH, NO. FRAUD IS ILLEGAL IN OUR SOCIETY.
WHAT I MEAN IS I'M GONNA BE REALLY BUSY COMBING THROUGH MY FINANCIAL RECORDS FOR THE REST OF THE NIGHT, AND I DON'T HAVE TIME TO WATCH A TEENAGE GIRL.
DO YOU MEAN SCRABATHA OR ME?
WHY WOULD I MEAN YOU?
I'M 13!
I DON'T KNOW WHAT 13 MEANS
WHAT DO YOU THINK "TEENAGE" MEANS
LOOK—
CAN I TRUST YOU TO KEEP AN EYE ON HER TONIGHT?

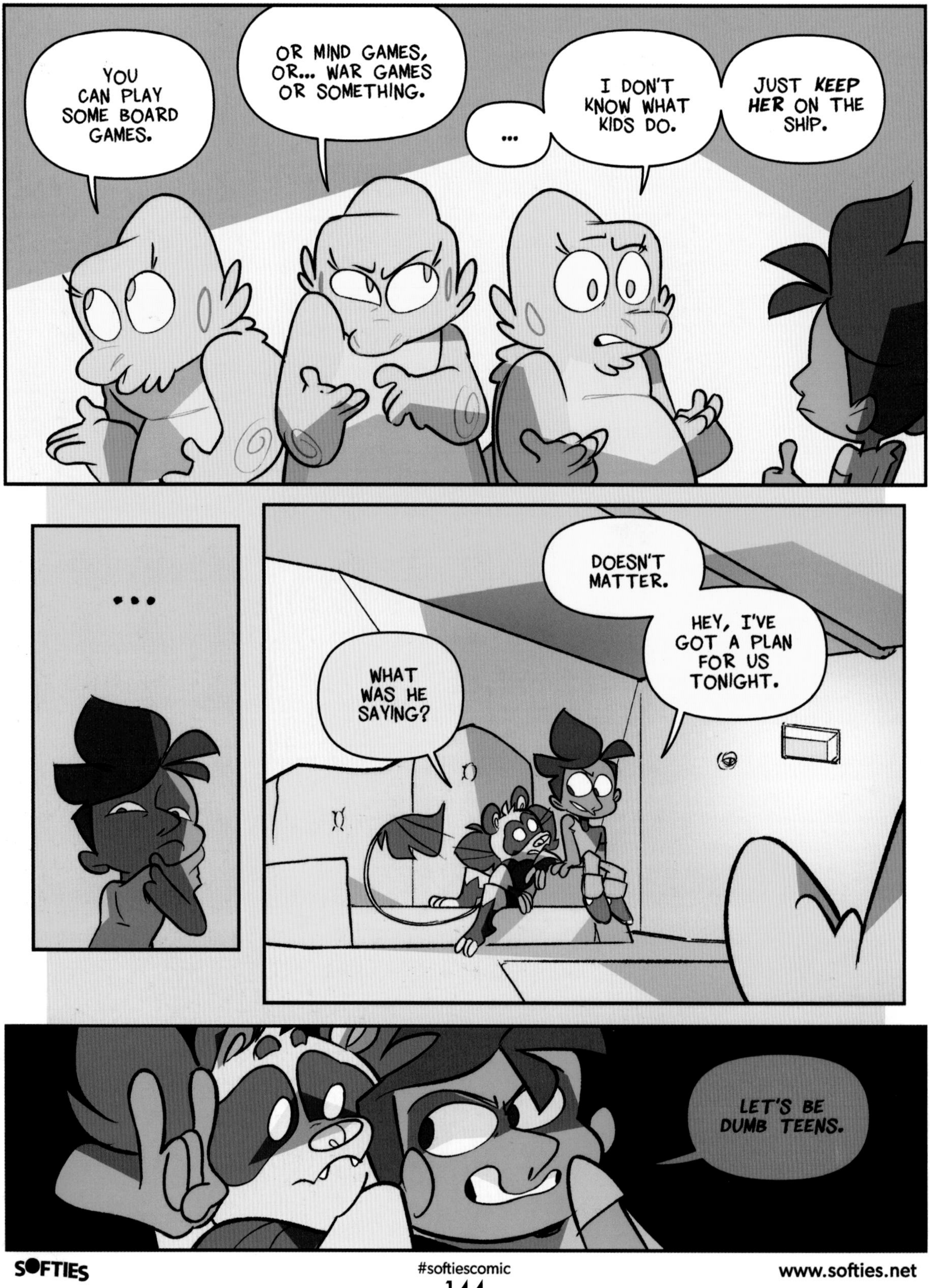
YOU CAN PLAY SOME BOARD GAMES.
OR MIND GAMES, OR... WAR GAMES OR SOMETHING.
...
I DON'T KNOW WHAT KIDS DO.
JUST KEEP HER ON THE SHIP.
...
DOESN'T MATTER.
WHAT WAS HE SAYING?
HEY, I'VE GOT A PLAN FOR US TONIGHT.
LET'S BE DUMB TEENS.

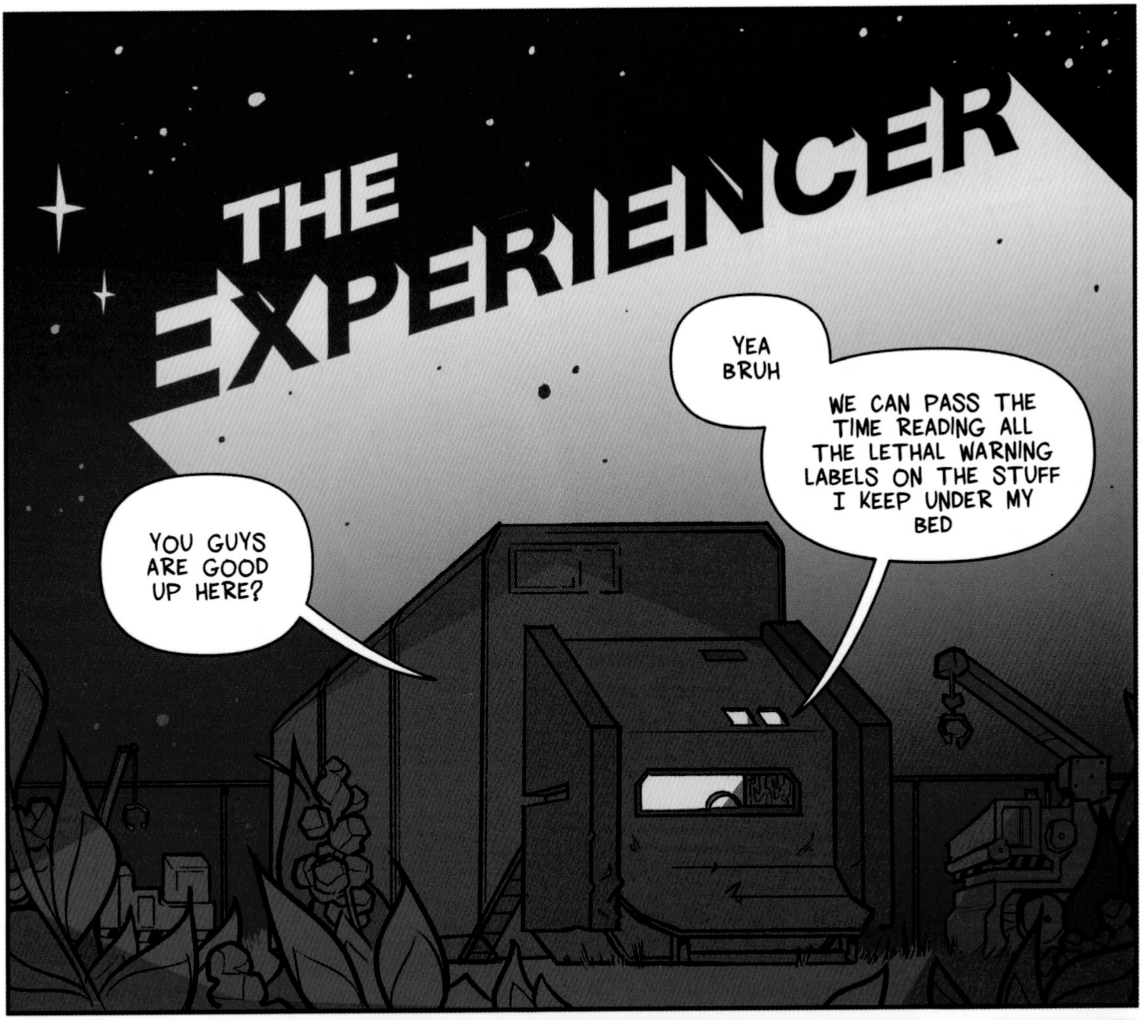
THE EXPERIENCER
YOU GUYS ARE GOOD UP HERE?
YEA BRUH
WE CAN PASS THE TIME READING ALL THE LETHAL WARNING LABELS ON THE STUFF I KEEP UNDER MY BED

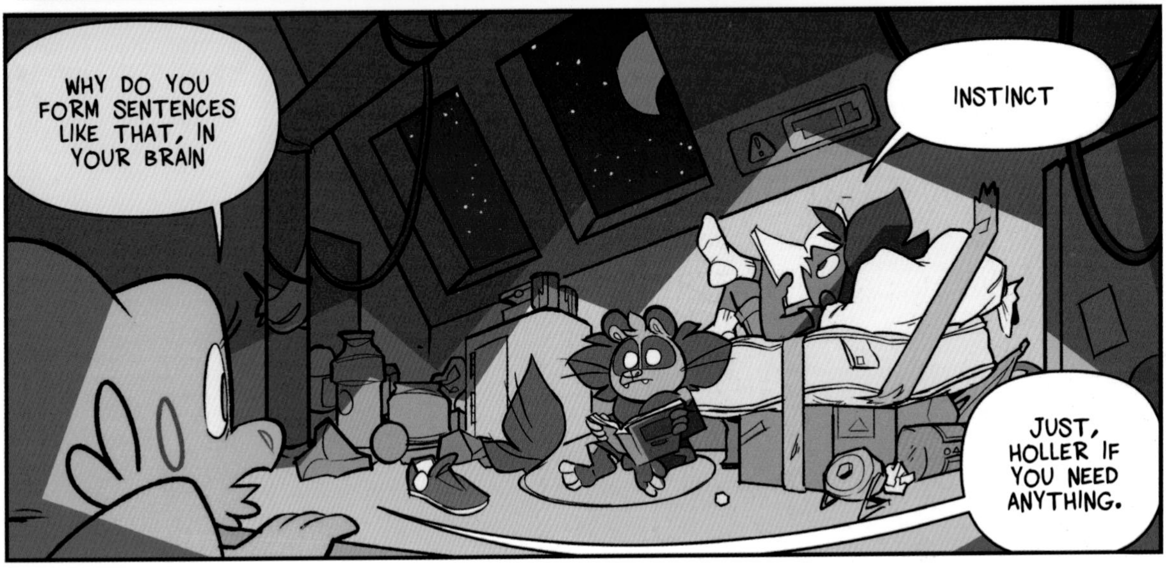
WHY DO YOU FORM SENTENCES LIKE THAT, IN YOUR BRAIN
INSTINCT
JUST, HOLLER IF YOU NEED ANYTHING.

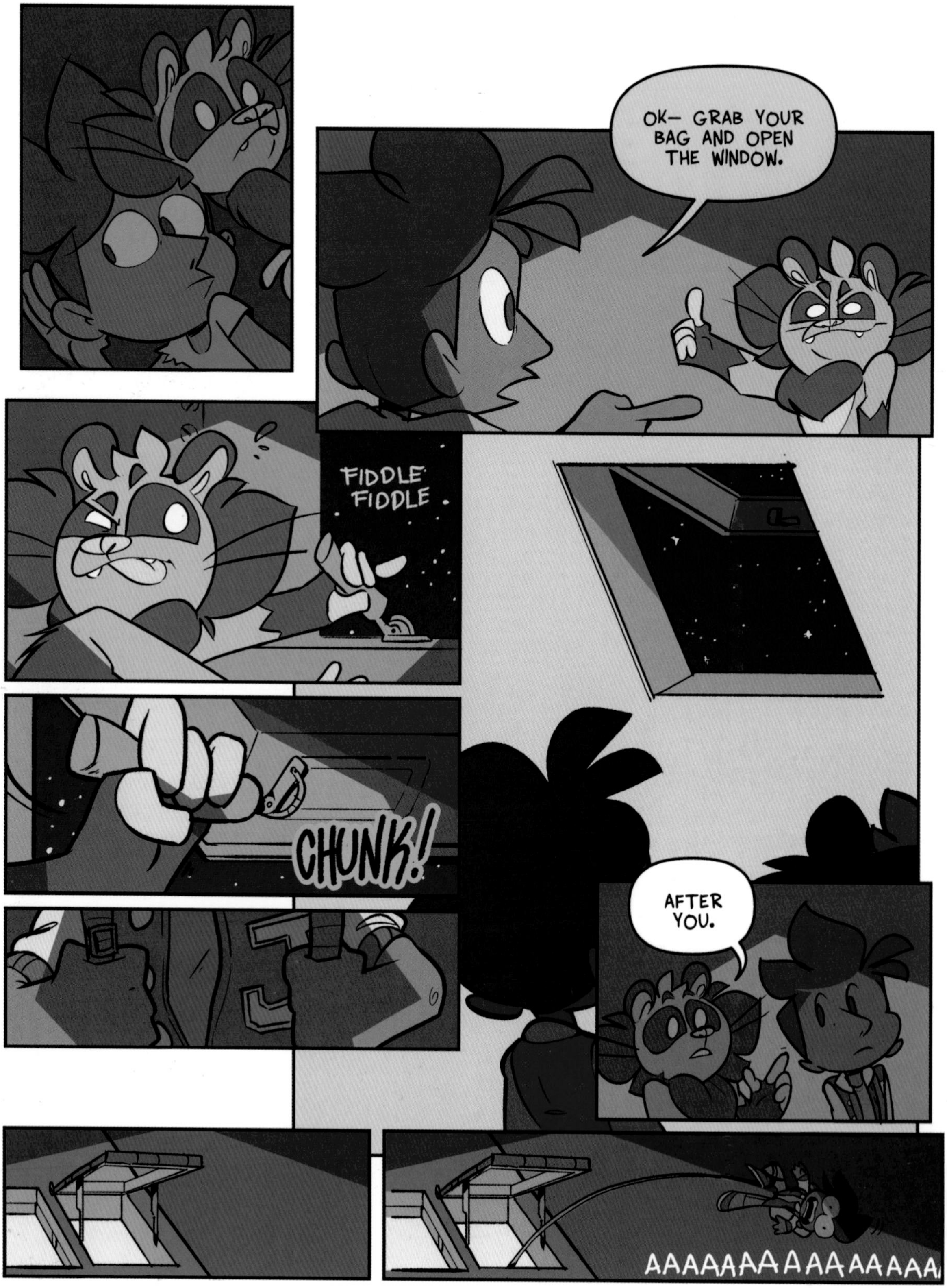
OK– GRAB YOUR BAG AND OPEN THE WINDOW.
FIDDLE FIDDLE
CHUNK!
AFTER YOU.
AAAAAAAAAAAAAAA

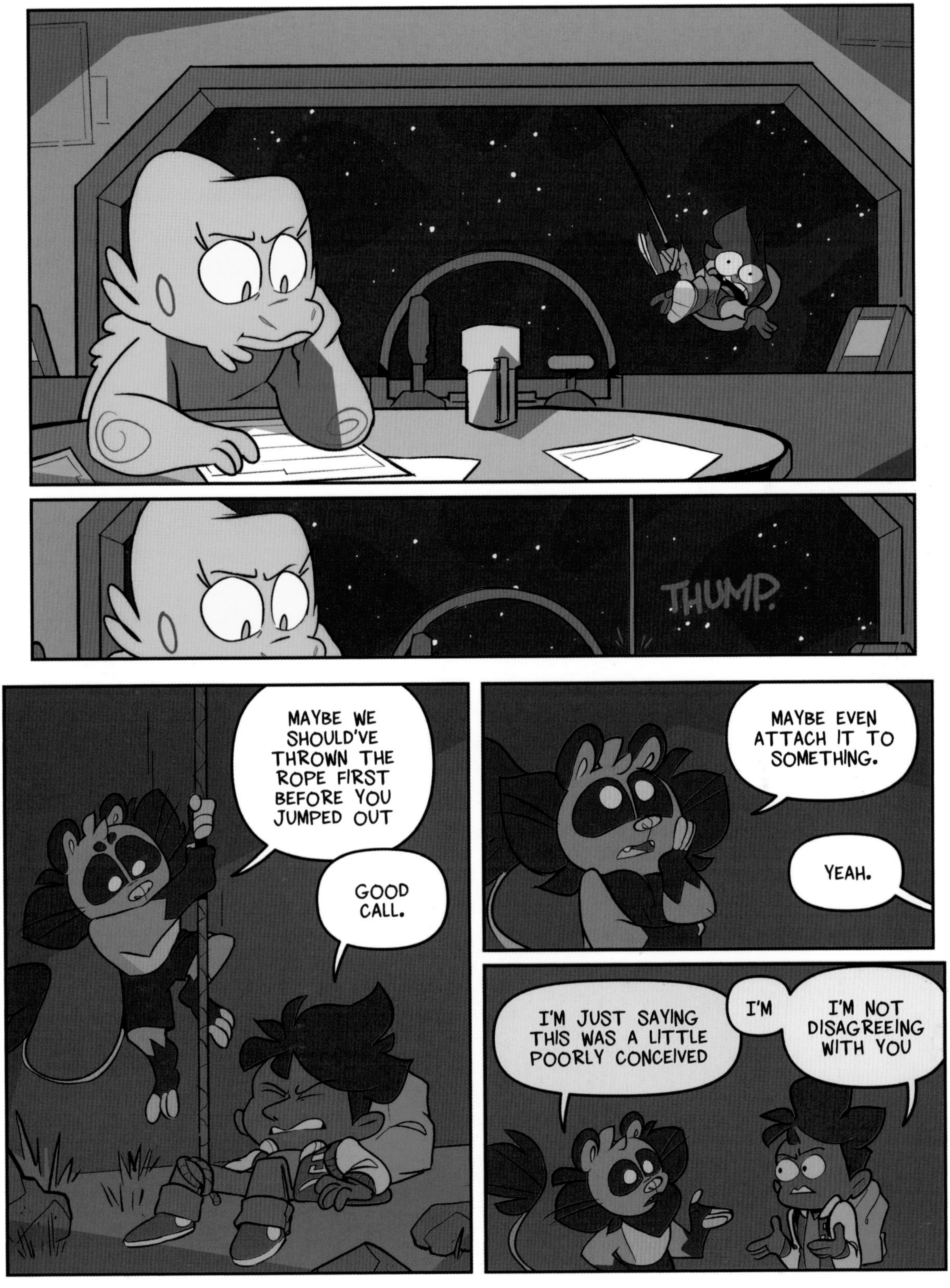
THUMP.
MAYBE WE SHOULD'VE THROWN THE ROPE FIRST BEFORE YOU JUMPED OUT
GOOD CALL.
MAYBE EVEN ATTACH IT TO SOMETHING.
YEAH.
I'M JUST SAYING THIS WAS A LITTLE POORLY CONCEIVED
I'M
I'M NOT DISAGREEING WITH YOU

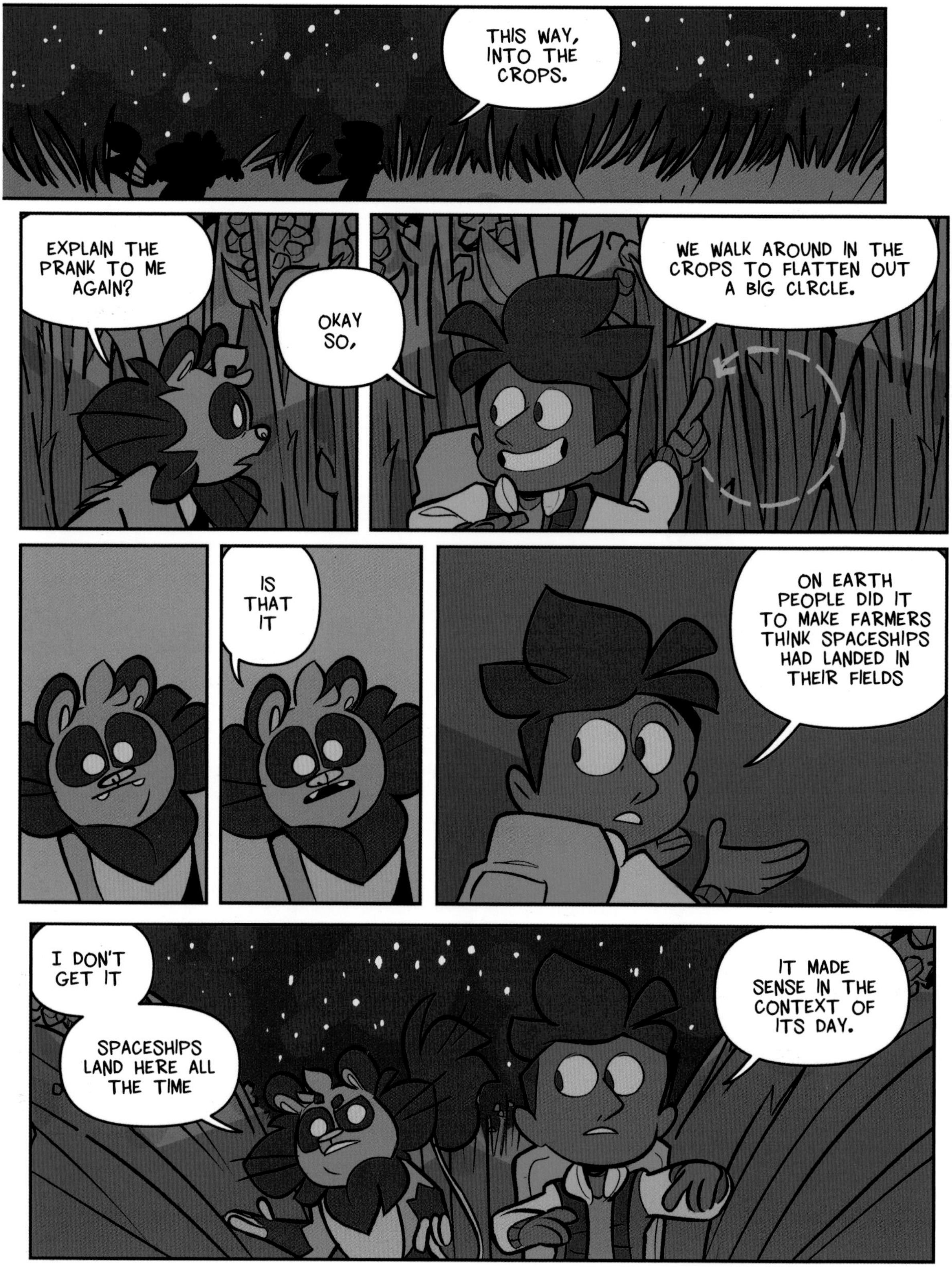
THIS WAY, INTO THE CROPS.
EXPLAIN THE PRANK TO ME AGAIN?
OKAY SO,
WE WALK AROUND IN THE CROPS TO FLATTEN OUT A BIG CIRCLE.
IS THAT IT
ON EARTH PEOPLE DID IT TO MAKE FARMERS THINK SPACESHIPS HAD LANDED IN THEIR FIELDS
I DON'T GET IT
SPACESHIPS LAND HERE ALL THE TIME
IT MADE SENSE IN THE CONTEXT OF ITS DAY.

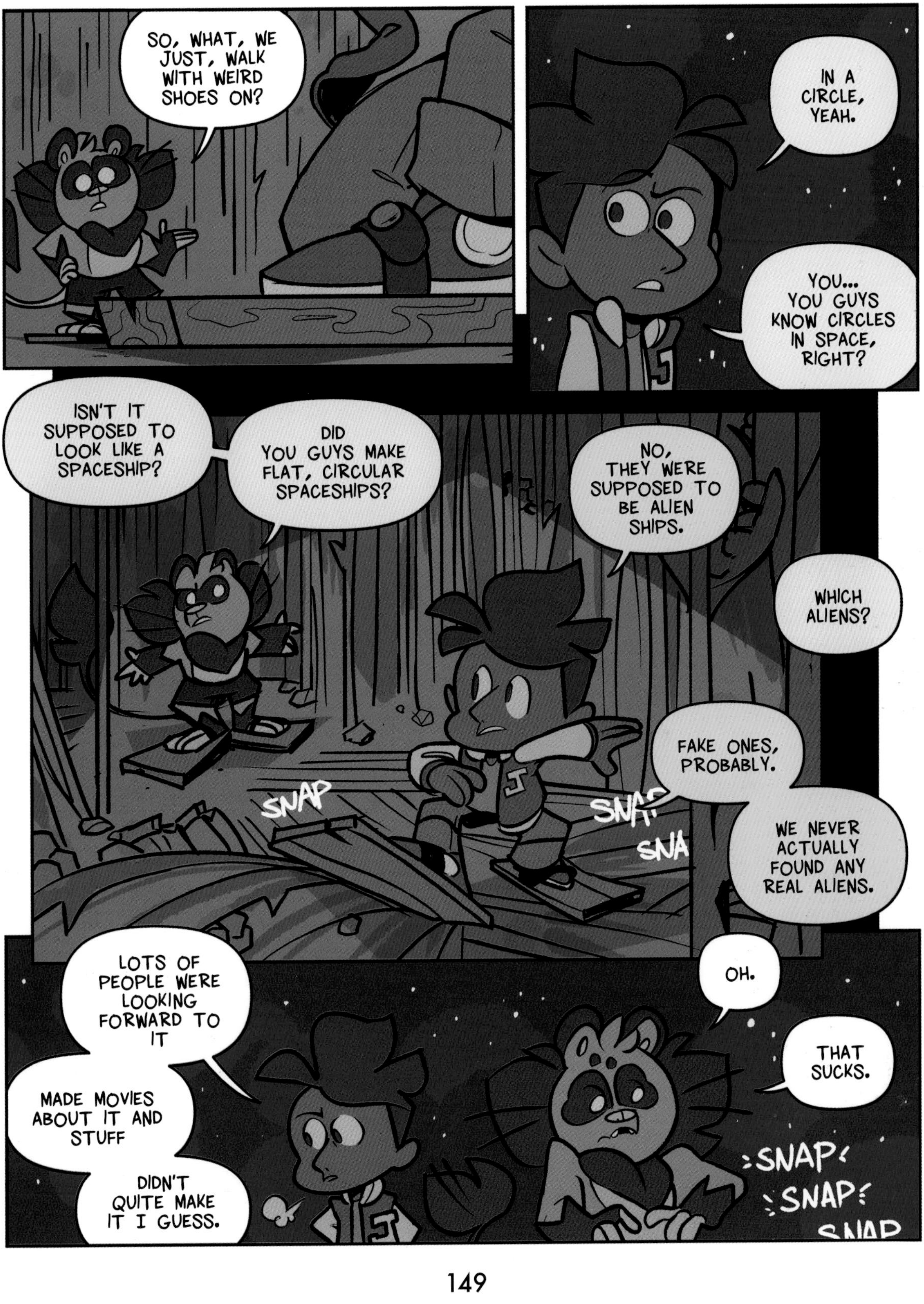
SO, WHAT, WE JUST, WALK WITH WEIRD SHOES ON?
IN A CIRCLE, YEAH.
YOU... YOU GUYS KNOW CIRCLES IN SPACE, RIGHT?
ISN'T IT SUPPOSED TO LOOK LIKE A SPACESHIP?
DID YOU GUYS MAKE FLAT, CIRCULAR SPACESHIPS?
NO, THEY WERE SUPPOSED TO BE ALIEN SHIPS.
WHICH ALIENS?
SNAP
FAKE ONES, PROBABLY.
SNAP
SNA
WE NEVER ACTUALLY FOUND ANY REAL ALIENS.
LOTS OF PEOPLE WERE LOOKING FORWARD TO IT
MADE MOVIES ABOUT IT AND STUFF
DIDN'T QUITE MAKE IT I GUESS.
OH.
THAT SUCKS.
SNAP
SNAP

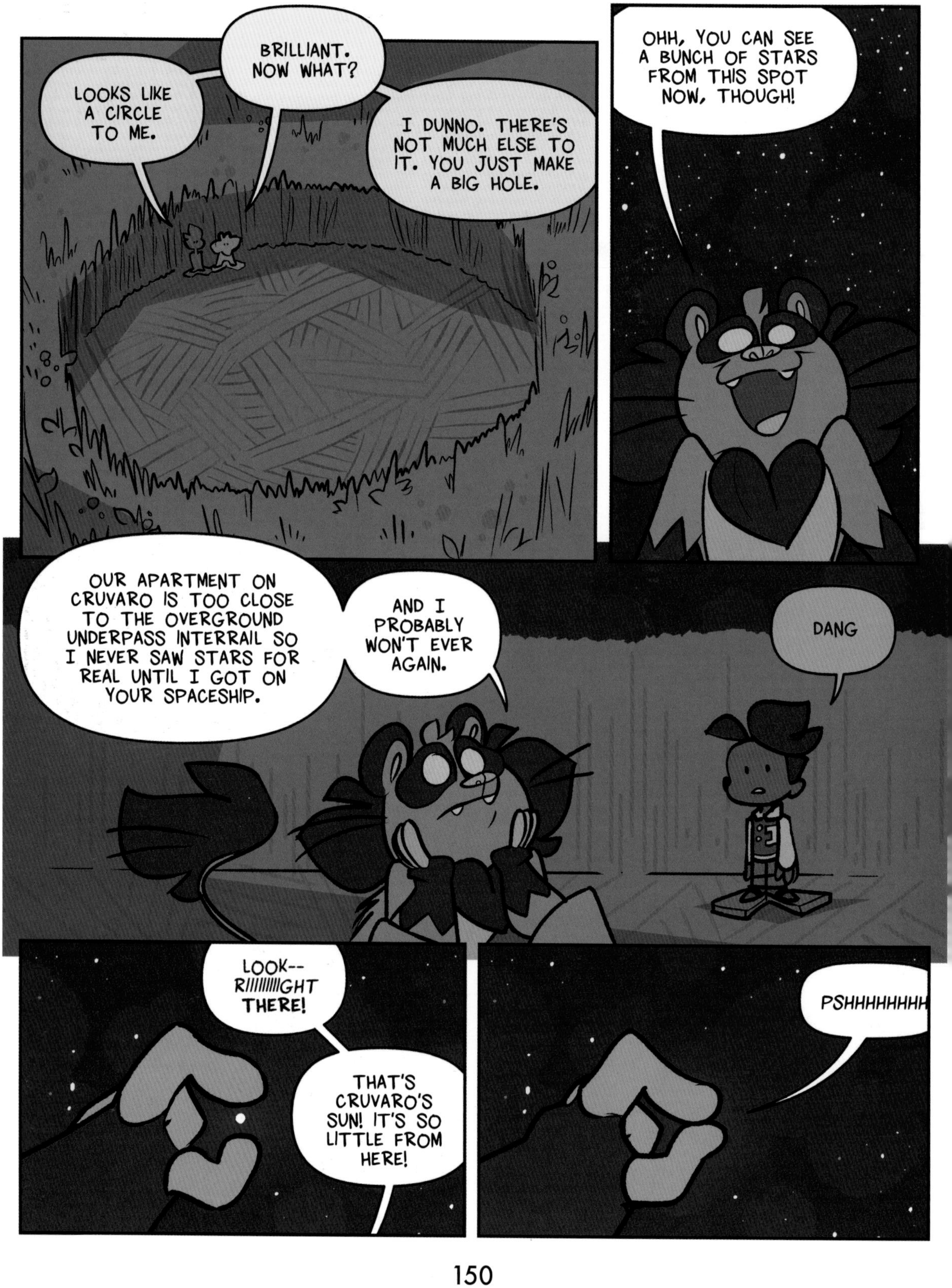
BRILLIANT. NOW WHAT?
LOOKS LIKE A CIRCLE TO ME.
I DUNNO. THERE'S NOT MUCH ELSE TO IT. YOU JUST MAKE A BIG HOLE.
OHH, YOU CAN SEE A BUNCH OF STARS FROM THIS SPOT NOW, THOUGH!
OUR APARTMENT ON CRUVARO IS TOO CLOSE TO THE OVERGROUND UNDERPASS INTERRAIL SO I NEVER SAW STARS FOR REAL UNTIL I GOT ON YOUR SPACESHIP.
AND I PROBABLY WON'T EVER AGAIN.
DANG
LOOK-- RIIIIIIIIGHT THERE!
THAT'S CRUVARO'S SUN! IT'S SO LITTLE FROM HERE!
PSHHHHHHHH

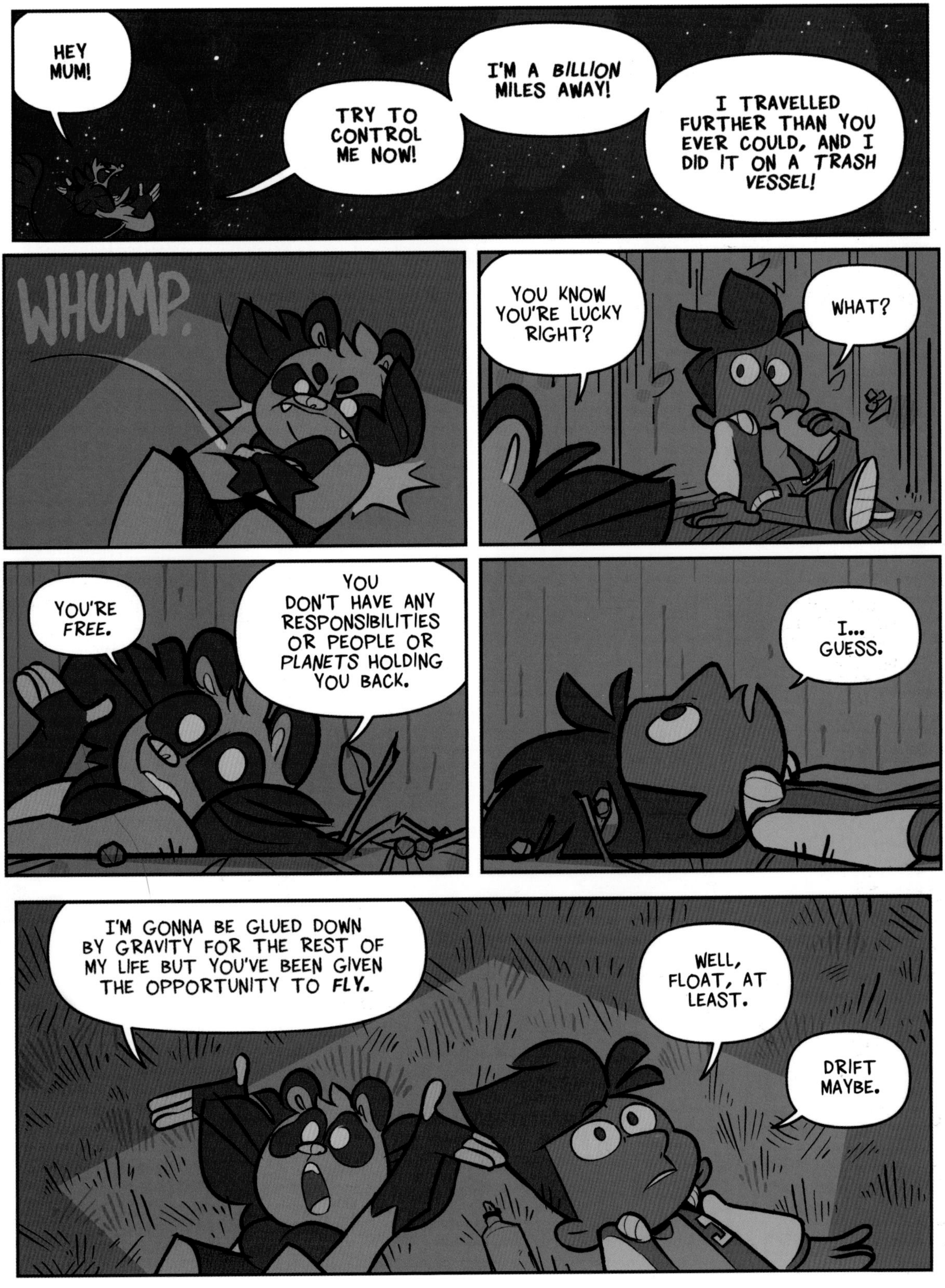
HEY MUM!
TRY TO CONTROL ME NOW!
I'M A BILLION MILES AWAY!
I TRAVELLED FURTHER THAN YOU EVER COULD, AND I DID IT ON A TRASH VESSEL!
WHUMP
YOU KNOW YOU'RE LUCKY RIGHT?
WHAT?
YOU'RE FREE.
YOU DON'T HAVE ANY RESPONSIBILITIES OR PEOPLE OR PLANETS HOLDING YOU BACK.
I... GUESS.
I'M GONNA BE GLUED DOWN BY GRAVITY FOR THE REST OF MY LIFE BUT YOU'VE BEEN GIVEN THE OPPORTUNITY TO FLY.
WELL, FLOAT, AT LEAST.
DRIFT MAYBE.

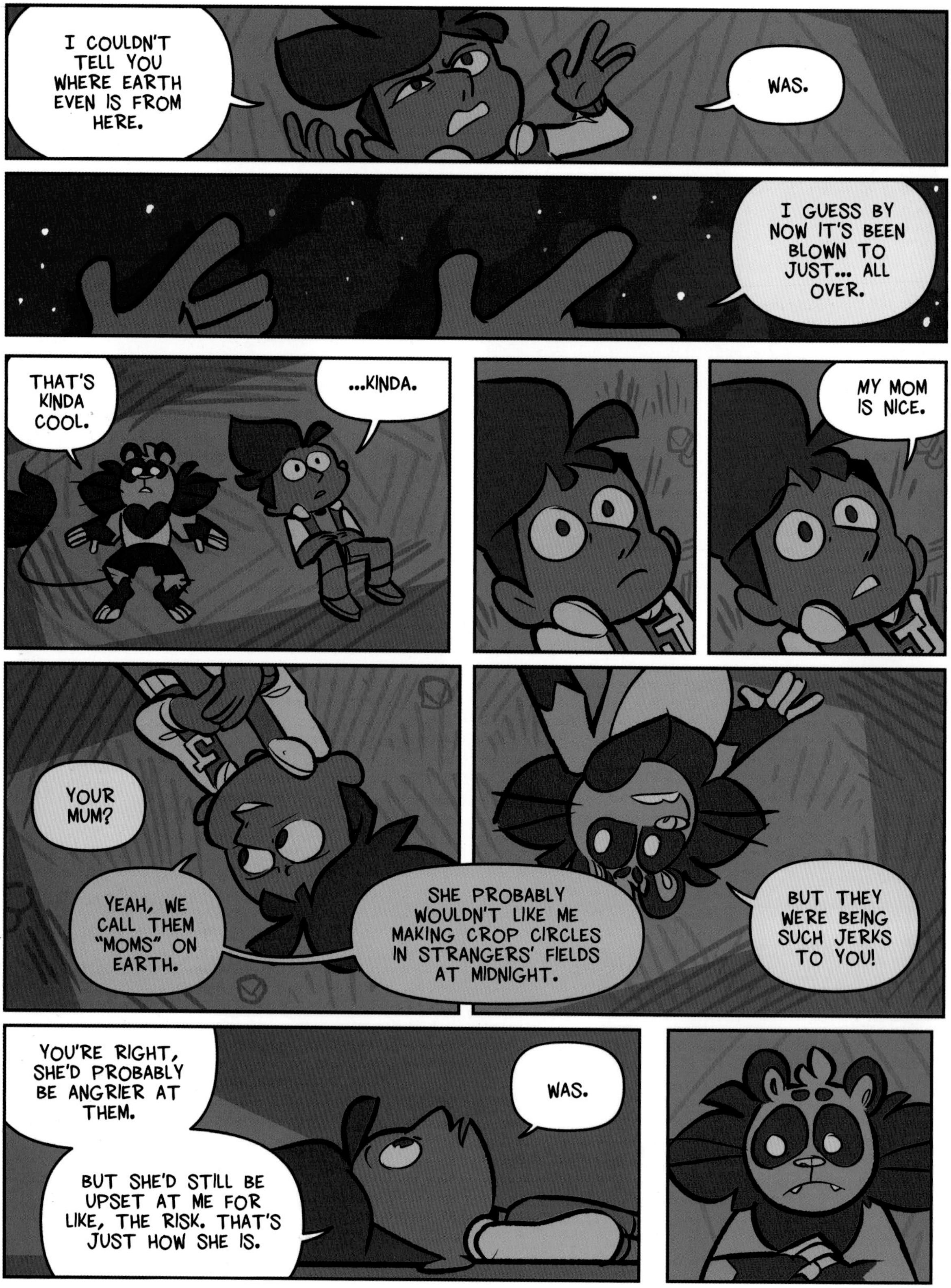
I COULDN'T TELL YOU WHERE EARTH EVEN IS FROM HERE.
WAS.
I GUESS BY NOW IT'S BEEN BLOWN TO JUST... ALL OVER.
THAT'S KINDA COOL.
...KINDA.
MY MOM IS NICE.
YOUR MUM?
YEAH, WE CALL THEM "MOMS" ON EARTH.
SHE PROBABLY WOULDN'T LIKE ME MAKING CROP CIRCLES IN STRANGERS' FIELDS AT MIDNIGHT.
BUT THEY WERE BEING SUCH JERKS TO YOU!
YOU'RE RIGHT, SHE'D PROBABLY BE ANGRIER AT THEM.
BUT SHE'D STILL BE UPSET AT ME FOR LIKE, THE RISK. THAT'S JUST HOW SHE IS.
WAS.

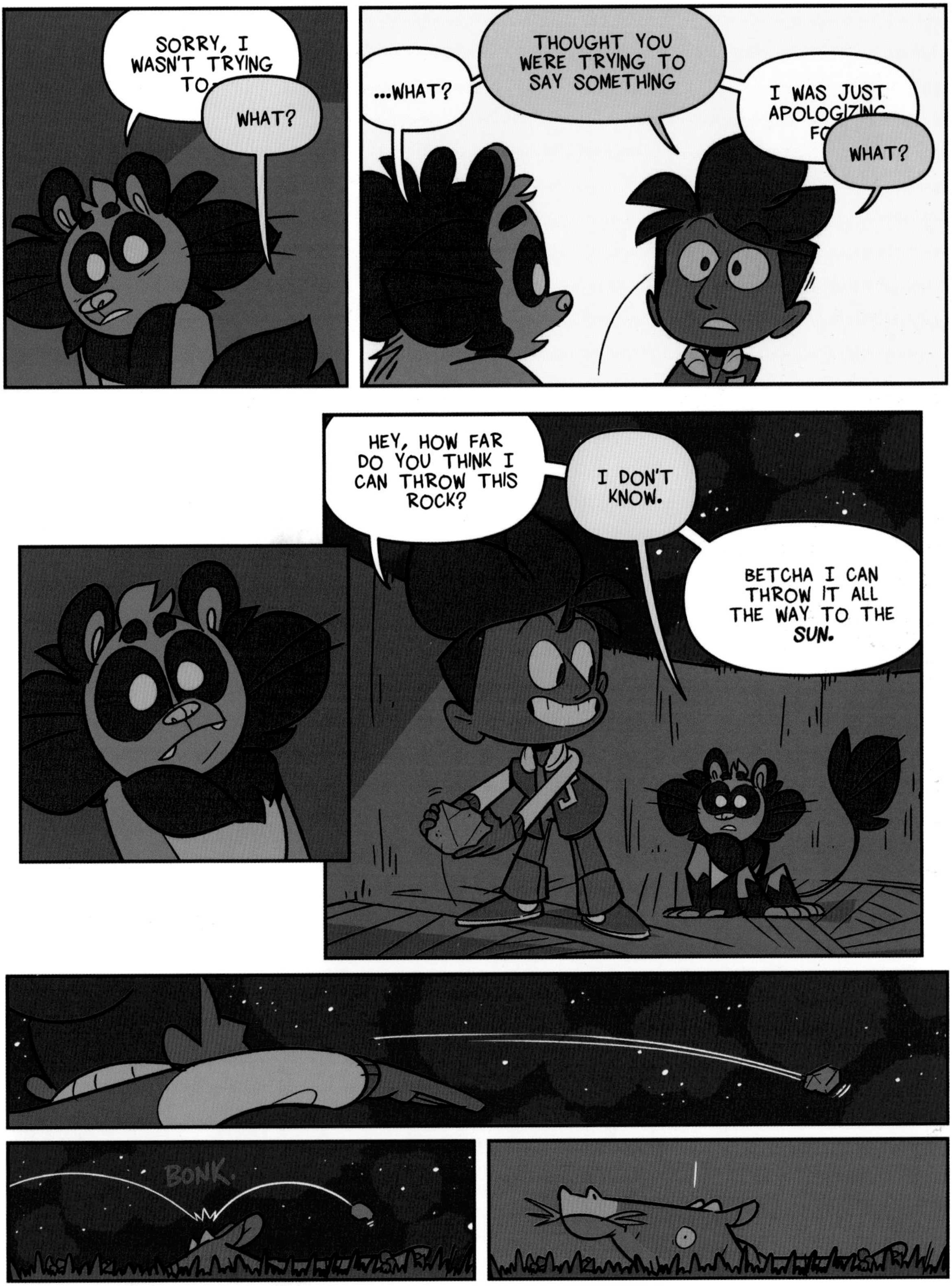

SORRY, I WASN'T TRYING TO-
WHAT?
...WHAT?
THOUGHT YOU WERE TRYING TO SAY SOMETHING
I WAS JUST APOLOGIZING FO-
WHAT?
HEY, HOW FAR DO YOU THINK I CAN THROW THIS ROCK?
I DON'T KNOW.
BETCHA I CAN THROW IT ALL THE WAY TO THE SUN.
BONK.

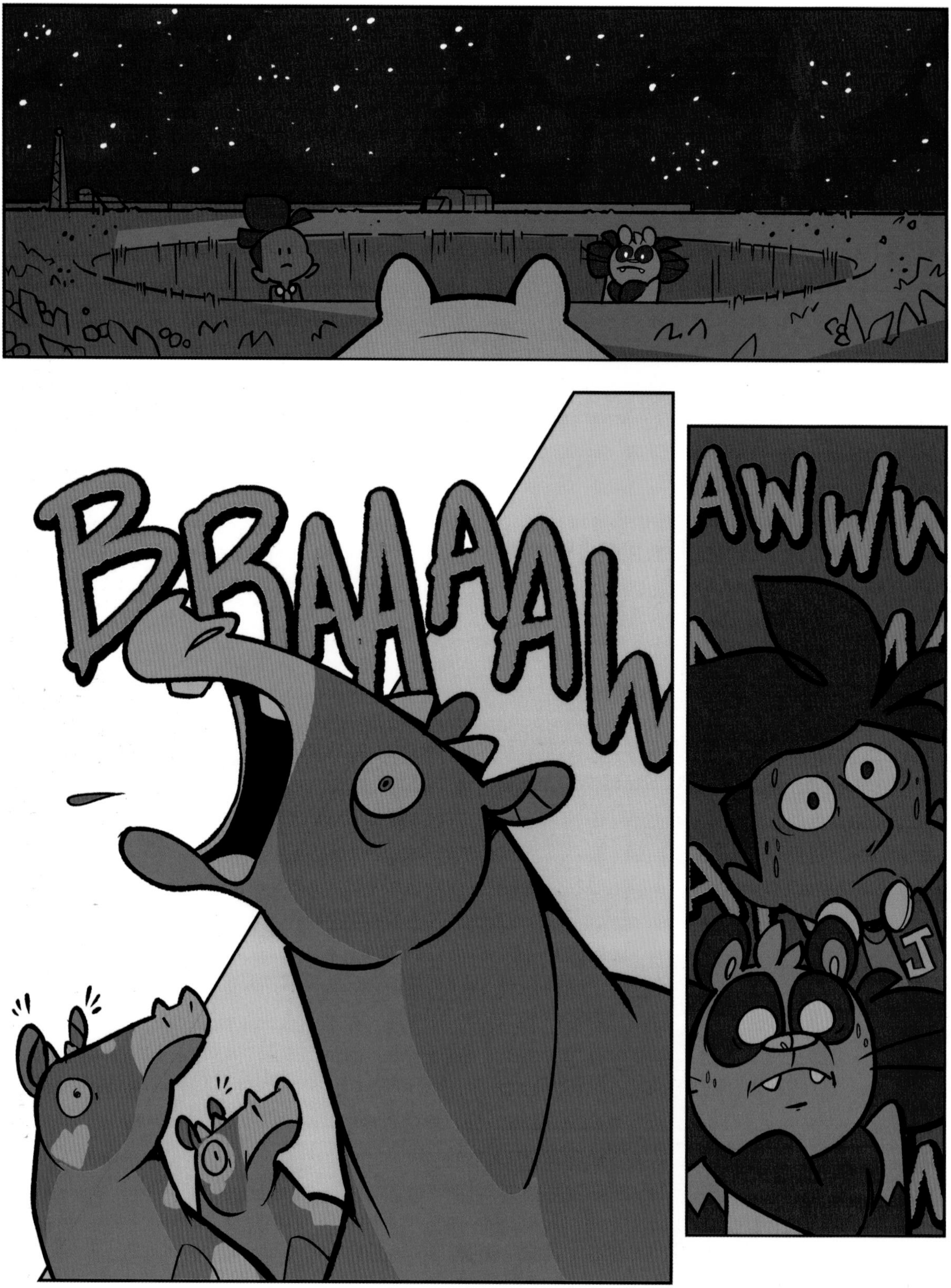
BRAAAAW
AWWW

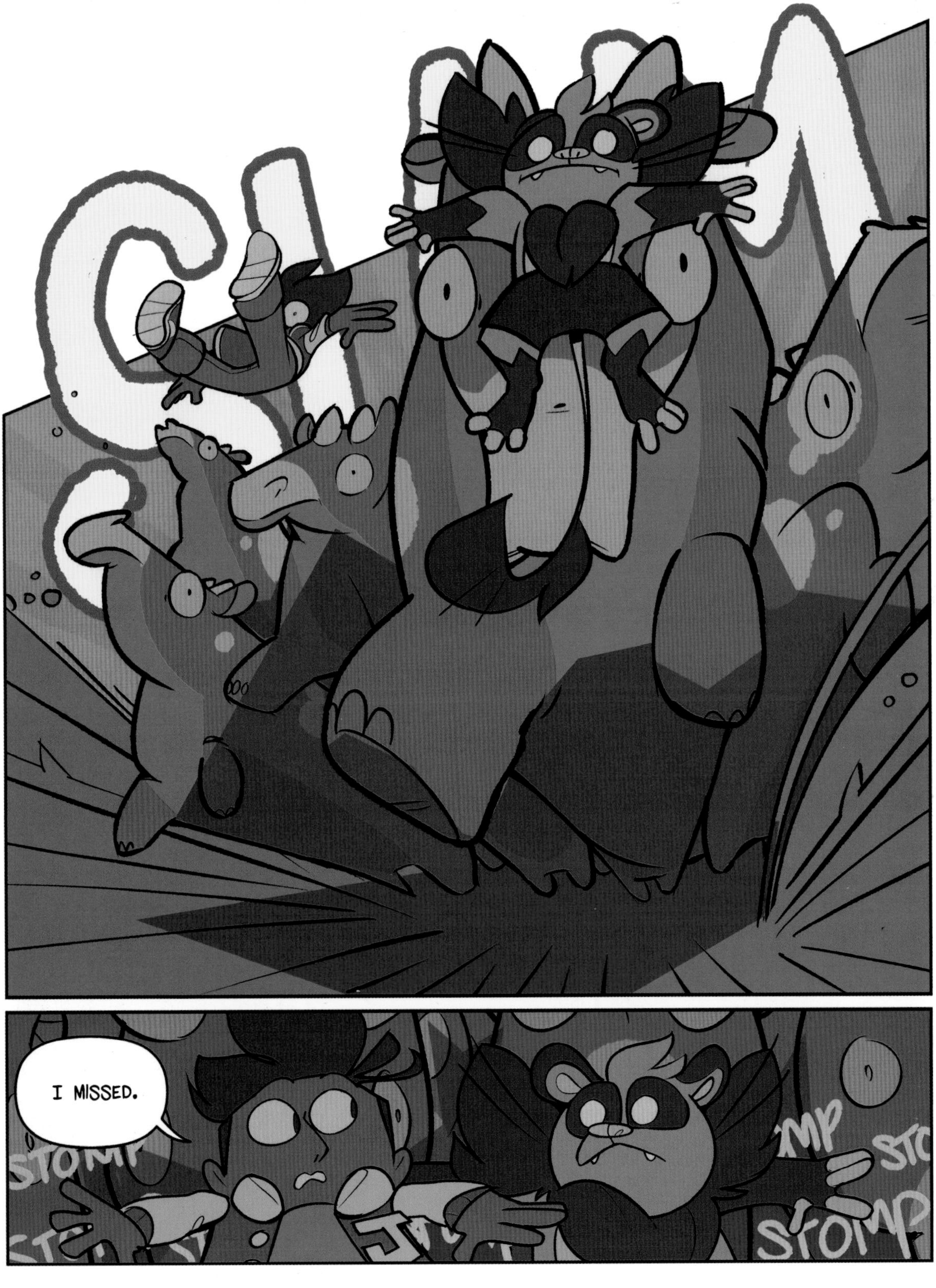
I MISSED.
STOMP
STOMP

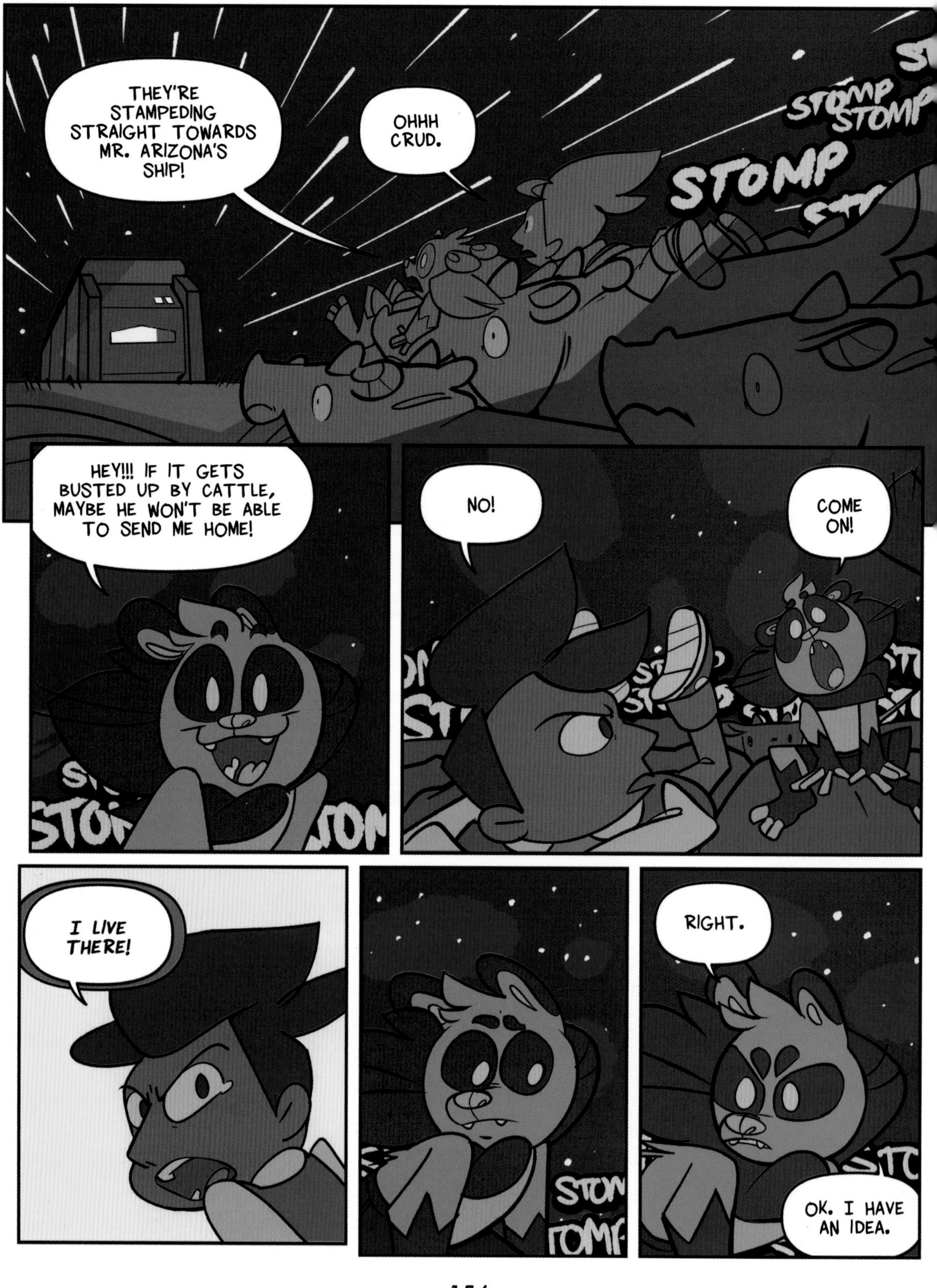
THEY'RE STAMPEDING STRAIGHT TOWARDS MR. ARIZONA'S SHIP!
OHHH CRUD.
STOMP STOMP
STOMP
HEY!!! IF IT GETS BUSTED UP BY CATTLE, MAYBE HE WON'T BE ABLE TO SEND ME HOME!
NO!
COME ON!
I LIVE THERE!
RIGHT.
OK. I HAVE AN IDEA.

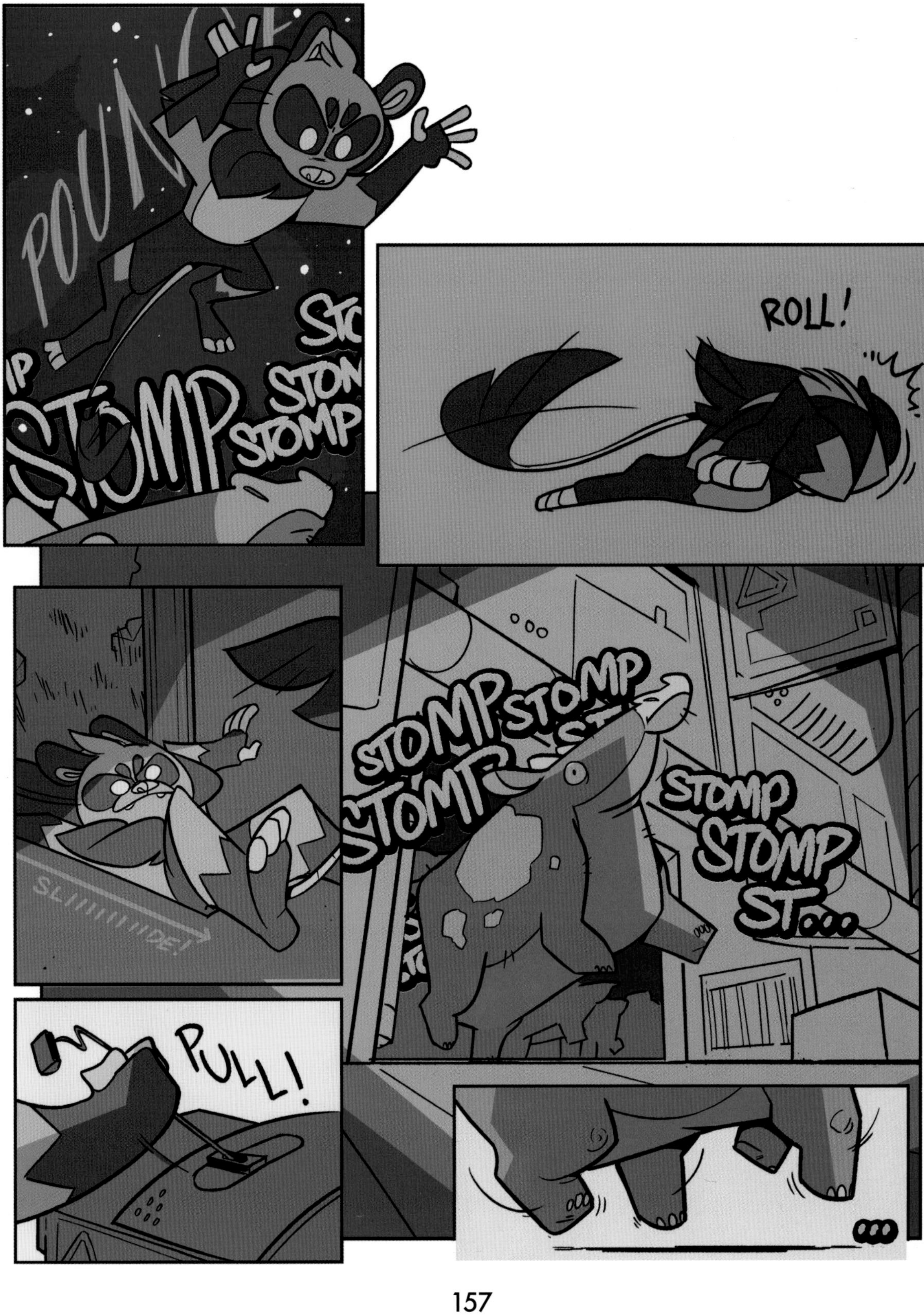
POUNCE
STOMP
STOMP
STOMP
STOMP
ROLL!
SLIIIIIIIIDE!
STOMP STOMP
STOMP
STOMP
STOMP
ST...
PULL!
...

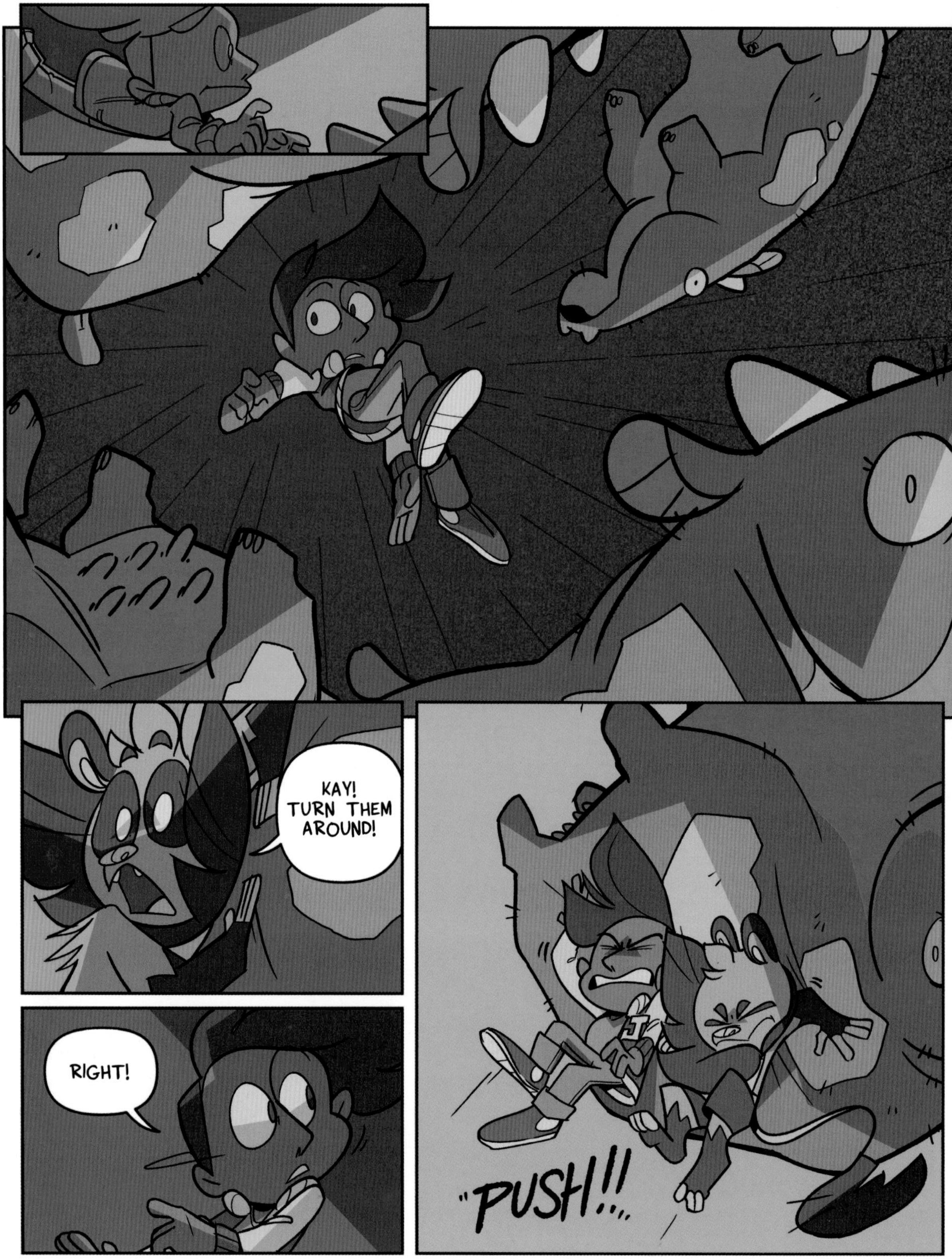
KAY! TURN THEM AROUND!
RIGHT!
PUSH!!

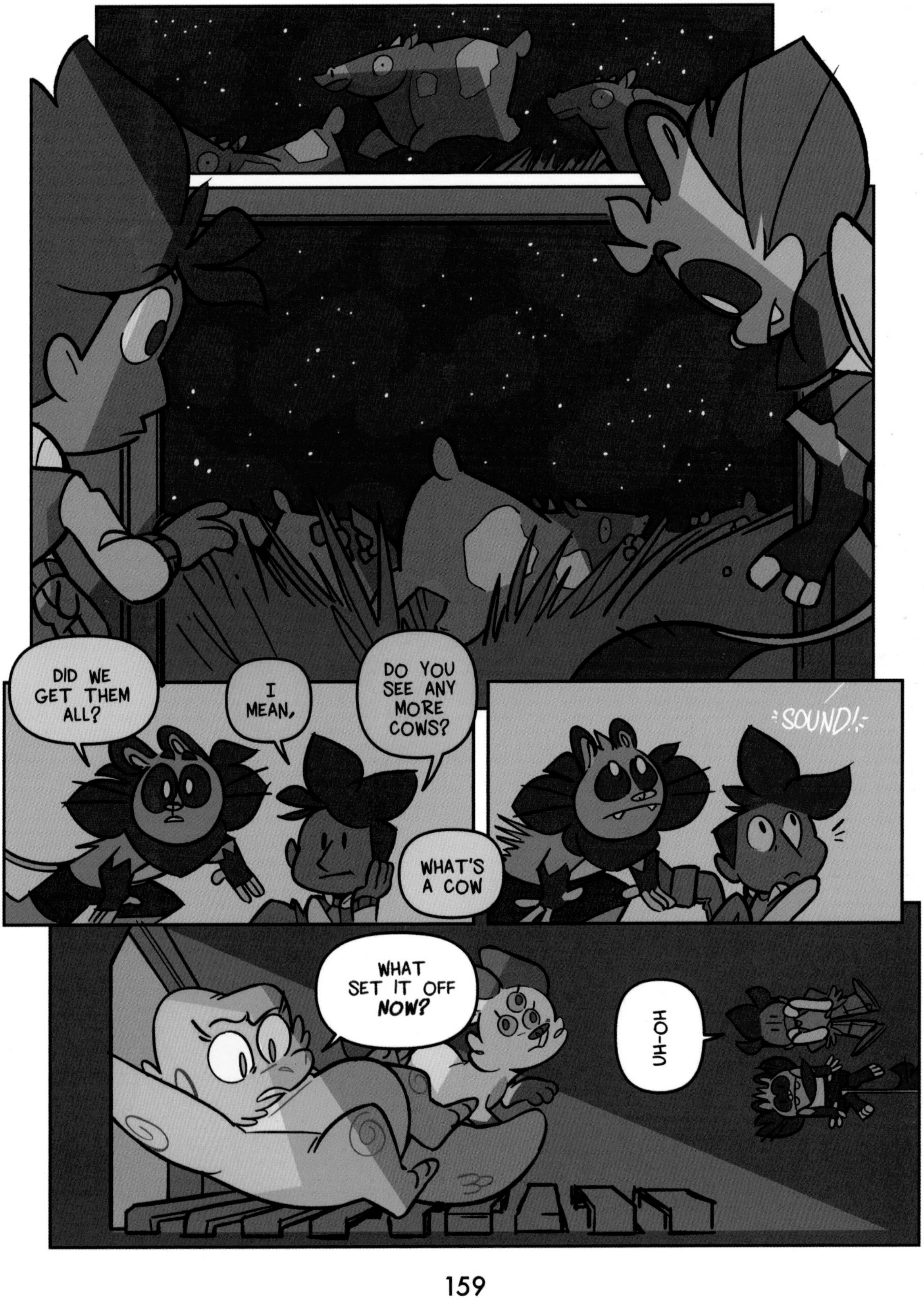
DID WE GET THEM ALL?
I MEAN,
DO YOU SEE ANY MORE COWS?
WHAT'S A COW
SOUND!
WHAT SET IT OFF NOW?
UH-OH

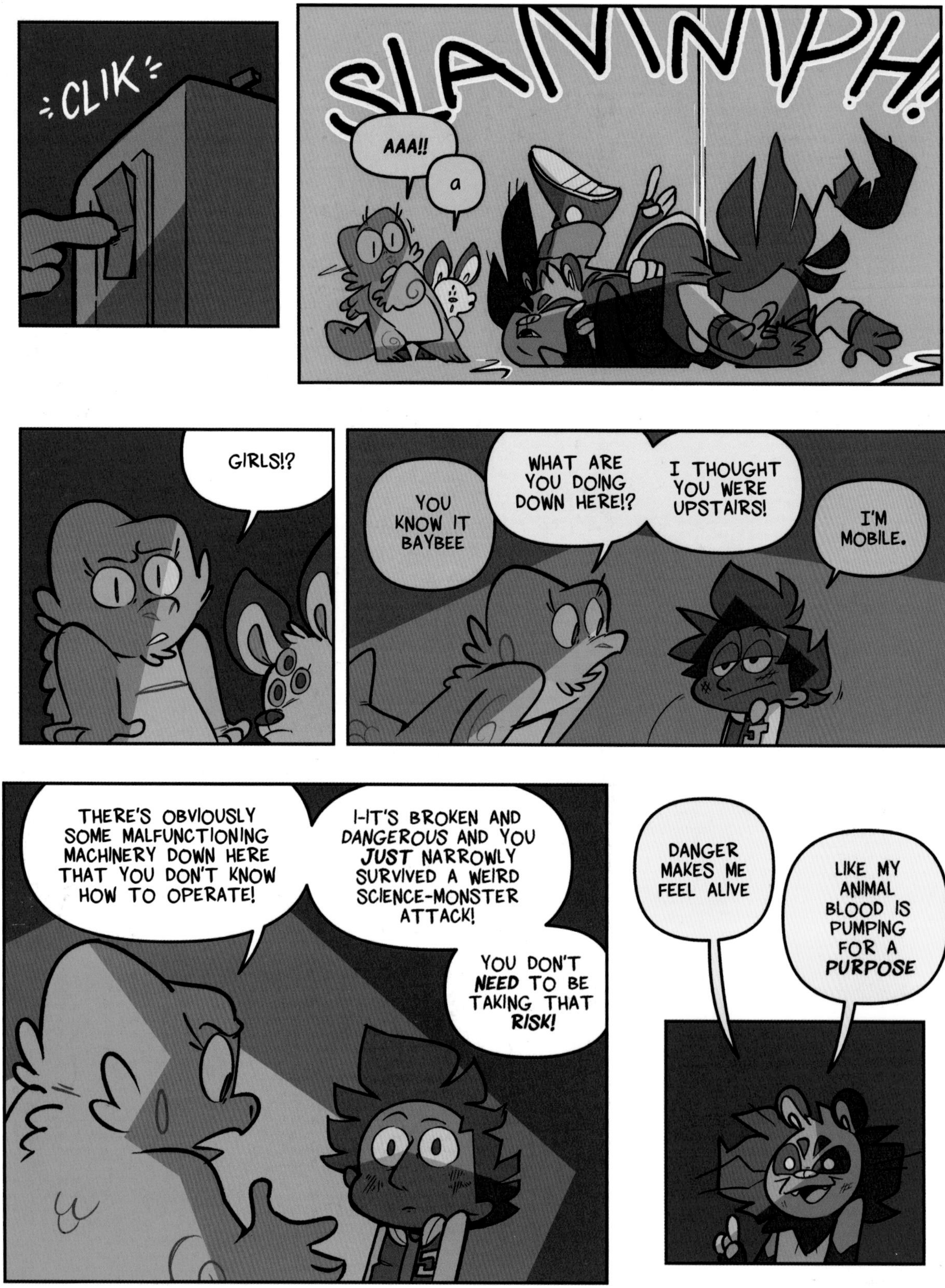
CLIK
SLAMMPH!
AAA!!
a
GIRLS!?
YOU KNOW IT BAYBEE
WHAT ARE YOU DOING DOWN HERE!?
I THOUGHT YOU WERE UPSTAIRS!
I'M MOBILE.
THERE'S OBVIOUSLY SOME MALFUNCTIONING MACHINERY DOWN HERE THAT YOU DON'T KNOW HOW TO OPERATE!
I-IT'S BROKEN AND DANGEROUS AND YOU JUST NARROWLY SURVIVED A WEIRD SCIENCE-MONSTER ATTACK!
YOU DON'T NEED TO BE TAKING THAT RISK!
DANGER MAKES ME FEEL ALIVE
LIKE MY ANIMAL BLOOD IS PUMPING FOR A PURPOSE

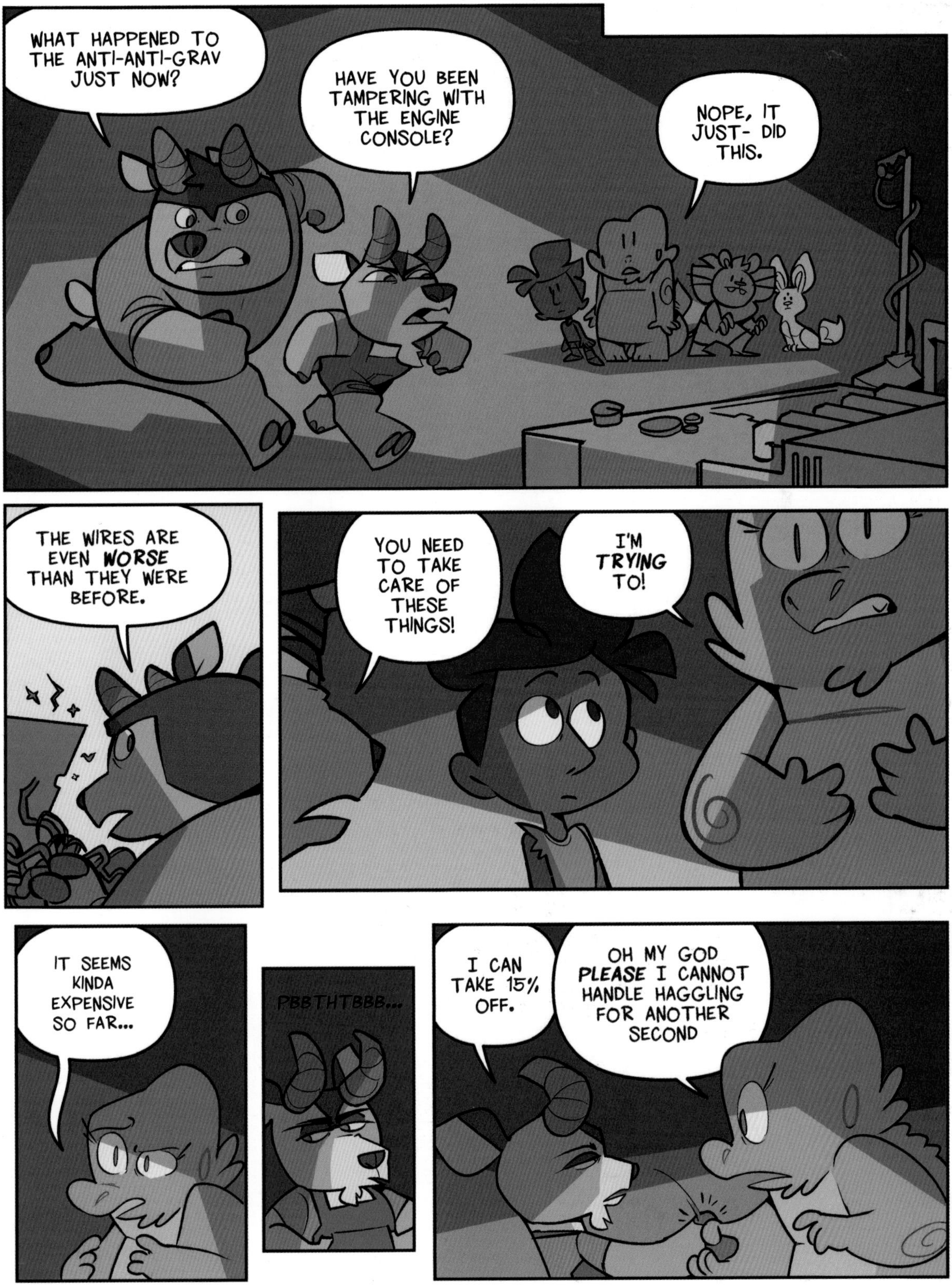
WHAT HAPPENED TO THE ANTI-ANTI-GRAV JUST NOW?
HAVE YOU BEEN TAMPERING WITH THE ENGINE CONSOLE?
NOPE, IT JUST- DID THIS.
THE WIRES ARE EVEN WORSE THAN THEY WERE BEFORE.
YOU NEED TO TAKE CARE OF THESE THINGS!
I'M TRYING TO!
IT SEEMS KINDA EXPENSIVE SO FAR...
PBBTHTBBB...
I CAN TAKE 15% OFF.
OH MY GOD PLEASE I CANNOT HANDLE HAGGLING FOR ANOTHER SECOND

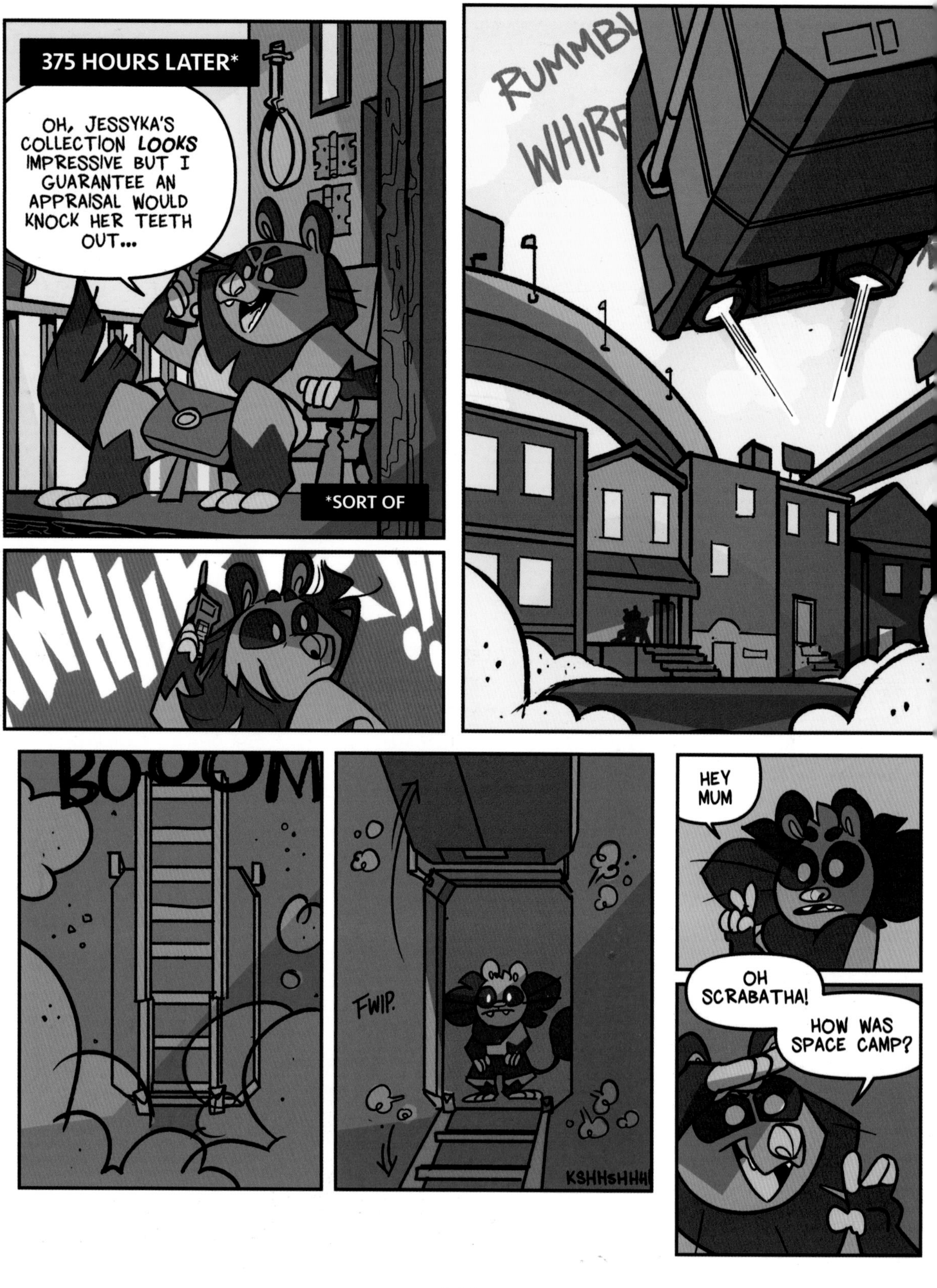
375 HOURS LATER*
OH, JESSYKA'S COLLECTION LOOKS IMPRESSIVE BUT I GUARANTEE AN APPRAISAL WOULD KNOCK HER TEETH OUT...
*SORT OF
RUMMBL
WHIRR
BOOOOM
FWIP.
KSHHSHHH
HEY MUM
OH SCRABATHA!
HOW WAS SPACE CAMP?

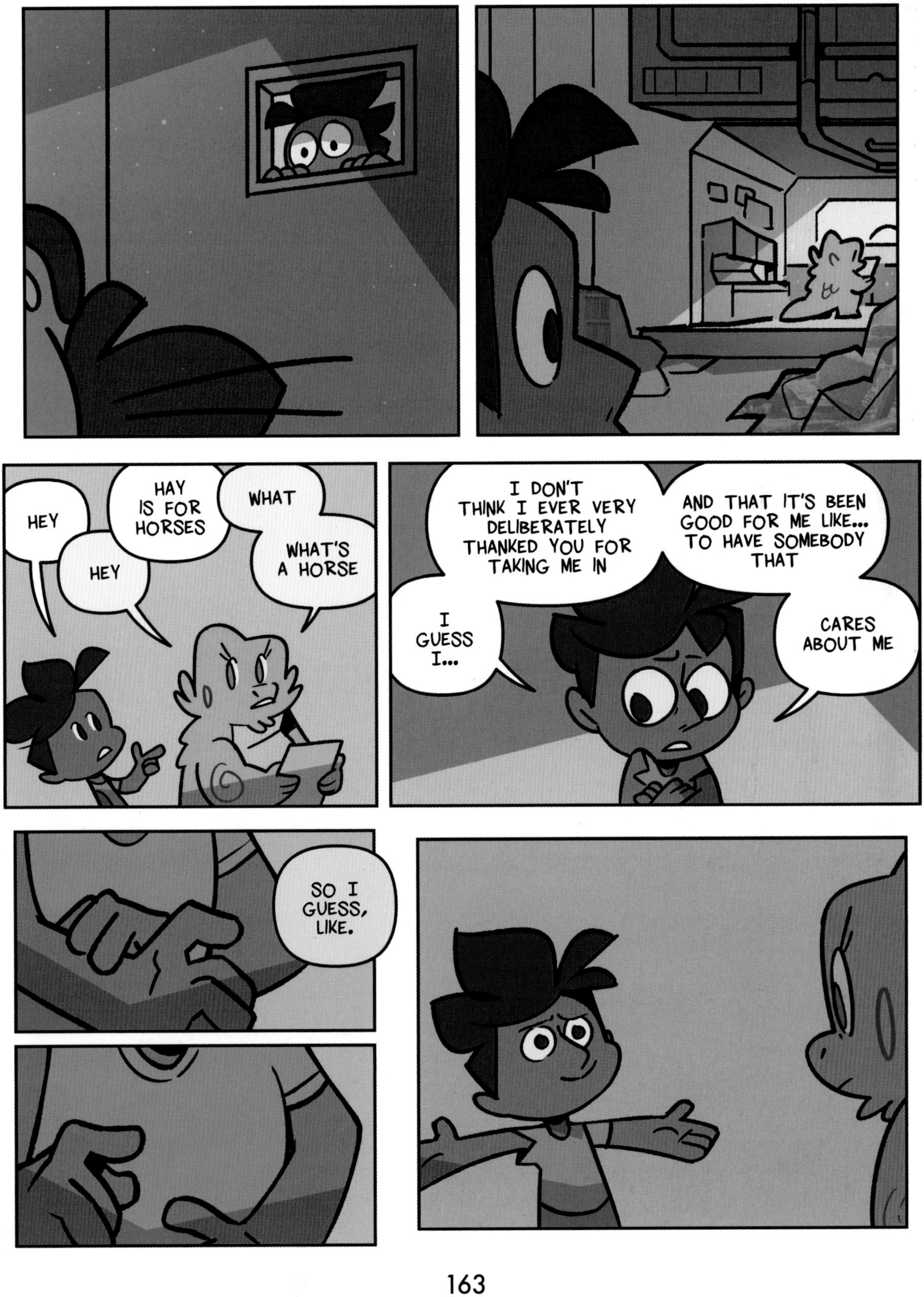
HEY
HEY
HAY IS FOR HORSES
WHAT
WHAT'S A HORSE
I GUESS I...
I DON'T THINK I EVER VERY DELIBERATELY THANKED YOU FOR TAKING ME IN
AND THAT IT'S BEEN GOOD FOR ME LIKE... TO HAVE SOMEBODY THAT
CARES ABOUT ME
SO I GUESS, LIKE.

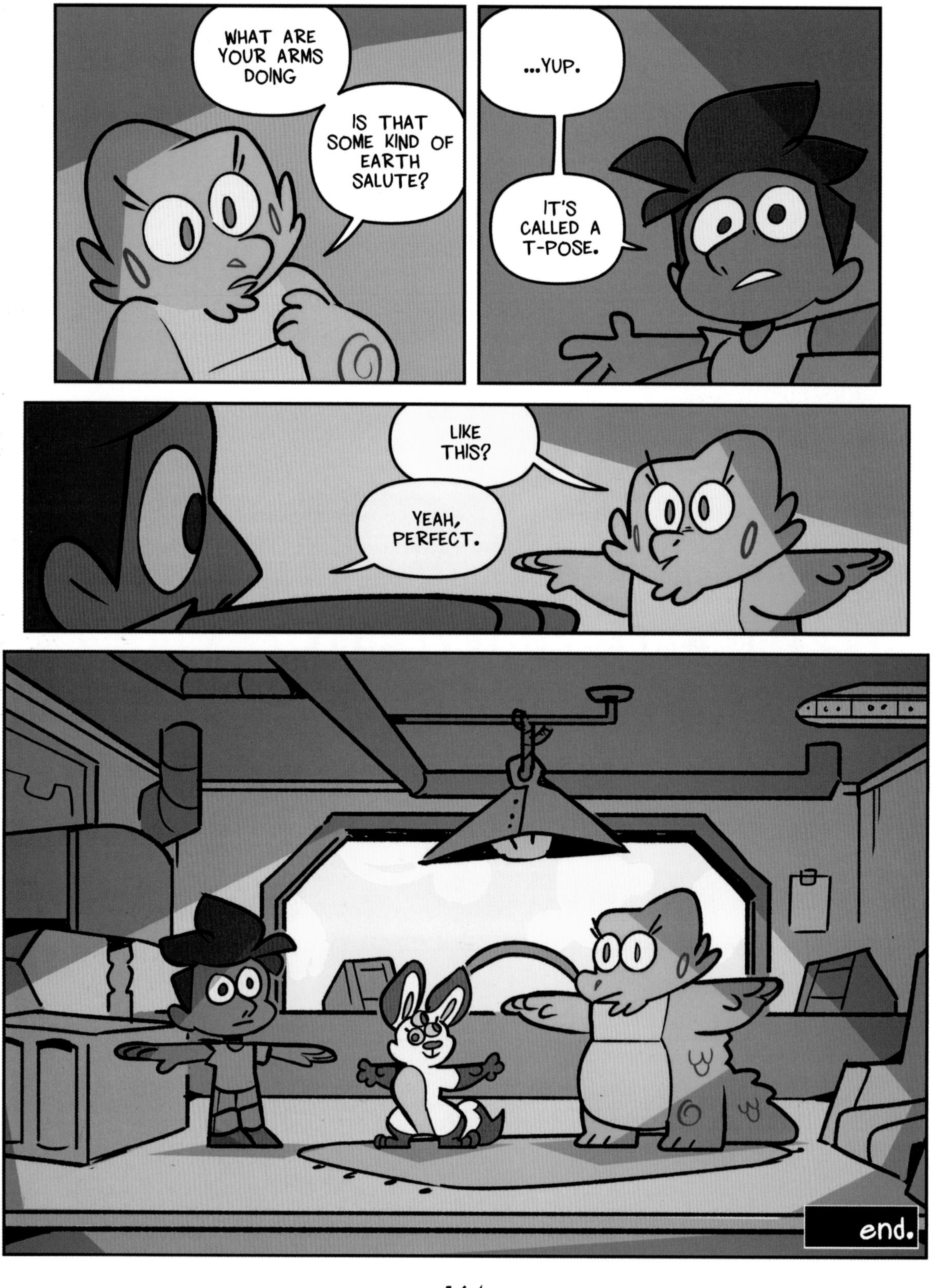
WHAT ARE YOUR ARMS DOING
IS THAT SOME KIND OF EARTH SALUTE?
...YUP.
IT'S CALLED A T-POSE.
LIKE THIS?
YEAH, PERFECT.
end.

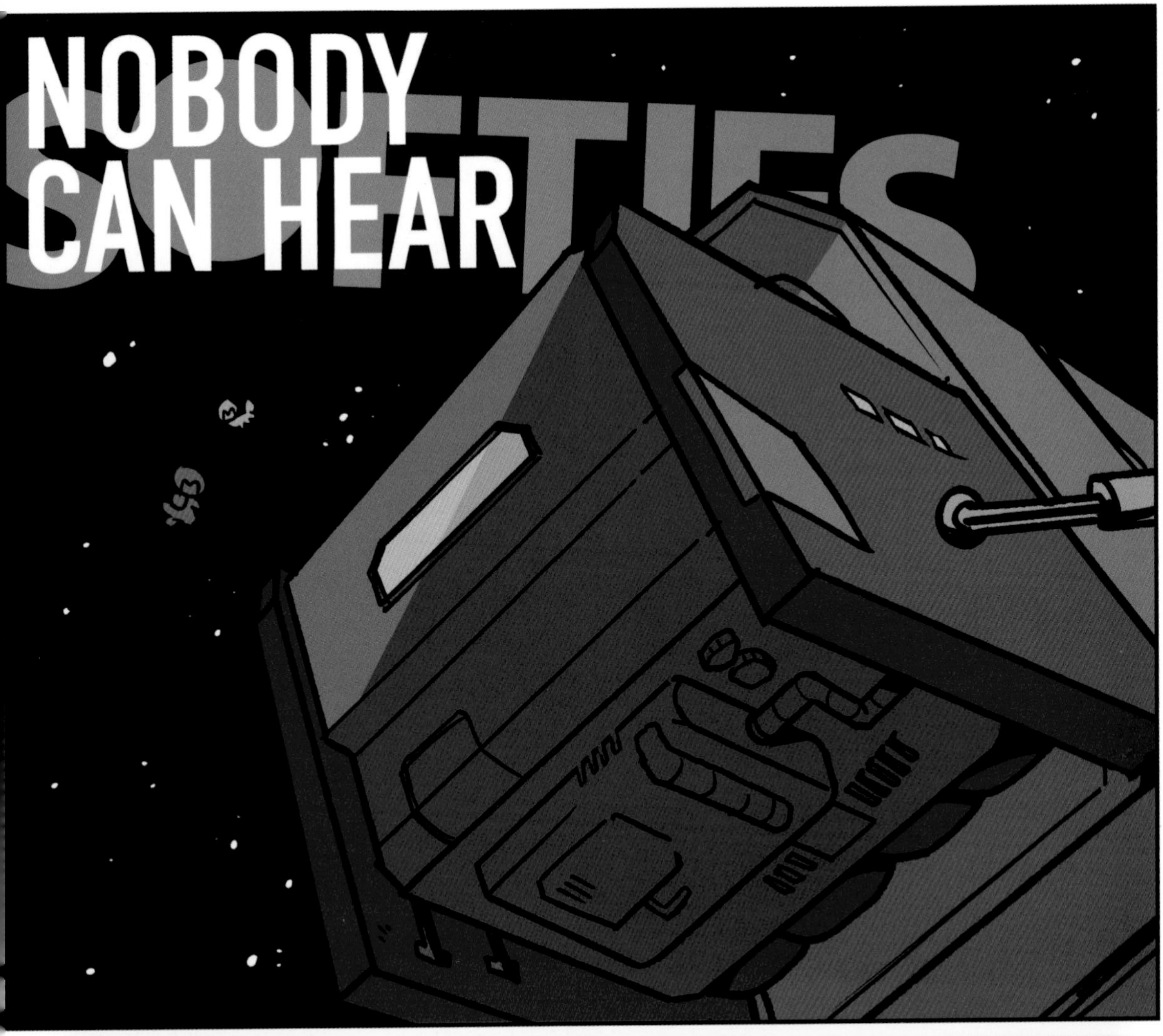
NOBODY
CAN HEAR

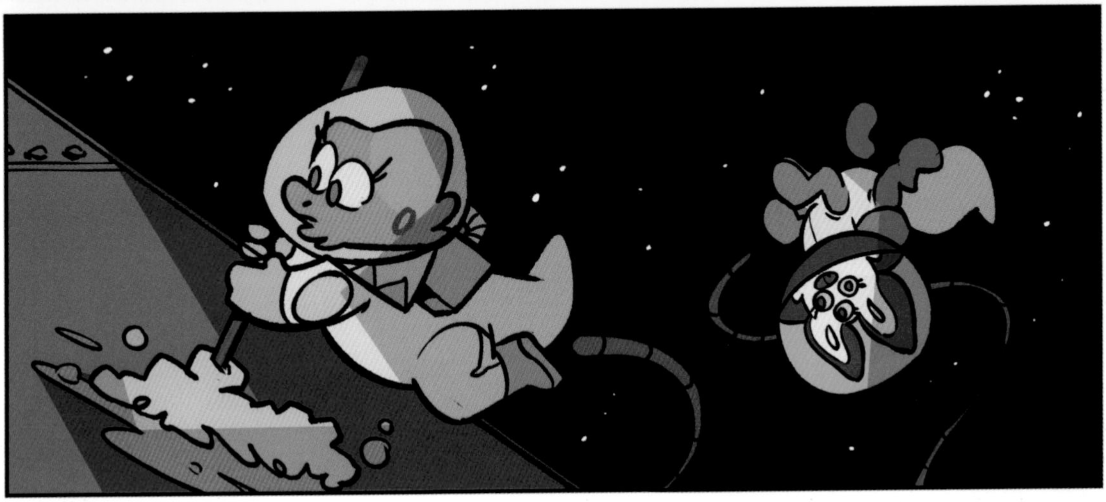

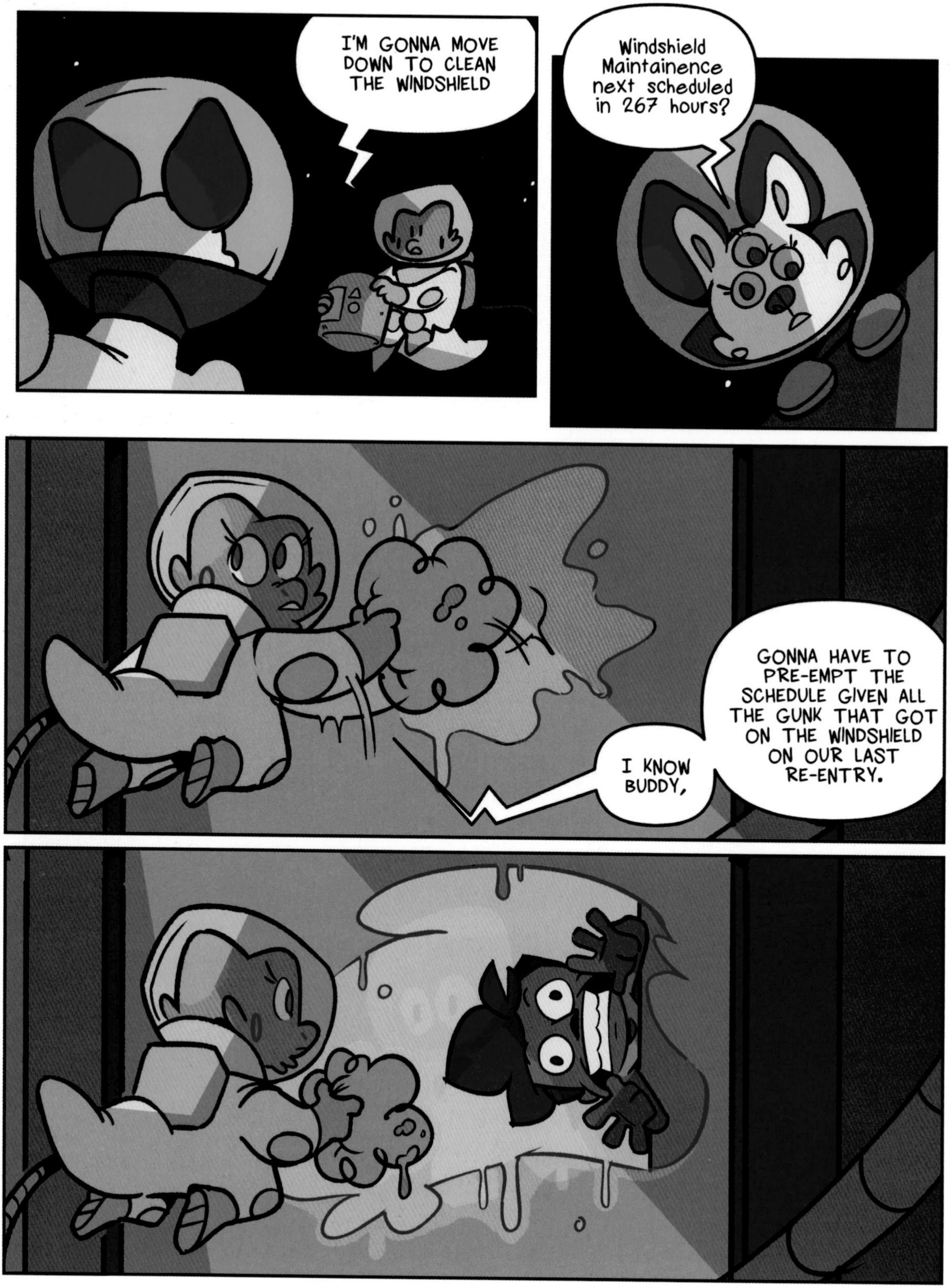

I'M GONNA MOVE DOWN TO CLEAN THE WINDSHIELD
Windshield Maintainence next scheduled in 267 hours?
I KNOW BUDDY,
GONNA HAVE TO PRE-EMPT THE SCHEDULE GIVEN ALL THE GUNK THAT GOT ON THE WINDSHIELD ON OUR LAST RE-ENTRY.

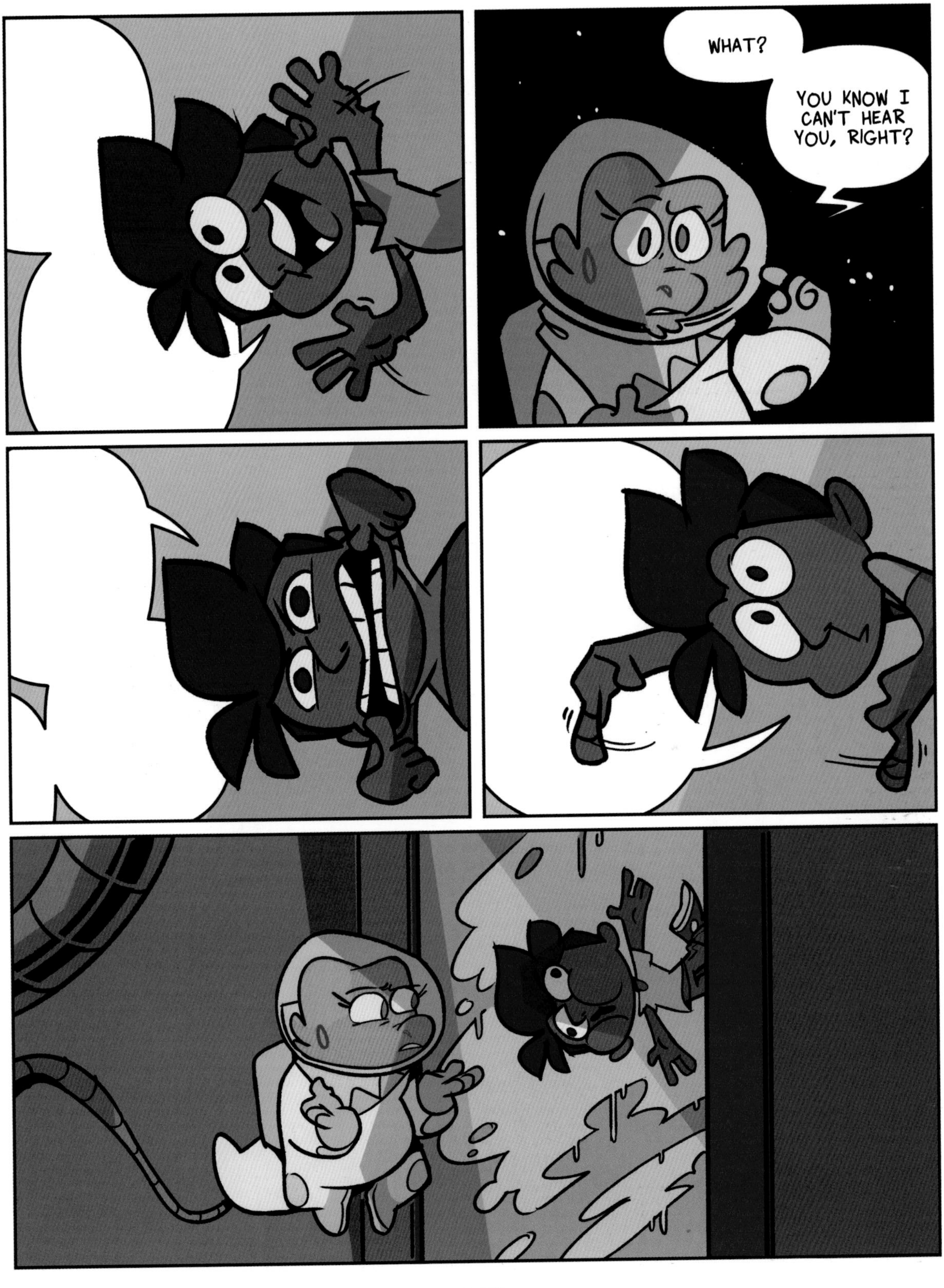
WHAT?
YOU KNOW I CAN'T HEAR YOU, RIGHT?

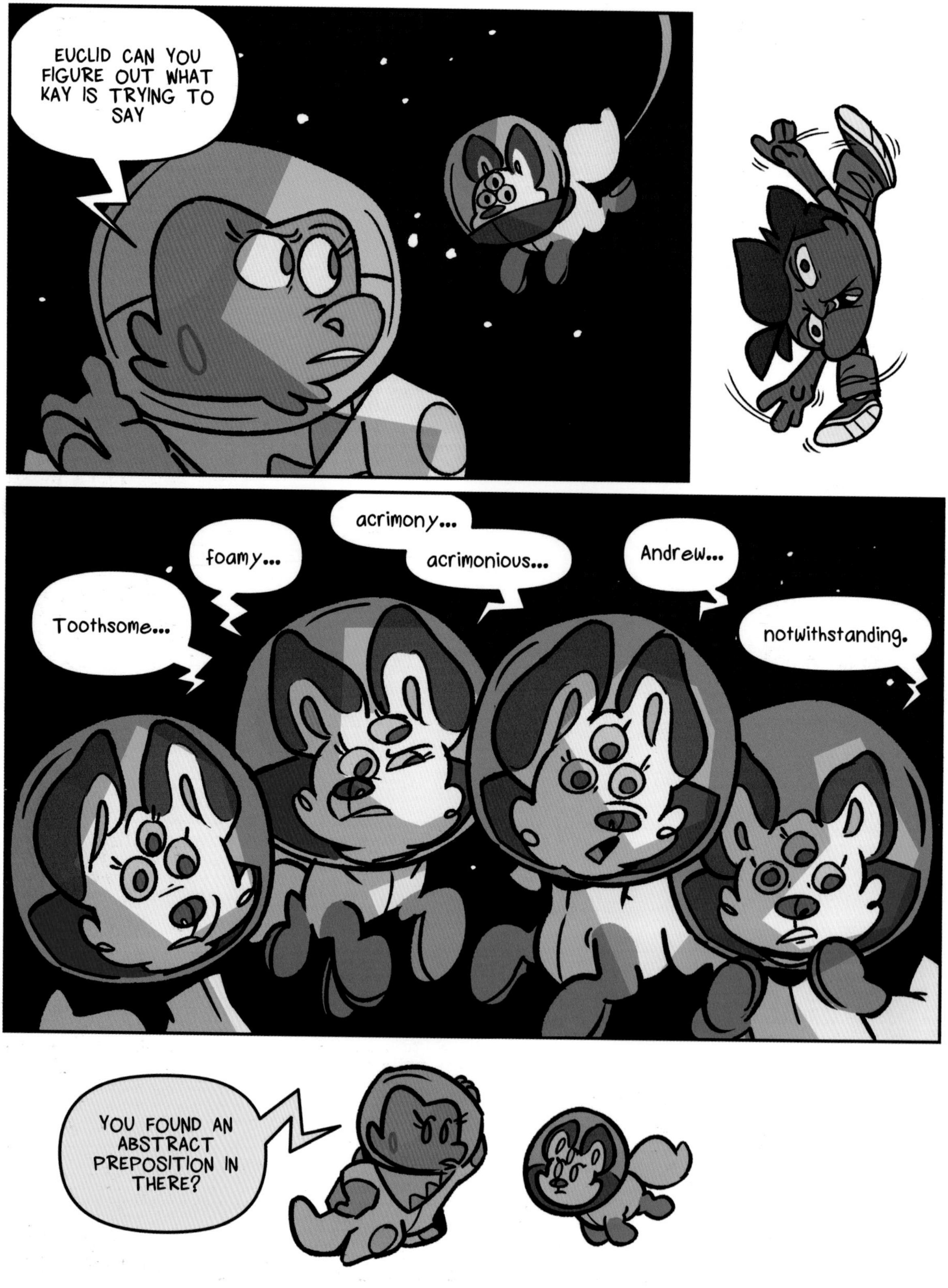
EUCLID CAN YOU FIGURE OUT WHAT KAY IS TRYING TO SAY
Toothsome...
foamy...
acrimony...
acrimonious...
Andrew...
notwithstanding.
YOU FOUND AN ABSTRACT PREPOSITION IN THERE?

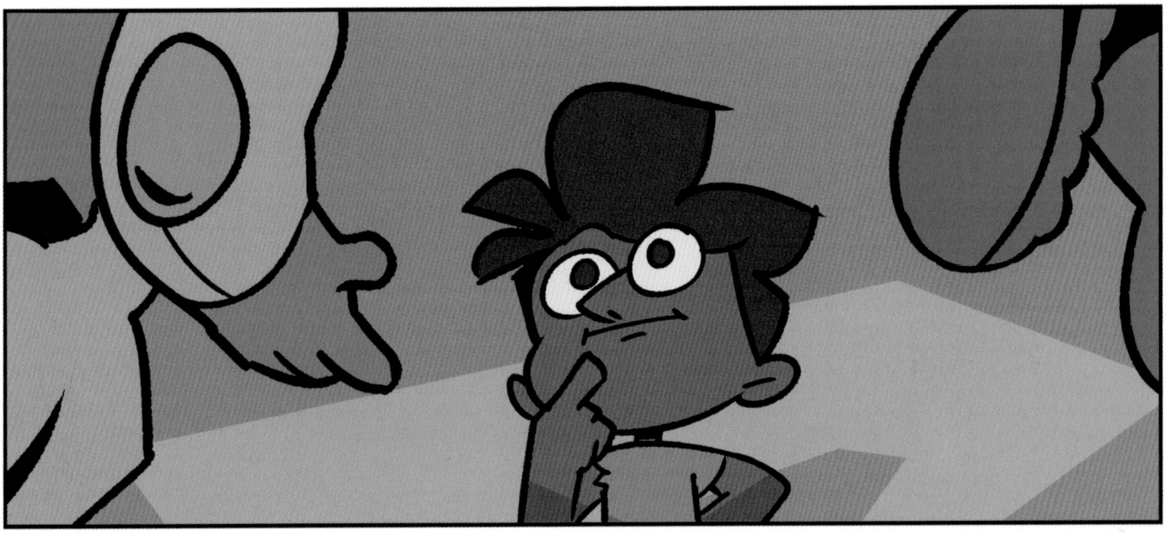

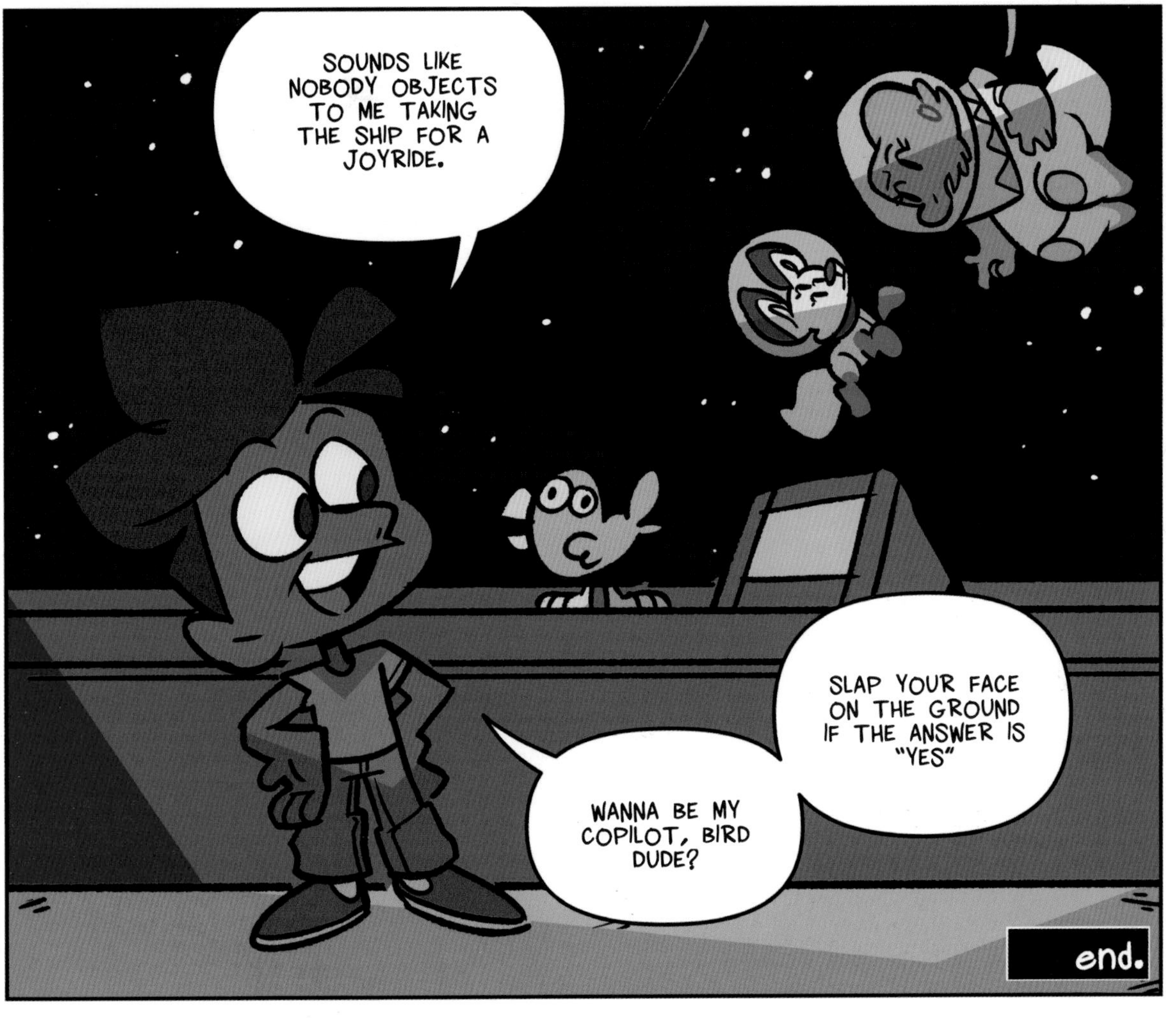
SOUNDS LIKE NOBODY OBJECTS TO ME TAKING THE SHIP FOR A JOYRIDE.
SLAP YOUR FACE ON THE GROUND IF THE ANSWER IS "YES"
WANNA BE MY COPILOT, BIRD DUDE?
end.

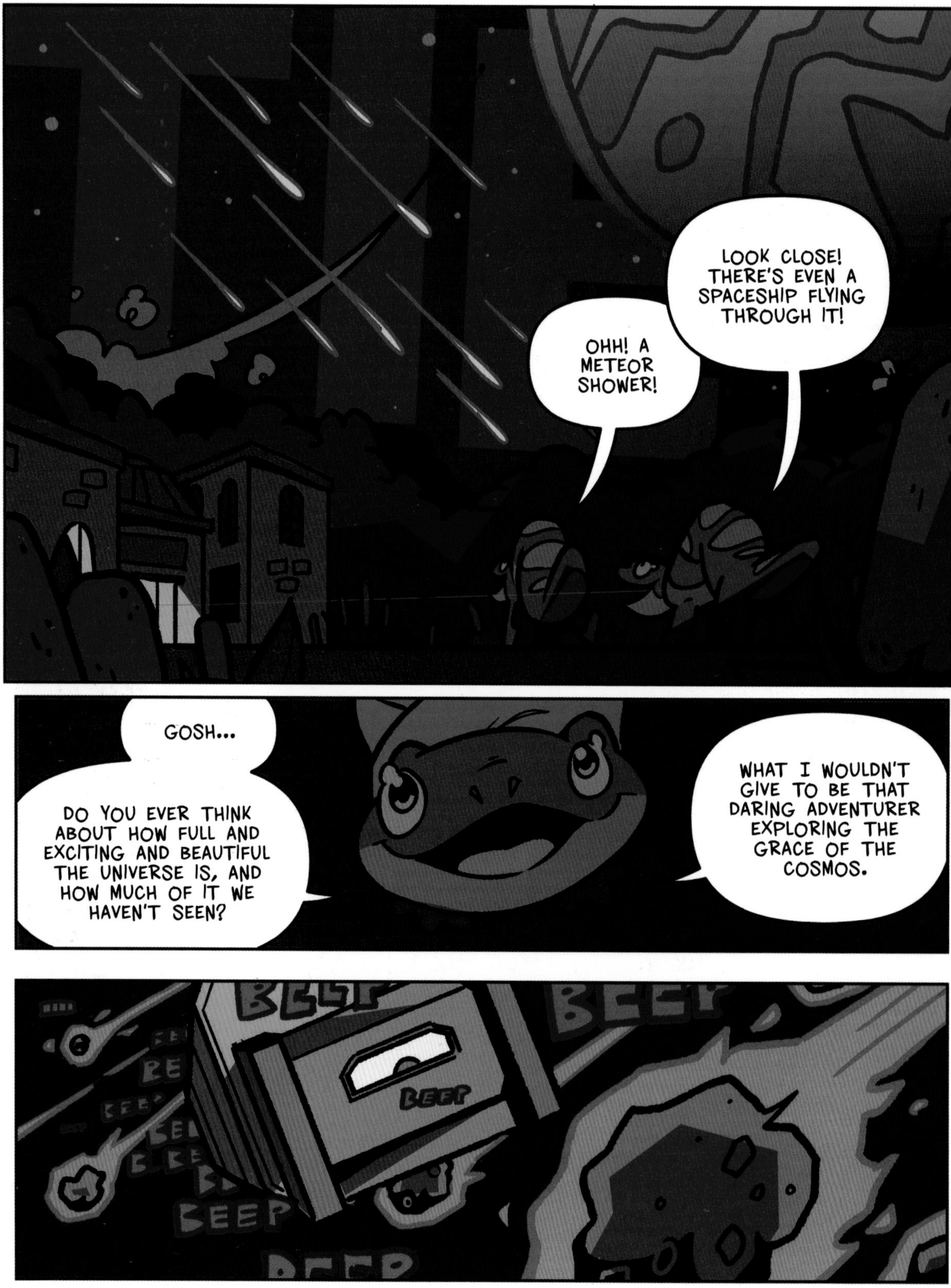
LOOK CLOSE! THERE'S EVEN A SPACESHIP FLYING THROUGH IT!
OHH! A METEOR SHOWER!
GOSH...
DO YOU EVER THINK ABOUT HOW FULL AND EXCITING AND BEAUTIFUL THE UNIVERSE IS, AND HOW MUCH OF IT WE HAVEN'T SEEN?
WHAT I WOULDN'T GIVE TO BE THAT DARING ADVENTURER EXPLORING THE GRACE OF THE COSMOS.
BEEP
BEEP
BEEP
BEEP

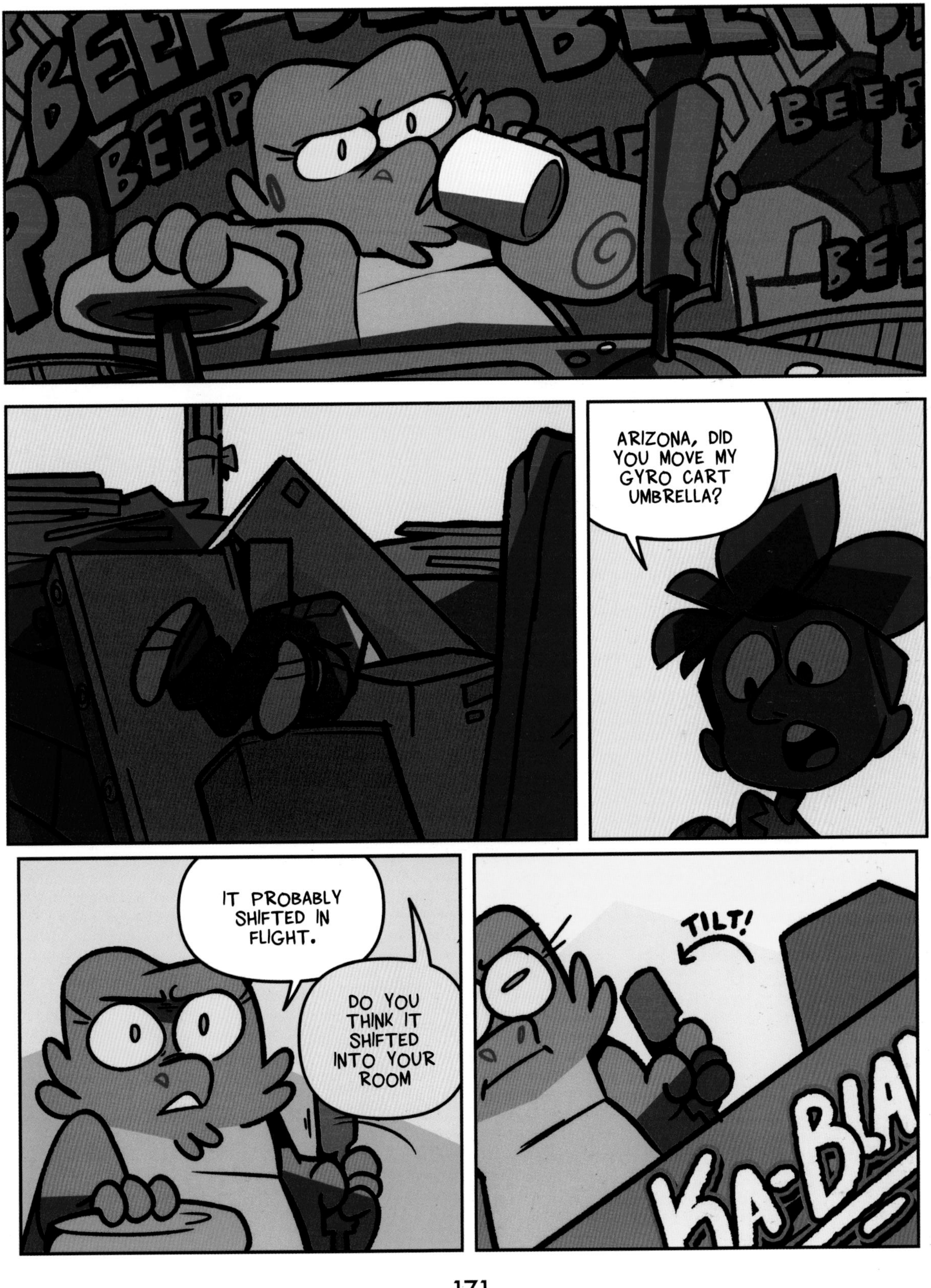
BEEP
BEEP
BEEP
BEEP
BEEP
ARIZONA, DID YOU MOVE MY GYRO CART UMBRELLA?
IT PROBABLY SHIFTED IN FLIGHT.
DO YOU THINK IT SHIFTED INTO YOUR ROOM
TILT!
KA-BLA

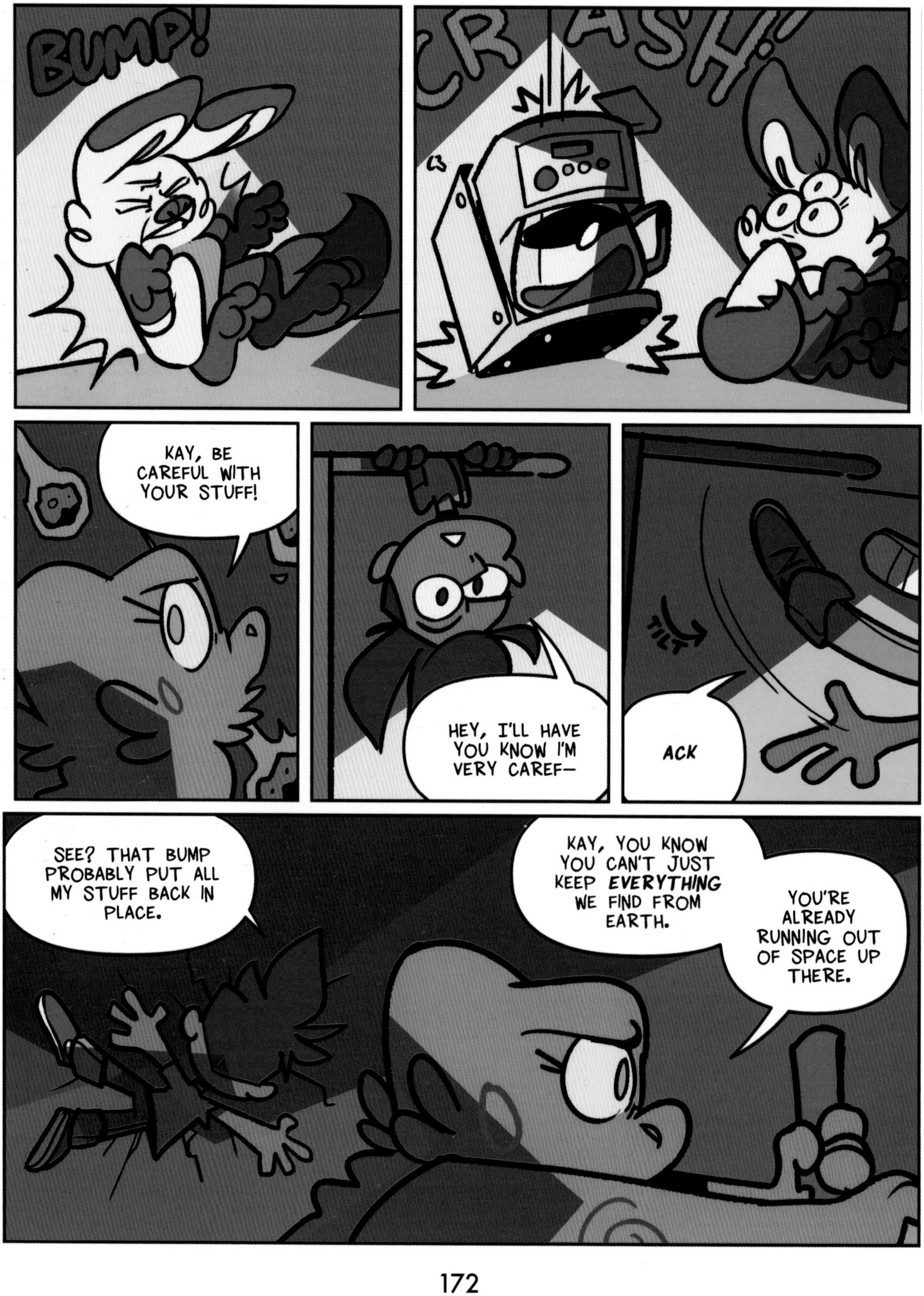
BUMP!
CRASH!!
KAY, BE CAREFUL WITH YOUR STUFF!
HEY, I'LL HAVE YOU KNOW I'M VERY CAREF—
TILT
ACK
SEE? THAT BUMP PROBABLY PUT ALL MY STUFF BACK IN PLACE.
KAY, YOU KNOW YOU CAN'T JUST KEEP EVERYTHING WE FIND FROM EARTH.
YOU'RE ALREADY RUNNING OUT OF SPACE UP THERE.

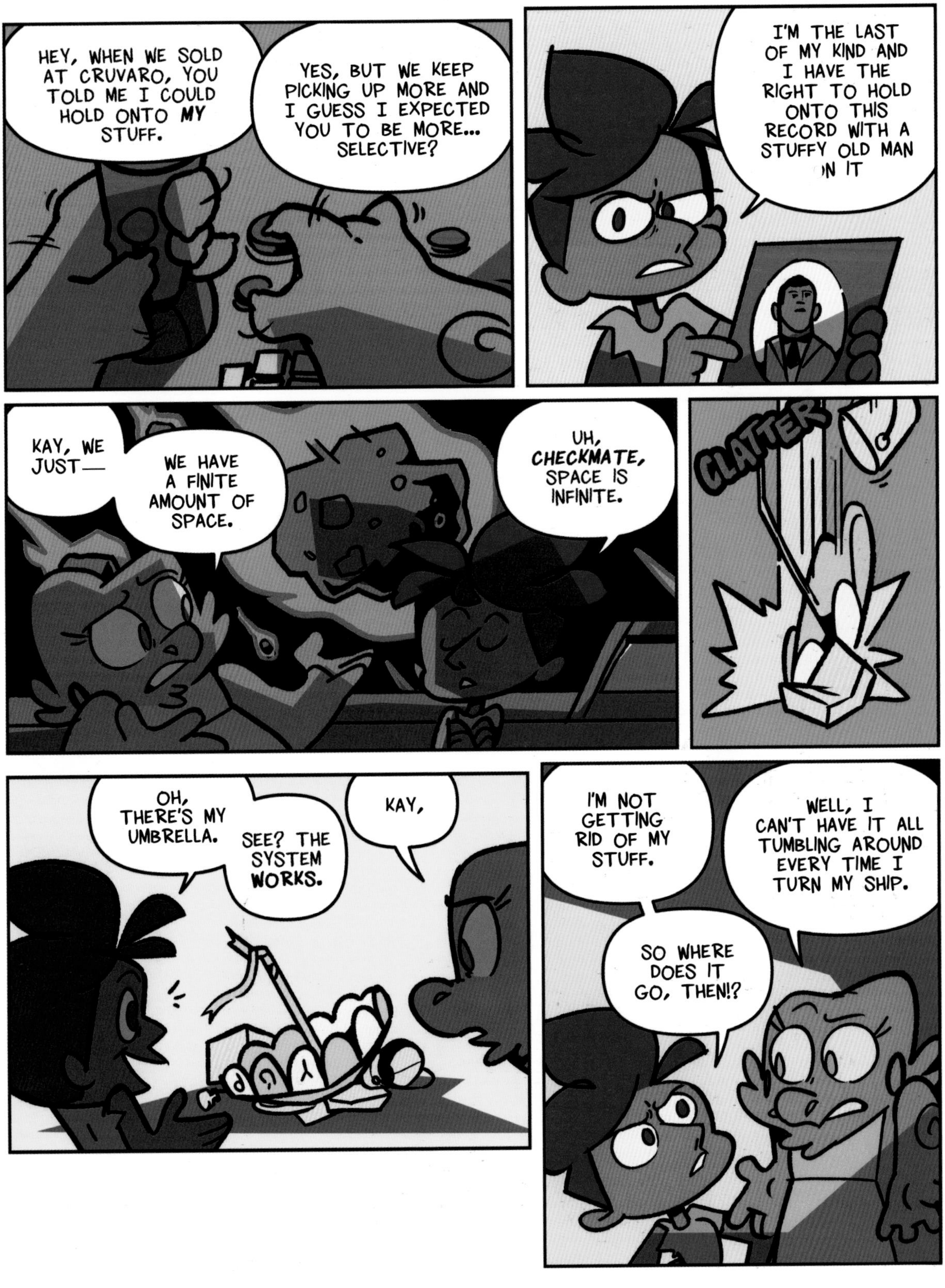
HEY, WHEN WE SOLD AT CRUVARO, YOU TOLD ME I COULD HOLD ONTO MY STUFF.
YES, BUT WE KEEP PICKING UP MORE AND I GUESS I EXPECTED YOU TO BE MORE... SELECTIVE?
I'M THE LAST OF MY KIND AND I HAVE THE RIGHT TO HOLD ONTO THIS RECORD WITH A STUFFY OLD MAN ON IT
KAY, WE JUST—
WE HAVE A FINITE AMOUNT OF SPACE.
UH, CHECKMATE, SPACE IS INFINITE.
CLATTER
OH, THERE'S MY UMBRELLA.
SEE? THE SYSTEM WORKS.
KAY,
I'M NOT GETTING RID OF MY STUFF.
WELL, I CAN'T HAVE IT ALL TUMBLING AROUND EVERY TIME I TURN MY SHIP.
SO WHERE DOES IT GO, THEN!?

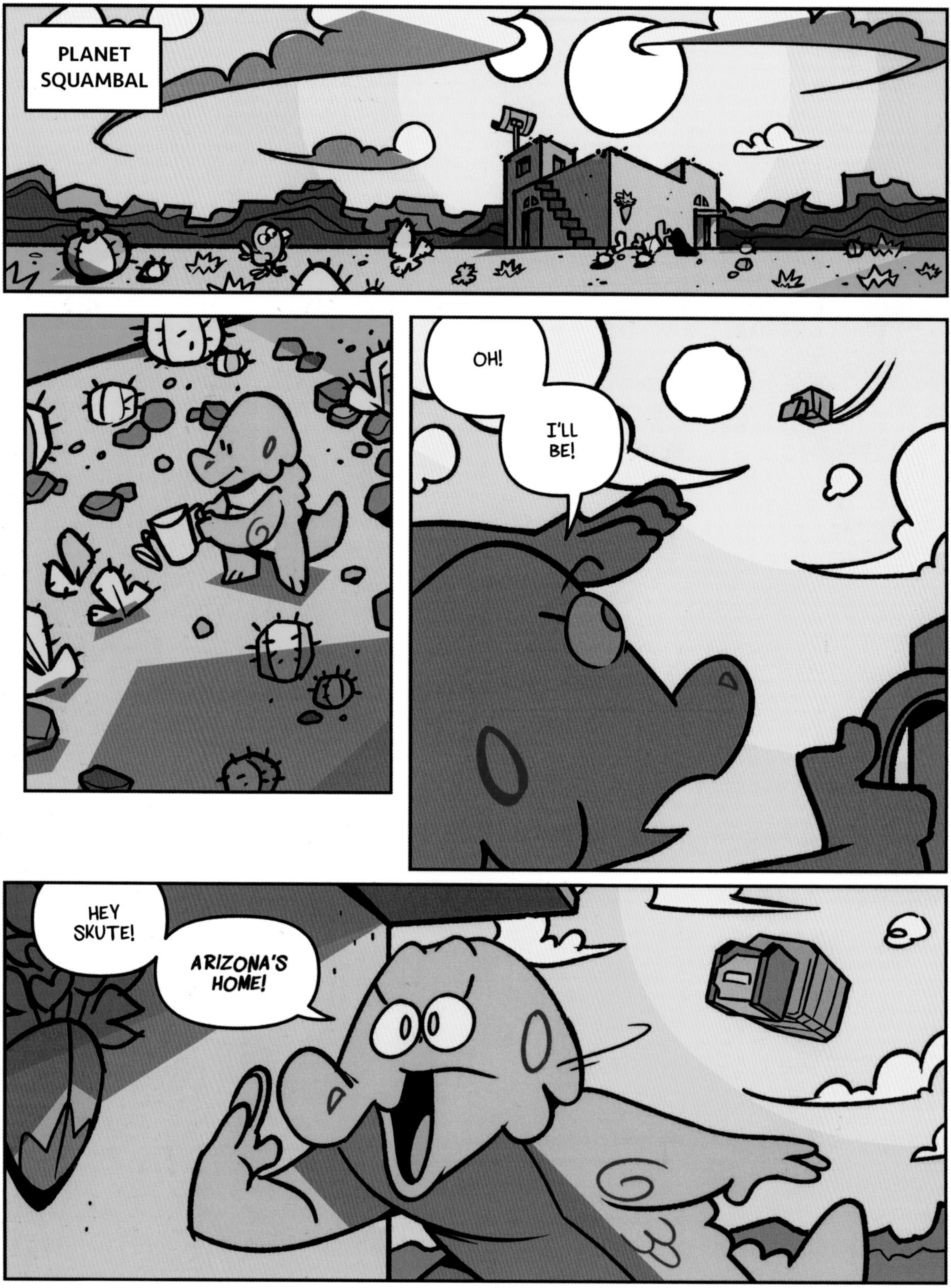
PLANET SQUAMBAL
OH!
I'LL BE!
HEY SKUTE!
ARIZONA'S HOME!

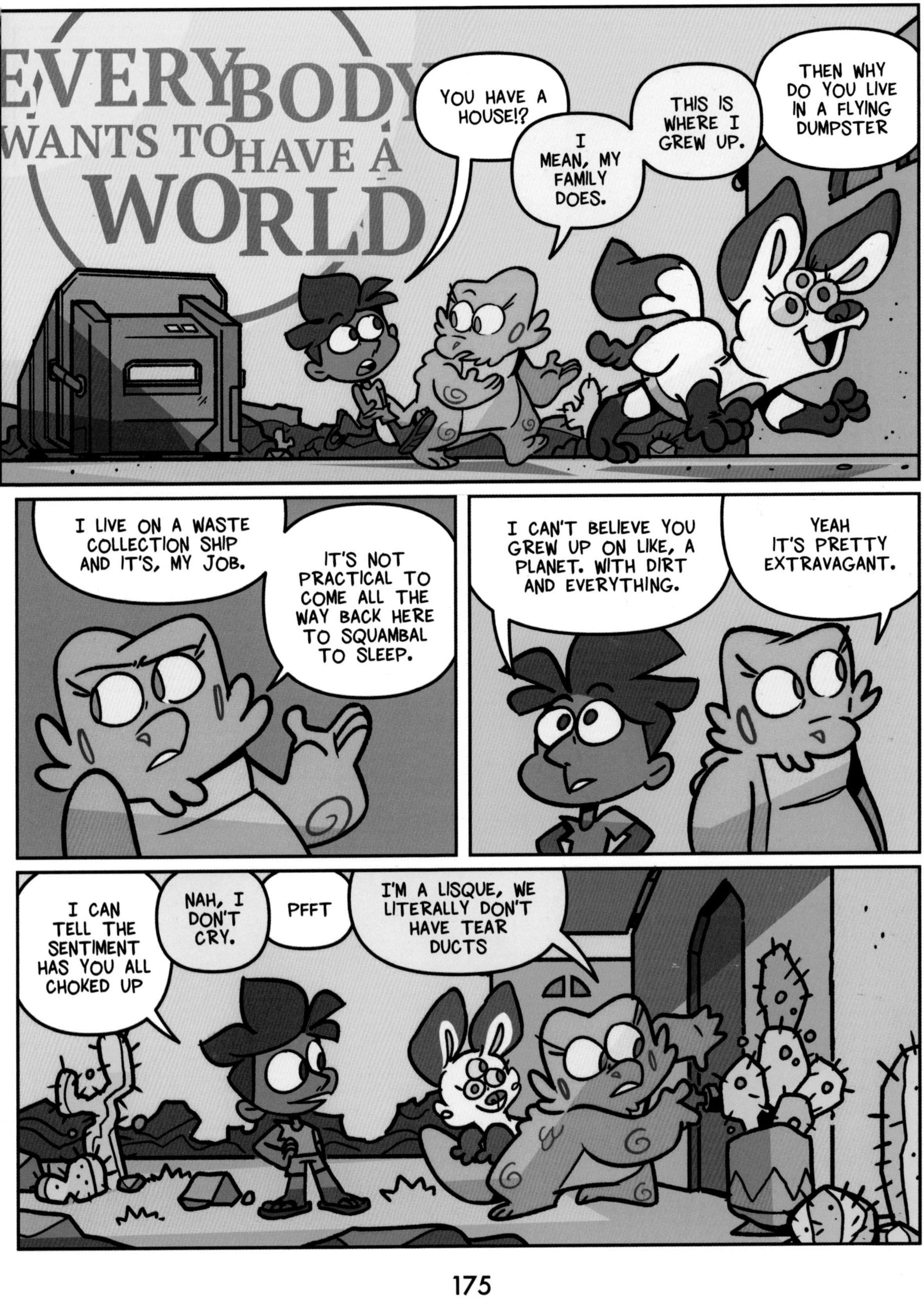
EVERYBODY WANTS TO HAVE A WORLD
YOU HAVE A HOUSE!?
I MEAN, MY FAMILY DOES.
THIS IS WHERE I GREW UP.
THEN WHY DO YOU LIVE IN A FLYING DUMPSTER
I LIVE ON A WASTE COLLECTION SHIP AND IT'S, MY JOB.
IT'S NOT PRACTICAL TO COME ALL THE WAY BACK HERE TO SQUAMBAL TO SLEEP.
I CAN'T BELIEVE YOU GREW UP ON LIKE, A PLANET. WITH DIRT AND EVERYTHING.
YEAH IT'S PRETTY EXTRAVAGANT.
I CAN TELL THE SENTIMENT HAS YOU ALL CHOKED UP
NAH, I DON'T CRY.
PFFT
I'M A LISQUE, WE LITERALLY DON'T HAVE TEAR DUCTS

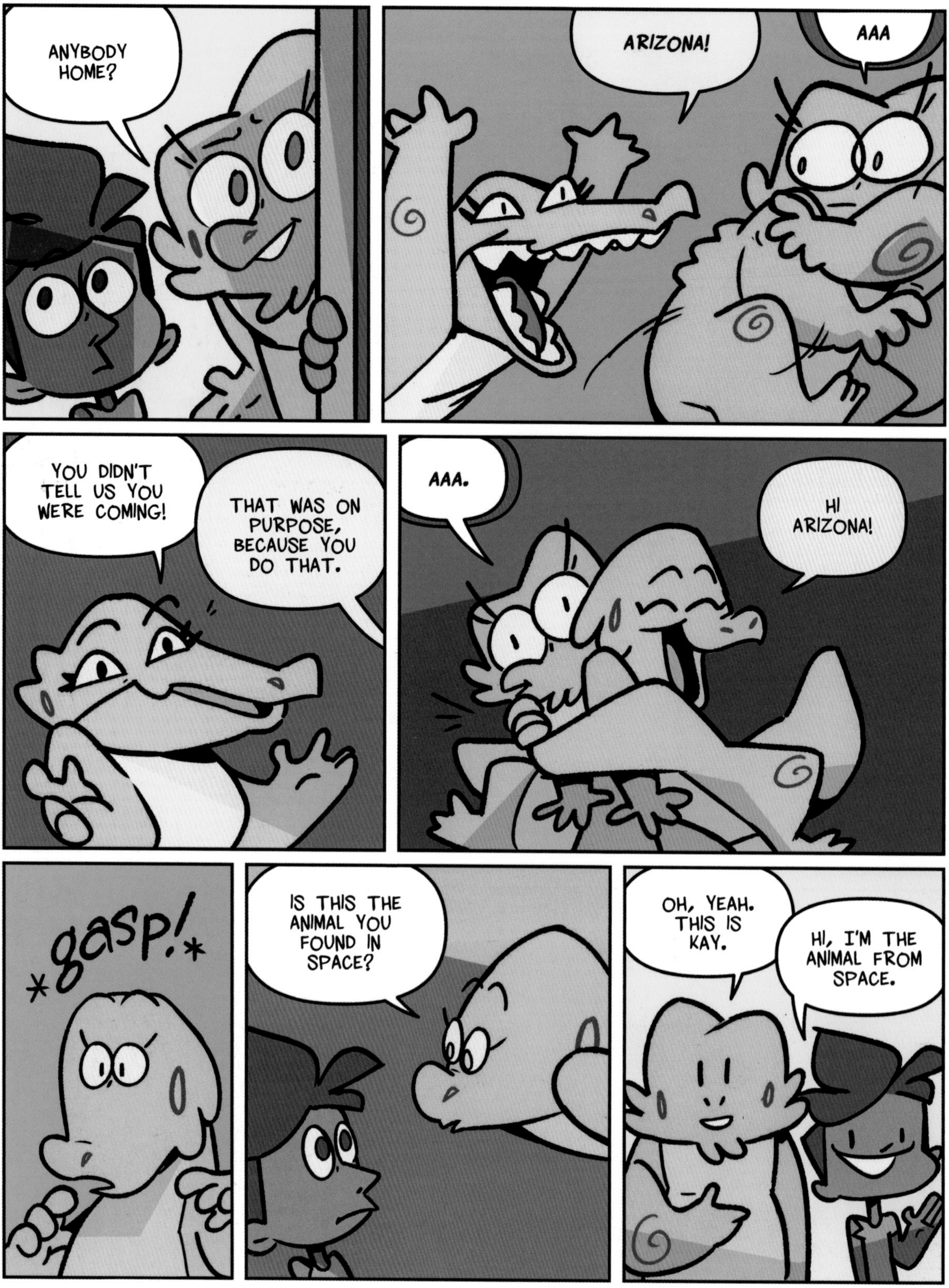
ANYBODY HOME?
ARIZONA!
AAA
YOU DIDN'T TELL US YOU WERE COMING!
THAT WAS ON PURPOSE, BECAUSE YOU DO THAT.
AAA.
HI ARIZONA!
gasp!
IS THIS THE ANIMAL YOU FOUND IN SPACE?
OH, YEAH. THIS IS KAY.
HI, I'M THE ANIMAL FROM SPACE.

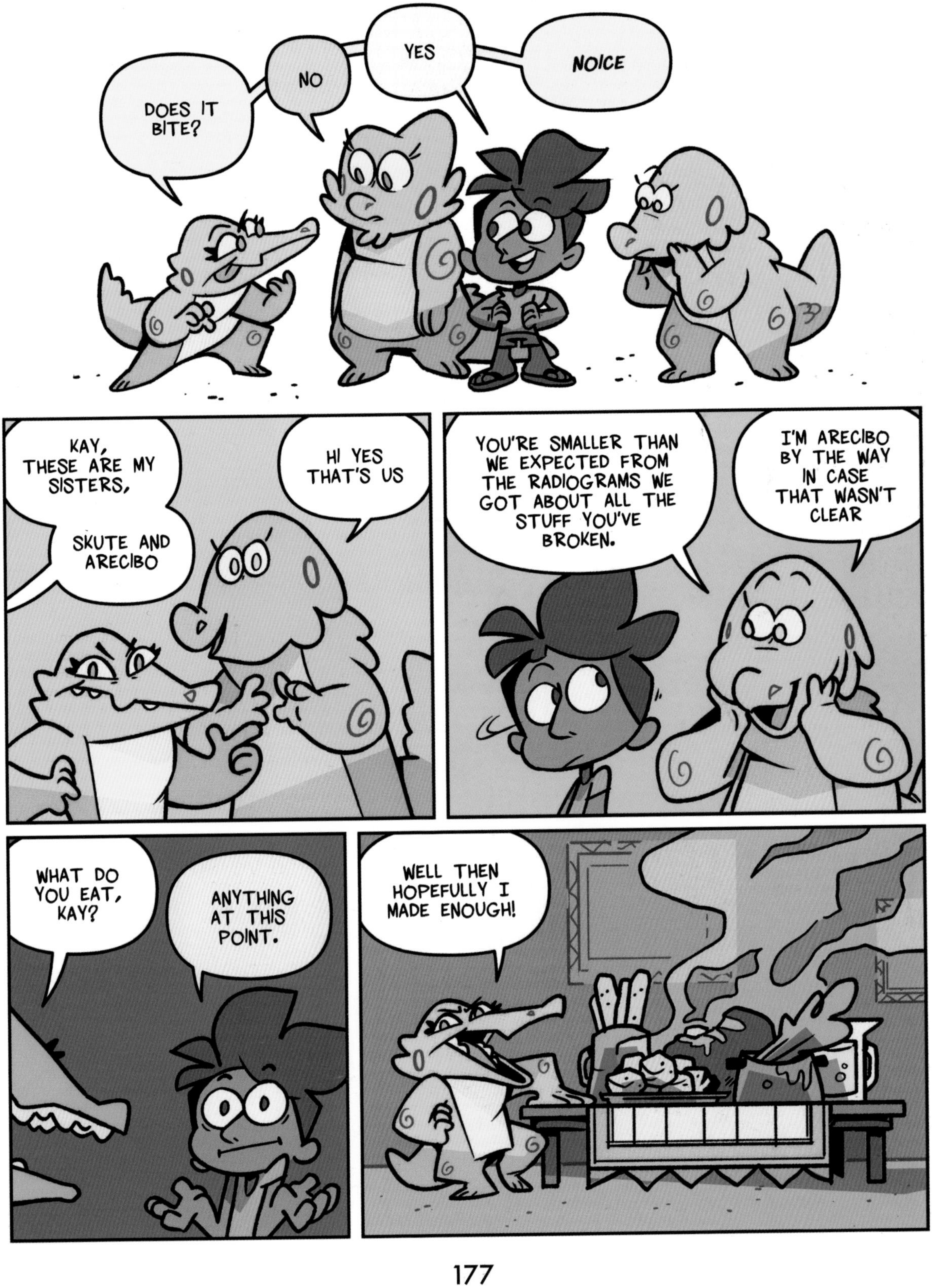
DOES IT BITE?
NO
YES
NOICE
KAY, THESE ARE MY SISTERS,
SKUTE AND ARECIBO
HI YES THAT'S US
YOU'RE SMALLER THAN WE EXPECTED FROM THE RADIOGRAMS WE GOT ABOUT ALL THE STUFF YOU'VE BROKEN.
I'M ARECIBO BY THE WAY IN CASE THAT WASN'T CLEAR
WHAT DO YOU EAT, KAY?
ANYTHING AT THIS POINT.
WELL THEN HOPEFULLY I MADE ENOUGH!

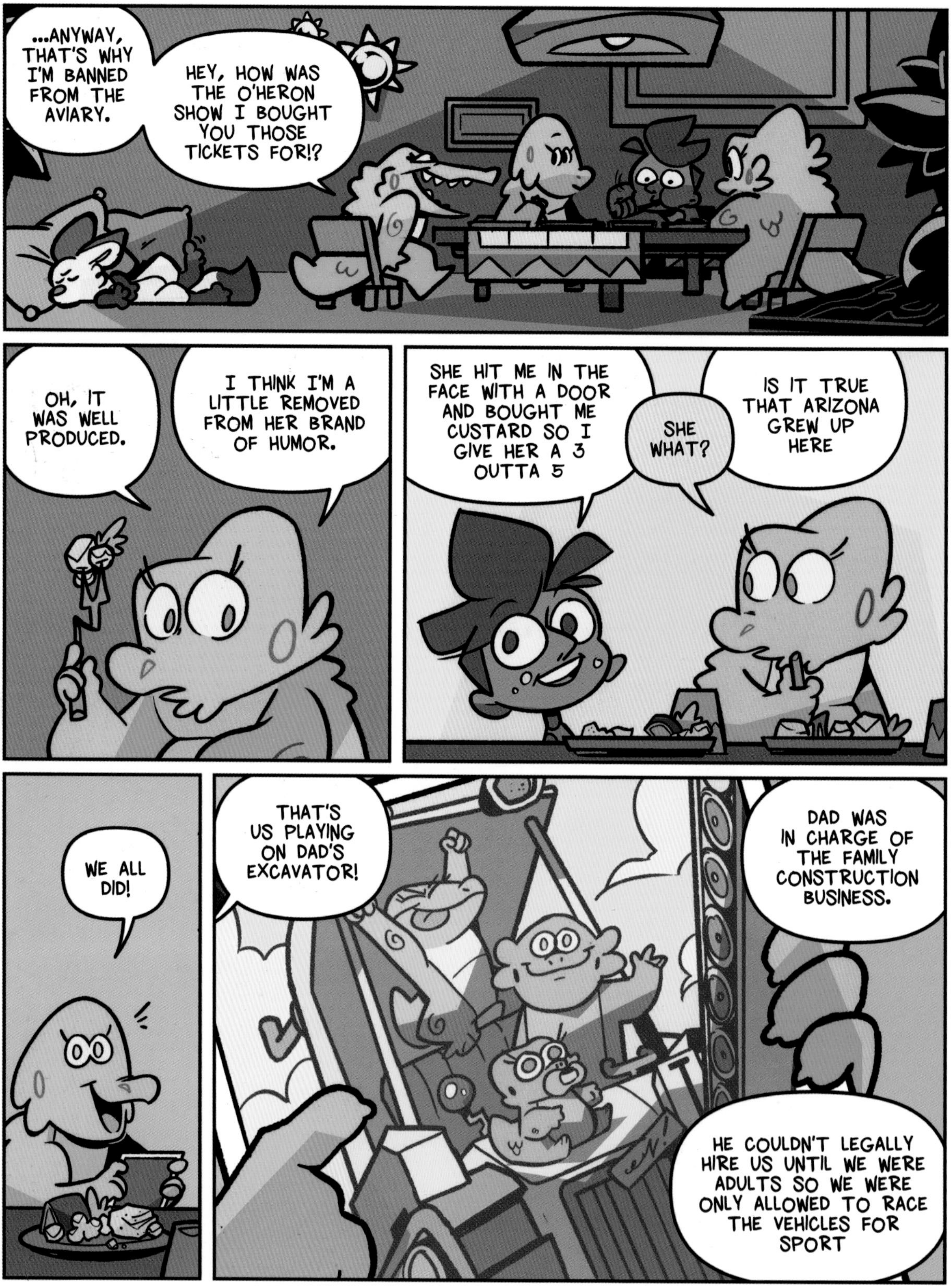
...ANYWAY, THAT'S WHY I'M BANNED FROM THE AVIARY.
HEY, HOW WAS THE O'HERON SHOW I BOUGHT YOU THOSE TICKETS FOR!?
OH, IT WAS WELL PRODUCED.
I THINK I'M A LITTLE REMOVED FROM HER BRAND OF HUMOR.
SHE HIT ME IN THE FACE WITH A DOOR AND BOUGHT ME CUSTARD SO I GIVE HER A 3 OUTTA 5
SHE WHAT?
IS IT TRUE THAT ARIZONA GREW UP HERE
WE ALL DID!
THAT'S US PLAYING ON DAD'S EXCAVATOR!
DAD WAS IN CHARGE OF THE FAMILY CONSTRUCTION BUSINESS.
HE COULDN'T LEGALLY HIRE US UNTIL WE WERE ADULTS SO WE WERE ONLY ALLOWED TO RACE THE VEHICLES FOR SPORT

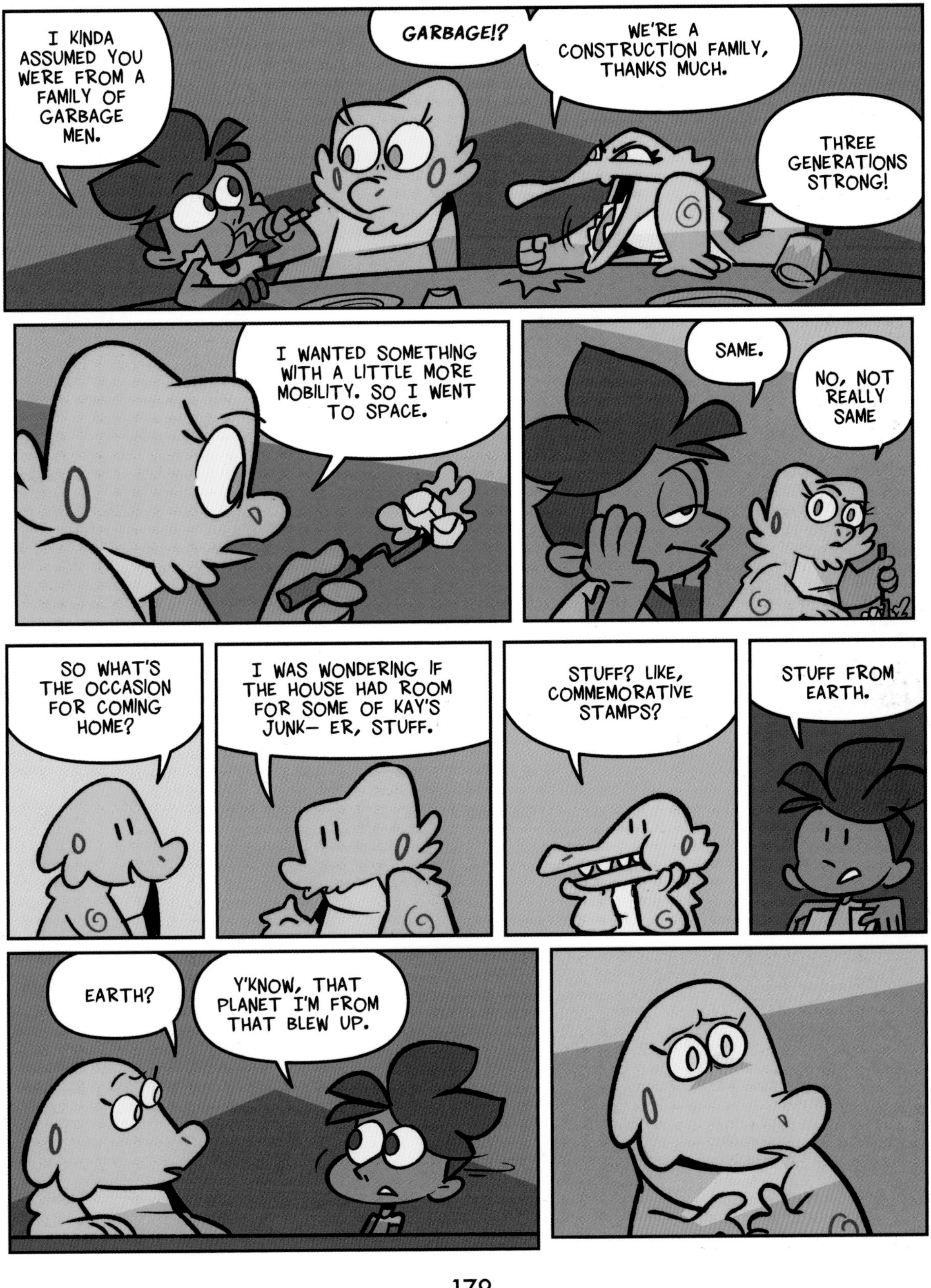
I KINDA ASSUMED YOU WERE FROM A FAMILY OF GARBAGE MEN.
GARBAGE!?
WE'RE A CONSTRUCTION FAMILY, THANKS MUCH.
THREE GENERATIONS STRONG!
I WANTED SOMETHING WITH A LITTLE MORE MOBILITY. SO I WENT TO SPACE.
SAME.
NO, NOT REALLY SAME
SO WHAT'S THE OCCASION FOR COMING HOME?
I WAS WONDERING IF THE HOUSE HAD ROOM FOR SOME OF KAY'S JUNK— ER, STUFF.
STUFF? LIKE, COMMEMORATIVE STAMPS?
STUFF FROM EARTH.
EARTH?
Y'KNOW, THAT PLANET I'M FROM THAT BLEW UP.

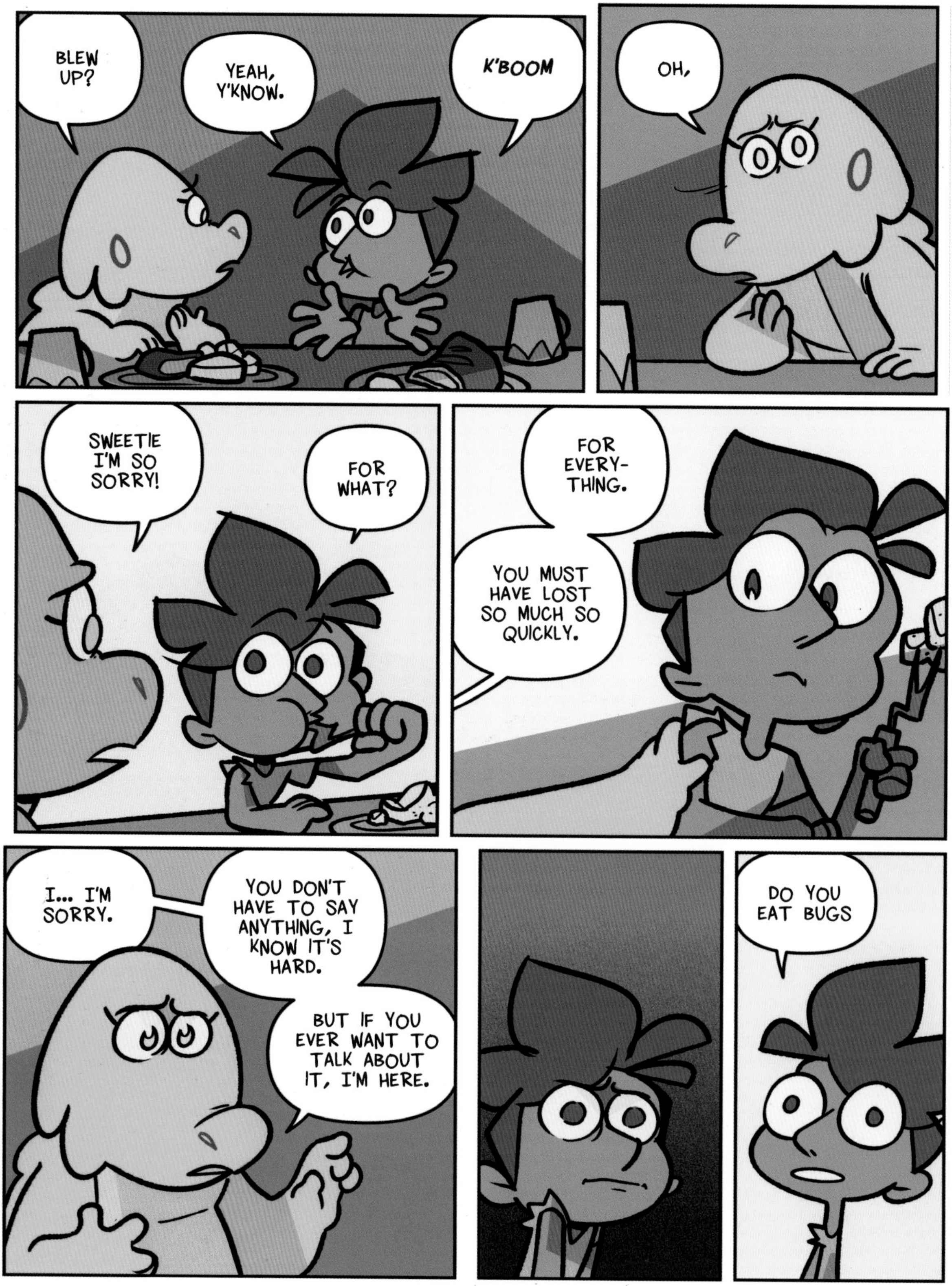
BLEW UP?
YEAH, Y'KNOW.
K'BOOM
OH,
SWEETIE I'M SO SORRY!
FOR WHAT?
FOR EVERY-THING.
YOU MUST HAVE LOST SO MUCH SO QUICKLY.
I... I'M SORRY.
YOU DON'T HAVE TO SAY ANYTHING, I KNOW IT'S HARD.
BUT IF YOU EVER WANT TO TALK ABOUT IT, I'M HERE.
DO YOU EAT BUGS

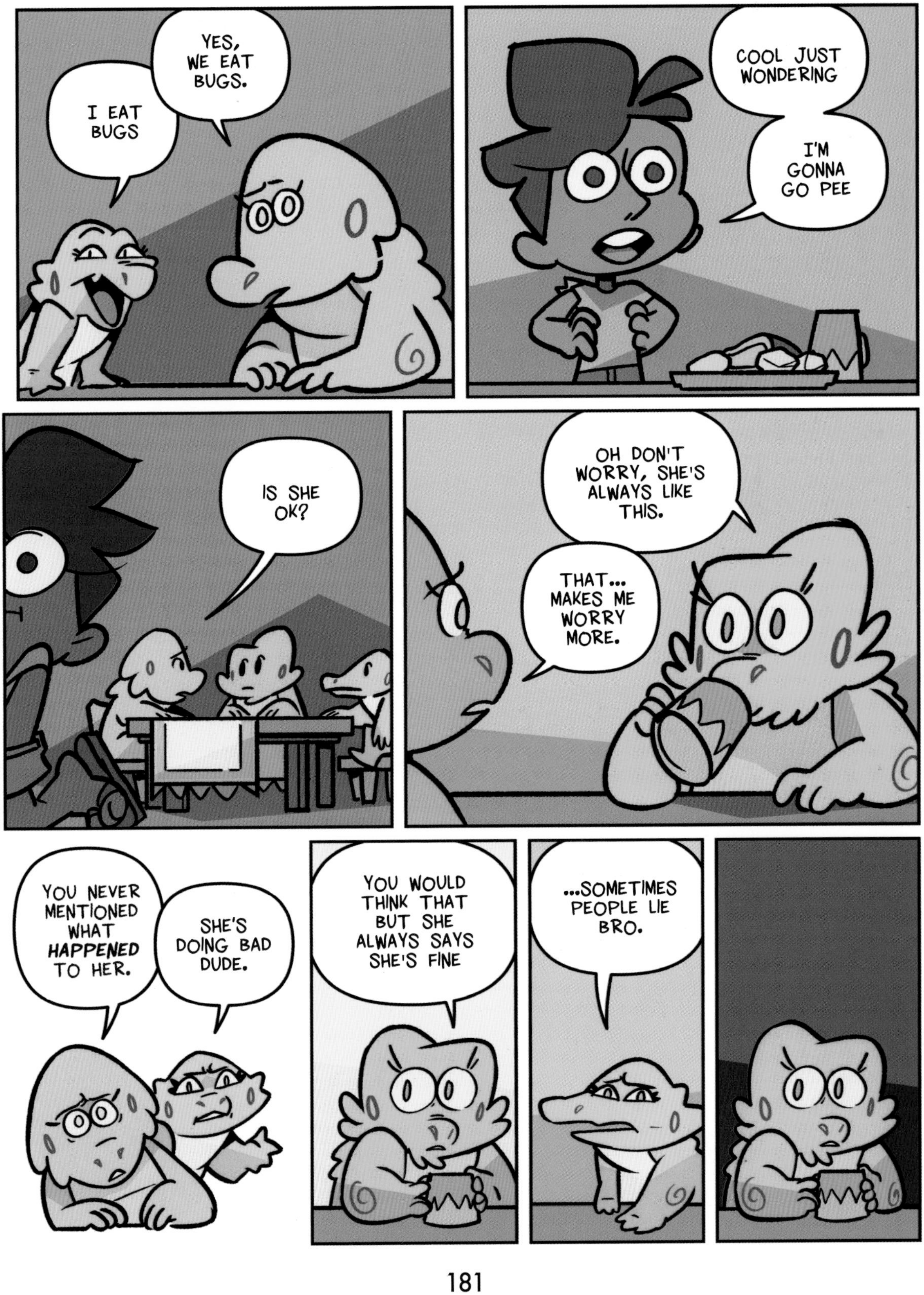
I EAT BUGS
YES, WE EAT BUGS.
COOL JUST WONDERING
I'M GONNA GO PEE
IS SHE OK?
OH DON'T WORRY, SHE'S ALWAYS LIKE THIS.
THAT... MAKES ME WORRY MORE.
YOU NEVER MENTIONED WHAT **HAPPENED** TO HER.
SHE'S DOING BAD DUDE.
YOU WOULD THINK THAT BUT SHE ALWAYS SAYS SHE'S FINE
...SOMETIMES PEOPLE LIE BRO.

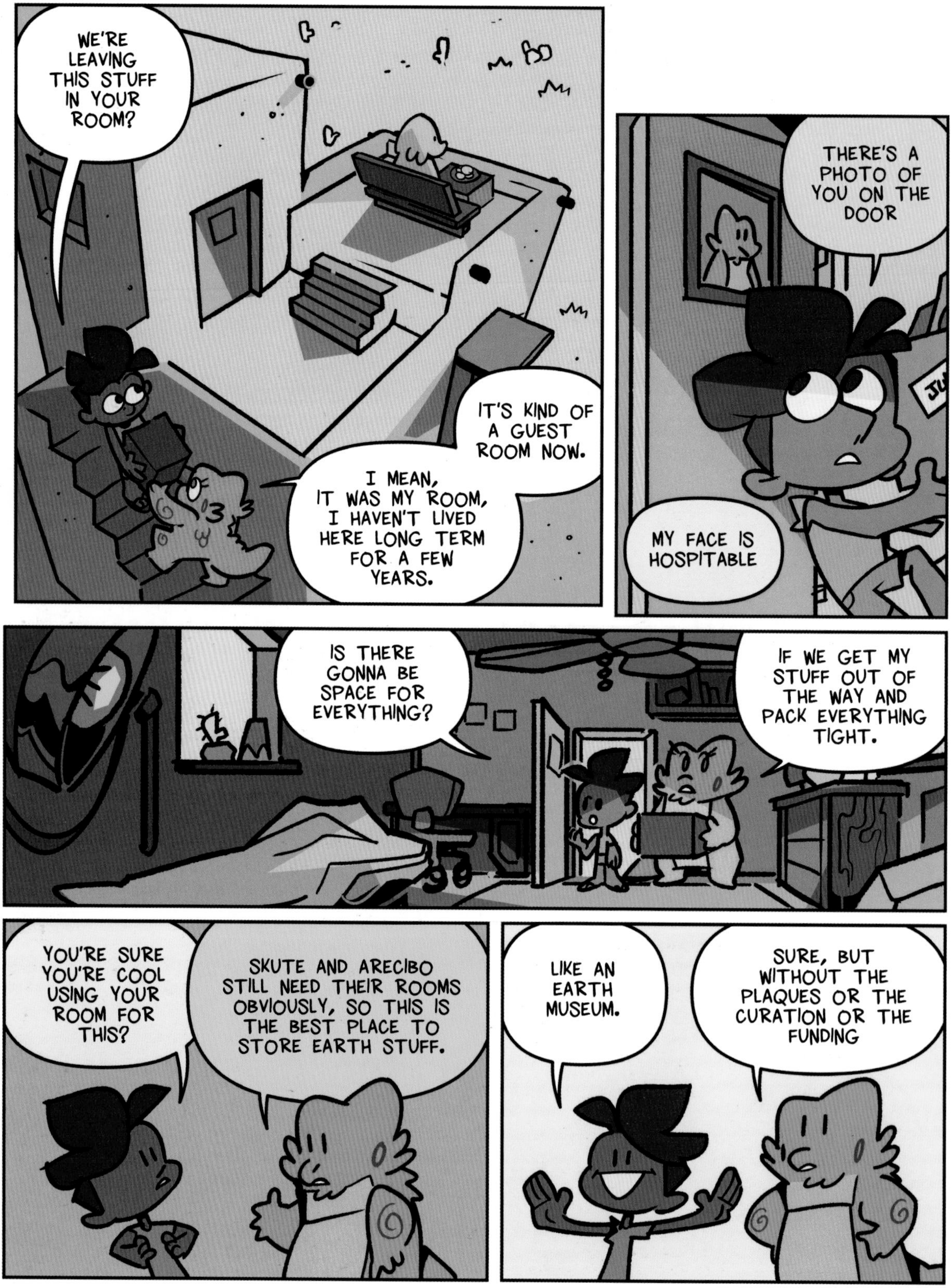
WE'RE LEAVING THIS STUFF IN YOUR ROOM?
IT'S KIND OF A GUEST ROOM NOW.
I MEAN, IT WAS MY ROOM, I HAVEN'T LIVED HERE LONG TERM FOR A FEW YEARS.
THERE'S A PHOTO OF YOU ON THE DOOR
MY FACE IS HOSPITABLE
IS THERE GONNA BE SPACE FOR EVERYTHING?
IF WE GET MY STUFF OUT OF THE WAY AND PACK EVERYTHING TIGHT.
YOU'RE SURE YOU'RE COOL USING YOUR ROOM FOR THIS?
SKUTE AND ARECIBO STILL NEED THEIR ROOMS OBVIOUSLY, SO THIS IS THE BEST PLACE TO STORE EARTH STUFF.
LIKE AN EARTH MUSEUM.
SURE, BUT WITHOUT THE PLAQUES OR THE CURATION OR THE FUNDING

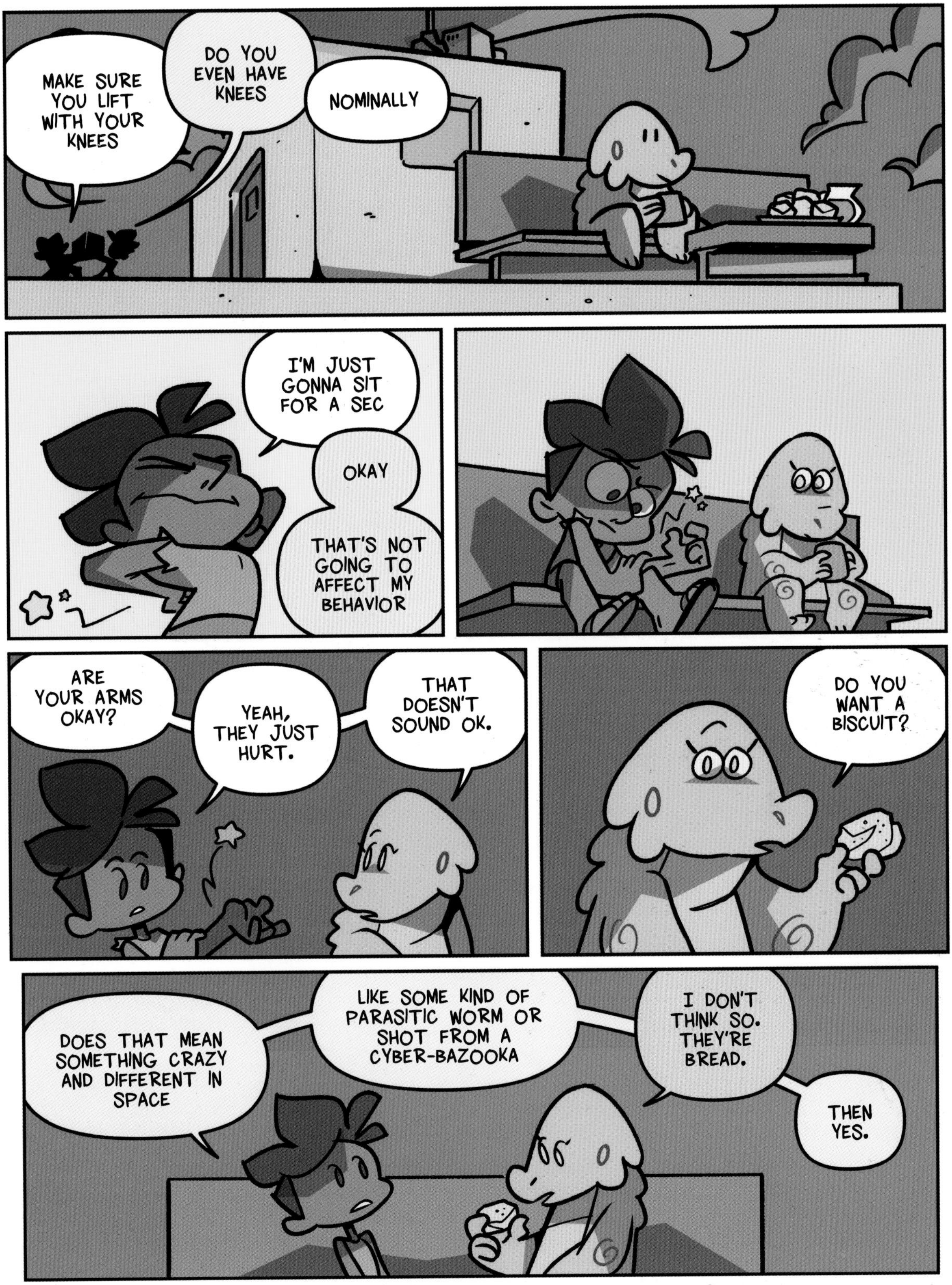
MAKE SURE YOU LIFT WITH YOUR KNEES
DO YOU EVEN HAVE KNEES
NOMINALLY
I'M JUST GONNA SIT FOR A SEC
OKAY
THAT'S NOT GOING TO AFFECT MY BEHAVIOR
ARE YOUR ARMS OKAY?
YEAH, THEY JUST HURT.
THAT DOESN'T SOUND OK.
DO YOU WANT A BISCUIT?
DOES THAT MEAN SOMETHING CRAZY AND DIFFERENT IN SPACE
LIKE SOME KIND OF PARASITIC WORM OR SHOT FROM A CYBER-BAZOOKA
I DON'T THINK SO. THEY'RE BREAD.
THEN YES.

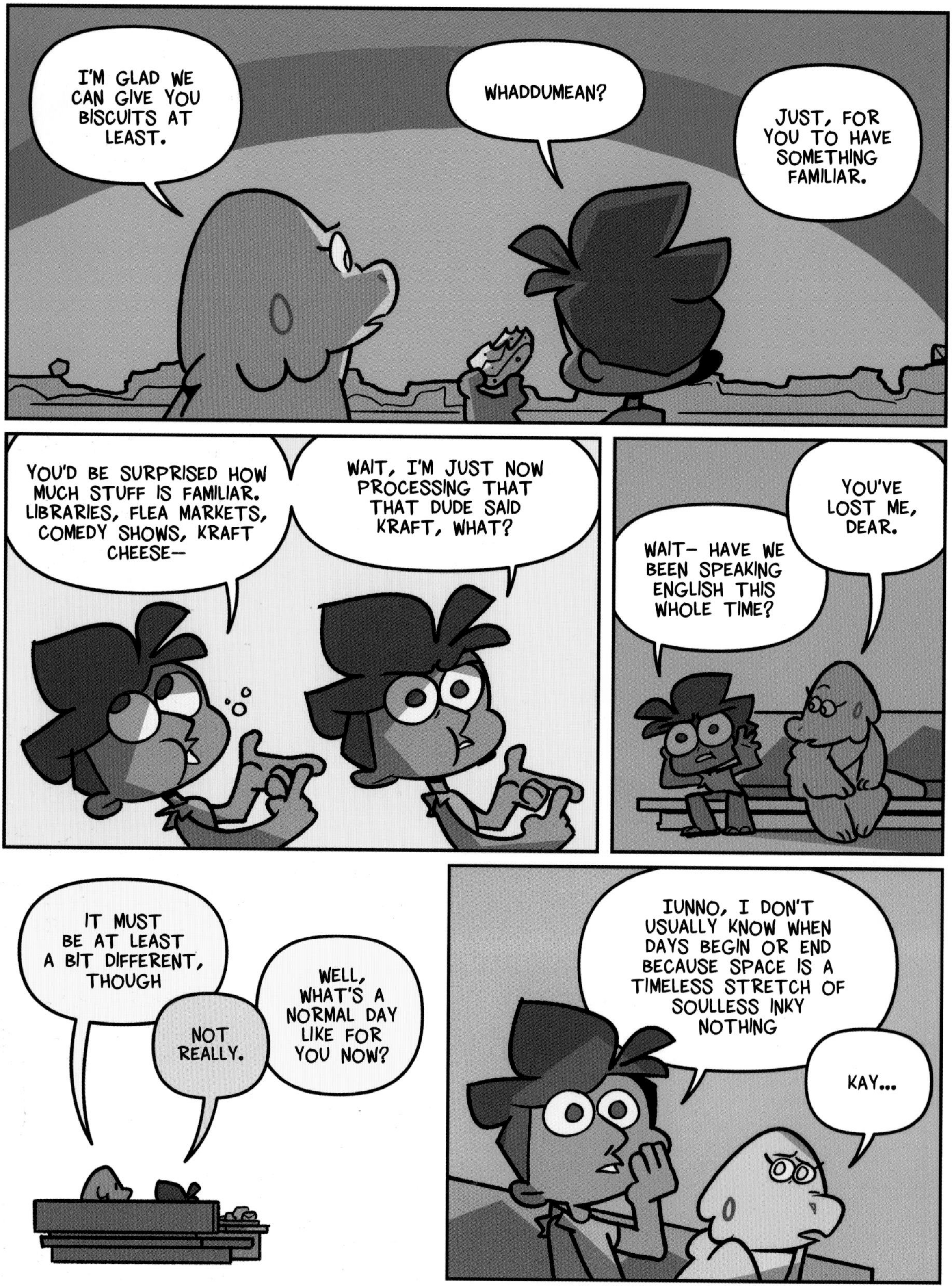
I'M GLAD WE CAN GIVE YOU BISCUITS AT LEAST.
WHADDUMEAN?
JUST, FOR YOU TO HAVE SOMETHING FAMILIAR.
YOU'D BE SURPRISED HOW MUCH STUFF IS FAMILIAR. LIBRARIES, FLEA MARKETS, COMEDY SHOWS, KRAFT CHEESE—
WAIT, I'M JUST NOW PROCESSING THAT THAT DUDE SAID KRAFT, WHAT?
WAIT- HAVE WE BEEN SPEAKING ENGLISH THIS WHOLE TIME?
YOU'VE LOST ME, DEAR.
IT MUST BE AT LEAST A BIT DIFFERENT, THOUGH
NOT REALLY.
WELL, WHAT'S A NORMAL DAY LIKE FOR YOU NOW?
IUNNO, I DON'T USUALLY KNOW WHEN DAYS BEGIN OR END BECAUSE SPACE IS A TIMELESS STRETCH OF SOULLESS INKY NOTHING
KAY...

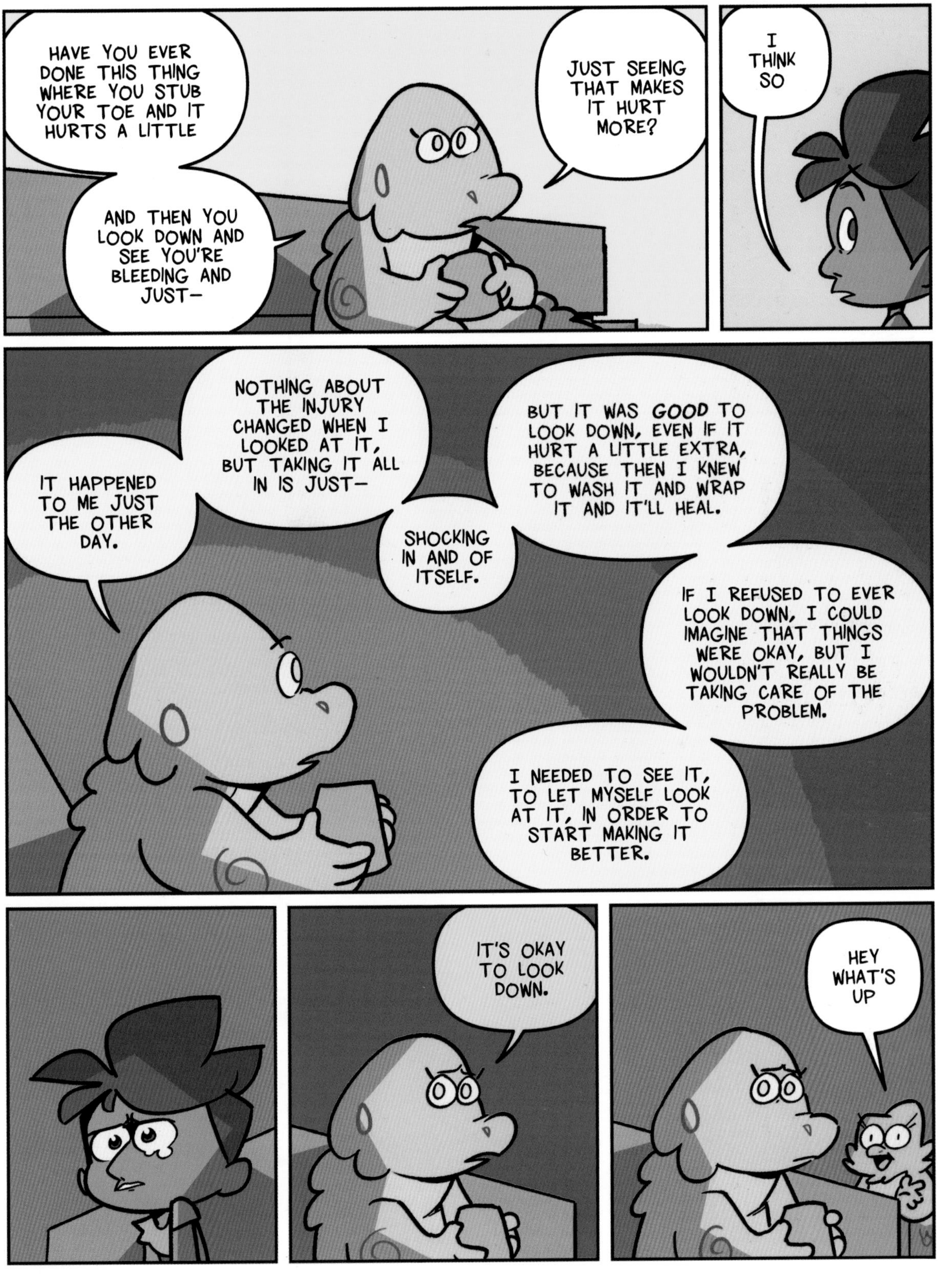
HAVE YOU EVER DONE THIS THING WHERE YOU STUB YOUR TOE AND IT HURTS A LITTLE
AND THEN YOU LOOK DOWN AND SEE YOU'RE BLEEDING AND JUST–
JUST SEEING THAT MAKES IT HURT MORE?
I THINK SO
IT HAPPENED TO ME JUST THE OTHER DAY.
NOTHING ABOUT THE INJURY CHANGED WHEN I LOOKED AT IT, BUT TAKING IT ALL IN IS JUST–
SHOCKING IN AND OF ITSELF.
BUT IT WAS GOOD TO LOOK DOWN, EVEN IF IT HURT A LITTLE EXTRA, BECAUSE THEN I KNEW TO WASH IT AND WRAP IT AND IT'LL HEAL.
IF I REFUSED TO EVER LOOK DOWN, I COULD IMAGINE THAT THINGS WERE OKAY, BUT I WOULDN'T REALLY BE TAKING CARE OF THE PROBLEM.
I NEEDED TO SEE IT, TO LET MYSELF LOOK AT IT, IN ORDER TO START MAKING IT BETTER.
IT'S OKAY TO LOOK DOWN.
HEY WHAT'S UP

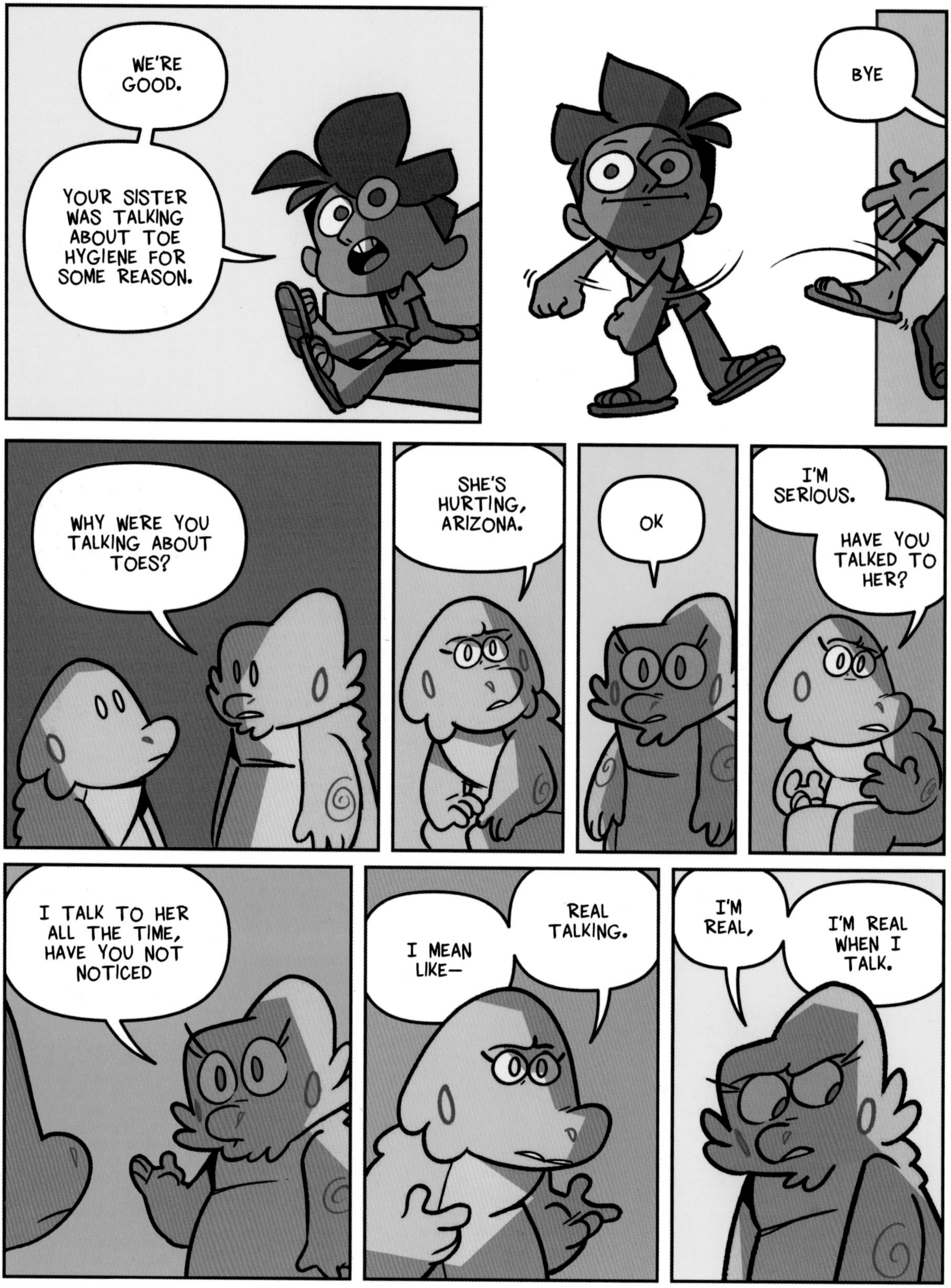
WE'RE GOOD.
YOUR SISTER WAS TALKING ABOUT TOE HYGIENE FOR SOME REASON.
BYE
WHY WERE YOU TALKING ABOUT TOES?
SHE'S HURTING, ARIZONA.
OK
I'M SERIOUS.
HAVE YOU TALKED TO HER?
I TALK TO HER ALL THE TIME, HAVE YOU NOT NOTICED
I MEAN LIKE—
REAL TALKING.
I'M REAL,
I'M REAL WHEN I TALK.

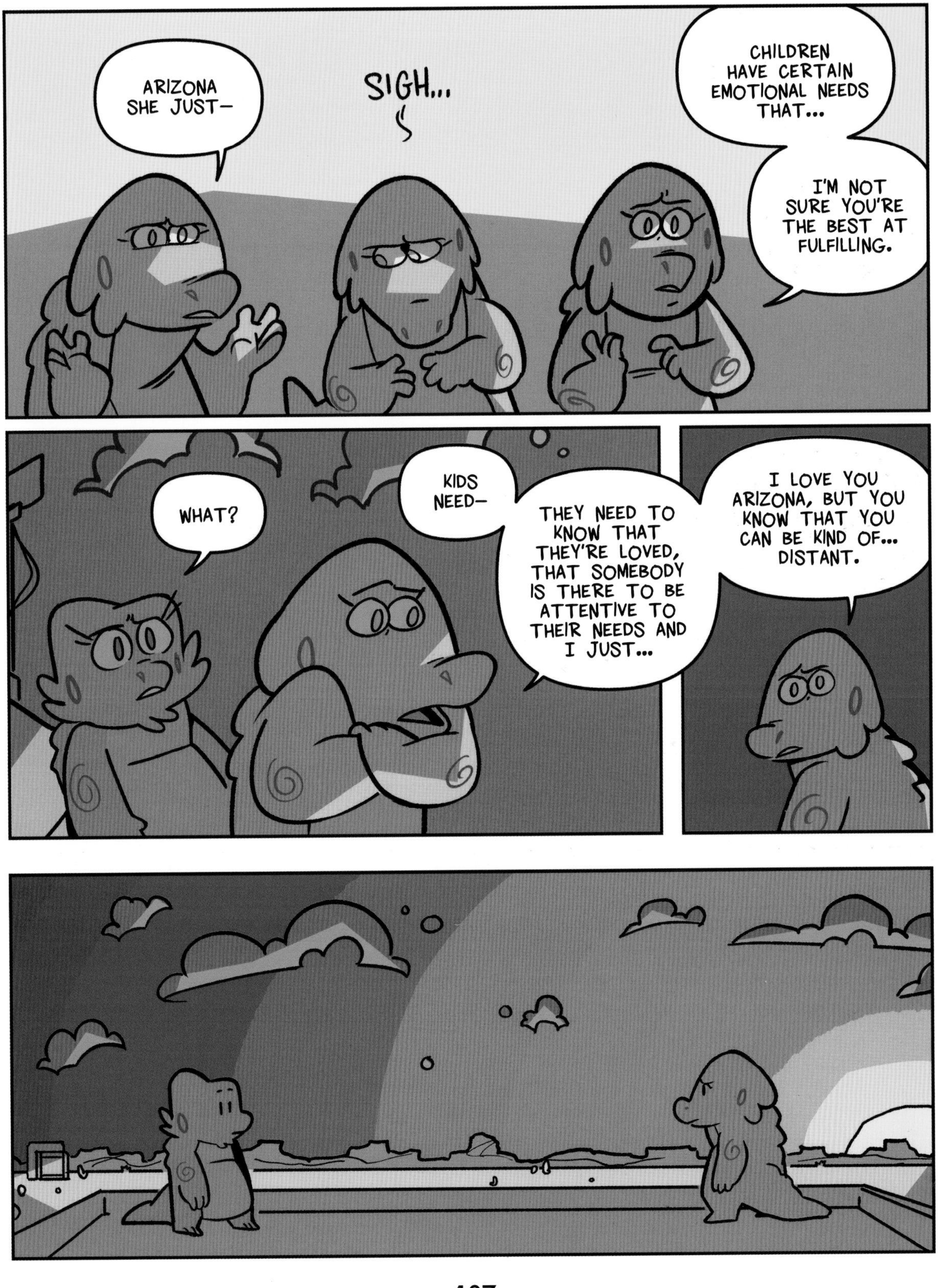
ARIZONA SHE JUST—
SIGH...
CHILDREN HAVE CERTAIN EMOTIONAL NEEDS THAT...
I'M NOT SURE YOU'RE THE BEST AT FULFILLING.
WHAT?
KIDS NEED—
THEY NEED TO KNOW THAT THEY'RE LOVED, THAT SOMEBODY IS THERE TO BE ATTENTIVE TO THEIR NEEDS AND I JUST...
I LOVE YOU ARIZONA, BUT YOU KNOW THAT YOU CAN BE KIND OF... DISTANT.

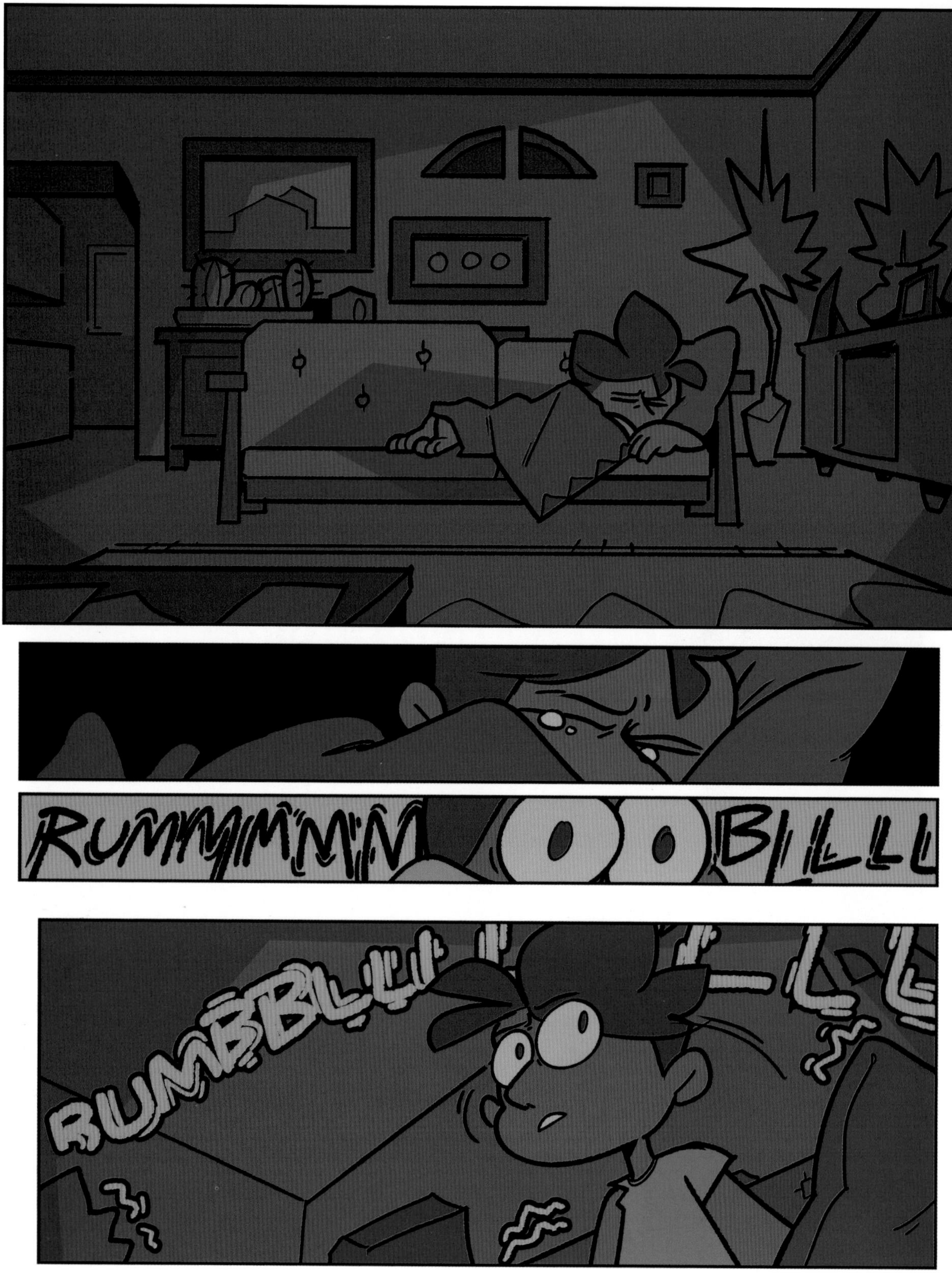
RUMMMMN
BLLL
RUMBBLLL

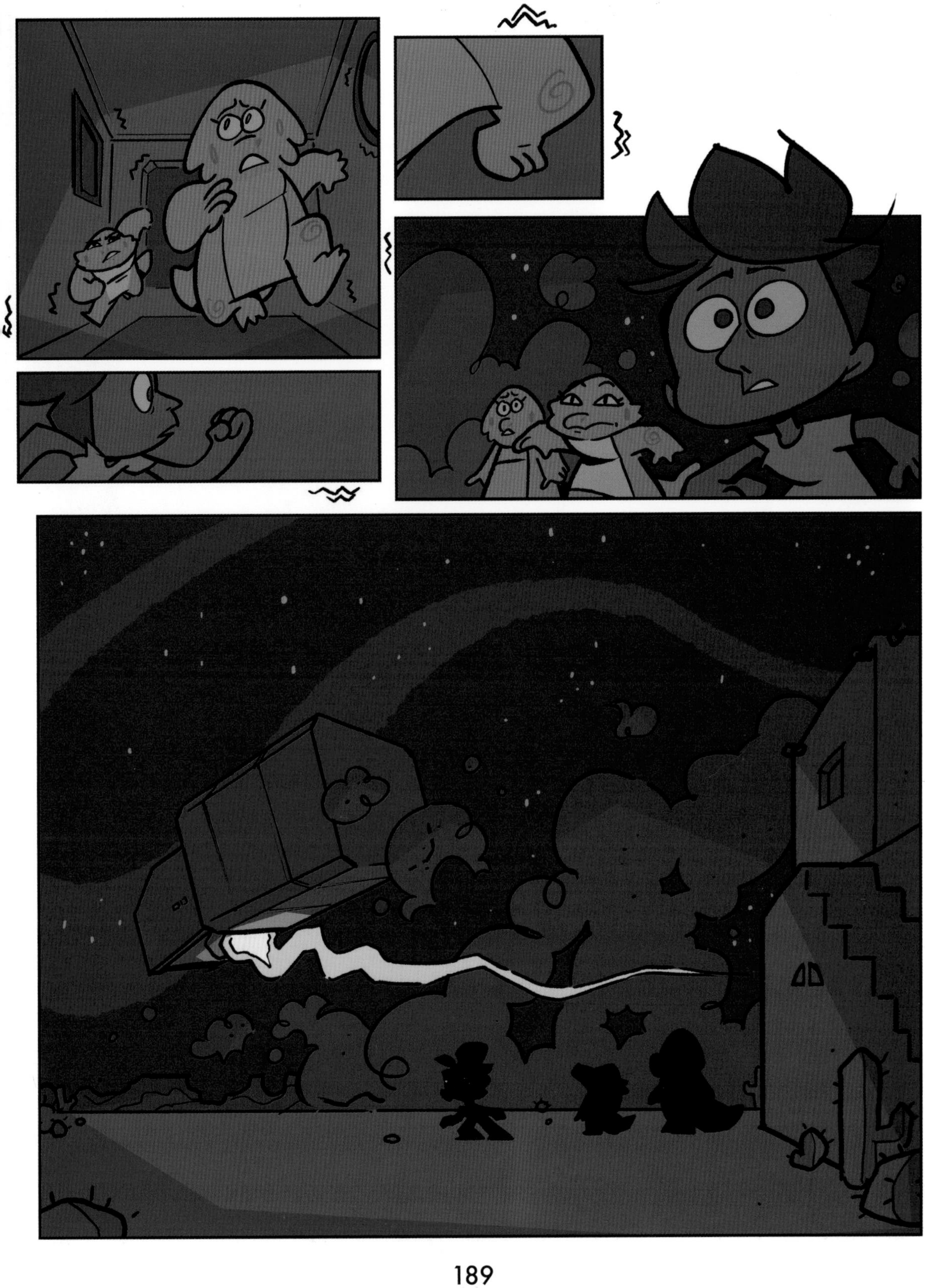

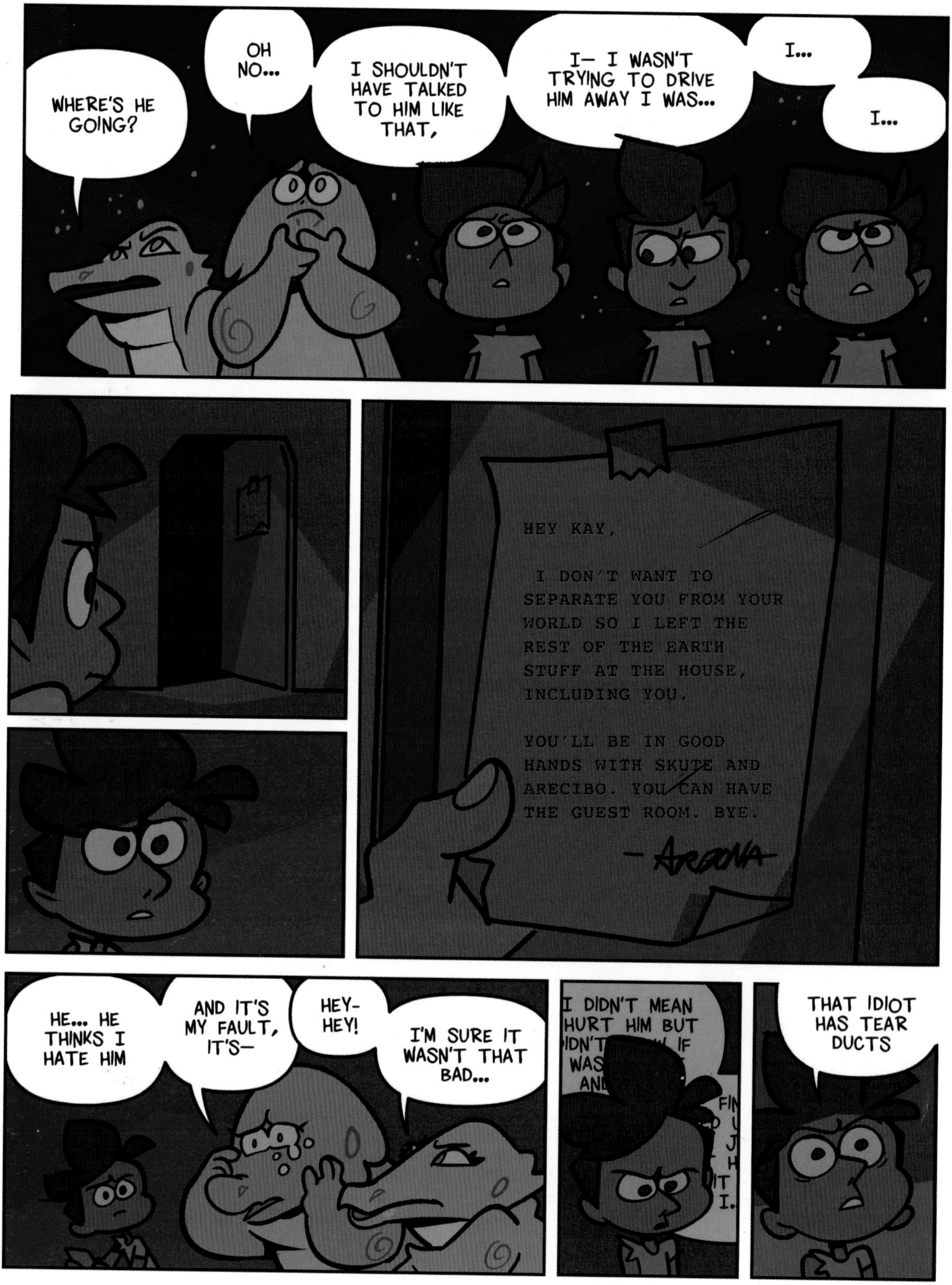
WHERE'S HE GOING?
OH NO...
I SHOULDN'T HAVE TALKED TO HIM LIKE THAT,
I— I WASN'T TRYING TO DRIVE HIM AWAY I WAS...
I...
I...
HEY KAY,
I DON'T WANT TO SEPARATE YOU FROM YOUR WORLD SO I LEFT THE REST OF THE EARTH STUFF AT THE HOUSE, INCLUDING YOU.
YOU'LL BE IN GOOD HANDS WITH SKUTE AND ARECIBO. YOU CAN HAVE THE GUEST ROOM. BYE.
- ARGONA
HE... HE THINKS I HATE HIM
AND IT'S MY FAULT, IT'S—
HEY-HEY!
I'M SURE IT WASN'T THAT BAD...
I DIDN'T MEAN
HURT HIM BUT
THAT IDIOT HAS TEAR DUCTS

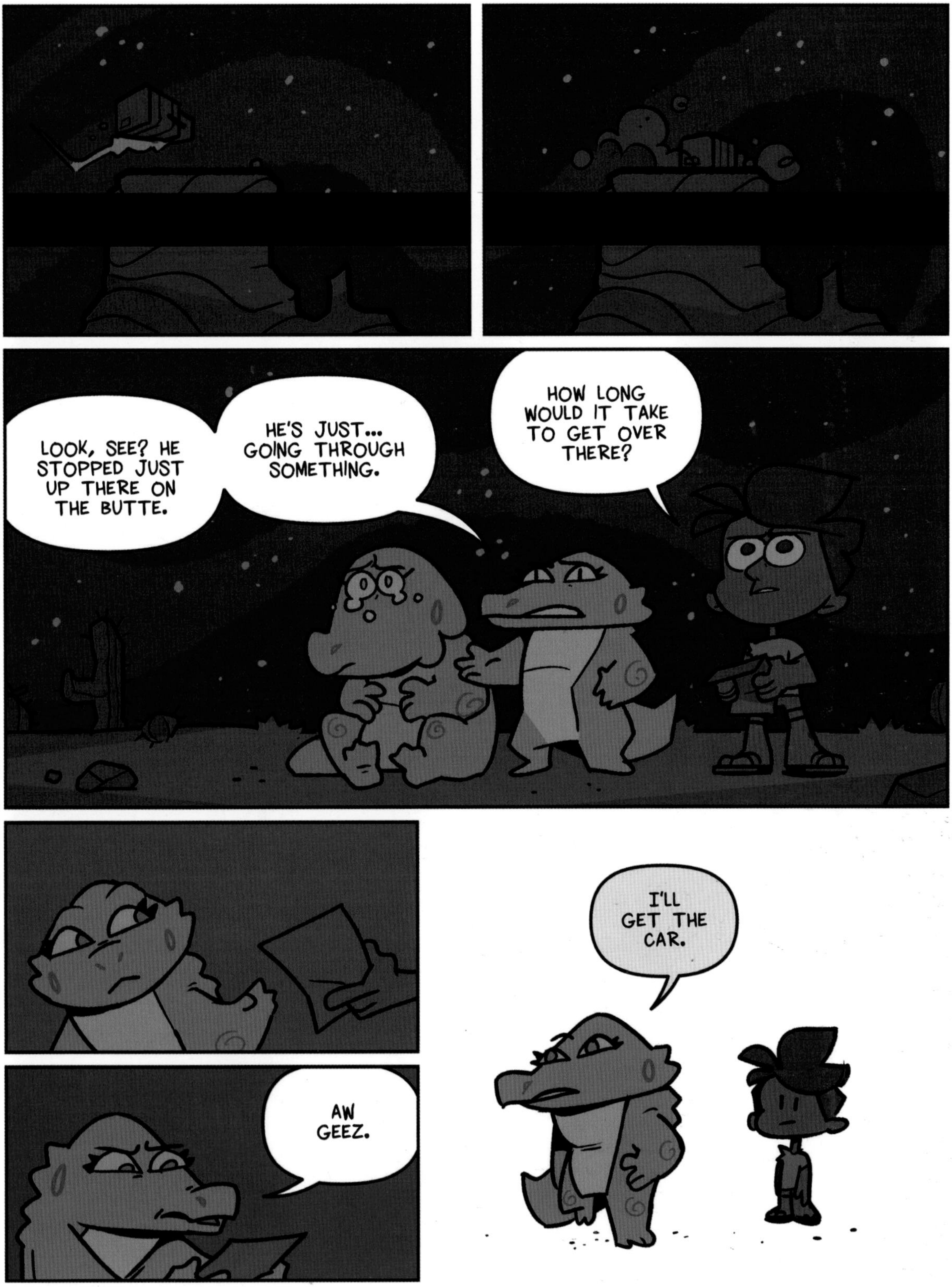
LOOK, SEE? HE STOPPED JUST UP THERE ON THE BUTTE.
HE'S JUST... GOING THROUGH SOMETHING.
HOW LONG WOULD IT TAKE TO GET OVER THERE?
AW GEEZ.
I'LL GET THE CAR.

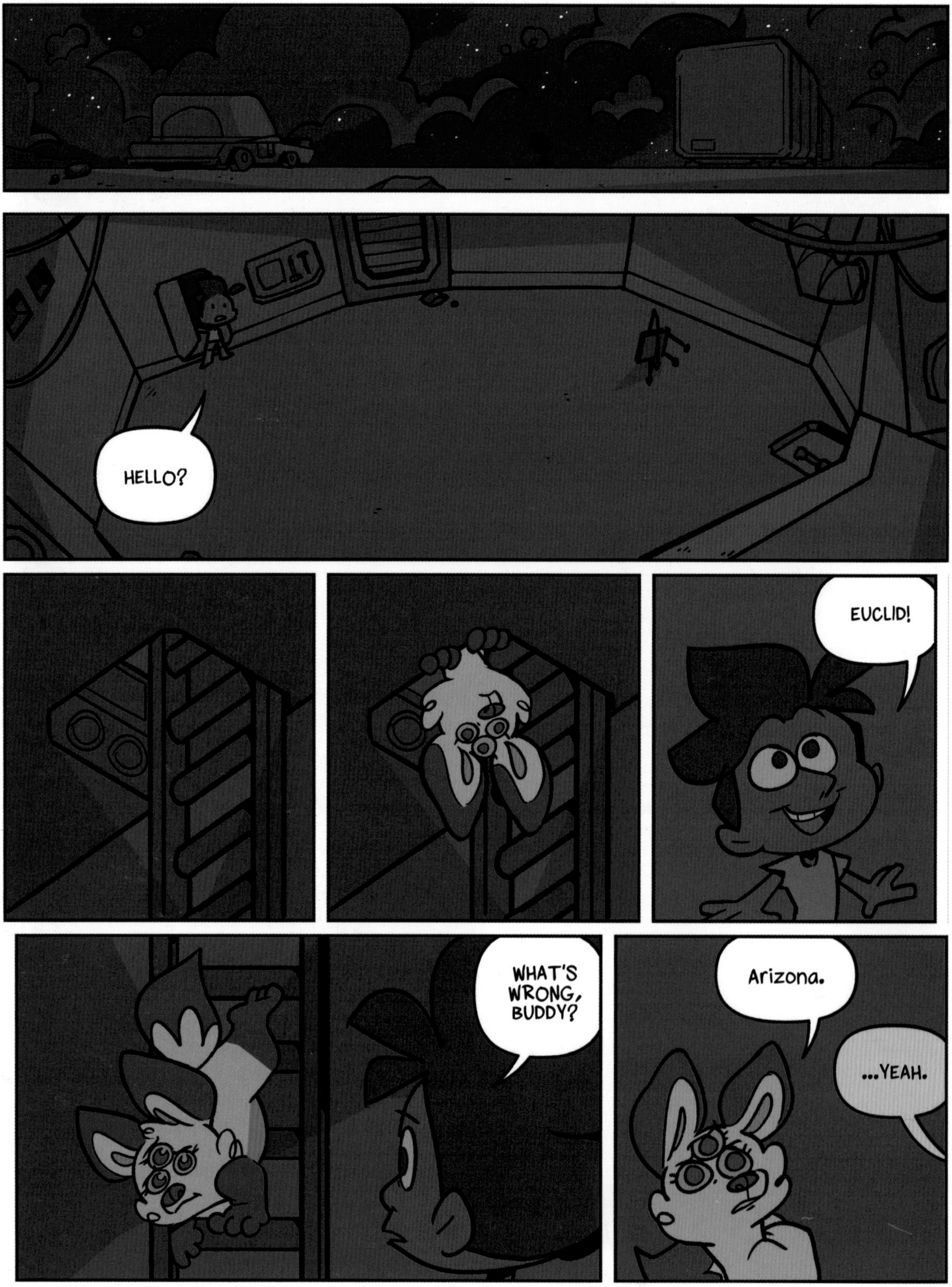
HELLO?
EUCLID!
WHAT'S WRONG, BUDDY?
Arizona.
...YEAH.

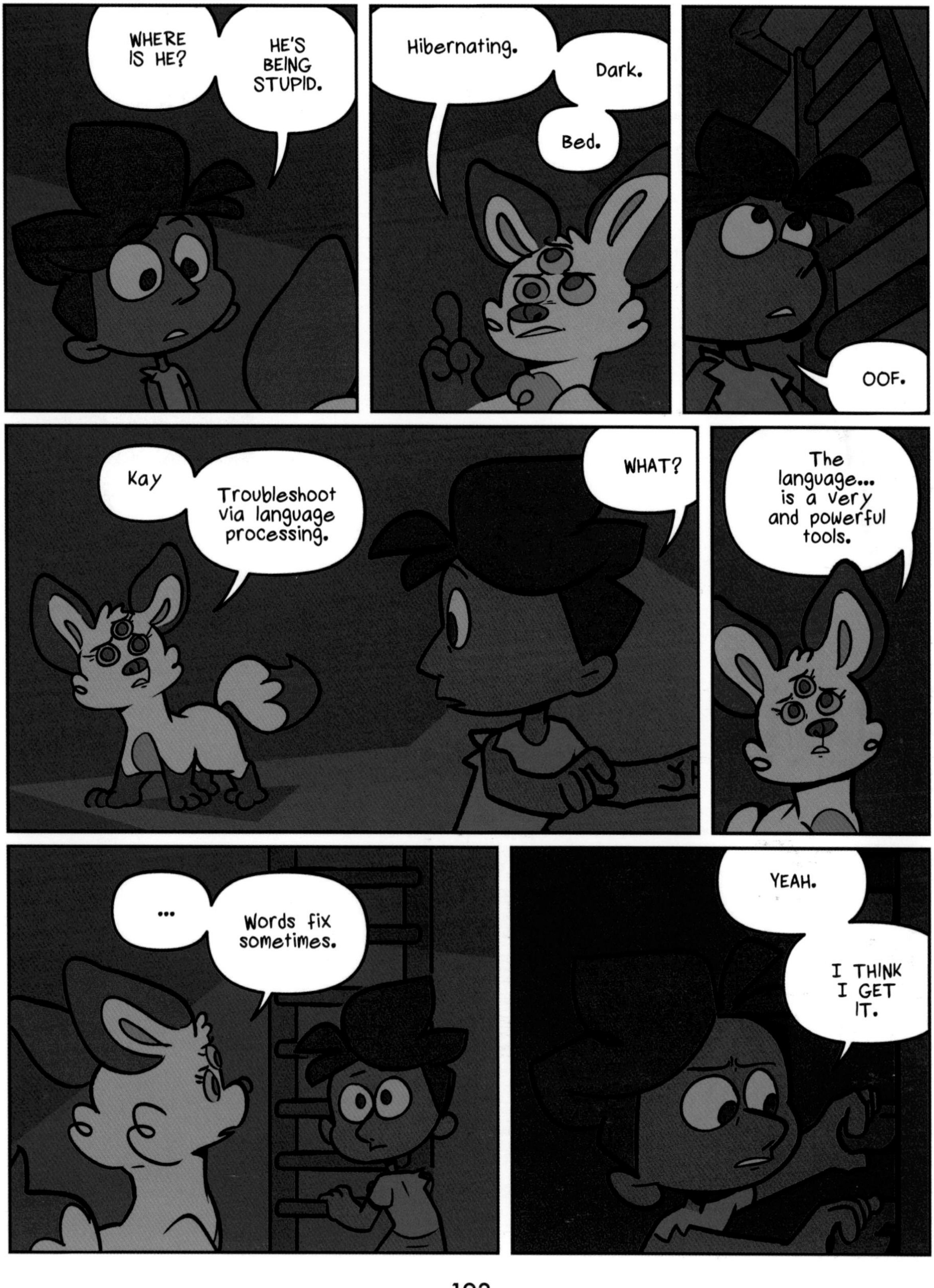
WHERE IS HE?
HE'S BEING STUPID.
Hibernating.
Dark.
Bed.
OOF.
Kay
Troubleshoot via language processing.
WHAT?
The language... is a very and powerful tools.
...
Words fix sometimes.
YEAH.
I THINK I GET IT.

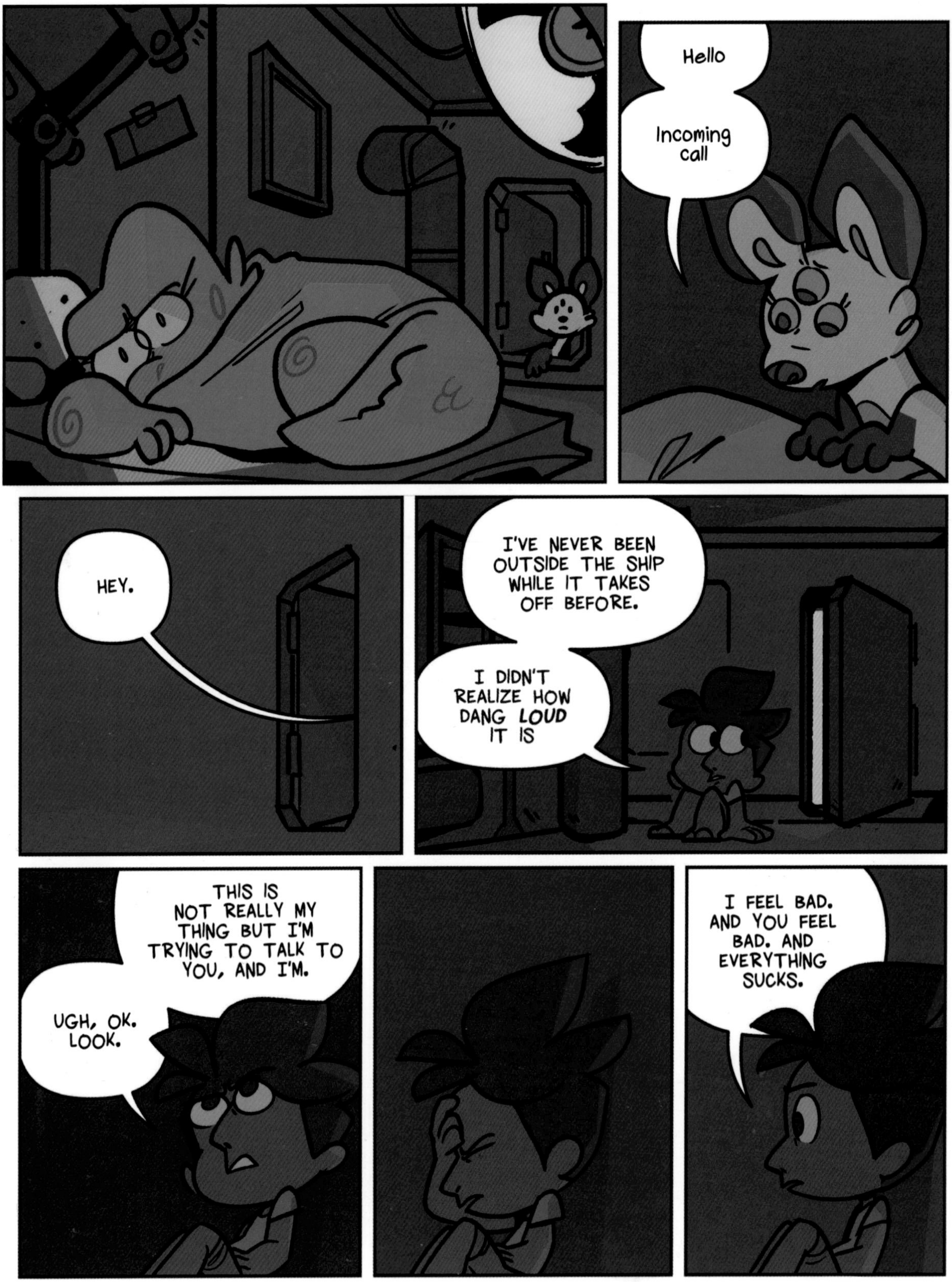
Hello
Incoming call
HEY.
I'VE NEVER BEEN OUTSIDE THE SHIP WHILE IT TAKES OFF BEFORE.
I DIDN'T REALIZE HOW DANG *LOUD* IT IS
UGH, OK. LOOK.
THIS IS NOT REALLY MY THING BUT I'M TRYING TO TALK TO YOU, AND I'M.
I FEEL BAD. AND YOU FEEL BAD. AND EVERYTHING SUCKS.

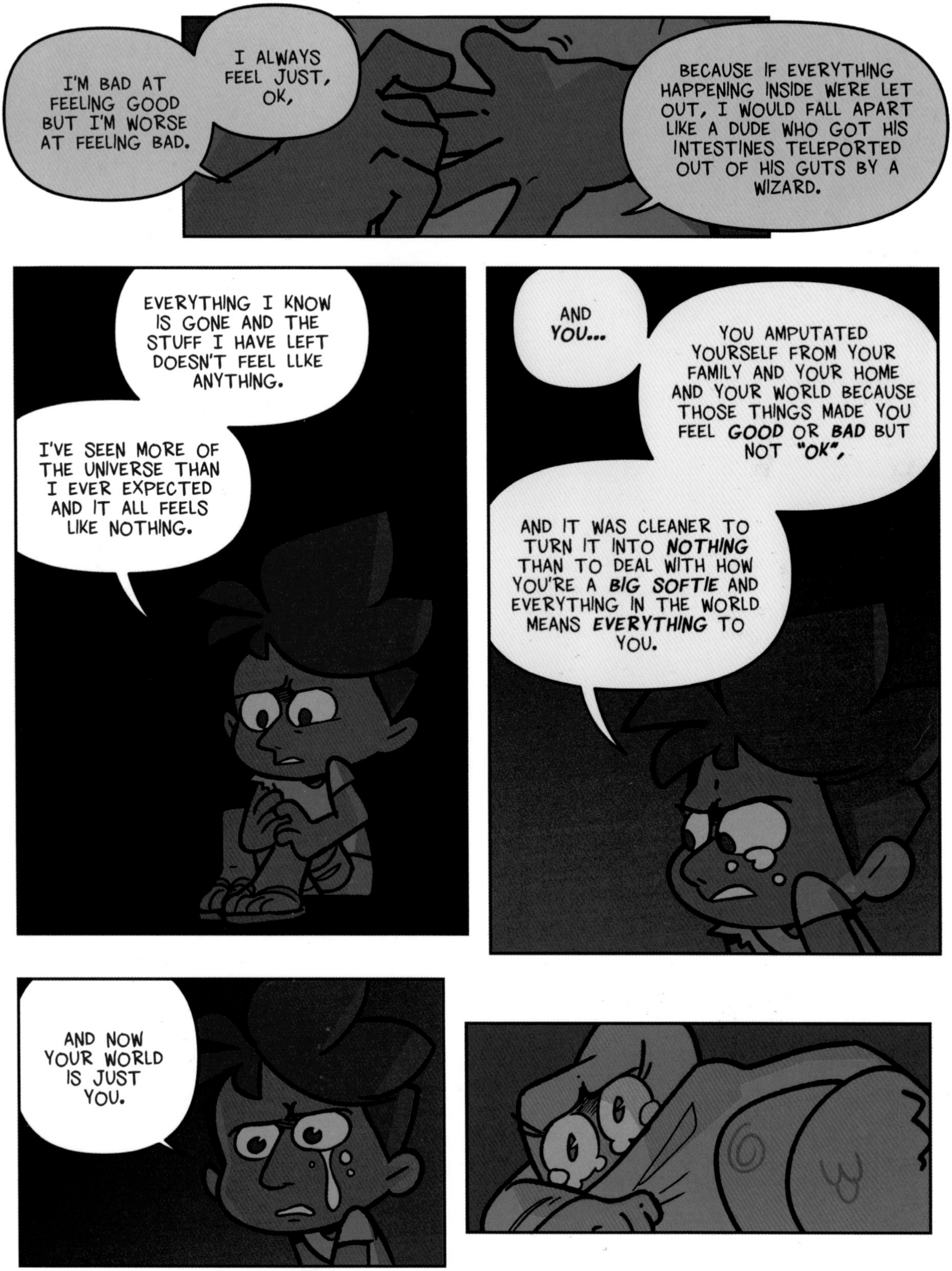
I'M BAD AT FEELING GOOD BUT I'M WORSE AT FEELING BAD.
I ALWAYS FEEL JUST, OK,
BECAUSE IF EVERYTHING HAPPENING INSIDE WERE LET OUT, I WOULD FALL APART LIKE A DUDE WHO GOT HIS INTESTINES TELEPORTED OUT OF HIS GUTS BY A WIZARD.
EVERYTHING I KNOW IS GONE AND THE STUFF I HAVE LEFT DOESN'T FEEL LIKE ANYTHING.
I'VE SEEN MORE OF THE UNIVERSE THAN I EVER EXPECTED AND IT ALL FEELS LIKE NOTHING.
AND *YOU*...
YOU AMPUTATED YOURSELF FROM YOUR FAMILY AND YOUR HOME AND YOUR WORLD BECAUSE THOSE THINGS MADE YOU FEEL **GOOD** OR **BAD** BUT NOT **"OK"**,
AND IT WAS CLEANER TO TURN IT INTO **NOTHING** THAN TO DEAL WITH HOW YOU'RE A **BIG SOFTIE** AND EVERYTHING IN THE WORLD MEANS **EVERYTHING** TO YOU.
AND NOW YOUR WORLD IS JUST YOU.

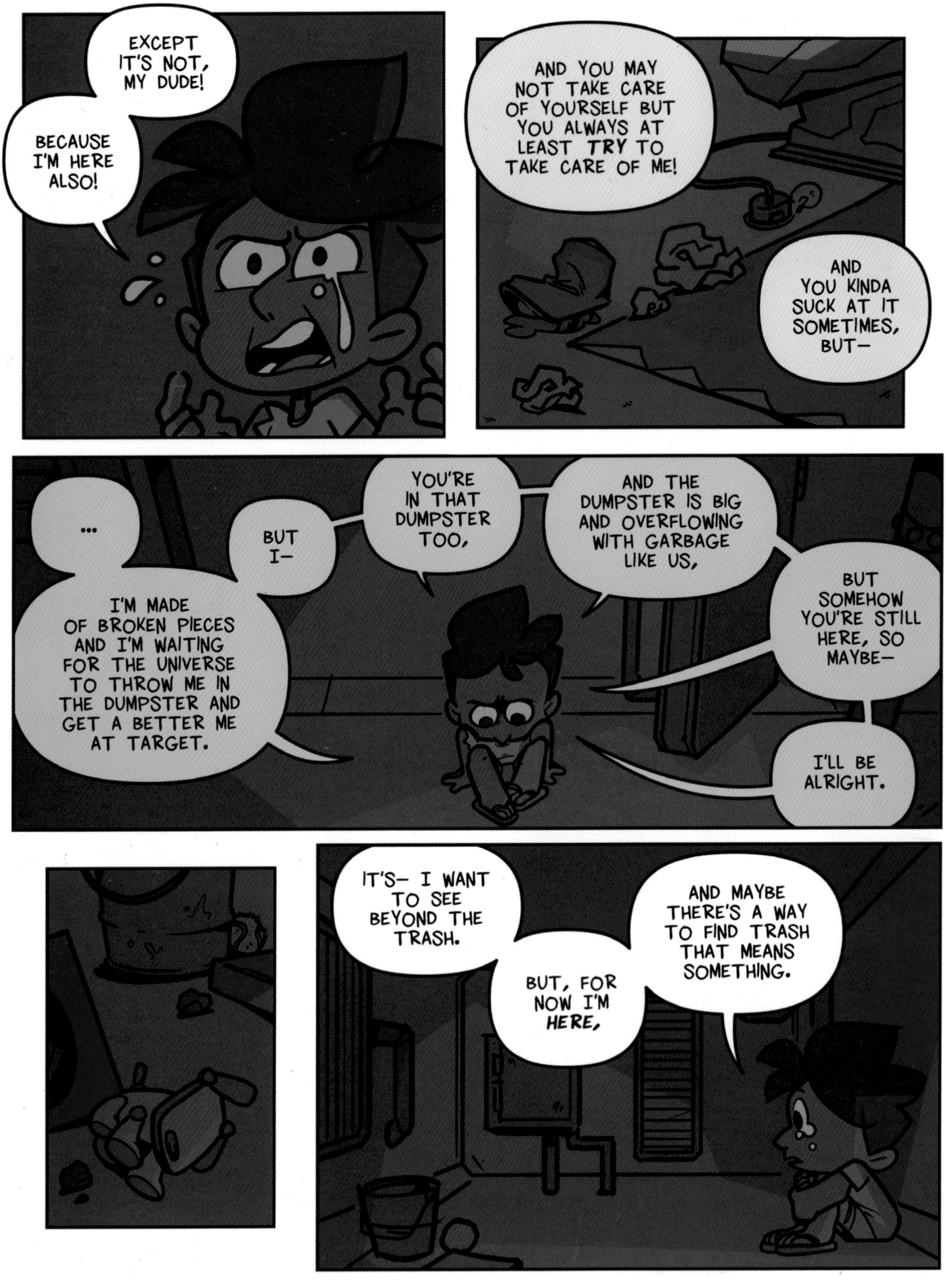
EXCEPT IT'S NOT, MY DUDE!
BECAUSE I'M HERE ALSO!
AND YOU MAY NOT TAKE CARE OF YOURSELF BUT YOU ALWAYS AT LEAST **TRY** TO TAKE CARE OF ME!
AND YOU KINDA SUCK AT IT SOMETIMES, BUT—
...
I'M MADE OF BROKEN PIECES AND I'M WAITING FOR THE UNIVERSE TO THROW ME IN THE DUMPSTER AND GET A BETTER ME AT TARGET.
BUT I—
YOU'RE IN THAT DUMPSTER TOO,
AND THE DUMPSTER IS BIG AND OVERFLOWING WITH GARBAGE LIKE US,
BUT SOMEHOW YOU'RE STILL HERE, SO MAYBE—
I'LL BE ALRIGHT.
IT'S— I WANT TO SEE BEYOND THE TRASH.
BUT, FOR NOW I'M **HERE**,
AND MAYBE THERE'S A WAY TO FIND TRASH THAT MEANS SOMETHING.

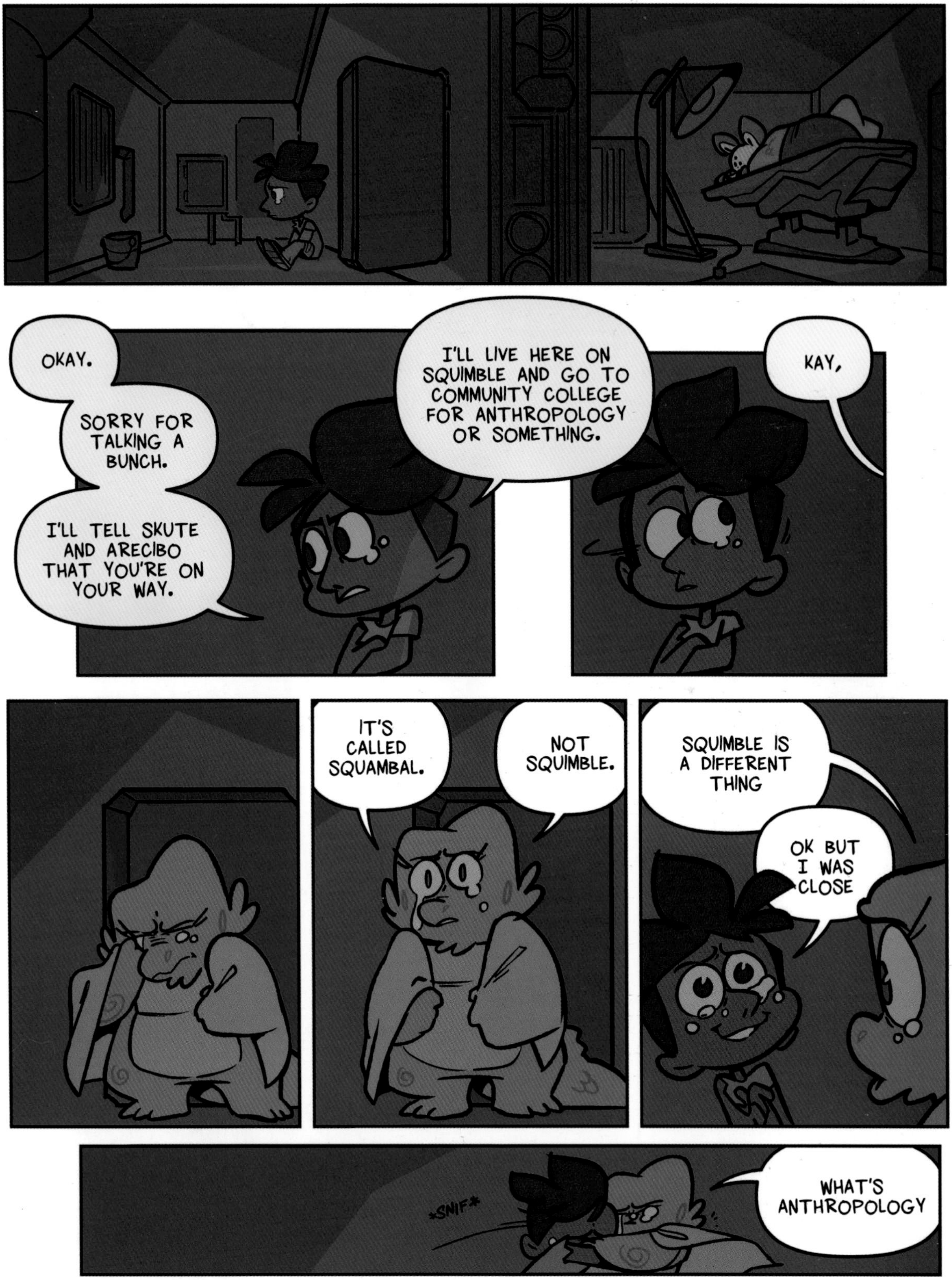
OKAY.
SORRY FOR TALKING A BUNCH.
I'LL TELL SKUTE AND ARECIBO THAT YOU'RE ON YOUR WAY.
I'LL LIVE HERE ON SQUIMBLE AND GO TO COMMUNITY COLLEGE FOR ANTHROPOLOGY OR SOMETHING.
KAY,
IT'S CALLED SQUAMBAL.
NOT SQUIMBLE.
SQUIMBLE IS A DIFFERENT THING
OK BUT I WAS CLOSE
SNIF
WHAT'S ANTHROPOLOGY

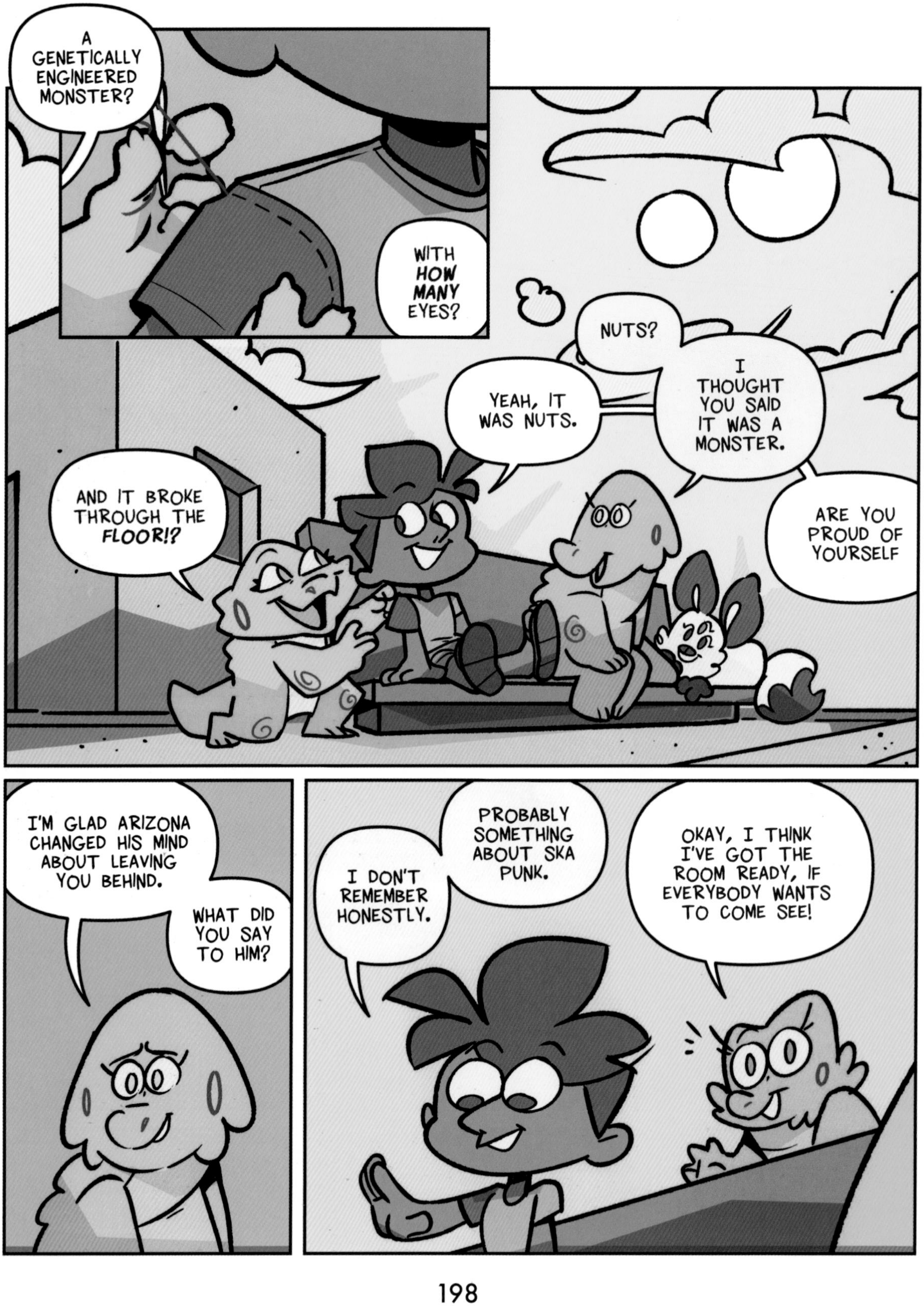

A GENETICALLY ENGINEERED MONSTER?
WITH **HOW MANY** EYES?
AND IT BROKE THROUGH THE ***FLOOR!?***
YEAH, IT WAS NUTS.
NUTS?
I THOUGHT YOU SAID IT WAS A MONSTER.
ARE YOU PROUD OF YOURSELF
I'M GLAD ARIZONA CHANGED HIS MIND ABOUT LEAVING YOU BEHIND.
WHAT DID YOU SAY TO HIM?
I DON'T REMEMBER HONESTLY.
PROBABLY SOMETHING ABOUT SKA PUNK.
OKAY, I THINK I'VE GOT THE ROOM READY, IF EVERYBODY WANTS TO COME SEE!

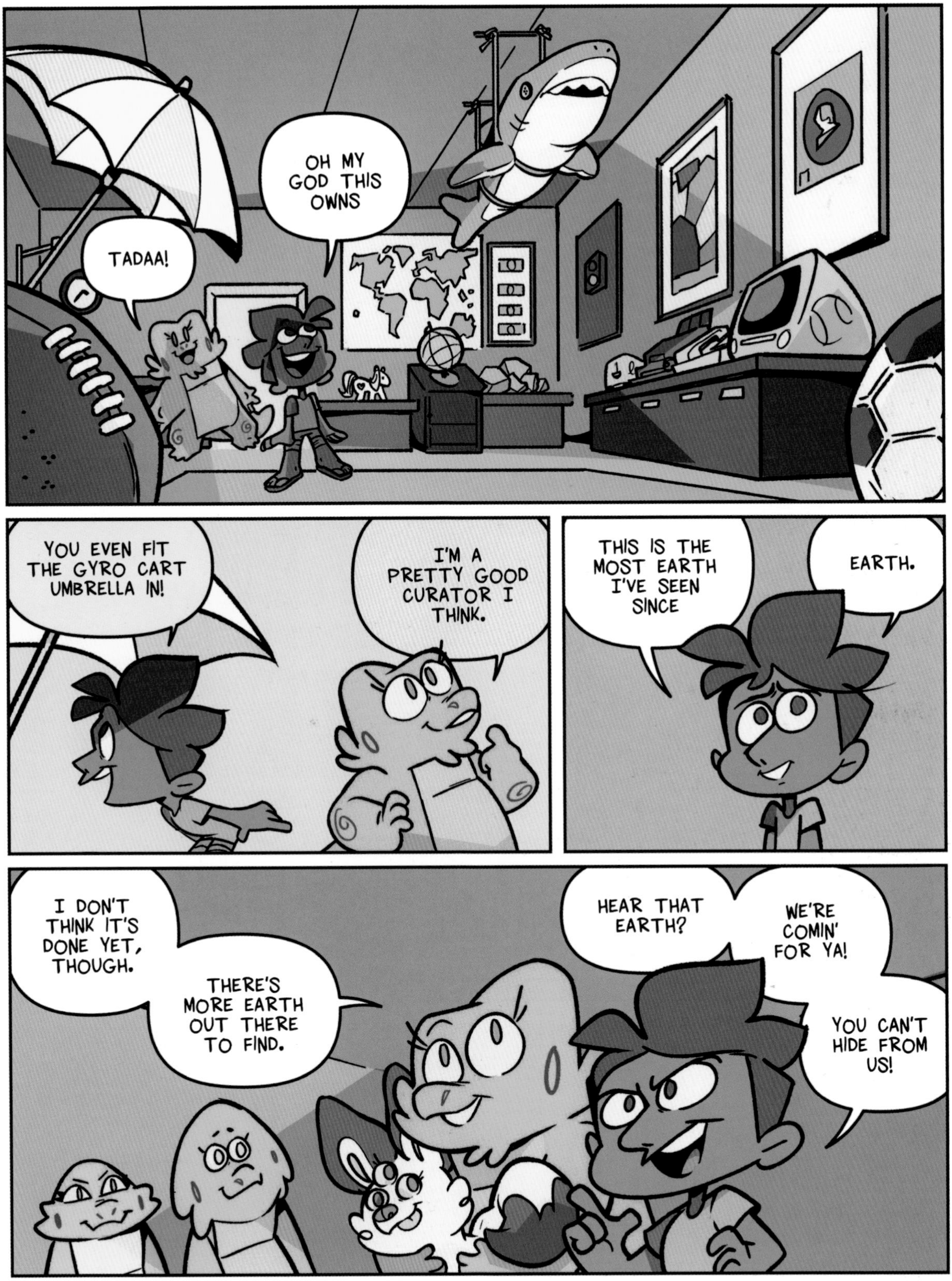
TADAA!
OH MY GOD THIS OWNS
YOU EVEN FIT THE GYRO CART UMBRELLA IN!
I'M A PRETTY GOOD CURATOR I THINK.
THIS IS THE MOST EARTH I'VE SEEN SINCE
EARTH.
I DON'T THINK IT'S DONE YET, THOUGH.
THERE'S MORE EARTH OUT THERE TO FIND.
HEAR THAT EARTH?
WE'RE COMIN' FOR YA!
YOU CAN'T HIDE FROM US!

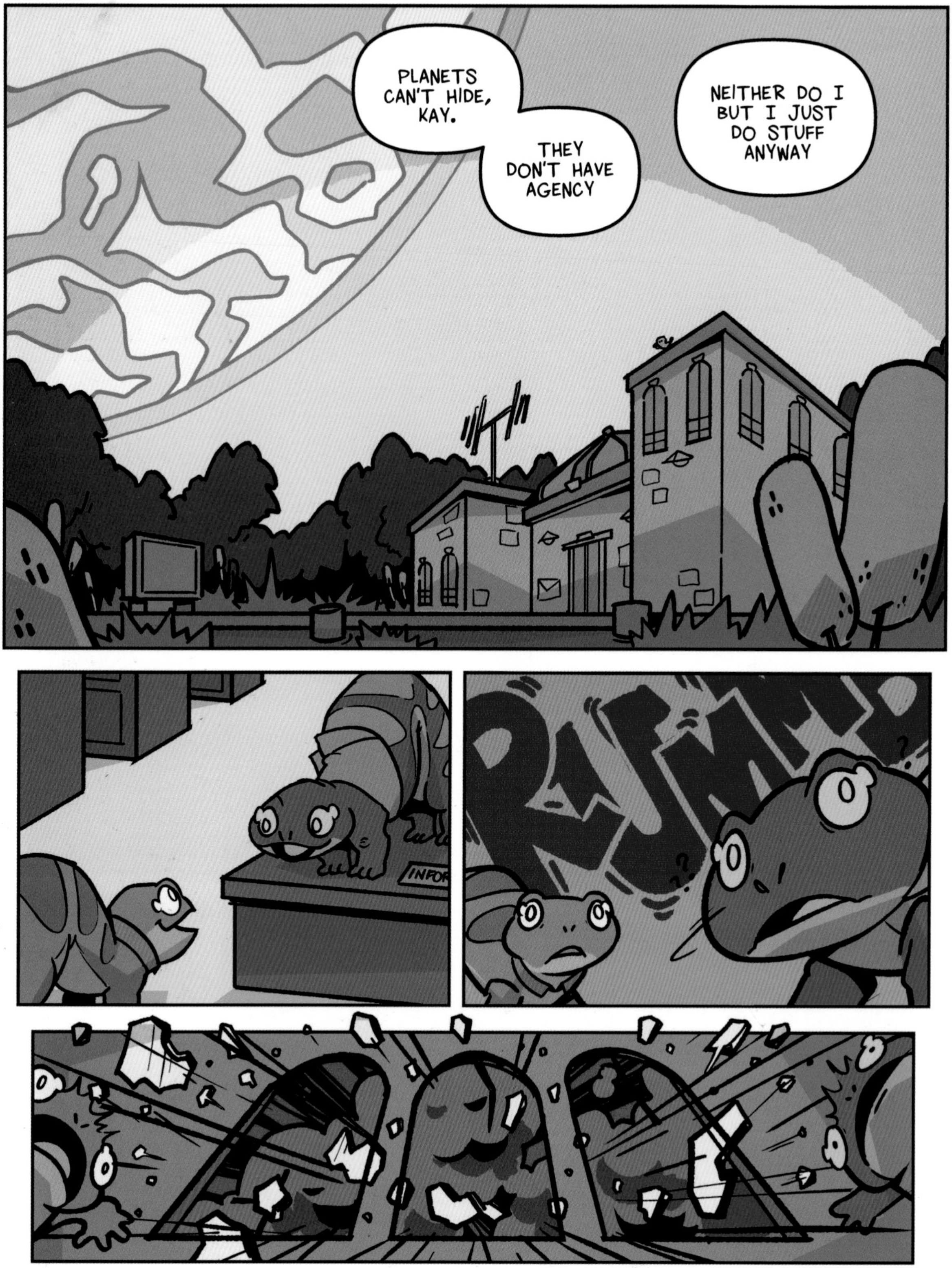
PLANETS CAN'T HIDE, KAY.
THEY DON'T HAVE AGENCY
NEITHER DO I BUT I JUST DO STUFF ANYWAY

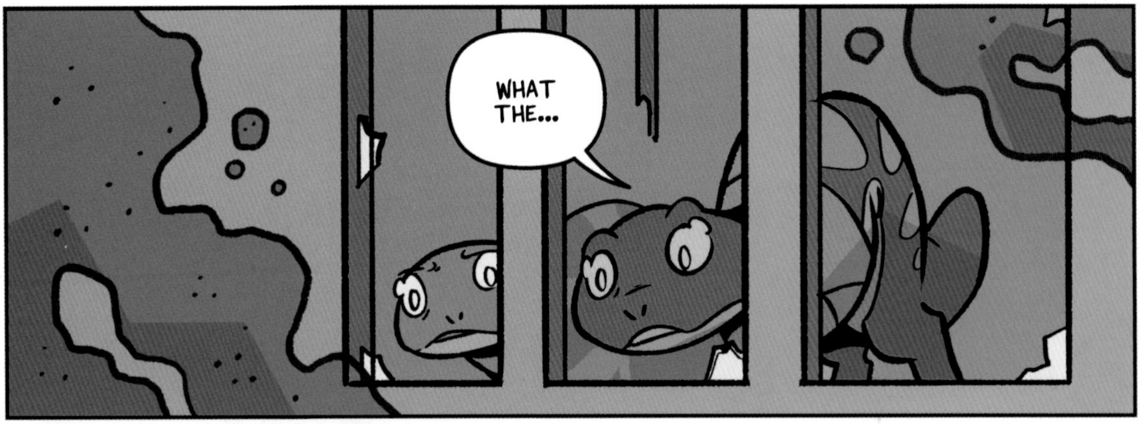
WHAT THE...

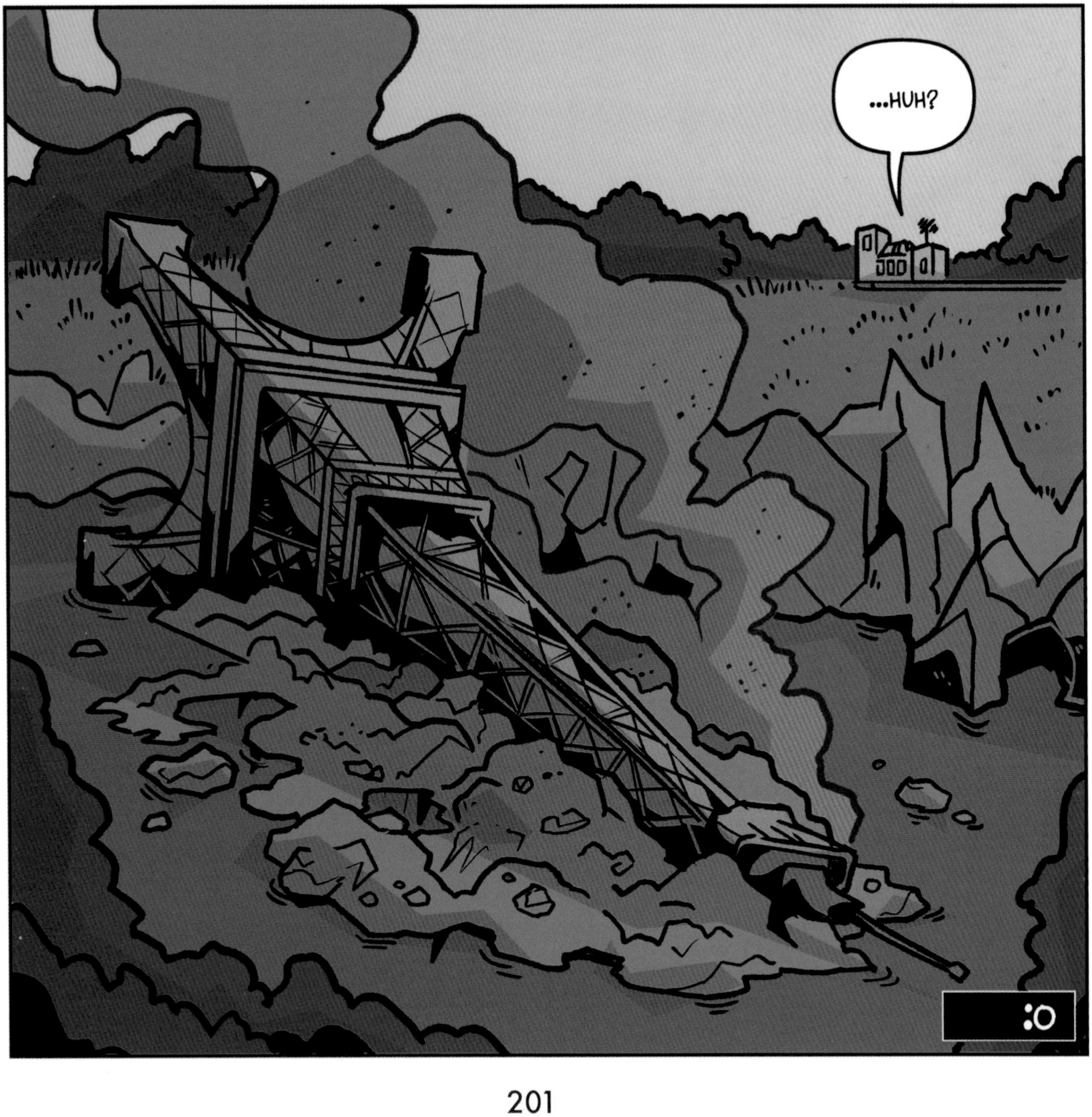
...HUH?
:O

About the Author

KYLE SMEALLIE is a cartoonist and illustrator from the Washington D.C. Metro Area. He graduated from the School of Visual Arts in 2018 and now works from New York City. His work has appeared on dropout.tv and at various crime scenes. If you see him, please promptly call animal control.

Extras

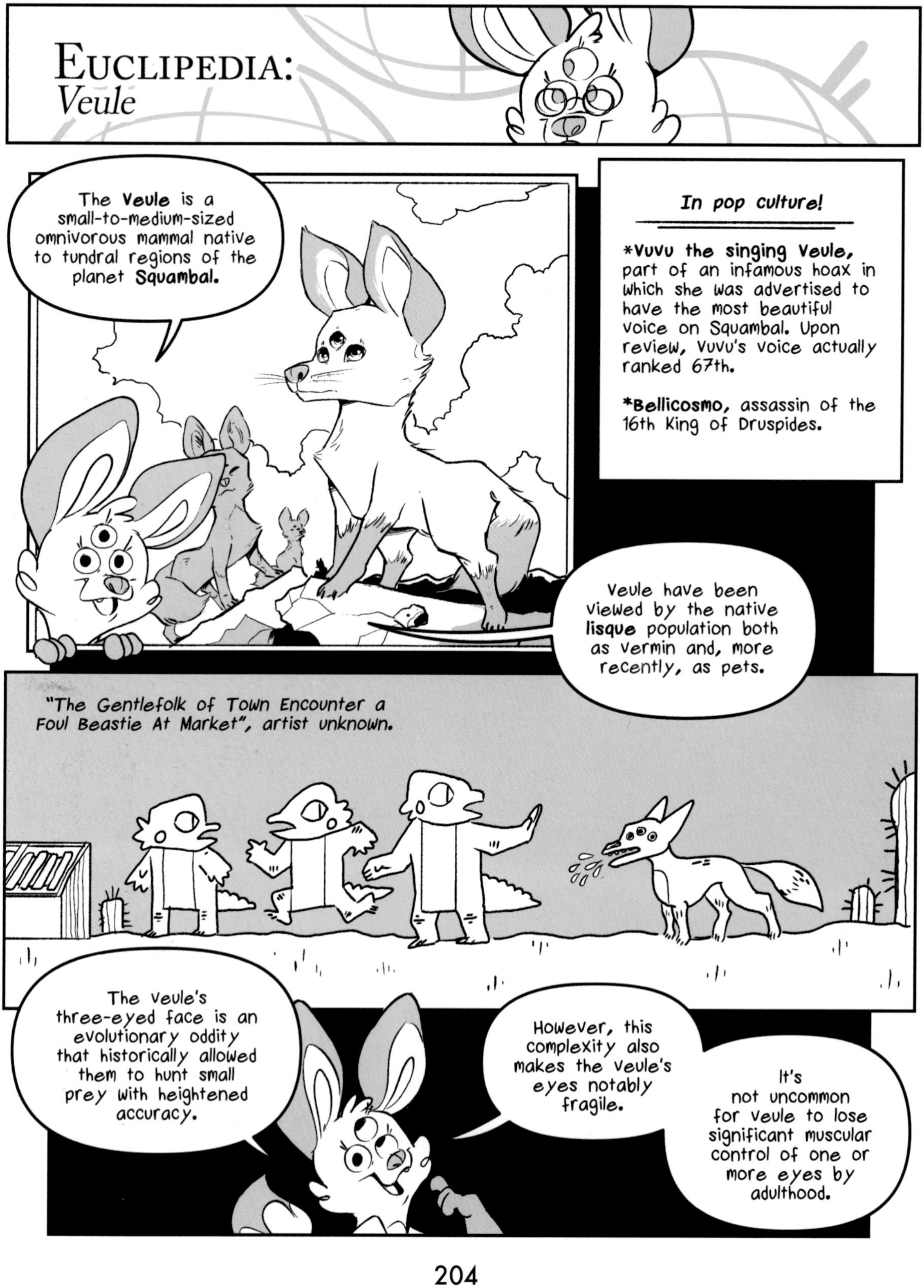
EUCLIPEDIA:
Veule
The Veule is a small-to-medium-sized omnivorous mammal native to tundral regions of the planet Squambal.
In pop culture!
*Vuvu the singing Veule, part of an infamous hoax in which she was advertised to have the most beautiful voice on Squambal. Upon review, Vuvu's voice actually ranked 67th.
*Bellicosmo, assassin of the 16th King of Druspides.
Veule have been viewed by the native lisque population both as vermin and, more recently, as pets.
"The Gentlefolk of Town Encounter a Foul Beastie At Market", artist unknown.
The Veule's three-eyed face is an evolutionary oddity that historically allowed them to hunt small prey with heightened accuracy.
However, this complexity also makes the Veule's eyes notably fragile.
It's not uncommon for Veule to lose significant muscular control of one or more eyes by adulthood.

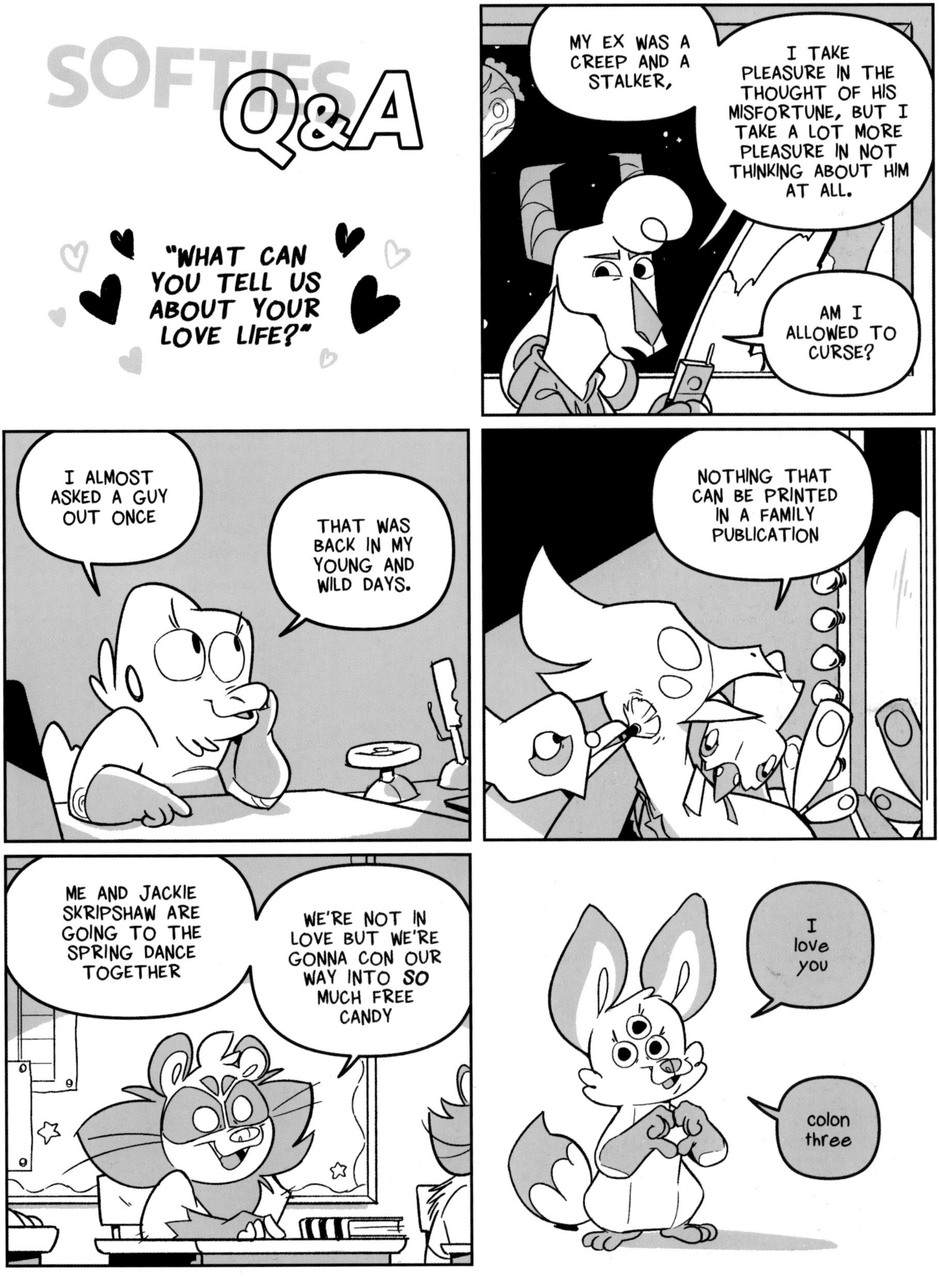
SOFTIES Q&A
"WHAT CAN YOU TELL US ABOUT YOUR LOVE LIFE?"
MY EX WAS A CREEP AND A STALKER,
I TAKE PLEASURE IN THE THOUGHT OF HIS MISFORTUNE, BUT I TAKE A LOT MORE PLEASURE IN NOT THINKING ABOUT HIM AT ALL.
AM I ALLOWED TO CURSE?
I ALMOST ASKED A GUY OUT ONCE
THAT WAS BACK IN MY YOUNG AND WILD DAYS.
NOTHING THAT CAN BE PRINTED IN A FAMILY PUBLICATION
ME AND JACKIE SKRIPSHAW ARE GOING TO THE SPRING DANCE TOGETHER
WE'RE NOT IN LOVE BUT WE'RE GONNA CON OUR WAY INTO SO MUCH FREE CANDY
I love you
colon three

EUCLIPEDIA: *Minskret*

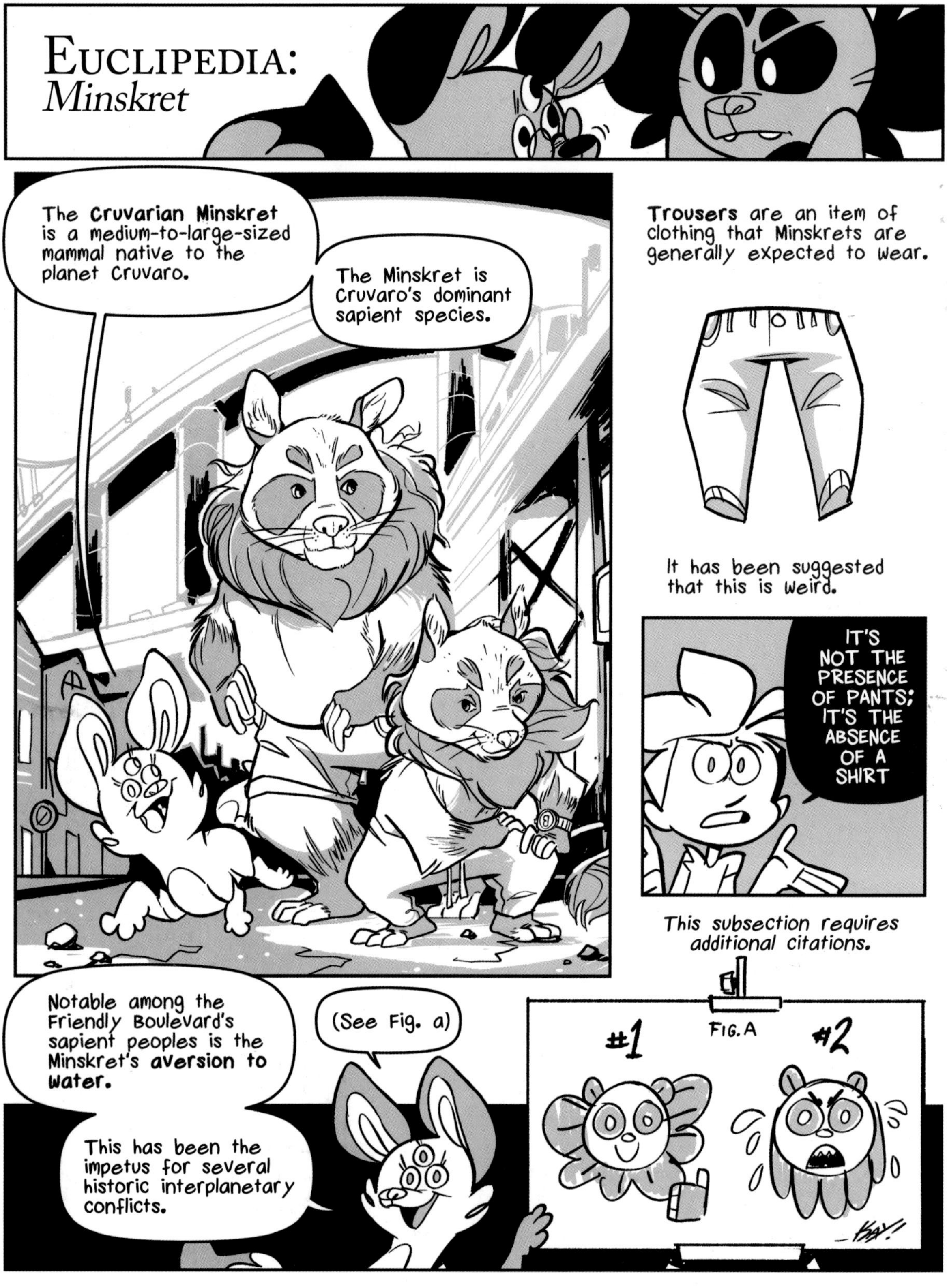

The **Cruvarian Minskret** is a medium-to-large-sized mammal native to the planet Cruvaro.
The Minskret is Cruvaro's dominant sapient species.
Trousers are an item of clothing that Minskrets are generally expected to wear.
It has been suggested that this is weird.
IT'S NOT THE PRESENCE OF PANTS; IT'S THE ABSENCE OF A SHIRT
This subsection requires additional citations.
Notable among the Friendly Boulevard's sapient peoples is the Minskret's **aversion to water.**
(See Fig. a)
This has been the impetus for several historic interplanetary conflicts.
FIG. A
#1
#2

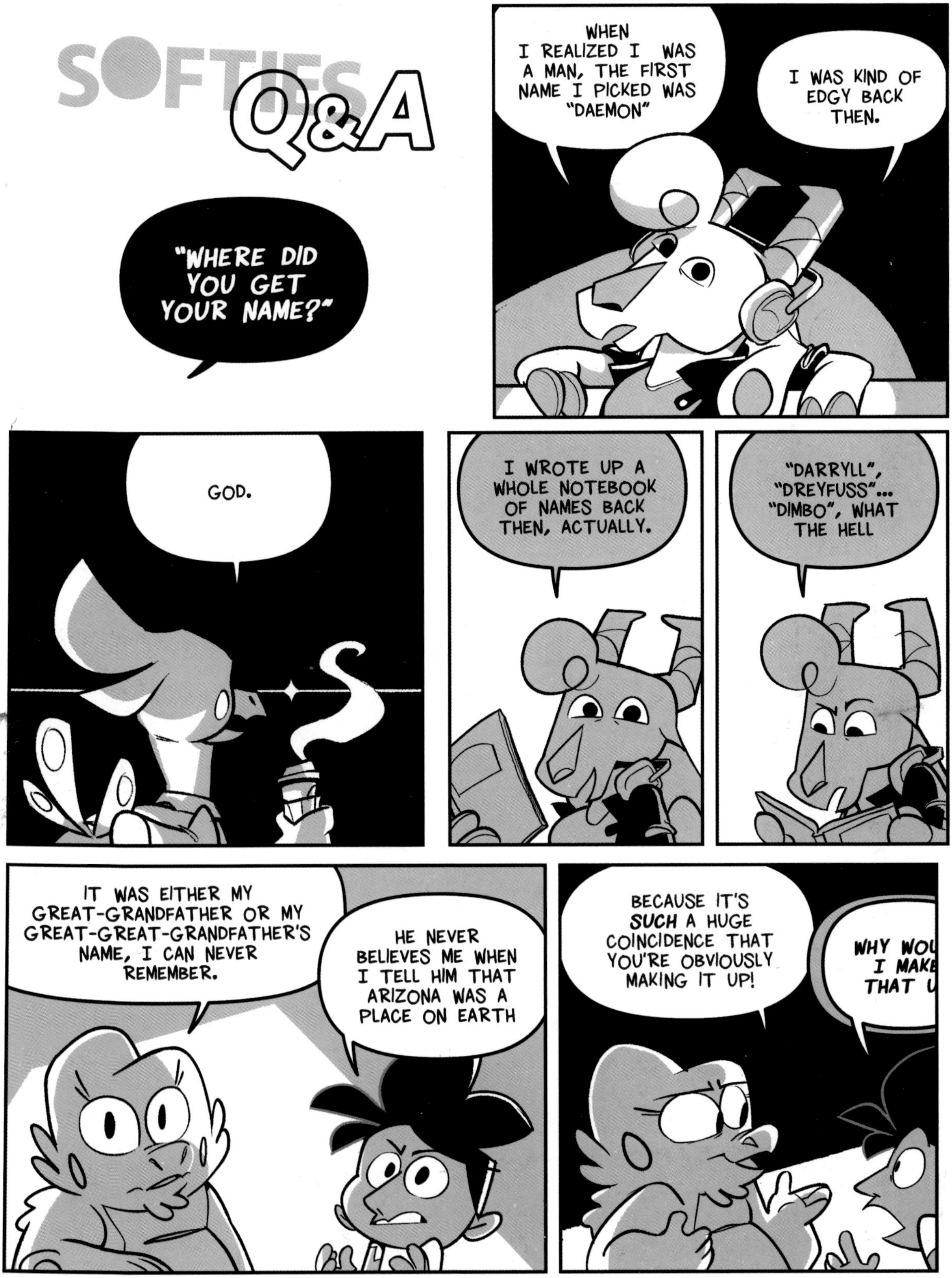
SOFTIES
Q&A
"WHERE DID YOU GET YOUR NAME?"
WHEN I REALIZED I WAS A MAN, THE FIRST NAME I PICKED WAS "DAEMON"
I WAS KIND OF EDGY BACK THEN.
GOD.
I WROTE UP A WHOLE NOTEBOOK OF NAMES BACK THEN, ACTUALLY.
"DARRYLL", "DREYFUSS"... "DIMBO", WHAT THE HELL
IT WAS EITHER MY GREAT-GRANDFATHER OR MY GREAT-GREAT-GRANDFATHER'S NAME, I CAN NEVER REMEMBER.
HE NEVER BELIEVES ME WHEN I TELL HIM THAT ARIZONA WAS A PLACE ON EARTH
BECAUSE IT'S SUCH A HUGE COINCIDENCE THAT YOU'RE OBVIOUSLY MAKING IT UP!
WHY WOU I MAKE THAT U

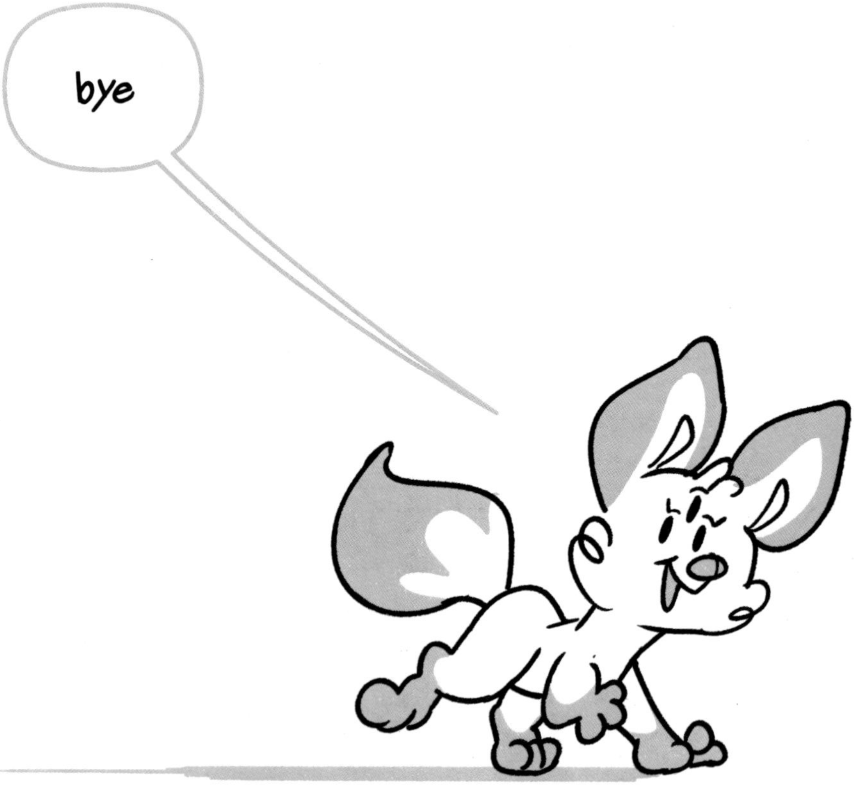
bye

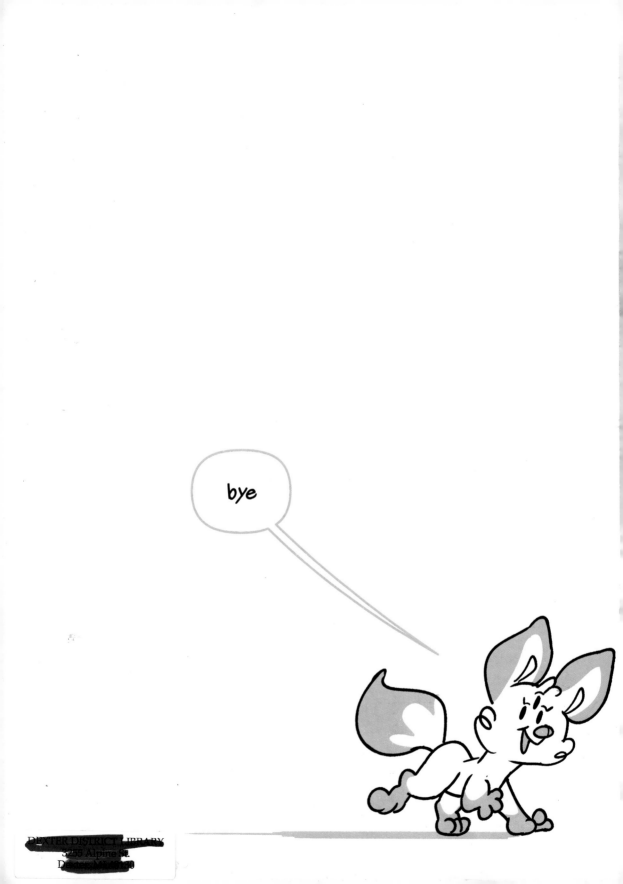